The Treasures of
B. Traven

The Treasures of B. Traven

JONATHAN CAPE
THIRTY BEDFORD SQUARE LONDON

This collection first published 1980
Jonathan Cape Ltd, 30 Bedford Square, London WC1
The Treasure of the Sierra Madre was first published in 1934
and *The Death Ship* and *The Bridge in the Jungle* in 1940

British Library Cataloguing in Publication Data

Traven, B
The treasures of B. Traven.
I. Title
823'.9'1F   PS3539.R314
ISBN 0 224 401830 2

Typeset by Inforum Ltd, Portsmouth
Printed in Great Britain by
W. & J. Mackay Limited, Chatham

Contents

The Treasure of
the Sierra Madre

1

The seat on which Dobbs was sitting was a thoroughly bad one. One rail was missing and another had caved in. It was a punishment to sit on it. It did not occur to Dobbs to consider whether he deserved this punishment or whether, like the majority of punishments, it was unjustly inflicted. Probably he would not have realized he was uncomfortable unless someone had asked him how he liked his seat. His preoccupation was the one usual with so many of us – how to get hold of some money. If you have a little money already it is easier, because you have some to lay out. But when you have nothing whatever, there are difficulties in arriving at a satisfactory solution of the problem.

Dobbs had nothing. It may safely be said that he had less than nothing, for he was not even adequately or completely clothed, and clothing, to those in need, is a modest start towards capital.

But there is always work for those who want it. Only it is as well not to go to the man who says so; for he never has any work to offer and never can point to the man who has. He makes his assertion merely to prove what a lot he knows of the world.

Dobbs would have wheeled stones if he could have got the job. But he could not even get navvy work. There were too many after it, and the natives always stand a better chance of getting it than a foreigner.

At the corner of the Plaza a shoe-black had his high iron chair. The other shoe-blacks, who could not afford a chair, ran about round the Plaza like weasels with their little boxes and folding stools and left no one in peace whose shoes did not shine like the sun. Whether you sat on one of the numerous seats or walked about, you were pestered all the time. It wasn't easy, then, even for the shoe-blacks to make a living, and compared with Dobbs they were capitalists; for they possessed an outfit which might cost three pesos at least.

Even if Dobbs had had the three pesos, he could not have been a shoe-black. Not here among the natives. No white man has ever attempted to clean shoes on the streets, here at least. The white man who sits on a seat in rags and starves, the white man who begs of other white men, the white man who commits burglary is not despised by other white men. But if he cleans shoes in the streets, or begs from Indians, or lugs round ice water for sale in buckets, he sinks far below the dirtiest native and starves all the same. For no white man will patronize him and the natives will treat him as an unfair competitor.

A gentleman in a white coat took his seat on the high iron chair at the corner, and the shoe-black set to work on his brown shoes. Dobbs got up and strolled across and muttered a few words in a low voice. The gentleman scarcely looked up, but feeling in his pocket he took out a peso and gave it to Dobbs.

Dobbs stood still for a moment, quite taken aback. Then he returned to his seat. He hadn't reckoned on anything at all, or only on ten centavos at most. He kept his fingers on the coin in his pocket. What should he do with it? A dinner and a supper, or two dinners, or ten packets of Artistas cigarettes, or five glasses of coffee and milk with a pan Frances, which is an ordinary roll?

After a short time he left his seat and followed the two or three streets that led to the Hotel Oso Negro.

The hotel was really only a Casa Huéspedes, a lodging-house. The front of it was occupied on one side by a shop selling shoes, shirts, soap and musical instruments, and on the other side by a shop selling wire mattresses, easy-chairs and photographic apparatus. Between these two shops was the wide entrance leading to the courtyard. In the courtyard were the mouldering wooden huts which formed the hotel. These huts were all divided into small, dark, windowless compartments, and in each of these cabins there were from four to eight bunks. Each bunk was provided with a dirty pillow and an old worn blanket. Light and air came in through the doors, which were always open. In spite of this the air in the rooms was always stale, for they were all on the ground level and the sun could penetrate only a short way into them. There was no current of air either, because the air in the courtyard was stagnant; and it was not improved by the latrines, which had no water system. Besides this, a wood fire burned night and day in the middle of the yard, and on it clothes were boiled in large jam tins. For the hotel also accommodated a laundry run by a Chinaman.

On the left of the entrance passage which led into the courtyard was a small room occupied by the porter. Leading out of it was another room with a grill which went up to the ceiling. The trunks, chests, packages and cardboard boxes which were left in charge of the hotel were stored here on shelves.

There were trunks belonging to people who had perhaps only slept there for a night, and many of the trunks and chests were thickly coated with dust. The money perhaps had only run to one night. The next night the man had slept out somewhere and the following nights too. Then one day he would come and take out a shirt or a pair of trousers or whatever it might be, lock the trunk and leave it in charge again. Later he might set off on a journey. As he had no money to pay for a ticket either by rail or ship, he had to go on foot; and so his trunk was no use to him. By this time he was in Brazil, perhaps, or had perished long since of thirst in a desert somewhere, or starved, or been killed on a forest track.

After a year, when the storage space became so congested that there was no room for the effects of new arrivals, the proprietor made a clearance. Sometimes there was a label on a chest or package, but often the owner of it forgot what name he had given and, having changed his name in the meantime, he could not recover his chest, because he was unable to recall the name he had used at the time. He might point out the article. The porter then asked the name, and when the name did not tally with the label which was stuck on to the chest with a pin, he refused to give it up to him.

Often too the label had fallen off. Sometimes the name was written in chalk and had got rubbed out. In other cases, the porter had been in a hurry and had forgotten to ask the name, and there was a cardboard box with nothing but the number of a bed written on it in blue chalk. Its owner, however, had never known the number of his bed, and if he had, he wasn't likely to have remembered it. A note of the date was never included.

It could never be ascertained, therefore, how long a chest or a trunk had lain in store. The length of time was judged by the thickness of the layer of dust which had collected on it. And according to its destiny the proprietor could say pretty accurately how long a trunk or a sugar-bag had been in his keeping. No charge was made. But when there was no more room, the articles which had the thickest coating of dust to show were thrown out. The proprietor looked through the contents and sorted them. They were mostly rags. It very seldom happened that anything of value was found; for no one who possessed anything of value put up at the Oso Negro, or he only stayed there a night. The proprietor gave these rags away to the more ragged of his patrons, who eagerly begged for them, or to any other tramps who passed by. No trousers are so ragged and no shirt so worn and no boots so trodden down that no one can be found who thinks them still good enough; for no one on earth is so poor that there is not another who can say he is poorer still.

Dobbs had no trunk to give in charge, nor even a cardboard box or paper bag. Even if he had owned anything of the kind, he would not have known what to put into it; for all he possessed was in his trouser pockets. It was months since he had had a coat.

He entered the porter's office. True, it had a counter in the wall which divided it from the passage, but no one, not even the porter himself, ever made use of it. On this counter, just in front of the sliding-window, stood a water-bottle and a small earthenware jug. This water-bottle was for the use of the whole hotel. If anyone was thirsty he had to come to this window shelf to drink. There was no water and no water-bottles in the sleeping compartments. Some of the more experienced lodgers, particularly those who were often thirsty during the night, took old Tequila bottles full of water to bed with them.

The porter was a young man, not yet twenty-five perhaps. He was small and thin and had a long sharp nose. His hours of duty were from five in the morning to six at night. At six the night porter took on; for the hotel was never shut, night or day. This was not on account of arrivals by train, as no trains came in after nightfall, unless they were late. It was because there were men sleeping in the hotel who were employed in restaurants or other trades where the working hours ended late at night, or sometimes in the early morning.

At all hours of night and day there was somebody stirring in the hotel. At any hour there was somebody who had to get up and go to work. Among those who slept there were private night-watchmen, bakers, paviours, newspaper sellers, bakers' roundsmen and many more for whose occupations there is no precise description. Many of them could have afforded to rent a room where they would have slept more comfortably and in cleaner surroundings and without the company of strangers, foreigners and tramps. But for the sake of being called and getting off punctually to work they preferred to sleep in the hotel, where they could rely on being called to the minute. Both porters were very efficient. Every day there were arrivals and departures. Every day there were changes. All nationalities were represented. White, yellow, black, brown and reddish-brown faces passed by the porter's window. But the porter on duty always knew whether they had paid or not. If he had any doubt he looked at once in his book and followed the man from the window which looked on to the courtyard, to see into which room he went.

There were a few smaller rooms available in which there was only one fairly wide bed with a mattress. The mattress was very hard, but the guests were not particular. These rooms were for two persons and each paid a peso. They were taken by those who were accompanied by a woman. For women and girls who came alone there were huts with a number of bunks at fifty centavos apiece. There were two doors to them, but they did not lock and hung so askew from the hinges that they would not even shut. The bunks, however, were furnished with mosquito-nets under which the girls could conceal themselves and undress. Indian girls and others of humble origin are astonishingly adroit at dressing and undressing under these nets and can pass the night under them as invisibly as though they were within the four walls of a house. The ones who stayed there were mostly kitchenmaids and scullerymaids from the restaurants.

A girl slept in this hotel, where not a door was ever locked or shut, much more safely than in many places which have the name of good family hotels, for the men were far too much occupied with their own concerns to take any notice of them; and the tramps and vagrants of the Oso Negro would have killed the man who dared to interfere with them.

There were clients of the hotel who had been there for two, three and even five years. As they always occupied the same bunks in the same corners, they were able to live here as cleanly as in a private house. Only, of course, their companions changed most nights. But sometimes there were enough of these permanent lodgers to fill a whole room. Their life there was much freer than in a private house. They could come in when they liked without putting a landlady into a temper, and they could go out when they liked without anybody bothering about them; and if they came home very drunk no one took the slightest notice of them.

The rooms had no cupboards. You hung your clothes on nails in the walls. Many of those who had been there some while and were in regular work kept their Sunday clothes in wooden boxes which they could padlock. Others made a curtain of sacking to protect their clothes from the dust. Others again laced them across and across with thick string so tightly that it would have been a difficult

13

matter to abstract a pair of trousers. It was very seldom that anything was stolen; if a man went past with anything under his arm he was scrutinized suspiciously by the porter, and if he was carrying another man's trousers, the porter would know it and not let him go far. And the porters were very well acquainted with the coats and trousers of the regular inmates.

The porter had very little room in his office, for it was crowded out with all manner of things – small packets and boxes and handbags for which it was hardly worth while opening the iron cage, as they were only handed in for a short time. It might be for half an hour or so, and generally they were called for within the time stated, but sometimes they were left for weeks and then forgotten. The owner left the town unexpectedly, perhaps as a seaman on a ship bound for the other side of the world. For if a ship just about to sail found itself shorthanded, the man had to go aboard in what he stood up in, or else lose the job.

This confined space also accommodated some high pigeon-holed shelves for towels, soap and loofahs, which were supplied to those who wanted baths. There were only shower-baths. The water was not heated and there was little of it.

Then there were pigeon-holes for letters and papers of all sorts, on which the dust accumulated.

Lastly, there was a safe. To this were consigned the articles of value handed in by the visitors to the hotel – money, watches, rings and valuable instruments. Among the latter were compasses, surveyor's instruments and others used by prospectors for gold, silver and minerals generally. For even owners of such instruments were often down and out and turned up here for a bed. Rifles, revolvers and fishing-tackle, too, were hung round the walls.

The thick hotel register occupied the only part of the table which was not littered up with papers, packets and boxes. Every visitor was entered in it, but only the surname, the number of his bunk and the sum paid. What his other names might be, or his nationality or calling, or why or whence he came, did not interest the proprietor at all. These particulars interested the police even less. They never so much as looked at the book. It was of interest at most to the revenue authorities when the proprietor desired to prove that his receipts were assessed at too high a figure. It is only when state-paid officials tumble over each other for something to do that the police find nothing too paltry for their notice and want to know, even to the colour of the one hair on a mole, who the arrival at an hotel is, where he has come from, what he is there for and where he intends going when he leaves. These officials would not know otherwise what to do with themselves, and the taxpayers would soon find out that they were superfluous.

Dobbs went in to the porter and, putting down his peso on the table said: 'Lobbs, for two nights.'

The porter turned the pages of the book until he found a vacant bunk, wrote down 'Jobbs' because he had not quite caught the name and was too polite to have it repeated, and then said: 'Room seven, bed two.'

'Good,' said Dobbs and went out. There was nothing now to prevent him lying down right away and sleeping for the rest of the afternoon and all night and all next day and the night after and on till the following midday, if he wanted to. But he was hungry and so had to go hunting or fishing.

But the fish were not biting. No one gave him anything. Then walking in front of him he saw a gentleman in a white coat. He overtook him and muttered a word or two, and the man gave him fifty centavos.

With these fifty centavos he went to a Chinaman's for dinner. It was long after midday, certainly. But there is always dinner going at a Chinaman's, and if it is too late to call it Comida Corrida, then the same meal is simply called Cena, and that turns it into supper, even though the Cathedral clock has not yet struck four.

Then Dobbs took his ease on a seat for a bit and finally thought of coffee. His stalking was fruitless until he saw a gentleman in a white coat. And this gentleman gave him fifty centavos. A silver piece.

'I'm in luck with gentlemen in white coats today,' thought Dobbs, and went to the round coffee kiosk on the side of the Plaza de la Libertad nearest to the customs and passenger quay.

He sat down on the high bar-stool and ordered a glass of coffee and two croissants. The glass was three parts filled with hot milk and then hot black coffee was added until it was full to the brim. Then the sugar-bowl was set before him and the two lovely brown croissants and a glass of ice water.

'Why have you robbers put another five centavos on the coffee?' asked Dobbs, while he stirred the mountain of sugar which he had shovelled into his glass.

'Costs have gone up,' said the waiter, busying himself with a toothpick. After which he leant indolently against the bar.

Dobbs asked the question merely for the sake of something to say. It mattered a lot, certainly, to a man like him, whether coffee cost fifteen or twenty centavos. But he wasn't going to excite himself over the raising of the price. If he could run to fifteen, he could run to twenty; and if he hadn't got twenty, he certainly wouldn't have fifteen. So really it all came to the same thing.

'I'm not buying any tickets, damn you. Leave me alone, can't you?' he shouted at the Indian youth who for the last five minutes had been fluttering the long, thin lottery tickets in front of his nose.

But the boy was not so easy to shake off.

'It's the Michoacan State lottery. Sixty thousand pesos first prize.'

'Get out, you thief. I'm buying no ticket.'

Dobbs dipped his roll in the coffee and pushed it into his mouth.

'The whole ticket's only ten pesos.'

'Curse you, do you think I've ten pesos?' Dobbs wanted to drink a mouthful of coffee, but the glass was too hot to hold.

'Then take a quarter. That's only two fifty.'

Dobbs had managed to get the glass to his mouth. But just as he was going to drink, he burnt his tongue and had to put it down again quickly, because it was getting too hot for his fingers too, after holding it so long.

'If you don't get out with your stolen tickets, you'll have this water in your face.'

Dobbs was in a temper by this time, not so much with the boy's importunate salesmanship as because he had burnt the tip of his tongue. He could not take vengeance on his tongue, nor on the coffee, which he took the greatest care not to spill. So he vented his rage on the boy.

This did not worry the boy at all. He was used to such outbursts. Also he was a good salesman and knew his man. A man who could drink coffee at that time of day and eat two fancy rolls with it was well able to buy a lottery ticket for the benefit of Michoacan State.

'Take a tenth then, señor. Only one peso.'

Dobbs took the glass of ice water and gave the boy a threatening look. The boy saw it, but did not budge from the spot.

Dobbs drank a mouthful of the water. The boy waved the tickets about in front of his nose. With one flick Dobbs threw the water in his face and the tickets were soaked.

The boy was not in the least put out. He only laughed as he shook the water from his tickets and his torn shirt. He took the shower-bath more as a friendly way of opening up a deal than as an expression of hostility and he had it firmly fixed in his small head that the man who could have a glass of coffee and milk and two rolls was bound to buy a lottery ticket as well, in order to win a prize and so find the means to repeat such extravagance.

The largest glass of coffee comes to an end in time. Dobbs drained his to the last drop, and when he had also picked up the last crumb of the rolls, he pulled out his fifty centavo piece. He got twenty back in small silver coin. The boy had only been waiting for this moment, apparently.

'Now señor, just buy a twentieth in the Monterrey lottery. Only twenty centavos. First prize twenty thousand pesos. Here you are. This is a lucky number.'

Dobbs weighed the silver piece in his hand. What should he do with it? Cigarettes? For the moment on the top of the coffee he had no desire for a cigarette. Money was thrown away on lottery tickets. All the same, once gone never missed, and for a day or two you could hope. It wasn't a matter of months. The draw was in a few days.

'Give me your ticket then, you son of a bitch – if it's only to see the last of you and your tickets.'

The little salesman tore the twentieth part of a ticket off the long slip without the loss of a moment. The paper was as thin as a gossamer – so thin that the print showed as clearly on the back as on the front.

'That's a very lucky number, señor.'

'Why don't you try it yourself, then?'

'I haven't the money for that, señor. Here it is. Many, many thanks, señor. Remember me next time.'

Dobbs put it in his pocket without looking at the number. Then he went off to have a bathe. It was a long way out of the town, beyond the cemetery, and then down the hill to the river. You had to jump ditches and pools and wade through morasses before you got there.

There were Indians by the dozen splashing in the water as well as white men of the same social level as Dobbs, men who lived on what others let fall. No one was in bathing drawers, but there was no one either who worried about that. Women and girls went past these bathing-places, and thought nothing of men bathing entirely naked. They saw nothing in it to offend or disgust them. Only the smart American and European women would have thought it beneath their dignity to walk past. They watched the bathers with good prismatic glasses from the balconies and windows of their houses high above. Ladies who lived on the other side of the Avenida Hidalgo, in the Colonia Guadalupe and in the other colonies, got themselves invited to tea by the ladies who lived here. Each one brought her prismatic glasses, so as to have a better view of the landscape from this commanding height. That is why the colony here had the name of Colonia Buena Vista.

The bathe was refreshing and Dobbs saved the five and twenty centavos he would have had to pay for a shower-bath in the hotel. But bathing here had its disadvantages too. There were the gigantic crabs which lay in wait in the mud. These crabs sometimes thought the toes of bathers were tasty morsels which they could not afford to despise, and it hurt like the devil when a fine full-grown crab got a proper hold on your toe and tried to make off with it.

The river was divided into many channels and the crab-fishers were dotted about on the different banks. It was a wearisome business, and only those whose patience was quite inexhaustible could do any good at it.

The crab-fishers were mostly Indians or the very poorest of half-breeds. The bait was decaying, stinking flesh. The more it stank, the better it was. A big bit of meat was put on the hook with a very long line, then the bait was thrown far out into the channel.

It was left lying there a good while. Then the fisherman began to draw it in slowly, very slowly, so slowly that the movement was scarcely perceptible. It took an eternity before the baited hook reached the bank again. Then the line was still drawn slowly up the flat slope of the muddy shore. A dozen times it might be all to no purpose. The hook had to be thrown out again, often with fresh bait, because the old one had been eaten off; and then once more with infinite patience it was drawn slowly in.

The crabs seized the lump of flesh in their claws and held on to it with such a fierce tenacity that they let themselves be drawn out of the water with it rather than release their grip. But if the pace were too fast the crab could not keep up, or else became suspicious and let go. Often it took such a firm hold of the bit of flesh that it severed it from the hook, and then the crab had won.

With patience a fisher could do a good day's business, for many of the crabs weighed half or three-quarters of a kilo, and the restaurants paid good prices, as crab is esteemed a great delicacy by the gourmet.

Dobbs watched the fishermen, but decided it was not a job for him. He had not got the patience for it. One little jerk and the booty was lost. It was a kind of fishing which required calmer nerves than Dobbs, who had been brought up in the racket of a large city in America, could command, even though he were offered five pesos for every crab he landed.

He strolled back to the town. The bathe and the walking to and fro had given him an appetite and now there was his supper to think of. Again for a long time he had no luck, and all he got in reply were insulting remarks which he had to put up with in silence. But a man gets callous when he's hungry and when his supper depends on a thick skin.

At last he saw a gentleman in a white coat. He thought to himself: 'I'm in luck today with gentlemen in white coats, I'll try it on again.' He guessed right – fifty centavos, and there was his supper at last.

Afterwards, while he took his well-earned repose on a seat, it came into his mind that it would be just as well to have something in his pocket, because you never know when you may need it. This thought did not come quite unprompted. It was the sight of a gentleman in a white coat going by on the other side of the Plaza. Dobbs went straight up to him.

Sure enough he put his hand into his pocket and brought out a fifty centavo piece. Dobbs held out his hand, but the man kept a tight hold on his coin.

'Now, listen to me, young man,' he said with annoyance. 'I have never in the whole course of my life come across impudence to equal this, and if anyone had told me such a thing could happen, I wouldn't have believed him.'

Dobbs stood there dazed. He too had never in the whole course of his life had such a lengthy speech made to him. He scarcely knew whether to stand his ground or to make off. But as the coin was still in the man's hand, he felt that sooner or later it was destined to come into his own and that the old boy was only enjoying the excuse for a sermon. I can very well, he thought to himself, listen to a sermon for the sake of fifty centavos, and that's all I have to do. And so he stayed where he was.

'This afternoon,' the man went on, 'you told me you'd had no dinner. Whereupon I gave you a peso. Then I came across you again and you say you had no money for a bed. Whereupon I gave you fifty centavos. Then you came along again and said you had had no supper, and again I gave you fifty centavos. Now just tell me what it is you want money for now?'

'For breakfast tomorrow,' Dobbs replied with presence of mind.

The man laughed and gave him the fifty. Then he said: 'This is the last time I'll give you anything. You can go to somebody else now for a change. It's beginning to get monotonous.'

'You must pardon me, sir,' said Dobbs, 'but I never knew you were the same person. I never looked at your face till this moment. I won't come to you again.'

'I'll give you another fifty to make sure you keep your word and don't plague me any more. That will give you a dinner tomorrow. After that you must support yourself without my assistance.'

'Then that well's pumped dry,' said Dobbs to himself; and he came to the conclusion that he had better leave the town and see what he could make of it farther afield.

2

That night a man in Dobbs's room said to another that he thought of going to Tuxpam, but he had no mate to go with. The words were scarcely out of his mouth before Dobbs said: 'I'll go with you to Tuxpam.'

'Are you a driller?'

'No, pumpman.'

'Right,' said the other, 'we can go along together if you like.'

Next morning they set off intending to scour the numerous oil-fields in the Tuxpam district in search of work. Before starting they had their glass of coffee and two rolls at a coffee stall.

It isn't so easy, though, to get to Tuxpam. There is no railway. You can only go by air. And that costs fifty pesos. But there are plenty of lorries going that way, and perhaps they might get a lift on one of them. As for doing it on foot – it is more than a hundred miles under a blazing tropical sun and very little shade all the way.

'First of all, we have to get across the river,' said Barber, 'and that's the least of our troubles.'

The ferry cost twenty-five centavos and they had no wish to spend this sum.

'There's only one thing to do,' said Barber, 'we must wait for the Huasteca freight ferry. They'll take us over for nothing. But one may not come until eleven o'clock. They go when they have a load, not by time-table.'

'Then we'll sit on the wall here and wait,' Dobbs replied.

He had bought himself a packet of fourteen cigarettes for ten centavos with the change he got when he paid for his breakfast, and they brought him luck. In the packet was a coupon for fifty centavos, which he cashed at once at the tobacconist's. So now he had, all told, one peso ten centavos.

Barber had about one fifty. They could have paid the fare, but as they had plenty of time and no occasion to hurry, they thought they might just as well wait for the freight boat and save the money.

It was a lively scene at the ferry. Motor-boats by the dozen, big and small, stood by for passengers. Special ones, for which a higher fare was charged, brought over the directors and managers of oil companies who were in too much of a hurry to wait until the ordinary boats collected the five or six passengers without whom they would not start. And as there were always people waiting, particularly work-people, who lived on this side and worked in their hundreds, and even thousands, on the other, the banks near the ferry, at certain hours of the morning and evening, were like a perpetual fair. There were stalls where you could get a meal, or coffee, or roasted bananas, or fruit, or cuchilladas, or hot tamales, or cigarettes, or sweets. All this trafficking owed its life to the ferry. Motor cars and trams were always discharging passengers for the ferry in a ceaseless stream. It went on all day and all night without stopping. There on the other side were the hands, here on this side the brain – the head offices and banks. On the other side it was labour, and here refreshment, rest and enjoyment. On the other side lay the wealth, the gold of the country – oil; but over there it was worthless. It was here on this side, in the town, in the tall blocks of offices, in the banks, at the board meetings, in the All American Cable Service that oil, which on the other side was quite valueless, acquired its value. For oil, like gold, is worthless in itself. Its value is only the result of a commercial process.

Dollars by the milliard were ferried across. Not in notes, not in coined gold, not even in cheques. These milliards went across as figures jotted down in little note-books, or sometimes merely on scraps of paper, by men who generally – but not always – took a special boat plying for hire at a fare above the prescribed tariff.

At half past ten the freight boat came over, loaded up with barrels, cases and sacks. A number of Indians, men and women, crossed in her, heavily laden with baskets, in which they had country produce for the town, mats, bast bags, poultry, fish, eggs, cheeses, flowers and kids.

21

Barber and Dobbs climbed in, but they had an hour to wait before the return journey was made. It was a long crossing, as the quay was a long way down stream. Up stream, one behind another, lay the tankers ready to take in the oil and carry it across the ocean.

On the far side the scene was just as lively, and the appearance of a fair in full swing quite as striking. Down stream too there were tankers, reaching almost to the river's mouth. Back from the river bank were the huge tanks filled to the brim with the precious oil. It was taken from the tanks to the river's edge by numerous pipes. From here it was pumped into the tanks of the ships through wire tubing. While the oil was being taken in, or when a ship was loaded with it, the red flag was flown as a danger signal. For the raw oil gives off a gas, and if there is any carelessness with a match or a naked flame the ship may burn out to the water-line.

Sellers of fruit, parrots, tiger cats, tiger and lion skins, monkeys, buffalo horns, and models of palaces and cathedrals formed of shells were here in crowds, offering their wares to the sailors. If they could not get money they would take clothing, waterproofs, leather trunks or anything else they valued in exchange.

The refineries discharged clouds of smoke and gas. The gas got into lungs and windpipes and stung like sharp needles. Then everybody coughed, and when the wind carried these fumes over the city the whole population felt it lived in a lethal chamber. Newcomers who were not used to it felt apprehensive and nervous. They clutched their throats all the time and tried to sneeze or snort it out, and wondered what was up. Many of them felt as though they would die of this smarting poison in the throat and lungs.

But those who knew it of old were glad to put up with it. So long as this acrid poison gas pervaded the town, gold ran through its streets and life was rosy. Look at it how you liked.

The saloons were on this side too, one touching another. They all lived on the ships' crews. The American seamen were their best customers, for in their own country they could get neither beer, wine nor brandy. They found here all they lacked at home, and they took in enough to keep them going for long enough in their own dry and stupid land. They were used to paying through the nose for bootleggers' brandy, and so here where prices were normal they felt that whisky and beer cost nothing at all and were simply being given away. One dollar went the way of the last in the canteens and bars. And not far off were the beautiful ladies who relieved them of what was left. But the sailors never thought they were being taken advantage of. They were happy, and if anyone had forbidden them their drink and their beautiful ladies they would have cursed him all sides up. They had the utmost contempt for the Mission to Seamen, which thought only of offering the sailor a clean bed and a comfortable room where he could read the newspapers. Anyone who wants to go to church can always find a church to go to, and there is no need to bring it to the sailor at his dinner time or to his bedside and sicken him here too of what little religion his schooldays have left him. Seamen and prisoners are always regarded as fair game by those who want to stuff in religion to the retching point. But overfeeding never comes to any good. And because it does no good and produces a result the opposite to what is hoped of it, the convict and the seaman only get more and more religion pumped into them. The convict in prison and the sailor on land, once all his money is spent, fall an easy prey to religious exploitation. They would both prefer a rousing film, but they cannot have that for nothing.

'It's just midday,' said Barber, 'we might board a tanker. Perhaps we might find dinner going.'

'Not a bad notion,' Dobbs agreed. 'We can only be fired out at worst.'

They saw two men with shirt sleeves rolled up standing at a fruit stall. Barber went straight up to them and asked: 'Which is your ship?'

'The *Norman Bridge*. Why?'

'Have you had dinner?' Barber asked.

'No, we're just going to have it now.'

'What about dinner for us two?' asked Barber.

'Come along. They're all across in the town. Tons of it.'

When Dobbs and Barber left the ship an hour later they were so full they could hardly walk. They leant against the side of a hut to give time for digestion. But they soon became restive, because they wanted to get on and make sure of shelter for the night.

'There are two roads we might go,' said Barber. 'We might take the big road here, keeping close to the lagoon. But I don't advise it. It's the road everybody travels on. There'll be nothing for us in the camps as they're all overrun with tramps; and we'll find no work either, because they get men in plenty.'

'Then what did we come across at all for if there's no point in it?' Dobbs asked in annoyance.

'No point? I didn't say that,' Barber said indignantly. 'I only say that on this road where all the traffic goes there isn't much doing because there are too many others already. In my opinion we'll do better on the inland road. We'll come on more oil-fields, which no one knows of and which lie off the beaten track. We'll hit on camps too which are just being started. There, there's always a job to be got. We'll follow the river up for a bit, then turn left, and half an hour'll bring us to Villa Cuauhtemoc.'

'Off we get then if you think that way's the best,' said Dobbs.

The whole way it was oil and nothing but oil. To the left on the high gradient the tanks were marshalled like soldiers formed up in line. The river was on the right. Soon there were no more ships and the river banks were vacant. But the water had a thick film of oil, the banks were covered with it and any object which the river or the incoming tide had thrown on to the banks was coated too with black glutinous oil. The road they walked on was turned to mud in many places where an abandoned pipe still exuded thick oil or where oil oozed from the ground. Oil and nothing but oil wherever you looked. The sky itself was shrouded in oil. Thick black clouds of smoke heavy with oil gases belched out from the refineries.

Then they came to higher ground which had a more pleasing aspect. Here were the wooden dwelling-houses of the engineers and clerks. They had good air and pleasant surroundings and made up for the lack of town life by gramophones and the radio. For it was difficult to get back from the town at night and not always very safe. The neighbourhood was infested by ruffians who were on the look-out for easy chances and thought little of doing a man in.

Villa Cuauhtemoc is the old town, a prehistoric Indian town, which was there before the Spaniards came. It has a healthier situation than the new town and it occupies the shores of a large lake which abounds in fish, duck and geese. The drinking-water is better there than in the new town. But the new town quickly left the old town far behind. For the new town is close to the sea at the mouth of a river which takes the largest ocean-going ships right up to the railway terminus, and they can anchor there as safely in the wildest hurricane as though they lay in an enclosed dock. In the new town the old town is scarcely ever mentioned. Thousands even tens of thousands, of the inhabitants of the new town have no idea that the real and original town lies across the river and only half an hour's journey inland. These two, mother and daughter, drift farther and farther apart. The new town, just a hundred years old, with its hundred thousand inhabitants and its chronic shortage of houses, is in Tamaulipas State, while the old one is in Vera Cruz. The old town becomes more and more provincial, the new one takes a more and more important place among the great cities of the world and its name is known to the ends of the earth.

The two were now in a hurry to get on and had reached the end of the town facing the lagoon where the road climbs up into the hills; and there they saw an Indian crouching by the roadside. He was wearing good trousers, a clean blue shirt, a tall conical straw hat and sandals. A large bast bag containing almost all he possessed was in front of him on the ground.

They paid no attention to him and went on without slackening their pace. After a time Dobbs looked round. 'What does he want, that Indian? He's following on behind us.'

Barber turned round. 'Looks like it. He's stopped now and he's pretending to look for something in the bush.'

On both sides of the road was thick impenetrable bush.

They went on, but when they turned round they saw the Indian following them. He seemed to be walking faster and catching up.

'Had he a revolver?' Barber asked.

'Not that I saw,' Dobbs said.

'I didn't see one either, but I wondered if you had seen anything of the sort perhaps. Doesn't seem to be a bandit, then.'

'We can't be too sure,' Dobbs said after looking round again, and seeing the Indian still on their tracks. 'He may be a spy of bandits who've told him to keep us in sight. When we camp for the night he'll fall on us or else the rest of the gang will come up.'

'Don't like the look of it,' Barber went on. 'We'd do well to go back. You never know what these fellows may be up to.'

'But what can they get from us?' Dobbs asked to reassure himself.

'Get?' Barber answered. 'But we don't carry a placard to say that we have only a peso apiece. And if we did they wouldn't believe it. They'd fall on us first, hoping to find we had bags full of it. Anyway, two pesos are a fortune to these fellows, not to mention boots, trousers, shirts and hats. All worth something.'

But they went on. Whenever they looked round the Indian was behind them, now only about fifteen paces away. When they stopped the Indian stopped. They began to feel nervous. The sweat broke out on them.

Dobbs breathed hard. 'If I had a revolver or a rifle,' he said at last, 'I'd shoot the fellow. Then we should be quit of him. I can't stand much more of this. How'd it be, Barber, if we caught him, tied him up to a tree and gave him one on the head. He wouldn't come after us any more then.'

'No,' Barber said. 'But perhaps he means no harm. I'd be glad to be rid of him, though.'

'I'll stand still and let him come up,' Dobbs said suddenly. 'I can't go on like this. It drives me crazy.'

They halted as if they wanted to knock something down from a tree – a fruit or a bird.

The Indian stood still too.

Dobbs now had an idea. He got more and more excited about this tree, as though there were something up there of uncommon interest. As might be expected, the Indian was taken in by the ruse. He came slowly nearer, step by step, with his eyes fixed on the tree. As soon as he was close up to them, Dobbs shouted out in great excitement: 'There it goes!' He caught hold of Barber and pointed to some creature which had apparently made off.

Then he turned abruptly to the Indian and asked him what he wanted. 'Why do you keep on following us?'

'I want to go there,' said the Indian, pointing in the direction in which Barber and Dobbs were going.

'Where?' Dobbs asked.

'There. Where you're going.'

'You don't know where we're going,' said Dobbs.

'Yes, I know all right,' the Indian replied quietly. 'You're going to the oil-fields. I want to go there too. I might find work.'

Barber and Dobbs were relieved. That was the truth, no doubt. The man was only after a job. He had not the look of a bandit either.

But to set their minds completely at rest, Dobbs asked: 'Why don't you go by yourself? Why do you run after us?'

'I've been sitting for three days from morning till night at the end of the town there, waiting for white men on their ways to the camps.'

'You know the way yourself though, surely?'

'That's true,' said the man, 'but I'm scared of tigers and lions. There are so many round here. That's why I can't go alone. They might eat me.'

'I don't see that we're any safer from tigers ourselves,' Dobbs said.

'Oh, yes,' replied the Indian. 'They don't like white men. They'd rather have Indians. But if I'm with you they won't come for me and won't eat me.'

Barber and Dobbs laughed over their fears now they knew that the Indian whom they had been afraid of was more afraid than they were themselves.

26

The Indian now kept pace with them. He spoke little and trotted along beside or behind them as the path allowed.

Just before sundown they came to an Indian village and counted on shelter for the night in one of the huts. The Indians are very hospitable, but in this case they were passed on from one man to the next always with the same excuse, that there was no room. There were only a few huts in the village, and when they came to the last one they met with the same refusal.

The man seemed troubled and upset and said: 'It will be better for you to go to the next village. It's a big one of more than thirty huts. There you'll find all you want.'

'How far is it?' Dobbs asked anxiously.

'How far? It is not far,' said the Indian, 'only two kilometres. You will be there long before tonight. The sun hasn't gone down yet.'

There was nothing for it but to go on to the next village. They walked the two kilometres, but they saw nothing of any village. They went on two more kilometres, and still there was no village in sight.

'That fellow was making fools of us,' Barber said angrily. 'I'd like to know why they wouldn't let us stop there instead of sending us out into the wilds.'

Dobbs, no less annoyed, said: 'I know something of Indians. And I should have known better. They never refuse anybody shelter. But they are afraid of us. That was the whole trouble. There are three of us and we might have made short work of the whole family in a hut during the night.'

'What bunk!' Barber replied. 'Why should we kill the poor devils? They have nothing, less even than we have, I dare say.'

'All the same, they were afraid. There's no other way of looking at it. They don't estimate wealth the way we do. It's a matter of a horse or a cow or two or a few goats. That's their wealth. We might have been bandits. How were they to know? And they fear bandits more than they fear the devil.'

Barber nodded and said: 'Maybe so. But what'll we do now? Here we are in the bush, and in ten minutes it'll be pitch dark.'

'All we can do now is to make a halt where we are.'

Dobbs saw no other way out of it. 'Surely there's a village not far off. The track is well trodden, and ox and horse dung about. But it may be an hour away, and we can't go on in the dark. We might get off the track and land in a marsh or a thicket and lose our-selves. And if we did come on the village they'd set the dogs on

27

us. It would only be looking for trouble for three men to arrive at a village at this time of night and ask for shelter.'

By the light of matches they examined the ground to find a suitable spot where they could lie down and sleep. But there was nothing but great cactuses and other varieties of prickly scrub. The ground itself was creeping with insects which would make rest or sleep unlikely. The Indian, too, had spoken of tigers and lions being common in the district. The Indian belonged to the district and must know what he was talking about.

They stood about for a time, and then when standing tired them they lay down after all. Dobbs lay next to Barber, but they had scarcely settled down before the Indian squeezed in between them like a dog, cautiously and slowly, but persistently. He did not feel safe until he lay between the white men; for the tiger would not go straight for the one in the middle. He would take one from the outside. And one would be enough for that night.

Dobbs and Barber, however, were not at all willing to make room for him. Their shouldering and elbowing must have bruised him all over. But he let himself be buffeted to and fro without protest. If they ejected him with their fists and feet, he only waited until he thought they had fallen asleep, and as soon as one or the other of them turned on his side, leaving the least space, he forced his way in again and kept on till he lay extended full length between them once more. At last they gave it up as useless.

Barber was awakened by some animal crawling over his face. He sat up and brushed it away, but while he sat listening to the singing and chirping in the darkness of the bush, he suddenly caught himself together in a spasm of fright.

He heard quite distinctly the cautious approach of a prowling beast. It was without doubt some large animal. When he heard it again and knew he was not deceived, he gave Dobbs a shake.

'What's up?' Dobbs asked sleepily.

'There's a tiger or lion on the prowl. Just behind us.'

'You must be dreaming,' Dobbs said, waking by degrees. 'It isn't likely that a tiger would venture to attack us.'

He listened. When he too heard the sound he sat up. 'I believe you're right. It's some large beast. A man wouldn't be creeping about here at night. He'd be more afraid than we are. It's an animal, and a big one judging from its tread.'

If the Indian had been awake all this time, he must have thought it safest to say nothing and lie quiet. But now he sat up with a jump and then sprang to his feet. Nothing could be seen of his face in the blackness of the night, but no doubt it was distorted by fear. From the sound of his voice the other two could imagine what his face must look like.

'It's a tiger close to us,' he said in a shaking voice. 'We're finished. He'll spring any moment. He's there in the undergrowth, waiting.'

Dobbs and Barber held their breath. The Indian knew the tread and smell of a tiger. He belonged to the country.

'What can we do?' Dobbs asked.

'We'd best shout and make all the noise we can,' Barber suggested.

'No good. Noise won't worry a tiger. It'll only aggravate him all the more.' They stood there breathless and listened. For a minute nothing was to be heard, and then two or three steps . . .

'I know,' Dobbs said softly. 'We'll climb up a tree. We'll be as safe there as anywhere.'

'Tigers can climb a tree too,' Barber said, also in a whisper. 'They're cats. They climb and jump like nothing on earth.'

'All the same, it'll be the safest place.' Dobbs stuck to his plan.

He felt his way and after a step or two came to a mahogany tree. Without thinking twice about it he started to climb.

When the Indian realized what was going on, he was up the tree after Dobbs in a flash, if only not to be the last and lowest. But he took his bag with him.

Barber did not wish to be left all by himself down below, and so finally he climbed up after the other two.

When they had settled themselves as comfortable as they could in the darkness, they breathed again and took a calmer view of the situation. They felt safer up there than on the ground. Barber was quite right when he said: 'Down on the ground the tiger could drag you away. Here you can hold on.'

'Hold on, yes,' said Dobbs. 'But he can take an arm or a leg away with him.'

'Better than if he took all the lot,' said Barber.

Gradually weariness got the better of fright. The Indian was again in the middle, with Barber below and Dobbs above. He felt doubly secure. They had all strapped themselves to branches with their leather belts in case they fell off in their sleep.

The night was long in spite of oppressive dreams and half-waking visions. At last the day dawned.

In the light of the sun everything looked perfectly normal and nothing remained of the night's horror and dread imaginings. Even the surface of the ground looked much more inviting than it had seemed at night. Only thirty yards away there was a clearing and the grass there looked very reassuring through the trees.

They climbed down and each had a cigarette by way of breakfast. The Indian brought out a few dried tortillas and gave one to each of the other two.

While they sat there smoking and munching in silence, again they heard the tiger's tread. All three jumped. They knew its tread as well as if it had been the step of their nearest and dearest. If ten years had elapsed they would have known it every bit as well; for it had eaten into the very fibre of their beings, and could never be dislodged.

A tiger in full daylight? Why not? But so close to three human beings? That seemed very improbable.

Dobbs turned in the direction from which the sounds came the night before and came now too. He peered through the trees at the clearing, and there was no tiger.

They could all see it distinctly now. It was grazing, tethered by a long rope to the stump of a tree in case it ran away. It was an amiable tiger, who was glad to be left to graze in peace. It was a donkey.

The Indian said nothing. He knew a tiger, and he knew that it was a tiger he had heard in the night.

Dobbs and Barber looked at each other. They said not a word, but they went red in the face. Then they laughed till they cried.

At last Dobbs said: 'Don't you ever tell this to a soul, or we'll never dare to show our faces anywhere again.'

3

The village, of which the Indians had told them the evening before, was not twenty minutes away. The discovery of a tethered donkey was already an indication that a village was not far off. But it is not always a certain indication, for it may easily be a donkey belonging to a woodcutter or a charcoal-burner.

In the village they were given something to eat, beans, tortillas and tea made out of citron leaves. Late in the afternoon they came to the first camp. Dobbs went straight to the foreman, but there were no jobs going.

'Do you want anything to eat?' asked the foreman.

'Yes,' said Dobbs. 'And we should be glad to spend the night here too, if we can.'

'We'll find room for you,' said the foreman, and went back into his hut after showing them the kitchen with a jerk of the head.

The Indian stuck closely to them. He might have been spliced to them. So when they went across to the kitchen, the Chinaman who ran it gave them a look and then decided that they would have to have their meal in the kitchen. It was on the Indian's account. Had Barber and Dobbs been alone they would have had their food in the white men's canteen. But, with the Indian, that was impossible, because the Indians had their own kitchen quarters.

'We must give him the shove,' said Dobbs, while he chewed. 'We can't take him round all the camps with us. It's got to stop.'

'We'll send him home first thing tomorrow morning,' replied Barber, who did not want to spoil his appetite by a more immediate solution of the problem.

Later Barber and Dobbs had a talk with the workmen, to hear what was going on here or in camps near by.

'Nothing doing,' said a tall Swede. 'All dud wells. Four have salt water, two sand and eight nothing but clay. They're all closing down. You needn't go any farther. New borings farther south. But you can't get there from here. You'll have to go by Panuco, or else by Ebano, if you want to reach that district.'

They dossed down in a store shed on old sacks, where they were safe from donkeys, and made up for the sleep of which the tiger had deprived them the night before.

In the morning they were given a light breakfast and then they set off again.

'Now then,' said Dobbs, when they were barely an hour from the camp, 'before we get to these other two camps, where there may be a job for us or at least our grub, we've got to settle this Indian.'

'Listen to me,' Dobbs went on, addressing the Indian, 'we're going on alone now. We've no use for you.'

The Indian looked up in alarm and said: 'But the tigers, Señor!'

'You must settle with tigers on your own,' Barber interposed.

'We want to be quit of you.'

'That's the fact,' said Dobbs, 'and if you don't go peaceably, then you'll get it in the neck.'

The Indian stood there, irresolute. It did not enter his head to plead or expostulate. They had told him to leave them and with that he had to be content. There was nothing to show whether he understood that he was a nuisance to them, and that they had a perfect right to choose their company for themselves. He quietly stood there and said nothing.

Dobbs and Barber went on. But the Indian still followed behind like a dog which, though it has been driven away, refuses to be parted from its master. It was not from devotion or loyalty or any such feelings. He knew that the two were bound for the oil-fields; he knew that they would always contrive to get something to eat; and he knew that as long as he hung on to them he could never starve. If he went alone he would not get even a crust in any of the camps, not even from his fellow Indians, many of whom he was sure to find working there. The fear of tigers, too, was genuine. At any cost he had to get to the camps in order to look for work; but he was afraid to go alone or in the company of other Indians. He knew the terrors of the bush and jungle better than the white men did.

After they had proceeded for half an hour, Barber turned round. 'There's that brown devil slinking along behind us still,' he said.

Dobbs picked up some stones and began to bombard the Indian with them. But he dodged them, and after that kept farther behind so as to be out of range whenever Dobbs or Barber picked up a stone and hoped to fire it off at him unawares.

'We shall never be quit of him,' said Barber. 'I don't know what else we can do.'

'Kill him like vermin,' Dobbs said in a rage, picking up another stone.

Sure enough, when they came to the next camp the Indian trotted into the cook-house with them and got his grub too. The foreman made a face when he saw the two coming along with the Indian at their heels.

Dobbs and Barber told him that the Indian followed them wherever they went, but he only shrugged his shoulders. He did not know what to make of two white men who went from camp to camp with an Indian.

Now was their chance to get hold of him and give him a good thrashing. But it wouldn't have answered, for the foreman would have thrown all three out on the spot if they came to blows; and

Dobbs and Barber had no desire at all to spend the night in the open.

It was the same thing next day. The Indian jogged along happily behind them, always keeping out of range; and it was useless to say anything, because he gave no sign of understanding what they said. He merely stuck to them.

So at last they made up their minds to take the shortest way back to the town. There did not seem to be much prospect of finding work in any of the camps round about, and there was no other way of getting rid of the Indian.

Towards evening they reached Villa Cuauhtemoc where they had come on the Indian on the road that led to the oil-fields. He showed no surprise that the trip was so soon at an end. He squatted down again where they had found him three days before, and waited there for new victims on their way to the camps.

That night Dobbs and Barber reached the river bank. It was too late to cross. They slept by the riverside under the shelter of a large tree, where they came on three more who had picked up a living there for the past four weeks, sleeping under the tree in the open and cadging their meals from the tankers. They had had lean days and days of plenty. There were days when not a ship would give them a bite of bread, and there were days when there were three or four they could go to for dinner and supper. It was a toss-up.

Next morning, the two of them crossed to the town by the ferry. Nothing had changed there during their brief absence. At the bank, in front of the Imperial and the restaurants which the oil magnates patronized, there were just the same people coming and going and firing off the same wisecracks as they had two and three and six weeks before.

Barber went his own way again and Dobbs had gained nothing in the interval except the knowledge that work was as hard to find in the oil-fields as in the city. That was something. He did not need to reproach himself with having left a stone unturned in his search for it. He could not do more than he had done. But in the oil-fields there were no more jobs going than there were here.

But one morning a job turned up. Loading machine parts. It was hard work and he earned only three pesos a day, which left him nothing over. And after five days the job came to an end. Then one day he was standing near the ferry which crosses to the railway station for the Panuco line, when up came five men who were apparently in a great hurry.

One of them, a thick-set, weather-beaten fellow, saw Dobbs

standing there. He stopped and after a word to the others called out to Dobbs: 'Say – do you want a job?'

'Yes,' Dobbs shouted back and came a step nearer.

'Come here – sharp! I can give you a job if you're not afraid of work.'

Dobbs had now come up to him.

'I've got a contract to rig up a camp. I'm a man short. Got fever or malaria or something, and I can't wait for him. So you can have his job.'

'Right,' said Dobbs. 'I'll come. What's the pay?'

'Eight dollars a day, keep deducted; that'll come to one-eighty or two dollars. Can't say for sure yet. Six dollars clear anyway. Well, what do you say?'

'I'll come.'

Dobbs, who ten minutes before would have given his eyes for a job worth two dollars a day, now spoke as though he did the contractor a favour.

'But you've got to come right now,' the contractor said sharply. 'Just as you stand. There's no time to go after your kit. The Panuco train starts in a quarter of an hour and we're not across the river yet. So pick 'em up, my lad, and come along.'

He gripped Dobbs by the arm and pulled him towards the ferry.

4

Pat McCormick, the contractor, was an Irish-American, and no longer a young man. He had spent most of his life among the oil-fields of Texas and Mexico. He had worked as driller, tool-dresser, truck-driver, teamster, timekeeper, bodegaman, pump-man and in every other capacity the oil-fields had to offer. Of late years he had worked on his own, rigging up camps as a contractor. He made a tender after a careful inspection of the site where the camp was to be erected; and it needed a man of his long experience to make a proper inspection of the ground. You had to reckon the distance from the nearest railway station, the distance from a road on which lorries could be driven and also whether the site was bush or jungle or prairie. Then there was the question of water and a supply of cheap native labour. Everything had to be taken into account before the price was fixed. If it was too high, the contract probably went to another man; if it was too low, the contractor lost money by cutting things too fine. But the American companies are not niggardly; if it could be shown that circumstances had been overlooked, or had arisen since, which justified an addition to the estimate, they were willing to pay it.

From Panuco they went on south by lorries loaded up with material, until the road, which was already bad enough, came to an end. From here a track had been cut through the bush for another three miles. This track was just wide enough for the pack-mules of the Indians employed on the job. The track ended in a clearing with a diameter of about a hundred metres, which had been cut in the bush. This was the site on which the camp was to be erected, for the company's mineralogists had come to the conclusion that oil was in all probability to be found there.

Twenty Indians from villages a few miles away had already cleared the site and were now employed in widening the track to the road, so that lorries could come along it.

For the first few days the six men slept in a tent. Two Chinamen cooked their meals.

Timbering and planks, tools, nails and screw-bolts had already been brought along on mules and donkeys, and every two hours a fresh caravan arrived. The caravan drivers also worked by contract. They got paid so much a load, not by time. If they had been paid by time, they would have lain down for a sleep on the way. The clearing of the bush was also done by contract. The men earned good money, much better than if they had been paid by the day. And now the first job was to erect a hut for the accommodation of the white workmen. Then came the kitchen and canteen. That was all completed in two days.

One of the workmen was now put in charge of the whole gang of Indians and set to work erecting the rest of the huts, while the remaining five constructed the derrick under Pat's orders.

That was a hell of a job. Dobbs had never before taken a hand in erecting a derrick. He had to carry timbers weighing a hundred-weight on his shoulders while the sun beat down without mercy. After three days his shoulders were raw. The skin, grazed by the timber and burnt by the sun, hung in strips about his neck.

When the timbering had been carried, there were the holes for the screw-bolts to be drilled. And all at top speed. There was scarcely time to eat, as not a moment of daylight could be wasted. From the first gleam of the sun to the last glow of red in the sky they hauled and toiled like slaves. Even after sundown the work went on by lanterns if there was anything that could be done by artificial light. There was no electric light till much later when all the machinery was installed.

The more experienced men put the timbering in position, riveted it with bolts and fixed the struts, and as the framework rose higher and higher the work went on at a dizzier and more dangerous height. The derrick builders gripped a strut with their knees, while with hands and arms they hoisted another of the massive balks, supporting it with their thighs, until hanging by their knees at this dizzy height, they directed the swaying bulk to the required position and there had to hold it fast while the bolt was pushed in and screwed tight. They had to be as nimble as monkeys, or they would have fallen headlong and broken their necks, or their arms and legs.

At last the derrick, the boring tower, was built and could be equipped. The heavy iron rollers, over which ran the stout wire cable that raised and lowered the chisel and scoop, were hoisted by a windlass and fixed in position.

The most arduous labours were now completed. Next came the machine-house, then the tool and store sheds.

Meanwhile, the road had been cleared and the first lorry came through on a straight run from the railway.

There was a small stream three miles away in the bush. Pipes were laid to it and a shed erected on the bank to accommodate a motor pump. Up to then, water for the camp had been carried in tins by donkeys. Now it was pumped and stored in tanks.

Next, the steam engine arrived, loaded on a powerful tractor. The following day, the tractor, with a commotion which could be heard for miles across the bush, fetched the boiler.

The next day, again, the great wooden driving-wheels were hauled along. They were like the wheels of a water-mill, and the cables and chains for the chisel, scoop and pipe were coiled on them. And the dynamo came, the wires were connected, and one evening there was an island of brilliant illumination which turned night into day, where only a few weeks before the bush had lain undisturbed in its tropical isolation since the creation of the world. The quiet of night was destroyed and all life in the bush within the radius of the perpetual illumination began to sicken. In the morning million upon millions of insects were piled up in heaps beneath the electric globes.

The rattle of machinery, which now never ceased day or night, drove the occupants of the bush from their homes, and they had to invade new territory in search of food and rest.

After this the real work of oil-getting began. The work of the camp riggers was done. They went back to the city and waited for a new contract, which might turn up in three days, or in six weeks; or again, they might still be waiting for it when six months had gone by. Oil is a gamble. Ten, twenty, or fifty thousand may be sunk in an oil-field, and then, when the boring has been taken to the utmost practicable depths, there is no oil – nothing but salt water, or sand or clay. The bush is restored to its rightful owners, who resume possession so swiftly and thoroughly that within a year every trace of human occupation has been swept away.

Oil is a gamble. You can lose a fortune or make five million dollars with five thousand. Hence all who have to do with oil are rich today and poor tomorrow. For weeks and months they labour in the heart of the bush or the jungle. And then they squander in three days in the town all that their hard work has earned them. The prudent and saving who do not squander it lose it just as surely. They wait and wait for work until their last peso has gone; then they beg from the people who go in and out of the Imperial, the Southern, and the banks. In the oil countries it is just as much a matter of luck to find work as to strike oil.

So it was with Dobbs. There he stood with no thought of a job. And then a job dropped from the sky.

'What about my money?' Dobbs asked the contractor.

'What's up with you?' said Pat. 'Don't be in such a hurry. You'll get your money. I shan't run away with it.'

'Well, give me some of it, anyway,' Dobbs asked.

'Right you are,' Pat replied, 'you can have thirty per cent.'

'And the rest?' asked Dobbs.

'Can't say. I haven't been paid myself yet.'

Dobbs got thirty per cent of his earnings. The others had not been paid up either. Those who pressed hard enough got forty or fifty per cent. Two others who wanted to stand well with Pat, so as to be taken on for the next contract, got only five per cent, and that only when they told him very humbly that they had not had a meal that night and could not pay for a bed.

'I'd just like to know whether the stiff has had his money or not,' Dobbs said to Curtin, who had worked on the contract too.

'Yes, if we knew that,' Curtin replied. 'The companies are often slow in paying because they're short of the ready and when the boring starts it eats money.'

For a week neither Curtin nor Dobbs could run McCormick to earth. He was not in his hotel. But one day they saw him on the other side of the street.

'On to him,' Curtin called out to Dobbs, and shot across the street. Dobbs was after him like a streak.

Curtin caught Pat by the sleeve of his shirt. He had no coat on.

'Where's our money, you swine? If you don't pay up we'll smash your face in. See?' Curtin took care to speak loud and flourished his fists.

'On the nail and no more of your put-offs,' Dobbs shouted. 'It's three weeks we've waited for our money.'

'Don't make such a damned noise about it,' said Pat in a low voice, and taking them into a bar, he ordered three large glasses of Habanero without delay. 'We can settle up quietly. Listen to me, I've another contract next week, and another after that's done; one in Amatlan, the other in Corcovado. I'll take you both on. You're good workers and I'd be glad to have you. Here's to it!'

He raised his glass and they all drank. Then Curtin said: 'It's all very well taking us on for your new contracts. But we don't work for nothing. Where is our money?'

'I haven't had it myself yet. I'm still waiting for the cheque.' He turned to the barman as he spoke and ordered three more large Habaneros.

'Look here,' Curtin said impatiently, 'you're not going to get away with it like this and put us off with a drink or two.'

'Put you off?' Pat said in astonishment. 'I put you off with drinks? That's not very . . . '

'What it is doesn't matter,' said Dobbs. 'We want our money. We've worked hard enough for it. What's the good of being taken on again for your next contracts if you don't pay?'

'Damn you, where's our money?' Curtin suddenly bawled out as if he had lost his senses. Perhaps the spirits had had an effect just the opposite to what Pat had expected.

'I haven't had my money myself yet, I tell you.'

Curtin took him by the throat and shook him. 'Pay up, you thief, or I'll smash your skull on the bar counter.'

'Quietly, gentlemen, quietly,' the barman put in, but took no further notice of the proceedings. He wiped away the rings left by the glasses and then lit a cigarette.

Pat was a hefty fellow, and he defended himself. But Curtin had the advantage of rage. Dobbs came nearer and made as though to join in.

But now Pat got loose from the grip on his throat and, stepping back, said mulishly: 'You're nothing but a couple of bandits, and I ought to have known it before. But I'll see myself cut to pieces before I take on such a pair of scoundrels in future. Take your money and don't let me see you again.'

'We don't want your permission for that,' said Curtin.

Pat pulled out a handful of crumpled dollar bills from his trouser pocket.

'Here's your money,' he said to Dobbs. In a moment he had counted out the correct sum. He knew in his head to a cent what he owed each of them. He pushed the money over to Dobbs, and then, dealing out the bills with one hand, he counted Curtin's and shoved the heap towards him.

'There,' he said in the tone one uses in getting rid of importunate beggars for charity. 'Now be so good as to leave me alone. You have your money and I shall be very careful in future not to take on any more odd-job fellows who know nothing.'

He threw down three pesos for the drinks. Then he shoved his hat on to the back of his head and went out, ignoring them as though they had deeply insulted him.

5

'What do you stop at the Cleveland for?' Dobbs asked Curtin when they were in the street again and mooching past the Southern Hotel. 'You pay three pesos the night there, at least.'

'Four,' Curtin replied.

'Come along with me to the Oso Negro. Fifty centavos,' Dobbs advised him.

'It's too dirty there for me, and nothing but beachcombers and such guys,' said Curtin.

'As you please. When your money's gone you'll land up at the

Oso Negro like the rest of us. I don't need to go there myself either, but I want to make what I've got go as far as I can. Who knows when we'll touch any more. I'm going to eat at a Chink's, too, as per usual.'

They had got to the corner of the Plaza, where there was the big jewellery store, La Perla. They stopped and looked at the display in the window. It was a blaze of gold and diamonds. There was a diadem that cost eighteen thousand pesos. They said nothing, but, as they looked at the treasure collected there and thought of its value, they thought too of the money some people in the town must have to be able to buy such things.

Perhaps it was the sight of all this that finally turned their thoughts from oil. For to live here was to think of oil and nothing but oil. There was not a way of gaining a living which was not oil, directly or indirectly. Labour or speculation, all was oil. They leant against the big plate-glass windows and looked indolently across the Plaza, beyond which the masts of the shipping could be seen. That took their thoughts to voyages and reminded them that there were other lands than this and other resources than those which this city offered.

'What's your notion now, Curtin?' asked Dobbs after a while. 'It's a poor look-out to stand about and wait for something to turn up. You can wait and go on waiting, while your money runs out. Then it's the old story again – begging from fellows who have come in from the camps for a day or a night. I've a damned good mind to try something different. Now's the time while we have the dough. Once it's gone, you're planted.'

'It's not the first time I've thought the same thing,' Curtin answered. 'I know all about that. But I'm damned if I know what to do – unless it's gold-digging.'

'That's the very ticket,' Dobbs agreed. 'I was just thinking of it. Come to look at it, it's no more of a speculation than waiting for a job in the oil-fields. There's no country on earth with so much gold and so much silver waiting to be scratched up as this country here.'

'Let's go over and sit on that seat,'Curtin said.

'I don't mind telling you,' Curtin began when they had sat down, 'that I didn't come down here for oil, but for gold. I only meant to work in the oil district till I had the money to go after gold. It costs a bit. There's the journey, and the shovels and picks and washing-pans and the rest of the outfit. Then you've got to live for six or eight months before you make anything. Then when all's said and done, it may be that you've lost everything, your money and your labour, because you find nothing.'

Dobbs waited for Curtin to go on, but Curtin said no more. Apparently he had no more to say. So Dobbs spoke up.

'It isn't the risk. There's just as much risk in hanging round for work. With luck you may earn three hundred dollars a month, perhaps more, for six or eight or eighteen months together. If you don't have luck you don't get work, and then you've lost everything just the same. We all know that gold's not lying about in heaps to shovel into a sack. I know that. But if it isn't gold, it may be silver; and if it isn't silver, it may be copper or lead or precious stones. If you can't work it yourself, there's always a company that'll buy you out, or take you into partnership on good terms. Anyway, it's worth thinking over.'

They went on to talk of something else. It is not a very serious matter, here, to talk of going to look for gold. Everybody speaks of it, everybody plans it, and of ten thousand there's only one who goes and does it, for it isn't quite such a simple matter as going out to shoot rabbits. There's not a man here who hasn't once at least made up his mind to go and look for gold; and of all the hundreds of mines worked for other metals there is not one which was not found and started by men who were on the search for gold and took what came. Many a mine which produces neither gold nor silver yields its owner greater riches than an ordinary gold-mine could. With the extension of electricity the value of copper increases. The time may come when gold will be quite superfluous; one can scarcely venture to say the same of copper, lead and several other metals.

No man has ever originated an idea. Any new idea is the crystallization of the ideas of thousands of other men. Then one man suddenly hits on the right word and the right expression for the new idea. And as soon as the word is there, hundreds of people realize that they had this idea long before.

When an enterprise takes definite shape in a man's mind, one can safely say that numbers of men all round him cherish the same or a similar plan. That is why movements catch on and spread like wildfire.

Something of the sort was occurring here.

Curtin determined to stay one more night at the Cleveland and moved into the Oso Negro the day after. When Dobbs turned in, there were three Americans in his room besides himself. The other bunks were not occupied, apparently. One of the newcomers was an elderly man whose hair was turning grey.

When Dobbs came in the three men stopped talking. But after a while they went on. The old man was in bed, one of the others was lying down in his clothes and the third was sitting on the edge of his bunk. Dobbs began to undress.

At first he did not gather what they were talking about. But soon he found that the old man was telling the younger ones about his experiences as a gold-digger. These two had come to search for gold; for in the States they had been told marvellous tales of the abundance of gold in this country.

'Gold is the devil,' said Howard, the old man. 'It alters your character. However much you find, even if it's more than you can shift, still you think of getting more. And for the sake of getting more you forget the difference between right and wrong. When you set out you make up your mind to be content with thirty thousand dollars. When you find nothing, you put it down to twenty thousand, then to ten thousand, and lastly you declare that five thousand would be quite enough if only you could find them, no matter how you have to labour. But the moment you come on gold, you are not to be contented even with the thirty thousand you originally hoped for, your expectations mount higher and higher and you want fifty, a hundred, two hundred thousand dollars. That's how you get entangled, and driven this way and that, and lose your peace of mind for good.'

'That's not my game,' said one of the other two. 'I can take my oath for that. Ten thousand and then I'm finished. Finished even though another million lay there to be picked up. That's the exact sum I need.'

'Nobody believes it till he's been out himself,' Howard replied in his leisurely way. 'It's easy to get away from a gambling table, but no man has ever got away from a heap of gold which was his for the taking. I've dug for gold in Alaska and found it, I've dug in British Columbia, in Australia, in Montana, in Colorado. And made my pile, too. Well, here I am in the Oso Negro and through with it. I've lost my last fifty thousand in oil. Now I have to beg from old friends in the street. Perhaps I'll go out and have another try, old as I am. But I haven't the money. Then there's always this to consider: if you go alone it's the best, but you must be able to stand the solitude. If you go two or three together, there's always murder at your elbow. If it's a dozen of you, then each man's share is diminished, and you have quarrelling and murdering without any disguise. As long as you find nothing, you're all brothers. But as soon as the little heaps of dust get bigger and bigger, the brothers turn cut-throats.'

In this way the old man got going on those tales about gold which are listened to more eagerly by those who drift in and out of such places as the Oso Negro than the most bawdy love stories. When an old gold-digger like this began on his stories he might keep it up all night. Not a man would sleep a wink and not a man call out: 'Give us a chance to get to sleep.' In any case, whether the tales were of gold or robbery or love, such a request would be in vain. A man might express his desire to sleep. But if he expressed it too often or too emphatically there was trouble, because the story-tellers maintained they had as good a right to be there as those who were there to sleep. A man has the right to spend the night telling stories if he chooses. If you don't like it you have the right to go and find a quieter place. No one should travel at all or put up in hotels who can't sleep in peace amid the thunder of guns, the rattle of wheels, the chumping of motor engines, and the coming and going and laughing and singing and chaffing and quarrelling of his fellow men.

'Have you ever heard the story of the Green Water Mine in New Mexico?' asked Howard. 'You can't have. But I knew Harry Tilton who was there, and I had it from him. A band of fifteen men went off to find gold. They didn't go quite in the dark. There was an old tradition that in a certain valley there was a prolific gold-mine which the Mexicans had found and worked and which later on the Spaniards took from them after the Indians had been forced by merciless tortures – tongues pulled out, skulls gimleted and other such Christian attentions – to betray its whereabouts.

'Close to the mine in a hollow among the mountains there was a small lake, and the waters of it were as green as an emerald. That's why the mine was called the Green Water Mine. La Mina del Agua Verde. It was an uncommonly rich mine. The gold was in thick veins, you had nothing to do but extract it.

'The Indians, however, had laid a curse on the mine, so the Spaniards said, because every Spaniard who had anything to do with it came to grief. Some by snake-bite, others by fever, others again through terrible skin diseases and other diseases of which the cause could never be discovered. And one day the mine was lost. Not a man could be found who had ever been there.

'When the consignments of gold ceased and no report either came through, the Spaniards sent an expedition. The position of the mine was accurately marked on maps and the way to it was easy to follow, and yet the mine was not to be found. And there was no difficulty in locating it. There were three sharp rocky peaks, and when you had them in a line with each other you were on the right track, and when a fourth peak, of a shape you couldn't mistake, came into view and stood at a particular angle to the line of march, then you were so close to the mine that you could not miss it. But though the search went on for months, neither the mine nor the mountain tarn was ever found. That was in 1762.

'This prolific mine has never been forgotten by anyone interested in gold-mining.

'When New Mexico was annexed by the Americans, there was a new rush to find it. Many never returned. And those who did were half crazed by the vain search and the delusions that came on them while they hunted around among the rocks in that valley.

'It was in the 'eighties, 1886, I believe, when some more went to look – these same fifteen men I am speaking about. They had transcripts from the old reports and copies of the old Spanish maps. There was no trouble with the four hilltops. But however they took their bearings by them, there was nothing to be seen of the mine. They dug and blasted here and there and not a trace could they find. They worked in gangs, three men to each, so as to quarter the whole territory. Their victuals began to run short, but they would not give up.

'One evening one of the parties of three was preparing a meal. The fire burnt up, but the coffee didn't boil, because the wind was strong and cooled the can. So one of them started to scoop a deeper hollow for the fire. And as he dug and got down a foot or a foot and a half he came on a bone. He threw it aside without looking at it and then pushed the fire down into the hole after he had made flues to give it air.

'While they sat eating their food, one of them took up the bone without thinking and drew a figure with it in the earth. The man nearest him said: "Let me have a look at that bone." After a look he said: "It's the bone of a man's arm. How did it get here?"

'The one who had dug the hole now said that he had come on it while digging and thrown it out.

' "Then there must be a whole skeleton here. Why should there be just an arm bone?" the other said.

'It was now dark and they wrapped themselves in their blankets and lay down to sleep.

'Next morning, the man who had found the arm bone, whom I'll call Bill, because I don't know his name, Bill, then, said:

' "Where that arm bone came from there must be a skeleton. Now I had an idea in the night. I asked myself, how came this skeleton to be here?'

' "That's easy," said one of the other two. "Someone killed or died of hunger."

' "That's possible, of course," Bill said. "There have been plenty of guys about here. But I don't believe they were killed or died of hunger just here. It's occurred to me that the mine was buried by a sandstorm or an earthquake or a landslip or something of the kind, and that explains why not a Spaniard ever came back. They were all buried close to the mine. It's true this bone may just as well belong to someone who was searching before us and lost his life here, but it's just as likely it belongs to one of the buried Spaniards. And if his arm is here so is his skeleton. And if we dig down to the skeleton we'll perhaps come on the mine. What I say is, let's dig a bit here where the fire was."

'They dug and, sure enough, they found the skeleton, bone by bone. They dug in a circle round about and found another, and further on a third. And so they got the direction which the landslide or the earthquake had taken. They followed it and came on tools and at last on nuggets of gold which had clearly been scattered abroad.

' "We've got the mine all right. And what now?" asked Bill.

' "Let's call the others," said one.

' "I never credited you with a lot of sense," said the third, "but I didn't know you were quite such a dam' fool. We'll hold our tongues and go back with the rest in a few days. Then in a few weeks we'll come back, us three by ourselves, and open the mine up."

'They all three agreed to this. They collected the few nuggets and pocketed them. With the proceeds they would be able to fit themselves out well for the job. Then they shovelled all the earth carefully back. But before they had done, one of the other gangs came up. They looked suspiciously at the signs of digging and then one of them said: "Hey, you guys, what's the game here? You want to keep us out of it, do you?"

'The first three stoutly denied having found anything and having meant to play a dirty trick. There was a quarrel, and as though the very air had betrayed them, two of the other gangs came up in the midst of the argument. They were just in time, for the first two gangs were on the point of coming to terms and agreeing to shut out the other three.

'Now, of course, the second gang drew back and accused the first of its treachery. A man was sent to summon the remaining one and when it arrived a council was held. It was resolved to hang the three members of the first gang for having intended to conceal their find.

'The three were hanged. There was none to dissent from the verdict, for now there were their three shares to divide among the remaining twelve.

'Then they set to work and the mine was opened up, and sure enough it was almost inexhaustible. But very soon provisions ran so short that five men were sent off to replenish them.

'Harry Tilton, who told me the story himself, decided that as he was satisfied with his share up to date, he would not go with these five men. So he took his share and went. A bank paid him twenty-eight thousand dollars for his gold, and he bought himself a farm and settled down.

'The five men bought pack-horses, good tools and a plentiful supply of provisions and had the claim registered. Then they returned to the mine.

'But when they got there they found the camp burnt to the ground and all the men who had stayed behind murdered, or, rather, killed by the Indians. There were signs of a terrible fight having taken place while they had been absent. They buried the bodies of their dead comrades and started working the mine again.

'They had not been at it more than three or four days when the Indians came back. They were more than sixty strong. They attacked at once and killed them all. One of them, however, was not killed outright but severely wounded and left for dead. When he recovered consciousness he set off to crawl away – for days or weeks – he didn't know. At last he was found by a farmer who took him to his house. He told his experiences, but he died of his wounds before he had been able to give an exact account of the place where it had all happened. The farmer set off to find the mine. He searched for weeks, but he never found it. Harry Tilton, who was in one of the northern states, heard nothing of all this. He was content to live on his farm and bothered no more about it; he imagined that all his comrades on the expedition were wealthy or prosperous men, who after they had got all the gold they wanted had gone east. He himself was a silent man. He had spoken of having made his money gold-mining. But there was nothing uncommon in that. And as he made little of his gold-digging days, the existence of this rich mine was again forgotten.

'But as time went on, the rumour grew that Tilton had made his money in a very few days. He did not deny it. And so it was plain that the place where he had dug must have been very rich in gold. He was pestered more and more by gold-diggers to work out a map that would make it possible to find the mine again. This at last he did. But more than thirty years had passed. His memory was no longer fresh. I set out with one of the parties which went by his map.

'We found all the places which Tilton had described. But the mine itself we never found. Perhaps it had been buried again by a landslip or earthquake, or else the Indians had obliterated all trace of it, and done it so well that nothing was to be seen. They did not want anyone in their territory; for a mine like that would have drawn men in hundreds to the spot, and thrown the whole neighbourhood into such a tumult that nothing would have been left of the life they were accustomed to.

'Yes, if one could find a mine like that,' Howard ended, 'one would be a made man. But you might search for it for a lifetime and find nothing. It is the same in any other line of business. If a man hits on the right business and has luck, there's his gold-mine. Anyway, old as I am, if anyone's after gold, I'm his man. But you need capital first, just as for all else.'

The story Howard told had nothing in it to act either as an inducement or a deterrent. It was the usual gold-digger's story; true, no doubt, and yet sounding like a fairy story. But all stories which tell of great winnings sound like fairy stories. If you want to win a fortune, you must take a risk. If you want gold, you must go and look for it. And Dobbs determined that night to go and look for gold, even though he were armed only with a pocket-knife.

There was only one perplexity. Was he to go alone, with Curtin, with old Howard, or with them both?

6

Next morning Dobbs told Curtin the story he had heard from Howard. Curtin listened attentively and then said: 'I dare say it's true.'

'Of course it's true. Why should he have been telling lies?'

Dobbs was surprised that any should doubt the truth of the story. But the doubt which Curtin implied made an effect upon him. Its truth had seemed to him to follow as obviously as night after day. There was nothing in the story which need have been invented. Yet the doubt which lay behind Curtin's words turned it into an adventure story. And though so far Dobbs had looked upon the search for gold as no more than the search for a pair of boots in the various stores of a town, or as the search for work, he now suddenly realized that looking for gold must necessarily have something mysterious about it. He had never before had this queer feeling of something uncanny, mysterious and strange when the talk fell on gold-diggers. When Howard told the story in his matter-of-fact way, he had not felt that there was any difference between gold and coal. They were both in the ground, and coal could make a man just as rich as gold.

'Lies,' said Curtin. 'I didn't say that. The story itself is no lie. There are hundreds such stories. I've read them by the yard in the newspapers that print such yarns. But, whatever else in this story may seem improbable, I'm certain that bit of it's true where those three fellows try to get away with it and put the rest of them off the scent.'

'You're right.' Dobbs nodded. 'That's the curse that hangs over gold.'

As he said it he realized that he would not have made such a remark an hour before, because the thought of a curse resting on gold would never have occurred to him.

Curtin had not undergone this change, perhaps only because he had not been confronted by such an unexpected doubt as the one with which he had just confronted Dobbs.

This inner experience of Dobbs parted the two without their knowing it. It was a parting within their emotional life. From now on their lives sought different goals. The destiny of each began to define itself.

'A curse on gold?' said Curtin. 'I don't see that. Where's the curse? There's just as much of a blessing on it. It depends who has it. It's the character of the man turns it to a curse or a blessing. Give a knave pebbles or dried sponges and he'll be up to some knavery with them.'

'Greed – that's the thing gold brings out.' Dobbs wondered how he came to say that. But he persuaded himself that it was only for the sake of contradicting Curtin.

'It's silly to talk like that,' Curtin replied. He spoke his intimate thought unintentionally, and Dobbs did the same without appearing to notice the change.

'It just depends,' Curtin went on, 'whether a man loves gold for itself or whether he regards it as a means to an end. There are officers in the army who are so keen on seeing a belt well polished that they forget what a belt's really for. Gold is not necessary in itself. If I can make a man believe I have plenty of gold, it's as good as if I really had it. It isn't gold that alters a man's character. It's the power gold gives him; and that's why people get excited when they see gold or even hear it talked about.'

Dobbs leant back on the seat. He looked up and on a roof opposite he saw two men laying telephone wires. Their footing was so precarious that you might have expected to see them fall headlong any moment. All for four pesos or four-fifty the day, Dobbs thought, and with the prospect of a broken neck or broken bones. It's just the same building a derrick, except that the risk is rather better paid.

He went on to think what a dog's life a labourer lived, and pursuing the thought, he asked: 'And would you do the dirty on your pals and get all the gold for yourself, like those three wanted to?'

'I can't tell you before hand,' Curtin replied. 'I don't believe there's a man who can say for certain what he might do if he had the chance of getting a heap of gold for himself by jockeying his pals out of their share. I'm pretty sure no man ever behaved as he expected when he came in for a lot of money, or saw the chance of raking in a heap of gold by a movement of his hand.'

Dobbs was still looking up at the men laying the wires. Although he wished them no harm, he had half a hope that one of them might fall, if only to break the monotony of life.

When none of them fell, it occurred to him that he was uncomfortable and that the seat hurt his shoulders. He straightened himself and lit a cigarette. He watched the smoke and then said:

'I'd do like Tilton. That's the best way, and then you don't need to slave and hang around and starve. I'd be content with a little and then go my way. The others might fight it out as they liked.'

Curtin had nothing to say in reply. They had said their say, and now they talked about something else, just for the sake of saying something instead of sitting there like dummies.

In the afternoon, however, after they had come back from bathing in the river, grousing all the way because they had to walk the whole length of the dusty Avenida just to save the fifteen-centavo tram-ride, the topic of gold came up again. The thought of gold was intertwined with the longing for a square meal, the thirst for a glass of ice water, the discomfort of bad nights on the hard bunks. It was really the thought of their present situation and how to alter it. Only money could alter it, and money was closely connected with gold. Thus the thought of gold gained on them until they thought of little else. Finally they saw that money was no use. Only gold, a great mountain of it, could release them from a life in which, even if they didn't starve, they could never eat their fill. The country they were in held an untold wealth of gold. They saw it gleaming in front of their eyes even when they shut them in the blinding glare of the white and dusty Plaza. Perhaps it was not gold. Perhaps it was the white streets, the white dust, the white houses that made them so impatient. But whatever they thought of they always came back to gold. Gold was ice water, gold was a full belly, gold was a suite of cool rooms in the tall and smart Riviera hotel. Gold and only gold could put a stop to the loitering about for ever in front of the American Bank in the hope of cadging a stray peso or a job from the manager of an oil-field. It was a degrading, shabby life. You couldn't go on like that for ever. It had to end. After three days had passed, and when there was still no prospect of a job, and when as far as they could see months might go by without any prospect of one, Dobbs said to Curtin: 'I'm going after gold, even if I have to go on my own. What does it matter whether I'm done in here or by Indians in the Sierra? I'm off.'

'I was going to make the same suggestion to you,' said Curtin. 'I'm ready for anything.'

'You don't care whether it's robbery or Santa Maria?'

'Santa Maria? I'm not a Catholic.'

'They won't ask whether you're a Catholic or not. But if you come to grief picking pockets you'll soon know who Santa Maria is. That's the penal settlement on an island off the west coast. They don't ask what your religion is – only how many years you've got. When you make the acquaintance of this particular Santa Maria you'll know why the Holy Virgin there has a blade of a knife in her heart. A man who got away live from the island drove it in.'

'We must get off tomorrow.'

Dobbs thought over this and then he said: 'I was thinking we might take old Howard with us. We'll ask him tonight what he thinks of it.'

'Howard? Why? He's too old. We might carry him on our backs, perhaps.'

'He's old,' Dobbs agreed, 'but he's as tough as the sole of a boot. When it comes to a pinch he'll stand more than both of us put together. I don't mind saying I know damn all about gold-digging, and shouldn't be any the wiser if there was gold in the ground under my eyes. Howard knows what he's about, he's been gold-digging and has made his fortune at it. He's lost it all in oil. It's half the battle to have an old hand with us. The only thing is, would he come?'

'We can ask,' said Curtin.

They went to the Oso Negro. Howard was in bed reading stories of bandits in the 'Western Story Magazine'.

'Will I come?' he said at once. 'There's no need to ask. Of course I'll come. You've only got to say gold and I'm your man. I've still three hundred dollars in the bank. I'll put up two hundred. It's all I've got. When that's gone, I'm finished. But one must risk something.'

After they had pooled all their money, Dobbs remembered his lottery ticket.

'Don't be superstitious,' Curtin was laughing. 'I've never seen anyone yet who won anything in a lottery.'

'Never mind,' said Dobbs. 'I'll go and look at the list all the same. That can't do any harm.'

'I'll come along with you. I'd like to see the long face you'll pull.'

The list was everywhere. It was in every street where lottery tickets were for sale. It was printed on linen. As no one ever bought a list the lottery could make no profit from the sale of them, and each list was handled by hundreds of people. They had to be very strong to withstand the eager grasp of all those who were sure that they must have won at last.

They found one of these lists at the corner of the Madrid Bar. It was the size of a handkerchief.

Dobbs glanced at it and said to Curtin: 'It's you to be laughed at for superstition, not me. Do you see that number there in heavy type? That's my number. For my twentieth part I get a hundred pesos.'

'Where from?' Curtin asked in astonishment.

'We go and cash it at once at the Agency.'

Dobbs put his ticket on the table. The agent examined it and without making any deduction handed Dobbs two fat gold fifty peso pieces.

When they were in the Plaza again Curtin said: 'Now I'll put up a hundred dollars. Then we'll have enough. I have a friend in San

Antonio over in Texas. He'll send me the money.'

He telegraphed and the money came by return. They took the night train to San Luis and from there the next train on to Durango.

Here they studied maps of the district.

'There's no use going anywhere near a railway,' Howard said. 'It's not worth while. Where there's a railway or even a good road, every corner which might yield anything is already known. We must go into the wilds if we want to get anything. We must snoop round where there's no tracks, where no mineralogist has ever been, where nobody has ever heard of a motor car. That's the sort of place to hit on.'

He fingered his way about the map and then said: 'Round about here. Just where, doesn't matter. Once we're there we must keep our eyes open. That's all. I knew a man once who could smell old gold as a thirsty donkey smells out water.'

'Right,' said Dobbs. 'And that reminds me, we must buy donkeys in one of the villages hereabouts to carry our traps.'

7

Curtin and Dobbs soon saw that they would have been helpless without old Howard. You don't find gold so thick on the ground as to trip over it. You must know how to see it. You can easily walk right over it and never know it's there. But Howard saw the least trace of it, if any trace was to be seen. He saw from the look of the ground whether there was the likelihood of gold or not, and whether it was worth while untying the shovels from the pack and panning a few shovelfuls of sand. Whenever Howard gave a blow with a pick and turned up the ground, or even washed a little earth in the pan, at once they were in the promised land, which ought by rights to be rich in gold. Four times they found gold. But the quantity was so small that it would hardly pay them a day's wage. Once they came on a very promising spot, but the water which they would need for the washing was six hours away, and so they had to give it up.

On and on they went, deeper and deeper into the mountains.

One morning they found themselves wedged in a narrow track. They crawled and clambered and panted, and could hardly get the donkeys forward. Their tempers were getting short.

And Howard made things no better by saying: 'I've taken two fine passengers on, damned if I haven't.'

'Hold your jaw!' Dobbs shouted angrily.

'Fine passengers,' Howard repeated scornfully.

Curtin had a powerful retort on the tip of his tongue, but before he could let loose Howard continued: 'You're so damned silly that you can tramp on millions with both feet and see nothing.'

The other two, who were in front, stood still and did not know whether Howard was making fools of them or whether the exertions of the last few days had affected his mind.

But Howard grinned and said quietly without any sign of excitement: 'There you go, walking on naked gold and can't see it. Till the end of my life I'll never know how I came to go looking for gold with such a pair of skunks as you two. I'd just like to know what I've done to have to put up with you.'

Dobbs and Curtin stood there. They looked down at the ground at their feet, then they looked at each other, and then at Howard with an expression which left it doubtful whether they were barmy themselves or only thought Howard was.

The old man bent down and scooped up a handful of loose sand. 'Do you know what I have in my hand?' he asked, and added without waiting for an answer: 'Gold dust. And there's more of it than we three could carry away on our backs.'

'Let's see,' they both yelled at once and started forward.

'You needn't come any nearer. You only need to bend down and pick it up. Then you'll see it and have it in your hands.'

Incredulously they picked up handfuls of sand.

'Perhaps you can't see it,' Howard said, grinning. 'But you can tell by the weight what's there.'

'That's true,' Dobbs shouted out. 'I see it now, too. We could fill our sacks and go straight back.'

'So we could,' said Howard with a nod. 'But that would be bad business. Better to wash it out clean. Why drag a lot of useless sand about with us? We shan't get anything for that.'

Howard sat down. 'The first thing is to fetch a few bucketfuls of water. I'll test the percentage of gold.'

And now the real work began. They had to find water. They found it, but it was about a hundred and twenty metres lower down

53

and had to be carried up by the bucketful. To carry the sand down and wash it straight away would have been more laborious and certainly more wasteful of time; for the water could be used again and again. And though it was diminished by each washing, there was only this loss to make good; whereas all the sand would have to be carried down every time, and it might be that in two heavy sacks of sand there would be scarcely a grain of gold.

They made their camp, made the cradle and the puddling trough, dug channels for the fall of water, excavated a tank, which they lined so well with chalk and clay that the leakage was not worth talking about.

After two weeks they were able to proceed to productive work.

Work it was, without any doubt. They toiled like convicts. It was very hot by day and bitterly cold by night. They were high up in the mountains of the Sierra Madre. No road led there, only a mule track as far as the water. The nearest railway station was ten or twelve days distant by donkey. And to get there you had to go over steep passes, by mountain paths, through water-courses and ravines, along the edges of precipitous cliffs. The whole way there were only a few small Indian villages.

'I've never had to work like this in my life,' Curtin said one morning when Howard knocked him up before sunrise. However, he got up, saddled the donkeys and fetched the day's supply of water, although it was seven o'clock before he got a bite of food.

By that time they were all three sitting at breakfast.

'I wonder sometimes,' Howard said, 'what you two actually imagined gold-digging was. I've come to the conclusion you thought the gold would be lying around like pebblestones, and nothing to do but bend down and pick it up and go off with it by the sackful. But if it was as simple as all that, gold wouldn't be worth more than pebblestones.'

Dobbs growled to himself. 'All the same,' he said after a while, 'there must be places where there's more of it and you don't need to break your heart to rake an ounce together.'

'So there may be, but they're like first prizes in a lottery,' the old man replied. 'I've seen places myself where you come on gutters with nuggets as big as my fist turned up with the pick or puddled out. I've known three, four and eight pounds got in the day. And I've known it when, in the same place, four men have racked their guts for three months and ended up with less than five pounds among the four of them. Take my word for it – the safest is washing out productive dirt. It's hard work, but when you've done your eight or ten months you pocket a good sum. And if you can stick it for five years, you're made for the rest of your life. But I'd like to see the man who'll do his five years of it. Generally speaking, the yield gives out altogether after a few months, and then you have to go on trek again to find a fresh place.'

The two greenhorns had never thought gold-digging was such hard work; and this was rubbed into them four times every hour. Digging and digging from sunrise to sunset in the sweltering heat; then up with the dirt into the trough; then rock and puddle and sift. And all to do over again three and four and five times – back and back with it into the cradle, because it did not come out clean.

So it went on day after day without a break. Their backs were so stiff they could neither stand nor lie nor sit. Their hands were like horny claws. They could not bend their fingers properly. They did not shave, nor cut their hair. They were too tired and they couldn't be bothered. If they tore shirt or trousers, they sewed a patch on, but not unless the things would otherwise fall to pieces.

There was no Sunday; for the only day of rest they had was a necessity in order to tinker up their primitive machinery, to wash themselves, to shoot a few birds or a buck, to find new grazing for the donkeys and to go to an Indian village for eggs, ground maize, coffee, tobacco, rice and beans. They were lucky if they could get such things at all. Flour, bacon and white sugar were not to be thought of except when one of them made a day's journey to the larger village where these rarities could sometimes, by no means always, be procured. When one of these expeditions produced a bottle of Tequila as well, it was a red-letter day.

Next, the question arose what they were to do about a licence. Prospecting was permitted without a licence, but not digging and washing out. But there were difficulties connected with a licence. You had to go to a government office and say exactly where the diggings were situated and pay a good sum. You also had to surrender a percentage of the yield. And it might take weeks before it was all settled.

All that might not have been so bad. The worst was that by taking out a licence, however careful you might be, you were pretty sure to bring bandits about your ears – those bandits who reap without sowing, who lie in wait for weeks and months while their victims do the hard work, and then fall upon them as soon as they load up to go, and take their gold from them. And not only their gold, but their donkeys and even the shirts from their backs. It is not easy to find the way back to civilization without donkeys or

55

trousers or shirts or boots. Often the bandits, realizing this, are kind enough to take their lives too rather than leave them in such a perplexity. Who is to say where the poor wretches have got to? The bush is so vast and so impenetrable and its dangers so many. Sometimes there is a search for a missing man. And before the search is even on foot, the bush has disposed of the body almost to the last bone. For this last bone it has to be made out who the man was to whom the bone belonged. And the culprits, of course, will be brought to justice. But for that, they must first be caught. And because of this, the bandit's trade is an easy one, much easier than getting gold by the sweat of his brow.

Whenever a licence is taken out, the news gets round. It has happened before now that the robbers are not bandits, but the representatives of a large and respectable mining company, who put the fortunate prospector out of the way. Then when the gold-field is not worked, the licence lapses after a few months, and the company take it up. The licence will be given them on the ground that the first licensee has lost his rights owing to absence.

It is far better therefore not to bother with a licence. When you decide to give up and be content with what you have got, you can convey your treasure unobtrusively away. No one will think of searching such ragged vagrants, and if you meet with bandits, or any who might turn bandits for the occasion, you can disarm them by begging for tobacco.

So much for a licence. If you have one, bandits will take your gold. If you haven't one, and the government gets to know it, they take half your little pile or the whole of it as a penalty. There you are in the vast silence of the bush. But there is so much else as well. The moment you possess anything, the world takes on another aspect. In any case, from that moment, you belong to the minority, and all who have nothing, or who have less than you, become your deadly enemies. From that moment you must be continually on your guard. There is always something to keep you on the alert. As long as you have nothing, you are the slave of an empty belly and of any who can fill it. But when you have anything, you are the slave of your possessions.

8

These three men whom chance had brought together had never been friends. They had scarcely ever given a thought to the possibility of being friends. At best, they were partners in an enterprise. They had come together simply from motives of gain. And as soon as this motive ceased, their partnership would be dissolved. They got across each other and quarrelled as it was, and as always happens after a time when people are thrown together. Their quarrels might have ended by making them friends. It would not have been very surprising. When people who are not friends begin to quarrel and dispute, it is often the beginning of an enduring friendship.

The common labours and worries and hopes and disappointments ought, according to all the laws of human intercourse, to have made friends of these three men during the months they spent together. They were war comrades, closer comrades, indeed, than any war could have made them. There was not one of them who had not saved the life of each of the other two on more than one occasion. Each was always prompt to help another and to risk his life or broken bones to rescue him from danger. Anything might happen. Once a tree they were felling fell too soon, and Dobbs caught it on his shoulder and sent it to one side; otherwise Curtin would have been crushed. As it was, Dobbs's shoulder was badly bruised.

'Bully for you, Dobbs,' was all that Curtin said. What else was there to say?

Two weeks after this, the slabbing gave when Dobbs was in the trench and Curtin rushed forward and hauled him out, although a great slice of gravelly earth swayed above him. Had it fallen a moment sooner, Curtin would have been so completely buried that Howard, who was trying to pin the slabbing at the other end, would have been too late even to guess where the two of them had got to.

When Dobbs had been pulled out and had got his senses and his breath back, he said: 'If you two had stopped to spit on your hands. I would never have spat on this heap of dirt any more.' As he spoke he spat out a mouthful of soil.

No words were wasted over incidents of this kind. It was all in a day's work and brought them no nearer together. If they had saved each other's lives for ten years together, they would never have become friends.

They could not see themselves with unprejudiced eyes, but if anyone else had seen them sitting round the fire before turning in, he would have had the impression that they were ready to spring at each other's throats at the first opportunity. Yet it was not murder that gleamed from their eyes. Perhaps it was jealousy. And yet if any one of them had been asked what he felt, he would not have said it was jealousy or greed. It certainly was not that. Each had the same as the others, each knew that the other two, like himself, had sunk their all in the common enterprise, and, like himself, had toiled and suffered privations and put up with every expected rebuff in order to achieve their common purpose. How could they feel jealousy or covetousness? A normal man doesn't have such unnatural feelings.

Every evening before the light began to fail, the day's yield was carefully weighed up and divided into three shares, and each took his share. They had done this from the start. 'We'd best share out every evening and each take his share,' Curtin suggested on the second evening after their labour began to show its first results.

'Then at least I won't need to be treasurer,' said Howard.

The other two looked up at once.

'Who the devil asked you to take charge of the funds? We'd think twice before trusting the lot to you.'

'Is that how the wind blows?' Howard said laughing. He was not at all put out. He had been through too much to be worried by such outbreaks. 'I was only thinking,' he said good-naturedly, 'that I was the most trustworthy man here.'

'You?' Dobbs shouted. 'And what about us – escaped convicts, I suppose?'

And Curtin joined in. 'How do we know where your palmy days were spent?'

Howard was not to be put out.

'You don't know that, of course. And it doesn't count for much between the three of us out here. I haven't asked either of you where you come from or where you spent the days of your innocence. It wouldn't have been at all polite of me. You should never tempt a man to tell lies. Out here, where not a cock crows, what's the use of deceptions? Whether we tell each other lies or the bleeding truth doesn't make a cent of difference. But of the three of us, I'm the only one to be trusted out here.'

The other two grinned, but before they had time for a juicy reply, Howard went on: 'You needn't excite yourselves. What I'm saying's right. We've only facts to think of here. Suppose we'd put the lot in your charge,' he said with a jerk of his head at Dobbs. 'But then when I was in the bush cutting props and Curtin had ridden down to get provisions, you'd pack up and clear out.'

'It's an insult to say that,' Dobbs broke out.

'Maybe. But it's just as insulting to think it. And if you wouldn't think it, you're the first man I ever came across who wouldn't. Out here it goes without saying that a man will make off with the lot, if he has the chance. He's a fool who doesn't. You're only a couple of hypocrites not to confess it. But let me see what you think about it when we have twenty kilos of pure gold in our hands. You're no better and no worse than the common run. And if you tie me to a tree one of these days and pack up and clear out, leaving me to my fate, so as to have my share, you'll only be doing what any man would do, unless the thought came to him that perhaps it mightn't pay him in the end. I can't get away with your two lots. I'm not quick enough on my legs. You'd be on me within twelve hours and hanging me from the nearest tree without scruple. I can't clear out. I'm at your mercy. That's why I say I am the only trustworthy man among us.'

'Looked at that way,' Curtin said, 'no doubt you're right. But in any case it'll be best to divide out every evening, and each man can look after his own share and go when he likes.'

'No objections to that,' said Howard. 'It is not a bad idea at all. Then we'll all be afraid of the others spying out our hiding-places.'

'You must be a proper bad 'un, Howard,' said Dobbs, 'if you have such ideas always running in your head.'

'That doesn't worry me, my boy,' Howard replied. 'I know what men are and what pleasant things they can think and do when gold's in the question. At bottom all men are alike when there's gold to reckon with. One's as big a scoundrel as the rest. When there's a chance of being caught, they're more prudent and lying and hypocritical. But here there's no occasion for hypocrisy. It's all clear and above board. In the towns there are all kinds of obstacles and restraints. Here there's one obstacle – the life of the other man.

And here there's only one thing to consider.'

'What?' asked Dobbs.

'I'd like to know what that is,' Curtin asked in the same moment.

'You need only to consider whether one day the memory won't weigh on you. Deeds don't trouble a man. It's always the memory that eats into you. But to come to business, we'll share out every evening and each man can look out a good hiding-place. When it comes to five kilos we shan't want to have it dangling round our necks any longer.'

9

Great care and ingenuity had been spent in concealing the diggings; and the camp where they cooked and slept was half a kilometre away. The diggings could only be approached from one direction, and here they were screened off so effectually by bushes and large stones that no one who passed by was likely to come across them. After a week the screen of bushes, the mounds of earth, the excavations and the blocks of stone were so entirely overgrown that even natives out hunting would have noticed nothing to suggest that work was in progress there.

They had no intention, however, of concealing their camp. It lay open to view, and in order to explain their presence there they stretched the skins of animals and birds on wooden frames. That showed at once that they were hunters who were collecting skins and rare birds. Not the least suspicion would be aroused, as hundreds of people carry on this profitable trade.

A secret path led from the camp to the diggings. To reach the path they had to crawl for the first ten metres. When they were through, the way they had come was screened by green prickly scrub. On their return to the camp, they first observed it carefully to see if there was anyone in the neighbourhood. If that had ever been the case, they would have made a wide circle and approached the camp from another direction, as though they had come in from hunting.

But they had never seen a soul, white or native, all the time they had been there. It was very unlikely that anyone would ever be wandering about in this wild spot. But they were too knowing and too prudent to leave it to chance. Even wounded game followed by a hunter would never have sought refuge where they were working. It would have smelt them and taken another course. Dogs, too, are nervous in the bush and never leave their masters to hunt on their own.

The life these three live here was more wretched than that of a Lithuanian factory-hand in Detroit. It was the most miserable existence you can imagine.

Dobbs said one evening that he had felt more of a human being in the worst trenches in France than during these weeks. Curtin and Howard could say nothing about that, because they had not had the honour of defending tender and innocent babes at the breasts of American mothers from the bayonets of the Huns. But every day they spent here made their life more intolerable. The monotony of their food, which they were too tired to cook properly, sickened them. The dreary sameness of their work made the labour of it even heavier than it was in any case. Digging, sifting, rocking, hand-picking, water-carrying, slabbing. One hour like another, every day like the last. And it had gone on now for months.

Perhaps they could have stood the labour. Hundreds of thousands of men spend their whole lives labouring in the same way and feel none the worse for it. But here there were other influences at work.

They had spent the first few weeks without realizing what they were in for. They never suspected for a moment that influences, of which they had had no experience, would sap their endurance. Each day at first brought something new. There was something to plan and carry out. Each of them, too, had a few jokes to tell, or some experience of life unknown to the others. Each was a study for the others, and had some peculiarity which interested or repelled, and at least occupied the attention of his fellows.

But now they had nothing more to tell. There was not a word in their vocabularies with which each was not familiar, even to the gesture and intonation which accompanied it.

Dobbs had a habit of half closing his left eye now and again as he spoke. At first Curtin and Howard found this very amusing and chaffed him about it. Then one evening, Curtin said: 'If you don't leave off winking that left eye of yours, you son of a bitch, you'll get

61

an ounce of lead in your belly. You know it annoys me, you jail-bird.'

Dobbs leapt to his feet and pulled out his revolver. If Curtin had got his out as quickly, there would have been a shooting match. But he knew that if he put his hand to his hip he would get six bullets in his belly.

'I know what you are,' Dobbs shouted, balancing the revolver from his wrist. 'You were flogged in Georgia for rape. You are not here in Mexico for your health, I know.'

Dobbs knew as little whether Curtin had ever been in Georgia as Curtin knew whether Dobbs had ever been in jail. They had drawn these conclusions from their pipes and chewed them out of their bacon, and came out with them now merely to excite each other to the highest pitch of rage.

Howard took no notice of them. He puffed out thick clouds of smoke and stared at the fire. When the two were silent for lack of further abuse, he said: 'Now, boys, leave shooting out of it. We've no time here for hospital work.'

After a while Dobbs put up his revolver and lay down to sleep. Curtin sat with Howard by the fire and lit another pipe.

One morning, not long after, Curtin prodded Dobbs in the ribs with the muzzle of his gun. 'Say a word, you toad, and I'll shoot.'

It happened in this way. Dobbs said to Curtin: 'Don't munch like a hog with acorns when you eat. What sort of a reformatory were you brought up in?'

'It doesn't concern you any more than a dog's turd whether I smack my lips or run at the nose. Anyway, I don't suck a hollow tooth like a whistling rat.'

Whereupon Dobbs replied:

'Have the rats in Sing Sing hollow teeth?'

Sing Sing, for those who don't know it, is the residence of all New Yorkers who get caught. The rest have offices in Wall Street.

This friendly joke was more than Curtin could stand, and he pushed his revolver between Dobbs's ribs.

'Damn you,' Howard shouted, losing patience, 'you behave as if we were all married to each other. Put that gun away, Curtin.'

'Who spoke to you?' Curtin shouted back in a rage. He let the muzzle fall and turned on the old man. 'What do you want to give orders for, you cripple?'

'Orders?' Howard replied. 'I'm not giving orders. But I came here to dig for gold, not to scrap around with two young fools. Each of us needs the others, and if one is shot to hell the two that are left can pack up, for two could do nothing, or no more than would amount to a fair day's wage.'

Curtin had now shoved his gun back in his hip pocket.

'And I may as well tell you,' Howard went on, 'I've had enough of your carry on. I don't want to be left here with either of you, and I'm going. What I've got will do for me.'

'But it won't do for us,' Dobbs shouted in a fury. 'It may be enough for the six months you have to live. But not for us. And if you sneak off before we've puddled the lot – we'll soon find a way of keeping you here.'

'Stow that, you old bag of bones,' Curtin said, joining in. 'We'll get you within four hours if you try that on. Do you know what we'd do with you then?'

'I can imagine it, you stiff,' Howard sneered.

'No, you can't,' Curtin replied with a grin. 'We'd take your belt off and tie you to a tree, tight and proper, and then we'd go and leave you there. Perhaps you thought we'd do you in? No, that's not the game.'

'Not a bit of it. You're too pious and I might be on your innocent consciences. Tie me up and leave me – you're not worth spitting on. And yet you weren't too bad when I met you down there in the town.'

All three were silent for a bit. Then Dobbs said:

'This is a lot of bullsh. But, damn it, when you never see a fresh face month after month, it's more than you can stand. It must be the same with married people. At first they can't be apart for half an hour, and as soon as they have to live together and haven't another word to say that the other hasn't heard a hundred times already, all they want is to poison each other. I know that from my sister. At first she wanted to drown herself because she couldn't get the man, and then when she'd got him she wanted to drown herself to get away from him. Now she's divorced and wants to try it on with someone else.'

'How much do you think we've got now, Howard?' Curtin asked unexpectedly.

The old man thought it over for a moment. Then he said: 'I can't say offhand. We don't get it all washed out clean. There's bound to be other metal along with it now and then. But I should say we'd got from fourteen to sixteen thousand dollars apiece.'

'Then,' said Dobbs, 'what about putting in another six weeks at it and then shutting down and quitting?'

'That'll suit me,' Curtin threw in.

'We shall have got all there is by then, anyway,' Howard said. 'By what I see of it, we shall be so far through even in four weeks that it won't pay for the labour. Have you noticed that, ten paces higher up in the direction we're digging now, the soil alters? There's no more sand. Either the stream must have fallen over the cliff at this spot, or else taken its rise at the foot of it. You can't tell which at this distance of time. No doubt there's been a landslip at some time or other and after that the stream took another course, or else the spring found another outlet.'

Peace was now restored to the camp. There were no more quarrels like the last one. They now had a fixed aim, and the day on which they would abandon their camp was settled. This so entirely altered their mood and their attitude to life that they could hardly understand how they had come to quarrel so bitterly. They were now preoccupied with plans for the future. There was the question of getting away unnoticed and conveying their dust into safety, and where, when that was done, to settle down, and what use to make of it when they had turned it into money. All this gave them something fresh to talk about. They looked forward already to living in a town among all the resources of civilization. And knowing that it wouldn't be long now, they found it easy to put up with each other's peculiarities; instead of being exasperated, they were tolerant of each other. If Curtin perseveringly scratched his head and then absentmindedly surveyed his fingernails with satisfaction, Dobbs, who also had bad habits of his own, did not tell him off. He said with a laugh: 'Are they biting, Curtin? Well, wait a bit, the meat's just roasted, and you'll have something else to worry at.'

And Curtin replied with a laugh: 'I'll have to break myself of this cursed habit, or they'll throw me out of the hotel.'

They got on better and better as the day drew nearer. Howard and Dobbs even spoke of going into partnership and opening a cinema together at Monterey or Tampico. Dobbs was to take charge of the artistic side, selecting the films, taking charge of the performances, writing the programmes and seeing to the music, while Howard was to be responsible for the business side, the café, the payments and receipts, the printing, the repairs and decoration of the building.

Curtin was in some perplexity. He couldn't decide whether to stay in Mexico or return to the States. He let fall once that he had a girl in San Antonio. It did not seem to worry him, however, though perhaps he gave that impression to avoid being chaffed.

Women were seldom mentioned among them, unless with con-

64

tempt. Why should they bother about them? One always speaks contemptuously of what cannot be had. It would have been difficult for these three to imagine themselves with a woman or a girl in their arms. It could only have been the runaway wife of a bandit. A decent girl would rather have drowned in a bog than trusted herself to any one of them, at least in their present situation and looking and behaving and expressing themselves as they did.

The gold that a beautiful and elegant woman wears on her finger, or a king in his crown, has been in strange company and washed in blood as often as in soap and water. A chaplet of flowers, a wreath of the leaves of a tree has a nobler origin, and though gold may be more durable this advantage is merely relative.

10

The day came when Curtin went to the village tienda to bring the last stock of provisions they would need before their departure.

'Where the devil have you been all this time?' Howard asked him when he dismounted and set to work unloading the pack-donkey.

'I was just going to saddle my donkey and go and look for you,' Dobbs put in. 'We thought something must have happened to you. You ought to have got back by two at latest.'

Curtin went on unloading the donkey without a word. Then he sat down and lit his pipe and handed out tobacco from the saddle-bags.

'I've had to come the devil of a way round,' he said at last. 'There's a guy down there in the village – says he's from Arizona.'

'What does he want here?' asked Dobbs.

'That's what I want to know,' Curtin replied. 'But the Indians only said that he'd been hanging around there the last few days. He asked the villagers whether there were any gold or silver mines in the neighbourhood. The Indians told him there weren't any, and no gold nor silver either, or anything else; and that they had a job to keep themselves by weaving mats and making pots. But then that half-wit at the tienda told him that there was an American somewhere in the mountains after game. He doesn't know that you are here too, he only knows about me. At least, I think so. And then he told the fellow that I came along now and again to buy provisions, and that I would probably be coming this week. So then the guy from Arizona said he'd wait for me.'

'And so he waited, did he, the dirty swine?'

'He did. As soon as I got down there he was on to me, and what was I after here, and was there anything doing, and he'd heard there was plenty of gold about and a lot more of the kind. I was pretty short with him and scarcely answered.'

'Didn't you put him right off it?'

'Sure. When I made any answer at all, I told him a lot of bunk. But that was no use. He was dead keen to come back to the camp with me. He said he was certain there must be gold in these parts, he could tell from the course of the dried-up streams, from the sand they had brought down, and bits of rock which had split off and come down from the cliff.'

'He's a great man,' said Howard, 'if he needs no more than that to tell him there must be gold here.'

'He knows nothing about it,' Dobbs broke in. 'He's a spy. Either a government spy or a spy of bandits who mean to hold us up when we start back. Even if they don't think of gold, there are the donkeys and tools and clothing, knives, revolvers and skins, as they think. All worth something. Enough to make it worth the while.'

'I don't think he's a spy,' Curtin said. 'I believe he's really after gold.'

'Then he has the outfit?' asked Howard.

'Not that I saw. He has a mule he rides on, a blanket, a coffee pot, a pan and a sack, with a few rags in it, I daresay, that's all.'

'He can't start washing out gold with his bare hands,' said Dobbs.

'Perhaps he'd had his tools stolen, or had to sell them. But what do we want with him nosing round?'

Curtin scratched his head and was just going to look at his nails. But when he saw that Howard and Dobbs had their eyes on him, he let his hand drop and decided once more to break himself of the habit. Howard and Dobbs however were not this time thinking of reminding him that in a few days he would be on his way to civilization. It was in their absence of mind that they followed Curtin's movements with their eyes. Their thoughts were busy with this mystery man from Arizona and they watched Curtin with the vague idea that it might help them to unravel the secret.

Curtin stared into the fire. Then he said:

'I couldn't make him out. He doesn't look as if he had anything to do with the government or bandits either. He looks innocent enough and speaks as though he means what he says. And whatever Dobbs says we have to do with him already. He followed me. At first he asked whether he could come back with me to my camp. I said no he couldn't. Then he rode after me. I stopped and waited for him and when he came up I told him to go to the devil and not bother me any more. He said he wouldn't be any bother to me only wanted company for a day or two as he was half crazed here in the mountains seeing nobody but these Indians. All he wanted was to sit by the fire for an evening or two with a white man and have a talk. Then he'd go. So I told him to look for another pal as I didn't want to have anything to do with him. I couldn't call him a hobo very well. He could have said the same of me, the way we both looked.'

'Where is the man?' asked Howard.

'He's not here by any chance?' Dobbs said, turning round.

'I hardly think that,' Curtin replied. 'I went all roundabout through the bush. But whenever I had him in view he was making straight here. If I'd been on foot I could have taken him right off the track. But try that with two donkeys. He only needs to know that there's somebody camping here in the mountains, and then if he has the direction roughly, he's bound to come on us today or tomorrow or the day after. And so he will. The only question is – what to do with him when he turns up? As long as he's here we can't go to the diggings.'

'It's a bad business,' said Howard. 'If it was an Indian I wouldn't mind so much. He wouldn't stay long. He'd be off home to the village. But this guy'll stick to us like a pitch plaster. He won't need telling either, to know that we've got something on here. For what should three white men be lying low here for – here in the mountains? We can only say we're robbers and murderers who are here in hiding. But then as soon as he's down in the village again we shall have a regiment of soldiers along, and that'll be the end of all our nice plans for the future. And if there's an officer and he believes the story of our being here because of robbery and murder, he'll perhaps have us shot on the spot to be sure we don't escape.'

'It's simple enough,' said Dobbs. 'We'll soon be even with the fellow. As soon as he comes we'll tell him to quit the neighbourhood, unless he wants a few ounces of lead in his carcase.'

'We'd look the fools then,' said Howard. 'Back he'd go and talk a lot of bunk and perhaps run across some mounted police, and then we'd be properly in the soup up here. You might as well tell him right off that we're escaped convicts from Santa Maria.'

'Well, there's still the straight way with him,' and Dobbs looked resolute. 'As soon as he comes, snipe him and be done with it. Or else hang him from that tree yonder, and strip the bark of it. Then we'll have peace.'

For a time nothing was said to this proposal.

Howard got up and looked at the potatoes (a rare treat), and after poking about among them sat down again.

'There's no sense in shooting the man down at sight. For all we know, he's a poor devil of a tramp who'd rather walk the wide world than rack his guts for a bare wage in the oil-fields or the mines. It'd be a crime to snipe a harmless hobo.'

'But how do we know he's harmless?' Dobbs protested.

'We shall find out,' said Howard.

'How?' Dobbs was only the more convinced that his plan was the best one. 'We'll bury him out of sight. If anyone down there says he saw the man come up here, it's easy enough to say we saw nothing of him. We can tip him down the gully there. And he might have fallen down there by accident.'

'Will you do it, then?' asked Howard.

'Why should I do it? We can draw lots who does it.'

The old man grinned. 'Yes, and the one of us who does it will have to crawl on his knees to the other two all his life long because they saw him do it. It's all right enough if you're by yourself. But as things are, for myself I say: No.'

'And I say no, too. It's too risky and too little sense in it. We must think of some other way.' Curtin now took his part in the discussion again.

'Are you downright sure he followed you and'll come here at all?' Howard asked.

Curtin looked down on the ground in front of him and said with resignation: 'I know he'll come and I know he'll find us. The impression he made on me was . . .' here Curtin raised his eyes and looked towards the narrow opening in the scrub. 'There he is,' he said in a weary voice.

Neither the old man nor Dobbs asked where. They were so astonished that they even forgot to curse. They followed the direction of Curtin's eyes and there in the dusk, fitfully lit up by the camp fire, stood the stranger, holding the bridle of his mule.

He stood quite still and did not even utter the customary Hallo. He did not say good evening. He simply stood there and waited, like a hungry man who is too proud to beg.

When Curtin was describing his encounter with the man in the village, each of his listeners formed a distinct idea of his appearance; but each had formed quite a wrong one. Dobbs had imagined a man with the coarse and bestial features of a vagabond in the tropics who ekes out a living by robbing travellers, thinking nothing of murder if it pays him or if his own safety requires it. Howard, on the other hand, had imagined the stranger as a regular gold-digger, impervious to any weather, with a face like tanned hide and hands like gnarled roots, afraid of no danger and undeterred by any difficulty, never at a loss, whose mind and body are undeviatingly fixed on the single aim of finding gold and working his find to the last ounce. He had imagined a gold-digger of the real honest sort, who will never be guilty of a crime and will commit murder for nothing short of defending his find or his share of the colour.

And now they were both taken by surprise. The stranger fitted neither Dobbs's conception of him nor Howard's. If neither of them spoke nor uttered an exclamation of surprise, it was partly because he looked so different from what they had imagined, and partly because he had made his appearance so suddenly and so much more speedily than they had expected.

The stranger still stood motionless in the small opening which led to the camp. He seemed to be just as much surprised as the three who sat round the fire. He had expected to find only one man, Curtin, and there, to his astonishment, he saw three. His mule nuzzled the bushes. Then it scented the donkeys and began to whinny. But in the middle it stopped abruptly, as though the silence of the human beings made it afraid.

Still the three men did not utter a word. They paid no heed to the fire, nor to their supper simmering over it. They kept their eyes fixed on the stranger as though they waited for him to say or do something. But he did not stir.

Then Dobbs got to his feet and strode with long strides up to the intruder. It was in his mind to ask him roughly what he wanted and how he had come there, and who he was. But when he was up to him all he said was Hallo, and the stranger likewise said Hallo.

Dobbs's hands were in his pockets. He had no idea what to say next. Finally he said: 'Come over to the fire.'

'Thanks,' the stranger said shortly.

He came nearer, but first lifted the old saddle with its two saddle-bags off the back of his mule, and after hobbling one of its forefeet gave it a clap on the hind-quarters. It ambled slowly away in the direction where the donkeys were grazing.

Then he said good evening and sat down by the fire.

Only Howard replied. 'How's things?' he asked.

'Hm!' the stranger answered.

Curtin stirred the beans and shook up the potatoes. Howard turned the meat, and Dobbs, who had not yet sat down again, chopped wood and threw it on the fire.

'I know I'm not welcome here,' the stranger said.

'I made that clear enough when I saw you down yonder,' Curtin did not look up as he spoke.

'I can't be for ever hanging around with no one but Indians. I want to see what Christians look like for a change.'

'Then go somewhere else and see for youself.' Howard did not trouble to be polite. 'We don't know any more than you do.'

'It doesn't interest us either,' Dobbs put in sourly. 'We've something else to think about. If you want to know, it's you we're worried about. We've no use for you here, not to light the fire for us or anything else. You'd best make yourself scarce as soon as it's daylight. Otherwise you may not find us too pleasant.'

The stranger said nothing to this. He sat still and watched the preparations for supper. When it was ready Curtin said: 'Help yourself. For tonight it'll go round. As for tomorrow, that's another thing.'

The meal was eaten in silence, or if anything was said it was only about the food – that the meat was not up to much, or the beans too hard, or the potatoes watery. The stranger did not join in, and he ate little.

When they had done, the other three lit their pipes.

'Got any tobacco?' asked Dobbs.

'Yes,' he replied quietly and began to roll a cigarette.

The others, for the sake of saying something and also of putting the stranger further off the track, spoke of hunting. But what they said did not sound very convincing, because it was not their real job. They felt, too, that the stranger knew more of hunting and of skins and the rest of it than they did. This made them uneasy and they began to talk of breaking camp and going to another district where there might be more game.

'It's no place for game here,' the stranger said, joining abruptly in the discussion. 'But it's a fine place for gold. There's gold here. I saw that some days back from the old dried-up water-courses which came down from the mountains here.'

'There's no gold,' Dobbs replied. 'We've been here long enough to know that. Do you think we'd hunt if there was dirt to wash? You must be bughouse,' he added, laughing derisively. 'We weren't born yesterday and we can tell a lump of gold from a pebblestone as well as you. We don't need your advice.'

He got up and went to the tent to turn in.

No one said any more and the stranger appeared to take Dobbs's ill-mannered remark in good part. Perhaps he was accustomed to that style of conversation.

Howard stretched himself and yawned. Curtin knocked out his pipe. Then they got up, one after the other, and went slowly over to the tent. They neither bade the stranger good night nor invited him into the tent.

The stranger got up too. He whistled, and after a moment his mule came hobbling up. He went up to it and patted its neck and spoke to it and then sent it away with a clap of his hand.

Next he put more wood on the fire and sat down and hummed to himself. Finally he got up and went to his saddle. He brought one of the saddle-bags over to the fire, pulled out a blanket and, rolling himself up in it, settled down to sleep with his head on the bag and his feet to the fire.

Talk went on in the tent. It was too far from the fire for the stranger to hear what was said. They spoke in low tones, too, but very emphatically all the same.

'I said it before and I say it again,' said Dobbs. 'Get rid of him. It doesn't matter how.'

'We don't know yet what sort of a guy he is,' the old man said it in a conciliatory tone. 'He seems harmless enough. I don't believe he's a spy either. He hasn't the look of one. He wouldn't be alone and he wouldn't be so hungry. I believe he has something on his conscience. They're after him for something or other.'

'We could start an argument with him,' Curtin said, 'and then lay him out once and for all.'

'That sounds amusing,' said Howard, 'but it isn't very commendable. It's a dirty trick.'

'Dirty or not,' Dobbs said in a rage, 'we've got to be quit of him, that's all. He's had his warning.'

They talked on, but always came back to the same thing – that the man had to get out of it, but that there were various objections to doing him in. At last they fell asleep on it.

11

Next morning they all assembled round the fire in a very bad humour. The stranger had already fetched wood and made the fire up. He had filled his kettle and put it on to boil. Dobbs greeted him at once: 'Where did you get the water, my good friend?'

'Out of the bucket.'

'Oh – out of the bucket. Very kind of you. But don't kid yourself we're going to carry water for you.'

'I don't. I'm going to fill the bucket again.'

As he spoke Curtin came up to the fire, in a worse temper if possible than Dobbs. He too said at once: 'Pilfering wood and water, eh? That's the notion, is it? If you lay a finger on anything of ours again, we'll put a bullet through you, see?'

'I took you for decent fellows who wouldn't grudge a drink of water.'

Dobbs went for him at once: 'What's that, you vermin? We're not decent fellows – bandits, I suppose?' And he gave him a well-directed punch in the face.

The man dropped and lay full length. Slowly he got up again.

'I might do the same for you now. But what's the use against the three of you? You're only waiting for the excuse to do me in. But I'm not such a fool. The time will come, perhaps.'

Howard meanwhile came to the fire and asked the man quietly whether he had anything to eat.

'I've got a tin of tea and some beans and rice and two tins of milk.'

'You can have some coffee with us. Some grub too – for today. Tomorrow you must look after yourself.'

'Thanks,' the man replied.

'Tomorrow?' Dobbs questioned. His temper was noticeably improved by the success of his knock-out. 'Tomorrow? Look here, do you think you're settling here for good?'

'That's the notion,' the man replied quietly.

At this Curtin shouted: 'Settling down here? Not without our leave.'

'The bush and the mountains are open to all comers.'

'Not so fast, young man,' said Howard. 'The mountains and the bush are free and the jungle below and the desert beyond. It's all free. But we're the first here and the first-comers have the right as settlers.'

'That's good enough. But how do you know you're the first here? Perhaps I was here before you ever thought of squatting here.'

'Have you registered a claim?'

'You've no claim either.'

'It's up to you, as we're in possession. If it's true you were even here before, you didn't stake any claim and you gave the place up again, so you've lost any rights you had.'

The stranger made no reply. The three others began to get breakfast ready. They didn't hurry because they didn't know what there was to do when it was over. They couldn't go and work, because then the stranger would have discovered their diggings. They couldn't go hunting and so deceive the stranger about their real occupation, because one of them would have had to stay behind to prevent him nosing around and perhaps coming on the mine by accident; and he might be a match for the one of them who stayed behind. There was only one way out of it. Two of them might reach the mine by the secret approach and work there, while one stayed behind to keep a watch on the stranger. But he wasn't likely to sit doing nothing. He would scout around. And as soon as he was told not to, he would know for sure that there was more going on than met the eye.

Curtin at last came to a conclusion.

'We'll go hunting, you and I, after breakfast,' he said to the stranger. 'We could do with some fresh meat.'

The stranger looked up at them to see if he could read the meaning of this proposal in their faces. If he went after game alone with one of them, he might easily meet with an accident; and that would be one way of getting rid of him. But then he said to himself that if they meant to put him out of the way they would do so in any case. Excuses are never lacking.

'I can go with you today,' he said, 'and then we'll be supplied. But tomorrow I shan't have much time.'

'Why not?' they all asked at once, and looked at him with astonishment.

73

'Well, I'm starting to look for gold here tomorrow. There's gold here. And if you haven't found any it only shows what dam' fools you are.'

This got the old man's goat and he blabbed out: 'Perhaps we aren't such dam' fools as you think. Perhaps we have found gold.'

'That wouldn't surprise me,' said the stranger. 'But you haven't found any. Or, if you have, it's just a few handfuls you've scratched up from the surface of the ground. But there's more than that here, close here somewhere. There's a good million.'

'A million?' Howard asked, opening his eyes wide.

Dobbs and Curtin could not speak for excitement.

'You haven't come on the placer, I know,' the stranger went on with composure. 'I know you've been a year here. The Indians down there told me a man had been up here that long. If you had struck the placer, you'd have been gone long since. For you could never have hoped to get away with all the lot without attracting attention. Or else you'd have opened a regular mine, with a licence and machinery and two or three dozen men.'

'We've nothing, not a cent,' said Dobbs.

'Call me what you like. But I'm not an infant. And if you three have been up here all these months, it isn't for your health. What I say is, let's be open and put our cards on the table. What's the good of this hole-in-corner business? I'm not a crook. To say the least, I'm as straight as any of you. I won't say I'm any better. We're all on the make, whether out here in the bush or back in the towns. Of course, you can put me out of the way, I know that. But that may happen any day. I have to risk that. So why can't we be open with one another?'

'Spit it out, then,' said Howard.

'You're right, Howard,' Dobbs answered to this. 'What I say is, let him have the chance to prove he's not a spy and isn't keeping anything else back that doesn't suit our book.'

He then turned to the stranger.

'We can't tell by looking whether you're a crook or not. It's true we've done a few months' hard labour here, honest work though, you can take our word for it. If we let you into it, you might easily make yourself a nuisance, and that might cost us all we've got for our hardships and privations. But I tell you this – we'd have you, even though you went as far as Hudson Bay first. We'd have you, and we'd show no mercy. So out with it. What d'you want and what's your game?'

The stranger drank up his coffee and then he said: 'I've been

74

honest with you from the start. I've told you there's gold here and that I've come to dig it.'

'What else?' asked Curtin.

'Nothing else,' the stranger replied.

'Good enough,' Howard put in. 'But what if we've found the muck? You don't suppose we're going to account to you for it. We've done our bit without you. So there you have it. We've found it and we're pretty well through.'

'So far so good,' the stranger replied without hesitation. 'You've been straight with me and I'll be straight with you, and we'll see if we can work together. For a start, then, I've a claim on this place. Wait now before you chew the fat. Of course I've no registered claim and no licence or anything of the sort. My claim lies in the fact that I know something that you don't. That is better than any licence, stamp and all. You've found nothing. A few grains, I dare say. You can keep them.'

'So we shall, don't you worry,' said Curtin.

'That's how it stands,' the stranger went on, speaking very slowly. 'I can't carry on alone. I want men, and it seems to me that you're the best men for the job. It's as much to your interest as mine to keep it dark; and you have tools and I haven't. I might sell my secret to a company. But it'd be a job to get more than a hundred dollars for it. They'd want it under their eyes and that they could only have here on the spot. Besides, I've good reasons not to shout about it, for then someone might come along with mining rights. I put it up to you. What you have, you keep. Of what you get after today through working on my plan, I take two-fifths.'

The three looked at each other and laughed. Then Howard said: 'We don't need you to tell us the tale, my boy. We can do that for ourselves. What do you say?' And he turned to the other two.

Dobbs said: 'What does it matter? We're as good as through and done with it. We've nothing to lose by giving him a day or two.'

'That's what I say. We lose nothing. We may as well see what there is in it now we're here,' said Curtin.

'I'm not on for it,' the old man said. 'It's a try-on and I've had enough of the wilds. I want to be in a proper bed again. I've got all I need. But of course if you're for it, then I've nothing to say. I can't trek two weeks through the bush on my own.'

'Listen to me, old cock,' said Curtin. 'I'm not out for overtime any more than you are. I've someone waiting for me. We'll give him a week. If in a week we come on the business this fellow's talking about, well and good, and then we can see if it's worth it. If

75

in a week we've come on nothing, then I'll go with you. Is that agreed?'

They all agreed, and now it was for the stranger to lay his plans before them.

'What's your name, for a start?' asked Howard.

'Lacaud,' he said. 'Robert Lacaud from Arizona.'

'Any relation to the Lacauds in Los Angeles, furnishing store?'

'Yes, on my grandfather's side. But I don't have any truck with them. We wouldn't be seen dead with them, and if we thought they were going to heaven we'd burn half a dozen churches to a cinder just to be sure of going to hell. But there's no need to worry. They'll never get to heaven.'

'Then you'll have to make it a dead cert that you do.' Dobbs said laughing. 'As you're shaping at present you'll hardly keep out of the way of those relations of yours.'

'I don't know,' said Curtin. 'If I'm not misinformed, there are different boiling departments down there, and he'll be able to put in a word at the right moment, so as not to be popped into the same cauldron as the other worthy members of his distinguished family. That can always be arranged, for Satan has a good heart. If he hadn't, how could he be up to so much fun and mischief?'

Howard had gone to see that the donkeys didn't stray too far, and in order to get a better view he had climbed on to a shoulder of the mountain side.

'Hallo!' he shouted.

'What's up?' Dobbs and Curtin shouted back. 'Have the donkeys gone?'

'Come here, quick. Quick as you like.'

The two of them jumped up and ran across to Howard. Lacaud too hurried after them.

'What's that over there coming this way?' the old man shouted. 'Perhaps you can tell better than I can.'

'Soldiers or mounted police,' Dobbs said. Then he whipped round on Lacaud. 'So now we have it, you skunk. So this was your secret.'

In a second he had him covered, but Howard, who was standing behind, knocked his arm up.

'You're wrong,' said Lacaud. Dobbs's sudden action had sent the blood from his face. 'I've nothing to do with them – police or soldiers.'

'Listen, my lad,' Howard said to him. 'We don't want any of that here. If they're after you, clear out of it – quick. And let them see you. We don't want any police up here. So down you go, quick march and where you like. Otherwise we'll take good care they get you. We can't do with you up here.'

Curtin had climbed higher up for a long and careful scrutiny.

'Not so fast,' he said. 'I don't think they're soldiers. Nor police either. They're not clothed alike and their firearms are all sorts and sizes. One of them, as well as I can see, has a great blunder-buss that must be a hundred years old at least. I know what they are – bandits.'

'Damn!' Howard shouted. 'Then it's out of the rain into the sump. We could do with mounted police ten times better than bandits. The police would tie us up and if there was no more in it than escaping taxes we could come to terms. But bandits – that's another story.'

Then a new idea struck him and he turned to Lacaud. 'Now then, cough it up. It's you we've got to thank. You're a spy of theirs. That's what I thought a time back.'

'I have nothing to do with bandits either,' Lacaud said. 'Let me have a look.'

He climbed up beside Curtin and took a careful look at the figures far below.

'They're bandits, and I know what bandits, too. I heard of them at Señor Gomez's Hacienda. And there was the account in a newspaper there. I can see one with a bronzed straw hat that was mentioned in the description of them. He's a good plucked one not to have changed it for another. But he won't know it was men-tioned. They never see a paper and couldn't read one if they did. That's the very last band I'd choose to run across.'

And now, while all four watched the movements of the bandits, waiting to see whether the leader would turn into the track which in all probability would bring them up to their part of the mountains, Lacaud told them all he had read in the paper, and all that the people in the Hacienda had been able to tell him. For though few Indians and Indian workers on the Haciendas can read, the news of such events as these spreads through the length and the breadth of the land with the speed of a prairie fire.

12

At a small station, where the night express stops for two minutes to drop and collect the mail, and to pick up or set down a couple of passengers, twenty or twenty-five men got into the train. It was between seven and eight o'clock and already pitch dark.

It never happened that so many people got in at this little station, but neither the station-master nor the officials on the train thought anything about it. They might be men going to market somewhere, or men on strike from one of the mines or on their way to another mining district to look for work.

They were all mestizos, wearing their large straw hats, trousers and shirts, and sandals or boots on the feet. All were wrapped in blankets, as the night was chilly. No tickets are issued in small stations after nightfall, but they could get them on the train. The station was unlighted and quite dark. Only the station-master and the officials who got out, and ran hastily along the train had lanterns. No one, then, had a sight of the men's faces, which in any case were shrouded up to the eyes by their blankets; and this, being the usual thing, caused no remark.

They all got into the first coach of second-class compartments, in front of which was the luggage van. In this coach as usual were the twelve soldiers and an officer, all with loaded rifles, to protect the train against bandits.

Most of the men remained in the first coach, but some, after the train had started, passed along into the next one, apparently to look for better seats. Both these second-class coaches were pretty full. There were peasants, tradespeople and Indians taking their wares to the next town. Behind these two coaches came a coach of first-class compartments which was also fairly full, and behind this, at the end of the train, was the Pullman sleeping-car.

The train quickly got up speed. It was twenty minutes or a little more to the next station. And now the train was in full career and the attendants were busy with the tickets for the passengers who had just got in, and who were blocking all the doors on to the corridor, where they had been standing from the start as though they were not going to sit down until they had found themselves good seats.

The next moment, without a word or any warning, they pulled rifles and revolvers from under their blankets and opened rapid fire. It was directed particularly on the soldiers, whose rifles were between their knees or leaning against the sides of the carriage, while they studied spelling-books in order to learn to read and write, or munched their supper or dozed.

The firing lasted only about ten seconds; by that time the coach was a shambles and all the soldiers were either dead or at the point of death. The train attendants too were either shot dead or mortally wounded and lay about on the floor or the seats. Twenty passengers were hit. Many were dead; others bleeding to death of their wounds. Babies at their mother's breasts, women and children were bleeding and dying in a scene of wild confusion. Men and women begged on their knees for mercy, mothers held up their weeping children in the hope of arousing the bandits' pity, while others offered their wretched belongings to pay for their lives. But the bandits went on shooting until no one stirred any more.

Then they turned to plunder, and took all that seemed to them of any value. Part of the band went to the first class and plundered without shooting. Watches and purses, rings, ear-rings, necklaces and bracelets – and if the booty did not come up to their hopes, a prod from a rifle or revolver quickly reminded their prey of a gold coin or two in a trouser pocket or a diamond ring in a dressing-case.

Next the lights were switched on in the Pullman, the passengers turned out of their beds and stripped of all they had with them.

All this while the train sped on its way. Perhaps the driver had not heard the shots, or else he hoped to reach the next station at such speed that the bandits would be unable to jump from the train.

But now the bandits returned to the front of the train, passing through the two second-class coaches, where the panic of the passengers, when they saw them coming back, rose to an indescribable pitch of terror. The bandits didn't turn their heads or move an eyelid. They went on into the luggage van where they broke open the trunks or else threw them overboard, to sort out at their leisure later on. They murdered the guard and climbed along into the mail van, where they shot down the two men in charge and ransacked the mail bags.

Meanwhile the driver realized that something was wrong or else saw some of the bandits clambering from the mail van on to the tender. The station was still far away and there was no hope now of reaching it. He put on the brakes and the train came to a sudden stop with the violence of a collision.

The fireman jumped clear and tried to reach the bush at the foot of the embankment. But he was hit by half a dozen bullets and rolled to the bottom. Four men climbed into the cab of the engine before the driver had time to jump and grabbed him. The bandits had found a large number of tins of petrol and gasolene on the train which were being sent express to the owner of a tienda. They poured it over the coaches and in at the broken windows and then threw lighted brands after it. Instantaneously, like an explosion, the flames shot up into the darkness of night.

The passengers trapped in the burning train uttered heartrending cries and surged against the windows in a frenzied effort to escape. If they succeeded, they fell burnt and singed from the height of the windows to the track and broke or sprained their limbs. Those who were too severely wounded, and could not in the panic find anyone to help them, were burnt to death.

In front, two of the bandits had the engine-driver covered with their revolvers; they forced him to uncouple the engine and drive off, with the whole band crowded on the tender, until they told him to stop. The burning train and its occupants were left to their fate. The wildly leaping flames shed a ghastly light upon the scene, while the victims ran backwards and forwards, crazed with horror and pain and fright, gesticulating and crying aloud and praying, and making last frantic efforts to rescue those who had been left behind in the raging furnace. Less than seven minutes all told had elapsed and the station towards which the engine was now racing was still far away. Suddenly one of the men told the driver to stop. The engine stopped and the men jumped down. The last shot the driver and pushed him with a kick down the embankment. Then he followed his comrades.

After a time the driver came to, and though on the verge of death he crept up the embankment and pulled himself into his engine. In spite of the pain he was in and the fear that he would collapse at any moment, he managed to get the engine started and reach the station. The station-master, who was already surprised by the delay – for the train had long ago been signalled from the last station – was amazed now to see an engine arrive by itself, and running up to it he found the driver wounded and bleeding.

Passengers waiting for the night train helped him to carry the man into the station building and here the dying man was just able to give a bare outline of the disaster before he died.

The station-master telegraphed immediately to the stations on both sides of him. He got them both and heard that a relief train would be sent immediately. There was a goods train on a siding in the station waiting to let the passenger train through. Two empty wagons were shunted and coupled to the engine, and the first relief train was ready.

But who was to drive it and go in it? The bandits were undoubtedly still on the line, collecting all that they had thrown out of the train. They would attack the relief train at once, if only to make sure of their booty. Probably they had torn up the rails or blocked the line.

'Better wait for the other train,' the station-master said. 'There's sure to be soldiers on it.'

But the driver of the goods-train engine broke in at once. 'I'll drive it,' he said. 'There are women and children bleeding there, and comrades of mine, and some of them may not be past help. I'll drive the train. What do you say, mate?' he asked the fireman.

The railwaymen of Mexico are all without exception members of a first-class union, radical to the backbone and never averse from a strike; and they hang together to a man. Their organization and the spirit prevailing in it make self-respecting men of them, who are eager to improve themselves as citizens of their country. Courteous and helpful, always laughing and joking, they bear no resemblance at all to the growling and snarling N.C.O.s who, disguised as railwaymen, make travelling in Central Europe such a disagreeable experience. They are not the subordinates of arrogant superior officers, for all share as comrades in the pride of their organization. The fireman may be president and spokesman of the group at whose meetings the chief of the line sits modestly on the same bench as shunters, pointsmen and wheel-greasers and listens quietly and attentively to the proposals the fireman has to make, as chairman, for improving the conditions of the railway worker. And in the event of a strike, the chief of the line, whose pay is ten times that of a wheel-greaser or shunter, does not organize the technical staff as an emergency gang. On the contrary, he gets out the bills and posters which inform the public of the reason and the necessity for the railways strike, because he is better at writing than the fireman, though the fireman is chairman and spokesman. The chief of the line and the shunter eat from the same spoon, so to speak; by virtue of their organization the dirty wheel-greaser is more to the chief of the line than the state can be, or the interests of trade and industry, or the common weal, all of which come second to the aim of securing the necessities of existence for the points-man, his comrade. For this reason the engine-driver need not have asked his fireman what he had to say; for he might have known what answer he would make; and what answer all the other rail-waymen who were standing about waiting for the goods train to start, would make also.

It was a question first of all of their own union members; but even if they had all been safe and sound, still they would have gone, because there were the passengers in desperate straits. Even though they put the members of their union first, the passengers came second. Indeed the railwayman feels a greater responsibility for the welfare of the passengers than for the welfare of his own family. For that is what his union teaches him. And his union is never wrong whatever anyone, the archbishop included, may say.

So the fireman spoke up: 'I'll take the passenger engine along first to see if all's clear. You follow at five hundred metres, and that'll give you time to stop if I come to grief through the rails being up.'

The engine was started, a wheel-greaser jumped in as fireman, and then they went backwards out of the station.

The small relief train meanwhile got up steam, and all the railwaymen, though they all had wives and children, jumped on board. So did some of the other people standing round; and then the train forged ahead into the darkness.

The scouting engine found the rails in order. The line was clear. But when it approached the scene of the disaster rapid fire was opened on it.

The bandits had had their horses concealed near the spot where they had made the engine-driver stop and they were still collecting their plunder. Those of them who were standing by with the horses, opened fire at once on the engine, hoping to bring it to a standstill, so that the rest of the band could carry on with the looting.

The driver was hit in the leg and his fireman grazed on the ear. But they went full speed ahead, signalling the all-clear by lantern to the train behind. It too was fired on. But some of the railwaymen had revolvers and returned the fire. The bandits could not be sure in the darkness whether there were soldiers in the unlighted wagons. Apparently they thought so; for they made their mounts in a hurry and left everything lying that they had not had the time to sort out. They mounted and rode away into the depths of the jungle, making for the hills.

With the help of the passengers who had escaped serious injury, the dead and wounded were lifted into the wagons, and the train returned to the station with its pitiful load.

A telegram had come to say that a hospital train was on the way. It could not, however, be on the spot before dawn. There were telegrams also from the government and the nearest garrison. All the detachments of mounted police of the neighbouring district were on the march, and four regiments of cavalry of the Federal Army were mobilized and would be dispatched by special trains to the scene of the outrage before daybreak, in order to pursue the bandits.

It is not easy to find a needle in a haystack. But if it has to be found it can be done, whatever the size of the haystack. Its eventual discovery is a mathematical certainty. But to find a bandit who has a good start of his pursuers along jungle tracks which he knows well and his pursuer does not know at all, and who, after traversing the jungle has the mountains, the high mountains of Mexico, before him is incomparably more difficult than finding a needle in a haystack.

But the soldiers are for the most part Indians themselves. That means a lot. Also they knew that the bandits at a given time had been at a given spot on the line between those two stations. And it was not very long before the officers ascertained that the bandits had split up into small parties each of which had taken its own way. The needle in the haystack had, in fact, been broken into small pieces.

A superficial description of the bandits had been telegraphed in all directions. But even though one of them rode through an Indian village, and even encountered soldiers there and roused their suspicions, the description would be worthless unless in his pockets or on his person there was something to connect him with the hold-up of the train. He could always advance an alibi and say that he was sleeping on that night twenty kilometres away from the scene of the hold-up under a tree on the road to Chalchihuites. No one could disprove it.

However, a troop of Federal Cavalry was riding through Quazamota. Two mestizos were squatting in front of a hut, wrapped in their blankets and smoking. The troopers rode quietly past. One of the men got up to go behind the hut. But at a wink from the other he turned back and squatted down again.

The troop had aready gone by when the officer turned and halted it. He was thirsty and he rode up to one of the huts. After drinking he rode across to the other side and dismounted just where the two men sat smoking.

'Do you live here?' the officer asked.

'No, señor, we don't live here.'

'Where are you from, then?'

'Our home is in Comitala.'

'Right,' said the officer, and put his foot in the stirrup. He was going to mount and ride off with his troop.

He was tired and the horse danced round. He could not get his foot into the stirrup. One of the two mestizos got to his feet because the horse was almost on top of him. He came up and took hold of the stirrup to help the officer. His blanket fell from his shoulders.

The officer put his foot to the ground again.

'What's that in your trouser pocket?' he asked the mestizo.

The man looked down at the bulge in his pocket. He turned half round as though to enter the hut or to seek some way of escape. Then his eyes wandered to the troopers and back to the officer, and drawing at his cigarette and taking it from his lips again he blew out a small puff of smoke and smiled.

In an instant the officer had him by the open neck of his shirt, while with his left he made a grab for his pocket.

The other mestizo by this time was on his feet too. He shrugged his shoulders, as though annoyed by the disturbance, and looked about for another spot where he could squat and smoke in peace. But a sergeant and two troopers had dismounted, and neither of the men could escape.

The officer let go of the man's shirt collar and looked at what he had pulled out of his pocket. It was a nice plump, handsome leather purse. The officer laughed and the mestizo laughed too. Opening the purse, the officer shook the contents into the palm of his hand. Not a great deal – a little gold, some big silver pieces. About twenty-five pesos all told.

'Is this money yours?'

'Of course it's mine.'

'It's a lot of money. You might have bought yourself a new shirt.'

'So I shall tomorrow. I'm going to the town.'

But there was also a first-class ticket to Torreon in the purse. Mestizos never travel first. Moreover the date was the day of the hold-up.

They searched the other man. He had money on him too, but loose in his pocket. But there was a diamond ring in the watch pocket of his trousers.

At a wink from the sergeant the rest of the troop had dismounted.

'Where have you got your horses?'

'Behind there,' said the first mestizo, shaking tobacco on to a cigarette paper. Then he drew the string of his pouch tight with his teeth and rolled his cigarette. He was not nervous at all and not a flake of tobacco was spilt. Smiling calmly, he lit his cigarette and smoked, while another N.C.O. went through all his pockets.

The horses of the two were brought along and searched. Wretched saddles and bridles and a worn lasso.

'Where are your revolvers?' asked the officer.

'Where the horses were standing.'

The sergeant went there and kicked up a revolver and an old pistol out of the ground.

'What are your names?'

They gave their names and the officer wrote them down with an entry of what he had found.

People of the village had now come round. 'Where's your cemetery here?' the officer asked one of them.

The officer, and the troopers with the two mestizos among them, followed the villagers along the road to the cemetery. The rest of the villagers followed on behind, men and children and women with babies in their arms.

A spade was brought, and while the mestizos dug their graves the soldiers stood at the corner of the cemetery.

The officer smoked, the troopers smoked and chatted with the villagers. When the holes were deep enough, the two mestizos sat down and rested and rolled themselves another cigarette. After a while, the officer said: 'You can say your prayers now if you want to.'

He then told off six men and they fell in.

The two mestizos showed not the faintest concern or alarm. They crossed themselves, muttered a few words and crossed themselves again. Then lit one more cigarette, and without waiting to be told, stood up side by side.

As the officer gave the order to fire, the two bandits smoked another puff or two and threw their cigarettes away.

When the grave had been filled in the officer and troopers took their caps off and stood in silence for a moment. Then they put on their caps again, left the cemetery, mounted and rode away.

Why should the state go to further trouble when the ultimate aim is the same?

Another troop of cavalry caught sight of eight men on horseback among the foothills in front of them. Apparently the men saw the soldiers, for they abruptly broke into a trot and vanished. The officer pursued them with his troop, but he could not make out in what direction they had gone. There were so many hoof marks on the sandy track, leading in so many different directions, that the officer was at a loss which of them all to follow. He chose those that seemed to be the freshest.

After some hours the troop reached a lonely Hacienda. They rode into the spacious farmyard and dismounted in order to rest themselves for a bit. The owner of the Hacienda came out and the officer asked whether he had seen anything of a party of mounted men. The man declared that no one could have ridden past the place without his knowing it. Whereupon the officer informed him that he would have to search the Hacienda, and the owner replied that he might do as he liked, and went back into the house. The troopers were about to follow him when they were met by a volley from different parts of the house. By the time they had retreated through the yard gates they had four wounded and one dead.

A Hacienda is a large farm, and being enclosed by a stout high wall it stands up like a small fortress in the country round.

The soldiers were no sooner outside, carrying the dead and wounded with them, than the gates were shut and the defenders continued firing over the top of the wall.

A desperate fight now began, which, as both sides knew, could end only with the total annihilation of one side or the other, unless the ammunition gave out. The besieged had nothing to lose. They would be shot in any case, and their only hope of altering the situation lay in defending themselves to the last.

The first thing was to take the horses back out of range, and the bandits, having no ammunition to spare, wasted none on the horses during this operation.

The soldiers were up against it. The Hacienda stood in open country with arable and pasture round it. They could not hope to starve the bandits out, and to wait for artillery would have been too g at an indignity for either the officer or his men to stomach. There was nothing for it, then, but to take the place by storm.

The Hacienda was attacked from all four sides at once in a thoroughly professional style. Each detachment in turn made short rushes and then lay down and opened fire while another made a jump forward. They could not scale the walls; the objectives were the two gates, one in the front and one in the rear. After a three hours' engagement the officer contrived to concentrate the defence on the one in front, while he himself climbed the one in the rear, which was only defended by three men, and broke it open.

The bandits, however, did not give up the fight. It was continued in the yard and then the battle raged from the house itself. It was late in the afternoon before the soldiers were undisputed masters of the Hacienda. They had four dead, and eleven wounded, two seriously. In the yards and the house there were not only the eight men they had caught sight of, but several others of the train bandits as well.

Seven were dead and five wounded. These were immediately shot. The owner of the Hacienda was among the dead, and it was not known whether he was a bandit or whether he had been forced to harbour them under threat of death. The farm hands had kept out of harm's way and they now crept out again. It was certain they at least had nothing to do with the business. The farmer's family was away on a visit in the town. A search of the men's clothing brought to light a number of objects which could have come only from the plunder of the train.

In this way more and more of the bandits were taken, singly and in bands. But it is not easy in such cases to bag the lot in a short time, and the difficulties increase as time passes; and those who finally escape are not likely to spend the remainder of their days in the calm of contemplation.

'And you,' said Lacaud when he came to an end, 'you seriously believe that I could have anything to do with bandits who committed such a horrible crime as that?'

'It'll be no tea party if they come up here. That's one thing we can be sure of,' said Howard.

'Then those fellows must be the last of the gang,' said Dobbs.

'That's what I think. It was mentioned in the report that one of them was wearing a bronzed straw hat, and they take him to be the ringleader, and the bloodthirstiest of the lot.'

'Then it won't be any tea party if they come up here,' Curtin put in. 'But I don't see them any longer.'

'You can't see them, they're in the bend,' said Dobbs. 'When they come out of it we'll be able to see whether they turn up hill or down the valley.'

13

They sat up there on the cliff, keeping a watch to see when the men on horseback came out of the bend.

'How many did you count?' asked Howard.

'Ten or twelve,' said Curtin.

'There can't be that many of the bandits left according to your tale,' Howard said to Lacaud.

'No fear. They've caught most of them. But the four or five who were left will have come on some others and formed a new band with something else in view.'

'Bob's right, I dare say. And if that's so and they come up here, we're for it. They're after revolvers and ammunition. You know the village and the people down there,' Howard went on, turning to Curtin. 'Perhaps they searched the village for revolvers, and the Indians, to get rid of them, said that you were up here with a rifle because you were hunting here.'

'Damn it, you're right. That's how it will be. They'll be up here for sure after the rifle.'

'Then we don't want to lose any more time,' said Dobbs. 'Curtin, you can stay here as you've good eyesight and keep a look-out to see if they're coming. We'll go and get everything under hatches.'

They caught the donkeys and took them into a thicket on the other side of the cliff and tied them up securely. Then they got their firearms and two buckets of water and the bags of biscuits, and took them to a dry gully close up against the perpendicular face of the cliff. This gully was well fitted for defence, for they could neither be taken in the rear nor outflanked, and in front there was open ground, where any movement of an attacker could be seen and every man would offer a clear target.

'There'd be the time,' said Curtin during their preparations, 'to climb up the cliff and creep into a cleft and wait till they'd gone.'

'Oh, you fathead,' said Dobbs, 'then they'd come on the mine and we'd never get back there again to lift the colour we've got hidden there.'

'I've seen no mine here,' said Lacaud.

'We know that,' replied Dobbs. 'We must make a clean breast of it now, however. Of course we have a mine here, and as long as we're in possession they won't get to it. But if we slink off, then they'll look for Curtin and his rifle and come on the mine today or tomorrow. There's no time to shift our stuff now, and anyway we could never get away with it once there was anyone at the mine. No – we've got to watch out here and not give way to them. There's nothing else for it. Even if they don't know we have the fine stuff here, by the sackful too, they'll strip us to the soles of our feet and leave us to die.'

'That's so,' Howard agreed. 'If there was any other way out of it, I wouldn't come to grips with them. But we've no choice.'

'They've turned this way,' Curtin shouted. 'They're coming up!' He sprang down from the ledge. 'We've no time to lose.'

'How long will it be before they're here?' Howard asked. 'You know that better than we do.'

'Fifty minutes and they're here. If they came on foot and knew the short cuts, it might be ten minutes under.'

'You're quite sure they're coming up?' asked Dobbs.

'Once they've taken the turn up hill they can't go anywhere else. They've got to come up. There's nowhere they can turn aside.'

'They might turn back again.'

'They could do that, of course. But we'd best not wait to see.'

'We'll take down the tent,' Dobbs advised. 'Then they won't see at once that there's more than one of us here. Besides, it looks too prosperous.'

The tent was taken into a gully. Then they made openings to fire through, so as to have a clear field of vision without needing to raise their heads above their cover. They were discussing plans of action when they heard voices at the last bend of the path, and their hearts stood still.

A minute or two later the men emerged from the bush on the edge of the clearing. They had left their horses behind, no doubt at the last bend, for after that the path was too steep for horses. But perhaps there was another reason as well for leaving their horses behind. There were seven of the men; the remaining three were presumably with the horses, or posted where they could keep a look-out. All were armed. Every man had a revolver, and some rifles as well. They all wore their large straw hats and brightly coloured neckcloths, but apart from this they were a ragged crew. Two had sandals on and two were barefoot; one had a legging and a yellow lace boot on one leg, and a gumboot on the other. Not one had a whole shirt; but several had leather jackets and three wore long tight brown leather trousers reaching to the ankle. All were provided with one or more cartridge belts, and some had blankets thrown over their shoulders. Probably the blankets of the others, as well as the knapsacks containing provisions, were with the horses.

The open space they stepped on to was bounded on the further side by the perpendicular cliff and on the two other sides by thick and apparently impenetrable bush and thorny scrub, out of which rose an occasional tree. They looked about them with curiosity; and what they saw was apparently not quite what they had expected. It was obvious, however, that the clearing had very recently been a camping-place. There was wood lying about, the places where fires had been were still fresh, and the ash not yet dispersed; empty tins, broken crockery and bits of paper were scattered here and there; and then the patch where the tent had been was still clearly defined. The whole clearing was an irregular square of about sixty paces. It had been gradually enlarged by the daily wood-cutting and felling of trees for firing. The fresh stumps of felled trees showed that the camp had been recently occupied.

The men stood in a group and began to smoke. Some squatted down, while the others talked. The man with the bronzed straw hat seemed to be the leader, for they all looked towards him whenever he spoke.

They came forward a few steps and then stood still again and talked. It was easy to see that they did not know what to do next. One or two were clearly of the opinion that they were too late. The gringo had gone. Finally the leader too, whom they called Ramirez, came to the same conclusion.

The talk grew louder as they separated and addressed each other from a great distance; and the four in the gully were able to gather what their plans were and to take counsel accordingly. Perhaps the bandits after a few hours' rest would go their way and leave them in peace.

Although some of the bandits as they wandered here and there went close to the sides of the clearing, there was not much fear of them finding the path to the diggings; for Dobbs and Curtin had occupied the last hour in screening it, and as long as the scrub they had stuck into the ground did not wither the secret was safe.

At last after a lengthy pow-wow the bandits appeared to have come to some conclusion. They spoke so loud and with such emphatic gestures that the beleaguered men quickly learned what it was they thought of doing. They had decided to make this their headquarters until the hue and cry over the train robbery had died down and the soldiers had carried the pursuit further afield. The place seemed to them exceptionally favourable. There was water not far below, grazing for the horses near at hand, and food could be stolen from the cultivated lands in the valley if they tired of eating game. A little way down there was a point from which they could have an open view of the track in the valley below, and if soldiers were seen actually approaching, they could still escape, as long as in the meantime they could discover a bolt hole; for there was no way on into the mountains, and once the soldiers were on the way up they would be caught in a trap.

They had already made a thorough reconnaissance, and all they wanted was another way out, and this they were sure to come upon, if not there at the top, anyway lower down – perhaps near the spring.

'I was just thinking,' Howard whispered to Curtin, 'that we'd been fatheads not to hide ourselves at the mine. But I see now it would have been the silliest thing we could have done. If they're going to settle down here, they'd soon have come upon us at the mine. We couldn't have done better than we have.'

'Darned if I know, all the same, what we're to do if they make this their headquarters,' Dobbs whispered back. 'Not one of us thought of that. I thought myself they'd have a look round and then clear out again.'

'Wait a bit,' Lacaud put in. 'Perhaps they'll change their minds and go.'

'It wouldn't be a bad idea,' Howard suggested, 'if we scattered along the length of the gully. If they did happen to come nosing round they needn't find us all in a bunch and shoot us down like rabbits. They don't know there's more than one of us up here, and if we let them have it from several places at once they may get the wind up and quit.'

Howard and Lacaud took the two ends of the gully. Each had a good rifle. Curtin and Dobbs took the middle and placed themselves so that anyone approaching the gully would be unable to see both of them at once.

The bandits squatted here and there in the open not far from the narrow path out of which they had just emerged. They smoked and talked and laughed; two lay full length, asleep or dozing. One had gone to the horses to tell the men in charge of them that they were going to stay where they were and that they were to look out a place lower down where the horses could graze. Another had been sent to join the man on look-out, so that the two of them could watch the valley. And now the same thought came to all of them in the gully – here was their chance to draw a bead on those five devils who were still in the clearing, and loose off. Then when the five others came to their help, they could give them a warm reception from the safety of their ambush. In this way they might hope to be rid of the lot. Each of the four cursed himself for not having advised this plan of action while there was time. It could hardly be called murder, they thought: for the bandits were not men. They were vermin.

Dobbs kept thinking it over, until at last he could not keep it to himself any longer. He crept along to Howard, who was nearest.

'That's just what I was thinking,' the old man replied. 'But then we'd have their carcasses lying all about.'

'We can bury them, though,' Dobbs whispered.

'Course we can. But I don't want to turn the place into a cemetery. We may have to stay on here a week or two yet. Cemeteries are all right, but you don't want them in front of your windows day and night. Otherwise, I'm all for it; that fellow with the pock-marked face has such a villainous look that a grown man would be afraid to sit with him in church.'

'You won't meet him in church.'

'Won't you, though? Him and all this bloodthirsty lot. I take my oath it is just these fellows who hang up the most silver legs and arms at the feet of the Holy Virgin of Guadalupe and St Anthony. They crawl on their knees from the door to the altar and three times round the four walls. Go and look. You'll find each man with his little picture or medal hanging round his neck. The government here in Mexico knows what it's about when it takes the Church in hand so roughly. These people are ten times as superstitious as the blackest heathen of Central Africa. They're – but what's that fellow up to? He's coming straight across. Back to your post.'

Dobbs crept back as nimbly as a cat. One of the men was, in fact, strolling across towards the gully and making straight for the spot where Curtin sat. He was not looking at the gully in front of him, for his head was thrown back in order to survey the whole extent of the cliff above it. He seemed to be searching for their means of escape. Perhaps, too, he had an idea that the gringo they were after might be hidden there somewhere, or had made his way along the cliff and down into the valley. They had seen nothing of him on the way up.

He saw, however, that there was no foothold there. It was like a wall. He whistled to himself and turned to go back. Looking down, as he did so, he noticed the gully. For sure, he thought, there was the path they might yet have need of. He went nearer, almost to the edge of the gully, and there he saw Curtin.

Curtin had had his eyes on him all the time, so it was no surprise when he saw the man almost on top of him.

'Caramba!' the bandit called out. 'Come here. Here's the bird on its nest, sitting on its eggs.' He laughed loudly.

The rest of them jumped up and started forward in astonishment. But when they were half-way across, Curtin shouted: 'Halt, you bandits, or I'll shoot.'

The bandits stopped at once. They did not dare put a hand to their revolvers. They didn't know what might be coming.

The man who had discovered Curtin held his hands up at once and went back, still with his hands up, to the middle of the clearing where the others were.

Not a word was spoken for some time, and then they all began to talk at once in great excitement.

At last the leader stepped forward.

'We're not bandits, we belong to the police and it's the bandits we're after.'

Curtin raised his head a little. 'Where are your badges, then? If you belong to the police, one of you at least must have a badge. Let me have a good look at it.'

'A badge?' the leader replied. 'I haven't any badge. I don't need one and don't need to show one either. Come out of it, we've something to say to you.'

'You can say it where you are. I can hear you all right.'

'We'll arrest you. You're hunting here and have no licence. We are going to arrest you and take away your revolver and rifle.'

Curtin laughed. 'Where's your badge? You've no right to carry arms yourself. You've no badge, and you don't belong to the Federal Police or the State Police either. You've no power to arrest me.'

'Listen,' the spokesman said, coming a step nearer. 'We shan't arrest you. Only give us your revolver. Your rifle you can keep. We want your revolver and the ammunition for it.'

He came forward one more step, and the rest followed him.

'Not another step,' Curtin called out, 'or I'll fire.'

'Why not be a little more polite, señor? We shan't hurt you. We only want the revolver.'

'I need it myself.'

'Throw the thing over to us, then we'll go away and not bother you any more,' one of the others called out.

'You'll get nothing here, so clear out.'

Curtin had raised himself a little higher, to have a better view of the ground.

The men consulted again. They saw that the gringo had the advantage of them for the time in the ditch; he had good cover. The moment they drew their revolvers, he would drop his head, and before they could reach the cover of the bush he could shoot six times and shoot the lot if he shot straight. So they retreated and sat down on the ground. It was ten o'clock and their next thought was for warming up their tortillas and tamales and whatever else they had brought with them. They made a small fire and crouched round it to prepare their scanty meal.

They had naturally convinced themselves that the gringo was bound to fall into their hands in the long run. He could not get away and as they were going to make their camp there it could only be a matter of two days at longest before he gave himself up. Besides, he would fall asleep some time or other, and then they would have him.

After they had eaten they lay down for the midday sleep. It was two hours before they came to life again and began talking. They wanted something to do, and their need of occupation prompted the notion of capturing Curtin by a trick and passing a pleasant afternoon at his expense. The victim does not find this way of passing the time so pleasant. Sometimes he does not survive this game of forfeits. You see, in the churches these people look at so many images and pictures of the most bloodthirsty tortures: figures of saints and martyrs standing up there lacerated and stuck about with spears and arrows, mouths gaping to show the stump of a tongue, hearts torn out and dripping with blood and emitting red flames, nailed and gory hands and feet, broken knees and crushed knee-caps, backs flogged with fish-hooks, and heads on which crowns of thorns are planted with blows of a heavy wooden mallet. These images and wooden statues are so realistic that the sight of them is unspeakably terrible. They are a waking nightmare and before them for hours together the faithful and pious kneel on their knees with arms extended and open palms, weeping and groaning and praying and droning their Ave Marias by hundreds and five hundreds. And when the time comes and they want to have a pleasant hour with a victim, they have no need to exercise their powers of invention. They only need to copy what they have seen from their tenderest years in church. And they make a careful and faithful copy of the originals, for all the imagination they have has its origin in religion, in a religion which influences them only through material and realistic representations and ceremonial magic. It is here, in this country, that the whole hideous crucifixion story is acted during Easter week in all its minutest details, with life-sized figures and a shocking truth to nature, before the eyes of credulous multitudes. It is no passion play; the representation is taken in all its literal crudity by these wretched people, who have been left for centuries in ignorance and superstition by the powers of darkness in pursuance of their narrow aims and selfish interests. And a government which strives in a progressive spirit to lift the curse from this tormented land, and is forced, therefore, to wage war against these unholy powers, must also send cavalry regiments to capture and treat as criminals men who do nothing but copy what they see. Is it possible that the incredible cruelties of that train robbery could be committed by normal men? The heathen Indians of the Sierra Madre of Oaxaca, Chiapas and Yucatan are incapable of such bestialities. But the mestizos and Mexicans, who before undertaking a crime pray to the Mother of God and kneel for an hour to St Anthony, begging for his help in it, and who after the crime again throw themselves on their knees before the Mother of God and promise her candles if she will see that they are not caught, these men do not know a crime of a cruelty which they are not capable of executing. Their consciences can never be troubled, for they lay the burden of their sins on the backs of these images, which in their scheme of things were fashioned for that very purpose.

So now the bandits began to think of a pleasant afternoon's entertainment, with the innocent diversion of forcing glowing embers into their victim's mouth as the first item. They talked about it, too, quite openly, and so clearly and circumstantially that Curtin was able to understand what awaited him.

One of them pulled out his revolver and put it under his open leather jacket in such a way that no one would notice that he had it there ready to fire; and Curtin could not see the movement from where he was. But Lacaud saw it.

The men got up one after another, stretched, and went to the middle of the clearing.

'Listen, señor,' the man with the bronzed straw hat called out, 'we'll do a deal. We wanted to get off now. We have nothing to eat and we want to be at market early tomorrow. Give up the revolver. I've a gold watch and chain here. You can have it for your revolver. It's worth a hundred and fifty pesos. Good business for you.'

He pulled the watch from his trousers pocket and swung it about by the chain.

Curtin was on his feet again. He called out: 'Keep your watch and I'll keep my revolver. Please yourselves about going to market. But you won't get the revolver. And that's the end of it.'

He was just going to drop down again when the man with the revolver under his jacket took aim at him. He stood behind one of the others and even if Curtin had seen him he could not have seen that the gun was levelled at him. But before the bandit pulled the trigger a shot rang out and the revolver fell from his grasp. He threw up his arm and shouted out that he was hit.

When the shot rang out all the men turned in astonishment to the gully. They saw a small puff of smoke ascending into the air. But it came from the left-hand corner, not from where Curtin had been seen. Yet they could see nothing of the marksman or his revolver.

They were so astounded that not a sound came from them. They retreated warily to the edge of the clearing and as soon as they got there they sat down and began talking again. The men besieged in the gully could not hear what they said, but they could see that they were in the utmost confusion. Could it be the police in ambush there?

And now the three who were posted as look-outs came up in a hurry. They had heard the shot and thought they might be wanted. But the leader sent them back again, because everything pointed to the need of having their horses ready.

After they had talked together for some time they suddenly laughed aloud. They got up and came back to the middle of the clearing, laughing uncontrollably.

'Listen, señor, you can't play your tricks on us,' the leader called out. 'We saw your game. You've got a fixed rifle in the corner there and you fired it with a string. But you don't come it over us like that.'

They all laughed at the joke and in an instant each man had his revolver in his hand.

'Come out of it, you fool, before we pull you out,' the leader called. 'You've no time to lose. One, two, three! Now then!'

'I'll see you to hell first,' Curtin shouted. 'One step and I'll shoot.'

'We'll soon show you.'

With one accord they all dropped to the ground and with their revolvers in their hands they began to stalk Curtin's hiding-place from different directions. But they did not get far. Four shots rang out along the gully, and two of the men shouted that they were hit. They only had flesh wounds, certainly; for they all turned and crept back into the bush.

There they discussed what to do next. It was obvious now that the gully was held by more than one man, and perhaps by four or five. And what else could they be but a detachment of police? And in that case there would be more of them posted on the track to bar their retreat. There was nothing for it, then, but fighting it out. Nevertheless, they showed no disposition to begin the battle. Apparently they wanted to see what the party in the ditch were going to do. And when no attack followed and not a sound was to be heard, they became once more uncertain and wondered whether it might only be the gringo playing another trick on them. For if there were soldiers there, they would not wait. They would attack and drive them into the arms of the police ambushed below.

But the men on look-out had reported nothing, and when one of them came up he shook his head and maintained that there were no soldiers lower down. The track was clear.

Next, one of the men apparently urged a regular siege of the gully, for whether the garrison were soldiers or hunters it was now clear that there was more in it than they had thought at first. If there were several of them, they must all have arms, as well as provisions and a lot else, all of which would come in handy. At the same time, there could only be a few of them – otherwise they would have followed up their advantage and come to grips at the moment when their fire had thrown their opponents into confusion.

The four men in the gully now found time for a council of war, for they could see that the bandits were not going to take any action just yet. They all crept to the corner where Howard was and discussed what to do. They had something to eat, drank some water and took their ease and smoked as the bandits had done for hours past.

'If we only knew what they'll be up to next,' Curtin said.

'It comes to the same whether we know it or not,' said Howard. 'We can't do anything until they begin.'

'We could get out and go for them,' Dobbs suggested.

'Then they'd have us.' Howard shook his head as he filled his pipe. 'They don't know how many of us there are. But then they could split up. We can command the clearing, but we can't reach the track – they'd have us ambushed. And we can command the clearing only by staying quietly in the gully here. We don't know either whether there isn't another gang on the way up.'

'That's my advice – stay quietly where we are,' said Lacaud. 'They won't be here for ever.'

'But how long will the water and bacon biscuits last us?'

'Three days if we're careful.'

At this moment the donkeys began to bray. The bandits listened, but took no further notice. Perhaps it convinced them that they had not got soldiers to reckon with, for soldiers would not have come on donkeys. Even if they thought of taking the donkeys away with them, they would have to get possession of the open space before they could get to them.

Howard now said: 'We've got the night to think of. They've the chance to stalk us.'

'Not tonight nor tomorrow night,' said Lacaud. 'It's full moon and as light as day. I know that from last night.'

'That's true,' Howard agreed. 'We're in luck there. We'd best hold the two corners, two and two together for the night. Then one can sleep and the other watch out. If both sleep, then not one of us will ever wake again.'

Nothing more was seen of the bandits in the open. They kept in the bush, where they could be heard talking and occasionally seen moving to and fro in the undergrowth.

'Now's the time for two of us to get in a little sleep,' said Howard half an hour later. 'They won't come any more today. We can be sure of that. But I don't mind betting they come before dawn.'

They now took turns to sleep, and the night passed without incident except for a stealthy approach at nightfall. But before more than two of them were out of the bush a shot barked out and they gave it up. A little later the moon was so bright that a cat could not have crossed the open without being seen.

But at three in the morning Lacaud gave Curtin a nudge, and Howard prodded Dobbs.

'Are you awake?' Howard asked.

'Sure.'

'They're stirring. They're crawling out from four sides.'

'Seems to be all ten of them,' said Dobbs after looking out for a moment.

'Yes, they mean business this time. Let's hope the other two are on their guard at the other end. I tell you what, Dobbs – as soon as they're half-way, we'll fire. Pick a man and shoot straight, so they get it hot straight away. Then if the other two are nodding – that Curtin's a glutton for sleep – they'll wake up when we fire. And they'll still have time.'

But before the enemy reached the middle of the clearing, two shots came from the corner where Curtin and Lacaud were. For it had occurred to them too that it might be as well to rouse Dobbs and the old boy before the bandits got too close.

The attackers, however, were not to be scared off. They crawled on. None of them had been hit – at least not seriously. Not a curse nor a cry escaped them.

Dobbs and the old man now loosed off and one of the bandits cursed; so he no doubt had got one.

Apparently they thought the fixed rifles had now all been fired off – but whatever they may have thought they decided anyway to make a quick end of it, for after crawling a little way they jumped up and made for the gully in open order, crouching as they ran.

Now, naturally, they offered a far better target. Three were hit at once. Two of them clasped a wounded arm and the third limped back with a bullet in the leg. Fire was kept up without a pause from the gully, while the attackers could make no use of their weapons because they could see nobody to shoot at.

They dropped to the ground again and passing the word along began creeping back to the bush.

After this it was soon daybreak. Experience had taught them that a daylight attack was not to be thought of.

When the four assembled in one corner for breakfast, Howard said: 'They'll come back tonight. And they'll have some other plan of attack. There's no chance now of their giving it up. We've shown what a good fort this ditch makes. They couldn't find a better place for their headquarters. Then there's our firearms and the rest of our traps. We must think out what we're to do.'

But four against ten who could retreat when they liked, four, whose drinking water had to be eked out, against ten who had water in their rear as well as provisions and even fresh forces – what plans were they to make? And the attackers had the further advantage of being able to sleep or not as they chose.

Curtin, who was standing sentry while the rest ate, suddenly called out: 'Come here. What are they up to? This looks bad.'

The other three went at once to the openings they had scooped out for firing through, and they all saw at once the danger they were in.

The bandits were very busy. They were breaking off branches and pulling down young trees and beginning to construct a movable palisade after the fashion of the Indians. Concealed behind it they would be able to stalk the ditch at their leisure and rout out the besieged without further trouble. A shot or two might be exchanged at close quarters in the ditch, but the end was certain.

Even Howard could think of nothing to counter this manoeuvre. They could do nothing but sell their lives as dearly as possible in the hand-to-hand fight at the finish. Any one of them who was taken alive would have little to rejoice about.

'The only thing that surprises me is why they haven't done it before this,' said Curtin. 'It's an old Indian trick.'

'Too much trouble,' Howard replied.

They talked it over, but they could think of no way out of the plight they were in. They might hack a way through the bush, but they'd be seen at once. They thought, too, of the mine. But that would not delay their fate very long. At last they came back to the idea of making an attack, in spite of the hopelessness of it – considering that they would attack across the open while the others would be in cover and in command of the track. Finally they dropped this idea too, for even Dobbs, who had urged it more eagerly than any of them, saw that it was sheer folly.

If only the cliff gave a foothold – but it was too steep, and even if they made the attempt in the hope of finding foothold higher up above the projecting shoulder, there would be nothing gained. The attempt could not be made in the night, and by day they would be shot down without trouble and without the chance of putting up a fight.

They could do nothing but sit and watch the enemy at their work. It would be completed by four in the afternoon, and then they might expect the attack, unless the night were thought a better time for it.

It was getting on for eleven. The bandits sat eating their midday meal near the entrance to the clearing. They were in good spirits and laughing. The four in the gully were clearly the objects of their mirth, for whenever they thought they had made a good joke they looked across at the ditch. Then there was suddenly a shout:

'Ramirez, Ramirez, pronto, muy pronto, quick here!'

One of the look-outs came running up the path and rushed up to the leader. All jumped up and disappeared down the path. They could be heard talking excitedly as they went farther and farther away.

Then no more could be heard and the besieged men wondered what to make of it.

'It's a trick,' Dobbs said. 'They want us to think they've gone – to fetch us out. Then they'll be lying in wait for us farther down.'

'I don't think so,' Howard put in. 'Didn't you see how excited the look-out was when he ran up?'

'That's part of the ruse, so as we'll think they've cleared out in a hurry.'

But Howard shook his head. 'They don't need any ruse once they'd hit on that Indian trick.'

Dobbs, however, was not to be persuaded. 'That Indian trick's all right. But it might cost them a few men, dead and wounded, and perhaps they're short of ammunition. If they can catch us without needing to fire a shot, and without our firing off our ammunition, which they regard as their own now, they'd be fools not to try it on. If it doesn't succeed, they still have their screens in reserve.'

'You may be right,' Howard admitted. 'It may be they want to save our ammunition; for if they come for us, naturally we loose off all we've got.'

Curtin had not joined in the discussion. He had crawled cautiously farther along the gully and then climbed up the projecting shoulder of the cliff. As there was nothing to be seen of the bandits and their voices came from a distance, he ventured to make use of it as a look-out.

He crouched on the shoulder of the cliff and looked down into the valley. He sat there for a good while. Then suddenly he called out: 'Hallo – out with you. There's a squadron of cavalry down below there. They're after our friends here.' The other three crept forward and all climbed up to the look-out; and a lively scene greeted their eyes. The troopers, in six detachments, were sweeping the plain in all directions. No doubt they had heard that the bandits were somewhere in the neighbourhood; and as they knew that the bandits had horses, they would not be thinking of the mountains where it was scarcely possible for a horse to go.

Lacaud, however, was of another opinion. 'Seems to me they know already where they're hiding. But they have more sense than to run into an ambush. Once they started climbing, shut in by thick bush and sheer rock, they couldn't do much – or only with heavy losses. Either they're going to bottle them up in the mountains or else they have some wheeze – and I think it's that.'

The soldiers swept on – five or six kilometres out into the valley. Till then the bandits had been sure their hiding-place was discovered. But now when they saw the soldiers riding farther away they began to think they were safe. A stretch of the track up the mountain could be seen and Curtin observed that the bandits came riding back to resume possession of their headquarters.

But the officer of the Federal Troops was by a long way more wily than they.

When the detachments were far enough off they began, as could easily be made out even at that distance, to pick up a trail. With wide circling movements and a vigorous riding to and fro, they let it be seen that they had at last discovered for sure that the bandits were among the crags. They reformed in column, without great haste, and made for the mountains and the track leading up into them. This was a feint. They knew that the bandits would do anything rather than allow themselves to be shut up in their mountain fastness, as long as the least chance was left of reaching other ground. Once their retreat was cut off, they would never extricate themselves from the wilderness of rock, and the troops had only to hold the approaches without needing to attack or expose themselves on the mountain paths to the bullets of the bandits ambushed in the thickets and rocky clefts.

Every movement of the troops was carefully noted by the bandits' look-outs. As soon as they realized that their hiding-place was discovered, they decided to take advantage of the start without a moment's delay and break away into the open country under the perfect cover afforded by the bush. Once there they could make themselves scarce, and even if they were discovered it would not be until their well-rested horses had so increased their start that the soldiers would perhaps lose the trail again.

But a small detachment of mounted troops lay concealed in the bush towards the side of the country which the bandits made for. This detachment had taken up its position the night before, when it was impossible for the bandits, who were in any case occupied with their night attack up above, to know anything about it. Shots had been heard in the night, echoing far down the valley from the face of the cliff, and this had convinced the ambushed soldiers that they were on the right track. They had no idea, of course, what the shooting was about, but they supposed either that the bandits were drunk or that they had accounts to settle among themselves.

The four men sat up there and waited for the fight; they reckoned that it would be an hour before the curtain went up. Once the show was over, they would be able to go back in peace to their interrupted labours.

Now the first shots were heard, and the main body, after entic-ing the bandits from their lair, wheeled and went for them at the gallop. The bandits were now cut off from the mountains, and uttering wild cries and waving their arms they raced for the open, urging their horses on by brutally goring their sides with their long spurs; and the horses fled down the valley at headlong speed.

Behind them followed the troopers who had been lying hidden in the bush. They had first had to mount after being disappointed in their hope that the bandits would pass close enough to give a good target. Thus the bandits got the start here too. On they rode, and as they rode they shot at their pursuers.

'All the better if they get a good start,' Howard said.

'Why?' Dobbs asked in surprise.

'We'll be quit of the soldiers too. They might pay us a visit to see if any more bandits were in hiding up here. They've got us out of a tight corner, but we don't want them here all the same. I'd rather keep our thanks until we're well on the way home.'

On and on they rode; the sounds of firing grew fainter; and soon the watchers on the cliff could no longer see how the race would end, for the riders disappeared into the quivering horizon.

14

The camp was once more in going order; they had cooked and eaten a meal and lain for a long time round the fire. There were still several hours of daylight, but not one of them suggested doing any work that day.

When it grew dark they were still round the fire, drinking coffee and smoking.

'Howard's right,' said Curtin. 'We'd best give up and shut down the mine. We might perhaps get another thousand, but we'd do better to be content with what we have. Some more uninvited guests may blow in and we may not come out of it so well next time.'

At first nobody answered. Then after a pause Dobbs gave his opinion:

'That'll suit me, for one. Tomorrow we'll shut down the mine, and next day early we'll sort things out and pack up and get the donkeys in, and early the day after we'll get off. I've had my bellyful too.'

Lacaud listened and made no remark. He smoked and looked with apparent indifference into the fire. Now and then he got up and broke a branch across his knee, and those he could not break he threw whole on the fire.

'Do you know the story of the Cienega Mine?' he asked abruptly.

'We know so many stories of mines,' Howard said wearily. He was absorbed in dreaming over his plans for employing his share of the takings to the best advantage, so as to have an easy life of it while his money doubled of its own accord, and then increased by stages to a hundredfold. Lacaud's question disturbed the computations by which he was arriving at the hundredfold. He was afraid he had made a mistake in his figures, and as he was too tired to go over the rows and columns again in his mind, he said: 'Sure – we'd forgotten all about you.'

At this Dobbs and Curtin looked up too, and Curtin laughed. 'That only shows what a damned lot you mean here. You'd dropped right out, although you fought with us and sit here now with us over our food and drink. Fact is, we've our own affairs to think about, and you don't come in there.'

'Weren't you saying something about some plan?' Dobbs asked. 'You can keep it. I don't give a damn for it – not if there's another ten thousand in it. I don't want them. I want the towns and to see some girls and to sit at a table with a cloth and a waiter to put the food down on it. I want to see how other people cook, for a change, and slave for a starvation wage.'

'There's more than ten thousand,' said Lacaud.

'Where?' asked Curtin.

'In my plan.'

'Oh – in your plan,' Curtin replied, and yawned.

'The stuff's there to see.' Lacaud tried to get them interested, but without success, for Dobbs said: 'If it's there to see, then pick it up. Don't leave it lying. Otherwise you may be sorry later. You're just the man who's always regretting something and always has something to regret. Well, I'm going to turn in.'

Howard and Curtin too got heavily to their feet, stretched and yawned, and went over to the tent. Curtin stopped on the way there, lost in reflection; then turned round, and stretched himself again as he looked up at the moon.

A thought struck him and he called into the tent: 'Howard, did you block the path when you let the donkeys loose this afternoon?'

'Sure,' Howard called back. 'At the bend beyond the grass patch, where we always do, near the pool.'

Lacaud meanwhile brought his bags along and lay down by the fire.

Curtin went up to him.

'You can come into the tent, man. There's room for a little one.'

But Lacaud replied that he was all right where he was. 'I'd always rather sleep by the fire than under cover. But say – won't you come in on it? Trust my word, there's something in it?'

'Come in on what? Oh yes – your plan. No, I'm too keen to be gone. I can't stand any more of it. We've got all there is to find here, and I won't do another hand's turn.'

Curtin went across to the tent and crept in.

'What did the guy want from you?' asked Dobbs.

'On about his plan, but I put him off.'

'I don't know what to make of him,' said Howard. 'I shouldn't be surprised if he had a screw or two loose. If I knew what he's been up to the last six months, I could tell you whether he's the wandering digger or just bush crazy. Perhaps both.'

'The wandering digger?' Curtin asked curiously.

'Yes, one of those who're always prospecting for gold, and know fairy tales by the dozen of lost and buried gold-mines, and has plans and drawings by the dozen too in his pocket or in his head, which show him the way to a forgotten mine, and dozens of silly yarns told him by Indians and mestizos about places where gold and diamonds are to be found. He looks and looks, and the more wild and untrodden the mountains and the greater the danger, the more convinced he is that he's on the track of a lode as thick as your arm. But he never comes on a grain though he knows for sure that he's right on top of it and must strike it next day. It's a kind of lunacy which can make a man as dangerous to his fellows as any other kind. And the victims are more to be pitied than other loonies, because they're always roaming without rest and without end. They're nearly dead of hunger one day, and of thirst the next; one time they have to defend themselves against mountain lions; rattlesnakes and other poisonous beasts and reptiles, another time against Indians; then again they fall and break their bones, and there they lie till they're found by some Indian or by bandits who take the trouble to fix them up again. But nothing stops them. They always know they're sure to find a gold-mine tomorrow.'

'That's not how he strikes me,' said Dobbs. 'There's something else in him besides that.'

'Maybe so,' Howard agreed. 'He can be what he likes for all I care. All I worry about is what to do with him if he tries to hang on to us when we go. We can't have that.'

'He'll see the mine tomorrow,' said Curtin.

'Doesn't matter now if he does,' Howard replied. 'We'll shut it down and if he likes to stay and open it up again, that's his own affair.'

Next morning, after breakfast, Howard, Dobbs and Curtin got to work in earnest. To their surprise Lacaud showed no disposition to crawl along with them to the mine. Certainly they hadn't asked him to, but they took it for granted that such a thing as a gold-mine would not be beneath his notice. He did not even ask a question about it. As soon as he had drunk up his coffee, he got up and went down the path.

Curtin followed him because he thought he might be going down to the village to let them know there that the time had come to rob the nest before it was too late. Lacaud did not know that Curtin was following him. He went his way unsuspectingly, stopping only to note the bigger trees and every rock, as though he were looking for some landmark. Now and then he bent down to examine the ground. At last he came to the grassy patch where the donkeys were. He crossed it to the pool. After inspecting it carefully he looked up at the face of the cliff. He went to the foot of it and, stooping down, began to poke about there.

Convinced now that Lacaud had other designs and was not proposing to cook their broth for them, Curtin went back to the other two and told them what he had seen.

'What did I tell you?' said Howard. 'The wandering gold-digger. We don't want to have any truck with him.'

He and Dobbs were busy breaking up the plant, and Dobbs had scratched his hand. Losing his temper, he said: 'What are we taking it down at all for? Why not leave it standing and clear out?'

'We agreed at the outset that if we found the fine stuff, we'd take our plant to pieces and fill in the trenches.'

'It's only delaying us and I don't know what's the good of it,' Dobbs growled.

'Well, boy, for a start I think the least we can do is to show some gratitude to the ground which has been so generous to us. We can close the wounds we've inflicted on it and not leave it disfigured. It's not decent to leave it cluttered up with our gear and turn its garden into a builder's yard. The mountain has earned of us the right to have its beauty respected. I'd rather remember the place as it was when we came than have it always before my eyes as the rubbish shoot we've made of it. It's bad enough that we can do no more than show our good intentions. This spot will still be an eyesore when we're gone.'

'It's a bit far-fetched what you say about the mountain,' said Curtin, 'but all the same I agree that you should sweep out the room that was clean when you came, even though there's no one there to praise you for it.'

'There's another reason, too,' the old man continued. 'It might be that someone came up here while we were on our way back. He'd see in a flash what we'd been up to and he'd be on our heels with half a dozen more. If we make things as shipshape as we can, it'll only look as if we'd been camping here a long time for some reason or another – not that it was washing dirt and nothing else. So lend a hand, Dobbs; we worked many a day for nothing till the mountain opened its hand, and the day's work is worth it even though it brings nothing in. When you make a garden for your home, it isn't with the idea of a cash return.'

The midday meal in the course of months had become short and simple. They made a tin of tea and ate a bit of leathery pancake, cooked early in the day. As soon as the tea was drunk and each had smoked a pipe, they went back refreshed to their labours. Not a moment of daylight could be wasted; breakfast had to be over by the time the sun rose and supper begun only when it had set. Otherwise they could never have got through all they had. The length of the days was pretty well the same all the year through, and what difference there was they scarcely noticed. Nor had the rainy season had much effect on their labours. Now and then the rain had poured down in regular cloudbursts; but there was always something else they could turn their hands to. The rain, in any case, was of some help, for it filled the tank they had dug out so as to have enough water for washing the sand, and saved them the labour of carrying water.

'It's been a dog's life,' said Curtin, sitting down a moment to rest.

'You're right,' the old man agreed. 'But when you look at it, none of us has ever worked for higher wages than we've earned here.'

Dobbs too had put his spade aside and sat down to fill a pipe. 'It strikes me,' he said slowly, 'that there's not much to shout about yet. I don't mean as regards what we've got, but until we have the whole box of tricks safely stowed away in a town and sit quietly in a hotel bedroom with it all in front of our eyes, we can't say it's actually ours.'

'That's what I've been thinking too these last weeks,' the old man said. 'It'll be touch and go getting back with it, what with bandits, and accidents on the road, and the police who may be inquisitive and want to know what we have with us. And if they catch sight of the yellow stuff, then either we've stolen it, or killed and robbed somebody, or we've dug it without a licence and evaded paying the tax. All that needs thinking about. Yes, you can turn it over in your minds, how we're to come to port with our cargo of pepper.'

The two younger partners were silent. Then they wrinkled up their foreheads in the effort of thought and groaned, for it cost them more than the hardest navvy work; and finally with deep sighs they got up and went on levelling the heaps of earth.

Late in the afternoon they collected all the dismembered equipment into a heap and burnt it. Next day the charred patch was to be strewn with soil. Then a few shrubs, young trees and turf were to be planted here and there.

'It might happen, you see,' the old man remarked, 'that one of us didn't get home with it, or else blued it all in a few weeks, or came to grief one way or another. Then he could come back here and puddle again. There'd be something left for him to get. That's another reason for leaving no traces behind us, which might put someone else up to having a look round here.'

Dobbs and Curtin understood this better than the old man's notion of showing gratitude to the mountain and not leaving the face of Nature disfigured. Dobbs was of the opinion that Nature could look after herself. She had more time and patience than he had; and he was not night-watchman of the lonely mountain landscape. But they had promised the old fellow, and so they did it; he was old, and even after all these months he still seemed to them a bit of a freak.

By the time they downed tools, no one would have supposed from a casual glance that there had ever been a mine there. There was only the bonfire still glowing and smoking. Next day the last signs of it would disappear.

Lacaud had not been by the fire at midday, and none of them knew whether he had been in the camp either before or afterwards. They had forgotten all about him. They were too much occupied with their own affairs to think of him. It was not until they came creeping out from their concealed track and saw him crouching over the fire and making it up that they remembered he was still there.

'Have you found your gold-mine yet?' Dobbs asked him as he came up to the fire with the kettle of water.

'Not yet,' Lacaud replied. 'But I don't know when I've been so close to it as I've been today.'

'Then I wish you the best,' Curtin laughed, bringing the frying-pan.

Lacaud had a pot of his own rice on the fire.

'You needn't make yourself any coffee,' Howard said good-humouredly. 'You can share ours. We don't put any more coffee in, only more water, and we needn't go easy with the water any more now.'

'Thanks,' Lacaud said shortly.

They washed and ate and sat by the fire. Howard, Dobbs and Curtin felt like factory hands on a Saturday night. They knew that they had nothing worse in front of them than a pleasant hour's work first thing in the morning, planting up the vacant space where the mine had been, followed by the even more pleasing job of packing up; and after that there was only getting donkeys ready for the journey. It was all light and welcome labour over which they could smoke and sing and chat.

And so for the first time for months past they sat in comfort and good humour round the fire.

The thought that they were soon to separate, after sharing for nearly a year the anxieties and labours and privations of their life together, made them more tolerant of one another than they had ever been. They felt for the first time that they were bound together by a bond of friendship, comradeship and brotherhood. They felt that they would stand by each other even at the cost of their lives. They felt closer to each other than actual brothers. Without saying so, they were sorry for all the petty and yet very contemptible malice and spite they had so often been guilty of towards each other.

Lacaud was excluded from this brotherhood. He could not read and understand their feelings as they, who knew each other off by heart, could. They could make no secret of what went on inside them; but they could keep it a secret from Lacaud if they wanted to, and even deceive him and lead him astray. This they could never do among themselves. Each during the past months had had no study but the study of each other. Neither books nor news-papers nor change of scene or faces had distracted them from this common study. It often happens that as soon as one of them began a sentence, the others knew how it would conclude, even the exact words and their exact sequence. Hence a remarkable habit had arisen of never concluding a remark at all; there was no need, for the other replied as soon as three or four words had been spoken. That was one reason for their getting so much on each other's nerves that they could have committed murder just to be spared the irritation of being forced to know beforehand what the other man was going to say. But what was there to enrich their vocabulary or enlarge their ideas? They were concerned always with the same circumstances and the same tasks, and without knowing it they had evolved a method of communication entirely their own which left an outsider stranded.

They had constructed a paddle-wheel, and this was set in motion by means of a primitive capstan to which a donkey was harnessed. This contrivance scooped up the water into the gutter which conveyed it to the washing-troughs where the dirt was puddled. Howard used to take charge of the capstan, as it was lighter work. Originally, they shouted: 'Howard, pump the water along. We're ready for it.' This had been abbreviated to: 'Pump'. And this word, pump, had finally come to mean water, because it was shorter and easier to say pump than water. When they meant water for making coffee or for drinking, they said simply: 'Pump a fire?' which meant: 'Is there water on the fire?' A spade, for reasons which none of them could explain later, was a cat, a pickaxe a shrike, and a dynamite cartridge a Mary. When a Mary was to be detonated, two words were used. One was Mary; the other cannot, for reasons of politeness and also on other grounds, be given here, although in a certain context and in certain conditions it can well apply to any Mary. The same word was used in reference to lighting a pipe or the fire. Eat, besides referring to meal times, acquired a meaning almost the opposite and stood for a word seldom employed by polite persons and not even alluded to without great caution.

Howard was never called by his name. He was called Olb, and this had been evolved from old boy. Curtin was Cow and Dobbs Pamp. Why, none of them could have said.

It was the same with all the words and phrases they used. They could talk for ten minutes without Lacaud's understanding a word they said; and of course it never occurred to them that he couldn't follow them and sometimes felt he was among foreigners. They

were so used to talking as they did that it would have seemed to
them ridiculous to talk in any other way.

15

'Yes, as for getting back . . .' Howard picked up the discussion
where they had left it at midday. Instead of getting back he said
kipping, but their talk must be put into a form which can be
understood by those who are not of the brotherhood.

'Yes, as for getting back, it's the devil. We'll get back all right, I
don't doubt. But even when you think you've got home with it,
you're a long way from having opened a bank account. Did you
ever hear the story of Donna Catalina Maria de Rodriguez? I'm
sure you didn't. With her too it wasn't just a question of the gold
and silver, but of getting away with it and putting it somewhere
safe. At Guadalupe there's the miraculous image of Our Lady of
Guadalupe, the patron saint of Mexico. You can go there by train
from Mexico City. Every Mexican and Indian who has anything on
his mind makes a pilgrimage to this wonder-working image in the
certain hope that his desire will be granted, whether a man wants
an acre of his neighbour's land, or a girl has lost her lover, or a wife
is in fear of its coming out she's poisoned her husband to get
another one instead of him.'

'It's all eyewash and superstition,' Dobbs put in.

'Not a bit of it,' replied the old man. 'It's no eyewash as long as
you believe in it. If a man believes in a God, for him there is a God;
and if he doesn't, then for him there's no such thing. But there's no
need to argue about that. I'm not saying what I think. I'm telling
you the sober truth.

'It was about a hundred and fifty years ago, just about the time of
the American Revolution. There was a prosperous Indian living
near Huacal, a descendant of the chiefs of the Chiracahuas. He had
all the land he wanted and took no part in the raids and murders of
the neighbouring tribes. His own tribe was settled on the land there

111

and found more pleasure and profit in cultivating it than in ever-lastingly scrapping with the Spaniands. This chieftain had only one sorrow in the world: his only son and heir was blind. In earlier days the child would have been killed: but now that he and his tribe had settled down and all the tribes been converted to Christianity, their ideas were more humane. Added to that, the child was strong and shapely and unusually beautiful.

'A wandering monk, who wanted to exploit the liberality of the chief to the last inch, advised the father to make a pilgrimage with the boy and his mother to the miraculous Virgin of Guadalupe, and not to be sparing of his offerings; for the Mother of God was greatly pleased by generosity and well able to appreciate the worth of what was given her.

'The chief left his estate in his uncle's charge and set out on his pilgrimage. He was not allowed to employ horse, donkey or wagon and had to make his long trek of nearly two thousand kilometres on foot with his wife and child. He had to say three hundred Ave Marias in every church he passed by and offer large numbers of candles and silver eyes.

'At last he reached Mexico and after offering up prayers and petitions in the cathedral, for several hours he prepared for the last stage of his painful ordeal. It is five kilometres from the cathedral to the miraculous image of Guadalupe. He and his wife with their little boy had to go on their knees for these five kilometres, each of them holding a lighted candle which had to be kept alight in spite of wind and rain. When one candle came to an end, another had to be lighted from it, and as they were consecrated candles they cost more than ordinary ones. It took all night to get there. The boy fell asleep, and even in his sleep he cried for a little piece of maize cake and a drink of water. But they were forbidden to eat or drink. They waited until the child was quieter and then the procession went on. All who met them, Spaniards and Indians, got out of their way and crossed themselves, for they thought the family must be guilty of some unusually discreditable sin if they had to expiate it by such a terrible pilgrimage.

'They were utterly exhausted when they got to the foot of the Cerrito de Tepeyacac, the hill on which in the year 1532 the Mother of God appeared three times to the Quauhtlatohua Indian, Juan Diego, and printed her picture on his ayate, or outer garment. Here they spent three days and nights on their knees, praying and imploring. The chief had promised the Church his cattle and his whole harvest if the Mother of God came to his help. But the miracle did not happen. At last, following the monk's advice, he promised his land and all he had, if the Virgin gave sight to his son.

'But even now there was no sign of the miracle he awaited and had been so confidently promised. The child was so exhausted with his long fast and the fatigue of the journey that it took all his mother's care to keep him alive.

'The chief, not knowing what more he could do, began to doubt the power of the Mother of God and of the Christian religion in general, and he said that he would now go to the medicine men of his race who had often enough proved to his forefathers that the old Indian gods had power to work miracles. The monk forbade him to speak in so blasphemous a manner, and threatened him that more disaster would fall on his family if he gave utterance to his doubts. And they told him that the fault was his own. The miraculous Virgin knew very well, what no one else might know, that he had done wrong on his journey – passed over a church here; purposely miscounted his Ave Marias there, to be quicker done; eaten when he ought not and on various occasions drunk water in the morning without first kneeling down and praying. The chief was forced to confess that he might now and then have said two hundred and eighty instead of three hundred Ave Marias, because of the difficulty of keeping count. And, said another monk, he had no doubt omitted to confess various sins, when he confessed in the cathedral; for to all who deserved it the miraculous Mother always granted help in their need. Therefore he had better repeat the pilgrimage in six months.

'Perhaps this was too much for the chief, or else – and this seems more probable – he had lost his faith in the miraculous power of the image. In any case, he returned to Mexico, ate heartily and took his young wife in his arms again, as, in obedience to the task he had been set, he had not done during the whole journey. Then he made inquiries in the town and was recommended to go to the house of a certain Don Manuel Rodriguez. Don Manuel was a famous Spanish doctor, but avaricious and greedy of power. He examined the boy and told the chief that probably he would be able to give him his sight. What would the Indian pay?

'The chief said he had a farm and many cattle. But that, said Don Manuel, was not money. "I want money, a lot of money." The chief then told him that he would make him the richest man in all New Spain if he gave his son his sight. How, asked Don Manuel, could he do that out of his farm? The chief replied that he knew of a rich gold- and silver-mine, and he would take him to it when his son could see. And they made the terrible contract that Don Manuel should have the right to put out the eyes of his son, if the mine either did not exist or by this time belonged to someone else.

'Don Manuel gave his whole attention to the boy for two whole months, working on him and performing operations, and neglecting all his other patients, even the Viceroy's private secretary. And after two months the child could see like an eagle. Don Manuel told the chief that the cure was permanent. And so it was.

'The chief was overjoyed and his gratitude knew no bounds. "Now I will prove, Don Manuel, that I did not lie to you," he replied when Don Manuel asked about the payment. "The mine belongs to my family. When the Spaniards came my ancestor covered it up, because we wanted no Spaniards in our country. We hated them and knew that the white men loved gold and silver more than their Son of God. The existence of the mine was betrayed to the Spaniards, and they came and tore out the tongues of my ancestor and his wife to make them say where the mine was. But though his mouth was full of blood and he was nearly frantic with agony, my ancestor laughed in their faces and they never got hold of the mine. And my ancestor wrote the words down, and after his death they went by word of mouth from father to son, until they came to me, and these are the words: 'If some great service is done to you or your family or your race, greater than the feather-crowned god of our people or the blood-crowned god of the white people was able or willing to perform, then give the treasure to the man who performs it and let it be his.' You, Don Manuel, have, in the person of my son, done to me, my family and my race that service which the god of the white people was too weak to do, in spite of all my pains and prayers and offerings, and therefore the mine is yours. Follow after me, on the road I will tell you, in three months' time, and speak to no one of what you know, and I will make you the richest man in all New Spain."

'The Indians,' Howard said, continuing his tale, 'don't know of many more mines than we do. At one time they knew the exact position of all the hidden mines of which, after the conquest of Mexico, the Indians obliterated every trace in revenge for the cruelties inflicted on them. But the Indians have not been stationary since the days of the conquest. Thousands of them were carried into other districts by the Spaniards as workpeople and slaves; others in the course of rebellions and wars were driven from their homes into the hills and the jungle; others perished of the poxes and epidemics which the white men introduced into their country in the cause of civilization; the families of chiefs died out or were murdered before they could hand on their knowledge to those who followed them. Hence it is very seldom now that an Indian knows of a buried mine. Sometimes he thinks he knows of one, but what is known in his family about this mine or the other has become so legendary, so mixed up with mines already discovered and known, that the actual site can never be identified, all the more as the site is described by words and landmarks and directions which in the course of time have lost their original meaning and are bound to put you on a false track. This story I am telling you goes back to a time when the traditional memory of the Indians was fresher and less influenced by the trade and commerce brought by the railways. These have caused the Indians to move about much more freely. They leave their homes and go wherever there are better opportunities of making their living.

'As soon as Don Manuel had wound up his affairs in Mexico he and his wife Maria made the long and difficult journey to Huacal. He found the chief and was welcomed by him like a brother. "It occurred to me on the journey," Don Manuel said to his host, "that it's a very strange thing you didn't work the mine yourself, Aguila. You could have given me a hundred thousand gold gulden, and for that I'd have done whatever you asked."

'The chief laughed.

' "I want no gold and I want no silver. I have enough to eat, I have a good and beautiful wife and a son whom I love and who is strong and well formed. What is gold to me? The earth brings a blessing; the fruits of it and my herds of cattle bring blessings. Gold brings no blessing and silver brings no blessing. Does it bring the blessing to you white Spaniards? You murder each other for gold. You hate each other for gold. You spoil the beauty of your lives for gold. We have never made gold our master, we were never its slaves. We said: Gold is beautiful. And so we made rings of it and other adornments, and we adorned ourselves and our wives and our gods with it, because it has beauty. But we did not make it into money. We could look at it and rejoice in it, but we could not eat it. Our people and also the peoples of the valleys have never fought or made wars for gold. But we have fought much for land and fields and rivers and lakes and towns and salt and herds. But for gold? Or silver? They are only good to look at. I can't put them into my belly when I am hungry, and so they have no value. They are only beautiful like a flower that blooms, or a bird that sings. But if you put the flower in your belly, it is no longer beautiful, and if you cook the bird it sings no longer."

'Don Manuel laughed.

' "I shan't put the gold in my belly, Aguila. Trust me for that."

'The chief laughed too.

' "I believe you. I can work for the earth, but I cannot work for gold, because then I should have nothing to eat, no tortillas and no camotes. You don't understand what I say, and I don't understand what you say. You have another heart. But all the same I am your friend."

'For three days they searched about in the mountains and the bush, scratching about and digging. Don Manuel was inclined to be suspicious of this long search and to believe that the Indian had cheated him of his reward. But then again, when he saw how cleverly and methodically the chief examined the neighbourhood, how accurately he noted the position of the sun and also the shadows which were thrown by the mountain tops, he was forced to recognize that he was not taking his course at random. "It is not as simple as you thought," said the chief. "There have been earthquakes, and a few hundred years of rainy seasons and cloud-bursts and landslides; rivers have changed their beds, streams have vanished and new ones risen. Little trees have grown into big ones, and big ones which were landmarks have died. It may take a week longer, Don Manuel, you must have patience."

'It took longer than a week before the chief said one evening: "I can give you the mine tomorrow; for tomorrow I have it under my eyes."

'Don Manuel wanted to know why he should not have gone straight home with the chief when he left Mexico.

' "We should still have had to wait till tomorrow, because the sun was not in the right line. Now it is right. I have known for some days where the place is, but tomorrow I shall have the mine and I can give it you."

'Sure enough, on the next day they found the mine in a gully. "There has been a bit broken off from the mountain here, as you can see. That is why it was so hard to find the place. There is the mine and it is yours. But now you must leave my house."

' "Why? I would leave it in any case, because I shall build myself a home near the mine."

' "Yes, my home is no more good to you. You have the rich mine and you bring no blessing."

'The chief held out his hand, but Don Manuel said: "Wait, Aguila, I want to ask you one more question. If I had asked you for

116

a hundred thousand gold gulden to heal your son, would you not have opened up the mine?"

' "Certainly I would have done so. But as soon as I had got the sum you asked I should have buried it again because gold is not good. For what could I have done? The Spaniards would have heard of it and murdered me and my wife and my son to get possession of it. According to your customs, murder is always committed for gold. So be careful, Don Manuel, that you are not murdered, when your people know that you have a mine. When they know that you have nothing but bread and tortillas, you are never murdered. I shall always remain your friend, but now we must part."

'Don Manuel began at once to make a camp there, and Aguila returned to his home, which was a day's journey away. Before he set out Don Manuel had procured the Certificados from the government which entitled him to search for precious metals and gave him mining rights over the places where he found them. He had left his wife in the last town they had passed through and he went back to fetch her, and also engaged workmen and bought the necessary machinery and tools and explosives for blasting. And now he got to work opening up the mine. It exceeded his wildest hopes. It was rich in silver that it surpassed all mines of which there was any knowledge. Its chief product was silver, but there was gold too, as a by-product.

'He knew enough of what went on to know that a man should never say too much about his mine, or put too high a value on it. Not only ordinary persons but even officials of the Crown and the highest dignitaries of the Church were very ready to cheat a man of his mine if he had not enough power behind him to defend his possession. The owner suddenly vanished and no one knew where he had gone, and the mine, having no owner, came into the hands of the Crown or the Church. The Inquisition, which kept its unholy power much longer in Mexico than anywhere else on earth and only disappeared at last when the Revolution triumphed and the country became a free and independent republic, was then in full and untrammelled vigour. It was enough for a bishop to hear of a wealthy mine for the discoverer and possessor of that mine to be dragged before the Inquisition on a charge of blasphemy, heresy, sorcery, or lack of reverence for the miraculous powers of an image. The Viceroy himself, the most powerful man in the country, trembled before the tribunal. If he was bidden to attend it, he went with a heavily armed bodyguard and made the announcement that his troops and the artillery had orders to open fire on the building of the Inquisition at once if he was not in his palace again within a given time and had shown himself to the soldiers. What then could an ordinary citizen do? Ten or twenty witnesses got up and took their oath that he had not kneeled down before the Pyx, or had said he found it hard to believe that a son could be his own father, or that the Pope could never be in error. And once this was sworn to, the miscreant was burnt and might take it as a special favour if he was strangled first instead of being burnt alive. But whatever his punishment, as long as his guilt was sworn to, all his possessions went to the Church. So it is not at all surprising that the wealthy who declined to make a voluntary offering of their land and their mines to the Church and the monasteries were summarily accused and found guilty of heresy, while poor Indians were usually treated by the Inquisition with far greater indulgence; for who, in their case, was to pay the high costs of the complicated judicial inquiry? The costs of the tribunal were by no means light. It proceeded against no one for nothing, as the documents prove; and the witnesses were the last people to make themselves cheap out of regard for the holiness of the end in view. But the power of every religion has its limits, and no religion can defy them without dying out. A religion which becomes too rigid to adapt itself to changing conditions and the passing of time, dies. Nations whose religion forbids them to draw the sword and enjoins on them to do no murder cannot go on waging wars for ever with impunity.

'Don Manuel had been made wise by the experiences which had so frequently befallen others. He sent away no silver or gold. He hoarded it up and bided his time. In spite of the rich yield of the mine, he treated his Indian workmen as shabbily as possible, paid them wages on which they could scarcely live and made them work till they dropped or died; if they did not work hard enough, he encouraged them with the lash. With niggers this method may answer for a long time, but not with Indians. During the three hundred years of Spanish rule in Mexico, the Spaniards never at any time had undisputed possession of the whole country. There was always rebellion somewhere. And if in one place it was stamped out with inhuman brutality, it blazed out somewhere else. If it was so in large, so it was in little; and one day there was a mutiny at Don Manuel's mine. His wife, Donna Maria, was able to fly in time, but he was killed. His treasure was not plundered. As soon as Don Manuel was dead, the Indian workers left the place and went back to their villages.

'When Donna Maria heard that the mine was safe again, she went back to it to carry on. She found all the treasure safe and undisturbed where it had been buried; and what she already possessed would have been enough to keep her in comfort for the rest of her days.

'But she had got it into her head to return to Spain, and to figure there as the richest woman in the land. As she was still young, and beautiful besides, she cherished the ambition of buying a castle and a nobleman's estate and appearing at court as the wife of a marquis. Grandees of Spain had married the daughters of Aztec, Tezcuc and other Indian princes of Mexico and Peru solely for their wealth. Why should not she, who came of a good Spanish family, get a marquis for her husband much more easily than they with the assistance of her boundless fortune?

'She was even better at figures than her deceased husband. She reckoned up how much a castle and a princely estate would cost in Spain, how much it would cost to keep up and the cost of servants, carriages, horses and travelling; how much the marquis would need and how much she would need herself day by day in order to make a brilliant appearance at court. But still she found that there was much she had not thought of. There would be disbursements to the government, and a church to build, in order to put the lofty personages of the Inquisition in good humour and stay their avarice. And then she still carried on until the sum total she had reckoned could be doubled, and thus insured herself against any possible error in her calculations. They were hard years she had to battle through. She was far from civilization and deprived of even the barest comforts; she was on the alert night and day, keeping a vigilant eye on the workmen to see that their wages were not too high, and on the other hand not so low that they gave out and mutinied. She had to think, too, of raids and the armed bands of criminals and deserters and escaped convicts and the dregs of the towns, which went about marauding and spreading terror among Indian and white people alike.'

16

'Even envy itself could not grudge Donna Maria the credit of being a better match for her formidable task than her deceased husband had been. She feared neither death nor the devil, neither marauding bandits nor mutinous Indians, and she would assuredly have been a match in one way or another for the Inquisition itself, if she had been summoned before it. She was robust, indefatigable and energetic; but if she met with a check, she fell back on her gift for diplomacy and triumphed all the more certainly. She could laugh when it suited her book; she could weep if that seemed more profitable; she could curse like a footpad and she could pray more devoutly than a Franciscan monk. She could do the work of six Indians, and when things did not go as she wished she went at it with her own hands, and the Indians, who were not used to seeing a woman do heavy labour as if it were child's play, were so dazed with astonishment that they had to do whatever Donna Maria required of them. So it went on for years. But at last she felt such a longing for Spain, for a clean house, for a good kitchen, a soft bed and a husband to fondle and caress that one day she decided to pack up and go. When she surveyed her hoard she found that it was enough for even the most fantastic luxury.

'She had got together an armed guard which watched over and defended the mine and her treasure. It consisted of Indians and a few mestizos and two Spanish soldiers who had either deserted or been dismissed. One of the two Spaniards took command by day, and the other by night.

'The metal, of which about one-sixth was gold and all the rest pure silver, she had run off into rough bars and ingots, so that it would be easier to transport. These bars were securely packed in boxes. How great the riches were which she had got from the mine may be judged from the fact that sixty mules, each one laden to the limit of its strength, were required for the transport of her treasure.

'The caravan with its escort of twenty armed men set off on the journey of two thousand kilometres to the capital city of Mexico. There was no proper road and their way led over deserts and steep mountains, through rivers and gullies and defiles, through primeval bush and forest and stretches of jungle; now in the ice-cold winds of the sierra and high snow-covered plateaux, then again in the blazing heat of belts of fever-haunted jungle.

'And then one evening after they had camped for the night it seemed to her that something unusual was going on. She went to see and found that one of the Spaniards had made an attempt to arrange matters to suit himself. He came up to her and asked: "Will you, or will you not marry me, Donna Maria?"

' "I marry you, a common thief who only escaped hanging because the hangman used a bit of rotten rope instead of a good new one?"

'Whereupon the fellow replied: "I'm quite ready to take it without you. I'll find a prettier girl than you."

' "What will you take without me?"

' "What's in the boxes."

' "Not as long as I'm here, you bastard."

'The man pointed across to where the men were encamped and said with a grin:

' "If you take a look over there you may change your mind. I can wait an hour."

' "You can wait your whole life or until you're hanged."

'However, she went across to the men and found that the fellow had done a fine bit of business for himself. The other Spaniard and the Indians were bound, and the mestizos had joined the mutiny, hoping to go shares. There they stood with pistols in their belts and looked at her with impudent grins on their faces.

' "Very fine," Donna Maria remarked to the fellow.

' "That's so," he replied. "And now perhaps you'll make up your mind and say yes nicely."

' "You're right that I'll make up my mind, you hound," she said, and at the same moment she seized hold of a whip lying with the saddles on the ground, and before the man saw what she was up to she blinded him with a merciless cut across the face. He staggered and like lightning she followed it up with a half dozen more. He fell in a faint and lay motionless. But she had only begun. The mestizos were so astonished that it did not enter their heads either to make off or to shoot. And as soon as they realized what had happened to their leader the whip was already being slashed across their faces. Some fell, others began to run, putting up their arms to shield their

121

faces. Donna Maria sprang to the other Spaniard and cut his cords with a few rapid jerks. He at once released the Indians, and in a moment they had jumped on to their horses and lassoed the mestizos.

' "Hang the bastard," Donna Maria called out, pointing to the Spaniard who had designed to marry her and now got heavily to his feet. Half a minute later he was hanging.

' "What did I tell you?" she called out to him as the Indians hoisted him up. "I told you you'd hang first. And as for you," she turned to the mestizos, "I ought to hang you too. But I'll let you off. You all have the hangman's noose round your necks, and I don't want to spoil his trade. But I warn you that if you try it on again I shall flog you myself until the flesh hangs in strips from your carcasses, then I shall roast you and then hang you. There is no need for you to stay, you can go if you like. You will get no wages and you will give up your arms. But if you choose to stay on, I will give you your pistols, your saddles and the horses you are riding on when we get to Mexico. Listen, you – what is your name?" she went up to the Spaniard who had taken her part. "Rügo, yes. When we get to Mexico, you shall have –" she was about to say a mule and its load, but she checked herself in time "– you shall have the right-hand load of that mule there, and the Indians half of the left-hand one between them." With this the mutiny was at an end.

'But there were still the marauding bands against whom the caravan had to be defended at all costs. These bands cared nothing for life or death. They fought to the last, for they had everything to gain; and the lives they staked they had already forfeited as criminals long ago. Not once but many times over.

'Then one animal fell with its load into a cleft and its load had to be salvaged. Another sank in a bog with all its treasure. A third disappeared while fording a river.

'It was a question whether it was easier to get the metal out of the mine or to transport it in safety to Mexico without Donna Maria's laying down her life in the attempt.

'The journey was a gruelling experience for her, and when she looked back to the long hard years at the mine, could she say they had been any better? She had never had a moment's joy since the mine came into her possession; and she could not recall a single hour when she had felt quite sure of her life or her treasure. In fact taking it day by day and reckoning up all she had been through, her life had been wretched beyond words, more wretched than the life of a beast. Fear and anxiety had never left her. Dread pursued her

122

into her dreams and there was no respite from the tormenting thoughts which harried her all day. There was one, and only one, ray of light in the misery of her dreary existence – the thought of the moment when she handed over her treasure to the safe keeping of His Majesty's Government in Mexico. This moment, the moment for which she had lived such a pitiful life for years past, came. She reached Mexico City without having lost very much of her precious load. She was received by the Viceroy in person, and he paid her the high honour of a private audience and talked to her for a long time. Her joy and gratitude exceeded all bounds when the mighty personage said that the fortune she had won at the cost of such arduous toil and severe privations should be received into the vaults which were exclusively reserved for the royal treasure.

'This was more than Donna Maria had ever dared to hope. Nowhere in all the Spanish dominions, not in the crypt of the Cathedral or in a monastery, could her treasure be so safely lodged, and from nowhere else could it be so certainly recovered. It was in the vaults of the government itself, and the Viceroy, the greatest power in the land, was personally answerable for its safety. Here her treasure was lodged in security at last, until she could convey it under military escort to a ship and carry it with her to the land of her longings. For his forethought and the gracious condescension he had shown her, she begged the Viceroy to accept a share which was large enough to seem a princely one even to a Viceroy of the Spanish dominions.

'Next she paid her men off and discharged them; and then retired to her Inn, the best in the town.

'And now at last after so many years she could lie down without a care and sleep. For the first time for years she could draw her breath in peace, eat in peace and allow her thoughts to wander. At last she could dismiss the cares which had ceaselessly revolved all those years in her brain, and welcome other and more delightful ones.

'But then something happened, something she had never expected. Her treasure did not disappear. It was not stolen from the vaults under cover of night and mist. Something else disappeared. Donna Maria lay down to sleep, safe in a beautiful white bed; but no one ever saw her get up. No one has ever seen Donna Maria again. Nothing has ever been heard of her. She vanished and not a soul knew where she had gone.

'That is easily explained,' Howard said, as he concluded his tale. 'Donna Maria had forgotten one thing only – that gold often makes a person invisible. And the only reason why I wanted to tell you the story was to prove to you that the difficulty of transport is just as great as the difficulty of the finding and digging. And even when you think you have got the loot safely home, even then it is not certain whether you will be able to buy yourself so much as a cup of coffee with it. It all goes to show why gold is so dear.'

'Is there no chance of finding where the mine was?' Curtin asked. 'The woman can't have exhausted it. There must be plenty left.'

'You can find the mine very easily,' Howard replied. 'But you'll come too late. It is worked by a big company, and it has yielded the company ten times the amount the vanished señora got out of it. It seems it is inexhaustible. You can easily find it. It is called the Donna Maria Mine, and it is not far from Huacal. You can work there for a weekly wage if it would give you any satisfaction.'

The men sat on round the dying embers, and then got to their feet. They stretched, stamped their feet on the ground and thought of turning in.

'That story is over a hundred years old,' Lacaud said.

'Nobody said it wasn't,' said Dobbs.

'But I know a story that is only two years old, and just as good, or perhaps better.'

'Oh, shut your mouth,' Dobbs said with a yawn. 'We don't want to hear your story, not if it's only a week old. We know it already and it doesn't interest us any more than you do. You'll do best to say nothing at all. You're only a wandering . . . '

'What?' asked Lacaud.

'A hobo,' said Dobbs and went after the two who had gone across to the tent.

Next morning, the last but one they were to spend there, the three of them were so excited that they could scarcely stop to have breakfast. They slunk off to their secret hiding-places and brought out the fruits of their labour – grains of gold and sand and dust, carefully wrapped in old canvas tied with cord. Each possessed a good heap of these packets. The task now was to pack them up safely and in a manner not to arouse suspicion. They put dried skins round them and tied them up in bundles which looked as though they consisted of skins and nothing else. The bundles were then put into sacks ready to load on the pack animals.

Dobbs and Curtin then went off to shoot some game for the journey. Howard made wooden pack saddles for the donkeys and looked the straps and ropes over, so as to avoid delays on their journey owing to packs giving way. Lacaud again went off on his own, pottering about in the bush in the neighbourhood of the level grassy patch. But he did not say what he was looking for and none of the three asked him. They showed neither pity nor contempt for his occupation. Pity was not in their line, and he did not interest them sufficiently to earn their contempt. It was a matter of complete indifference to them now what he did, so long as he did nothing to hinder them. Even if he had found a mountain of solid gold they would have hesitated to put off their departure by a day. They were so set on getting off that nothing could have stopped them. They were suddenly so sick of the drudgery, the privations and the solitude; and if Lacaud had tried to persuade them that he was on the track of something good and that they ought to stay a week longer, they would have fallen on him and beaten him half to death. When Howard let fall the remark that Lacaud seemed to know too well what he was after to be the wandering gold-digger, Curtin said: 'Nothing can make me alter my mind. If he brought me a lump of gold as big as my fist I wouldn't have it.'

'Not have it? Why not?' said Dobbs. 'I'd have it all right. But we can hardly get what we have away as it is. Let him bring it me in Durango. Then I'll have it. But now – I'm off.'

That evening they sat round the fire saying little. Each was too much preoccupied with his own thoughts and plans to tell a yarn or disturb the others' meditations. It was still dark when they struck camp and got ready to move off.

'You stay here, then?' Curtin asked Lacaud.

'Yes, I'm not done here yet,' he said.

'Good luck then, my boy. Perhaps another time we'll have time to listen to your fine story,' Dobbs said laughing. 'Then perhaps you'll have proofs to show us.'

Lacaud put his hands in his pockets. 'Proofs? Proofs, do you say? I can give them now. But you've no time.'

'We have not,' Dobbs replied. 'That's why we have to get off. We're in a hurry to get under cover.'

Howard shook Lacaud's hand.

'I've left you some salt, pepper and one or two other things that would only be in our way. They'll come in handy perhaps. There's a bit of tent cloth as well. You can have it. It's good for a wet night.'

'Thanks,' Lacaud said.

Dobbs and Curtin shook hands with him too. Dobbs gave him some tobacco, and Curtin a handful of cartridges. Now that they were parting they felt friendly of a sudden. It was on the tip of

Curtin's tongue to ask him to accompany them instead of leaving him there alone in the bush, where he had not a hope of finding anything; they had been there long enough and turned every stone over and they knew what was to be found and what wasn't. But instead he only said: 'Good-bye.'

Howard felt the same desire. He wanted to urge him to come with them, and thought of giving him a job in the Cinema, as operator or manager. Then he kept it to himself and only said: 'Good luck.'

And Dobbs thought that a man more for the journey would do no harm. It would be an added defence against bandits, and their loads would excite less suspicion if they were divided among four. But he only shook his hand heartily and said: 'So long.'

Lacaud was as brief as they were, and then he stood and looked after them for a time. When they were out of sight, he turned to the fire and stirred the embers with the toe of his boot. 'Pity,' he said aloud.

17

They had to make a long detour with their train of pack animals in order to avoid the village where Curtin used to go for provisions; for as long as they were not seen, the inhabitants would think that he was still up there in the mountains. Even after leaving the village behind they still kept away from the roads and followed paths on which they were unlikely to meet anybody. The farther they got from this district the better hopes they had of reaching the town unobserved. Once there, they and all they possessed were in safety. They would go to an hotel, and continue their journey by train after packing their stuff in cases such as any traveller might have.

For the time they had scarcely any ready money in their pockets, a few pesos only, and these had to last until they reached the town. There they could sell the donkeys and whatever else they had no longer any need for, and the proceeds would buy their tickets. But first they had to reach the town. This distance was not very formidable. But they did not want to travel by the roads, where bandits and police were more likely to be encountered than on the hidden and winding paths. The fewer people they met the better.

But the paths did not always lead in the direction they wished. All paths led to villages or some human habitation. Sometimes they suddenly ran into a village when they least expected or wished to. And they could not very well turn back once they were in sight of it. It would look suspicious.

That was how they got into an Indian village on the second day. They had been unable to avoid it. It is not very unusual for a donkey caravan to pass through a place. To see it driven only by white men is unusual, certainly; but no one thought much about it, because white men have so many extraordinary ideas. But when they reached the middle of the village they saw four Mexicans standing in front of a hut. Three of them had bandoliers buckled round them and revolvers at their hips.

'That's police,' Dobbs said to Howard. 'We're for it.'

'Does look like police,' the old man replied.

Dobbs stopped the donkeys, but Howard gave him a push. 'Don't be a fool,' he said. 'If we stop all of a sudden like that, or even turn round, we're finished. That'll tell them at once there's something wrong. Keep going ahead as if we had a clear conscience. So we have, too. It's only the taxes and not having taken out a licence.'

'May cost us the whole bag of tricks all the same,' Dobbs cursed.

Meanwhile Curtin came up.

'Who's the guy with spectacles?' he asked with a jerk of his head towards the fourth man, who was armed and stood in the door of the hut apparently talking to some of the villagers.

'Probably he is a government inspector,' said Dobbs. 'The devil knows what's up here. Let's go quietly on.'

The Mexicans had not seen them approaching. It was not until they got to the village square where the hut stood that one of the police turned and looked after them. Then he spoke to the others and they too turned their heads and looked after the caravan which was quietly jogging on. When it had nearly crossed the square, one of the police suddenly called out:

'Hallo, señores, one moment!'

'That's done it,' Dobbs said in a low voice.

'I'll go across alone,' Howard proposed. 'You two stay with the donkeys. I'll find out what they want.'

Howard went across and politely asked what he could do for them.

127

'Have you come down from the mountains?' one of them asked.

'Yes, we've been hunting.'

'Have you all been vaccinated?' he asked next.

'Have we what? Been vaccinated?' Howard said it with obvious relief. He knew now what they were up to.

'Sure, we've all been vaccinated as children. That's obligatory with us. I've been vaccinated ten times at least all told.'

'When was the last time?'

'Two years ago.'

'Have you got the certificate on you?'

Howard laughed.

'I don't carry that about in my pocket.'

'I should say not,' the man said. 'But in that case you must be vaccinated right now. We are the vaccination commission and we have to vaccinate everyone we come across in the villages.'

The man with the spectacles went into the hut and came out again with his case. He opened it. Howard bared his arm and the man scratched it with the needle.

'We have an easier job of it with you than with the people here,' he said with a laugh. 'We have to lie in wait for them. They run off to the mountains and into the bush. They think we want to cut their heads off.'

'Yes,' said one of the police, 'it takes more to vaccinate the people here than catching a whole gang of bandits. But if we don't get them all done the smallpox will get the upper hand. It's the worst with the children. The women make an uproar as if we were going to murder the brats, and fight like wild cats as soon as we touch them with the needle. Look at my face, how they've scratched me. And my mate here has a great bruise on his head where a woman hit him with a stone. We've had four days here. They've all slunk off and we'll have to starve them out before they'll come back. But they're coming back by ones and twos when they find that the children who've been vaccinated haven't died of it. But how are we to explain to them that we only do it for the good of them and their children?'

While he spoke he turned the leaves of a book till he came to the first empty page.

'Write your name here, in both places.'

Howard wrote it and gave the book back.

'Your age?'

The official entered it, wrote his signature and tore off half the page along the dotted line and gave it to Howard.

'That's your certificate. The other half we keep in the book. Now send the other two across. It'll do them no harm even if they've been done ten times already.'

'What do I pay?' the old man asked. 'We're a bit short of money.'

'There's nothing to pay. It costs nothing. It's the government pays.'

'Then it's a cheap do,' Howard said laughing, and pulled down his sleeve.

'We know you've all been vaccinated,' said one of the other officials, 'or at least we take it you have. But we're only too glad to have a shot at you. The inhabitants watch every movement we make from their hidden places. That's why we chose this hut in the open here. When they see that we make no difference between Indians and white men and that you hold out your arms as if you did it every day, it'll give them confidence. They see it won't cost them their lives.'

Howard went back and sent Dobbs and Curtin to be vaccinated too.

'That's the best news I ever heard,' Curtin said laughing. 'I thought every moment they'd come and ask a lot of dam' fool questions.'

'If you like you can tell them all you've been doing for months past,' said Howard. 'It won't interest them any more than your family tree. They are the vaccination commission, and anything that hasn't got to do with vaccination leaves them cold. They'd vaccinate a bandit if he came by and let him go again. It's not any part of their job to catch bandits.'

'Now then,' Dobbs broke in, 'stop that blather. We'll be vaccinated and then get on quick.'

'Did I say we were going to spend the night here?'

'No, but you talk as though we had to fall on their necks over there,' Dobbs said, and hastened across to the hut.

Howard shook his head with a rueful expression and turned to Curtin.

'That Dobbs has no sense of humour, as I've said more than once. I'd rather fall on the necks of a vaccination commission than into the hands of a police detachment going their rounds on a mining control. Now off with you, Curtin, and get your certificate so as we can go on again.'

In the evening they camped near Amapuli. They had to stop there, because they were told they would not find water again before night.

While they were preparing their meal, four Indians came to their camp from the village, and after a polite greeting asked whether they might sit down.

'Como no? Why not?' Howard replied. 'You won't be in our way at all.'

The four Indians sat for some time watching how the strangers roasted their meat and cooked their rice.

'You've come a long way, no doubt,' one of them said at last, 'and no doubt you have a long way still to go. You are very clever men, that's sure.'

'We can read books,' Curtin replied, 'and we can write letters, and we can reckon with figures.'

'With figures?' another of the four asked. 'Figures? We don't know that.'

'Ten is a figure,' Curtin explained. 'And five is a figure.'

'Oh,' said another of their guests. 'That's only half of it. Ten is nothing, and five is nothing. You mean ten fingers or five beans or three hens. Is that it?'

'That's so,' Howard put in.

The Indians laughed, because they had understood, and one of them said: 'You can't say ten. You must always say ten what. Ten trees or ten men or ten birds. If you say ten or five or three without saying what you mean, there's a hole and it's empty.'

Then they laughed again. After they had been silent again for a good time, one of them said: 'My son has fallen into the water. We pulled him out again at once. I do not believe, though, that he is dead. But he does not wake up. You have read books and know what to do.'

'When did your son fall into the water? Yesterday?' asked Howard.

'No, this afternoon. But he does not wake up.'

'I will go with you and have a look at your son. I will see if he is dead.'

The men got up and Howard went with them. They took him to a house built of sun-dried bricks. There was a mat on the table and on the mat lay the boy.

Howard examined him carefully. He raised his eyelids and put his ear to his chest and felt his hands and feet. Then he said: 'I'll just see if I can bring him round.'

For a quarter of an hour he worked the boy's arms up and down, and then had hot poultices put on his stomach and chafed his hands and feet; and when he put his ear to the boy's chest again he found

130

that his heart was beginning to beat. After an hour the boy began to breathe by himself and a few minutes later he opened his eyes.

The men and women who were in the hut had been watching what the stranger did without uttering a sound. The women who heated the poultices communicated with each other by gestures or in low whispers. Even now, when the boy was fully awake, not one of them dared speak.

Howard got his hat and putting it on went to the door. No one stopped him and no one spoke. Only the father of the boy went after him and held out his hand and said: 'Señor, I thank you.' Then he went back into the house.

It was now quite dark and Howard had difficulty in finding his way back to the camp. But finally the light of the fire put him on the right road.

'Did you manage to do anything?' Dobbs asked.

'Nothing much,' said Howard. 'Artificial respiration, and he came to. He'd just had a shock. He'd have come round by himself in a few hours without help. It was just a mouthful of water. Have you left me a bit of meat?'

Before sunrise they were on their way again. They were in a hurry to reach Tomini, and from there they hoped to find their way over the mountain range. After they had had their midday rest, they loaded up the donkeys again and were just getting them on to the path when Curtin said: 'What's this? Looks as if we had something on the line.'

'Where?' asked Dobbs. 'Yes, you're right. Indians on horseback. But it doesn't mean we've hooked them. They may be out riding or going to market.'

It was not long before the Indians came up with them, and they were the same four who had paid them a visit the evening before, and with them were two others whom Howard had seen in the house.

The Indians greeted them and then one of them said: 'But, señores, why have you run away from us?'

Howard laughed. 'We didn't run away, but we have to get on. We have to go to the town. We have important business there which cannot wait.'

'Oh,' said the father of the boy whose life had been in danger, 'business can always wait. Business is never in a hurry. There are days after today and days after tomorrow and days after that. But first you must be my guests. I cannot let you go. You have given his life back to my son. In return you must be my guests – for two weeks. No, that is too little. You must be my guests for six weeks. I have land and plenty of maize. I have cows. I have many goats. I will give you every day a good turkey cock to eat and eggs and milk. Every day my wife will make you tamales.'

'We thank you with all our hearts,' said Howard, 'but if we do not reach the town in time, our business is lost.'

'Business does not run away,' one of the other Indians replied to this. 'Business is tough, like the flesh of an old goat. Business makes trouble. Why do you want to make trouble for yourselves when you can have all you want with us? You will have no troubles, and we have music and dancing as well.'

'No, we have to go. We must get to the town,' Dobbs said, beginning to show annoyance.

'We have taken your gift,' the father said, 'and you must take our gift.'

When the Indians saw that the strangers made more difficulties than they expected over the invitation to be their guests, one of them said: 'The two young men can go if they like, but you – ' and he pointed to Howard ' – you may not go. My brother's son would die for certain, if we did not have you for our guest. We must pay for your medicine, because you were good to the boy.'

All their annoyance and all their protestations went for nothing. There was no escape. They were surrounded by the six men and in their power.

Finally Dobbs had an idea.

'There's no undoing last night's foolery. If you stay, they're content. It's only you they want to keep back. We'll go on and you can follow later. There's no other way out of it.'

'It's all very well to talk – but what about my packs?'

'They can stay with you,' said Curtin.

Dobbs was against this.

'I don't advise it. They'll rummage through them and take the stuff from you, or they'll start talking and it'll get about, and if they don't kill you, bandits will get to know and lie up for you.'

'Then what am I to do?' asked Howard.

'We'll take your lot and bank it in your name. Or perhaps you don't trust us.'

It was Dobbs said this.

'Trust you? Why not trust you?'

Howard laughed and looked from one to the other. 'We have lived together getting on for a year and worked together all that time. That's meant trusting each other, I should say.'

And since there was nothing else for it, they had to take the only decision with which the Indians could be satisfied. They were concerned only in showing Howard their gratitude. So the only thing to do seemed to be for Howard to hand over his share to the other two. They both made themselves answerable and both gave chits on which they acknowledged the receipt of so many packages, each of about the same weight in grams of washed sand.

'And where will you hand it in?' Howard asked.

'We'll put it in a safe with the Banking Company of Tampico in your name,' Curtin said.

'It's only a few weeks, old boy,' said Curtin. 'Whatever comes, I'll wait for you in Tampico. You'll find me at the Southern, or the Imperial. I'd stay with you, but there's the waste of time, and, as you know, I have someone waiting for me.'

Howard was given one of the horses, and the Indian whose horse it was got up behind one of the others. Then they returned laughing and talking to their village, carrying Howard along with them in triumph.

18

This delay meant the loss of half a day; for the Indians were in no hurry at all to end the discussion, however pertinaciously they stuck to their guns. They had made it quite clear that they were not particularly eager to rope in Howard's two companions. If Howard had wished, they would have been ready to include them, and they would have offered them the same hospitality. But they did not seem to take to them. Perhaps they did not like their expression. Indians take more stock of a man's expression than of anything else about him.

It was owing to this delay that Curtin and Dobbs did not get as far even as the Indian hamlet, Cienaga, and so they had another day's journey before they could reach the pass by which they meant to cross the range. The whole affair had annoyed them, and they were so bad-tempered that they scarcely spoke a word. If they had to say anything they spoke in a growl. They were furious at having Howard's load on their hands and his donkeys to drive, loading and unloading them at every stop. He had failed them and shirked his share of the job. It was just his donkeys that broke away from the caravan, and just his packs that were not properly roped and shifted on the pack saddles during a journey. With curses they made them fast again, and meanwhile the other donkeys scattered and had to be rounded up. When there were three of them none of this happened. All they could do was to curse and revile Howard from afar. They soon saw how ridiculous this was; he could not hear them, and it was a mere waste of energy to curse at him. So then they cursed the donkeys – who could not understand and paid no attention. They trotted on, snatching a bite of grass here or a twig from a branch there, if ever there was a second's space in which to reach out their tongues without the beast behind rudely barging into them.

Finally there was nothing left but to grouse at one another, blaming each other senselessly for the most remote and trivial matters merely in order to produce a reply and to find in it further cause of aggravation. It is always the replies that made the quarrel. But whoever has the philosophic composure to refrain from replying to reproaches, accusations and ridiculous assertions?

Curtin took the head of the caravan and Dobbs the rear, and they directed their amiable and well-meant remarks at each other over the backs of the donkeys in between them. The donkeys twitched their ears forwards to pick up a flaming oath from Curtin, then backwards to hear how Dobbs would take it and how violent his retort would be. The donkeys which were next to each other put their noses together and snuffled and whispered something and grinned with open mouths. If the path was too narrow to go two by two, then the one behind snuffled at the rear of the one in front, and he in turn looked round and nodded and grinned, and made it very clear that he understood and had come to the same conclusion. And so, snuffing and looking back and nodding and grinning and wagging and twirling their long ears, they passed the word along the line. If Dobbs and Curtin had only spared a moment to observe what the donkeys thought about it, they would certainly have acquired the rudiments of true philosophy. But who would sink so low as to learn from a donkey?

'I'm stopping here,' Dobbs said suddenly. 'I'm not plodding on like an ox all day.'

'It's only three o'clock, man,' Curtin answered.

Dobbs got into a temper at once. 'I didn't tell you, did I, to camp here?' he shouted over the donkeys' backs. 'You can go on till morning and bust yourself for all I care.'

'Tell?' Curtin roared back. 'You've nothing to tell me about. You are not the boss yet.'

'Perhaps it's you, then. I've just been waiting to hear you say it.'

Dobbs went purple in the face.

'All right,' Curtin said more quietly, in spite of his annoyance, 'if you're beat . . . '

'Beat?' Dobbs shouted. 'I can see you beat any time.'

'Well, anyway – if you don't want to go any farther, we can unload and camp here. I don't mind.'

'There's water here, for one thing,' said Dobbs, calming down also. 'Who knows whether we'll find water again before night?'

Eating generally mends the temper, unless there's a discussion about what it's costing. And so it was here, although it was no feast. There was even a toast proposed, a toast to the absent member. Dobbs was toast-master.

'What'll the old fellow be doing now?' he said, and as he said it he thought of himself and his own interests, not of Howard's at all. At first he thought of Howard, but even before the words were out of his mouth he realized that there was something nearer to him than Howard. He looked across at the packs, and his eyes rested for a moment on the old man's.

Curtin too looked across at the packs, but he misinterpreted the toast-maker's look. For he said: 'We'll get home all right with the whole cargo. We are far enough from the mountains. There's nothing suspicious about us now whatever. In two days, if we get a clear view from the top, we'll see the smoke of the trains.'

Dobbs said nothing to this. He stared into the fire and then looked away at the dark shadows of the grazing donkeys, and as he didn't want to go on watching them nor to stare any more into the fire, his eyes went back to the packs and fastened upon Howard's.

Suddenly he gave Curtin a dig with his fist and laughed out loud. His laugh was tumultuous and unsteady.

Curtin looked at him in astonishment; and, though he had no idea what the joke was, he caught the infection and laughed a little, looking round at the same time to see what had suddenly made Dobbs so merry.

'What makes you laugh like that?' he asked.

Dobbs burst out louder than ever.

'It's so damned comical.'

'What is?'

'That fool of a man giving us all his bronze. Out here in the wilds. What's easier? He can whistle for us. He'll never find us, the old bag of bones.'

Curtin had stopped laughing. 'I don't understand what you're talking about, Dobbs.'

Dobbs laughed and gave him another dig. 'Don't understand, you poop? Where were you brought up?'

'I'm damned if I do understand,' Curtin said, shaking his head.

'What's there to understand? Don't be so thick-headed. We clear out. That's all.'

Curtin showed no sign of understanding what was expected of him.

'We clear out,' Dobbs explained. 'Land home with it, share out and each go his way.'

'Now I begin to see what you are after.'

'You've taken your time about it,' said Dobbs, and slapped him on the shoulder.

Curtin stood up, walked about and came back to the fire. He did not sit down, but stood there looking up at the sky. Then he said dryly: 'If you mean we're to jockey Howard out of what he's got by his labour . . . '

'Of course I do. What else do I mean? And I mean it good and proper.'

'Yes. Well, if that's what you mean,' Curtin went on, as though Dobbs had not interrupted him, 'then I'll have nothing to do with it. I'll take no hand in that game.'

'If it comes to that,' Dobbs now said, getting up and planting himself in front of Curtin, 'I don't need your permission. It's none of your business. If you don't come in on it, it's your own look out. Then I take the lot, and if you don't like it you can lump it. Do you understand now?'

'Yes, I understand you now.'

Curtin shoved his hands in his pockets and took a step back out of Dobbs's way.

'And?' asked Dobbs sharply. 'And what?'

'As long as I'm here you won't touch a bean of the old fellow's. I signed his chit . . . '

'So did I and spit on his chit. He's got to find us first. Then I'll tell him bandits robbed us. It's clear as daylight.'

'I signed the chit,' Curtin went on undeterred, 'and I gave him my word, apart from you altogether, that I'd bank his share. It's

136

not just the chit and the signature, or the promise either. There's a lot you promise and put your name to that it'd take you all your life and longer to carry out. It's not that. It's another thing altogether. It isn't as if he stole it or picked it up, or won it in a lottery or in the money market or at Monte Carlo. He got it out of the ground by honest labour and hard labour too. There's not much I respect. But I have some respect for what a man has got by the toil of his own hands.'

Dobbs made a contemptuous gesture.

'You can keep your Bolshie notions for someone else. They don't go down here. I know them off by heart.'

'It's nothing to do with Bolshies,' Curtin replied. 'It may be true that it's the object of the Bolshevists or Communists to put some respect for the earnings of labour into the heads of those who don't need to work and have money already and to give the worker the full benefit of his labour instead of cheating him of it on all kinds of pretexts, and applying it to schemes that don't interest him at all. But that's another story. Whatever you think about it, that's not what I'm talking about. But I tell you straight, as long as I'm with this caravan or anywhere near it, you don't lay a finger on anything that belongs to the old man. You don't go near his bronze as long as I stand upon my two feet. So now you know.'

Curtin sat down and, taking out his pipe, began to fill it. He did his best to seem unconcerned.

Dobbs remained standing and looked steadily at Curtin. Then he laughed derisively.

'You're right, my boy. Now I do know. I know now what you're up to. And I've known it for some time.'

'What have you known for some time?' Curtin asked without looking up.

'That you've had it in mind yourself to put a bullet through me tonight or tomorrow night, and bury me like a dead dog, and then make off with Howard's lot and mine too, and laugh at us for a couple of fatheads.'

Curtin lowered his pipe, which he was just lighting, and looked up. His eyes were wide and vacant. This accusation robbed him of all power to give them any expression. He had never for a moment thought of acting the part that was foisted on to him. He did not call himself a pattern of integrity. He could help himself with the best, if it came to that, and he was not the victim of his conscience. The oil magnates and steel kings and railway lords could never get where they do if they were troubled by consciences. Why should an insignificant creature like him have more exalted views and a more sensitive conscience than those who are pointed to as the great ones of the earth and extolled in newspapers, magazines and story books as the highest examples of energy, will-power and achievement? But, nevertheless, what Dobbs now attributed to him was more than he could stomach. Perhaps if he had thought of it himself he might not have thought so hardly of it. But thrown at him in this rancorous and disgusting way, he thought it the dirtiest action he had ever heard of. And if Dobbs thought him capable of it, it showed what Dobbs himself could sink to. How could he have thought it of anyone, unless it had been in his own mind? And in that case, Curtin was a dead man; for Dobbs would not think twice about destroying him in order to get the whole lot for himself. It was the consciousness of the peril he was in that deprived his eyes of all expression. He saw that from this peril there was no escape. He was helpless – about as helpless as a man can ever be. For what defence had he against Dobbs? They had four or five days' journey before them. And even if they met anybody it would be no help. Dobbs had only to hint at the reward and he would have anyone they met on his side. And if they met no one, so much the better for Dobbs. Curtin could keep awake for one night and save his skin. But the next night he would only sleep the sounder. There would be no occasion for Dobbs to waste a bullet. He could tie him up and knock him on the head and bury him. He could even spare the knock on the head.

There was only one way out. Curtin had to do with Dobbs what Dobbs meant to do with him. Slay or be slain. There is no other law.

I won't have his bronze, thought Curtin, but I must put him out of the way. The old man shall have his share and I shall have mine, and that swine's I'll bury with him. I won't be the richer for him, but my life is worth as much as his.

His left hand with his pipe in it was on one knee, and his right hand on the other. Now his right began to travel slowly to his hip pocket. But in the same moment Dobbs whipped out his revolver.

'You stir, my boy, and I shoot,' he shouted.

Curtin kept his hands still.

'Up with 'em!'

Curtin stretched his arms above his head.

'I wasn't far out,' Dobbs jeered. 'Your fine talk was only a smoke-screen. But you don't get past me like that. Stand up!' he said, coming nearer.

Curtin did not utter a word. His face had gone white. Dobbs went up to him and reached round to his hip pocket to disarm him. Curtin whipped round. Dobbs shot. But owing to Curtin's sudden movement the bullet missed him; and before Dobbs could fire again Curtin laid him out with a powerful punch to the chin, and flinging himself on top took away his revolver. Then he jumped up and retreated a few steps.

'The boot's on the other foot, Dobbs,' he said.

'So I see,' Dobbs replied. He sat up, but stayed where he was.

'I don't mind telling you now that you're altogether mistaken,' Curtin told him. 'It never so much as entered my head to take a thing off you or to put you out of the way.'

'That's easy said. But if you're such a good boy you can give me my gun back.'

Curtin laughed. 'It had better stay where it is. It's no toy for you.'

'That's the game, is it?' Dobbs said, and went to the fire.

Curtin took the cartridges out of Dobbs's revolver and put them in his pocket. He thought of handing it back to Dobbs and Dobbs held his hand out for it. But thinking better of it, Curtin put both revolvers in his trouser pockets. Then he sat down by the fire, taking care to give himself room in case of an unexpected attack.

And now he lit his short pipe. Dobbs said nothing and Curtin had ample leisure to pursue his thoughts.

He was no better off than he had been half an hour before. He could not keep a watch over Dobbs for four days and nights. He would have to fall asleep some time and then Dobbs would overpower him. And he would show no mercy, for he was now convinced that his suspicions of Curtin were correct and that if he put him out of the way it would be in self-defence. There was only room for one of them. Fear and exhaustion would drive them both half crazy. Whoever first fell asleep would fall a victim to the other.

'What about separating first thing tomorrow – or tonight and each going his own way?' Curtin asked.

'It would suit you well.'

'Why me?'

Dobbs laughed rancorously.

'You'd get me from behind, eh? Or put bandits on my track?'

'If that's what you think,' said Curtin, 'then I don't know how we're to get quit of one another. I'll have to tie your arms together, day and night.'

'Yes, that's what you'll have to do. So come and do it. Here I am.'

Dobbs was right. It was not so easy to do. It might mean that the boot came on the other foot again. And it would be for the last time. Dobbs was the stronger and the more unscrupulous. He was the stronger owing to his robuster conscience. The unscrupulous man survives the man who hesitates. Those who put their trust in acting quickly rather than in carefully considering and weighing their actions are the winners. But the others conquer in the end and possess the land. Here, however, it was a question only of winning, because the life of each depended on overpowering or destroying the other. Curtin was in the stronger position, but he dared not make use of it. He was political by nature, but no doer. Dobbs on the other hand could waste, but he could not spend; he could destroy, but not overthrow. And therefore he too was no doer; for the doer can both spend and overthrow.

19

The night that now began was terrible for Curtin, but not for Dobbs. Now that he had discovered Curtin's weak side, he felt perfectly sure of himself. He could play with Curtin as he chose.

Curtin sat close enough to Dobbs to keep an eye on him, but not so close that he would not have time to lift his revolver if Dobbs thought of attacking him. He set himself with all his strength to the task of keeping awake. He was tired by the day's journey and felt that to hold out all night would not be easy. He could not walk about because it would tire him more. For a time he sat upright, but that too was tiring. Then he came to the conclusion that it would be better to get under his blanket and lie down. It would rest his limbs. Also Dobbs would not be able to see so clearly if he dozed off for a moment.

After about an hour when Curtin had not stirred for a long while, Dobbs sat up and began to crawl. Instantly Curtin levelled his revolver. 'That'll do,' he shouted.

'You're a good night-watchman,' Dobbs replied with a laugh.

Later, after midnight, Dobbs was wakened by the braying of one of the donkeys. He made another attempt to stalk Curtin, but Curtin held him up at once.

Dobbs knew now that he would win. By his two feints he had prevented Curtin from sleeping, and now he slept on himself. The next night would be his.

Next day Dobbs had the head of the caravan. So there was nothing he could do. Then came the evening; and then the night. Soon after midnight Dobbs got up quietly and went over to Curtin and took his revolver. Then he gave him a kick in the ribs.

'Up, you swine,' he said. 'The boot's on the other foot. And now it'll stay there.'

Curtin was dazed with sleep and asked: 'Boots? What about boots?'

Then he understood and began to get up.

'Sit where you are,' Dobbs said and sat down facing him. He pushed the burnt-out brands into the fire and the flames shot up.

'There's not a lot to say,' he went on. 'I'm not going to play the night nurse for you as you have for me tonight and last night. I'm going to make a clean end of it. I don't mean to live in fear of my life from now on.'

'Then it's murder you mean.' Curtin said it without a tremor. He was too tired to realize all that had happened.

'Murder?' Dobbs replied. 'Where's the murder? I've got to save my own skin, I suppose. I'm not your captive. I'm not bound to hang on your mercy for every day you leave me lingering.'

'You won't get out of it like that,' Curtin said, slowly coming to his senses. 'The old man won't let you get away with it so easy.'

'Won't he, though? Why, it's simple. You tied me to a tree and went off with the whole cargo. Nothing simpler. You'll be the skunk of the two of us. You can leave it to me to see he never finds you. Get up and now and – quick march.'

'Where to?' Curtin asked.

'To your burial place. Did you think you were going to dance somewhere? You don't need to pray. There's no one to hear your prayers. You'll find the right place, don't worry. I'm only sending you there a little earlier than you thought. So up you get – quick march!'

'And suppose I won't?' Curtin asked. He was still tired out and dazed with sleep. He knew well enough now that it was deadly earnest. But he was too tired to think beyond the shot he was soon to hear, too sleepy to grasp with the shot his existence would be ended. It all seemed to him like a dream, a dream in which he never quite lost the consciousness of its being only a dream out of which he would wake in the morning with nothing but a faint recollection of what the dream had been about. And yet he tried to impress on his memory all that went on in his dream so as to be able to recall it clearly to his mind when he woke. He felt that it was important not to forget his dream because it gave such a clear insight into Dobbs's character, clearer than he had ever had, or thought possible. He remembered distinctly having heard once that sometimes you get to know a person better through a dream than in waking life, and he made up his mind to be more effectually on his guard against Dobbs, as soon as day dawned than he had been hitherto.

'I can just as well go on sitting here,' he said with closed eyes. 'What have I to get up and march anywhere for? I'm tired. I want to sleep.'

'You'll have time enough to have your sleep out. Up you get now – step out.'

The loud and harsh command tortured Curtin. Swaying and stumbling he got to his feet, merely to avoid hearing it again.

Dobbs drove him forward with blows of his fists for fifty or sixty paces into the bush. Then he shot him down.

Curtin collapsed and fell. Dobbs bent over him and when he heard neither a breath nor a sigh he put the revolver back into his pocket, and returned to the fire.

He sat there for a time and tried to think out what to do next. But not a thought would come. He felt quite vacant. He stared into the fire, heaping on more wood or pushing bits further into the glow with his feet. Then he lit a pipe.

After drawing a few puffs, suddenly a thought flitted across his brain. He thought that perhaps he had missed Curtin. Perhaps he had only stumbled and fallen at the very moment the shot was fired. He turned about towards the bush where Curtin lay. For a time he looked intently into the darkness as though he expected to see Curtin coming for him.

Next he found sitting uncomfortable and got up. He walked once or twice round the fire, kicking at the branch ends with his toes. He sat down and pulled his blanket round him; then rolled himself up in it and lay down. He drew a long breath in the hope of getting off to sleep, but he checked it in the middle. He was certain he had not hit Curtin and that suddenly he would see him standing over him with a revolver in his hand. The thought was intolerable. He could not sleep for it.

142

Snatching a stout and fiercely burning branch from the fire, he went with it into the bush. Curtin lay there on the same side as before. He did not breathe and his eyes were shut. Dobbs put the flaming brand to his face, but Curtin did not stir. His shirt over his chest was soaked in fresh blood.

Reassured now, Dobbs was about to go. But before he had gone three steps he turned and, drawing his revolver, he fired another shot into him. Then he went back to the camp.

He put the blanket round his shoulders and sat down by the fire.

'Damn it,' he said, laughing to himself, 'it gave me a prick of conscience to think that he might be alive still. But now I'm satisfied.'

The word conscience, however, stuck fast in his mind. It made itself at home there and any sentence that took shape in his mind hinged on this word, conscience. Not as a conception so much as a naked word.

Now I'll just see, he thought, whether conscience is playing a trick on me. Murder is the worst crime you can commit. So my conscience should be lively at present. But I never heard of a hangman who was troubled with his conscience. Mr McDollin in Sing Sing has put a hundred and fifty in the electric chair, and he seems to enjoy it. He sleeps quietly in his bed every night without his conscience pricking him. Perhaps there may be four switches and four men to press a button each and none of them knows which button did the damage. But all the same, Mr McDollin must clap the fellows in the chair. He has accounted for a hundred and fifty and perhaps more, and yet he is a respected man and an officer of the state.

And how many Germans did I kill in France? Fifteen? Twenty-three, I believe. 'Fine,' said the Colonel. And I've always slept well. Not one of those Germans ever appeared in my dreams and not one of them ever disturbed my conscience. Neither their mothers nor their wives, nor their little children ever bothered me night or day. There was that time in the Argonne. A German machine-gun nest. Lord, how they stuck it! With two full companies we couldn't get near them. At last their losses were too heavy and they showed a rag of white. There were eleven of them still alive. As we went forward they put their hands up and laughed. They were true soldiers, and thought us the same. We bayoneted the lot like so many cattle. The worst of us was a fellow called Steinhofer. He went mad and wouldn't spare even the wounded. He had been born in Germany and only left it when he was seventeen. His parents and brothers and sisters are all in Germany to this day. And it was he who showed no mercy. There were one or two who begged for their lives because they had so many children. What did this fine Steinhofer say to these fathers? What was it? Anyway, it was a swinish thing to say and he followed it up with the bayonet. I believe he got a medal. But an English artillery officer came along just as the slaughter was over. And the Englishman said: 'You swine, you ought to be ashamed of your-selves.' If Steinhofer wasn't ashamed of himself and if so many more of his fellow-countrymen were not ashamed of themselves for crying murder on the Germans more lustily when war broke out than the most bloodthirsty Jingo, why should I be ashamed of myself? I've never felt a pang of remorse over those young Germans, let alone Steinhofer. Why should my conscience be upset over this skunk Curtin? As long as he's dead, my conscience is easy. Conscience is active only when the prison doors are open and the hangman is by. If you're acquitted, or if you've done your time, a murdered man will never worry you.

He worries you only if you're afraid it'll come out, or that you may be caught.

Soldiers and hangmen get their pay. That's why their consciences don't trouble them, however many they may do in. And what have I to be afraid of? I have the plunder and Curtin will never be seen again. I'd better bury him first thing in the morning.

Dobbs laughed out loud. It amused him that his thoughts were suddenly so lively and chased each other so fast through his head. It struck him as remarkable that he had grown so wise and had such clever ideas. If they were written down, he thought, they'd take him for a very learned fellow. He was surprised that he had never known before what a clear-headed, open-minded fellow he was. He went on to think how easy it was to be a match for preachers who twaddled on about conscience without ever having come up against it in any matter of importance. He could soon show them that all the stuff they talked and wrote about it to keep people in fear all their lives was nothing but humbug.

If you believe in conscience, then it is there, and it acts when you tell it to; if you don't believe in it, then you haven't one and it can't ever bother you.

Dobbs stretched himself at full length by the fire, and as he fell asleep he felt he would sleep better than he had for days. And in fact he slept right on till daylight.

He drank some coffee left over from the night before and began

144

to load the donkeys. It was only then it occurred to him that Curtin was dead. He regarded it as a fact, one which no longer concerned him any more than if Curtin had died of some sickness or than if someone else had killed him. He felt like an onlooker. Not for a moment did he feel any pity or even a pang of remorse. There was nothing to regret. Curtin had been put out of the way, and this was a matter only for satisfaction.

He wondered whether to take Curtin's stuff along with him or simply to leave it there. But he decided at once that it would be folly to leave the packs behind there. They would only fall a prey to bandits or marauding Indians. Curtin could never have any use for them now. On the other hand, what wouldn't it mean to himself to have the whole of the swag? He might, for example – but there was no good beginning to think of all he might do with it. It would be an exaggeration to say that the whole freight would make him stink of money. It would not even make a rich man of him. But it would put him beyond want. And he did not intend to sit and do nothing: no, he was going to start some enterprise, a factory or a ranch, or else speculate – but better not speculate perhaps. He might not be lucky. Why not, though? Because of his paltry life of want? Why, the most miserable specimens had most luck. It was just the most worthy and respectable people who always had bad luck, whatever they might touch or whatever they started on. Of course, if he left all the property of the other two behind, no one would be able to bring it up against him that he took to self-defence for the booty's sake. There were people, judges even, who could turn and twist things so that in the end it came out as downright murder. But then, suppose he left Curtin's share behind and someone else picked it up, not a soul would ever believe that he had taken nothing that belonged to Curtin. The best thing, all said and done, was to take it boldly and for the time think no more about it. If it came to light there would be plenty of time to say: 'What d'you mean? Here's the man's whole property. I stole nothing from him.' First, though, he would see how things went and how far he could go.

It was just the same thing with Howard's share. If Howard ever found him – well, there it all was just as it had been handed over. But first he'd have to find him. And if he did not find him until later, who could ever say? So many things happen. Bandits might have stripped him of all but his life and one sack which he had rescued with difficulty. There are so many bandits about. You can put anything down to them because they're capable of anything. It

145

was they who shot Curtin too. Perhaps it would be better to say that they had quarrelled and fought, and then separated. Curtin had gone another way and he couldn't say what had become of him. But, after all, it would be best to tell the story of the bandits. What was the use of flogging his brains to decide what he should say and what story he should tell. Once safe in the town, there would be plenty of time to put it all in order. He might wait for the old man in Tampico quite openly and rush to meet him with such a hair-raising tale that he would never think of questioning the truth of it. The pack or two which he had rescued from the bandits' claws could be shared with the old fellow. He'd be so glad that anything at all was left that he would not say another word. Perhaps, again, something might happen to the old swine on his tramp to the rail. If only he had a couple of mestizos handy. For twenty or twenty-five pesos, they'd lie up for the old man and put him out of sight; then no one at all would know a thing about the whole business.

20

The donkeys were loaded. They stood there patiently, moved a few paces and then stood still again. Now and then they turned around. They waited to be told to go on, and didn't understand what the delay was for. They were used to their programme and it was getting on for midday. Loading up had given Dobbs more trouble than he had expected. It was not so easy without help to load the animals in such a way that the packs would not slip; for he could not be on both sides of them at once. It was impossible to get both loads on to the pack saddle at once, because the packs were too heavy and he could not lift them high enough to get them both on at the same time so that they balanced. If only donkeys would kneel down to be loaded like camels. But, just because they are not camels, donkeys will not do this. Besides, they could never get to their feet again under such loads, although they can travel with them for hours up mountains and down again without showing a sign of fatigue. Finally, however, Dobbs succeeded in getting the animals loaded.

He was just going to give the donkeys a shout and a blow, when he thought of Curtin. He had been thinking of him the whole morning and particularly while loading up, but as of someone absent or gone away rather than dead. He had not yet so fully realized that Curtin was actually dead and done with as to be able to think of him only as a dead man.

Now, however, when the caravan was about to start, he thought of Curtin as a dead man. And then it occurred to him that he ought as a matter of prudence to have buried him before setting off. For a moment he was undecided whether after all to leave him lying where he was. The coyotes, mountain lions, vultures, ants and flies would dispose of the body quick enough. But then there would still be a few bones and rags left over. And it was not very advisable to leave them there as an advertisement of what had happened, or of what might have happened.

But these thoughts became entangled with another thought which until now had never come to him, and it made him irresolute. He thought that perhaps the sight of the corpse would make him lose his head. There was such an unearthly desolation and silence all around him. The scrub was so meagre that it looked as though the trees had never grown up. They seemed unable to decide whether they ought to grow a little larger or whether it was better to stay as they were. The droughts are so long and may cost them their lives if they need too much water. And since many of them from sheer cunning refuse to grow any bigger, the earth beneath them takes its revenge by making them grow crooked, stunted, askew and grotesque.

There was not a sound of beast or bird in the undergrowth. There was a wind. Dobbs felt it and saw the clouds moving overhead. But the trees did not stir. They stood as though turned to stone. They were not green, but grey-blue like brittle bits of lava. The air round them took on this same dead grey, and it seemed to Dobbs that the very air had turned to stone and could not be breathed.

The donkeys were now standing quite quietly as though they waited to be turned to stone like everything else around them. Sometimes with an unnatural slowness they turned their heads and gazed at Dobbs with their large black eyes. For a moment he was afraid of them, and to shake off his fear he went up to one of them and tightened its cords. Then, going up to another, he pulled at its load to see whether it was tight enough and wouldn't shift during the descent of the pass. But everything was fast enough. The puffing and blowing against the bodies of the animals and the feel of their hides calmed him, and he forgot the look from their great glassy eyes, shining, like flakes of coal.

Had he too, thought Dobbs, his eyes open, glassy, vacant and dim? Only natural, he told himself. Dead men's eyes are always open, and their eyes are always glassy and dim. But no, he thought again, they are not glassy and they do not shine like the donkeys' eyes; they are worn, dull glass. In fact, they are not glassy at all. They are glazed. It will be better to bury him. I might perhaps think of his eyes. Yes, I must certainly bury him.

He pulled out a spade from one of the packs. But as soon as he had it in his hand he thought again that burying the body was unnecessary and a mere waste of time. It might mean that he would just miss a train, and the sooner he left that neighbourhood behind him the better.

While he was pushing the spade back again through the cords he felt a curiosity to know whether the vultures had found Curtin out yet. If he were only sure of that, he thought, he would feel safe. Once more he pulled out the spade and walked away into the bush. He went straight for the spot where Curtin was lying. He could have hit on the direction, perhaps even the very spot, blindfold. But when he came to the place there was nothing there. He had made some mistake. The darkness of the night before and the uncertain light of a flaming branch must, he supposed, have made him mistake the direction. He began to look about, creeping through the undergrowth and pushing his way through the scrub. Suddenly he felt bad. He was afraid of coming on the corpse when he least expected it. He did not want that. It might even happen, he thought, that groping round he might unawares touch the corpse on the face. The thought gave him an eerie sensation. He now decided to give up the search.

All the same, when he was half-way back he said to himself that he would never have peace until he had seen the corpse lying there under his eyes and could be convinced that Curtin was really dead and past troubling him any more.

He began his search over again. He quartered the bush in all directions, then ran back to the camp to take up his direction again from there. Suddenly he found he could not any longer remember for certain in which direction he had driven Curtin out on the night before. Time after time he took his direction afresh. It was no good. The corpse was not to be found. Could he possibly have so completely mistaken the direction?

His excitement rose to fever-pitch. The sun was now straight above and blazed without mercy. He panted and broke out in a sweat. He was parched with thirst. But instead of drinking he poured water without thinking straight down his throat.

When he went back to grope through the bush he kept glancing nervously about. For a second he wondered whether it was fright. But he persuaded himself it was nothing but his nerves. Certainly it was not his conscience, he was sure of that. It was only excitement.

The donkeys had become impatient. The ones in front had begun to get underway. And soon the rest of the caravan followed as a matter of course. With a curse he was after them. This frightened the donkeys and upset them. They began to trot and he had to overtake the leaders before he could bring the caravan to a halt. Quite out of breath, he chased them back to the camp, where they stood quietly nibbling at the sparse grass. Now and again one of them turned and looked at him with large and wondering eyes. This terrified Dobbs and he decided to blindfold them.

Nevertheless, he began again on his search, and when for the hundredth time he had convinced himself that he was on the spot where he had shot Curtin down, he saw a piece of a charred branch. And now he knew that he was at the right place. It was a piece broken off from the branch which he had used to light his way the night before.

The ground looked disturbed. But that might just as well have been caused by his own trampling and groping about. He saw no blood. In any case it could scarcely have been seen on ground like that. Had Curtin been dragged away by some animal? Or had somebody found him and carried him away? He could not have crept away by himself because he was dead. Dobbs had convinced himself of this. It must have been an animal that had dragged him away.

All the better, thought Dobbs, because soon there would be nothing left of the corpse. And now, feeling calmer, he began to think of making a start. All the same, he kept turning round, and first he thought he caught sight of Curtin between the trees and then had as bad a shock when he decided that it was another man he had seen. Next he started up because he was convinced he heard voices. And if a twig snapped or a stone was dislodged he thought some beast was stalking him, the same one that had dragged Curtin away, and which, once having tasted blood, would spring on him from behind.

He shouted to the donkeys and they started off. But the journey was far more difficult than Dobbs expected, for if he went to the head, the tail of the caravan began to string out and even to take side paths and look for grass in the bush. Time after time he had to halt the caravan in order to round up donkeys which had been left behind.

So then he took the tail of the caravan, and now the donkeys in front went astray and the whole caravan went to pieces. He got out rope and tied each donkey to the pack saddle of the one in front to keep them together, and once more he took the head. But as soon as a donkey pulled on the pack saddle of the one in front, the one in front came to a standstill and the whole caravan halted.

He began now to give all his attention to the leading donkey, whipping him on and so forcing him to drag the others after him. This succeeded for fifty yards or so, but then the donkey thought better of it. He came to a stop, planted his forefeet firmly in front of him and putting back his long ears stood as fast as a rock. Dobbs might whip him or kick him in his tenderest spots, the donkey would not stir; for he had no idea what was up. He was supposed to go and at the same time he was dragged back from behind. Once more Dobbs changed his tactics and, getting in front, he dragged the leading donkey along. For a time all went well. The donkeys all followed. But when the leading donkey discovered that it was much easier and more convenient to be dragged along than to go of his own accord, he allowed himself almost to be carried, until Dobbs at last had such a weight to pull that a whole railway train might have been attached to the rope which was strained over his shoulder. He had to give it up and attempted once more to drive them along from behind, running the whole length of the caravan to collect any beasts who strayed.

Then there came a time when the caravan went along by itself without any trouble. The donkeys had settled down and kept well to the path. There was peace and quietness at last and Dobbs walked comfortably behind and lit a pipe. And as he had nothing else to do but stroll quietly along, he began once more to be busy with his thoughts.

I didn't make a proper search, he thought to himself. Perhaps he wasn't dead, only badly wounded. Now he's crawling through the bush and he'll end by reaching an Indian village. Then it's all up. Dobbs turned round with a start, for he thought he heard Indians close behind, pursuing him to give him up to the police.

But perhaps he won't get to a village. The villages are far apart and, even if he isn't dead, he's too hard hit to do more than drag himself along. I must find him and finish him off. In any case, it's attempted murder and brigandage, and that will mean twenty years in Santa Maria.

At last he saw nothing else for it but to go back and make a fresh search for Curtin, dead or alive. It occurred to him that there was one direction in which he had not looked at all. This was the opposite direction from the spot where he had left Curtin lying. He had never searched there at all, and it was quite clear that Curtin might have crawled off in that direction because it would lead him back to where they had seen that village at midday the day before. Dobbs had been fast asleep and neither seen nor heard anything. Perhaps, too, Curtin had avoided passing close by the camp in case he waked Dobbs and got finished off. He would have been defenceless. Yes, there was no doubt of it. Curtin had crawled off in that direction, and it was there he was to be searched for.

It was just before nightfall when Dobbs was once more back at the old camping-place. He did not wait to unload the donkeys, but began on his search at once. He searched in the new direction with the same feverish haste with which he had searched in the opposite direction during the morning.

But the night came quickly and Dobbs had to give up.

There was now only one thing left. He could not waste a single hour more on the search. He would have to get off at dawn and reach the railway at Durango with the utmost speed, sell the donkeys and tools at once and, taking the first train to one of the large towns, vanish from sight there. For the time he could not think of Laredo, Eagle Pass, Brownsville or any other station on the frontier, for, if Curtin had really reached a village or if Howard was on the road, then he would be looked for first of all along the frontier.

At noon, on the day before, Dobbs had seen from a bare mountain height the smoke of an engine in the far distance. It could not be so very far now.

21

Dobbs was on the way before daylight. The caravan went along fairly well once it had settled down. The beasts were more willing than on the day before, because they had not been kept standing so long and they were already familiar with the first part of the way. Nevertheless, one donkey broke away and Dobbs was unable to round it up. He had to let it go, as he had no more time to lose. Its load bumped against trees while Dobbs was chasing after it and the girths broke. The donkey cantered off without its packs. Dobbs took the trouble to distribute the load among the other donkeys, for the runaway would no doubt follow and join up again of its own accord at night.

Dobbs had now an almost unbroken view of the railway line in the distance, and the track led downhill the whole way towards the valley. That very afternoon he could easily have reached a station at Chinacates or Guatimape, but he would have caused too much of a stir with his caravan in these tiny villages, all the more now when he was quite alone. It would look suspicious. Besides, in little places like that no one would buy his donkeys, tools and the other stuff which he had to sell in order to buy a ticket and pay the freight charges.

So he had no choice. He had to go on to Durango, where he could transact his business without exciting much attention. This meant another two days' hard going, perhaps even three. If only he knew whether Curtin was dead or not, but after all one must always leave something to luck.

When Dobbs pitched camp for the night he felt calmer than he had for two days past. It was not really conscience that had vexed him. It was rather the uncomfortable feeling one has after leaving a job half done. And he had left his job less than half done and it took its revenge by making him feel uneasy. He ought to have smashed Curtin's skull, plunged his knife into his heart and put him under the ground there and then. That would have made a proper job of it and set his mind at rest. 'Do your job well and do it at once', he had been taught as a child, and yet when it had come to the pinch he had neither done it properly nor at once.

Anyway, there came the donkey which had broken away, trotting up to join its companions. Two of the grazing donkeys raised their heads and brayed. They were, no doubt, his intimate friends, but the runaway went up to one of the other donkeys and after snuffling and nibbling its neck began to graze beside it as unconcernedly as if it had only wandered away for five minutes instead of having trotted along miles behind the caravan for a whole day.

'That's a bit of luck,' Dobbs said with a laugh when he saw the donkey trotting up. 'That's fifteen pesos to the good. Another two days and I can write the old boy a letter to send the other swine a doctor. I can snap my fingers at them then.'

He was in such good spirits that he began to whistle and at last to sing, and he passed that night much more quietly than the night before, during which he had started up several times, frightened by every sound.

Towards noon of the next day when the path went over a hill, he could see Durango in the distance. Durango, the lovely jewel of the Sierra Madre, which, bathed in golden light and softly fanned by gentle breezes caressing it with the tenderness of a feminine hand, nestles between protecting hills. 'The Town of Sunshine' it is called by those who, once having seen it, are homesick for its endearing loveliness. Mother Earth, who is not stingy when once she has a mind to make a present, has placed on one side of it one of her miracles of nature, the 'Cerro del Mercado', a mountain of pure iron, six hundred million tons of pure iron ore.

That evening he camped for the last time. Next evening he would be in Durango and on the following morning in the train for Canitas. The sale of the donkeys and the rest of his gear would take little time, as he would ask no more than he stood in need of for his journey.

He was jubilant. He was in sight of port. When the wind was in the right direction he could hear the whistle of the goods trains in the silence of the night. And this shrieking whistle of the engines, which often sounds so mysterious and ghostly, made him feel that he was already in an hotel close to the station. It was the cry of civilization and this cry was his assurance of safety. He had a longing for law and order, for the solid masonry of the town, for everything which would serve to guard his treasure. Once within the sphere where property is protected by law and where strong forces make law respected, he was safe. There everything and every accusation had to be proved, and, if nothing could be proved, then the possessor was the lawful owner, whose property would be protected by the bullet and the prison. But he would certainly avoid putting himself in need of proving his title. He would carefully keep out of the way of every stone or pebble over which it is so easy to stumble when you have to keep a look-out on every side. What could Howard do? Nothing. If he attempted to invoke the police or the law he would be up against it himself, for he had dug for gold and removed it without the permission of the government. He had robbed the state and the nation, and so he would take good care before making any move against him. And Curtin? Even supposing he were alive, what could he do? Just a little. He too had robbed the state and could make no accusation without confessing it. Dobbs had not robbed the state. No one could prove it against him. Attempted murder? Curtin could not prove that either. There had been no witness. As for Curtin's wounds, who could say in what scrap or robbery he might have got them? Dobbs by that time would be a well-dressed and prosperous gentleman who could afford the services of an expensive lawyer. Everyone would believe him when, with a casual wave of his hand, he pointed to the other two as bandits. To look at them would be enough, and, besides that, they were by their own confession robbers of the state. He would hold that over them. They would never get at him, not when he once had the protection of the law. Law is a good thing after all.

It was only in the interval before he reached the station and before he could take shelter within the protecting arms of the law that the two could do anything against him. But they were far away and tomorrow he would be safe. Perhaps a long time hence they might by pure chance come across him somewhere, in the States or in Cuba or in Mexico or even in Europe. They could, of course, call him murderer, bandit and shameless swindler to his face. They could do that, but, though he could not stop them, he would not turn a hair. Or, if they went it too strong, he would bring a charge of slander against them. No court in any civilized country would ever believe that such things were done anywhere on the earth. Not nowadays. A hundred years ago, or even fifty, but not today, anywhere. Such lawless places are no longer to be found. Every judge knows that, and he would laugh at such slanders. And then the slanderer would have a heavy fine to pay, or else go to prison, for Dobbs is an honourable and prosperous man, who has made his money by perfectly lawful speculations.

The old man or Curtin might of course murder him. They could do that in spite of all the laws in the world, but they would hang for it or take their seats in the electric chair. They knew that all right, and therefore they would think twice about it.

The whistle of another engine sounded in the darkness. For Dobbs it was music, the music of security.

Strange that Curtin never made a sound when he shot him down, not a groan, not a whimper, not a rattle, not a sigh. Nothing at all. He collapsed like a felled tree, and lay there full length as though dead. Only the blood flowed and soaked thickly through his shirt. Nothing else moved. And when Dobbs took the burning branch to see him by, expecting something horrible, all he saw was that white staring face. He couldn't in any case have felt any horror, for Curtin lay so oddly cramped that Dobbs almost laughed at the grotesque appearance of his body.

And now Dobbs laughed aloud to himself. He thought it so funny, the sight of Curtin struck down and lying there dumb, so funny to think that a whole life can be quenched for ever with just a touch on the trigger of a gun.

Wherever could the body be? Carried away, found and brought into safety? Or dragged off by a lion or a tiger? But that he must have seen. Could it be that he wasn't dead?'

Dobbs grew restless and began to shiver. He raked the fire together. Then he turned round and looked across the bare expanses and beyond them to the bush. At last he could lie still no longer and got up to walk about. He told himself that he did it to get warm, but in reality it was because he could see on all sides more easily when he was on his feet. Sometimes he thought he saw someone stalking him. Then he felt sure he heard someone coming up to the fire. Suddenly he had the sensation of someone standing close behind him. He even felt his breath on his ear and the point of a long knife at his ribs. With a quick jump he sprang forward and whipped round with his revolver in his hand. But there was nothing to be seen. Nothing but the dark shadows of the donkeys, who were unconcernedly grazing or lying down. Dobbs excused himself on the ground that you have always to be on your guard. He had done nothing ridiculous, not anything that had any connection with fright or conscience. No one could travel alone through the wilds with such a valuable cargo and not be nervous. It was quite natural, and if anyone pretended otherwise he was only deceiving himself. He did not sleep quite so well that night as the nights before. But the reason was obvious. It was only because he was overtired. He was delayed in his start next morning, as some of the donkeys had strayed to a distance and had to be fetched. Dobbs had been careless when he hobbled them. He lost fully two hours.

The road improved and by midday Dobbs could reckon that three hours more would take him to Durango. It was not his intention to make straight for the middle of the town. He meant to halt at the first Fonda he came to on the outskirts and unload there. He would arrange with the owner of the Fonda to introduce him to buyers for the donkeys, unless the man would take them himself at a low price for the sake of a bargain. Then he would load all the rest, that is to say, the sacks containing the real goods, on a wagon and have it delivered at the express goods station. In this way he would avoid arousing suspicion. The stuff could be consigned as hides. He would pay the highest rate for merchandise and then no questions would be asked.

The track was deep with sand and dust. On one side there was open country, but on the other there was a steep bank of dry, friable clay and crumbling, weathered stone. Thorny bushes and maguey plants were dotted here and there, withered and parched and thickly covered with dust.

Whenever the wind rose or a sudden squall came over, a column of suffocating dust swirled up, and you could scarcely breathe. The fine sand was driven into the eyes, making them smart and blinding them for minutes together. When the squall had passed over, the still air weighed on the land with a metallic glare; then in the blazing atmosphere the dust seemed to singe and roast the skin. The earth, after waiting months for rain, could no longer bear the oppression of the sun and threw back its light with a tormenting brilliance. The dancing shimmer of the merciless sunlight struck through eyes and brain of man and beast, until they staggered on dazed, with closed eyes and not a thought for anything but the end of their torment.

The donkeys struggled on with half-shut eyes. Not one strayed or left the path. They walked like automatons, scarcely moving their heads. Dobbs too had his eyes shut. If he opened them by so much as a chink, the cruel glare flooded into them and he felt that his eyeballs would be burnt up.

Then through his eyelashes he caught a glimpse of some trees by the wayside. He decided to make a brief halt there, just five or ten minutes for the sake of leaning a moment against the trunk of a tree and opening his eyes in the welcome shade to rest them. The donkeys would gladly stand for the sake of a moment's rest in the shade.

When he came to the trees he ran to the front to turn the leading donkeys, and the caravan came to a halt. Of their own accord the animals thronged into the shade and stood quietly. Dobbs went to his water bottle and after washing the dust out of his mouth had a drink.

'Say, got a cigarette?' he heard someone ask him.

He gave a start. It was the first human voice he had heard for days.

For a moment he thought the voice must be Curtin's; then Howard's. But in the same second he realized that the words were Spanish and that therefore it was not either of his two companions. He turned his head and saw three men lying under the next tree. They were mestizos, down and out and in rags, fellows who perhaps had worked for some mining company long ago and now had been for months without work of any kind. They drifted to and fro on the outskirts of the town, sleeping, idling, begging, and if they saw the chance of some petty theft they took it as a gift from God, who allows no sparrow to starve even though it neither ploughs nor sows.

On the other hand, they might just as well be escaped convicts, or criminals not yet caught, who were lying in hiding until they had grown their beards and could hope to return to the town without being recognized. Whatever a town cannot do with, even on its rubbish heaps, it drives out on to the roads, which lead to it, out beyond the zone of rusting jam tins, broken bottles, leaky enamel ware, stoved-in buckets, yellowing newspaper and all the other refuse which a civilized town ejects day by day. It is just the same in the tropics as everywhere else. No beast produces such a mass of rubbish and filth as the civilized human being; and the disposal of this filth which he daily produces costs him as much trouble, labour and forethought as the production and use of all the things which he imagines he finds necessary.

Dobbs had been in the country long enough to know that he was now in as awkward a situation as any he could have looked for. He knew these outcasts from the towns, fellows who had less to lose than any destitutes in the world.

He saw now that he had made a bad mistake when he left the road to have a quarter of an hour's rest in the shade. Not that he would have been any safer on the road, but at least he would not have walked straight into the trap.

'I've no cigarettes. I haven't had a cigarette for ten months.'

That sounded all right, and he added that he himself was a poor devil who couldn't afford to buy any.

'But I've a little tobacco left,' he went on.

One of the men asked for paper to roll a cigarette.

They were all still lying indolently on the ground with their heads turned towards him. Two were propped on their arms and the third lay stretched on his front with his head turned askew to look at Dobbs.

'I've got a bit of newspaper,' said Dobbs.

He took his bag of tobacco and a bit of paper out of his pocket and handed them down to the one who lay nearest him; for the man did not bother to get up to take the tobacco.

They all tore strips from the paper and shook tobacco on to them. Then they rolled themselves cigarettes and the one in front gave the bag of tobacco back.

'Cerillos? Matches?' asked the one who gave the tobacco back.

Dobbs felt in his pockets and brought out some matches. They even returned his matchbox.

'Going to Durango?' asked one of them.

'Yes, to sell the donkeys. I want money. I haven't a cent.'

That was a cute answer, thought Dobbs, for now they knew that he had nothing in his pockets.

They all laughed. 'Money, that's just what we want, too, eh, Miguel? That's what we're waiting for, money.'

Dobbs leant against a tree and kept an eye on all three of them. He filled his pipe and lit it. All sense of fatigue left him. He was looking for a way out. Perhaps, he thought, I could hire them as drivers. It will look better when I reach the town than arriving quite alone with the caravan. Then they'll be sure of a job and look for a peso each and drop any other ideas they may have. They'll be sure of food in their bellies and a few glasses of Tequila.

'I could do with two or three drivers,' he said.

'Oh, you could?' One of them laughed.

'Yes, the donkeys give me enough to do. They don't keep together.'

'What will you pay?' asked another.

'A peso.'

'Among the three or each?'

'Each. Not till we get to the town, of course, and I can put some money in my pocket. At present I haven't a centavo.'

Again Dobbs thought what a cute answer he had made.

'Are you by yourself, then?' asked one who was propped on his arm.

What shall I say, thought Dobbs. In order not to let them wait for an answer and arouse their suspicions, he replied: 'No, I'm not by myself. There are two others behind with the horses.'

'That's a funny thing, Miguel, don't you think?' said the one who was stretched out on his stomach.

'Yes,' Miguel answered, 'that's very funny. Here he is by himself with all these donkeys and lets his friends come behind on horseback.'

'Can you see anything of his friends on the horses?' asked the third.

'I'll have a look,' answered the one who lay flat. He got up slowly and, walking away from the trees, looked up the road, which could be seen for a long distance a little further back.

When he returned he said: 'Those two with the horses are a long way off yet, an hour at least. That's a funny thing, Miguel, don't you think?'

'A decir verdad,' said Miguel. 'I think it's very funny too. What's all this in the packs?' he asked, and getting up went to one of the donkeys.

He punched one of the packs with his fist.

'Skins, I should say,' he said.

'Yes, there are skins there,' Dobbs admitted. He was feeling more and more uncomfortable, and wanted to get off.

'Tiger?'

'Yes,' said Dobbs indifferently, 'there's tiger among them.'

'They fetch money,' said Miguel with a knowing air, and stepped back again from the donkey.

To hide his uneasiness Dobbs went up to one of the donkeys and tightened its girths, although there was no need for it. Then he went to one of the others and gave a pull at the packs, as though to make sure they were fast. Next, he tightened his belt and pulled up his trousers to show that he was making ready to go.

'Well, I'll – yes, I must get on if I'm to be in the town by dark.' He knocked out his pipe against his heel as he spoke. 'Which of you will come as driver to Durango?' He looked at them and at the same time rounded up the donkeys.

Not one of them made any reply. They looked at each other and exchanged meaning glances. Dobbs intercepted one of these, and gave a push to one of the donkeys to get it going. The donkey trotted off and another lazily followed it, but the rest stood still and nibbled at the grass. Dobbs went up to one of them and shouted at it, and it too moved off.

The men were now on their feet. Without apparently meaning anything, they strolled up to the donkeys which had not yet moved and crowded them back or got in front of them if they made an attempt to follow the rest.

The animals, however, began to get restive when they saw the head of the caravan under way and already on the road, and so they pushed past the men. But the men had now come to life and seizing the reins they brought them to a halt without any disguise.

'Get off from those donkeys,' Dobbs shouted angrily.

'What's that?' said Miguel, impudently pushing out his jaw. 'We can sell them just as well as you can. They'll be none the worse because we sell them.'

The other two laughed and caught hold of another donkey.

'Leave go of those donkeys,' Dobbs shouted louder than before. He took a step back and pulled out his gun.

'You don't frighten us with your gun,' sneered one. 'You can only shoot one of us and he won't care.'

'Get back and let go,' shouted Dobbs.

Then he loosed off at the nearest man. It was Miguel. But there was only a hard, dry click. Again and again he pressed the trigger. Not a shot rang out. Dobbs stared and the men stared. From sheer astonishment they forgot to laugh or jeer.

But one of them bent down and picked up a large stone.

A pause of one single second followed. Yet his thoughts crowded upon Dobbs so quickly in this single second when his life was at stake that he could not help wondering how it was possible for anyone to think of so many things in one second. His first thought was how his revolver could have missed fire. But this brought a long story to his mind. On the night when he shot Curtin he had crept up to him while he was asleep, taken his loaded revolver from him and later shot him with it. Curtin had had both revolvers in his pockets, his own and Dobbs's. As both revolvers were marked and Howard could have identified them, Dobbs threw down Curtin's, with which he had fired the shots, beside the body after shooting him the second time. But he put his own revolver in his pocket. Thus it would appear, if Curtin's body were found, that he had been attacked and had defended himself. Dobbs's revolver was of a different calibre and the bullets could not have been fired from it. Dobbs forgot only one thing. He forgot, when he took back his own revolver, to load it. He forgot that Curtin unloaded it on the night when he took the revolver from him. Busy as his mind had been all these last few days, it had never once entered his head that the revolver was still unloaded.

Still in the same second Dobbs thought of another weapon. He was standing close beside one of the donkeys to whose pack a machete was tied. He made a grab to draw the machete and defend himself with it. This might have served him well, for with the machete in his hand he could perhaps have gained time to load his revolver with the few loose cartridges in his shirt pocket.

But the second had now run out and the stone came hurtling at his head. He saw it coming, but he did not turn his head aside quickly enough, because his mind was entirely taken up with the machete.

The stone stretched him out, more by the weight of its impact than the injury it did to him.

But before he had time to jump up again Miguel was on to the machete, to which his eyes were first directed by Dobbs's movement. With a practised hand he drew it in one sweep from its long leather sheath; the next moment he was above Dobbs, whose head with one short sharp blow he struck clean from his neck.

Less shocked than taken aback by the swiftness of it, they all three stared at the body. The head lay separated only by the thickness of the blade from the trunk, and the eyes quivered spasmodically and then, with a sudden jerk, remained three-quarters shut. The fingers of both hands stretched to their full extent and then were tightly cramped together. This they did several times, until, they gently opened and died, half closed.

'It's you who did it, Miguel,' said one of the other two in a low voice as he came nearer.

'Shut your mouth,' shouted Miguel in a passion and turned suddenly on the speaker as if to kill him. 'I know myself who it was who gave it him, you canary bird. If it comes out, you two will be shot as well as me. You know that, without me needing to tell the police. It's all one to me in any case and I am not your wet-nurse.'

He looked at the machete. There was scarcely any blood on it. He wiped it against a tree and pushed it back into its sheath.

22

Donkeys do not as a rule concern themselves with human affairs in the way that dogs are so ready to do, and the caravan had gone quietly on; and as they have more intelligence than those who have had nothing to do with them believe, it had taken the road for Durango.

In their excitement, the men had quite forgotten the donkeys. They stripped the trousers and boots from the body and pulled them on there and then. Neither trousers nor boots were worth much, for they had seen more service during the last ten months than was ever expected of them. All the same, they were magnificent acquisitions compared with the rags these men wore.

But not one of them would have the shirt or put it on, although all three, in place of shirts, wore what can only be described as a network of tattered remains.

'Why don't you take the shirt and put it on, Ignacio?' asked Miguel, giving the body a push with his foot. There was nothing on it now but the threadbare khaki shirt.

'It's not worth much,' answered Ignacio.

'You have reason to say that, you dirty hound,' observed Miguel. 'Compared with yours, it's better than new.'

'I don't want it,' said Ignacio and turned away. 'It's too close to his neck. Why don't you take it yourself?'

'I?' asked Miguel, frowning angrily. 'I'm not going to put on a shirt which is still warm from that hound of a gringo's body.'

But the truth was that for Miguel too the shirt was too close to the neck of the corpse. There were no bloodstains on it, but all the same none of them would put it on. They had a foreboding that they would not feel comfortable in it. They could not explain the feeling and contented themselves with saying that the shirt was too near the neck and that this was why they didn't want it.

'The swine is sure to have some shirts among his gear,' said Ignacio.

Miguel turned on him at once. 'You wait till I've had a look, and if there's anything left over we can talk about it.'

'Do you think you are boss here?' now shouted the third, who for the last few minutes had been leaning against a tree, taking no part in the discussion. He had good reason, for he had got the trousers and Miguel the boots. Only Ignacio had come out of it empty-handed, since he would not have the shirt.

'Boss?' yelled Miguel in a rage. 'Boss or no boss, what have you done up to now?'

'Didn't I plug the stone at his skull?' shouted the third. 'You wouldn't have lifted a hand to him otherwise, you skunk.'

'A stone,' sneered Miguel. 'About as much good as a toothpick. Which of you two mangy cats would have got to work and finished him off? You bastards. And in case you don't know it, I can make use of the machete a second time and a third too, for the pair of you. I don't want your permission for that.'

He turned round, meaning to go to the donkeys.

'Where are the donkeys? To hell with it!' he shouted in astonishment.

They saw now that the donkeys had gone.

'If they get to the town we shall soon have a lot of police buzzing round,' Miguel shouted.

They set off running after the donkeys. They had need to run, for the animals, finding not so much as a dried stalk to detain them, had trotted briskly on. It took more than an hour before the men got back to the trees with them.

'We'd best put him under the ground,' said Miguel, 'or else someone with nothing better to do might want to know what the vultures had found here.'

'Yes, and perhaps you'll leave a label behind with your name on,' Ignacio sneered. 'What does it matter to us whether the carcase is found or not? He won't be able to say whose company he was in last.'

'You are very smart, my little cock,' said Miguel. 'If they find the swine and us with his donkeys, we'll have nothing to say. But if they find the donkeys with us and no sign of the body, then someone has got to prove that we helped the gringo to hell. We can say we bought the donkeys from the gringo. But if they find what's left of him no one will believe we bought his donkeys. So get on with it.'

The spade that Dobbs had meant for Curtin was now used for his own burial. It was quick work. They didn't trouble themselves much. They did what was barely necessary and then left the matter to the ants and the worms.

After this they set off and drove the string of donkeys back into the mountains again. They didn't venture into the town for personal reasons, and also because they thought they might meet someone there who knew Dobbs and was waiting for him. It was also quite possible that Dobbs had spoken the truth and that two others were really following him on horseback. For it seemed to them very unlikely that Dobbs should have driven the whole string by himself. So, in order to avoid the risk, they turned off from the track which, according to their reckoning, Dobbs had followed and took another mule-track up into the hills.

As soon as they were in the bush they could not restrain their curiosity any longer. They wanted to know what the booty was and what was to be found in the packs. It was dark by then and the mist made the place where they had halted for the night still darker; and to avoid betraying their camp while they were still in the neighbourhood they refrained from making a fire.

They got busily to work unloading the beasts and undoing the packs. They found another pair of trousers and two pairs of light shoes. There were also cooking implements, but only a handful of beans and even less rice.

'It doesn't seem he was a millionaire after all,' said Ignacio. 'No wonder he had to get to the town.'

'There was no money on him either,' grumbled Miguel, while he looked into the pack he had undone. 'Only seventy centavos in his trouser pocket, the bastard. And the skins aren't up to much. They won't fetch above a few pesos.'

Then he came to the little packages.

'What's he got here? Sand, nothing but sand. I'd like to know what he lumps this sand around for all in little bags.'

'That's easy,' said Ignacio, who now came on the little bags in his pack too. 'It's clear enough. The fellow was an engineer from a mining company, who had been looking round the mountains and taking samples of soil back to the town, where it could be tested by the other engineers and the chemists in the office. Then the American companies know straight away where to stake out a claim.'

He shook the bag out. Miguel too emptied out the ones in his packs, and when he saw that the little bags were only made of worthless strips of canvas he cursed gods, devils and all gringos. It had got so dark that even if they had known more about it they would never have recognized the nature of this sand.

164

Angel also, the third man, found the same little bags in his packs. He gave another explanation. He said: 'The swine was a proper American swindler and liar, I can tell you that much. These little bags were all put nicely among the skins and then skins tied round them tight. D'you know why? He was going to sell the skins in Durango by weight, and to make them weigh more he put sand in with them, and so that the sand shouldn't run out he put it in little bags. He'd have sold the skins one night, and next morning, before the buyer found out, he'd have left by rail. We've upset his game for him, the swine.'

Miguel and Ignacio agreed that this was the best explanation and they made haste to get rid of the sand.

23

While it was still night they packed up and went on. By midday they came to a village and asked an Indian whom they found in front of his house, whether he knew anybody who would buy donkeys, as they intended to sell some of theirs because they had no use for them. The Indian looked at the donkeys, walked round them and inspected the marks branded on them; then he also looked at the packs and gave a casual glance at Miguel's boots and Angel's trousers, as though willing to buy them as well. Finally he said: 'I cannot buy any donkeys, I have no money. But perhaps my uncle will buy them. He has enough money. I have none. I will take you to my uncle and you can see what he says.'

The three ruffians thought this promising, for in general you can go the round of half a dozen Indian villages before finding anyone to buy a single donkey. Usually the people have no money, and a peso is a large sum to them.

A few hundred yards further on they came to the uncle's house. It was, like most of the others, built of sun-dried bricks and roofed with grass, and stood on the large open space in the middle of the village where the market, the Independence Day celebrations, the festivities commemorating the Revolution and political gatherings were held. In the middle there was a modest pavilion where music was played during public festivities and from which speakers gave addresses. From this pavilion, too, the heads of the Public Health Commission addressed the inhabitants when they toured the country to instruct the Indian population in matters of health and the care of children. The Labour Government does more in this direction than all other governments put together since the arrival of the Spaniards.

The Indian went into his uncle's house to speak to him about buying the donkeys. It was not long before the uncle came out and went up to the three bandits, who were squatting in the shadows of a few trees near the house.

He was an elderly man, already grey-haired, but strong and wiry. His copper-brown face was alert and his black eyes glanced like a boy's. He wore his plaited hair fairly long and drawn back from the face on each side. Holding himself very erect, he walked slowly up to the men. After greeting them he went straight to the donkeys and had a good look at them. 'Very good donkeys, señor,' said Miguel, 'very good, verdad, you could not buy better at Durango market.'

'It's true they are good donkeys,' said the uncle, 'over worked and in poor condition. You must have come a long way.'

'Not so very far, scarcely two days,' Ignacio put in.

Miguel punched him in the ribs. 'My friend here is not quite right, we have only come two days' journey since they were last rested. But we've been some weeks on the road.'

'Then it's no wonder they're a bit down. But we'll soon feed them up again.' As he said this he looked more closely at their ragged clothing and their scoundrelly faces. But he did not let it be seen that he was observing them; it was rather as though he looked at them without thinking while his mind was occupied with the deal. 'What would you want for them?' he asked without taking his eyes off them.

Miguel smiled and, bending his head confidentially, suggested that twelve pesos would not be too much.

'For the lot?' the Indian asked innocently.

Miguel laughed as though he had heard a good joke: 'Not for the lot, naturally. I mean twelve pesos for each animal.'

'That is a very big price,' the uncle said briskly. 'I can buy them in Durango market for that.'

'You'd be lucky,' Miguel replied. 'They're a lot dearer there, fifteen or even twenty pesos. And then you have them to drive home.'

166

'That's true,' the Indian nodded, 'but they pay their way on the road. I can load them up with goods to bring back.'

Miguel laughed aloud. 'I see we have a smart man to deal with, and we don't want to stick out for our price. We'll say nine pesos and that's my last word. I know things aren't too good for you either and we've had a long dry season this year.'

'Nine pesos,' said the uncle quietly. 'I cannot pay that. Four pesos and not a centavo over.'

'Make it five and the donkeys are yours,' said Miguel, putting his hands in his trouser pockets as though he had got the money already.

'Four pesos is my bid,' said the uncle quietly.

'You pull the skin over my ears, señor; I am not out to make a fortune, but strike me blind if I am not making you a present of the donkeys at the price.' As he said it, Miguel looked from the uncle to the nephew and then at his two companions in crime, who nodded with an air of doleful resignation to show that they were giving away their last possessions.

The uncle nodded likewise, but with the air of having known the evening before that he would buy donkeys for four pesos apiece next day.

He went up to the donkeys again and said: 'Are you going to take the packs away on your back?'

'Yes, you're right, there's the packs,' said Miguel, taken off his guard, and he looked at his two companions; this time not so cocksure as before, but rather as though he expected their advice and assistance.

Ignacio understood the look and said: 'We want to sell the packs as well, we're going on by rail.'

'That's true,' Miguel went on fluently. 'We're selling them too, that was what we meant to do.'

As a matter of fact they had forgotten all about the packs.

'What have you got in them?' the uncle went on, and gave one of the packs a punch with his fist.

'Skins,' said Miguel. 'Good ones. Also our pots and pans and some tools. You won't want to take the rifle. That's too dear.'

'What sort of tools are they?' asked the uncle

'All sorts,' Miguel replied. 'There are spades and pickaxes and crow-bars and a lot else.'

'How do you come to have tools of that sort?' the uncle asked casually, as though for the sake of conversation.

'Oh – the tools – well . . . ' Miguel was suddenly in a fix. He felt uncomfortable and swallowed once or twice. The question of the tools took him by surprise.

Then Ignacio waded in: 'We've been working for an American mining company. That's where we've just come from.'

'Yes, that's it,' Miguel put in quickly and threw a grateful glance at Ignacio. He would never forget his timely help.

'Then you must have stolen these tools from the mining company,' said the uncle dryly.

Miguel laughed and winked at the uncle, as if he were one of them. 'Not exactly, stolen, señor,' he said. 'Stealing is no business of ours. It's just that we didn't hand the tools in when we finished our last shift. No one can call that stealing. We don't want much for them, perhaps two pesos the lot, just to save lugging them to the railway.'

'Of course, I can't buy all the donkeys myself,' the uncle now said slowly. 'I have no use for so many. But I'll get the rest of the villagers along. Each has a bit of money, and I can promise you, you'll soon be quit of the donkeys and the other gear as well. I will do my best. Sit down. Do you want water or a packet of cigarettes?'

Angel went in to the house with him and came back with a jug of water and a packet of Supremos.

The uncle said a word to his nephew, and the nephew went off to summon the men of the village.

The men came, old and young, singly and in twos. Many had their machetes at their sides, others carried them unsheathed in their hands, and others again carried nothing at all. All of them went first into the uncle's house and spoke to him. Then they came out again and after looking the donkeys over carefully they looked at the three strangers too. Perhaps they looked even more closely at the donkeys' owners than at the donkeys themselves, but very much more unobtrusively. The strangers did not notice that they were being so carefully examined. They took it for the ordinary curiosity of the Indian peasant.

After a while the men's wives came along too, creeping up slowly and a little shyly. They all brought their children. Some of the women carried their children slung on their backs, others had them in their arms. The children who could walk ran about round their mothers like chicks round a hen.

At last it seemed that all the men were assembled, for no more came up. Only an occasional woman slowly drew nearer to the house. The uncle now came out followed by the men who had last been in the house with him. They stood in a group. But the rest,

168

who had come out earlier and had been examining the donkeys, remained where they were. Thus the bandits, without noticing it, were unobtrusively surrounded. Wherever they might turn, their escape was cut off. And yet there was nothing in it, since the men had only come to look over the donkeys.

'You are selling them very cheap,' the uncle said. 'The only thing that surprises us is how you can sell such good donkeys for so little.'

Miguel replied with a broad grin. 'You see, señor, we need the money, that's why, and so we have no choice but to sell.'

'Are the donkeys branded?' the uncle asked casually.

'Of course,' said Miguel, 'they're all branded.' He looked round at the donkeys to see what the brand was but the men got in front of the donkeys, so that not one of the bandits could see how they were branded.

'What mark are the donkeys branded with?' the uncle asked.

Miguel began to feel extremely uncomfortable, and his companions started turning this way and that to see the mark. But the Indians, apparently without design, edged them further away from the donkeys.

The uncle looked steadily at Miguel, and Miguel became more and more uncertain of himself. He felt the approach of something which would have a decisive effect on his continued existence, and when the uncle, without repeating his question, continued to look him straight in the eye, he knew that he had to answer. He hesitated a moment and swallowed hard and then said: 'The mark – yes, the mark, it's a ring with a stroke under it.'

The uncle called out to the men standing by the donkeys:

'Is that the mark?' he asked them.

'No,' they called back.

'I made a mistake,' Miguel said. 'It's a ring with a cross over it.'

'That is not the mark,' the men said.

'No, I'm wrong again,' Miguel said, almost beside himself. 'Of course, it's a cross with a ring round it.'

'Is that right?' asked the uncle.

'No,' the men said, 'it's wrong.'

'Yet you told me that they were your donkeys,' the uncle said quietly.

'So they are,' Ignacio broke in, unabashed.

'It's odd then that none of you knows how they are branded.'

'We never troubled to notice,' said Miguel, trying to look unconcerned.

The uncle turned to all the men present.

'Have any of you,' he asked them, 'ever seen a man who owned donkeys or any other cattle without knowing how each one was branded, even if the brands were different and the animals came from different breeders?'

The men all laughed and said nothing.

'I know very well,' the uncle said, 'where these donkeys come from.'

Miguel glanced at his two companions. They were all looking round for some way of escape, when they heard the uncle say:

'The donkeys come from Señora Rafaela Motilina of Avino, the widow of Señor Pedro Leon. I know his brand mark. It is an L with a P backwards on the stroke of the L. Is that right?' he called out.

And the men standing near the donkeys called back: 'That's right, that is the brand mark.'

The uncle looked about among them and called out: 'Porfirio, come here.'

One of the Indians came forward and stood beside him.

The uncle now went on to say: 'My name is Alberto Escalona. I am the Alcalde of this place, regularly elected, and installed by the governor. This man here, Porfirio, is the policeman in this place.'

There are differences between countries and climates, and differences in upbringing and in the influences to which people are subjected. In any case, if anyone in Europe announces his office and title, his object is to arouse a tremor and feelings of awe, so that the man he addresses, impressed by the sublimity of the occasion, shall respectfully incline himself and pay the holder of the title the honour due to his rank. Here, on this continent, a title counts for nothing, a name for little and personality for all. No one inclines himself unless on occasion before a woman. And anyone who calls the President 'Your Excellency' would be as ridiculous as a president who expected it. The president is much less usually addressed as Mr President or Señor President than as Mr Coolidge or Señor Calles, as indeed the rule is almost without exception, and anyone who has business with the president shakes his hand when he arrives and when he goes, and talks to him as if he had eaten from the same spoon all his life. This is something that the freshly starched, top-hatted presidents of the brand-new European republics have still to learn. For European presidents take absolute rulers as their patterns, whereas presidents here take no one for their pattern, or, if they need a pattern, they take themselves as a pattern and so they are just such men as anyone else in the country. And if anyone here says: 'Our president is a great fathead', the president does not sentence him to a five months' imprisonment; rather, if he hears of it, he says to himself or his friends: 'That fellow knows more about me than I do myself, he seems to be a smart man.'

If anybody here mentions his office and says: 'I am a magistrate of this place and this man here is the chief of police', it has quite another meaning than it has in Europe.

The three bandits knew at once what it meant and that there was an end of hand-shaking. They started up and tried to make their escape without taking their donkeys with them.

They would have sold the lot now for a peso or given them away for nothing, if only they could have left the village behind them; but there was no question of that now.

Miguel felt for his revolver. But he found his pocket empty. In his excitement he had not noticed that Porfirio had relieved him of it. The revolver would certainly have been of little use, for it was still unloaded. But the Indians could not have known that and might perhaps have let him go if he had threatened them with it.

'What d'you want, then?' Miguel shouted.

'Nothing so far,' the Alcalde said. 'We're only wondering why you're in such a hurry to be gone without taking your donkeys with you.'

'We can take our donkeys or not, we can do what we like with our donkeys,' Miguel replied in a rage.

'Yes, but they are not your donkeys. I know the history of these donkeys. Señora Motilina sold these donkeys ten or eleven months ago to three Americans who were going hunting in the Sierra. I know the Americans.'

Miguel grinned and said: 'That's quite right. It's from these Americans we bought them.'

'At what price?'

'Twelve pesos apiece.'

'And now you want to sell them for four. It seems a bad bargain.'

The Indians laughed.

'You told me,' said the Alcalde, 'you had had the donkeys a long time. How long?'

Miguel thought for a moment and then said: 'Four months.' It occurred to him that he had said they had been working in a mine and had come a long journey.

'Four months?' the Alcalde remarked dryly. 'That is a funny

thing. The Americans came down from the mountains a few days ago. They were seen in the villages. And they had all the donkeys which you bought from them four months ago.'

Miguel tried on his confiding smile once again.

'The truth is, señor, we bought the donkeys from these Americans two days ago.'

'That sounds better. So you bought them from the three Americans?'

'Yes.'

'But it cannot have been the three Americans, for I know that one of them is in a village on the other side of the Sierra. He is a doctor.'

'It was only one American we bought them from.' Miguel scratched his head.

'Where was it you bought the donkeys?' the Alcalde continued relentlessly.

'In Durango.'

'That is scarcely possible,' said the Alcalde. 'The American could not be in Durango by this time, and if he was you could not have got here.'

'We travelled all night.'

'Maybe, but why should the American sell his donkeys to you in particular when he was already in Durango where he could find plenty of other buyers?'

Ignacio now joined in: 'How do we know why he wanted to sell his donkeys to us and not to others? That was his affair.'

'Well, he must have given you a receipt,' said the Alcalde. 'A receipt with the price and the brand marks; otherwise Señora Motilina can claim the donkeys any time, because they are branded with her mark.'

'He didn't give us a receipt,' Miguel answered. 'He didn't want to pay the stamp.'

'You might have paid the few centavos yourselves in order to have a proof that you'd bought them,' said the Alcalde.

'Damnation,' Miguel shouted, clenching his fists. 'What is it you want from us? We go quietly about our business and you surround us. We'll make a complaint to the governor and have you removed. Do you understand?'

'That's a bit too much,' the Alcalde said, smiling. 'You come to our village and want to sell us donkeys. We want to buy the donkeys and we agree about the price. But after all we have the right to know where the donkeys come from. Otherwise, early tomorrow morning perhaps soldiers may turn up and say we are bandits and have taken the donkeys from their rightful owner after killing him, and then we should be shot.'

Miguel turned to his friends and gave them a look. Then he went on: 'We don't want to sell the donkeys now at any price, not even for ten pesos. We want to go on.'

'But you might sell us the tools and the skins, all the same?' asked the Alcalde.

Miguel thought this over, and as it occurred to him that the skins and the tools had no brand mark, he said: 'Right, if you want the skins and the tools – what d'you think?' turning to his friends.

'Very well,' said they. 'Let them go.'

'They belong to you, I suppose?' asked the Alcalde.

'Course they do,' Miguel replied.

'Why didn't the American sell his skins in Durango? Why are you carrying skins back here? You are only carrying water to the river.'

'Prices were not good in Durango and we thought we'd wait for a better time.' Miguel began to walk to and fro, though the Indians left him little room.

'Did the American go naked to the railway?' The Alcalde threw in this question unexpectedly.

'What do you mean?' Miguel went white.

'Well, you have his boots on and that other has his trousers on. Why has none of you got his shirt on? It was quite good. In any case, it was as good as new compared with the rags you're wearing.'

Miguel was silent.

'Why didn't any of you take it?' repeated the Alcalde. 'I can tell you,' he went on, 'why none of you wanted to put that shirt on.'

Neither Miguel nor either of the other two waited to hear what the Alcalde would say next. Each of them leapt upon the men nearest him. It was so sudden that the Indians were not quick enough to get hold of them, and they made their escape and ran down the village street, making for the open.

The Alcalde nodded to some of the men, and a few minutes later five of them were in pursuit of the runaways on horseback. They didn't even wait to saddle the horses. They only threw halters over their heads. The thieves had not got far. The Indians overtook them before they had reached the last house of the village. They were lassoed and brought back to the village square.

'Now we'll go and find the American and ask him what he sold you the donkeys for, and why he let himself be stripped naked and made you a present of his boots and trousers. We will bring his shirt, which none of you wanted, back with us.' The Alcalde said this as though it was for their information and required no reply.

The three were bound and then guarded by Indians, who squatted down opposite them with their machetes across their knees.

The other men saddled their horses, put tortillas in their bast pouches and set off. The Alcalde and Porfirio rode with them.

24

It is very difficult for anyone to travel for long in these parts without being seen. Even though he tries to avoid all habitations and all encounters on the way, there are always eyes which see him, follow him on his way and observe all his doings. He himself as a rule does not know that he is observed. Long before he has seen them, the Indians have left the tracks and crept into the bush, where they wait for him to go by and do not come out again until he is out of sight. They have seen him, little as he thinks it, and so thoroughly inspected him from head to foot that a few hours later the whole village knows just what he looks like and all that he has with him. From water channels, from behind hillocks and rocks and bushes the eyes see every movement and every step the stranger makes.

The mounted men followed the track which Dobbs had gone and not the one which the bandits had taken. As they were on horseback and riding light, they reached the place where Dobbs had halted by midday. The spot was easy to find.

Two of the men followed the trail on towards the town. But they soon found that the donkeys had merely strayed and then been driven back again.

It was now a simple matter for the Alcalde, himself a full-blooded Indian, to reconstruct the whole affair. The donkeys had gone on by themselves, so no one had had time to bother about them. Hence something must have been going on at that spot which so absorbed the attention of all those who were present and whose footprints could be recognized, that they had not noticed when the donkeys began to stray. And whatever had happened must have been of some importance, for otherwise the donkeys would not have got so far.

The footprints of the American were not to be seen either from the trees to the spot where the donkeys were overtaken, or from this spot on towards the town. Even if he had gone barefoot it would have been easy to recognize his tracks. The form of his foot would not be so beautiful as that of an Indian's foot, because he wore boots which cramped the toes. Besides this, the feet of white men are much larger than those of Indians, whose feet are usually neat and small.

As the American's tracks did not lead on, it followed that he must be there. And as he had not been very deeply or carefully buried and as no rain had fallen, the men in a few minutes came on his grave.

No one can be accused of murder unless the body can be produced, as Miguel had said. In this he was right. This is the law, and one may call it a good law, for in such vast countries men can vanish so completely that a corpse is more easily found than a man who disappears of his own accord.

The body was found, and as the three bandits were in possession of the dead man's property without being able to produce any title to it, there was no need for further proof.

The Alcalde gave one glance at the body and then observed: 'Machete.'

Then the men took the shirt off the body and the Alcalde took possession of it. After this the Indians buried the body once more. They worked with bare hands and when they had filled in the grave, which they dug deeper than before, although they had only their machetes, they stood for some while round the mound without their hats. They did not pray, but with bowed heads all looked down upon the mound.

While they were standing there the Alcalde went to the nearest tree and cut off a small branch with his machete and then cut it in two pieces. He tied the two pieces together with string in the form of a cross and planted it in the ground at the head of the grave.

Next morning they were back in their village. The Alcalde showed the shirt to his captives, who looked at it and shrugged their shoulders.

Meanwhile two men were dispatched to the nearest station of mounted police and a detachment arrived during the morning. The inspector, when he had seen the men, said to the Alcalde: 'There's a reward for that one,' pointing to Miguel. 'I think it is three hundred pesos or two hundred and fifty. I don't know exactly. He's a bandit and has committed two murders already. The other two are no doubt birds of the same feather. I don't know them. The reward will come to you, señor, to Porfirio and the rest of the men here. Now what will you do with the donkeys and their packs?'

'Tomorrow we shall restore them to their owners,' said the Alcalde. 'I know where they are. One of them is a doctor and they won't let him go on the other side of the mountain. We want him here too for a week. He'll have his gear now and will not be in such a hurry to go on.'

The three bandits were now taken over by the police. They were no longer on the lasso. They went on foot surrounded by the mounted soldiers. There is the shirt, there are the trousers, there are the boots, there are the donkeys, there are the packs, there is the cross on the mound. It is not likely, then, that the further procedure will take more than two hours. There will be no costly scaffold erected and no white gloves put on. The state has not got the money for all that. Money must be saved for more important matters.

25

Howard was a very busy man. He was not able to enjoy the leisure he had hoped for. He was famed far and wide as the great medicine man. The Indians of the uplands are all very healthy and live to an age which seems fabulous to the European. They are defenceless only against diseases brought in from outside. But though they all enjoy most enviable health they suffer, all the same, from ailments and infirmities into which they persuade themselves by dint of hard talking. They only need to hear of an illness and to have its symptoms described in order to be sure within three days that they have it themselves; that is why doctors, medical and clerical, do such good business in the country.

A woman came to Howard and wanted to know why she had lice, while her neighbour had none. What was Howard to prescribe? An ointment would have been the right thing. But as soon as it was used up, the lice would return, and the question would be repeated: 'Why have I got lice and my neighbour none?' Howard got out of the difficulty by a simple expedient, for he was a genuine medicine man. He said: 'It is because you have very good healthy blood and lice are fond of it, whereas your neighbour has very poor and sickly blood.' Whereupon the neighbour, a woman bursting with good health, came and asked him to prescribe for her poor and sickly blood. If she had gone to a qualified doctor in the town, he would have prescribed salvarsan, although she had not the least symptoms of any illness requiring it. But people imagine that salvarsan is good for the blood and so the doctor prescribes it.

Howard had no salvarsan by him. He had, indeed, no medicine whatever. His one and only prescription was hot water, two litres every day. For the sake of variety he might prescribe three litres or one and three-quarters or one and a half; then again hot water with lemon juice or with orange juice or with any herb or vegetable he was acquainted with and knew could do no harm.

Those who do not know the healing power of water may find it remarkable that the men, women and children who besieged the medicine man all got well. At least, so they said. And it is the case with all illnesses that, if you are convinced that you are ill no longer, you are immediately cured.

In the case of bodily pains when, as the people said, death lurked immediately under the skin and they could plainly feel it when they pressed on the place, Howard prescribed hot compresses, and again for the sake of variety, cold compresses, compresses on the head, on the neck, on the palms of the hands, on the pulse, on the pit of the stomach, on the soles of the feet or wherever the place might be. And in these cases too the people all got well. Death crept back again from under the skin, because it grew too hot or too cold for it, as the case might be.

As for fractures of arms or legs, strains or sprains, here the people needed no assistance. They had nothing to learn from any doctor. And there was no need, either, for Howard to act as midwife. They had no trouble with childbirth.

Howard's fame increased daily, and if he had more taste and liking for a life among a primitive people he might have been content to stay on here for ever in peace and happiness; but every day his thoughts were set on his departure. He thought again and again of his two companions, wondering whether they would duly hand over his share and whether they would get safely to the railway. His consolation was that there was nothing he could do, except rely upon their honesty and resource.

Then, one morning, an Indian came riding to the village and asked for the house where the great medicine man lived. He spoke first to Howard's host and then the two went up to Howard.

His host said: 'Señor, this man here is from a village over the mountains and he has a story to tell you.'

The Indian sat down, rolled and lit a cigarette and then began to tell his story.

'Lazaro was in the bush burning charcoal. He is a charcoal burner. It was early in the morning. He had just stacked up his wood. Then he saw something creeping on the ground. And when he looked more closely he saw that it was a white man crawling along. He was covered with blood and could go no further. Lazaro gave him water to drink. Then he left his stacked wood and got the white man on to his donkey and took him to his house in the village.

'When the man had been laid on a mat in the house he was dead. But then another man came and looked at the white man and said: "He is not quite dead. He is only very sick and very weak. Filomeno must ride over the mountain to the white medicine man because Filomeno has a horse and a donkey does not go so fast."

'I am Filomeno, señor, and I have a good and fast horse and here I am. You can certainly help the sick white man if you come at once.'

'What does the white man look like?' asked Howard.

Filomeno was able to describe him as clearly as though he stood beside him and Howard knew that it was Curtin.

He got ready to go at once. His host and three other Indians accompanied him.

It was a long and hard ride. But when they arrived Curtin had recovered a little and seemed to be out of danger. Curtin had told the people of the village no more than that he had been shot on the road, by whom he did not know. He wanted to avoid Dobbs being followed, because in that case all would be up.

'The dirty swine shot me down in cold blood,' Curtin told Howard, 'because I wouldn't go halves on your lot with him. He tried to pretend it was in self-defence. I saw at once what he was after. I might have agreed to the share-out and then, when we got to the town, put the matter to rights again. But you might perhaps have joined us before I expected and then you'd have believed I'd agreed to do you down. You'd never have believed I'd only made a pretence of it. He gave me one in the left side and left me lying in the bush to rot. But now I find I was shot twice, though I can only remember the once. I almost think the skunk came back when I was unconscious and put another into me, just to be sure of making a good job of it. I came round late in the night and dragged myself away from the place as fast as I could. I thought to myself: he'll be sure to come in the morning before he gets off and if he finds there's a breath left in my body, he'll finish me off. Then I came on an Indian burning charcoal in the bush. He was afraid and ran away at first. But I spoke to him and told him that I was at my last gasp, so he helped me at once and brought me here. Without his help, I was finished. I could go no further and no one would ever have found me.'

'Then he's made off with the lot?' Howard asked.

'Sure.'

The old man reflected for a moment. Then he said: 'Actually he wasn't a crook. At bottom he was a decent fellow. The mistake was his going on alone with you. It's a damnable temptation to travel day in and day out with a heap of gold, along tracks and paths through this Godforsaken bush, and only one man at your side. The bush keeps whispering and whispering and shouting its temptation in your ear: "I tell no tales. Here's your chance which will never come again and I am as secret as the grave." If I was as young as you two, I don't know that I could have resisted such a hellish temptation day after day. It is only a matter of a second, one single second, and you can count for yourself how many seconds there are in a day of four and twenty hours. For the flash of a second the mind loses its grip and before it grips the cogs again you have loosed off. Then there's no turning back and you have to finish the business.'

'The swine had no conscience,' said Curtin.

'He had just as much or just as little as the rest of us who know we have to use our elbows to get on top. When there is no chance of being run in, conscience is as silent as an empty brandy bottle in a dusty corner. Conscience only shouts when it has a good backing. That's the reason for prisons, hangmen and the pains of hell. Had the armament manufacturers, who made their money by helping the peoples of Europe to massacre each other, any conscience? Had Mr Wilson any conscience when he let fifty thousand of our young fellows be murdered because Wall Street was afraid of losing its

179

money and the munition makers wanted to do even better business? If he had, it's the first I've heard of it. It's only the small fry who have to have a conscience; the others don't need one. Our friend Dobbs will find his conscience very lively as soon as he knows that he only killed you by halves. You can leave conscience out of it. I don't believe in it. All we have to think of now is how to recover the goods.'

Howard's idea was to ride straight off to Durango in order to overtake Dobbs, or, at least, find him in Tampico before he fled the country. Curtin was to remain in the village getting well and come on afterwards.

When Howard explained to his host that he now must see to his property because Curtin lay there sick, they gave their consent to his departure even though it grieved them that he should go soon.

Next morning Howard was ready to set off for Durango. But his Indian friends refused to let him go alone. They wanted to accompany him and see him safe to the town, in case he might meet with the same fate as his friend Curtin. So they all rode along with him.

They had just reached the next village when they met the Indians, with the Alcalde at their head, who were on their way to take the donkeys and the packs to Howard.

'But where is Señor Dobbs, the American who was taking this string of donkeys to Durango?' Howard asked after looking round and seeing nothing of Dobbs.

'He has been killed,' the Alcalde said quietly.

'Killed? Who by?' Howard asked mechanically.

'By three bandits, who were taken up by the soldiers yesterday.'

Howard looked at the packs. They seemed to him to have shrunk strangely. Running up, he opened one of his own packs. The skins were all there but the bags were gone.

'We must overtake those bandits,' he shouted. 'I've got to ask them something.'

His escort was quite ready. They left the donkeys to go on to the village where Curtin was. All the rest of them made a bee-line after the soldiers.

The soldiers had not been hurrying. On such occasions they always visit every place lying off their route to hear what's going on and to show the peaceful inhabitants that the government does not forget to give them its protection. The prisoners whom they take along with them only deepen the impression made on the Indian peasantry that they can quietly pursue their labours and that the

180

government looks after the righteous and lays all bandits and footpads by the heels. Bandits, and any others who might have a thought of taking up the business, are warned by the sight of the prisoners, whose end is clear to all, that there are drawbacks to the career of robbery on the roads. Such warnings are more effective than reports in the newspapers – which are never seen in such places and which in any case no one could read.

They overtook the soldiers next day. Howard was introduced to the officer by the Alcalde as the owner of the donkeys and their loads and was given permission at once to question the bandits.

He didn't want to hear any more about their murder of Dobbs, as the Alcalde had already given him a full account of it. All he wanted to know was where the bags had got to.

'The bags?' Miguel repeated. 'Oh, those little bags – we emptied them all out. There was nothing but sand in them to make the skins weigh heavier.'

'Where did you empty them out?' Howard asked.

Miguel laughed. 'How am I to know? Somewhere in the bush. One bag here, another further on. It was dark. Then we went on during the night, so as to get away – we didn't put any crosses up where we emptied them out. You can get sand anywhere for the picking up. And if it's that particular sand you want, perhaps as a sample, I don't suppose you'd find a grain of it now. We had a terrible downpour the night before last, and even if we knew the place it'll all be washed away. Otherwise I'd tell you gladly enough for a bag of tobacco. But I don't know and so can't earn my tobacco.'

Howard did not know what to say. All he could do was to let out such a shout of laughter that the other men and the soldiers too could not help laughing as well, although they did not know what the joke was. But he laughed so heartily that no one could resist joining in.

Howard threw the bandit a bag of tobacco, thanked the officer and then rode back with his friends.

'Well, my boy,' he said, sitting on the edge of Curtin's bed, 'the gold is back where it came from. Those fine gentlemen took it for sand and thought we were going to cheat the dealers by having it weighed in with the skins, and the precious innocents chucked it all away. They don't know where, because it was dark. And anyway, the rain-storm the night before last has just put the lid on it. Otherwise, all we slaved ten months for was to be had for a bag of tobacco.'

He began to laugh so hard that he had to double up in case he hurt himself.

'I'm damned if I see what there is to laugh at,' Curtin said half angrily.

'I don't understand you,' said Howard, still laughing. 'If you can't laugh now till you burst, then you don't know what a good joke is, and that would be a pity. It's a joke worth ten months' hard labour.'

And he laughed till the tears ran down his cheeks.

'They have made me into a medicine man,' the old man chuckled, 'and I have more cures to my credit for less medicine than the best doctor in Chicago. And you were twice shot dead and are still alive, and Dobbs has so entirely lost his head that he will never be able to look for it again. And all this for gold which is ours and yet nobody knows where it is, and it's going begging for a bag of tobacco worth thirty-five centavos.'

Now at last Curtin began to laugh as hard as the old man had the whole time. But Howard put a hand over his mouth. 'Not so loud, my boy, otherwise you'll burst your lungs. And you must keep them, because otherwise we won't get to Tampico. We shan't manage it by railway. We shall have to ride the donkeys, and those we don't need for riding we must sell, so that we can have tortillas and frijoles to eat, the millionaires that we are.'

'What are we to do when we get there?' Curtin asked.

'Well, I had been wondering whether I wouldn't settle down here as a medicine man. We could run the show together. There's more than I can do alone. I need an assistant, and I'll make over all my prescriptions to you. They're good ones, I can promise you.'

When Howard began to look through all the packs one by one, he found one pack in which the bags had not been emptied out. Either it had been overlooked or else the bandit who had possessed himself of it was too lazy to empty it there and then and thought he would leave it over until later, when they were not in such a hurry to get on.

'This will just pay for – pay for what?' asked Howard.

'Not a cinema,' Curtin said.

'It wouldn't run to that. But I thought perhaps a little delicatessen shop?'

'Where? In Tampico?' Curtin said, raising himself on one elbow.

'Of course, where do you think?' Howard replied.

'But during the last month we were in Tampico, four big

182

delicatessen shops went bust in six months.' Curtin thought it important to remind the old man of this.

'That's true,' said Howard. 'But that was twelve months ago. Things may have altered. We must risk something.'

Curtin thought a moment and then said: 'Perhaps your first idea was best – we'll try the medicine business for a time first, then at least we're sure of board and lodging. Whether this would be so with the delicatessen shop, I shouldn't like to say.'

'But you sit right in the middle of it, you only need your tin-opener and you can open a tin of what you like.'

'That's all fine. But I'd like to know what you'll have to eat when they come and seal up your delicatessen shop. Then you won't get at your tins any more.'

'I hadn't thought of that,' Howard said sadly. 'It's true we couldn't get at the tins then, and the best tin-opener would be no use at all. I agree that it will perhaps be better to leave the delicatessen alone for the time and stick to medicine. Besides, it is a highly honourable profession. After all, any fool can be a grocer, but not a medicine man by any means. It's got to be born in you. And I have good right to say so. Come along to my village and you'll soon learn something. You'll take your hat off when you see what honour I'm held in. A few days ago they wanted to make me into a legislative body. But what they mean by that I haven't been able to find out.'

At that moment his host came in.

'Señor,' he said. 'We must now ride on. There is a man just arrived on horseback. He says there are so many people in the village wanting to see the doctor that the village is getting anxious. So we must get off at once.'

'Do you hear that?' Howard said, turning to Curtin and shaking his head.

Curtin laughed and said: 'In three days I'm coming to see the medicine man myself.'

Howard had no time to reply. The Indians had picked him up, carried him out and put him on his horse.

Then they rode off with him.

The Death Ship

THE FIRST BOOK

Song of an American Sailor

Now stop that crying, honey dear,
The Jackson Square remains still here
    In sunny New Orleans
    In lovely Louisiana.

She thinks me buried in the sea,
No longer does she wait for me
    In sunny New Orleans
    In lovely Louisiana.

The death ship is it I am in,
All I have lost, nothing to win
    So far off sunny New Orleans
    So far off lovely Louisiana.

1

We had brought, in the holds of the S.S. *Tuscaloosa*, a full cargo of cotton from New Orleans to Antwerp.

The *Tuscaloosa* was a fine ship, an excellent ship, true and honest down to the bilge. First-rate freighter. Not a tramp. Made in the United States of America. Home port New Orleans. Oh, good old New Orleans, with your golden sun above you and your merry laughter within you! So unlike the frosty towns of the Puritans with their sour faces of string-savers.

What a ship the *Tuscaloosa* was! The swellest quarters for the crew you could think of. There was a great ship-builder indeed. A man, an engineer, an architect who for the first time in the history of shipbuilding had the communistic idea that the crew of a freighter might consist of human beings, not merely of hands. The company who had ordered the ship to be built had, somehow, made the great discovery that a well-treated, well-fed, well-housed crew is worth more to the welfare of a ship and its ability to pay high dividends than a crew treated like bums. Everything was as clean as a Dutch girl. Showers whenever you wanted them. Clean bed-sheets and clean pillow-covers twice a week. Yes, sir. Everything was solid like rock. The food was good, rich, and you could have as much as you could pack. The mess-gear always polished like in a swell hotel dining-room. There were two coloured boys to attend to our quarters and mess to keep them spick and span like a peasant home in Sweden at Whitsunday. All for no other reason than to keep the crew in fine health and in high spirits. Yes, sir.

I second mate? No, sir. I was not mate on this can, not even bos'n. I was just a plain sailor. Deck-hand you may say. You see, sir, to tell you the truth, full-fledged sailors aren't needed now. They have gone for ever, I think, with the last horse-drawn cab in New York. A freighter of today isn't a ship at all. A modern freighter meant to make money for the company is only a floating machine. You may not know very much about ships, sir, but believe me, real sailors wouldn't know what to do with a modern ship. What such a ship needs is not sailors who know all about rigging; what she really cries for is men who are good engineers, mechanics, and working men who know machinery when they see it. Even the skipper has to be more of an engineer than a sailor. Take the A.B., the able-bodied sailor, who used to be more than anybody else a real sailor; today he is just a plain worker tending a certain machine. He is not supposed to know anything about sails. Nobody would ask him to make a proper splice. He couldn't do it for a hundred dollars. Nevertheless he is as good a sailor on a modern freighter as his grandfather was on a three-mast schooner. Yes, sir.

All the romance of the sea that you still find in magazine stories died long, long ago. You would look in vain for it even in the China Sea and south of it. I don't believe it ever existed save in sea-stories – never on the high seas or in sea-going ships. There are many fine youngsters who fell for those stories and believed them true, and off they went to a life that destroyed their bodies and their souls. Because everything was so very different from what they had read in those alluring stories. Life on the sea is not like they make it out to be and it never was. There is a chance, one in a hundred, maybe, that at some time romance and adventure did exist for skippers, for mates, for engineers. You still may see them singing in operas and making beebaboo in the movies. You may find them also in best-sellers and in old ballads. Anyway, the fact is that the song of the real and genuine hero of the sea has never yet been sung. Why? Because the true song would be too cruel and too strange for the people who like ballads. Opera-audiences, movie-goers, and magazine-readers are like that. They want to have everything pleasant, with a happy ending. The true story of the sea is anything but pleasant or romantic in the accepted sense. The life of the real heroes has always been cruel, made up of hard work, of treatment worse than the animals of the cargo get, and often of the most noble sacrifices, but without medals and plaques, and without mention in stories, operas, and movies. Even the hairy apes are opera-singers looking for a piece of lingerie.

I was just a plain deck-hand. What you might call a handy man aboard. I had to do every kind of work that came my way or that was pushed my way. In short, I was just a painter and brass-polisher. The deck-hands have to be kept busy all day long. Otherwise they might fall for some dangerous ideas about Russia. On a modern ship, once under weigh, there is little to do outside of the engine-holds. Sometimes repairs have to be made on deck or in the holds. Holds have to be cleaned or aired. The cargo has shifted, perhaps, and has to be put back into place to keep the ship from hanging down a fin. Lamps have to be cleaned. Signal flags set in order. The life-boats watered and inspected. And when nothing else can be done on deck, the hands paint. Always there is something to be painted. From morning to night.

There comes a day in the deck-hand's life when he feels convinced that there are only two kinds of people on earth, those who sail the high seas and those who make paint. You feel a sort of gratitude towards those good people who make all that paint, because should they ever stop, the second mate would surely go mad wondering what to do with the deck-hands. The deck-hands can't get paid for just looking around the horizon or watching the smoke of another ship coming up. No, sir.

The pay was not high. I have to admit that. The company could

189

not have competed with the German and the Italian freight rates had they paid us the wages of the vice-president of a railroad. They say the whole trouble is that sailors don't know what to do with their pay; otherwise they might easily own, after a couple of years, five or six sea-going freighters. For my part, not being under the influence of the success stories of the builders of our nation, I reckoned like this: if I would not spend a cent of my pay for twenty-five years and I would tuck it away in a trust or bank and if I would never have, during those twenty-five years, one week without pay, but work hard all the time, even then I could not retire and live on my dividends. Still, after another twenty-five years of equal pay and of equal good luck in always having a ship, I might by then call myself a useful and honest citizen and a member of the lower middle-class, ready to buy a gas-station somewhere on a highway. A fine and noble prospect – it convinced me to stay a plain sailor for a good long while and so prepare myself for the bread in heaven and leave for others the cake here on earth . . .

The other guys had gone ashore. I didn't care to see the city. I don't like Antwerp. There are too many beachcombers, bums, worthless sailors, and drunken ships'-carpenters around anyway. One should not mix with such people, being a sailor on a smart American freighter, and a freighter from New Orleans at that. Besides, I told Honey I wouldn't play around with any dames. At least not on this trip. No, sir. I mean, yes, sir.

I have learned that it is not the mountains that makes destiny, but the grains of sand and the little pebbles. Sounds philosophic, but it is the truth.

I was alone in the fo'c'sle. Everybody else had gone ashore to get a bellyful of port life before going home to be dry again. I was sick of reading true confession stories and ranch romances. I couldn't even sleep any more, which was strange, because I can sleep anywhere and any time. I didn't know what to do with myself. We had laid off work at noon, when the watches were assigned for the trip home.

I wandered from the quarters to midship and back again. Five hundred times or more. I spit into the water and speculated on how far the rings might go before they died. I threw crumbs of bread into the water to feed the fishes.

It made me so very miserable to look at the offices and buildings along the docks, by now all empty and closed. Office windows after closing hours make the same impression upon me as bleached human bones found in a desolate place in the open sun. From the height of the ship I could see right into the offices, where on dull desks were piled up all kinds of papers, blanks, bills. Blanks too can make me sick; they remind me of questions I have to answer to some official to whom I would like to say whose son I think he is.

All and everything about the docks and the buildings and the offices looked so utterly hopeless, like a world going to pieces without knowing it.

In the end I got a craving to feel a solid street under my feet. I wanted to see people hustling about. I wanted to make sure that the world was still going on in the usual way, doing business, making money, getting drunk, laughing, cursing, stealing, killing, dancing, falling in love, and falling out again. I really got frightened being alone there.

'Why didn't you come earlier in the afternoon like the other guys did?' the mate said. 'I won't give you any money now.'

'Sorry, sir, to bother you, but I sure must have twenty bucks advance. I have to send it home to my mother.'

'Five and not a cent more.'

'I can do nothing with a five, sir. Prices are high here in Belgium since the war. I need twenty, not a cent less. Maybe sir, I mean I might be very sick tomorrow. Who do you expect would paint the galley then? Tell me that sir. The galley has to be ready when we reach home.'

'All right. Ten. My last word. Ten or nothing. I'm not obliged to give you even a nickel.'

'Well then, sir, I'll take the ten. But I think it's lousy the way they treat us here in a foreign country.'

'Shut up. Sign here for the ten. We'll write it in the book tomorrow.'

The truth is I didn't want more than ten in the first place. But if I had asked for ten I wouldn't have got more than five. The fact is I couldn't even use more than ten. Once in your pocket and out in town, the money is gone, whether you have ten bucks or two hundred.

'Now, don't get drunk. Understand. There'll be plenty of work tomorrow and you've got to be ready to go on hand when we're putting out,' the mate said.

Get drunk? Me get drunk? An insult. The skipper, the other mates, the engineers, the bos'n, the carpenter haven't been sober for six consecutive hours since we made this port. And I am told not to get drunk. I didn't even think of Scotch at all. Not for a minute.

'Me get drunk, sir? Never. I don't even touch the cork of a whisky bottle, I hate that stuff so much. I know what I owe my country in a foreign port. I am dry, sir. I may be a Democrat, but I am dry. Ever seen me drunk, sir?'

'All right, all right, I haven't said a word. Forget it.'

'Thank you, sir.'

Ashore.

2

It was a summer twilight, beautiful and dreamlike. I was in full harmony with the world as it was. I could not understand how anybody on earth could be displeased with life. Communists, reformers, and hell-drummers ought to be kicked out of this beautiful world of ours. I strolled along the streets, looking at the windows where the riches of the world were on display, calling to be bought and carried away. All the people I met seemed so satisfied with themselves and with everyone else. The girls smiled at me, and the prettiest were the ones who greeted me best.

I came to a house that had a fine gilded front. It looked friendly, inviting, and very gay. The doors were wide open, and they said: 'Come in, good friend. Come in and be happy with the happy. Just drop in here, and forget all your worries!'

I had no worries. Yet I felt fine that somebody should call me and remind me that I might have worries. In I went. There was a jolly crowd there. Singing. Music. Laughter. Gay talk. Everything friendly.

I sat down on a chair, at a table. Immediately a young man came, looked me over, and said in English: 'How do you do, mister?' He put down a bottle and a glass. He filled the glass and said: 'Drink to the greatness of your country!' So I did.

For weeks I had seen only the guys of the bucket, and water and more water, and stinking paint. So I thought again of the greatness of my country. And again. There is really too much water on earth. And most of it is salty, at that. And paint is no perfume. Well, to the greatness of my country!

There was foggy weather around me. The longer I sat at the table, and the more I thought of my country, the thicker became the fog. I forget all the worries I could remember ever having had during my life.

Late at night I found myself in the room of a pretty girl. She was laughing and friendly. She was sweet.

Finally I said to her: 'Now look here, Mademoiselle whatever your name may be, you're a piece of sugar. That's what you are. Tell me, what time is it now?'

With her sweet laughing mouth she said: 'Oh, you handsome boy – ' Yes, sir, that's exactly what she said to me. 'Oh, you handsome sailor boy from the great and beautiful Amerique land, you want to be a cavalier, don't you? A real cavalier. You wouldn't leave a little defenceless lady alone in her room at midnight, would you? Burglars might come and rob me or take me away to dark Africa. They might even murder me or sell me as a slave to the wild Arabians. And I am afraid of mice, I am.'

'I am not afraid of a mouse,' I said.

'Oh, you bad sailor man. That's what you are,' the pretty lady said. 'Please don't leave me alone here at midnight. I am so afraid of terrible burglars.'

I knew what a real red-blooded American must do when he's called to rescue a defenceless lady. It was almost a daily sermon from the time I was a kid: 'When a lady asks you to do something, you jump up and do what she says, even if it should cost you your life. Just remember that every woman is a mother or may be a mother some day. That's a good boy.'

What else could I do? It's in the blood. You have to do what a lady asks you to do. Even if it should cost you your life.

Early in the morning, before the sun came up, I hurried to the docks. There was no *Tuscaloosa* to be seen. Her berth at the pier was abandoned. She had gone back home to sunny New Orleans. She had gone back home without me.

I have seen children who, at a fair or in a crowd, had lost their mothers. I have seen people whose homes had burned down, others whose whole property had been carried away by floods. I have seen deer whose companions had been shot or captured. All this is so painful to see and so very sorrowful to think of. Yet of all the woeful things there is nothing so sad as a sailor in a foreign land whose ship has just sailed off leaving him behind.

It is not the foreign country that makes him so sick at heart, that makes him feel inside like a child crying for its mother. He is used to foreign countries. Often he has stayed behind of his own free will, looking for adventure, or for something better to turn up, or out of dislike for the skipper or the mates or some fellow-sailors. In all such cases he does not feel depressed at all. He knows what he is doing and why he did it, even when it turns out different from what he expected.

But when the ship of which he considers himself still a useful part sails off without taking him with her, without waiting for him, then he feels as though he had been torn asunder. He feels like a little bird may feel when it has fallen out of its nest. He is homeless. He has lost all connection with the rest of the world, he thinks; he has lost his right to be of any use to mankind. His ship did not bother to wait for him. The ship could afford to sail without him and still be a good and seaworthy ship. A copper nail that gets loose, or a rivet that breaks off, might cause the ship to sink and never reach home again. The sailor left behind, forgotten by his ship, is of less importance to the life and the safety of the ship than a rusty nail or a steam-pipe with a weak spot. The ship gets along well without him. He might as well jump right from the pier into the water. It wouldn't do any harm to the ship that was his home, his very existence, his evidence that he had a place in this world to fill. If he should now jump into the sea and be found, nobody would care. All that would be said would be: 'A stranger, by appearance a sailor.' Worth less to a ship than a nail.

Pretty, isn't it? So I thought. But the depressed feeling that was looming up within me didn't grip me in full. Before it could get hold of me I knocked it cold.

— the bucket. There are lots of other ships in the world. The oceans are so very big and so full of ships. They have hardly room enough to sail without choking each other. How many ships are there? Surely no less than half a million. One of those half a million sea-going ships, one at least, will need, some time sooner or later, a plain sailor. My turn will come again.

As for Antwerp, well, it's a great port. All ships make this port some day or other. What I need is just patience. That's all. Who would expect that somebody, maybe the skipper himself, would turn up immediately and yell out: 'Hey, sailor, what about signing on? Union pay!' I can't expect anything like that to happen.

Thinking it all over, well, what's there to worry about a faithless bucket leaving me flat in Belgium. Like all women do – leave you the first time you try it out with another dame. Anyway, I have to

194

hand it to her, she sure had clean quarters and showers – and swell grub. No complaints about that. Right now they're having breakfast. Those guys will eat up all of my bacon, and the eggs too. The coffee will be cold again when I come into the mess. If they leave any coffee at all. Sure the cook has burned the bacon again. He'll never learn. I wonder who made him a ship's cook. Perhaps a Chinese laundry man. As for Slim, I see him already going through all my things, picking out everything he likes, before he hands the bag over to the mate. Maybe they won't even turn in my things to the mate. Those bums. Not a decent sailor among them. Just running around with dames. Using perfume and facial soap. How I hate them. Sailors? Don't make me laugh. But I'd never have expected this from Slim. Seemed to be a regular guy. You would not have believed Slim'd be that bad; no, sir. You can't trust anybody any longer. But then – he always used to steal my good toilet soap whenever he could lay his hands on it. What can you expect from a fellow who steals your soap when you're out on deck?

What's the use worrying about that bucket? Gone. It's all right with me. Go to the devil. The ship doesn't worry me at all. What worries me is something different. I haven't got a red cent in my pocket. She told me, I mean that pretty girl I was with during the night, protecting her against burglars and kidnappers, well, she told me that her dear mother was sick in the hospital, and that she had no money to buy medicine and the right food for her, and that she might die any minute if she didn't get the medicine and the food. I didn't want to be responsible for the death of her mother. So what could I do as a regular red-blooded American except give her all the money I had left over from the gilded house? I have to say this much, though, about that pretty dame: she was grateful to me for having saved her mother from an early death. There is nothing in the whole wide world more satisfying to your heart than making other people happy and always still happier. And to receive the thousand thanks of a pretty girl whose mother you have just saved, that is the very peak of life. Yes, sir.

3

I sat down on a box and followed in my mind the *Tuscaloosa* steaming her way home. I wished earnestly that she would spring a leak, or something, soon, and be forced to return and give me a chance to hop on again. I should have known better; she was too good a bucket to run foolishly on the rocks.

Another hope of mine went bluey. I had hoped that the crew might object to leaving me behind and make it tough for the skipper, or even engage in a mild form of mutiny. Apparently they didn't care. Anyhow, I wished that damned canoe all the ship-wrecks and all the typhoons any sailor ever heard of from old salts spinning yarns that made even drunken quartermasters get the shivers.

I was just about to doze off and dream of that little peach of a girl when somebody tapped me on the shoulder.

Right away, without giving me a chance to see what was going on, he talked to me so rapidly that my head began to buzz.

I got mad and I said: 'Rats, be damned, beat it, leave me alone. I don't like your damn jibbering. And besides I don't know what you want. I don't understand a single word of your blabbering. Go to the devil.'

'You are an Englishman, are you not?' he asked, speaking in English.

'Nope; Yank.'

'Then you are American.'

'Looks like it. And now that you know all about me, leave me in peace and go to your wifie. I've nothing to do with you, no business.'

'But I have some with you. I am from the police.'

'Your luck, old man. Fine job. How much do they pay the flats here? What's troubling you with a swell job like that? Something wrong?'

'Seaman, hey?' he asked.

'Aha. Any chance for me?'

'What ship?'

'*Tuscaloosa*, from New Orleans.'

'Sailed at three in the morning. A long way off, I dare say.'

That made me mad again. 'I don't need you to tell me any stale jokes.'

'Your papers?' he asked.

'What papers do you mean?'

'Your passport.'

'*What?*'

'That's what I said; let me have your passport.'

'Haven't any.'

'Then your sailor's identification card or whatever you call it in your home country.' He sort of pushed me.

'My sailor's card? Yes, yes.' Hell. My seaman's card. Where have I got it? I remember now, it's in a pocket of my jacket; and my jacket is in my sailor's bag; and the bag is stowed nicely away under my bunk in the fo'c'sle in the *Tuscaloosa*; and the *Tuscaloosa* is now – gee, where can she be right now? I wonder what they've got for breakfast today. Sure, that damned cook has burned the bacon again. I'll get him some day and tell him what I really think of him. Just let me be around, painting the galley. Guess I'm getting hungry.

'Well, well,' said the flat, shaking me, 'your sailor's card. You know what I mean.'

'My sailor's card? If you mean mine, what I want to say, my sailor's card – I'll have to come clean about the card. The truth is, I haven't got any.'

'No sailor's card?' He opened his eyes wide in sheer astonishment, as if he had seen a ghost. The tone of his voice carried the same strange amazement, as if he had said: 'What is that, you don't believe there is such a thing as sea-water?'

It seems that it was incomprehensible to him that there could be a human being with neither a passport nor a sailor's card. He asked for the card for the third time, almost automatically. Then, as though receiving a shock, he recovered from his astonishment and sputtered: 'No other papers either? No identification certificate? No letter from your consul? No bank-book? Or anything like that?'

'No, no, nothing.' Feverishly I searched my pockets, so as to make a good impression upon him. I knew quite well I had not even an empty envelope with my name on it.

Said he: 'Come with me.'

'Where to?' I wanted to know. Perhaps he was sent to fish up

197

some derelict sailors for a rum-boat. I could tell him right then that not even wild horses could drag me aboard one.

'Where? You will find out pretty soon. Just keep going.' He wasn't so friendly any more.

After some hopping we landed. Where? Yes, sir, you guessed right. In the police-station. Here I was searched, and how! When they had searched all over, and had left unsearched not even the seams of my clothes, one of the searchers asked, absolutely seriously: 'No arms? No weapons of any kind?' I could have socked him one right then, I was so mad. As if I could hide a machine-gun in my nostrils, and a couple of automatics under my eyelids. That's the way people are and you can't do anything about it.

The examination over, I had to stand up before a high desk behind which sat a man who looked at me as if I had stolen his overcoat. He opened a thick book filled with photographs. The guy that had pinched me acted as the interpreter. Without him I would never have known, until the end of my days, what the man behind the desk wanted. Funny that these people understood our language pretty well when they needed our boys to fight for them, and when they wanted our money.

The high priest at the desk looked at all the photographs, and after each photograph he looked at me. He did this a hundred times. He had that way of looking upwards with his nose kept close to the thick book that people have when they look over the rims of their eye-glasses.

At last he got tired of moving his neck up and down. He shook his head and disgustedly closed the book with a bang. It seems he hadn't found my photograph. I could have told him before that he wouldn't, if he only had asked me, because I knew damn well that I had never been photographed in Antwerp. I too got tired of this lame business, and I said: 'Now I am hungry. I want to eat. I haven't had any breakfast this morning.'

'Right,' the interpreter said. I was taken into a small room, with nothing in it that I would call furniture.

I wonder if all the Belgians call what I got a breakfast – coffee, bread, and margarine. It was the minimum in quantity and quality.

Then I was left alone to occupy myself with counting the bars at the window, a job I did rather well.

About noon I was again brought before the high priest.

'There are nine,' I said right away, 'exactly nine.'

'What nine?' the high priest asked with the help of the interpreter.

'Nine bars at the window,' I answered.

The high priest looked at the interpreter, and the interpreter looked at him, and then both of them looked at me, finally shaking their heads; and the interpreter said: 'Well, they are this way, sir. You know it from the war. There is something loose in their upper storeys. One cannot take them seriously.'

'Do you wish to go to France?' the high priest asked me.

'No, y'honour, I don't like France. Under no circumstances do I wish to go to France. I don't like war-mothers running wild about the battlefields. No, France is no place for me.'

'What do you think of Germany?' he asked.

'I don't care to go to Germany either, if you please, sir.'

'Why, Germany is quite a fine country. Take Hamburg for instance. You could easily find there a good ship to take you home.'

'No, I don't like the Germans. They often go out of their minds without warning.'

The high priest assumed a dictatorial attitude: 'Well, then, it is all settled now, once and for all. No more objections on your side, sailor. You are going to Holland. And understand, this is final?'

'But I do not like the Dutch,' I said, and I was just about to tell him why, when he cut me short: 'We do not care a rag if you like the Dutch or if you don't. You may fix this with the Dutch yourself, when you meet them in person. In France you would be best off. However, for a rich gentleman like you, France is not good enough. Too bad we have nothing better to offer you. You don't want to go to Germany either. The Germans also are not good enough for you. Hell, just tell me what people other than your own do you like? None apparently. So you are going to Holland, and that is that. We have no other border. We cannot, just to please you, acquire another neighbour who might find favour with you. And, just to make clear to you what we think of you, we don't even care to throw you into the water. That is the only border we have besides the others already mentioned. It's all right with me if you choose the water. We are at your service, mister. And so you are going to Holland and like it. That's all. Be glad you're getting off so easily. We have jails, and we have camps for people without papers.'

'But see here, gentlemen, you are all mistaken. I do not wish to go to Holland, because the Dutch – '

'Quiet now. This question has been settled, for good. How much money have you got?'

'Why, you searched me all over. How much money did you find

on me? That's how much money I've got.'

'Which means, in other words, not a single cent. Is that what you mean?' he asked.

'Exactly, y'honour. Right you are.'

'Take him back to the cell,' commanded the high priest. 'Let him have a bite to eat.'

A bite. I would like to know when these people really eat.

4

Late the same afternoon I was taken to a railroad station. Two men, one of them the interpreter, accompanied me. No doubt they thought I had never before been on a train, for they would not leave me alone. Not for a minute. One of them bought the tickets while the other remained standing near me. He took good care that no pickpocket should try to search again where they had searched without success. I'd like to see a smart pickpocket find a red cent in pockets that have been searched by the police.

Very politely they escorted me aboard the train and offered me a seat in a compartment. I thought the gentlemen would now take leave. They did not. They sat down. Apparently afraid that I might fall out of the window when the train was moving, they seated themselves on either side of me. Belgian policemen are courteous. I could find no fault with them. They gave me cigarettes, but no matches. They were afraid I might set the train afire.

We came to a very small town and left the train. Again I was taken to a police-station. I had to sit down on a bench. The men who had brought me told a long story to the high priest in charge.

All the policemen stared at me as if they thought me a murderer who had not been properly hanged and had escaped. Suddenly I conceived the idea that I was to be hanged and that they were all only waiting for the hangman, who could not be found for the moment because he had gone off somewhere to a wedding. This idea, that I was to be hanged, impressed me more and more every minute. Had not the high priest in Antwerp said clearly that they

200

wouldn't mind throwing me into the water? Why not hang me just as well? It's the easiest thing to do in a lonely spot.

There's nothing to laugh about; no, sir. It was a very serious matter indeed. Only consider, please: I had no papers; the high priest had not found in his thick book my photograph, either. Things would have been different if he had found my photograph because then he would immediately have known who I was, and that I was an honest sailor. Anybody could say that he had been left behind by the *Tuscaloosa*. Where are the proofs? I had signed in half an hour before the *Tuscaloosa* was leaving the port of New Orleans. The skipper had no time then to sign me on properly. I am sure he didn't even know my name. He never cared to know it. What was a plain deck-hand to him? He had other worries; he was not sure what his woman was doing when he was at sea. Therefore, even if somebody took the trouble to wire him, he would just answer: 'I don't know the bum; hang him if you wish.' He was that kind. Better for him to ignore me altogether than to run up expenses for his company bringing me back home.

Y'see, sir, I had no proof of any sort as to my legal existence. I had no established home anywhere in the world. I was a member neither of a board of trade nor of a chamber of commerce. I wasn't the president of a bank. The truth is I had no bank-connections at all. I've never heard yet of a sailor with a savings-account. It's not the sailor's fault. It's the wages, which never allow him to meet all his expenses ashore.

I was just a nobody. You can't blame the Belgians if they don't want to feed a nobody. You see, the Belgians already have to feed so many nobodies who are only half Belgian, while the other half is French, English, Austrian, German, American, or Scotch, on account of the trouble they had with the war and the occupation of their country. I would have been only another reason for not paying us back the money they borrowed from us when they were in a hole.

So hanging me was the simplest thing to do, and the quickest. There was no one in the world who would worry about me. No one who cared. One bum more or less, what does it matter? There was even no necessity to put my name in the thick book in which all hanged people are written up.

Now they were waiting only for the hangman, because without the hangman it would have been plain murder, and illegal, and it would have been a blemish on a civilized nation as the Belgians are.

I was right. They were waiting for the hangman. They made

preparations. One of the flats came along and handed me two packages of cigarettes. The last gift to a condemned man. Then he gave me matches, seated himself near me, and started to talk English. He slapped me on the back, laughed, cajoled me, and tried to tell me an Irish joke, which, as he explained, he had studied in a book that was supposed to teach English in six weeks without a teacher.

'Don't take it so hard, old man,' he said. 'Smoke your cigarettes and be happy. See, we all have to die some day. I was spared in the war. But one day I too have to swallow dirt. As for you, sailor, we have to wait until dark. We can't do it in bright daylight very well.'

Not take it so hard. I wonder if he ever was so close to being hanged as I was then. Perhaps he was the kind that doesn't take being hanged so hard. Maybe he was used to it. I was not; no, sir.

The cigarettes had no taste at all. Straw and nothing else. Damn it all, I don't want to be hanged. I looked around for a chance to make a clean get-away. Nothing doing. They were staring at me all the time. I was the first American sailor that ever had come their way. An interesting circus animal to them. How I hate these Belgians! I'd like to know why we ever helped them out when they had their pants full.

When darkness had fallen, about nine, someone brought me my last supper. Nasty people, these Belgians. So that's what they call the last supper for a poor condemned man. I can assure them I will never commit murder in Belgium. Potato salad, three slices of liver-wurst, each slice as thin as paper. Clever people, the Belgians, not cutting their fingers when slicing liver-wurst for the last supper of a poor devil. There were also a few slices of bread that was neither really black nor really white, and the inevitable margarine. Belgium has no cows and therefore no butter. Why don't they come to Wisconsin, where people throw butter into the fire to make coffee boil quickly. What a supper! That's the gratitude of these Belgians. And I was nearly wounded once when they were down on their knees begging for help.

The flat who had used up one hour and a half to tell me an Irish joke now came up with a bottle.

'What are you, feller? A good American or a bad one?' he asked.

I looked at the bottle in his hand, and I answered: 'I am a bad one, officer.'

'Exactly what I thought,' he laughed. 'And since you are a bad one I am allowed to give you this bottle of red wine to wash down your supper with. If you had said you are a good American, I would

202

have taken you to be a true believer in prohibition.'

'Prohibition?' I said. ' – prohibition. Let me have the bottle and I'll show you the real gargle of a real American sailor, a gargle such as, migud, you have never seen and never heard of in all your life.'

'That's right, old feller. I thought so all along. Your prohibition. Don't make me laugh out loud. Fine men like you Americans letting yourselves be bossed round by hysterical church-sisters. Not us Belgians, sailor. With us Belgians it is still the man who wears the pants. And if we men like to get a good shot, we damn well drink it and care the devil about women and sin.'

What a pity that a man like that is a cop! Why isn't he a sailor? And why doesn't he come to God's country? That's the kind of people we need back home. The Belgians are not so bad after all. I felt now rather glad that we loaned them our good money, even though there's no chance in the world of ever getting it back again. It pleased me a lot to see that our money helped to keep alive a spirit like this one. So our money was not altogether wasted.

About ten that night the cop who had made me feel at home with his bottle said to me: 'It's time now, sailor. We have to step on it. Come along.'

No use crying now: 'I don't want to be hanged.' It's fate. That's what it is. If the *Tuscaloosa* had waited only two hours more, this would never have happened. It seems I am not worth two hours. Well, let's go and get it over with.

Then something awakened within me. After all, I am not an animal that anybody can do with as he pleases. Where there's life there's hope. An old sailor's saying, and it has always been a good and truthful one.

I shook off the hands which were upon my shoulder, and I yelled: 'I'm not going. I'll resist. I'm an American. I'm an American citizen. I'm going to complain to my ambassador and to my consul. I haven't done anything wrong.'

Said the interpreter: 'You are going to complain? You? And just who are you? You are no American. Prove it. Come, come, show us your passport. Or your sailor's card. We'll even be satisfied with a letter from your consul. See, we are generous. Even a letter from your skipper will do. You have no passport. In any civilized country he who has no passport is nobody. He does not exist for us or for anybody else. We can do whatever we want to. And that is exactly what we're going to do right now. If we want to, we can even hang you or shoot you or kill you like a louse. Just like that; chip, and off you are.' He snipped his fingers and rubbed the nails of his thumbs one against the other. 'Out with him,' he commanded.

'And don't ever bring him back here,' shouted the high priest from behind his desk, where he had been asleep during the past few hours. He had just been awakened by the row I made. 'If any one of you,' he addressed the two men taking me, 'ever brings him back here, I will hang you instead of him. The least I shall do is to put you behind the bars for three years. Get him out now and execute him right in front of the station; what do I care?'

I said nothing more. The two flats were armed, and I was not. We three left the town, and soon we arrived in open fields.

The night was pitch-black. It was a bad road we walked, rough, broken up. When we had gone about a mile and a half, we turned off the road and entered a narrow path crossing a meadow. For another mile we walked only across meadows.

Suddenly we came to a halt. I wonder if Belgian cops are mind-readers. Just when I was about to swing out and land one on the jaw, one of them grasped my right arm. 'We are here now. We will have to say good-bye to each other; don't mind the tears.'

I had an ugly feeling in my throat now, when I knew the last minute had arrived. All my life I had wanted so badly to live in Australia and make good. Now my life was snatched away from me. There were hundreds of things I had planned to do some day. All over now. Too late. Terrible words: too late.

I felt so dry that I would have liked to ask them for a bottle of that fine stuff they used to prove that they still wore the pants. But really, I thought, what does it matter whether my throat's dry or not? What difference does it make whether I go to hell with a drink or without one? I had always pictured hangmen as morons, not the sort these two guys were. Anyway, hanging for money and as a profession is a dirty business. I don't know why people do it when there are so many other jobs in the world just as interesting, as, for instance, being a piano-player during the rehearsals of the Follies, or something like that.

Never before in my life had I realized how beautiful life really is.

'Oui, oui, mister. We have to say good-bye,' the interpreter said again. 'We have no doubt you may be a fine fellow and a good sailor, but right now we have no use for you here in Belgium.'

For such a simple reason they hang a man in Belgium. What people!

He raised his arm, apparently to throw the noose over my neck and to strangle me first so as to make me entirely helpless, as I could see that they had not spent any money to erect real gallows. I wasn't worth the gallows, because I had not committed a murder, and so no newspaper was interested about the way I was executed.

With his outstretched arm he pointed in a certain direction, and said: 'Over there, just where my finger points, there is Holland. The Netherlands, you know. You have heard of the Netherlands, haven't you?'

'Yes, officer.'

'You go right in the direction I am pointing out. See? I don't think you will meet a customs officer or patrol on the way. But if you should see someone hovering around, then take care not to be seen yourself. Keep out of his way and don't mind him at all. After going in this direction for about one hour you will come to a railroad track. Follow this track for a while in the same direction until you reach the depot. Hang around until dawn, but be careful. Avoid being seen. Early in the morning large groups of working men will come to take the train to Rotterdam, where they work. You go then to the ticket office and say: '*Rotterdam, derde klasse.*' Don't say one word more. There, take this money, five gulden.'

He gave me five coins and then said: 'Here is a bite to eat. Don't buy anything at the station. Your talk would betray you. Somebody might get suspicious and start to question you. Then everything would be lost and you'd be done for. Understand? Take this.'

He handed me a couple of sandwiches wrapped up nicely, two packets of cigarettes, and a box of matches.

'You see, you don't have to buy anything. Here is everything you need. Soon you will be in Rotterdam. Don't talk to anybody. Pretend you're deaf.'

I was overwhelmed with joy. Ordered to hang me, they helped me to make off and clear out. I am glad we helped them win the war. These Belgians are people who really deserved to be on our side during the war. I don't care if they never pay back the money we loaned them. I am paid in full, and whether others get their money or not certainly does not concern me any longer.

I jumped like a spring chicken and cried: 'Thank you, thank you ever so much, and if you should ever come to Cincinnati or some other place up there in Wisconsin, be sure and call me up. Thank you, boys.'

'Don't make a fuss,' he interrupted me; 'one of those bone-heads over there might hear you yelling. And I tell you that would be no good for you, nor for us either. Now, listen carefully to what I have to tell you.' He whispered, but he repeated every word three or five times so as to impress me with the full meaning of his warning. 'Don't you ever dare to come back to Belgium. I warn you, sailor. If we ever find you in our country again within the next hundred years, I swear we will lock you up for life, and ninety-nine years more. Life imprisonment. That's something, sailor, believe me. I have orders to warn you properly so that you can't say later you have not been warned. Because we don't know what to do with you. Bums and unemployed and other thieves we have aplenty. We don't need any more.'

I didn't want to leave these Belgian officers with a bad impression about a stranded American sailor. So I said: 'Maybe my consul could – '

'Hang your consul,' he broke in. 'Have you got a passport? You have not. Have you got a sailor's card? You have not. What could your consul, *your* consul, do with you without a sailor's card? He would kick you in the pants, and we should have you again to support at the state's expense. Don't try your consul. You have been warned properly – life imprisonment. So you'd better cut this consul business.'

I shook hands with them again and again, and said: 'You are right, gentlemen. I promise solemnly never again to set foot on Belgian soil.'

'That's a good boy.'

'Because,' I added, 'I am really happy to leave Belgium. I haven't got anything here. I suppose you are right, Holland is far better for me. I worked for a while in Pennsylvania. That's why I know I'll understand at least half of what the Dutch say, while here among you Belgians I never know what's wanted of me.'

'Don't talk so much nonsense,' the interpreter said. 'You'd better be going now. Be smart. Should you hear somebody popping up while on your way to the depot, you just lie down quietly until the danger has passed. Don't let them get you. Never forget the life imprisonment. We would make it tough for you, sailor, believe me. I mean well. Good-bye.'

They went like shadows.

I started off on my way to the depot.

5

Rotterdam is a beautiful city. If you have money. If you haven't any, you are better off in New Orleans. Besides, New Orleans is just as pretty, and more interesting.

I hadn't any money. So I found Rotterdam just a city like all others. To be sure, it is a great port. But there was no ship in dire need of a deck-hand or a plain sailor or an engineer. I would have taken the job of engineer at once if there had been an opening. The joke would have been on the ship as soon as she was out at sea. The skipper would not throw me overboard. That would be murder. Something in the line of painting or brass-polishing can always be found aboard, and you take it even if you have signed on as a second engineer. I would not have insisted on the pay for a second; no sir.

I would have taken any job on any ship, from kitchen-boy to captain and everything between. As it happened, not even a skipper was missing.

In these European ports it is hard to get a ship. To get one that crosses over to the home country is impossible. Everybody wants to go across to God's own great country. I simply can't get it into my head what all these guys are looking for there. They must have got the crazy idea that everybody lies on his back and needs only to open his mouth and in goes the roast turkey with cranberry sauce and all the trimmings; and no one has to work, everybody gets high wages just for doing nothing, sitting around watching baseball games.

What with hundreds of mugs hanging around waiting to take a job on a ship without pay, there was no chance for an honest, home-made sailor like me to get a bucket sailing home.

The Belgian cops had talked about my consul. Yes, why not? Why hadn't I thought of my consul before? My consul. The American consul. Good idea. Splendid. He, my consul, he clears scores of American ships. He makes out all kinds of papers for them. If there is any man who knows every American ship coming

207

or going, it is he. He is asked to supply sailors when the skipper is short of hands. There are always guys who would rather stay in a wet country with low wages than live in a dry country with heaps of dollars a week. If you get the heaps of smackers, I mean.

The whole affair passed by quicker than the time it had taken me to get the idea about seeing His Holiness the American consul at all.

'You are American?'

'Yessir.'

'Where is your sailor's identification card?'

'I have lost it, sir.'

'Passport?'

'Nosser.'

'Citizenship papers?'

'Never had any. Born in the country. Native state – '

'Never mind. Well, what do you want here?'

'I thought maybe, sir, I mean I was thinking, since you are my consul, that maybe you might – what I was going to say, you perhaps might do something to get me out, because, you see, sir, I am stranded, to make it short.'

He grinned at me. Rather nasty. Strange that bureaucrats always grin at you in a nasty way when they want to thumb you down.

Still grinning, he said: 'Your consul? My good man, let me tell you something: if you wish to address me as your consul, you will first of all have to prove that I am really your consul.'

'I am American, sir. And you are the American consul.'

'Right-o. I am the American consul. But who are you to tell me that you are American? Have you got any papers? Birth-certificate? Or passport? Or authorized sailor's identification?'

'I told you already that I lost it.'

'Lost. Lost. Lost. What do you mean by lost? In times like these one does not lose such important papers. Ought to know that, my good man. You cannot even prove that you have been on the *Tuscaloosa*.'

He pronounced 'have' like *hauve* and 'know' like *knouw*, trying to make us poor Middle West guys believe that he came from Oxford or Cambridge or I don't know what.

'Cawn you prove thawt you hauve been on the *Tuscaloosa*?'

'No.'

'Then what do you want here? I might cable the *Tuscaloosa* provided she has wireless. But who pays for the cable?'

'I thought you could do it.'

'Sorry. I am not provided by the government with funds out of which I could pay for such cables. Did you sign on in New Orleans in the shipping offices of the company?'

'No. I did not. There was no time to do so, because the ship was already up and down when I came aboard, because two men had made up their minds to stay off.'

The consul meditated for a few seconds. Then he said: 'Suppose you could prove that you really shipped on the *Tuscaloosa*; that is no proof that you are an American citizen. Any Hindu or even Hottentot may work on board an American merchant vessel if the mawster of the ship needs men and he is not in a position to get American sailors.'

'But, sir, Mr Consul, I am American, sure.'

'That's what you say, my good man. That's what you've told me several times. But you have to prove it. With papers. That's a rule. I cawn't accept your declaration as sufficient evidence. By the way, how did you come from Antwerp to Rotterdam? And without papers? How did you cross the international lines without papers?'

'But, Mr Consul, haven't I told you, the Belgian police – '

'Nuts. Don't try to pull my leg or I am through with you right here and now. The Belgian police; who ever heard of such a thing – that officials, state authorities, would send a man without papers, without his consent, across the international border in the middle of the night? To whom do you think you are selling that yarn? Authorities committing unlawful smuggling of aliens into foreign countries? Pshaw! Tsey, tsey, tsey. Nonesense. Where did you pick up that story? Out of a magazine? Come clean, come, come.'

While he was making this fine speech, he played with his pencil. When he had finished, he begun to hum 'My Old Kentucky Home', beating time with his pencil upon his elegant desk.

So I knew that no matter what he had said, his thoughts were somewhere else. Perhaps at a supper for two with a dame from Louisville.

I was extremely polite. Nevertheless, something inside me told me to take the inkstand and fire it right into the middle of his grinning plaster sponge. Yet I knew how an American has to behave in an American consul's office in a foreign country. Never forget it; as an American in a foreign country you are always representing your dignified homeland.

He looked at me with empty eyes for a long while. I was sure he was still at supper with his dame and was not quite sure if the time had now come to tell her why he had invited her to have supper

209

with him so late at night, and in his apartment, too, and all alone.

I didn't want to wait until he had reached breakfast with that Kentucky dame, so I said: 'Maybe, Mr Consul, sir, there might be a chance to get me a ship making for home. A skipper may easily be short a man.'

He came to, and snapped: 'Eh? What did you – ? No, no, of course not. There is no such possibility. An American ship without papers? Not from me, no, sir. Not from me.'

'Then, where can I get papers, if not from you, sir?'

'Not my concern, old man. Did I take away your papers? I certainly did not. Any bum might step in here and ask me to provide him with legal papers. No, sir.'

'Has it never happened, here in your office, sir, that people have come in to tell you that they have lost their papers or that their papers have been stolen?'

'Of course. Things like that do occur. But those people have money. They are not just bumming about the world like sailors, getting drunk and selling their papers to get the money to buy more booze.'

'But I tell you, sir, I lost my papers. They are on the *Tuscaloosa*.'

'Perhaps they are. Perhaps they are not. Even if you left them there as you say you did, how do you know a fellow-sailor of yours hasn't sold them? What do you say to that?'

'I don't think so.'

'Now, of course, if you had money, we could cable to Washington. But since you have no money, I can do nothing. My salary is not so high that I can afford to pay for a cable for you worth perhaps fifty or sixty dollars.'

'Won't you tell me what I can do?'

'Since you have no papers and no proof of your American citizenship, there is nothing I can do for you. I am only an official. I have to obey rules. It certainly is not my fault. I didn't make the law. By the way, have you had something to eat?'

'No, sir, I told you I have no money, and I haven't gone begging yet.'

'Wait just a minute.'

He rose from his chair and went into another room.

After a few minutes he came back and gave me a sort of ticket.

'With this ticket you will be provided for three full days with three meals each day and lodging. The address of the boarding-house is printed here. After this ticket has expired, if you are still without a berth, you may drop in here again for another one. You are welcome. Why don't you try some ship sailing under a different flag? There are a good many ships nowadays that are not so very particular as to papers. Some even go across to the Canadian coast. Of course, you understand I make no suggestions. Find out for yourself. My hands are bound in a case like yours. After all is said and done, I am nothing but a servant of the government. Really sorry, old man. Good-bye and good luck!'

I was almost convinced that that man was right after all. Maybe he was not to blame. Why, he has no reason to be that way with me. I never saw him before. I never did him harm. Why should he harm me? He was only a servant of that soulless beast called the state. He had every answer ready for me before I spoke. They must have been part of his education, and they had to be memorized before he could pass the examinations for his diplomatic career.

However, when he asked me if I was hungry, he really forgot for a second or two that he was nothing but a servant of the state. Then he became quite human and showed that he still had some soul left. Nothing strange about that. To be hungry is human. To have papers or not to have papers is inhuman. It is against nature's laws. That's the point. There is a good reason for being the way he is. The state cannot make use of human beings. It would cease to exist. Human beings only make trouble. Men cut out of cardboard do not make trouble. Yessir. Excuse me, I mean: yes, sir.

6

Three days are not always three days. Some three days are very long, some very short. But no matter how short three days really are, the three days for which I had a meal ticket were over before I had had time to realize how short three days can be.

I had made up my mind that, regardless of how hungry I might feel, I would not go again to my consul. I thought it silly to listen to his memorized sermon once more. He would not provide me with a ship. So what was the use of giving him the pleasure of having a man sit in front of him listening with attention to his speech? There

211

would be no change in his way of explaining how helpless he was and how sorry he felt for being unable to do something for me, except to give me another meal ticket – but this time with a sour look. No, before I would go again to see him, I would prefer to look for itching pockets.

I had another reason for not wanting to see him. His eyes, when he had asked me if I were hungry, had a look almost like my mother's used to have when she said: 'Like that pie, Gerry? Have another cut.'

This time he might tell me what my mother would never have said. 'Sorry, but it is the last time. There are too many asking for help. You understand.' No.

Oh, you forgotten goldfish, with the folks all off for a long vacation! Was I hungry? Bet your life I was. And tired. Migud, so tired from sleeping in gateways, in corners, in nooks. Always chased and hunted by policemen, striking matches or flashing their search-lights at me.

A civilized country means a country that sends to jail a man found asleep in the streets without evening clothes on. You have to have a house, or at least a room to sleep in. How you get it is of no concern to the police.

No ship in port short of hands. And if there was a ship that needed a man, fifty sailors, natives of the port, and all with excellent papers, came to apply for the job. A hundred jobless to one job. And none for a foreigner. Taking on a man whose papers were not in good shape, who was not in the country legally, was punishable with a big fine. It was punishable even with a prison sentence. It was the law that protected the jobless of their own country. If you don't belong to a country in these times, you had better jump into the sea. No other way out.

Each protects his own kind. Internationalism is just a word that sounds fine from a soap-box. Nobody ever means it; not the Bolshevists either. Stay with your own tribe. Or with your clan. The chiefs need you. If for some reason or other you cannot belong, you are an outcast. You cannot even stay with the dogs of the tribe. Any papers to identify you? No? Out you go and stay out; hell, we've got enough of your kind, get out of here. What's that? Don't let any more workers in. Keep wages up. What do I care if the workers of the other clan cannot even buy dry bread. That's why we call ourselves Christians – because we love our neighbours dearly; so let them go to hell or heaven, wherever they want to, so long as they don't try to eat their daily bread with us. We haven't got enough for ourselves; that's why we have to burn it to raise prices. When you are hungry, and chased when you want to sleep, you easily fall for the wrong religion.

So it happened.

A dame and a gent were standing in front of a shop-window.

Said the lady: 'Look, Fibby, how lovely these kerchiefs are!'

Fibby, apparently knowing nothing about kerchiefs and thinking about lunch, mumbled something that could be taken for an affirmation or for something concerning the stock-market.

The lady again: 'No, bless me. I've never seen anything so cute and so lovely. Must be old Dutch peasant art.'

'Yep. Right you are,' Fibby said, entirely uninterested. 'Genuine. Genuine old Dutch. But, in old English, it's probably copyright nineteen hundred and twenty-two.'

'Aw,' said the fine lady, 'zatso? Let me tell you something.'

I didn't wait to hear her tell him something, for now I was convinced that it was Forty-second or Times Square or Park Row. And it was music to me.

I went about the job rapidly and very cunningly. That's what I thought. But Fibby knew all the tricks. He must have been in the trade before he got into magazines. So we had a lively argument, and the lady, bored to death all day long, liked it immensely.

Fibby got interested in the story far more than did his wife, or his lady friend, or his – well, what do I care what she means to him – they've got their passport in fine shape and are unmolested sharing a double stateroom. As I was saying, Fibby got interested in my story far more than his wife or his lady friend – oh, hell, what do I care? – well, more than his lady could make him interested in old Dutch shawls.

He seemed to have a great time listening in to my story. He smiled, then he laughed, then he roared with laughter. People passing by thought another couple of Americans had gone crazy about nothing at all, as they usually do. He found no other expression to comment on my story with but 'Zat so! Zat so? Gee, zat so? Man, zat so!'

There may be stories that have no end, but mine had one. When I had finished, he was still roaring and bellowing.

'The greatest comedy in all of this lousy Europe couldn't have made me laugh like you did. Oh, boy; oh, boy! What a story! A whale of a story. That's what I've been looking for. What I came over for. Man, you don't know what you mean to me.'

On he went, laughing and laughing.

And I, ass that I was, I had thought he would weep about my sad tale and my hopeless fate. Of course, he only had to listen to it, not live it. He saw only the humour of it; he wasn't hungry, and he had an elegant room in a swell hotel where no policeman would ever kick him in the ribs.

'Listen, Flory,' he said to his lady friend. 'What do you think about the story that boy just told us? Isn't that story great? A birdy dropped out of its little nest. And says he was hungry. Imagine, Flory, here in Holland, where they throw cheese and butter in the ash-cans, and where the people have so much spare time that they haven't got anything else to do but grow flowers instead of cotton or wheat. What a country!'

'Oh, his story is wonderful! It's marvellous. It's peachy. I think it's the greatest, cutest little story I have ever heard.' That's what Flory, the lady friend, said. She went on: 'Wonderful. Just too wonderful for words. Where are you from? From New Orleans? My, my! What a town! Still French and Blackies there? Why, isn't that interesting? It's really thrilling. Why, Fibby, did I ever tell you I still have an aunt living there, down in Dixie, in New Orleans, I mean? Have I ever told you about Aunt Sophronia of New Orleans? Haven't I? Oh, I must tell you all about her. You know, the one that starts every sentence with: "When gran'pa, the colonel, you know – was still living in South Carolina." '

Fibby didn't listen to Flory. He had become accustomed to putting down the phone any time she called him up and letting her talk until he was sure it was time to hang up or to say: 'Yes, honey, I am listening.'

He fumbled about his pockets and fished out a bill. He gave it to me and said: 'Here, take this. It's not only for your story, but for your having told it so splendidly. It's a great gift, my boy, to tell a story the way you did, a story that is not true, but that sounds true. That's the point of story-telling. Making people believe the story is true. You are a great artist, you know. I feel it. A pity that you are bumming your way through the world. But some people, I think, have to do it this way. Can't help it. You know, my boy, you could make quite a pile of dough, the way you tell stories. You are an artist.' He turned round to Flory: 'Isn't he an artist, sugar?'

'He is a great artist,' the lady friend admitted, happy that she could say something again after such a long silence. 'He is a great artist. Why, I feel sure he is the greatest artist I have ever seen. Listen, Fibby, won't you ask him for dinner? Dear me, we would show those Penningtons something worth while. Calling them-

214

selves The Penningtons. Upstarts. The! I could just scream out loud. The! What were they anyway, only five years ago? The! I'm just waiting for the day when they say the word *Mayflower*. I'm only waiting for that day.'

They are married. With a licence, wedding march, church bells, and everything.

Fibby paid not the slightest attention to the onrush of Flory's eloquence. He kept on smiling and then again fell into heavy laughter. Once more he fished in his pocket and produced another bill.

He handed this one also to me, and now he said: 'Get that, my boy; one is for having told your story so very well; the other one is for having given me a most excellent idea for my money-making machinery; I mean my paper. You see, it's like this; in your hands your story is worth just one dime. In my hands your story is worth in the neighbourhood of five grand cold cash. I am paying you your dime with full interest. I am honest, you see; I do not steal plots, I pay what they are worth to the owner. Many thanks for your trouble. See me again some time. You may look me up in New York. Well, so long. Good-bye and good luck. It was a real pleasure.'

That was the first cash I ever received for telling a story. Yes, sir.

I went to a money exchange. I reckoned this way: for one dollar I'll get about two and a half gulden Dutch, so for two bucks I'll get five gulden. Welcome, little smackers; I haven't met you for a long time. I threw my two bills upon the counter. The man picked them up, looked at them quickly and then began to pay me out gulden one after another. When I had five I wanted to leave, but the man said: 'Wait a minute; won't you take all with you?' So I stayed and let him pay and pay as long as he liked. What did I care? When he had finished, he said: 'This makes it exactly twenty Americans.' Was I surprised! Fibby, may Wall Street bless his bank-account, had given me two tenners, and I had thought it was only two ones. I hope he makes a pile of money with the story I told him. He is a swell guy. Of course, he is from New York. People having New York for their home town are that way, not like the misers from Iowa.

It looked to me like quite a good bit of dough. But somehow, before I could realize what a good feeling it is to have some cash, it was gone. Only those people who have lots of money learn to appreciate the real value of money, because they have time to find out. On the other hand, how can people who have no money, or very little, ever find out what money really means? It is in their hands so short a time that they have no chance to see what it means. Certain people, however, preach that only the poor know the worth of a cent. This difference in opinion is the cause of class distinction.

7

Far sooner than I had expected came the morning which I knew to be the last one in a long time that would find me in a bed. I began already to hear the footsteps of policemen and night-watchmen.

I searched my pockets and found just enough coin to make possible a hasty breakfast. Hasty breakfasts are not at all to my liking, because they are but invitations to lunches and dinners that never come. Meeting a Fibby is not an everyday occurrence. Suppose I should have the good fortune to meet one again: I shall tell the same story, but this time I'll make it funny. It may just happen that the gent I tell the story to in a way befitting a musical comedy will receive it weeping bitterly and will get an idea contrary to Fibby's. And if this bird happens to have a magazine for railroad men and gas-station operators and girl stenos, he might easily be willing to spring another twenty bucks. Money can always be squeezed out of an idea, regardless of whether it makes somebody laugh or somebody else cry. In this world there are just as many people who like to weep and will pay two dollars for that pleasure as there are people who will pay for having lots of fun. Usually it costs more money to see a bad tragedy than to see a good comedy. People are like that, and nothing can be done about it. Anyway, I like people who prefer a good time better than –

A good time. What's the matter now? Can't a guy have his beauty nap for the last gulden he paid for a bed? I'd like to know where the next bed will come from.

'Leave me in peace, damn it all. Yes, I paid for my bed last night when I went upstairs. Yes, I paid for it all right, so let me sleep. I am tired.'

The knocking and banging against my door, however, does not cease.

'Goldfish in —, leave me alone. I want to sleep. You heard me. Get out of here. Get away from that door or I'll sock you.' I wish that bum would only open the door so that I could fire my shoe into his face. So they call the Dutch a quiet people.

'Open that door'; again the voice at my door. 'Open! Police. We want to speak to you for a minute.'

'All right, all right. Coming.' I begin to doubt that there are some people still left on this earth who are not policemen or who have no connection with the force. The police are supposed to maintain quiet and order, yet nobody in the whole world causes more trouble and is a greater nuisance than the police. Chasing criminals, and thereby killing innocent women. Keeping order, and throwing a whole town in the middle of the night into an uproar. Nobody drives more people crazy than the police. And just think, soldiers are also a police force, only with another name. Ask me where all the trouble in the world comes from.

'Hey you, what do you want of me? I'm not wanted anywhere.'

'We only wish to ask you a few questions.'

'Go ahead. I'm listening.'

'You'd better open that door. We want to see you.'

'Nothing interesting about my face. I've never been on the screen.'

'Come, come, or we shall have to break in the door.'

Break in the door. And these are the mugs paid by the taxpayer to protect him against burglars. Break in the door. All right. No getting away. So I open the door. Immediately one of the guys sticks his foot in so the door can't be closed again. The old trick of the master. It seems to be the first trick a cop has to learn on joining the force.

Two men. Plain-clothes men.

I am sitting on the edge of my bed and start to get dressed.

'Are you American?'

'Yip. Any objection in Holland?'

'May we see your sailor's card?'

It seems to me the sailor's card, and not the sun, is the centre of the universe. I am positive the great war was fought not for democracy or justice, but for no other reason than that a cop, or an immigration officer, may have the legal right to ask you, and be well paid for asking you, to show him your sailor's card, or what have you. Before the war nobody asked you for a passport. And were the people happy? Wars for liberty and independence are to be suspected most of all, ever since the Prussians fought their war for liberty against Napoleon. All peoples lost their freedom when that war was won, because all liberty went to that war and has been there ever since. Yes, sir.

'I haven't got a sailor's card.'

'Wha-a-a-t? You ha-a-a-a-ave no sailor's card?'

The tune of this long drawn-out question reminded me of the question with which I had been bothered not long before, and exactly at the same time – when I wanted to sleep.

'No, I ha-a-a-ave no sailor's card.'

'Then you have a passport.'

'No service, gentlemen. Gas-pump out of commission.'

'No passport?'

'No passport.'

They looked at each other, nodded, and felt well satisfied with the work they had done so far.

'I suppose you have no identification card from our police authorities either?'

'You hit it, gentlemen. I have not.'

'Do you not know, mister, that no alien is permitted to live in Holland without proper identification papers viséd by our authorities?'

'How should I know?'

'Do you mean to say that you have been living on a mountain on the moon?'

Both cops consider this so good a joke that they laugh and laugh until they cough.

'Get dressed and come along with us. The chief wants to see you.'

I wonder if the Dutch hang a guy without papers or just kick him in the buttocks and take him to the chain-gang.

'Has any of you gentlemen a cigarette?'

'You may have a cigar if you like. We don't smoke cigarettes around here. We are men, and mean to stay men. But if you wish, we'll buy you a package of cigarettes on our way to the station.'

'All right with me. Shoot the cigar.'

I smoke the cigar, which is rather good, while I wash and dress. The two cops sit close by the door and follow everything I do like dogs.

I am in no hurry. Anyway, regardless of how much time I take to get ready, there is finally nothing else to do but shove off.

Upon coming to the police-station I was searched. This was done with all the cunning they had. Tearing open even seams. Still thinking of spies, I thought. But later it dawned upon me that they were looking, whenever they caught a sailor, for Bolshevik ideas rather than for photographs of fortresses or warships.

They had more luck than their brethren in Antwerp. They found some twenty-eight cents in Dutch money, with which I wanted to buy a hurried breakfast.

'Is that all the money you have?'

'As you haven't found any more in my pockets, it must be all.'

'What money did you live on while here in Rotterdam?'

'On the money I no longer have.'

'Then you did have money when you came here?'

'Yep.'

'How much?'

'I don't remember right now how much, but it must have been in the neighbourhood of a couple of thousand dollars or so.'

'Where did you spend it?'

'With the dames. Where else could I?'

'Where did you get the money you had when you came here?'

'I had taken it out of my savings-account.'

The whole outfit roared with laughter. Somehow, they took good care to watch the high priest before they started to laugh. When they saw that he was laughing, they also laughed. As soon as he became serious again, they did exactly the same. It couldn't have been any better done if it had been commanded by a movie-director in Hollywood.

'How did you come into Holland? I mean without a passport? How did you pass the immigration and so?'

'Oh, that? Oh, well, I just came in, that's all there is to it.'

'Exactly. That is what we want to know. How did you come in?'

'How can a fellow come in? I came on a ship.'

'What ship?'

'Oh, you mean the ship? Well, she was – it was – sure, it was the – the – yes, it was the *George Washington*.'

'So? On the *George Washington*?'

'Yes, sir.'

'Sure? You are sure of that?'

'Bless my grandmother's soul.'

'When?'

'Oh, you mean when? Well, I don't quite remember the exact day. Musta been six or nine weeks ago or so.'

'And you came on the *George Washington*?'

'Yes, sir.'

219

'A rather mysterious ship, your *George Washington*. As far as I know, the *George Washington* has never yet come to Rotterdam.'

'That's not my fault, officer. I am not responsible for the ship.'

'That's all right. And so you have no passport? No sailor's card? No sort of paper to show who you are? Nothing to identify you? Absolutely and definitely nothing? Nothing at all to show that you are an American?'

'Evidently not, sir. What can I do about it? Certainly, my consul – '

'As you have no papers and no proof, what do you expect your consul to do?'

'I don't know. That's his business, not mine. I have never been a consul, to know what a consul's duty is in a case like mine. Sure, he will furnish me with papers.'

'Your consul? The American consul? An American consul? To a sailor? To, maybe, a communist? Not in this century, my boy. And most likely not during the next either. Not without papers. Not unless you are, let us say, a member of the New York stock-exchange or the first president of the Missouri Railroad. Never to a bum like you.'

If I had a million dollars, I would give half of it – well, one tenth of it – to know where this chief of police got such a fine understanding of God's great country. He cannot have collected his wisdom in Rotterdam.

'But I am American.'

'Why not? Fine. You see, it's like this. Suppose we take you to your consul. As you have no papers he will not recognize you. So he will, officially, hand you over to us. Then we have no way ever to get rid of you. I hope you understand? Do you?'

'I think so, sir.'

'So what could we do with you? The law is that anybody picked up without papers must be imprisoned for six months. When he comes out, he is deported to his native country. Your native country cannot be determined, since your consul does not accept you as a citizen. Then we have to keep you here with us, whether we like it or not. We cannot shoot you like a dog with a disease, or drown you in the sea, although I am not so sure but that sooner or later such a law will be passed in every country, above all in every civilized country. Why should we, having two hundred thousand unemployed, feed an alien who has no money? Now, listen, do you want to go to Germany?'

'I do not like the Germans.'

'Neither do I. All right, then, Germany is out. Well, my man, this will be all for the morning.'

What a man! He was a thinker. I wonder where the Dutch get people like that for their cops. Back home he would have the capacity of solving problems of national economy, or be dean of Princeton. That's the difference between those European countries and ours.

He called a cop to his desk and said: 'Take him to his cell. Fetch him breakfast. Buy him a few English magazines and newspapers and get him cigarettes. Make him feel at home.'

Feel at home with this sort of curtain at the window! All right, let's have breakfast first and do the thinking later.

8

Early in the evening I was taken in again to the chief of police. He ordered me to go with two plain-clothes men, who would take care of me.

We went to the depot, boarded a train, and left for the country. We came to a small town where I was taken to the police-station.

It was about ten o'clock when the two men in charge of my future said: 'It's time now. Let's get going.'

Across ploughed fields and swampy meadows we went, or, rather, staggered. I was not sure that this was not another road to execution. I should have inquired, while I was still a free man, if in Holland the noose is in vogue, or the hatchet, or the guillotine, or the chair, or just choking a man to death with bare hands. Now it worried me not to know how the Dutch would do it. Then again I thought that maybe the Dutch have the same system of doing away with sailors without passports that the Belgians have.

They have.

We came suddenly to a halt and one of the two cops said in a low voice: 'You go right on in that direction there. You won't meet anybody now. It's not their time. If, however, you see somebody coming, get out of the way or lie down until he has passed. After a mile or less of walking you will come to a railroad track. Follow this track in that direction, the one I am indicating here, look. You will come to the depot. Wait until morning. Be careful you're not seen by anybody, or it will be too bad for you. As soon as you see a train ready to leave, you step up to the window where they sell tickets, and you say: '*Une troisième à Anvers.*' You can remember those words, can't you?'

'Easy as pie. I know it's Spanish.'

'It isn't Spanish at all. But never mind. It's good French.'

'Doesn't sound like the language we have in New Orleans.'

'Quiet, now. You will do what I tell you or land in jail for six months. Don't answer any questions anybody might ask you. Just play deaf. You will get your ticket all right, and after a certain time you will come to Antwerp. Antwerp is a great port. Hundreds of ships there all the time. They are always badly in need of sailors. You will get a ship before you even have time to ask for it. Here is a mouthful to eat, and also cigarettes. Do not buy anything before you are safe in Antwerp. Understand. Here, take thirty Belgian francs. It will do for all you need.'

He handed me three packages of cigarettes, a few sandwiches wrapped up, and a box of matches.

'Don't you ever dare return to Holland. You sure will get six months of hard labour, and then afterwards the workhouse for vagrancy. I will see to it that you won't miss it. Well, shove off, and good luck.'

Good luck! There I was in the middle of the night, left alone in a foreign country.

The two cops disappeared.

I strolled along. After a while I stopped to think it over.

Belgium? In Belgium, I had been told by their police, I would get life if they caught me again. On the other hand, in Holland the worst that awaited me was six months, and after that the workhouse for sailors without identification cards. It may be that the workhouse in Holland would be for life. There is no reason why Holland should make it cheaper than her neighbour Belgium does.

After long thinking I made up my mind that, all circumstances considered, Holland was cheaper. Besides, the food was better. Above all, the Dutch speak a human language, most of which I can understand almost as well as the lingo on the road in Pennsylvania.

So I went, first, off the direction, and then I turned back into clean Holland.

Everything went fine.

So I was on my way to Rotterdam again. I couldn't go to the

222

depot to take a train. The two cops who had brought me to the border might take the same train back.

I tried hitch-hiking. I don't know if any American stranded in Europe ever tried the game there. It is different from what it is on the Golden Highway or the Lincoln Highway.

The first idea I got about how it is done was when I met a milk-wagon going to town. It was drawn by two mighty horses of the kind the breweries of St Louis used to have in the good old days.

'Hop on,' the driver said. 'So, you are a sailor? I have an uncle over in America. If you meet him, just tell him that four years ago we lost a cow; she fell in the canal and was drowned. He will remember the cow; she was sort of checkered. Welcome. I hope you have a pleasant trip home.'

Then I met another peasant who had hogs on his wagon. He gave me a lift and was friendly. It took me all day long to reach Rotterdam, but I saw quite a bit of the country. I told everybody who gave me a ride all about myself and all that had happened. None of them minded. No one said: 'What are you doing here in our country? Why haven't you got any papers? Out with all aliens.'

It was the other way round. I was invited here and I was invited there, to have a bite or a cup of coffee or a shot of gin. I got from this man two cents, from that woman three cents, and from another man one cent to help me along. They were not rich, but plain peasants. But they had a heart, every one of them. They all hated the police, and they cursed whenever I told what they had done to me.

I would give a second tenth of my million to find out who it is, in reality, that makes the laws about passports and immigration. I have not so far found an ordinary human being who would say anything in favour of that kind of messing up of people's private affairs. It seems to me governments have to mess up things to create new jobs for officials and to produce evidence of their God-given right to collect more taxes.

9

Thirty francs, no matter how you get them, don't last very long. Money always goes sooner than you expect it will. The same with really fine people.

Hanging around the docks one day, I saw two guys walking along and caught a few words of their conversation. There is something queer about languages. The English say that we can't speak English, while we say that what the English talk is a sort of ancient Scotch, because no serious-minded person can ever guess what they mean when they start talking about races or movies or, worse, politics. That's why the first English settlers couldn't get along as well with the Indians as we can, because the Indians are hundred-per-centers, and the English are not.

But whatever language the limeys talk, I am not crazy about them. They don't like us, either, and never did. It's been going on now for more than a hundred and fifty years – ever since the tea-party that had no bridge-partners. The war made things worse.

You come into a port where the limeys are thick, and they shout as though they owned the world. Maybe in Australia, or in China, or along the coast of the Indian Sea. You step into a tavern like a good and decent sailor who is ashore for a couple of hours and wants to wash down the salt from his throat.

You don't have to say who you are. You just step across to the bar and you say: 'Hello, pal, gimme a shot. No, straight. Make it two.'

That's all you need to say, and hell is let loose.

'Hey you, Yank. Who won the war?'

Now, as a decent sailor, what can you say to that? What has that to do with me? I didn't win the war. Of that I am sure. Those who say they won it would rather that nobody reminded them of it, true or not true.

Again: 'Hey, Yank, you're a smart sailor. Tell the world who won the war!'

What do I care? I am drinking my hard washer, and ask for

another, straight. Mother told me long ago not to meddle with boys who are not honest and who seek only trouble.

Now there are about two dozen of the limeys. Grinning and laughing. I am alone. I don't know where the other fellows from my can are right now. Not very likely to drop in here, anyhow.

'Make this one a doubler. Mother's son is thirsty.'

'Hey, submarine admiral, Nancy of the gobs. Tell us real sailors who won the war.'

I do not even look at the drunks. I punish them with my profound disrespect. But they cannot leave a guy in peace, especially since I am all alone. I don't even know if the barman will keep neutral. I guess I shall have to say something. The honour of my country is at stake. No matter what it may cost me.

Now what can I say? If I say: 'We,' there will be roaring laughter and a big fight. If I say: 'The Frenchies,' there will be a fight. If I say: 'I won it,' there will be a fight, and most likely the jail afterwards and then the hospital. If I say: 'The Canadians, the Australians, the Africans, and the New Zealanders,' there will be a fight. If I stay on saying nothing, it will be taken to mean: 'We Americans won it,' which, I know, will surely result in the biggest fight. I could say: 'You English, you won the war.' This would be a lie, and that reminds me again of my mother, who told me a thousand times never to tell a lie, and always to think of the cherry tree that was responsible for a president. So what else can be done about it? There is a fight on. That's the way they treat the fine guys whom they called, when they needed them badly, 'our cousins across the sea.' Not my cousins; no, siree.

So that's why I am not so crazy about the limeys. But whether I liked them or despised them made no difference now. I had to be friendly, for they were all I had to rely on.

'What bucket are you from, chaps?'

'Hello, Yankey, what're you doing here?'

'I was mixed up with a jane who had a sick mother. Had to take her to the hospital myself. So I was skipped, see?'

'Now it is too hot here for you, isn't it? Polishing anchor-chains, hey?'

'You said it. How about stowing with you?'

'It might be done. Always a free hand for a sailor feller.'

'Where are you making for?' I asked.

'Lisbon and old Malta, and then Egypt. Can't take ye that far, but welcome to Boulogne. From there on, you have to look out for your own future.'

'Boulogne will be okay with me.'

'See, the bos'n we have is a bloody devil, he is. If it were not for him, we could take you round the world sightseeing. Now, tell ye what we'll do for you. You come round about eight at night. Then the bos'n will be so filled up he'll be kicking over the rim. Doesn't see anything and doesn't hear anything. Now, you just come up. We'll wait for you at the railing. Just look at me. If I tip my cap over on to my neck, everything is shipshape and you just hop on. But if anybody finds you aboard, don't ever say who heaved you up. Sailor's word.'

'Understand. I'll be there at eight.'

I was there. The cap was cocked on to his neck. The bos'n was so well drenched that it lasted until Boulogne. There I got off, and that's how I came to France.

I changed my money for French coin. Then I went to the depot. I bought a ticket to the first station on the way to Paris. The Paris Express. I boarded it.

The French are very polite gents. No one molested me to show my ticket.

The train pulled in at what they call a *gare*, which means their depot. So I came to Paris, which is supposed to be the paradise for Americans who have become sick of God's country.

Now the tickets were asked for.

The police are quick in Paris. Since I had no ticket for Paris, and I had ridden all the way down from Boulogne on a very soft seat unmolested by anybody, I had become a case for the Paris criminal investigation police department, or something that sounded as high-falutin' as that.

I knew a few words of French, and I hoped that this would save me, but these cops knew more about the English language than I shall ever be able to pick up. They must have had better teachers than we usually have.

Where did I come from? Boulogne. How did I come to Boulogne? On a ship. What ship? The *Abraham Lincoln*. No *Abraham Lincoln* lately in Boulogne. Where is my sailor's card? Haven't got any.

'You mean to say you have no – '

'No, I have no sailor's card.'

I had become so used to that question that I would understand it even in Hindustani, whatever that may be. The tune of the words, and the gestures, and the lifted eyebrows that always accompany the question are so unmistakably alike among all the bureaucrats and policemen of the world that there never can be any doubt about what is asked.

'And I have no passport either. Nor have I an identification card of the French authorities. No immigration stamp. No customs-house seal. I have no papers at all. Never in all my life did I ever have the papers.'

I rattled off all this to spare them the work of questioning me for an hour. I could easily pass the toughest examination for immigration officers, because I have had the best schooling any guy ever can have.

The chief, who had wanted to spend an easy hour or two with me, became confused. He looked at me with dying eyes. He seemed to feel that I had taken from him all his upholstered authority. He pushed around some papers lying on his desk to find a few questions for me. After a while, trying to compose himself, he gave up for the day.

Next day there was a hearing, of which I did not grasp a single word, since everyone spoke in French. When it was all over, somebody tried his best to explain to me that I had got ten days in prison for cheating the French railroad out of the money for a ticket to Paris. I learned later that in France one might get for such an offence as much as two years, but someone in court had said that I was too dumb to understand the French law and it would be an injustice to load two years on me.

That was the welcome the French gave a good American who had been willing to help them win democracy.

I had never been in prison back home. When home I am very decent and dull, just like all the home folks. When living among baboons, do as the baboons do. Life is easier that way, and you may find a dame who thinks you are a great guy – in fact, the greatest guy on earth. But in foreign countries everything is different, and so am I. That's why travel is educating. You never get educated staying home, because you stay dumb like the rest. If you show only a bit of intelligence above the average, everybody says you must be a crank, or something else must be wrong with you, or else you would not act the way you do and upset everything. Back home in Sconsin I would never have told a good story. Everybody would have said that I was silly, and I'd better buy the gas-station Mr Jorgeson is offering for sale. So I do not know how prison life is at home.

In Paris it was this way:

First day: Registration. Bath. Health examination. Bedclothes

227

obtained. A book from the prison library. Cell assigned. Take possession of cell. First day gone.

Second day: The money they found on me was handed over to the treasurer of the prison. I had to make several statements as to whether it was my money, whether any of it was missing, whether the coins were exactly the same as far as I could remember. All this written in three thick books. Also information was asked as to other valuables found on my person, of which there were none, and which I had to testify to several times, signing my name about two dozen times in as many books and on as many blanks. Afternoon: Called for by the minister of the prison. Sort of Protestant or Calvinist. He spoke good English. It must have been the English William the Conqueror spoke before he landed on the coast of old England. I did not understand one word of his English. I was in France, therefore I was more courteous than at home, where one is thought silly when courteous; so I did not let the minister feel that I did not understand what he was talking about. Whenever he mentioned God, I thought he was talking about a goat. That was the way he pronounced it. Not my fault. So the second day came to an end.

Third day: In the morning I was asked by about fifteen different officers if I had ever in my life sewn strings on aprons. I said that I had not, and that I had not the slightest idea as to how it is done. Afternoon: I am called for by eight or nine prison officials who inform me that I have been assigned to the sewing department to sew on apron-strings. I have to sign my name on dozens of blanks, which takes all the afternoon.

Fourth day: I have to appear in the store, where I receive a pair of scissors, one needle, about five yards of thread, and a thimble. The thimble did not fit any of my fingers. I complained, but I was told to be quiet; they had no other thimbles to satisfy my peculiarities. I had to sign my name in books several times. Each time, before signing my name, I was asked if I had the needle, and if the needle was still good, or if I thought it looked as though it had a dull point. Afternoon: I was shown how to set up in the middle of my cell a little bench in such a way that it would be seen from the peep-hole in the door. On this bench I had to lay out in open view the scissors, the needle, the thread, and the thimble. These things were not laid out any old way. They had to be arranged in a special manner, which took me all afternoon to learn, because every time I thought it was right, the officer told me it was wrong and I had to do it all over again until he was satisfied. But he added that there was still something lacking in accuracy. Outside my door a cardboard sign was put above the peep-hole, which stated that the resident of the cell had scissors, a needle, a thread, and a thimble. When this sign had been put on my door, the fourth day was gone.

Fifth day: Sunday. Something said about good behaviour, and the Lord will do all the rest.

Sixth day: In the morning I am taken to the shop in which I have to work. Afternoon: I am given a place to sit and to work. Sixth day gone.

Seventh day: In the morning a prisoner is introduced to me as the professor who is going to teach me how to sew on apron-strings. Afternoon: The prof shows me how to use the needle, and how to get in the thread without biting up too much of it. Seventh day gone.

Eighth day: The prisoner in charge of my education shows me how he himself sews on apron-strings. Afternoon: Bathing and weighing. I am asked if I have any complaints as to treatment or food. I tell them that I am used to better food and a better sort of coffee. No one takes any notice of my complaints; they only say it is all right, they cannot grow a special coffee for me. The eighth day is gone.

Ninth day: During the morning I am sent for to see the chief warden. He asks my name, and wants to know if I am the guy whose name I said was mine. I answered: 'Yes, sir.' Then he asks me if I have any complaints. I tell him that I am not much satisfied with the food and the coffee. He says: 'The French law is the best law in the world, and there is no country more civilized than France.' I have to sign my name in two books. Afternoon: I am shown how to sew on apron-strings. The ninth day gone.

Tenth day: During the morning I sew on one apron-string. The guy who teaches me how to do it examines the string it took me an hour and a half, perhaps two hours to sew on. Then he says that it is not sewn as well as he had thought I would do it, and that he feels sorry that he has no other remedy but to cut off the string and have me do it all over again. Afternoon: When I am half-way through sewing on the string again, I am called to the chief warden, who tells me that tomorrow morning my time is up. Then he says that he is sorry that I have to leave, but it is the law; he has been satisfied with my good behaviour, and I have been an example to other prisoners. After this is over, I am weighed and examined by the doctor, who asks me if I am all right. Then I am called to the receiving hall, where I have to return the prison garment. For a

229

while I have to wait in an open cell without anything on but a towel. Then I have to go to a desk where I am handed my civilian clothes. I am asked if anything is missing. I say: 'No, sir.' Then I am allowed to dress in my own clothes. The tenth day is over.

I am called the next morning very early and asked if I wish to have breakfast here or if I want to get out in a hurry. I say that I would prefer to have breakfast in town. So everything is hurried up, and I don't have to wait until breakfast-time. I am taken to the treasurer, who returns my money. He asks if the amount is correct. I have to sign my name in three books. Then I am notified that I have earned fifteen centimes while working here. These fifteen centimes are paid out, and I have to sign my name again in three or four books. I am asked again if I have any complaints. I say: 'No, sir, thank you, mercy beaucoup,' which means the same. I am now discharged, and taken to the gate, where another warden looks me over, reads some papers, and then opens the gate and says: 'Marshey,' which means in French: 'Scram!'

I do not think that the French government made much money out of me. And there is still a question whether the French railroad will be convinced now that my ticket was paid for by sending me up.

When I had gone hardly twenty feet, two policemen met me and said that they had waited for me only to tell me that I had to leave France within exactly fifteen days by the same road I had come in, and if I am still found in France after the fifteen days have expired, the law will take care of me and not with very soft gloves; so the best thing for me to do would be to leave even before the last of the fifteen days. They did not tell me how the law would take care of me. Perhaps by shipping me to their Devil's Island and keeping me there until death do us part. Every age has its Inquisition. Our age has the passport to make up for the torture of medieval times. And unemployment.

'You ought to have some papers to show who you are,' the police officer advised me.

'I do not need any paper; I know who I am,' I said.

'Maybe so. Other people are also interested in knowing who you are. Of course, I can get you the prison release paper. Somehow, I think it would not do you much good. I have no authority to furnish you with any other paper.'

'But you have authority to put me in jail, haven't you?'

'That is my duty. That is what I am paid for. What did you say? I do not understand you. Now you may go. I have warned you officially that you have to be out of the country within fifteen days. How you manage it is not my business. You came in some way; you may go out the same way. If you are still here, then I shall find you, be sure of that. Why don't you go to Germany? A big country, and a very fine country at that. Try the Germans; they like fellows like you. Well, good luck! I hope never to see you again.'

There must be something wrong somewhere, that the police of all the countries I have been in want to ship me off to Germany. The reason may be that everybody wants to help the Germans pay off the reparations, or everybody seems to think that Germany is the freest country in Europe. How can that be, with a socialist president, who is more nationalistic than old man Bismarck ever was?

10

I stayed in Paris for several days. Just to see what would happen. Unexpected happenings often help you more and push you further ahead than plans worked out carefully. I now had a right to walk the streets and boulevards of Paris. My railroad ticket had been paid for, so I did not owe the French nation a cent, and I was entitled to make use of their sidewalks and their street illuminations. I have to admit that I did not see for a moment the American paradise that I had been sure I would find at every corner and in each nook.

I felt bored, and I did not know what to do, where to go, or how to entertain myself. So I hit upon the idea that the cheapest way to have fun would be to see my consul. I had a desire to find out if he had passed a different examination for his diplomatic career than had his brother in office in Rotterdam. I thought I might take up studying the representatives of our diplomatic service overseas. I had seen so many American consuls in the movies and in musical comedies like *Madam Butterfly*. Having a rare opportunity to do so, I thought it might be a good idea to learn whether the movie-makers have again lied, as they mostly, not to say always, do.

I had to wait the whole morning. Nor did my turn come in the afternoon. The class I belong to always has to wait and wait, stand long nights and days in long files to get a cup of coffee and a slice of bread. Everybody in the world, official or boss, takes it for granted that our sort of people have ages of time to waste. It is different with those who have money. They can arrange everything with money. Therefore they never have to wait. We who cannot pay with cold cash have to pay with our time instead. Suppose you get sore at the official who lets you wait and wait, and you say something about the citizen's right – it won't help you a bit. He then lets you wait ten times longer, and you never do it again. He is the king. Do not forget that. Don't ever believe that kings were done with when the father of the country made a revolution.

The waiting-room was crowded with people, with plain people like me. Some of them had already been sitting there four days. Others had been there scores of times. First a certain paper had been missing, then a certain certificate was not complete, then some record was not sufficient, and blanks had been filled in fifty times, and fifty times torn up and thrown into the waste-basket and done over again. The whole thing was no longer an affair of human beings; it had become an affair of papers, blanks, affidavits, certificates, photographs, stamps, seals, files, height-measuring, and quarrelling about the correct colour of the eyes and the hair. The human being himself was out and forgotten. A piece of merchandise would not have been treated so.

The good old flag spread all over the wall. A picture of the man who had said something about the country being created by the Lord to be the land of the free and for the hunted. Another picture of another man who had said great things about the right of human beings, even Negroes, to unrestricted freedom.

A huge map was there also. It was the map of a country great and large enough to give some space to an extra fifty million human beings eager to work and to find happiness on earth. I looked at the map and I was pleased to see that good old Sconsin was still on it.

I was still looking around when a lady came in like a clap of thunder. Short, unbelievably fat. In this room where everyone awaiting his turn had a lean and hungry figure, this lady had the effect of a loathsome insult.

The fat lady had curly, bluish-black, oily hair, done up in the manner affected by street-girls when they want to go with their men to the chauffeurs' ball. She had a pronounced hooked nose, thick lips, brightly painted, brown dreamy eyes that were larger than the holes they were set in and looked as if they might pop out any moment. The fat lady was dressed in the most elegant masterpiece of a French dressmaker. Looking at how she tried to walk like a human being on her immensely high heels, one had the impression that in a minute she would collapse under the weight of her heavy pearl necklace and the heavy platinum bracelets around her wrists. Her fingers were ridiculously short and thick. On all fingers, save on the thumb, she wore diamond rings; on some fingers she carried two and even three rings. It seemed that the finger-rings were necessary to keep her thick fingers from bursting open.

Hardly had she opened the door when she cried: 'For God's sake, I have lost my passport.' (She pronounced it 'pacepot'.) 'Where is that consul? He has to receive me immediately. I must have another pacepot. I take the Oriental Express in the evening.'

I had been made to believe that only sailors can lose their papers. Now I see that even well-dressed people can be without passports. Hello, Fanny, I can tell you that Mr Consul is going to say something very interesting to you about lost passports. I feel some sympathy for that fat lady. The sympathy of the galley-slave for his fellow.

The clerk jumped to his feet, all devotion. He bowed and said in a soft and very polite voice: 'Of course, madame. I will announce you right away to the consul. It will be a pleasure. Just one moment, please.'

He ran and brought a chair and begged the fat lady to be seated. He did not say: 'Sit down!' Just: 'Will you be seated, madame? Thank you.'

He helped the lady to fill in all the blanks. The hungry and lean people who had been waiting for weeks had to do this by themselves, and when it was not satisfactorily written they had to do it over and over again. The lady perhaps could not write. So of course the clerk had to help her. Or she was so great a personage that she did not need to write. At home she probably had a social secretary who did all the writing for her and told her all the gossip.

No sooner had the clerk filled out the applications than he took up the forms, ran to one of the doors, behind which the death-sentences were passed out, knocked softly, and went in. In less than half a minute he returned, ran up to the lady, bowed, and said: 'Mr Grgrgrgrs wishes to see you, madame. I am certain you have the three photographs with you.'

'Here they are,' the fat lady said, and handed the photographs to the clerk. Then the clerk sprang to the door, opened it with a bow, and let her in.

The lady was not long in the holy chamber. When she came out, she closed her hand-bag with an energetic gesture which announced better than her speech ever could: 'Thank heaven, we have money. And we do not mind paying for quick and good service. A consul cannot live by his salary alone. Live and let live.' Then she walked across the room wagging her hips like a dog that is pleased with itself.

The clerk rose from his chair and invited her to be seated again. The fat lady sat down, using only half of the chair, thinking this would indicate best how much of a hurry she was in. She went fishing in the depths of her hand-bag, took out a powder-puff, and began to powder her thick nose. She had taken out not only her powder, but something which distinctly crinkled in her hands. She pushed the crisp affair among papers lying on the table. As she did so, she gave the clerk a glance, which he caught all right. However, he made believe he did not know what the glance meant. When the lady had whitened her nose, she shut her hand-bag with the same energetic snap she had used on coming out of the holy chamber.

The hungry men and women waiting in the room had never been in God's country before. They merely wanted to go there and partake of the riches of the world. So they were still innocent and did not understand the universal language of snapping hand-bags. Since they did not know how to use this sort of language, and since they had no means of using it in the right way, no one offered them a chair, and they had to wait until their turn came.

'If it would please you, madame, will you call for your passport in half an hour, or do you wish us to send it to your hotel?'

'Never mind, mister,' the fat lady said. 'I shall drop in myself in an hour on my way to the station. I have signed the passport already, in the consul's office. Good afternoon.'

The fat lady returned in an hour. She received her passport with a bow from the clerk and with: 'Always a great pleasure to be at your service, madame.'

I was still sitting and awaiting my turn.

I apologized mentally for my unjustified bad opinion of American consuls. They are not so bad as I thought. It was nothing but national jealousy, what Belgian, Dutch, and French policemen had told me about American consuls being the worst of all bureaucrats alive. Here, at this consulate, I certainly would obtain the passport that would help me get a ship to go back home and be an honest worker after all. I would settle down somewhere in the West, get married, and do my bit to populate my country and make the kids bigger and better citizens.

11

I was asked to 'come in'. All the other people waiting here had to go, when their number was called, through a different door from the one I used. I passed through the same door through which the fat lady had passed. So I was, after all, to see Mr Grgrgrgrs, or whatever his name was. Exactly the gent I was most eager to see. A person so kind as to give a lady in need, in so short a time, a new passport would understand my troubles better than anybody else.

The gentleman I met was short, lean, and rather sad, or worried about something. He was dried up to the bones. He looked as though he had been working in an office before he had reached fourteen. I had the impression that, should it ever happen that he could no longer go to an office at a certain hour in the morning and work there or sit there until a certain hour in the afternoon, he would die inside of six weeks, believing himself a failure.

'Sit down. What can I do for you?'

'I would like to have a passport.'

'Lost your passport?'

'Not my passport. Only my sailor's identification card.'

'Oh, then you are a sailor?'

When I said: 'Yes, sir,' he changed the expression on his face, and his voice took another tone. He narrowed his eyes, and from then on he looked at me with suspicion written all over his face.

'You see, sir, I missed my ship.'

'Drunk, eh?'

'I never drink, sir. Not a drop. I believe in prohibition.'

'But did you not tell me you are a sailor?'

'Exactly. My ship got under weigh three hours before the time we were supposed to sail. I had presumed that we would go out with high water. As we had no cargo and were going home in

235

ballast, the skipper didn't have to wait for high water to come in, and so he ordered the ship to make off early in the night.'

'Your papers were left aboard, I suppose?'

'Right, sir.'

'I might have known this before. Do you remember the register number of your sailor's card?'

'No, sir. I am sorry.'

'So am I. Where was the card issued? By what shipping board?'

'I don't remember where it was. You see, I have shipped in coast traffic, Boston, New York, Philly, New Orleans, Galveston, and all along the Mexican Gulf. You see, sir, a sailor does not look every day at his card. In fact, I have never looked at all at what it said. Often it is not even asked for by the skipper when he signs you on. He takes it for granted that a guy has his card. More important to the skipper is what ship you have been on before, and under which master, and what you know about the job.'

'I know. You don't have to tell me.'

'Yes, sir.'

'Naturalized?'

'No, sir. Native-born!'

'Birth registered?'

'I do not know, sir. When this happened, I was too small to remember exactly if it were done or not.'

'Then your birth has not been registered.'

'I said I do not know, sir.'

'But I do know.'

'Well, sir, if you know everything beforehand, why do you ask me?'

'Now, don't you get excited here. No reason for that. Was your mother married to your father?'

'I never asked my mother. I thought it her own business, and that it concerns nobody else.'

'Right. Excuse me. I was only thinking that the marriage licence might be found somewhere. Your father was also a sailor, like you?'

'Yes, sir.'

'I thought so. Never came home again, I suppose?'

'I do not know, sir.'

'Any relatives alive?'

'I do not know, sir. Never knew any.'

'Know somebody in the States who has known you since you were a boy?'

'I think there ought to be lots of people who ought to know me.'

He took up a pencil and got ready to write down names and addresses. 'Will you, please, name any of these people who have known you for a long time – let us say fifteen years or so?'

'How could I recall any of them, sir? They all are people of no importance. Just plain people. Working folks. Changing places whenever their work calls for it. I would not know their full names or even their real names, only the names we knew them by or called them.'

'Have you a permanent address back home?'

'No, sir. I could not pay for one. You see, I live on my ships, like most sailors do. When laid off for a while I stay in a sailors' home or just in any cheap boarding-house near the waterfront.'

'Your mother still alive?'

'I think so. But I do not know for sure.'

'You do not know for sure?'

'How can I know for sure, sir? While I was away, she changed her address several times. Perhaps she's married to somebody whose name I do not know. You see, sir, with us working people and sailors everything cannot be done as fine and smooth as with the rich guys that have an elegant house of their own and a swell bank-account and a telephone and a lot of servants. We have to look out first for a job, and afterwards we worry about other things. The job means eating. Without a job we are just like a farmer without a farm.'

'Ever gone to the polls to vote in any state election?'

'No, sir. I never had any time to mix with politics.'

'You are a pacifist?'

'A what, sir?'

'Well, I mean you are communist. You do not want to fight for the country.'

'I did not say so, sir. I think that as a sailor who works hard I am fighting every day for the greatness of my country. Our country would not be a great country if there were no sailors and no working men.'

'Didn't you say you shipped in New Orleans?'

'Yes, sir, that's right.'

'Then, of course, you are a member of the – now, what is the name? Yes, of the Industrial Workers of the World. Syndicalism and such things?'

'No, sir, never heard of it.'

'But you said you shipped in New Orleans?'

237

'Yes, sir.'

'Never in Los Angeles?'

'No, sir.'

For a long while he looks at me with dull eyes. He does not know what more to ask. He drums the desk with his pencil. Then he says: 'Well, I cannot give you a passport, and that is all there is to it. Sorry.'

'But why, sir?'

'Upon what proofs? Your statement that you claim American citizenship is no proof. Personally, I believe that you are American. However, the Department of Labour in Washington, to which I am responsible for making out passports and other identifications, does not wish to know what I believe and what I do not believe. This office in Washington accepts only unquestionable evidence and no mere beliefs of a consul abroad. If you bring proper evidence, it will be my obligation to issue a passport to you. How can you prove that you are American, that I am obliged to spend my time on your case?'

'You can hear that, sir.'

'How? By your language? That is no proof.'

'Of course it is. It is the best proof.'

'Here in France there live thousands of Russians who speak better French than the average Frenchman does. That does not make a Russian a Frenchman, does it? In New Orleans, on the other hand, there are several thousand people who speak only French and very little if any English. Nevertheless they are as true Americans as I am. Texas and southern California are full of people who speak Mexican and Spanish, but they are Americans in spite of their foreign language. So what proof is the language you are speaking?'

'I was born in the States.'

'Prove that and I will give you a passport within two days. But even if you were born in the States, I would still have the right to question your citizenship, because it might have happened that your father, before you were of age, certified on your behalf for another citizenship. I would not go that far, of course. Just prove to me that you were born in the States. Or name me a few persons who will testify that you are native-born.'

'How can I ever prove anything, then, since my birth was not registered?'

'That is not my fault, is it?'

'It looks, sir, as though you would even doubt the fact that I was born at all?'

'Right, my man. Think it silly or not. I doubt your birth as long as you have no certificate of your birth. The fact that you are sitting in front of me is no proof of your birth. Officially it is no proof. The law or the Department of Labour may or may not accept my word that I have seen you and that, as I have seen you, you must have been born. I know this is silly, it is nonsense. But I did not make the law. Do you know that I might get fired or discharged from public service for having given you a passport without any other evidence than your word and your presence in person? Frankly, in your case I do not know what to do.'

He pressed a button. In came the clerk. The consul writes my name on a scrap of paper, asking me how I spell it. 'Look up this name, please, Gerard Gales, last residence New Orleans, sailor, *Tuscaloosa.*'

The clerk leaves the door partly open. I see him going into a small room where all the files are located. I know what he is looking for: the deported, the undesirables, the criminals, the anarchists, the communists, the pacifists and all the other trouble-makers whom the government is anxious to refuse re-entry into the country.

The clerk returned. The consul had been standing at the window in the meantime, looking out into the street, where life went on as busy as ever, papers or no papers.

The consul asked: 'Well?'

'Not on file. No records.'

'You gave your right name, did you?' the consul asked. 'I mean the name you were living by in the home country?'

'Yes, sir. I never had any trouble back home.'

The clerk left the room and I was again alone with the consul.

There was silence for a long time. I looked at the pictures on the wall. All faces familiar since I was a kid. All great men. All lovers and supporters of freedom, of the rights of human beings, builders of a great country, where men may and shall be free to pursue their happiness.

The consul rose and left the room.

After five minutes he came back. A new question had occurred to him: 'You might be – I do not insinuate you are – an escaped convict. You might be wanted by the police at home, or in any other country.'

'You are quite right, sir. I might. I see now that I have come in vain to my consul, who is paid to help Americans in need. I see it is

239

hopeless. Thank you for your trouble, sir.'

'I am very sorry, but in your case I simply do not see any way I could do anything for you. I am only an official. I have strict regulations by which I have to work. You should have been more careful with your papers. In times like these nobody can afford to lose his passport or similar important papers. We are no longer living in those carefree pre-war times when practically no papers were asked for.'

'Would you, please, and if you do not mind, tell me one thing, sir?' I asked.

'Yes?'

'There was here, yesterday afternoon, a very fat lady, with a dozen heavy diamond rings on her fingers and a pearl necklace around her fat neck which might have cost ten thousand dollars at least. Well, that lady had lost her passport just as I have. She got a new passport here in less than an hour.'

'I see, you are referring to Mrs Sally Marcus from New York. Surely, you have heard the name before. That big banking firm of New York.' This the consul said with a gesture and a modulation of his voice as though he wanted to say: 'My good man, don't you know, this was His Royal Highness the Prince of Wales and not just a drunken sailor without a ship.'

He must have noticed by the expression on my face that I had not taken the information as he had expected I would. So he added hastily: 'The well-known banking firm, you know, in New York.'

I still did not satisfy his hope of seeing me turn pale when such a great personage was mentioned in my presence.

But Wall Street, the house of Morgan, the richness of the Rockefellers, a seat on the stock-exchange has never made any, not even the slightest, impression upon me. It all leaves me as unimpressed as a cold potato.

So I said to the consul, 'I do not believe that this lady is an American. I would think her born somewhere in Bucharest.'

'How did you guess?' the consul opened his eyes wide and almost lost his breath. 'Sure, she was born in Bucharest, in Rumania. But she is an American citizen.'

'Did she carry along her naturalization papers?'

'Of course not. Why?'

'Then how could you tell that she is an American citizen? She had not even learned to speak the American language. Her lingo is not even East Side. I bet it is not even accepted at Whitechapel.'

'Now get me right. In the case of that lady I do not need any

240

evidence. Her husband, Mr Reuben Marcus, is one of the best-known bankers of New York. Mrs Marcus crossed in the most expensive state-room on the *Majestic*. I saw her name on the list.'

'Yes, I understand. You said it, Mr Consul. I crossed only as a plain deck-hand in the forecastle bunk of a freighter. That, I see, makes all the difference. Not the papers. Not the birth-certificate. A big banking-firm is the only evidence needed to prove a man a citizen. Thank you, sir. That's exactly what I wanted to know. Thank you, sir.'

'Now, look here, mister sailor. Let's talk this over and get it straight. I do not wish you to leave here with the wrong impression about me. I have told you that, under the circumstances, I have no power whatever to do anything for you. I am not to blame. It is the system of which I am a slave. If I had the power – let us say if I were going to leave office anyway during the year to retire – I promise you, upon my word, I would be pleased to give you any paper you need. But I cannot do it. My hands are bound. Entirely. Frankly, I believe your story. It sounds true. I have had cases similar to yours. The same result. Could do nothing. I believe you are American. I almost think you are a better American than certain bankers ever will be. You belong with us. You are the right blood. But I tell you just as frankly: should it happen that the French police bring you here before me, to recognize you, I would deny vehemently your claim to American citizenship. I might say, as a man, I would do it with a bleeding heart, but I would do it, because I have to, as a soldier in war has to kill even his friend when he meets him on the battlefield clad in the uniform of the enemy.'

'Which means, in fewer words, that I may go to hell.'

'I did not say that. But since we have become frank with each other, I might as well admit, yes, it means exactly that. I have no other choice. I might, of course, write to Washington and present your case. Suppose you could produce the names and addresses of people back home who know you. It would nevertheless be from four to eight months before your citizenship would be established satisfactorily. Have you got the means to stay that long in Paris to wait for the final decision of Washington?'

'How could I, sir? I am a sailor. I have to look for a ship. There are no ships in Paris. I am a high-sea sailor, not a sailor of vegetable boats on the river Seine.'

'I knew that. You cannot wait here in Paris for months and months. We have no funds to provide for your staying here. By the way, would you like to have a ticket for three days' board and lodging? When it expires you may drop in again to have another one.'

'No, thank you just the same. I'll get along all right.'

'I suppose you would rather have a railroad ticket to a port where you might pick a ship sailing under another flag, or you may have the good luck to find a master of an American ship who knows you.'

'No, many thanks. I shall find my own way.'

He sighed. For a while he went to the window looking out again. Nothing new seemed to come into his mind. It would have been a rare thing anyhow for an official to come upon an idea that is not provided for in the regulations.

So there was nothing left for him to say but: 'I am so sorry. Well, then, good-bye and all the luck!'

After all, there is a great difference between American officials in general and European officials in general. The office hours ended at four, or even at three. When I was out in the street again I noticed that it was five. But at no time during my conversation with the consul did he show any sign of impatience or make me think that he was in a hurry and had to go home or to the golf links. Not all American officials are like that, yet there are still some. In Europe, however, I have never met any official who did not, fifteen minutes before his working hours terminated, start showing me my way out regardless of how important my business might be.

Now I had really lost my ship.

Goodbye, my sunny New Orleans! Good-bye and good luck to you.

Well, Honey, you'd better stick up with somebody else now. Don't wait any longer on Jackson Square or at the Levee. Your boy is not coming home again any more. The sea has swallowed him. I could fight gales and waves, be it with fists or with the paint-brush. But I have lost out in my fight against the almighty papers and certificates. Get another boy, sweetheart, before it is too late, and ere all your blossoms have fallen off in the autumn winds. Don't waste the roses of your sweet youth waiting for the guy who no longer has a country, for the man who was not born.

Damn the skirt! Ship ahoy! Fresh wind coming up! All hands, hear, get all the canvas spread! Sheet home! And all of it. Up and high! A fresh wind is coming up!

12

The Paris-Toulouse Express. I am on the train and have no ticket. Just before we reach Limoges, tickets are examined. I have very urgent, and private, business to attend to, and disappear. The conductor notices neither my presence nor my absence. I am still on the train after it pulls out of Limoges, and I still have no ticket.

I don't understand why train officials always have to examine tickets. There must really be many railroad cheaters. Well, I won't say cheaters; let us say, people who cannot afford to buy tickets. Oh, of course, there must be some kind of inspection. Who would pay dividends to the stockholders if everybody rode free?

French trains are different from ours. There is a long corridor on one side that runs the length of the car. From this corridor doors lead into small compartments in which five or six persons can be seated.

All of a sudden the conductor walked through the corridor and opened the door to the compartment in which I was sitting. I had no time to attend to my urgent private business. So I sat there and looked him straight in the face. I used mental influence, or what is called telepathy. I looked at him as if I had a ticket. He caught my stare and closed the door. I knew telepathy was a great science, and it worked fine. He was absolutely convinced that I had a ticket.

I was just about to think it over and decide how to use telepathy in other things, particularly with my consuls, when the conductor returned. He opened the door, looked at me doubtfully, made a gesture as though to close the door again, and then said: 'Excuse me, sir, where did you say you wanted to get off or change trains, please?'

He said this in French. I could grasp the meaning, but not the exact words. So I had no answer ready. I tried to think up a few French words to answer him with.

The conductor, however, gave me no time to explain. He pleaded: 'Will you, please, let me have your ticket again?'

He spoke very politely. Yet he could not get from me what I did not have.

Satisfaction with his own cleverness spread all over his face when he said: 'I thought so.'

Since I was sitting next to the door and as there were only two more passengers in the same compartment, sitting by the window, they did not notice the tragedy that was happening right under their noses.

The conductor took out a notebook, wrote something in it, and went his way. Perhaps he has a good heart and will let me slip by? I shall never forget his kindness. Maybe some day his grown-up sons will come to Cincin, and I shall treat them fine.

In Toulouse, right in front of my car, I was awaited and received. The conductor made a slight gesture towards me, and two gentlemen said in a low voice: 'Please follow us, quietly.'

Nobody seemed to notice what was going on. The gentlemen put me between them exactly as though they were friends meeting another friend who had just arrived at the depot.

Outside, a motor-car is waiting. French motor-cars, as I now notice for the first time, are different from our flivvers. They are fire- and burglar-proof. There are tiny little compartments inside, just big enough so you can sit down without spreading your elbows in comfort. Each compartment has a door. I am let in and the door is locked from the outside. The car, after a while, makes off. There is one little window close to the top. I can see nothing from it but the upper floors of the houses we pass. It's an important car, because a whistle from the chauffeur gets it the right of way over all other vehicles.

I have a feeling that the car will take me to some place I do not like. I have gathered sufficient experience by now to know that whenever I run up against certain strange customs anywhere in Europe, then I am on my way to the police-station. I never had anything to do with the police back home. In Europe everything is different. I may sit quite satisfied with myself on a box by the docks, and, sure enough, a cop comes up, asks me questions, and takes me to the police-station. Or I may lie in bed, doing nobody any harm, and somebody knocks at the door, and half an hour later I am again in a police-station. There are still people who say you cannot sin while you're asleep. But the police in Rotterdam insisted that I did sin while asleep that morning. Then again I may sit in a train, speaking to nobody, looking into nobody's purse, asking no one for his paper. It doesn't help me a bit. I find myself in the

244

police-station as soon as the train has pulled in. I think that must be the trouble Europe is suffering from. These people simply cannot attend to their own affairs. The police will not allow them to do so. Seven-eighths of their short lives have to be spent, some way or other, with the police. Whenever they move from the second floor to the third floor in the same house, they have to notify the police that they have done so, and they have to fill in three blanks, in which they specify their religion, the names of their grandfathers, and where their grandmothers were born. And that is only the brighter side of their intercourse with the police. They can do practically nothing without asking the police for their kind permission. Even closing or opening your own window in your own home is regulated by the police. And heaven knows for what reason, they are for ever acting like sergeants with liver trouble; they never act like human beings who receive their salaries from the very same people they push around day and night. You cannot even dance in your own home, or in a public dance-hall, without a special permit from the police. All Europe is a paradise for bureaucrats. Under such circumstances it is no wonder that our bankers will never collect from any European countries the debts they ran up fighting for democracy and civilization and humanity. All the money these people earn goes to building up a better bureaucracy and a bigger police force. I hope only that somebody will come up to me again to offer me liberty bonds in the instalment plan.

'Where do you come from?'

A uniformed high priest is sitting behind a very high desk, in front of which I stand like a two-legged mite. They are all alike, be they in Belgium, Holland, Paris, Toulouse. Always asking questions. Always asking the same questions. Always doubting every answer given them. I cannot get away from the idea that if some day a sailor without a passport should land in hell, he would have to pass the same kind of desk before he is admitted.

Now, of course, I might just ignore their questions and say nothing. Yet who is he that could stand a hundred questions and answer none? An unanswered question flutters about you for the rest of your life. It does not let you sleep; it does not let you think. You feel that the equilibrium of the universe is at stake if you leave a question pending. A question without an answer is something so incomplete that you simply cannot bear it. You can get crazy thinking of the problems of an unbalanced solar system. The word 'Why?' with a question mark behind it is the cause, I am quite certain, of all culture, civilization, progress, and science. This

245

word 'Why?' has changed and will again change every system by which mankind lives and prospers; it will end war, and it will bring war again; it will lead to communism, and it will surely destroy communism again; it will make dictators and despots, and it will dethrone them again; it will make new religions, and it will turn them into superstitions again; it will make a nebula the real and the spiritual centre of the universe, and it will again make the same nebula an insignificant speck in the super-universe. The little word 'Why?' with a question mark.

So what could I do, a sailor without papers, against the power of the word 'Why?'

'Why are you here? Where do you come from? What's your name?'

I have given no answers as yet. But now I can no longer resist the question mark. I have to say something. I do not know what might be better, to tell him that I came from Paris or to tell him I came from Limoges. Since Limoges is nearer, the railroad hasn't got so big a claim on me as it would have if I said I came from Paris.

'I took the train at Limoges.'

'That is not correct. You came from Paris.'

Let's see if they are smart.

'No, officer, I was not on the train since Paris, only since Limoges.'

'But you have a station ticket here from Paris, good only for the first suburb out.'

With this I realize that my pockets have been searched again. I hadn't noticed it at all. I seem to have become so accustomed to being searched that I have lost my capacity to take account of it. It must be the same with married people and their kisses; divorce proceedings begin when they take account again.

'This ticket? Oh, you mean this ticket from Paris? I have had this for a long time.'

'How long?'

'Six weeks or so.'

'Strange ticket. Rather a great miracle. The ticket given out to you six weeks ago bears yesterday's date.'

'I am sure, then, that the clerk must have post-dated it by mistake.'

'We have this fact clear now. You boarded the train at Paris.'

'I paid from Paris to Limoges.'

'Yes, you are a very good payer. You even buy two tickets. Because you would not have needed this ticket if you had bought a ticket to Limoges. Where is your ticket from Paris to Limoges? Since you did not leave the train at Limoges, the ticket must still be in your possession.'

'I gave it to the conductor on reaching Limoges.'

'Then where is the ticket from Limoges? How could you get into the train after you handed in the ticket at the collection gate at Limoges?'

'I do not know.'

'Let us now take your name.'

I could not spoil my decent American name. Some day I might belong to society. It is only a question of making money. So I gave him a name which I borrowed for this occasion from a grocer I used to know in Chic, who once threw a stick after me. For that he is now on the police blotter in Toulouse, France. A warning to all grocers never to throw sticks after little boys when they catch them with their dirty hands in the barrel of maple syrup.

'Nationality?'

What a question! It has been testified to by my consuls that I no longer have such a thing as nationality, since there is not the slightest proof that I was born. I might tell here that I am French. My consul told me there are lots of people who speak excellent French but are not Frenchmen, so there must also be lots of people who do not speak any more French than I do, but who are nevertheless French citizens. I should like to know for whom it would be cheaper to ride on a French railroad without a ticket – for a Frenchman, or for an American, or for – ?

That's an idea! A German! A Boche! Right now, only a few years after the war. All France is still filled to the brim with the most terrific hatred against the Heinies. Might be a new experience. One should never cease to learn. If you cannot go to college because you have no money and you have to sell papers to make your own living, you should nevertheless not miss any means by which you can get educated. Travelling, and having lots of experiences in life, are the best education for any man. Profs are as dull as last week's morning paper. I wonder what they'll do to a German caught riding on their express trains so soon after the war.

'I am only a German, sir.'

'A German? What do you know about that! A German! I suppose from Potsdam, too?'

'No, not from Potsdam, officer. Only from Vienna.'

'That is in Austria. Anyway, it is all the same. They are all alike. Why have you no passport?'

247

'I had one. But I lost it.'

'You do not speak the hacky French of a German. What district are you from?'

'The district I was raised in is situated in a region where Germans still speak an old English tongue.'

'That is right. I know the district well. It is where English kings had a great influence up to the middle of the last century.'

'Yes, sir, you are right. It is called Saxony.'

For the first time I learned that it is a good thing not to have a passport. If you haven't any, nobody can find one in your pockets; so nobody can look up your record. Had they known that I had already robbed the French national railroad, it might have cost me two years, or even Devil's Island. I got only two weeks.

When the first day in prison was over, taken up with registration, signing my name in dozens of books, bathing, weighing, medical examinations, I felt as though I had done a long and hard day's work.

Kings and presidents don't rule the world; the brass button is the real ruler.

Next morning, right after a poor breakfast which did no justice to the overestimated French cuisine, I was taken to the workshop.

In front of me was a pile of very peculiar-looking nameless things stamped out of bright tinned sheet iron. I wanted to know what they were. Nobody could tell me, neither my fellow-prisoners nor the wardens. One said that he was sure they were parts of a dirigible manufactured in different sections throughout the country. The day after the declaration of the new European war all these parts would be gathered together, and within less than a week about five thousand dirigibles would be ready for service. Others denied this and insisted that the little things had nothing to do with dirigibles, but were parts of secretly manufactured submarines. Again, others said they were parts of a new machine-gun, one as effective as the best in existence, but so light that a soldier could carry it like a rifle. Others, that they were parts of a tank that would have a speed of about seventy miles an hour. Another fellow told me that they were parts of a new type of airplane, each carrying no less than two hundred gas-bombs, fifty heavy nitroglycerine bombs, and three machine-guns, and having a speed of six hundred kilometres per hour, and a service-time of eighteen hours without refuelling. Not one person, warden or prisoner, ever suggested that they might be parts of machinery or something else useful to mankind. Such an idea occurred to no one. It was the same everywhere in France.

Whenever something was made that nobody knew anything about, everyone concluded that it was to be used in the next war to end war.

I myself could form no idea as to what these little things might be good for.

The warden in charge of the shop came up and said: 'You count off this pile one hundred and forty-four pieces. Then you make a new little pile of a hundred and forty-four pieces. Then again you count off one hundred and forty-four pieces, pile them up neatly, and put them aside. That is your work.'

After I had counted the first pile, the warden returned. He looked at the little pile and said: 'Are you sure there are exactly one hundred and forty-four pieces, not one more or less?'

'Yes, officer.'

'Better count them again. I trust you fully. But, please, I beg of you, count them with the greatest care. That's why I gave you this special work. You look intelligent. I think you are the only man here who has the intelligence to do work with his brain and not with his hands.'

'You may be assured, officer, I shall do my best.'

'Please do. That's a good boy. You see, suppose my superior checks up and finds one piece above or below the hundred and forty-four I have to deliver; I might get a terrible rebuke. I might even lose my job here. I would not know what to do, with a wife sick at home and three little kids; and my mother and the mother of my wife also depend upon me. I could not afford to lose the job. Please be careful when counting.'

I counted them first in one heap; then I made twelve dozens, counting carefully each dozen, then all the dozens twelve times. After that I counted them all over in heaps of ten each, making fourteen heaps of ten, and adding at the end four single pieces. Having done that, I counted them in piles of twenty, making seven piles all together, and again four extra.

The warden came up, looked at what I was doing, and said: 'That's the way to do it. You are the first one that ever could do it right. I knew that you had brains, and that you know how to use them. I can depend upon you. Thank you.'

When finally I had decided that I had one pile of one hundred and forty-four pieces, I laid them aside and reached out to count off a second pile of one hundred and forty-four. No sooner had I started than the warden, who had been watching me all the time from a seat in the corner, came up and said: 'Better count them once or twice more. There might easily be a mistake. I would commit suicide if I lost my job for such a grave error.'

I took the pile and began to count the pieces again, one by one. The warden stood for a while watching me, and said: 'That's exactly the way it has to be done. Just use a little brain, that's all. I will see to it that you get some cigarettes for good behaviour.'

After two hours I decided once more to start counting off another pile. The warden came. He looked with a worried face at the pile I had shoved off to make room for the new one. I took profound pity on him. I thought he would break out crying any minute. I could not stand it. So I took back the first pile and began to count it all over again. His face immediately began to brighten up, and I noted even a faint smile around his lips. So pleased was he that he tapped me on my shoulder and said: 'You have brightened up my whole life as nobody else ever did around here. I wish you could stay here for a few years.'

When at last my time was up, I had counted the grand total of three piles, of one hundred and forty-four pieces each. For months afterwards I still wondered whether perhaps one of the three piles was not counted incorrectly. I trust, however, that the warden gave my piles to a newcomer to count over.

I received fourteen centimes in wages. I didn't want to ride on a French railroad again without a ticket. It was not that I was afraid of being caught once more. No, it was just that I could not burden my conscience with the thought that on my account the French railroad or the French nation would go bankrupt. It might come to a point where the French government would say that I was responsible for their failure to pay their debts. (By the way, these are the same people that make such a fuss about the Russians not paying their debts.)

To tell the truth, I must say that it was not my concern for the welfare of the French nation that made me decide to leave France and go elsewhere. It was that when I found myself outside the prison there were again two gentlemen waiting for me to warn me seriously to leave the country within fifteen days or go back to jail for six months and after that be deported to Germany. I did not like to see the Germans go to war with France again, this time on my behalf. I do not wish to be responsible for another war. It will come anyway.

13

Going south, following the sun. I wandered along roads as old as the history of Europe. Perhaps older.

I stuck now to my new nationality, merely to see what would happen so soon after the war to a vagabond in France who said openly: 'I am a Boche.' It appeared that everybody took it good-naturedly, sometimes entirely indifferently. Wherever I asked I got food; and the peasants were always willing to put me up for the night in their barns, often even in their spare rooms inside the house.

Instinctively, it seemed, I had hit upon the right nail. Nobody liked Americans. The French peasants cursed us. We were the robbers. We coined our dollars out of the blood of the glorious French youth. We were the Shylocks and the usurers. We cut their throats; we made money out of the tears of the French orphans and widows. We took away from them their last cow and goat. We could not swallow all the gold we already had, but we wanted the last French gold coin found in the stocking of the poor grand-mother.

No matter where I met those small-town folk and village people, it was always the same: 'If we only had one of those damned Americans here, we would beat him up as we do all swindlers. They don't deserve anything better than to be treated like a filthy dog. Did they fight for us? The hell they did. They only ran after our women. They sold us ammunition. But what sort? We couldn't kill a single German soldier with their ammunition. Their shells killed our own soldiers, because they always came out backwards. Fought for us? Don't make me laugh. They sent their men over not to fight for us, but only to look after their money.

'Where do you intend to go now, boy? To Spain? That's right. A good idea, a splendid idea. Spain is pretty. And warm. They have more than we have to feed you. Just look what those Americans have done to Spain. They cannot leave any country alone. They

251

must put their fingers into every country on earth and make all the people in the world slave for their bankers. What have they done to Spain? I mention only Cuba, and the Philippines, and Puerto Rico, and Florida, and California. Always robbing us poor European countries. Now go on and eat, just help yourself. We have still a few potatoes left and a stale bread crust.

'And when a poor fellow saves up a little money, and wants to go to America to earn a few dollars and send them home to his poor parents, do they let him in? They do not. First they steal all the land from the defenceless Indians, and then they want to keep it all for themselves.

'Say, Boche, do you know what? Look here, you stay here with us for a couple of weeks and work. Spain is still far, far off. *Mon Dieu*, far off. Of course, we cannot pay you very much for your work, because the Americans haven't left us anything. Let's say thirty francs a month. Eight a week. Before the war we paid only three francs to our farm-hands. Then of course, our franc was worth a lot more than now. For a franc you could buy five times what you can buy now, or even ten times. We had a Boche here working with us during the war. He was a prisoner of war. I have to say this much about him, he was an industrious labourer. We were all very sad when the war was over and he had to go back to his country. Say, Antoine, wasn't that Boche a hard worker? I should say he was. Wil'em was his name. But he said he wasn't related to the emperor. Just his name. We all liked him a lot. People told us we were treating him too well, since he was only a prisoner who had killed perhaps a thousand of our boys. Anyway, he didn't look that way. He was tame and he knew how to work on a farm. He worked like three oxen, didn't he, Antoine? I should say he did.'

I stayed and worked there. Soon I learned that Wil'em must indeed have been a worker such as none other under the sun. Half a dozen times every day I had to listen to some remark like this: 'I don't understand, but Wil'em must have come from another part of the country than you. You cannot work as Wil'em could. Am I right, Antoine?'

Antoine answered: 'You are right, mother. He is surely not from the same province. He cannot work like Wil'em. I suppose even among you Boches there are differences, just as with us; some are good workers, some are so bad they don't even earn the salt they put in their soup.'

This soon got on my nerves. Wil'em must have understood more about farming than I. One doesn't learn agriculture in Lincoln

Avenue in Chic. At least I didn't. I am sure Wil'em worked so hard, not because he liked to work hard, but because he preferred to stay with these peasants rather than work on Algerian roads, as ten thousands of other German prisoners did. No matter how hard I worked, no matter how early I rose in the morning and how late at night I turned in, Wil'em had done better. But the peasant I was working for will never get a farm-hand as cheap as he got me. Other peasants in the same village had to pay their hands as much as twenty, twenty-five, and even thirty francs. I received eight. Of course, I was that poor Boche who had been found and picked up on the roadside half starved and nearly dying. They had saved my life, they told everybody. It was only fair that I worked for them for eight francs.

When finally Wil'em appeared in my dreams, I thought it time to leave. I explained I had to see relatives in Spain whom I had not seen since the Goths had left Germany for Spain.

'They sure will be pleased to see you looking so fine,' Antoine said.

Instead of eight francs a week, they made it eight francs for the six weeks of work. Mother said: 'It's easier to count a round number, so we'll make it even.'

I said: 'It's all right with me, mother.'

'Of course, you understand,' Antoine said, 'we cannot pay you your wages now. You will have to wait until after the New Year. Then we get our money for the crop. But the good food you got here has done wonders for you. You haven't overworked yourself. See, that Wil'em, he – '

'Yes,' I interrupted him, 'Wil'em came from Westphalia. I am from Southphalia. We don't work so hard. Everything grows there of its own accord. We only have to pray once in a while. We are not used to working hard. Everything is thrown into our laps.'

'You certainly are clever people. I must say that much of you,' the peasant said. 'We won the war, of course, as was expected. But we take it like good sports. The war is over now, so why should we be angry at each other? We all must live, mustn't we? Well, here, take a franc. The rest, after New Year. I hope you have a good time in Spain.'

14

The longer I wandered on, the more mountainous became the country, until I found myself in surroundings so desolate and dreary that I longed to see a human face. I would have been contented even with a bandit or a smuggler, in whom, I had been told the day before, this region was richer than in goats. And I saw plenty of goats.

'The border is not far off now,' the shepherd with whom I had stayed last night told me in the morning when I left. This shepherd, poor as he was, had shared with me his bread, onions, goat-cheese, and watery red wine.

Walking along a winding path, I saw something near by that looked partly like walls covered with mud, partly like the ruins of an ancient castle. I thought I might find a treasure left hidden there by the old Romans, so I went closer.

Suddenly two soldiers sprang up right in front of me, pointed their rifles at my stomach, and said: 'Vollevoo, where are you going?'

'To Spain,' I answered. 'It must be right over there, right behind this mountain.'

'It is,' they said. 'There is Spain. But first you will have to come to our officer in command. Don't you know where you are?'

'How should I know, messieurs, I am here for the first time in my life, and I wish I were in Spain.'

'You are within the French fortifications,' one of the soldiers said, 'and I might just as well tell you that if your story is not good, or if the old man has got a letter that he does not like from his lady, then there is a good chance of your being shot at sunrise, whether you like it or not.'

They gave me cigarettes and brought me to a gate that was so well hidden in the mud wall that I almost got a shock when it appeared before us as if it had risen out of the ground at the word of Aladdin.

I was led in, searched, and ordered to wait until called for.

Two hours passed. Then I was taken across a big yard where I saw a dozen heavy guns and soldiers lined up for drill.

Again I had to wait in a small room, always with the two soldiers at my side, with bayonets fixed.

A door opened and an orderly told my soldiers to bring me in. Behind a desk sat an officer. Rather young.

My soldiers made some report that I only partly understood, because they spoke in military language – which in all countries is different from the language of the people who pay taxes so that soldiers may live.

'You are Dutch?' the officer asked.

'No, I am Boche.'

'You look more like a Dutchman.'

I am sure he wanted only to know whether I was lying or not, because the soldiers certainly told him that I said I was a Boche.

'What are you doing in a French fortress?' the officer asked.

'I did not know that this is a French fortress. It does not look like one.'

'What did you think it was?' he asked.

'To me it looked like ruins left by the old Romans.'

'Can you sketch?' he wanted to know.

'No, sir, I cannot.'

'Know how to make photographs?'

'I never spent any money buying a camera. Really, I am not much interested in photography. I think it rather silly, because you can get photographs made anywhere for little money.'

'Did you find anything on him?' the officer asked the soldiers.

'No,' they said.

Then he said: 'Shershey!' which is French, and which means: 'Search him again.'

One really gets sick of so much searching.

'So during the war you were a German officer, weren't you?' he asked when the searching was done and nothing was found save a comb and a piece of soap, which they cut open to see whether I had hidden a machine-gun or something inside of it.

'No, sir. I wasn't even a common soldier.'

'Why not?'

'I am a C.O. I mean I was one of those birds who had to remain in prison while the war was on.'

'For spying?'

'No, sir. Only, the Germans thought that I would not allow them

255

to make war if they let me go free, so they put me in jail, and then they felt safe to do as they pleased.'

'You mean to tell me that you and a dozen more who were also in jail would have been able to prevent the war?'

'That's what the Germans believed. Before they put me away I never knew how important a person I was.'

'Which prison were you in?'

'In – yes – in – in Southphalen.'

'What town?'

'In Deutschenburg.'

'Never heard of such a place.'

'Nor have I. I mean not before I was in prison there. It is a very secret place, about which even the Germans themselves don't know anything.'

The officer took a book, opened it, looked for certain chapters, read them, and said, when he was through: 'You will be shot at sunrise. Sorry. On account of being in a fortification near the Spanish border. Since the Spaniards and we ourselves are still at war with the African colonies, the war regulations have not been cancelled. Nothing else for me to do but shoot you.'

'Thank you, officer.'

He stared. Then he asked: 'What are you thanking me for?'

'For the good meal you have to give me before you shoot me. Y'see, officer, I am hungry, very hungry; in fact, I am nearly dying. What do I care about being shot so long as I am sure of getting a good farewell dinner?'

At this the officer roared with laughter. He gave an order to one of the soldiers, and I was taken out and given coffee and cigarettes.

About six in the evening I was taken to still another room and ordered to sit at a table. I was hardly seated when two soldiers started bringing in plates, glasses, knives, spoons, forks. As soon as the table was laid, the two soldiers began to bring in the eats.

The officer who had sentenced me to be shot came in. He said: 'Don't ever think that we French are stingy, not even to a Boche. For your farewell dinner you will get the officers' Sunday dinner, in double portions. We don't want you to go – All right, I don't know where you will go, and I don't care either. What I mean to say is, we do not send anybody away, no matter where to, without giving him a good meal.'

I think the French are far more polite to the fellows they want to execute than the Belgians, who gave me only a bite of potato-salad and three slices of liver-wurst.

The French are really poets when it comes to cooking dinners. '*Mon dieu*, officer, sir, for a dinner like that I wouldn't mind being shot twice every day in the year. I am sorry that I have only one life to be shot; I wish I had a thousand.'

'I like to hear that, my boy,' he said; 'I take it as praise of my nation. Have two cigars and make yourself comfortable until sunrise. Good night.'

Funny, I couldn't feel like a condemned man who has only seven or eight hours to live. The dinner had been too good to let me have any foolish sentiments. I think the horror one has of being shot, hanged, electrocuted, strangled, beheaded, drowned, or killed by whatever other means people use to kill the condemned – I think that horror is not of the execution in itself, but of the stingy last dinner that one gets the night before. In China they get nothing; just kneel down, and off goes the head. Everything looks different when your belly is full of an elegant dinner. Of course, a hamburger and a cup of coffee won't do the trick. Nor hash.

15

Reveille awakened me. The sun was already out. I thought they had forgotten me and had shot somebody else instead. Or maybe the French have another notion as to what sunrise is than we have. But they'll let me know on time. Why worry?

A soldier opened the door.

'Breakfast?' he said. 'Washed up already? Fine. The officer wants to see you right after you have your coffee. Come along.'

After breakfast, which was a short affair, I was taken to the officer.

Said he: 'Still alive? How do you like it? We have delayed execution because I got a telephone call from headquarters concerning you. I shall have to ask you some more questions. All you have to do is just tell the truth regardless of the consequences.'

'All right, shoot, sir.'

'Suppose we let you go. Where would you go?'

'To Spain, and if I cannot go to Spain, I want to be shot – of course, with the understanding that I get another last dinner.'

He broke out into a terrific gale of laughter. Still giggling, he said: 'If I were not convinced that you are a Boche, I would think you an American. Only Boches and Yankees think of nothing but: When do we eat? So you are going to Spain?'

'Yes, colonel.'

'Captain to you.'

'Yes, captain colonel.'

'We would rather that you go back to Germany. Free railroad fare.'

'Not even in an aeroplane, colonel,' I said. 'Germany is entirely out. Not for the kisses of two French girls. Not me.'

'But then you would be at home.'

'Who wants to be home, colonel? I am happy that I am so far away from home.'

'What do you want to go to Spain for? There is no job waiting for you.'

'I don't mind the job, captain. You see, colonel, it's like this. Winter is coming on. I have not stored away any fuel. I thought it might be a swell idea to go to Spain, where there is always sunshine. And no worry about where the food will come from either. It's warm there all the time. One just sits in the sun and eats grapes and oranges and chestnuts and such things. Fruit grow wild there. You just pick them up wherever you see them.'

'I think,' the officer said after some meditation, 'we cannot let you go to Spain. Will you promise to go back to Germany if we let you go free?'

'I won't promise, and I won't do it either. Spain or death. I hate to help the Germans pay the reparations. And I don't want to go there. You are really nice people, you French people. But I shouldn't like to stay here in France either. You also have to pay too many debts. I don't feel like paying those debts, because I did not make them. I never like to pay the debts of other people. I am going to Spain. And if I cannot go to Spain, you may shoot me; it's okay with me.'

Another young officer, who was sitting in a corner of the room and had listened to our conversation, stood up and came over to the desk.

The two officers talked in the French soldier's lingo, which I could not understand.

When they had talked for a while, laughing, most of the time, the officer in charge said: 'Now listen here, fellow, we shall do as

258

you wish. We are not barbarians, and I think I can take the responsibility for what I am about to do. You are going to Spain. We shall bring you under guard to the border, and if the Spaniards have no objection to letting you into their country, you will be handed over to them. The Spaniards are fine people. They won't hurt you a bit. They are better off than we are. They like the Boches. Of course, if you were an American, you couldn't live in Spain for twenty-four hours. But a Boche – that's different. Dismissed until we call you.'

I did not heed his order. I shifted from one foot to the other.

'Anything else?' he asked.

'Yes, colonel, captain.'

'Well, what is it?'

'May I – I mean, can I – or rather, would I get another Sunday officers' dinner, double portions, before I leave? What I mean is, since this is the last dinner I'll get on French soil, may I have the Sunday officers' dinner, double portions, colonel, captain?'

Did the officers and the soldiers in the room laugh? I should say they did.

I could not see why they were laughing. What is there to laugh about if a guy is hungry and tries to get as much out of the army kitchen as he can? I stood amazed, and so they laughed all the harder.

Finally, the captain said: 'That's out, my good fellow, no Sunday dinner today, because it is Monday. But you'll get the officers' dinner, and double portions. I sincerely hope that it will be the last meal you ever eat in France. If I ever catch you eating another, I will see to it that you are shot, spy or no spy.'

They started laughing again.

16

Two soldiers, with bayonets fixed to their rifles, accompanied me to the border. With all military honours I marched into sunny Spain.

It was the turning-point of my life. I did not know it then, but I do know it now; yes, sir.

'He has no papers,' the corporal said to the Spanish customs officer, who appeared to be glad to get something to worry about, because the post was a quiet one.

'*Es alemán?*' the Spaniard asked.

'*Si, señor,*' I answered. '*soy alemán con mucho hambre.*' Which is Spanish and which means: 'I am a Boche and I am plenty hungry.'

'*Bienvenido,*' he said, which is the same as our 'Be welcome.' We, of course, seldom mean it, but the Spaniards really mean it and they act accordingly.

The soldiers presented a paper which the Spanish officer in charge signed. Then the soldiers, their duty done, sat down and talked with the Spaniards. They got wine and cheese, and they made merry, because after a while Spanish girls came along to pep up the lonely post. They played guitarras and accordions and danced. The wives of the customs officers were in the village and could not see what was going on here, where, they thought, their husbands sweated about the collection of customs and the writing of reports.

As soon as I was handed over to the Spaniards they pulled me, almost triumphantly, into the customs house. They shook hands and embraced me. Some kissed me on my cheeks.

War against the Americans, and you will find no better friends on earth than the Spaniards. If they had only known who I really was, that I had robbed them of Cuba and the Philippines and that I had cracked up some of their battleships! I still wonder what they would have done to me if they had known my nationality. I was a victim of circumstances, and I hope the Spaniards will forgive me, and besides I personally had nothing to do with Cuba and the battleships, because all this happened before my time.

My outward appearance was exactly what a Spaniard had imagined a German would look like. Since the *Tuscaloosa* had sailed, I had changed neither suit, cap, nor shoes, for there was nothing to change them for. My linen looked like linen when it had been washed in brooks, creeks, and rivers, sometimes with soap, mostly without. Yet my appearance was, to them, the best proof that I had come directly from Germany.

They were sure that I must be hungry as only a man who has been blockaded by the English can be. Consequently they gave me enough food to last a week. Whenever I tried to stop eating, they

260

used all kinds of tricks to make me go through the whole course again.

While I was eating, two of the officers went to the little town near by. When I was stuffed to the limit, the two officers came back with bundles. I got a shirt, a hat, shoes, half a dozen socks, handkers, collars, ties, a pair of pants, a jacket. I had to throw away everything I had about me, and I had to dress. When this was finished, I looked so much like a Spaniard that anyone who had known me back home would have thought I had turned bullfighter.

It was late. The French soldiers said they had to go home. So they left, saying good-bye to me. I told them to give my regards to their colonel, and thank the whole of France for what they had done to me. They won't pay their debts anyhow, so why shouldn't I send them my regards?

Now the customs officers started playing cards. They invited me to play with them. I did not know how to play with those funny-looking Spanish cards, but I was taught. Soon I played so well that I won quite a stack of Spanish pesetas, which pleased them immensely, and they urged me to go on playing. I felt like a robber. Whatever I did, when a play was over, they said I had won.

Oh, you sunny, wonderful Spain! May you prosper and live long! No one calls you God's country. It was the first country I met in which I was not asked for a sailor's card or for a passport. The first country in which people did not care to know my name, my age, my beliefs, my height. For the first time my pockets were not searched. I was not pushed at midnight across the border and kicked out of the country like a leper. Nobody wanted to know how much money I had, or what I had lived on for the last three months.

The Spaniards did not fight for liberty, and that's why they still have it.

I spent my first night in Spain in the customs house, because it was late when we had finished playing cards, and I was not yet used to the gallons of wine I had drunk.

From then on I had to pass every night in another house in the little town. Every family considered it partly the greatest honour, partly the highest duty, to have me. Each family wanted to keep me for a whole week. Most evenings there were fights going on over me. The family I was staying with did not want to give me up to the family whose turn it was next to have me. When all turns were up, the whole round started over again. Each family tried to do better than the former. I felt myself getting fat. Worse than that, I got sick. These people were all well-to-do. Smuggling is still a great business, and it is a very honourable business. The king of the smugglers was honoured by being made mayor of the town, and the vice-king was made chief of police. No wonder these jolly folks treated me like a bishop on a vacation.

I escaped one night. Like a thief. I am sure these good people think ill of me. They think me ungrateful for having left them without saying good-bye and many thanks. Anyway, only an imbecile or a feeble-minded individual could have stood it for long. Those folks would never understand it, good-natured as they are. They think a man treated as I was treated should feel as though he's in heaven. But even in heaven I should feel sick if I just had to sit around and eat and eat. Slavery results from such treatment. You forget how to work and how to look after yourself. I should feel unhappy in a communistic state where the community takes all the risks I want to take myself. In that Spanish town I could not even go into the back-yard without having some one yell after me if I were sure I had soft paper. Yes, sir. I mean, no, sir.

If I had not escaped, there might have come a day when I would have started to kill them, one by one, for having made me utterly useless and for making me hate myself.

17

When I got tired of Seville, I made for Cadiz. As soon as I began to dislike the climate of Cadiz, I returned to Seville. And when the hailing of a new-born torero was too much for me, I was again on my way to Cadiz. By doing so frequently enough, the winter passed. A winter balmier than most winters are in New Orleans. About good New Orleans – I could have sold that ole town now for a quarter without feeling conscience-stricken. There were lots of other sunny places in the world! Why, of all places, should it be just New Orleans?

My pockets were exactly as empty as they were when I arrived at the border. And still no flat ever asked me about papers or about the means I lived by. The cops had other worries. What did they care about a penniless foreigner?

When I had no money to buy me a bed for the night, I slept anywhere I found to stretch my bones. The morning found me lying there peacefully. The cop on the beat had passed by a hundred times, but he respected my slumber and he took good care that nobody should kidnap me. Here homelessness and poverty aren't crimes like at home, where they put a man in jail if he hasn't got a place to sleep. That is why at home a man who is expert at robbing is considered a respectable citizen whose property must be protected by the police.

Once I was awakened by a cop while asleep on a bench. He said that he was very sorry to disturb me, but he wanted to warn me that a heavy rain was on its way and that I had better go over to that shed yonder, where I would find straw and a tight roof, and where I would sleep a lot better.

I was hungry and I stepped into a bakery and told the man behind the counter that I had no money, but was hungry. I got all the bread I needed. No one ever bored me with the silly question: 'Why don't you work? A strong and healthy fellow like you!'

They would have considered such a question unbecoming. They had no job to offer – they knew that jobs were scarce – but they knew that men must eat to keep the world going.

Many ships sailed from here. Some days half a dozen at a time. Certainly there were ships amongst them that were short a sailor or two. That, however, did not worry me in the least. Why, there were other fellows who wanted the job. Why should I rob them of their chance? Besides, spring was here.

Life was beautiful. The sun was so golden and so warm. The country was lovely. People were friendly, always smiling, singing; and there was music in the streets, in the gardens, on the shore. The people who sang and made music and made love were mostly in rags, but they were smiling and friendly, and lovely. Above all, there was so much freedom. Do as you like, dress as you can afford, don't molest me, and to hell with everything. And don't you forget: Spain has no Statue of Liberty.

In Spain no one speaks of liberty, because people have it. Perhaps their political liberty is not much compared with that of other nations; but no one butts into the private lives of the people; no one tries to tell them what they must drink or eat, or with whom they have to spend the night.

When I was in Barcelona, one day I passed a huge, sinister-looking building, out of which came horrible shrieks.

'What's going on in there?' I asked a man who happened along.

'That's the military prison,' he said.

'But why do the people inside cry so heart-breakingly?'

'People? They are not people. They are only communists.'

'They don't have to cry because they are communists,' I said.

'Oh yes, they do. They are beaten up by the sergeants, and they are tortured. See?'

'Why are they beaten?'

'Didn't I tell you they are communists?'

'No reason to beat them up. Lots of them in Russia.'

'We don't want them here. That's why they are beaten until they die. Beaten and whipped to death. At night they are taken out and buried secretly.'

'Then they must be criminals?'

'No, they are not criminals. They haven't stolen anything. Some killed the minister. But those have been dead a long time. They are beaten and tortured just because they are communists.'

'I tell you again, amigo, I still cannot understand why they are killed in such a horrible way.'

'Can't you see? Those men are communists. They want to change everything in the whole world. They want to make slaves of everybody, so that nobody can do what he pleases. These silly people want the state to do everything, regulate everything, so we should be only slaves of the state. We don't want this. We honest people want to work when and how we wish to. And if we don't wish to work and we prefer to go hungry, then we don't work and we go hungry. We want to be free and to stay free. If we starve to death, that is nobody's business but our own. But the communists want to interfere with everything, with our private lives, with our occupations, with our marriages, and they say the state should command and order everything and leave nothing for us to worry about. That is why these communists are beaten to death, and it serves them right.'

There seemed to be a cloud over sunny Spain, but soon the cloud went away. Why should I condemn Spain because of what I had heard? I do not want to judge. Each age and each country tortures its Christians. That which was tortured yesterday is the powerful church today and a religion in decay tomorrow. The deplorable thing, the most deplorable thing, is that the people who were tortured yesterday, torture today. The communists in Russia are no less despotic than the Fascists in Italy or the textile-mill magnates in America. The Irish who came five years ago to the States

264

and who took out citizenship papers yesterday are today the most ardent supporters of all the narrow-minded God's country-praisers who want to ban from these United States everyone who did not ask his parents to be hundred-per-centers. Whose fault is it that a Jew was born a Jew? Had he a chance to ask to be born a Chinese? Did the Negro ask the English or the Puritans to bring him to the only country worth living in? Since the great George was not an Indian, he must have been an offspring of one of those goddamned immigrants, and to hell with them.

So why should I feel a furrener in Spain, where shines the same sun that shines on Sconsin. The moon is just the same, too; Honey may see it in New Orleans, when she thinks of me. If she does. The *Tuscaloosa* is back by now. I shall look into the matter later. Let us have Spain first. It's closer, anyway.

There is no reason why I should run after a job. I'd have to stand up before the manager like a beggar, cap in hand, as sheepishly as if I were asking him to let me shine his shoes with my spit. In fact, usually it is less humiliating to beg for a meal than to ask for work. Can the skipper sail his bucket without sailors? Or can the engineer, no matter how clever he is, build a locomotive without workers? Nevertheless, the worker has to stand with his cap in hand and beg for a job. He has to stand there like a dog about to be beaten.

Thinking of all the humiliation made it easy for me to go to a restaurant or hotel to ask for the left-overs. The cook doesn't treat me as degradingly as foremen and bosses do.

After all, why chase jobs when the sun is so golden and clear and the skies are so blue, so wonderfully blue, tinged with flares of white gold? Why hang around factory gates when people are so friendly and so polite even to me. As long as I don't commit murder or burglary, I am a decent citizen, and everybody respects me as such. No cop comes up and wants to search my pockets to see if he can find a lost formula for the manufacture of unbreakable wine-glasses.

One day I smelled fried-fish. When I came up to ask for the left-overs, the people begged my pardon for not having anything to give me.

I concluded that the best way to eat fried fish is to catch'm and fry'm. I was used to asking for a meal, yet I thought it rather unusual to go begging for hooks and a line to fish with. I waited at the pier until a passenger boat came in, and then I waited outside of the customs house. Somebody handed me a bag and told me to follow him to his hotel. He gave me three pesetas and his thanks.

I went to a hardware store and bought a line and a couple of hooks. It amounted to about a peseta. Just to make friends, I told the salesman that I was a stranded sailor in Spain, waiting for a ship to pick me up. He wrapped up the goods for me, and when I handed him my peseta he said: 'It's all paid for, sailor. Thank you very much for your patronage. Good luck in fishing. *Adios*.'

Such a country I should leave? Such people I should spoil by chasing jobs and looking busy and hustling? Not for the world.

Spain backward? Don't make me laugh, sir. Those folks know more about the values of life and the destinies of the human race than any prof of phil at the State U of Sconsin.

18

I was sitting on the quay with my hook and line in the water. The fish wouldn't bite. I did my best to feed them with black sausage, which I got from a Dutch that had come in the day before. She was going to Java or thereabouts.

I had gone cooking to the Dutch. 'To go cooking' is another way of saying 'to make friends with the crew' of a bucket that's in port – to get the meals so necessary for the health of a stranded sailor who is in Spain just to study the land and the people. To go cooking is not always a pleasure, sir. No, it is not.

The worker who has a job feels superior to a worker who is without one. Workers are not at all as chummy toward each other as some people think when they see them marching with red flags to Union Square and getting noisy about a paradise in Russia. Workers might have a big word in all affairs were it not for the middle-class ideas they can't shake off. The one who makes the delicate parts of an engine feels superior to the man who stands before a lathe making bolts by the ten thousand. And the man at the lathe feels superior to the poor Czech who gathers up the scraps from the floor and carries them in a wheelbarrow to the backyard.

Sometimes, while standing on the quay, looking up at the fore of a tub where the hands sit at lunch, I hear one of them yell out: 'Hey, you bums, you stinking beachcombers, nothing to swallow, hey? I suppose you want to come up here and lick spit, hey? All right, but only two of you, so we can keep an eye on you thieves.'

There were others who enjoyed throwing all the food – soup, meat, bread, beans, prunes, coffee – into one pot together with all their half-chewed left-overs, and then handing us this mess and saying: 'Well, if you are really hungry, eat that, and say thanks, buddy.' We were hungry and we had to eat it.

Or they gave us a huge bowl full of good soup, and then threw into it all the spoons they had, and we had to fish the spoons out with our dirty fingers, to the merriment of the comrades. They did not mean it, they just wanted to be funny. And funny, too, were those who saw us standing hungrily on the quay and yet would throw, before our eyes, half a dozen loaves of white bread into the sea, and potfuls of meat.

Since no working man can ever be sure of his job and of his superior standing, it happened often that one of those friendly fellow-proletarians was left behind when the ship sailed. He then had to go cooking with us to the buckets coming in, and he learned how it felt to be on the shore and to be treated that way by members of his own class.

They were not all of this sort. Most of them were really true fellow-workers who parted easily with a peseta or a pair of pants and with the best meals they could offer. There were some who even went to the cabins of the officers and stole soap and towels for us, and dozens of cans of meat from the galley. Once I got twelve roasted chickens for lunch – and I couldn't keep the left-overs for a rainy day because I had no refrigerator in my pocket.

The crews of the French and the American ships were the best of all. When there happened to be exceptions, they were foreigners to the flag under which they sailed. The German ships were, with very rare exceptions, the worst of all. It was not the crew that was nasty, although sometimes they were too. It was the officers who acted like little gods. The German ships, long before they put in, fastened at the railings huge wooden posters with gigantic letters: 'No Admittance'; and to be sure, they never forgot to hang out the same poster in Spanish. I still wonder what the Germans do with their left-overs. I suppose they can them and store them away for the next war. Yes, sir.

The fish would still not bite, and the black sausage from the Dutch got smaller and smaller. Perhaps that part of the ocean hasn't got any fish left.

While I was hanging around in Barcelona one day, sailors told me that there were many American ships in Marseilles that were short of hands, because lots of them had jumped to stay in France and study the French girls. The crew of a freighter stowed me away, and I landed in Marseilles all right. Like all tales about fine jobs that were just waiting for somebody to take them – and make your own price – it was the bunk. Nothing in it. Not a single Yank in, not even a rummer with a faked flag.

I didn't have a centime. Late in the evening I stepped into a saloon in which there were many sailors. I thought I might meet somebody willing to spring a supper.

A waitress, a pretty young girl, came up and gave me a menu. She asked what I wanted to have. I said I had no money and I was just looking around to find a friend. She asked me who I was and I said: 'Boche sailor.'

She asked me to sit down, and she added: 'I'll bring you something to eat.'

Again I told her about my not having any cash.

'That's all right,' she answered. 'Don't you worry, you will have plenty of money soon.'

Now I got seriously worried. I felt sure that there was a trap somewhere or that they needed a guy to frame for someone else. I tried to wind myself out. Before I could do it, however, the waitress was back at the table with soup, fish, meat, and a bottle of wine. Seeing this in front of me, I forgot all about traps and frame-ups.

After having eaten, and drunk the red wine, and a second bottle that was put on the table for me, the girl, all at once, cried out: 'Messieurs, here is a stranded German sailor who cannot pay for his supper; won't you help him out?'

I felt lousy hearing this. But it was too late now to skip. I expected that very second to be beaten up and my bones broken into bits.

I was wrong. Nothing of the sort happened. All the men in the saloon, sailors and longshoremen, turned around to look me over. One of them stood up, came over to my table, clinked glasses, and said: 'Here's to your luck, sailor.' He did not say Boche.

The girl passed a plate around, and when she brought it to my table, there was enough on it to pay for my supper and the two bottles of wine, and something was still left for breakfast the next morning.

When closing-time came, the girl asked me if I had a place to

268

sleep. I said I had not. Then she said: 'You may come with me for the night; I will put you up.'

She had only one bed in her little room. I wanted to lie down on the floor, the way they do it in the movies, to show the girl that I was a gentleman. The girl, however, did not seem to like it very much. She said: 'Don't make me ashamed of you. What do you think I brought you here for? You will have to pay for the night. And pay rather well or I shall be sorry in the morning that I believed you to be a good sailor.'

What else could I do? I had to do what she ordered.

'Do you think,' she said when the light was switched off, 'that I got you a good supper just for your belly's sake? No, my boy. You will have to pay for the supper also. I don't want you to catch cold on the floor, and, besides, I am afraid of burglars, and of mice, too.'

In the morning she said: 'Leave quietly. If the landlady sees you, she's liable to raise my rent, thinking that I made a little money on the side. Come again whenever you can, sailor. Always pleased to meet you, and supper will always be ready for you.'

I would have liked to tell her right then that she was wrong in thinking that a Boche was a good payer. Anyway, I am sure some fine day she will find out, because quite a few American buckets put in at Marseilles port, and there are lots of guys on them who like to pay well.

The same day I hopped another freighter and went back to Barcelona.

19

Have I sailed many ships, sir? I should say I have. And I have seen thousands of ships. Even the great unbeliever Saint Tom would believe that. But, migud, I have never seen a ship like that one.

The whole thing was a huge joke. Looking at it, one wouldn't believe that it could ever keep above the water. One would readily believe, though, that it might be an excellent means of transportation over the Sahara Desert. Yes, sir. A team of camels could pull her fine along the sand.

Her shape was neither modern nor pre-Roman. To try to place her in any period of shipbuilding was futile. She did not fit in any age I could think of. In no marine-museum anywhere in the world had I ever seen a model like that one.

On her hull was her name: *Yorikke*. The letters were so thin and so washed-off that I got the impression that she was ashamed to let anybody know her true name. *Yorikke*. Now what language could that be? Almost any language. It sounded Nordic. Perhaps she was a hang-over from the old Vikings, hidden for centuries in a lonely bay somewhere in Iceland.

I don't know why, but that ship got me like a spell. I couldn't get away from it; no, sir. I stopped fishing, and I went over to look at the stern. According to international agreements, the name of her home port should have been painted there clearly. Apparently she did not want to betray her birth-place. So you're like me, I thought, without a proper birth-certificate. Bedfellows, hey? Of course, there was something painted on the stern. But, I am sure, only a well-trained archaeologist could have deciphered what those spots meant.

There was a flag, of course, flying above the stern. The flag, however, was so pale, so flimsy, so shredded, that it might have represented any flag of any country in the world. It looked as if it had been flown from the battleships of all the fleets that had partaken in sea-battles for the last five thousand years.

I was interested in the colour of the hull. I couldn't make it out. It looked as if it had been snow-white when the ship was still in her baby-shoes. That, however, must have been some time before old man Abraham left Ur of the Chaldees with his wife Sarah. I could see that at least two hundred new layers of paint had been put on top of the original white. As a result there were as many different colours painted on her hull as are known to exist. Those layers of paint made her appear twice her true size.

No owner of the *Yorikke* had ever permitted all her paint to be taken off and an entirely new coat put on. Every patch of paint that was still good had been preserved so as to make the painting as inexpensive as possible. So there were a hundred square feet of sky-blue next to a hundred square feet of canary-yellow.

When I saw her first, I almost dropped my fishing line in my excitement at seeing that monstrosity of the sea.

Often an individual may be recognized as insane by his outward appearance. The more deranged his mind is, the more awkward or strange his way of dressing will be, provided he is left to do as he likes.

There was something wrong with the *Yorikke*. To call her a sane ship or a normal vessel would have been an insult to all the other ships that sailed the seven seas. Her appearance agreed perfectly with her mind, her soul, her spirit, and her behaviour. Only an insane ship could look like that. It was not alone her coat that made her look crazy. Everything on and about the bucket harmonized with her appearance.

Her masts were like branches reaching out from a fantastic tree in North Dakota in November. Her funnel was crooked and bent like a corkscrew. I couldn't figure out exactly how her bridge was connected with the rest of her.

As I sat on the pier, looking at this old maiden *Yorikke*, I laughed and laughed. I let loose such thundering laughter that *Yorikke* became frightened. She trembled all over and began to glide backwards along the bulks. She didn't want to go out into the open water. She was, obviously, afraid, knowing perhaps that she might never come back. She grazed and scratched along the heavy timbers of the pier, making a squeaking piercing noise. Seeing her struggling so hard against the orders of her skipper, I began to pity her. It was like dragging old Aunt Lucinda, who had never been away from her native town, Jetmore, Kansas, into a bathing-suit and out upon a diving-board thirty feet above the level of the ocean. I felt real sympathy for the frightened *Yorikke*, who had to leave the calm, smooth water of the sheltered port and be driven out into the merciless world to fight against gales and typhoons and all the grim elements under heaven.

None of her men had mercy on her. They were working like hell to get her going on her way, indifferent to her unwillingness and her shrieking. I heard the crew running about. I heard their shouting and their hustling. The windlasses were rattling and clanging. I knew they were giving that old girl the works and were beating her up to get her to do her best before the eyes of so many seafaring people staring from other ships.

What could an old defenceless jane like her do against the rough fists of so many rum-soaked guys? Scratch and squeal and squeak she might, and bite, but it won't do her any good. She simply has to snap out of it and get it over and make off.

She was always that way. Once safe in the open sea, she would start running like a young devil let loose for the first time from her grandmother's apron-strings. I found out later that she ran so fast only to get back that much quicker to a snug port, in which she could rest and dream of the days long ago when no one had to hustle to make as many trips as possible for the sake of the company's turnover.

She couldn't be blamed for her behaviour. She had begun to get heavy feet; she was no longer as young and springy as she was when she stood by to guard Cleopatra's banquets for Antony. Were it not for the many thick coats of paint on her hull, she would have frozen to death in the cold ocean, for her blood was no longer as hot as it was five thousand years ago.

20

There are people who seriously believe that they know something about ships, sailors, and oceans, simply because they've crossed on passenger ships a couple of dozen times. But a passenger really learns nothing and sees nothing about ships, salt water, or the crew. I might just as well include among the ignorant the ship's officers and stewards. Ships' officers are merely bureaucrats with a claim for an old-age pension, and the stewards are just waiters.

The skipper is in command of the ship. All right. But he does not know the ship. No, sir, believe me. The guy that sits on the dromedary and tells the driver where to go doesn't know the dromedary. The driver alone knows the animal and he alone understands it. It is he to whom the animal speaks and it is he who speaks to the poor beast. Only he knows the worries, the pains, and the joys of the dromedary.

The same holds true of a ship. The skipper in command always wants to do something the ship can't do and doesn't want to do. The ship hates him, just as all commanders are hated by those they kick around. When a commander is loved, or thinks he is, it is only because everybody under his command is clever enough to know that they can get along with the old man best by complying with his whims and caprices. Always consider your boss crazy, and you will always be right and stand in good with him.

272

The ship loves the crew. The crew are the only true comrades a ship has at sea. They polish the ship, they wash it, they stroke it, they caress it, they kiss it – and they mean it, because they are not hypocrites where their ship is concerned. The skipper has a home, sometimes a country home or an estate, and he has a family, a pretty wife, and lots of worries about his family. Some sailors too have wives and kids. They seldom make good sailors. They look at the ship just as a factory-worker looks at the plant he works in to make a living. The good sailors, the true sailors, the born sailors, have no other home in the world than their ship. It may be this ship or that one, but home is always a ship.

And the ship knows perfectly well that she couldn't move an inch without the crew. A ship can run without a skipper and officers. I have seen ships do it. But I have not yet heard of a ship that went along with only a skipper aboard.

The ship speaks to the crew, never to the skipper or to the officers. To the crew the ship tells wonderful stories and spins yarns of all sorts. The ship in turn likes to listen to the tales told by the crew. When old salts start to spin, all the rattling and crackling of a windjammer ceases. The ship gets quiet so as not to lose a single word of the story. All the sea-stories I know have been told to me by ships, not by people and the stories written by pensioned skippers are the bunk. I have seen ships chuckling on Sunday afternoons, when the crew were sitting on deck telling stories of the seven seas and cracking jokes about skippers and mates and chiefs. I have seen ships cry and weep when stories were told of brave sailors who had gone to the bottom after having saved a child or another fellow. And I once heard a ship sob bitterly when it knew it would go down to its last place on the next trip. It was that ship that sobbed so heart-breakingly and that never came home again that was listed four months later at Lloyd's as 'lost in unknown waters'.

The ship is always on the side of the crew and never takes the part of the skipper. Why? The skipper doesn't work for the ship, nor does he care for it; he works and cares for the company that pays him. Often the men don't even know which company the ship they are on belongs to; no, sir. They don't bother with such details. They are interested in the ship, and in the food that the ship gives them.

Suppose the crew mutinies – the ship immediately joins them, and the skipper does not know what to do with the bucket. It's a fact; strange, perhaps, but so it is. I knew a ship that went out with a crew of strike-breakers. She was still in sight of the coast, less than twelve miles off, when she went down, just to drown that gang. She did it so unexpectedly that not a single man was saved. Yes, sir.

Looking again at that old dame *Yorikke*, I could not understand how she could have a complete crew going out of sunny Spain, the land of the free and the happy. To go with that ship rather than stay behind in such a great country was beyond my comprehension. There was a secret hidden somewhere. Perhaps she was — but it could not be. Not here, so close to civilization. A death ship leaving a civilized port with clean papers? Well, it's out now. A death ship.

Why didn't I notice it at the first glance? But still, there is something about her that makes it not altogether definite that she's that sort of tramp. The bucket begins to interest me. I simply can't stop looking at her, if only to find out what the mystery is in back of her.

Finally she seemed to give in and make up her mind to go voluntarily. Thus I learned that she had personality. Her skipper didn't know it. He was a fool. *Yorikke* was more intelligent by far than her captain. She was, I could see now, like an excellent and experienced thoroughbred horse, the kind that has to be left alone if it is to show its best qualities. A skipper has only to present a stamped certificate, indicating that he has passed an examination, and there he is in command of a ship as delicate and as individualistic in character as the *Yorikke*! Another proof of the fact that a skipper doesn't know his ship; no, sir. Anyway, what does a skipper do all day long? Only worry where and how he can cut down expenses for the company — usually by cutting down the rations for the crew, which puts something in his own pocket, too.

The skipper tried to force *Yorikke* against the tide and wind. An old lady, with the experience of five thousand years, should not be forced. If you try it, she is likely to go off her track and bust right into a heavy flood-breaker. If she goes wrong, the pilot isn't to blame. The pilot is only supposed to know the waters of the port in which he is commissioned. He is not supposed to know the ship. That's the skipper's business. I could tell now what sort the skipper was who chased that dame around.

She scratched off hard against the quay. I had to draw up my legs or she would have taken them along. I had no intention of shipping my legs to Morocco while the rest of me remained in Spain.

She kicked at her stern like an old hussy trying to dance the rhumba. A whirlpool of muddy foam was stirred up by her propeller. From her side she spat and fiffed and pished and sissed like an old farm-mule with bladder trouble. Then she began swaying like a drunken society lion trying to avoid the lamp-posts, and never able to do so.

The skipper tried his hand again and succeeded in steering her clear of the wharf. Seeing her only now about two feet away, and noticing that her hull looked pock-scarred, I said to myself that even if I had a chance to escape the hangman by signing on for this bucket, I would prefer the hanging. For I could not remember ever having seen anything in the world, ship or no ship, that looked so dreadful and hopeless, and so utterly lost, as did the *Yorikke*. I shivered. It was better to be a stranded sailor and hungry than to be a deckhand on this ship.

21

While the bucket was still struggling asthmatically to come clear, I glanced up to the fore-deck, where a dozen men were standing – obviously part of the crew off duty.

I have seen in my time ragged men, filthy men, wretched, lousy, stinking, dirty, broken, drunken, besmeared, sticky, unwashed, uncombed, unshaven, pishy and pashy, slimy, dreggy, and smutty men, but, so help me, God, never before in all my life, not anywhere in the world, not even excluded Asiatic and South American ports, had I seen men like that crew hanging on the railing of that ship and staring down at the pier. A crew ship-wrecked and marooned on a god-forsaken island for two years might look – but probably not – like that. How was it possible for a crew on an outgoing ship to be so? It was inconceivable that a ship could sail with such a crew.

I certainly did not look elegant. Far from it. Oh, very far! A Scotchman seeing me might have thrown me a penny. Yet compared with these men I looked like the sheik of the most sumptuous baby on Broadway.

This was no death ship. May the Lord forgive me for the sin of mistaking the *Yorikke* for a death ship! They were pirates hunted for a year by all the battleships of all nations, buccaneers sunk so low that they had come to the point of looting Chinese vegetable junks.

One of them wore neither cap nor hat; no, he had wrapped around his head, turban-like, a rag from a woman's petticoat. Another – well, sir, you may not believe me, but may I be signed on as a stoker on an outrigger-canoe if I lie – well, he wore a high black silk hat. Figure that out, a sailor with a top-hat aboard an outgoing freighter. Perhaps there was a special regulation on the *Yorikke* that the funnel-sweeper had to wear a top-hat. There was another guy there who had on full evening dress, and very elegant too. Since he was only half the size of the clothes he wore, and since the man with the top-hat looked more like the former owner of the evening dress, I knew the whole story. The man with the top-hat had been to a ball at the French embassy, where he had picked up – let's presume 'picked' up – a pearl necklace belonging to the wife of a Chicago packer, and he had had to make his get-away quickly when the woman yelled. Or perhaps he had been to his own wedding, and when he saw, for the first time, his mother-in-law, he ran like hell and reached the *Yorikke* just in time to be signed on as a coal-drag. Others were clothed, or, better, bedecked, with ragged pieces of sacks. One wore instead of a man's shirt a kind of woman's blouse which was probably missing somewhere in the upper room of a tavern in a North African port. I would not have been surprised to see one of them wearing a mantilla. But maybe that one was right now in the stokehold firing the boilers.

Had I been sure that they were pirates I would have begged them to take me along to fame and riches. But piracy, nowadays, doesn't pay if you haven't got at least one submarine.

Somehow, I felt they weren't pirates. Therefore I preferred the hangman to sailing on the *Yorikke*. The ship that can take me away from sunny Spain has to be a hell of a lot more elegant than the *Tuscaloosa*. And I don't want to say anything against the *Tuscaloosa*. She was fine. Yes, siree.

I wonder where the *Tuscaloosa* is now? Panama? Or home again to New Orleans? New Orleans. Jackson Square. Levee. Honey. Oh, – . Well, let's put on another piece of black sausage. Maybe we'll yet get fried fish for supper tonight. Just one moment, until that old rusty bathtub has gone. If it isn't fried fish, maybe we'll get some paste soup in a restaurant or a good Hollandish supper on the Dutch yonder.

The *Yorikke* passed along like a snail that had overeaten.

When the faces of the crew on the fore-deck were right above me, one of them yelled down: 'Hey, you, ain't ye a sailor?'

'Yessir.'

'Want a dshop?' Not bad English he used.

Do I want what?

Chips and dancing grizzly bears, I hope he doesn't mean it! A job. If he should be serious! Gods and heathen in dark Africa, save my soul.

A job. Exactly the question I have been afraid of for months and months. The trumpets of the archangel Mike on Judgement Day wouldn't have put as much fear of God into me as that question. It is the eternal law that a jobless man has to chase around for a job. When since the days of Cain was it ever heard of that a job is offered to you without your asking for it?

I am superstitious, like all sailors. On the seas and on ships, dependent always on good luck, and on the weather, and on fair sailing ways between hidden rocks, cliffs, sandbanks, and oncoming ships in thick fog, one cannot help getting superstitious. Without some superstition to rely on in time of trouble, one would go mad, because praying doesn't do a sailor any good. Ask the skipper when he orders the life-boats down. He just shouts: 'Don't waste time, hurry up or the tub'll kick over.'

It is this superstitious character that makes me answer yes when I am asked if I want a job. Suppose I should say no – all my luck, for the rest of my life, would be lost. I might never again get a ship to sail on back home to New Orleans.

Besides, a day might come when I really needed cash. It may be that the girl says: 'Well, the doc figgers it will be about the middle of next week if it's late.' Then you need a job and need it badly. And then you feel sorry that once in your life you refused to take a job that was offered to you.

This damned superstition of mine has already played me plenty of tricks and put me in conditions that were not at all pleasant or interesting. It was pure superstition and nothing else that led me once to become a grave-digger's assistant in Guayaquil, Ecuador. It was superstition that led me to help sell splinters from the cross of Our Saviour at country fairs in Ireland, splinters from the very cross on which Our Lord breathed his last sigh. Each splinter was sold for a half-crown, and the magnifying glass with which to see the splinter set the believer back another half-crown. Since I played the Irish that nasty trick I have given up all hope of ever being saved and getting a chance to learn how to play the harp.

22

So, on account of my superstition, it was only natural for me to answer yes when asked if I wanted a job. I couldn't see my face, but I was sure that I was pale, pale from the horrible thought that I might have to sail on that bucket.

'A.B.?' the man asked.

Now, here was my chance. They were short an A.B. and I was not an A.B. I was careful not to say 'Plain'. In cases of emergency even a 'plain' can take the wheel, if it's a quiet watch.

Joyfully I answered: 'No, mister. No A.B. Black Gang.'

'Splendid!' the man cried out. 'Splendid! Exactly what we need. Make it snappy. Hop on. We're off.'

Everything was clear now. They would take on anything and anybody they could get. I was sure they were short half the crew. I might as well have said cook, or carpenter, or bos'n, or chief, or even captain; they would have answered: 'Just what we need. Hop on.'

I had still a few cards to play. 'Where ye bound?' I asked. A sailor has the right to refuse to sign on if he doesn't like the trip or if he knows he is wanted by the police or by a deserted jane with a child in the country the ship is bound for.

'Where ye want to go?' they shot back.

Smart folk. No getting away from them. Whether I say the South Pole or Mount Everest, the answer will be: 'That's exactly where we're going. Hop on.'

I knew one country where that bucket wouldn't dare to go. So I said: 'England.'

'Man, you're lucky,' yelled the guy. 'We have cargo for Liverpool. Small goods. You can be paid off there if you want.'

Here I had them. I knew that the one country in the world where a sailor could not be paid off if he wasn't English was England at that time. He had to be sick, or the ship had to lay off for repairs. But – how could I prove they were lying?

It seemed utterly ridiculous. No one in the whole world could force me to sign on with that ship, and yet – Guess it is always like that. If you are happy and contented, you want to be still happier. You want a change. I am convinced that ever since old man Adam was bored in Paradise – and, by the way, it was the only human virtue he ever showed – it has been man's curse never to feel perfectly satisfied.

Fate was again playing one of her many dirty tricks. I had said yes. Kings may break their word, but a good sailor cannot. This ship I had laughed at so heartily and so loudly now took her revenge. Didn't I say that the *Yorikke* had personality?

The trouble was that I had gone to look at outgoing ships. A sailor who feels satisfied at being stranded should keep his nose away from ships with the blue flag up. A ship putting out should concern a sailor only if it's his own ship.

Another thing: a sailor shouldn't dream of fish or fishing. It's a bad dream for a sailor. It's unlucky for a sailor. A sailor shouldn't even think about fish. Even when he's eating fish, he should eat it in the belief it is something else. I had neglected to obey that good old rule that has come down to us from seafaring people much wiser than we are.

I tried my last resort: 'What is the pay?'

'English money,' the guy yelled.

'How is the grub?'

'Rich and plenty. And listen, you sailor, hop on and get busy, or you won't make it. We're off.'

They threw me a rope. I caught it. With outstretched legs I swung over, bumping against the hull. They quickly hauled me up, and I mounted steadily until at last I swung over the bulwarks.

And there I was on the *Yorikke*.

And that very moment, as if the *Yorikke* had been waiting for me, the engine took a deep breath, and the ship got up full speed. With caressing eyes I looked back upon wonderful Spain, now vanishing from my sight, disappearing in a mist with such rapidity that I had a feeling she was punishing me for having betrayed her. Well, Spain, I am sorry, but a sailor has to play fair, and he has to keep his word better than a king.

When the last glimpse of Spain had been veiled from my eyes, I felt that I had entered that big gate over which are written the solemn words:

He who enters here will no longer have existence!

THE SECOND BOOK

Inscription over the crew's quarters
of the death ship

He
Who enters here
Will no longer have existence;
His name and soul have vanished
And are gone for ever.
Of him there is not left a breath
In all the vast world.
He can never return,
Nor can he ever go onward;
For where he stands there he must stay.
No God knows him;
And unknown will he be in hell.
He is not day; he is not night
He is Nothing and Never.
He is too great for infinity,
Too small for a grain of sand,
Which, however small,
Has its place in the universe.
He is what has never been
And never thought.

1

Now I could look closer at the shark-hunters. The impression I had
got when I was still sitting on the quay was not bettered. Nor did it
become worse. It simply became smashing and absolutely destructive. I had thought some of them Arabians or Nubians or a new
kind of Negro. But now I realized that they were whites and looked
like Swahili men only on account of the coal-dust and filth that
covered them.

Nowhere on earth except in Bolshevik Russia are deck-hands
considered members of the same social class as the skipper. Should
that ever happen somewhere else, it would lead to complications;
yes, sir. One fine day somebody might mistake the deck-hand for
the skipper and thereby find out that a deck-hand can be just as
intelligent as most skippers are. Which, by the way, would be no
evidence that the deck-hand in question is intelligent at all.

Here, on the *Yorikke*, there were, obviously, several ranks of
deck-hands. I got the impression there were deck-hands of the first
grade, of the second grade, and more. I noticed two men who,
doubtless, belonged to the class of deck-hands of the sixth grade,
which may be considered the lowest class of deck-hands. I don't
think these sixth-graders would have enough intelligence to help
the savages of New Guinea break open coconuts with a stone axe.

'Good day!' the gang-leader of the pickpockets said to me. 'I aim
de shecond enjuneer. Dat man here wat is mine nabor, now dat ish
our donkey-man.' Some English, I thought; henceforth I shall
have to translate their lingo if I want to understand what they
mean. He wanted to inform me solemnly that he was the second
engineer and that the horse-thief at his side was the donkey-man,
or, as we used to call him, the donk. He gets his name, not from an
ass, but from the donkey-engines which are used on ships to drive
the windlasses, the winches, the cranes, and such machinery.

'Thank you, gentlemen, and I,' I introduced myself, 'I am the
first president of the company that runs this tub here, and I have

come aboard to hustle you guys stiff.'

They must not think that they can put one over on me – telling me that one is the second and the other the donk. Not me, no siree. I had already sailed as a kitchen-boy when birds like these were still being chased by truant-officers. I know cinnamon when I get it in chocolate.

He didn't understand me, for he went right on: 'Go to the quarters afore, and get you a bunk.'

– ! Does he speak seriously? This escaped convict, is he really to be the second engineer, and the other pickpocket the donk? I tottered to the foc'sle as though I'd been clubbed over the head.

On coming to the quarters I found a few men lazily stirring about in their bunks. They looked at me with sleepy eyes, showing not the slightest interest in me. I figured that a new sailor was looked at with less interest than a new can of paint.

I am positive that the *Yorikke* had seldom, if ever, left a port with a complete crew. A nasty story was told about her always being short of men. It was rumoured, and I am sure the rumour was well founded, that the skipper had several times gone out of town to the gallows, where, in the silence of the night, with the help of the bos'n, he carefully examined the hanged to find one in whom there was enough life left to let him say: 'Yes, cap'n, sure I'll sign on.' I don't see any damn reason why I shouldn't believe this rumour. Other things have happened on the *Yorikke* that were a hundred times worse.

I asked for a vacant bunk. With a movement of his head, crooking the corner of his upper lip, a man indicated lazily an upper bunk.

'Did someone kick off in it?' I asked.

The man nodded, crooked his upper lip again, and said: 'The lower bunk is also for sale.'

So I took the lower. The man was no longer looking at me. I felt sure that if I asked him another question he would throw a knife at me, or at least his shoes.

The bunk was not only vacant, but also entirely free from any mattress, straw, sheet, blanket, or pillow. There was only dust and splinters and broken-off pieces of worm-eaten wood inside. The bunk was an example of how far an economical shipbuilder can go to save space without coming to the point where a labour-inspector would say: 'Not enough space left for the crew.' Labour-inspectors are very lenient as regards the builder and the company. In this bunk there was hardly space enough to lay two tightly folded umbrellas close to each other. A sailor, provided he was very lean, could lie in it only sideways. To sleep on his back was out of the question. The *Yorikke* took good care never to let a sailor get so fat around his hips that he would find it impossible to lie sideways in his bunk. Since every sailor coming from his watch was so tired that he couldn't even think of gin, it didn't matter, anyhow.

The aisle or, better, the gangway between the bunks was so narrow that you could sit way back in your bunk and you would still have your knees pressed against the opposite bunk. It was impossible to dress, but as a matter of fact there was little dressing ever done by the crew, for they had nothing to dress with. Everybody kept the few rags he was clothed in on his body, working or sleeping. Whoever would undress on lying down would never find again what he used to call his pants or shirt or shoes.

Besides, there were no blankets, and your clothes served to keep you at least a little warm when you slept.

In each of the bunks opposite the one I had taken there were a few pieces of ragged sackcloth and shredded scraps of old canvas and such remains of pants, jackets, and shirts as, regardless of how hard one might try, could no longer be used as clothes. These rags served as the mattresses. For pillows some guys used pieces of wood; others had old discarded cordage and junk. Now I knew it was possible to sleep on cordage, and soon I learned to envy those who had it.

Whenever a man skipped in port and was left behind or whenever one fell overboard or died, the survivors fought for those rags and cordage harder than hungry vultures fight with hyenas over a carcass.

2

The *Yorikke* had no electric light, and no machinery for it. In her immaculate innocence she evidently did not know that such a thing as electric light even existed. By many means I could discover the exact age of the *Yorikke*. One of those means was the light used to illuminate the quarters of the crew.

This apparatus we called the kerosene lamp. Newcomers, not yet initiated, called it more crudely the petroleum lamp. It was a kind of small tin kettle, pretty well shattered. The burner, which could be screwed off, had had, at the time it was bought, the appearance of brass, perhaps even bronze. Even a four-year-old girl, however, knows that brass cannot rust, but iron can and does.

The rust that had accumulated during the last five hundred years had destroyed the burner. Yet out of a habit acquired in long service, the burner still kept its original form, like a ghost. Each newcomer was warned not to touch the burner too hard when filling up the lamp, because the ghost might dematerialize, and no burner would be left.

The glass chimney of the lamp was only a short stump, always thickly blackened by smoke. By order of the bos'n the lamp had to be cleaned every day. So every morning the question was fired. 'Whose turn is it, damn, to clean the lamp?' I never heard anyone yell: 'It's me,' nor anyone say: 'Your turn, Spainy.' The 'you,' whoever it might have been, would have fought with words and fists to win a decision that it was not his turn. The lamp was never cleaned.

It was the same lamp, as could be seen from its antique shape, that had been used by the seven virgins when they went out into the night to guard their virtue. The wick had not been changed since the time it was made, by cutting off a piece of the woollen underwear of one of the virgins. One could not expect that a lamp used by virgins to guard their virginity would light up the quarters of the crew of the *Yorikke* sufficiently so that we could see each other.

The kerosene used in the lamp was called diamond oil. It was called so in the books which the skipper presented to the company when collecting his expenses. But I had seen the skipper's cabin-boy go into the enginehold when the engineer was called out by the skipper. The boy scratched up all the dropped oil and grease from the engine, brought it to the skipper, and the skipper mixed it with gas to make the diamond used in our lamp.

I asked upon arriving on the *Yorikke*: 'Where is the mattress for my bunk?'

'Not supplied here. Must have your own.'

'Pillows?'

'Not supplied.'

'Blankets?'

'Not supplied.'

'What is supplied here, then?' I finally asked.

'Work,' a man answered calmly.

I was really surprised to see that the company supplied at least the ship; and by no means would I have been perplexed if the company had demanded that the sailor bring his own ship along.

When I hopped on the ship, I had on me a pair of still decent-looking pants, a hat, a jacket, and one pair of shoes. I was considered the richest guy aboard, for the bird that owned the evening dress wasn't so well off as I had thought when I first saw him. The pants were cut short right under his knees, and the elegant-looking coat with its forked tail was busted in the back. Yet the front had looked grand.

After being on the *Yorikke* for a couple of weeks, I learned that those guys who had the least to call their own were liked best by the skipper and the mate. The skipper always looked with grim eyes at a man returning from shore leave with something new on his back. On the other hand, he never minded a bit seeing a man return so drunk that he had to be carried aboard. He tipped mugs who had helped the sailor find his ship; and many times he willingly paid the tavern debts for one of his own men. Yet never would he have paid a dollar in advance to a man if he knew that the man was going to buy himself a new shirt.

The quarter I was in had two compartments, which were separated by a thick wooden wall against which, on either side, were fixed two bunks. Two bunks, the upper and the lower, of my compartment were fixed against the gangway wall; the other two were fastened on that same wooden wall. The other compartment had two bunks on the wall and two on the hull of the ship. Thus what was built for four men served for eight.

Regulations demand that the crew must not eat their meals in the room in which they bunk. They must eat in the crew's mess. There was no such mess for the crew on the *Yorikke*, for the simple reason that when the *Yorikke* was built, all labour in Egypt, Greece, and Persia was still done by slaves, and to demand a special dining-room for them would have meant, in the Persian language, criminal syndicalism – for which being thrown to the lions was considered a very lenient punishment. Now, there are a few ports in the world where, occasionally, labour-inspectors come aboard to see if communists, who are always yelling that crews are treated like animals, are liars or racketeers. These labour-inspectors are mild-mannered with the shipping companies; they have a very sympathetic understanding of the companies' worries. These inspectors usually feel delighted to have the skipper throw sand in their eyes. The company that owned the *Yorikke* used for sand the strange fixing of a mess-room for the crew.

The wooden wall which divided the sleeping-quarters into two did not reach from one end of the place to the other. It ended two feet beyond the bunks, where it was fixed against an iron post. From this post on, in the direction of the bow, there was a little space left. Into this space a long rough table and two benches were set up. So there you had the required mess-room. To be sure, it was still the same room as the bunks, but it gave the impression that the mess-room was apart. You had only to use your imagination a little. Of course, there was no wall dividing the two bunk-spaces from the mess-space, and since there was no wall, there could be no doors. But since a sailor with a head could imagine a wall with a door in it, any labour-inspector with a head could also imagine it. So everybody was satisfied, and the report for the *Yorikke* was always okay.

In a corner, right by the crude dining-table, there stood an old bucket, which was always leaking. This weather-beaten bucket was the wash-basin, bathing-tub, shower-bath, and scrubbing-pail, all in one. It served, moreover, for lots of other purposes, one of which was to catch a couple of pounds of the insides of drunken sailors returning from shore leave, provided it was reached in time.

Crowded into the space called the mess-room were four closets. These closets were supposed to serve as wardrobes for the crew. Had it not been for the filthy rags and torn-up sacks that hung inside, these closets might have been called empty. Eight men lived in this quarter, yet there were only four closets. Still the shipbuilder had overestimated the chances of the crew owning something. Because at present there was nothing worth guarding in any of the closets.

By special order of the skipper the quarters had to be swept every day. Usually it was done by one who had remained stuck in the mud unable to get his foot out, or by one who had lost a needle or a button that he could not spare. Once a week the quarters were flooded with salt water. This we called scrubbing the foc'sle. No soap, no brushes were supplied. The skipper probably sent in bills for soap and brooms and brushes, but we never saw them.

The crew did not even have soap with which to wash their shirts. Soap was a rare and precious thing on the *Yorikke*, which was additional evidence that the *Yorikke* had not yet entered the stage where civilization begins. Happy the man who carried in his pocket a little piece of soap with which to wash his face when he became ashamed of himself. Nobody ever dared let even the smallest piece of soap lie around. It could be as tiny as a pinhead, yet someone would find it and hide it like a diamond. This appreciation of soap indicated that the crew were not savages and that they still kept slightly in touch with civilization.

The filth on the floor and the walls was so thick and so hardened that only an axe could break it off. I would have liked to try it – not out of any sentiment about cleanliness, which was wholly lost on the *Yorikke*, but for scientific reasons. I felt sure – and to this very day I still feel the same way – that if I had broken open the crusted filth and mud, layer by layer, I would have found Phoenician coins and medals near the bottom. I still feel excited when I speculate on what I might have found if I had gone still deeper. There is a great possibility that I might have found the bitten-off finger-nails of the great-grandfather of the Java man, so very essential to science for determining whether the cave-man had heard of Henry Ford and if early bank mathematicians had had sufficient intelligence to figure out exactly how much money old Rockefeller makes while he cleans his dark goggles.

Leaving the quarters, one had to pass a very dark and unbelievably narrow corridor or gangway. In the opposite wall was a door leading to quarters similar to ours in shape and arrangement, but ten times worse as regards filth and dirt. I would have sworn away my soul that nothing on earth could be filthier than the quarter I was in, but when I saw the opposite quarter I said: 'This is the worst.'

One end of the gangway led to the deck, the other to a kind of pitfall. Near the end of the gangway, not quite at the pitfall, there were two very small rooms, one at each side. These small rooms served as quarters for the petty officers, the bos'n, the carpenter, the donkey-man, and another man who had something to say aboard ship. There was a mystery about his position. Sometimes he helped the donkey, another time he lent the carpenter a hand, and sometimes he acted like a second bos'n, chasing the deck-hands about the aft while the bos'n was chasing them about the fore. Had we still lived in the days before the revolution, I would have thought him the whipper, the chainer, the hangman. He looked like a bos'n escaped from a captured pirate-ship.

The pitfall led down into two small holds. One was the chain-hold, or the chain-chamber, in which there were all kinds of chains, emergency anchors, and such objects as might be useful for repairs at sea.

The other room, to starboard, was called the hold of horrors, or, more often, the chamber of horrors. There was nobody on the *Yorikke* who could claim that he had ever been inside it. We tried several times to find a peep-hole or a crack through which we might see what was inside. But there was no peep-hole and no crack to be found, and when, once during the night, Spainy drilled a hole through the door, we discovered that the door was protected with armour-plate.

Once when for some reason or other somebody asked for the key to this hold of horrors, it came to light that no one on the whole bucket knew where the key was. The mates claimed the skipper must have it. The skipper, on the other hand, swore by his soul and by the safety of his unborn children that he knew nothing about the whereabouts of the key to that forehold. And immediately he gave strict orders against opening the door, adding that should anyone dare force this hold open, he would shoot him like a sick dog and sink his carcass in the sea without a prayer. We got scared stiff and avoided going even near it save when we were ordered to get something out of the hold towards port.

I have never met a skipper who had no whims. This one had them wholesale. One of his many whims was never to inspect the quarters of the crew, which, according to regulations, he has to do at least once a week. He always had some excuse for not doing it, saying he would do it the next day, because at the moment he didn't want to spoil his appetite, and, besides, he had to hurry to take the position of the ship.

3

There is a rumour along the coasts of the Mediterranean and the western African coast that two men were actually in this hold of horrors and saw with their own eyes everything inside. These men, of course, were no longer on the *Yorikke*. They had been fired the moment the skipper discovered that they had broken in. He was not the same skipper who was now in command, and who had sworn to shoot any man who dared look into this hold.

Nevertheless, fired or not fired, their stories remained on the *Yorikke*. The crew may leave a ship, their stories never leave. A story penetrates the whole ship and every part of it, the iron, the steel, the wood, all the holds, the coal-bunkers, the engine-hall, the stokehold, even the bilge. Out of these parts, full of hundreds and thousands of stories, tales, and yarns, the ship tells the stories over again, with all the details and minor twists. She tells the stories to her best comrades – that is, to the members of the crew. She tells the stories better and more exactly than they could ever be told in print. One has only to listen with an understanding heart and with love for the ship. Of course, those people who sign on for a trip the same way as they would take a job in an automobile plant never hear any of the stories told by the ship, and they sign off as dumb as they were when they came aboard. There's no use telling those guys that ships tell stories; they simply think themselves too smart to believe it; yes, sir.

This story about the two men having been in the hold of horrors remained on the *Yorikke* like all the others. The two men driven by an unquenchable curiosity had seen a number of skeletons in that hold. Frightened as they were, they could not count how many there actually were. To count them would have been, anyway, rather difficult since the skeletons had fallen apart and had mingled with each other. There was no doubt, though, that there were a lot of them. But these invaders of the hold were able to make out to whose bodies the skeletons had originally belonged.

They were the last remains of former members of the crew who had been eaten up by rats. These rats, huge as big cats, were often seen by us when they ran out of this hold through some hole which we could never find. The rats ran about the quarters trying to pick up food and old shoes; and they disappeared as quickly and strangely as they had shown up. We were all afraid of the big, savage animals, but we could never catch or kill one. They were too quick and too smart for us.

Why and for what reasons the unfortunate sailors had been thrown into the hold of horrors and given over to these terrible rats we, for a long time, could not see. But from the stories told about the *Yorikke* in the ports where we put in, we picked up here a word and there a word, and eventually we put the whole story together.

These sailors, of whom only the scattered skeletons told that they had ever been alive, had been sacrificed to cut down the running-expenses of the *Yorikke* and to keep high the dividends of the stockholders of the company.

Regulations require that a sailor must be paid overtime if he makes any by order of the skipper, because unions have had some bad influence even on the shipping business. Now, when a sailor signed off from the *Yorikke*, he naturally asked to be paid for his hundreds of hours of overtime. He relied on this pay, for his regular wages were always paid out long before in advance money.

So whenever he dropped the word: 'Sir, how about my hundred and sixty hours' overtime?' he was led right away to the hold of horrors and thrown in it before he had a chance to realize what was happening. The skipper had no other means to dispose of the sailor, because the skipper was under strict orders to keep the expenses for the *Yorikke* far below the possible minimum, or he would lose his job. Skippers have a tougher time to land a job than a plain sailor has, for everybody wants to be a skipper, and very few like to be deck-hands. On account of the difference in wages.

It always happened, of course, in port. No sailor has yet been found who asked to sign off in mid-ocean, without another ship standing by. Being in port, the skipper could not throw the man overboard. The port authorities would not permit such a thing to be done, because it would pollute the harbour, for which crime the skipper would have to pay a heavy fine. The port authorities were not interested a bit in what a skipper might do to his men so long as the port was kept clean. Suppose the skipper had let his man go without paying for overtime; the sailor (sailors are that mean) would have gone straight to the seamen's union, or, worse, to the Wobbly firemen's syndicate, or, in a mild case, to the consul. In any case the skipper would have been forced to pay the overtime, or the whole *Yorikke* would have been put under an embargo. The Wobblies in particular and the communists would have held the ship for half a dollar if the skipper had refused to pay it to a sailor when due.

So what else could the skipper, no matter how human he was, do? He simply had no other way out than to throw the sailor into the chamber of horrors.

He did not mean to do the sailor harm; he just wanted not to be troubled by the union or by the authorities, for he might miss his proper sailing-time and have to pay twenty-four hours more in anchorage taxes. When the ship was on the high seas again, the skipper went to the hold of horrors to release his man, whom he needed badly, because two or three men had, as usually happened on the *Yorikke*, skipped the bucket, or else they were somewhere in jail for being drunk or for a row or on account of some trouble about a dame with a baby.

But in the meantime something had happened in the hold of horrors that the skipper could not have foreseen. Certain rats in the hold had taken out marriage licences upon seeing a sailor come in to provide them with an excellent wedding feast. So the rats had every reason not to let that sailor go, once he came within their reach. No matter how elegantly and nobly the skipper gave battle to the rats, he always lost out, and if he had fought to exhaustion, there was every possibility that he might have had to share the lot of his sacrificed sailor. The skipper dared not shoot or call for help, for then his secret would have been revealed and he would have lost for all time his chance to get away with not paying his men for overtime. There was nothing else for him to do but leave the sailor to the wedding guests.

You could never make a man who had sailed the *Yorikke* believe those dreadful stories about slaves and the slave-ships; no sir. Never had slaves been packed as closely as we were. Slaves could never have worked as hard as we had to. Never could slaves have been as hungry and as tired and as down and out as we always were. Slaves had their festivals, their singing, their dances, their weddings, their beloved women, their children, their joy, their religious merriment, and hope. We had nothing. Senseless drunks and a ten-minute girl for half a peseta were all the recreation we ever had. We were as cheerless as a busted five-cent balloon in an ash-can.

Slaves were valuable goods, paid for in real money, goods that were expected to bring even higher prices if kept in good shape. They were goods handled like rare vases. Nobody would have paid even the cost of transportation of slaves that were starved to death, that were bruised from too many whippings, that were so overworked that they could hardly move a toe. Slaves were treated better than good horses, because they had a greater commercial value.

Sailors, on the other hand, are slaves that are not bought and that cannot be sold. Nobody is interested in their well-being, because if one of them falls overboard, or dies in the dung, no one loses any money on him. Besides, there are thousands eagerly waiting to take the place of him who is thrown into the ditch along the road to the progress and prosperity of the shipping business.

Sailors are certainly not slaves. They are free citizens, and if they have established residences, they are even entitled to vote for the election of a new sheriff; yes, sir. Sailors are free labourers, they are

291

free, starved, jobless, tired, all their limbs broken, their ribs smashed, their feet and arms and backs burned. Since they are not slaves, they are forced to take any job on any ship, even if they know beforehand that the bucket has been ordered down to the bottom to get the insurance money for the owners. There are still ships sailing the seven seas under the flags of civilized nations on which sailors may be whipped and lashed mercilessly if they refuse to ship double watches and half of the third watch thrown in.

Slaves had to be fed well, like good horses. The free sailor has to eat whatever is placed before him, regardless of whether the cook was yesterday still a tailor. The company cannot pay wages for a real cook, because the stockholders of the company want their dividends. Suppose a good cook comes aboard and wants to do something for the hard-working crew; he cannot do it, because the skipper has to economize on the expenses for the crew's fare.

There are wonderful regulations all over the world as to the treatment of sailors aboard ship. They look fine on paper, these regulations. There are also the most wonderful regulations as to the purity of food, especially in packing-plants. And just open a can in which you are supposed to find the pork and beans that the elegant label tells you about. Instead of pork and beans you find only the effective results of the pure-food regulations. Precisely the same is true of the five thousand regulations concerning the welfare of sailors aboard seagoing buckets. Whenever new regulations are made I think of the *Yorikke*, and right then, without the help of a communist meeting or a peace conference, I know exactly what the regulations will be good for and in whose favour they are enacted.

There are sea-stories and sea-stories, millions of them. Every week an output of at least seven hundred and fifty. If you look closely, however, at those interesting sea-stories, you notice that they tell of sailors who are opera-singers in disguise, who manicure their fingernails, and who have no other worries than their god-damned silly love-affairs. Even that heavenly, that highly-praised, that greatest sea-story writer of all time knew how to write well only about brave skippers, dishonoured lords, unearthly gentlemen of the sea, and of the ports, the islands, and the sea-coasts; but the crew is always cowardly, always near mutiny, lazy, rotten, stinking, without any higher ideals or fine ambitions. Of course the crew is that way. Why? What ambition shall the crew have ? For whom? The skipper has ambition, because higher wages and promotion and orders await him. His name flares over the front pages of the papers and is set perhaps in golden letters on tablets on the walls of the Board of Trade. The crew have nothing in the world but their wages, their food, their health, their lives. They have no promotion in sight and no share in the dividends of the company. So what earthly reason have they to be ambitious about anything? To save the lives of passengers in a shipwreck no crew have ever failed in their duty as human beings; but skippers have, to save the company's money. Sailors know that, and therefore they are the only people who know how to read a sea-story the right way, and how to read about the bravery of skippers in newspaper reports. Not the skipper, but the sailor is the one who is the first to risk his life, because he is always nearest the real danger, while the skipper on his bridge, like the general at headquarters, is farthest away from where he could lose something; yes, sir.

4

I hardly exchanged more than ten words with those sleepy men groaning in their bunks. When I had been told that there were no blankets, pillows, or mattresses for the crew on this bucket, there seemed to be nothing left to talk about.

Above me, on the fore-deck, I heard the rattling and banging of the chains, the clanging and scratching of the anchor against the hull, the screeching of the winches, the hustling and trampling of heavy feet, the commanding and swearing and cursing of the mates and the bos'n and of whoever thought he had somebody to chase around.

Noise like that always makes me sick at my soul. I feel best when the ship is out on the high sea. A ship in port is no longer a ship. It is merely a box to be loaded or to be unloaded. Nor is a sailor aboard a ship in port a sailor; he is just a hired man. Nothing better. The dirtiest work a sailor ever has to do is done while the ship is in port; the sailor works there exactly like a worker in a factory. No watches, only a full day's work. Cleaning, scrubbing, wiping, painting the hull, polishing, sweeping, washing, repairing. You get sick only thinking of it.

I didn't leave the quarter while I still heard the noise overhead. It isn't a good policy to go near where work is being done. No hurry for me. I don't get paid for it, anyhow. Work always comes your way, don't you worry. A long life of work is still ahead of you.

I have read a hundred times in the magazines stories of men who succeeded in life, who were never such horrible sinners as to be failures, with pictures and photographs taken from life, in which you saw the great gun first as a dirty baby, then as a farm-boy, then shining shoes, running errands, selling newspapers and uxtras in the streets, then working as an office-boy for three bucks a week, and soon afterwards becoming the president of the bank and owning all the savings-account deposits of the customers, and marrying Margaret Wackersford and in doing so becoming the son-in-law of the president of the First National and the brother-in-law of the vice-president of Bethlehem Steel and the nephew-in-law of the Secretary of the Navy, and everything is fine now, and all he does from now on is just collect money and more money. All this is in the success stories, with pictures, and therefore it is the whole truth and nothing but the truth, so help me. I have done exactly the same. When I was not yet seven, I was up at four in the morning working for a milk-man until six-thirty for forty cents a week; from six-thirty to nine I worked for a newsagent, who paid me sixty cents a week for running like the devil from residence to residence with an armful of papers; from nine to twelve I shined boots; then there were the afternoon papers; then chopping wood and running to the laundry for ladies; then came the evening papers, and so on until I fell like a stone on the bare floor of a room in Lincoln Avenue, Chic, in which I was allowed to sleep free of charge for washing dishes at night for a German clergyman who had fled from his country on account of having like a true gentleman, sworn falsely to save the reputation, if any, of a married jane. Before I was ten I shipped as a kitchen-boy on a Spanish tramp, making all the Pacific ports from Mexico down to Chile, after having had a hurried career as a dumb boy in a circus assisting a clown who couldn't be funny without pushing and fighting a half-starved boy. I certainly have always known how to work, and I have always worked four times more than I was paid for. But I am still far from being the first president of the California Railroad and Steamship and Fruit Corporation. Suppose I should really work for thirty long years in a steel mill, always doing more and more in the hope that I might at least become cashier. Then, one day, thinking that the time has come to cash in the promised reward, I would go to the office and ask: 'How about the job as assistant vice-president to begin with?' The answer is: 'Sorry, nothing doing right now, but just go on the same way as you have been doing during the last thirty years. We are watching you all right and taking proper notice of all you do. As soon as we need another president, we will think it over. Don't forget to punch the time-clock.' Meanwhile I have become forty, and soon out I go with the short but plain notice: 'We have to take in younger men; you will find something else.'

I don't know where jobs as presidents and as millionaires could be found for all the readers of success stories if they should try to cash in on the promises. A hundred and twenty years ago there was a saying: 'Every one of my soldiers carries a marshal's baton in his bag.' Today it is: 'Every one of our employees may become president of our company; look at Mr Flowerpot, he did it.' I think all these successful men must love shined boots of another sort than I, and the newspapers they sold must have been different from the papers I carried.

I waited until the noise on deck had ceased and I was sure that there was no more extra work left. When everything seemed quiet and the *Yorikke* went softly on her way, I left the quarters and went to look about the deck. The moment I stepped out, the pickpocket who had introduced himself as the second engineer hopped me and said: 'Just looking for you, guy; the old man wants to see ye and sign ye on. Just follow me.'

Rich experience has taught me that whenever somebody says: 'Just follow me,' or: 'Come along,' it means always: 'We shall take good care of you, and keep you here for quite a while. Take it easy and don't resist.'

The *Yorikke* was running like a devil flitting into hell. The pilot had left the ship long ago, and the first mate had taken the bridge.

The skipper was still a young man, hardly more than thirty-five. About five seven in height. Slightly fat without looking it. He certainly never over-ate, though what he ate was good. His face was healthy and red; he must have had freckles when a boy. His hair was brownish yellow; it might have been nearly red when he was ten. His eyes were light waterish blue, without a definite expression, and with the look of a man with very little energy. Later I learned that his eyes did not indicate his character. Very well dressed, one might say really elegant. The colour of his suit, his tie, his socks, and his smart shoes all matched well and showed him to

295

be a man of good taste. If one did not know his profession, one would never think him the captain of a tramp. He would have been the glory and essence of an ocean liner in which women between thirty and forty were sailing to get away from their rich and boresome husbands. But any person who was in a hurry to reach Europe safely would never have trusted a liner on which he was the skipper, looking as he did. From his looks one would not have guessed that he could ever bring even a three-hundred-ton bucket from one port to another in calm weather. Here again he betrayed his looks. I learned soon that he was one of the ablest skippers and the most daring and enterprising I have ever met. In war-time he would make a skipper of a torpedo-boat chaser such as there are very few of in the whole world.

He spoke a refined English, the kind one may learn in a good school in a foreign country. It was grammatically too correct for anybody American or English to think him a native of an English-speaking country. When speaking he selected his words with great care and good taste, giving the impression of a cultured individual, but at the same time an English-speaking person would feel that he was not trying to give that impression, but that he talked that way because he wanted to use only words of which he was absolutely sure of the proper meaning and of the correct pronunciation. Once when I was alone in his cabin I had a look at his library. There were only four or five books of such trash as detective or mystery stories. The rest of his books were so carefully selected that ever afterwards I wondered how that man came to be the skipper of a tramp. There must have been something back of it. Perhaps his wife was found in bed with another man, and a shooting resulted. Lost honour for abandoning a ship or crew, or something like that, it could not have been. He was not the kind to do that. Later, knowing more about human beings, I think I came pretty close to understanding him through and through. He was the type that refuses an offer to be the captain of a liner, for if he had taken it he would have been bored to death and would have resigned after two trips – after being chased by American women from the East and Middle West who stepped up behind him at three o'clock in the morning or at midnight and asked questions, already twenty-five million times correctly answered, about why a ship carried green lights at star and red lights at port, and why the propellers are at the stern instead of at the bow since an airplane has the prop at its bow, and why a liner is tugged out of port instead of going out under its own power – questions never asked to learn the facts, but to brag: 'Oh, my dear, I've just come from the master of the ship. I had a long talk with him about navigation. He told me all about it, and just think, oh, dear me, he's had that sort of job for fourteen years!'

The contrast between the skipper and his second engineer, who also ranks as a ship's officer, was not striking, but simply destructive in every way. If I had still been in doubt as to what kind of ship I was on, this contrast alone would have told me and convinced me without any other evidence.

'So you are the new drag?' the skipper greeted me when I stepped into his cabin.

'The what, sir?'

'The coal-drag, the coal-shoveller; you know, the man who hauls the coal from the bunkers to the fireman, to the stoker, if you understand that expression better.'

'I, sir? You mean me? I the drag, the shoveller? You are mistaken, sir, excuse me. I am no drag, I am a fireman.' The truth began to dawn upon me.

'I didn't say a single word to you about being fireman,' the horse-thief broke in. 'I said the black gang, the fire gang, didn't I? That's what I said.'

'Right,' I admitted. 'That is what you asked, and I answered yes. But in all my life I have never been a coal-drag.'

The skipper's face showed that he was beginning to be bored. He said to the pickpocket: 'That is your business, Mr Dils. This does not concern me. I thought everything was in shape.'

'I wish to be put ashore right away, sir,' I said to the skipper. 'It was never my intention to sign on as coal-shoveller. Not me, sir. I shall protest, and I sure shall complain to the harbour authorities of attempted shanghaiing.'

'Who shanghaied you?' the horse-thief yelled. 'Did I? It's a stinking, funking lie, it is. I haven't to shanghai anybody.'

'Dils!' the skipper fell in again with a warning tone in his voice. 'I will have nothing to do with this, you understand, Mr Dils.' He laid, this time, particular stress upon the 'Mister'. 'I am not responsible for anything of this sort, I want to make this as clear as sunlight, Mr Dils. You will have to stand for what you are doing. Straighten this out between you. Outside. Not here in my cabin.'

The pickpocket seemed not to mind what the skipper said. He asked me again: 'What did I say to you? Didn't I say black gang?'

'Yes, you said that. But you didn't say – '

'So what? Does the drag belong to the black gang or does he not? Just tell me your opinion,' the louse questioned.

'Of course, the coaler belongs to the boiler gang,' I answered, 'but, see here, mister, this does not mean – '

'All right then, this will do, this surely settles the issue,' the skipper said. 'If you really meant fireman, you should have said so. Then our Mr Dils would have told you that we are not short a fireman. Well, now we may write.'

He opened the book with the crew's register and asked my name.

My honest name in the register of a death ship? Not me. I have not come down so far yet. Never again in all my life would I have a chance to sign on for a decent ship. I sure would rather prefer a release paper from San Quentin or Leavenworth or some other honest mansion than the pay-book of a death ship. Every honourable skipper would shun me more than if I were coming full of syph ole Phillis.

So I abandoned my good name. I think it was anyway only my mother's name, since it had never been clear if my father had really his name added or not. I severed all family connections. I no longer had a name that was by right my own.

'When and where were you born?'

My name gone, I still had my country.

'In – in – in – ' I began to stammer.

'Where did you say?'

'Alexandria.'

'Alexandria what? In the United States?'

'No, Egypt.'

With this my country was also gone. For the rest of my life I would have for identification only the pay-book of the *Yorikke*.

'Nationality? British, I presume.'

'No, sir, without nationality.'

Can there be anybody in the world who would expect me to register on this ship my name and my nationality? On the *Yorikke*? It would give the *Yorikke* a chance to say: 'American? –. –. An American even came *here*, to shovel coal within my very hull, a dirty assistant to a Portuguese fireman who was an escaped convict from an Arabian pen.' No, sir. I couldn't do that. It was not patriotism. It was simply – well, I could not. It would have been like betraying my country to the enemy. Sell out my country to the *Yorikke*? Whatever the consuls or all the other authorities in all the world may say, it is still my country; and it is still my country with all her gangsters, bandits, corruption, red tape, unlimited mediocrity and hypocrisy, and with her political mandarins; it is still the country which nobody can ever take away from me. It's just love,

298

like the love for a mother whether she likes it or not. And it is so far, so very far away from all the loud jazz-patriotism and flag-waving. It is love. And against love there is no medicine and no death-penalty of any use. So for this love, and for her honour, I had to renounce my country, as if I had never heard of it.

So I repeated: 'No, sir. No nationality. Without a country. League of Nations, Geneva.'

He did not ask for a passport or for my sailor's card or for any paper or envelope with my name on it. He knew that men aboard the *Yorikke* must not be asked for papers. They might say: 'Sorry, sir, I have no papers.' Then what? In that case he would not be permitted to sign the man on, and the *Yorikke* would never have a crew. A man with any paper, whether his own or not, never shipped on the *Yorikke*. In the next port the list of the crew has to be verified by the consul of the country under whose flag the ship claims to sail. Since the man has made a trip already, the consul cannot refuse to acknowledge him a proper member of the crew. He has to accept him, paper or no paper. The man is now actually considered a resident of the country under whose flag the ship sails. But it does not give the man a country, or a nationality, or the right to claim a passport.

The consul does not know death ships, officially; and unofficially he does not believe in their existence. It requires certain talents to be a useful consul. Nor do consuls believe a person was ever born if said person cannot produce a birth-certificate.

Every skipper of the *Yorikke* knew how to get his men. He could never sign on a new man as long as the ship was still in port. In that case he had to take the man to the consul. The consul was obliged to ask for the passport or sailor's card. If he had none, the consul was not permitted to let the man sign on. Then the skipper would have been one man or many men short. The skipper always waited until the blue flag was up, the signal that the ship was sailing within two hours. The blue flag up, the ship is considered already out of port and on her way. From that moment on, the port authorities no longer have any jurisdiction over the ship, with certain cases excepted. Any man coming aboard now is regarded as having signed on under the emergency rules – a ship under weigh with crew incomplete. The skipper now has the right to sign on as many men as he wishes without being compelled to take them to the consul. After the man has made one trip, short or long, the consul must sign him on or the port authorities will report him. This, by the way, settles once and for all the question of how the skunk survived the flood. He hopped on when the ark was already under sail, leaving Noah no time to sign him on properly with the American consul, and, owing to international regulations, the skunk could not be thrown overboard, but had to be signed on under the emergency rules. That's why. Because these regulations are so old that long before Adam came to life, sailors who had sold their sailor's cards signed on that way to get away from a hot spot.

The skipper was still writing in his book.

After I had given up my name and my country, only my right to work was left. My work was the only thing the *Yorikke* wanted me for. Therefore I was going to sell my man-power as high as I could.

'The pay for coalers is forty-five pesetas,' the skipper said without looking up from his book.

'Hey! What's this? Forty-five pesetas?' I yelled.

'Yes, didn't you know that?' the skipper asked with a tired look at me.

'I signed on for English pay.' I defended my wages.

'Mr Dils?' the skipper asked sharply, throwing a stern glance at the second engineer.

'Did I – I mean me, myself – ever promise you English wages? Say it. Did I?' the horse-thief asked grinningly.

Right then I could have socked that son of a beachcomber, never mind, I could have socked him so that his own mother would have said: 'That is not my son, that must be the leftover of a twisted alligator.' But I came to in time. I would not have liked to be in chains on the *Yorikke*, eaten by the rats that had just taken out marriage licences. Just keep cool, my boy. I felt like ice dropped by the kitchen door at the back porch. And with an icy voice I said: 'Yes, you have. You have promised me English money.'

'Exactly, my man,' the pickpocket said, 'I have promised you English money. Exactly. But I haven't said a single word about English wages, have I?'

'Now what is this, Mr Dils?' the skipper interrupted. 'If you mean to hire men, I should suppose everything is straight.'

'It is straight, sir. I have promised this man English money, but not English wages. Have I or have I not?' he was addressing me again.

'Yes,' I answered, 'that is right, but I was of the opinion that you meant English wages, which would be about ten pounds a month.'

'We cannot take into consideration here what your opinion was,' the skipper said to me. 'We can only consider what was said and what was not said. If Mr Dils has said English money, then he was right. We pay the forty-five pesetas of your monthly wages, of course, in English currency. No mistake in that. In English pounds and shillings, at the rate of the day on which the payment is due. All overtime is paid at fourpence.'

Weeks later it came to me that I had not asked for how much overtime these fourpence are to be paid, for the hour, for the day, for the week, or for the year. When I found out it was meant for the week, it was too late to make any objections. Objections would have been overruled anyway, since overtime was never paid, and asking for it meant the hold of horrors.

'Where do you wish to sign off again?' the skipper asked without looking at me, keeping his eyes on the book and writing letters and figures.

'Next port of call,' I said quickly.

'You cannot do that, ' the horse-thief said.

'Oh, yes, I can do that and I shall.'

'You have it all wrong, brother, you cannot sign off at the next port of call,' the pickpocket said again. 'You signed on until we make Liverpool, didn't you?'

'That's what I meant,' I said. 'Liverpool is the next port we are putting in.'

'Not on your life,' the skipper said. 'We cleared papers for Saloniki, Greece, you see. But in the meantime, I have changed my mind. We are making North Africa. That's what I am going to do.'

Cleared for Greece and making North Africa. Aye, aye, sir. Now I get the whole course straight. Morocco and Syria right now are paying well for – for – All right, skipper, I get you. As soon as you have pocketed the money you are after, we make for the grand port, or, let's say, for the ground port. From now on, you cannot hide anything from me, an old salt. Nosser. Not from me. This is not the first smuggler and armer I have shipped in. But for the sake of fighting and for another chance to look behind the curtain, I did not give in.

'You have told me Liverpool, haven't you?' I said to the horse-thief.

'Not true, sir.' The horse-thief addressed the skipper with lips drawn wide, trying to grin like a hyena. 'I said, when offering this man a job, that we had a light cargo for Liverpool, and that he may sign off at Liverpool as soon as we make it.'

'I see,' answered the skipper, 'I see everything is in fine shape. We have eight cases of Spanish sardines for Liverpool. Low freight rate. Time to deliver not over eighteen months. I cannot make

301

Liverpool on account of eight cases of Spanish sardines at the rate of seven and six each. The fresh water I have to take in for this trip would cost me more than the freight these cases pay. But, of course, as soon as there is a chance to get a full cargo for Liverpool, I shall not hesitate to make that port.'

Since I am out of my baby-shoes for quite some time, I know damn well what those eight cases are for. Blindfolding for papers and clearances. Always good to have on hand for an excuse to change the course when it is necessary for some hot reason. I was sure he had small cargoes for Italian ports, French ports, Albanian ports, Turkish ports, Egyptian ports, Syrian ports. He may put in any port he wishes, without any chance for anyone to accuse him of having incorrect clearing papers. I do not know why, but I begin to like this man. I begin to understand why he, a man of culture, is running a ship like the *Yorikke*. At heart he is a vagabond, a pirate. Perhaps it is in his blood. He cannot help it. The times for pirates are gone. It doesn't pay any longer. In these times the career is too short. But there is still in modern times a sort of dangerous trading and shipping that the right man with the true pirate spirit can find far more adventurous than any pirate of old could ever have thought of. Pirates of old were brutes. They were never in need of intelligence. Sheer brutality did the job in those times. Modern pirates must have intelligence and quickness of mind, and more of it than the admiral of a fleet of battleships. For a man with brains and an adventurous spirit it is, by far, more thrilling to outwit clever customs officials and captains of gunboats who chase ships that run arms to Syrian and Moroccan rebels than it was for crude pirates to capture a defenceless merchant ship.

I see clearer every minute what kind of tub I am in. There is no escape. The company wants to get fat. It can't be done in decent business with ships like this one. But it can be done in a business that pays better than any decent business can ever do. Money must be made. That's religion. Because expenses must be met. The greatest disgrace is to fail to pay your debts and go into bankruptcy. A decent citizen pays his debts. And ships cannot run without sailors. What's the use anyway?

'Sign your name here,' the skipper said to me, breaking into my thoughts about economic problems.

He handed me his pen.

'Here? My name? Me? Never!' I protested.

'As you wish,' the skipper cut short. 'Mr Dils, will you, please, sign here as witness for a man who cannot write?'

I felt myself going wild. That pickpocket sign for me? Such a lousy leper sign on my behalf, as a sort of representative of a red-blooded American? Not he. And nobody else, as long as I have a hand to write with.

'All right, skipper, I shall sign myself. I see there is no way out. I am caught. My just punishment for betraying sweet sunny Spain.'

'Do not talk so much nonsense. Write your name and have done with it. I have got lots of other things to do than to taddle around with a stubborn coaler. Put it down and beat it. We cannot spare a coal-shoveller much time.'

I wrote with clear letters that will last until the trumpets of the Last Day are calling, and somebody then will be confused as to how to call me.

'Helmond Rigby, Alexandria, Egypt.'

There it now stands for ever. Black on white. I can't get away from it. Ahoy, *Yorikke*, ahoy, hoy, ho! Go to hell now if you wish. What do I care? It's all the same now to me. I am part of you now. Where you go I go, where you leave I leave, when you go to the devil I go. Married. Vanished from the living. Damned and doomed. Of me there is not left a breath in all the vast world.

> Ahoy, *Yorikke*! Ahoy, hoy, ho!
> I am not buried in the sea,
> The death ship is now part of me
> So far from sunny New Orleans
> So far from lovely Louisiana.

Hello, over there, beyond. Yes, I mean you there, you beyond. We are comrades now, gladiators. What was it you said? Yes. *Morituri te salutamus!* The modern gladiators are greeting you, O great Caesar, Caesar Augustus Capitalismus. *Morituri te salutamus!* The moribund are greeting you, O Caesar, great Imperator Caesar Augustus. We are ready to die for you; for you and for the glorious and most holy insurance. Send us to the grand port, to the ground port; you are welcome, thank you.

O times, O morals! How things have changed, boys, you there from beyond! The gladiators marched martially into the arena in an array brilliant and glittering and shining against which a circus-parade in Kansas City would look like the funeral of an inmate of a poorhouse. Gee, how they marched in! With the blaring of fanfares and trumpets and the beating of great drums and the playing of marches such as Sousa would have liked to compose, if only he had

had the right feeling for the tunes of true martial music. And the women! Those beautiful dames hailing the marching gladiators from their balconies, covered with carpets representing all the riches of Persia, those beautiful perfumed janes hailing and cheering the gladiators as if they were boxers in Madison Square Garden. Smiles and kisses were thrown from the ladies down to the victorious fighters. Amidst the rousing cries and hails and applause of the most excited crowds any world has ever seen, while the trumpets blared and the drums roared and the finest bands of the Roman Empire played emotional war-tunes, these gladiators breathed their last sighs, dying as no modern soldier ever has a chance to die.

We, the gladiators of today, we must perish in dirt and filth. We are too tired even to wash our faces. We starve because we fall asleep at the table with a rotten meal before us. We are always hungry because a shipping company cannot compete with the freight rates of other companies if the sailors get food fit for human beings. The ship must go to the ground port, because the company would be bankrupt if the insurance money would not save her. We do not die in shining armour, we the gladiators of today. We die in rags, without mattresses or blankets. We die worse than hogs in Chic. We die in silence, in the stokehold. We see the sea breaking in through the cracked hull. We can no longer go up and out. We are caught. The steam hisses down upon us out of cracked pipes. Furnace doors have opened and the live coal is on us, scorching what is still left of us. We hope and pray that the boiler will explode to make it short and sure. 'Oh, down there, those men,' says the stateroom passenger who is allowed a look through a hole, 'those filthy sweating devils, oh, never mind, they do not feel it, they are accustomed to the heat and to such things as a ship going down; it's their business. Let's have another cock well iced.'

Of course, we are used to all that may happen. We are the black gang. If you are hungry and you need a job, take it. It's yours. Others are waiting to take it for less.

We go to hell without martial music and without the prayers of the Episcopalian. We die without the smiles of the beautiful ladies, without holding their perfumed handkerchiefs in our hands. We die without the cheering of the excited crowd. We die in deep silence, in utter darkness, and in rags. We die in rags for you, O Caesar Augustus! Hail to you, Imperator Capitalism! We have no names, we have no souls, we have no country, we have no nationality. We are nobody, we are nothing.

Hail to you, Imperator Augustus! You don't have to pay pensions to widows and orphans. Not even as little as a coffin. We do not even ask for six square feet of the cheapest ground. We, O Caesar, are the most faithful and the most loyal of all the servants you have. The moribund are greeting you: Hail, Caesar!

5

At half past six a Negro brought in the supper. It was brought in two good-sized tin kettles, more or less of the kind used at camp-fires. These kettles were battered as if they had seen hundreds of battles. They were dirty and greasy, and they looked as if at least a full month had passed since they had last been cleaned.

The supper was a watery meagre vegetable soup with an ugly-looking layer of rancid fat on the surface. In the other kettle there were potatoes in their skins, the cheapest sort which could be found in a poor market. Then there was another tin can in which I saw hot brownish water. The Negro noted my look, and, as if he had heard of finger-bowls, he thought perhaps I might use this water for the wrong purpose. To avoid any misuse of it he said: 'That's the tea.' The tea smelled like the hot water mother used in the kitchen when rinsing the dishes in the sink.

'Where is the meat?' I asked the Negro.

'No meat today,' he said.

I looked up and saw that he was no Negro, but a white man. He was, as I learned right afterwards, the coaler.

'Getting supper to the fo'c'sle is your business,' he told me in a sleepy voice, and in a way as if I had offended him.

'I am not the mess-boy on this tub; you may as well know that right from the begin.'

'No mess-boys on this box, no mozos, no moises,' he informed me.

'And so?'

'Well, here the drags have to do it, the coal-drags.'

With this I received the first blow. The blows were now falling so quickly, and so hard one after the other, that I ceased to count them. Fate was on. Let's have it.

'Supper is brought in by the drag of the rat-watch,' he went on.

On decent ships this would be the dog-watch. Here, I assumed the dog-watch is the watch which on honest buckets would be the palace-watch. All right with me. Go on. I am caught fine. Let the blows rain thick and mercilessly.

Rat-watch for me. The watch from twelve to four. Bells were not known here. All terms were confused. Here one might even hear such terms as downstairs and upstairs. Because high-class sailors were rare on the *Yorikke*. And if there was one, he could not use the proper terms; he would have been taken for a high-brow and ridiculed. Most of the men would not have understood him at all.

Rat-watch. The most horrible watch that was ever invented to punish rebellious sailors. You come to the fo'c'sle at four, tired. You wash your face as well as you can. Then you have to get the supper for the whole outfit. After having had supper you wash the dishes, since there is no mess-boy to do it for you. The cook does not care how dirty the kettles are; he throws in your grub, dirty or not dirty. Now you lie down in your bunk to get some sleep. You have to eat all that your belly will take, because there is no other meal until eight in the morning. On this full belly, full of potatoes and a thin greasy soup, you cannot sleep right away. You just turn round and round. The other guys off duty are sitting there playing cards and telling stories to each other. You cannot yell at them to be quiet because you want to sleep. They might lose their ability to talk. Knowing that you need sleep, they are already only whispering. But whispering is more annoying than talking in a loud voice. Close to eleven you fall asleep. All the other boys have turned in meanwhile. Precisely at the minute you take the first deep breath in a profound sleep, it is twenty to twelve and the drag of the other watch is waking you up as roughly as he is able. Out of your bunk, down below into the stokehold. At four in the morning you return from your watch. You wash your face. Maybe you don't. You are too tired. Like a stone you fall into your bunk. At about a quarter past six the noise starts on deck; the day-hands are chased around, here hammering, there sawing, yonder shouting and commanding, rattling of chains and squeaking of winches. At eight somebody shakes you out of your sleep. 'Breakfast is ready,' he yells into your ear. All during the forenoon there is not one minute without that hard noise of work on deck. It beats into your brain without pity. Twenty to twelve nobody comes to call you, because no one on a ship would expect anyone to be asleep at that time. The little sleep you might be favoured with is also taken away from you because you have to be on time for your watch, and you must not oversleep or you will start your watch with such a row from the second engineer that anger eats you up, and your work will be twice as hard. You stagger drowsily below, and you almost fall against the furnace doors. No pity. The ship must go on, because a ship is under control only when under steam, just as an airplane is out of control when it has lost its minimum flying speed. So you go to your watch and work worse and harder than a Negro slave until four. And so it goes, on and on.

'Who washes the dishes?'

'The coal-drag.'

'Who cleans the — hold?'

'The drag.'

Cleaning privies and such things is, absolutely, an honourable work. Provided one hasn't got anything else to do. In this case it was what a Mexican would call: *la porquería y la cochinera mas grande del mundo entero*. Or something which cannot be explained well in good English with dames listening in. Anyone who would have come close to see would have said: 'This is the filthiest and dirtiest cave I have ever seen in all my life.' From my experience on a decent farm, and from experiences in tropical countries, I know that pigs are cleaner in fact than hundreds and thousands of human beings ever try to be. So it would do pigs, when left alone and not interfered with by miserable small farmers, an injustice if I said this here looked like a pig-sty. I could not blame the skipper for never wishing to inspect the fo'c'sle, as was his duty. He sure would not have been fit for two full weeks afterwards to eat a single meal. We had to look at it every day, and we had to eat also. No excuse for anything when there are only two points around which you revolve: Live or die. Yesser.

My punishment for having left sunny Spain is hard.

On ships like the *Yorikke* it is the coal-drag who has to do any work that comes along that no one else will undertake. No matter if the work is the lousiest, the filthiest, the most dangerous, the drag is called upon to do it. He has to do it. He has no right to refuse. Suppose there are three drags, one for each watch, when the crew is complete; the lowest of these three drags is the drag of the rat-watch. And suppose the two other drags refuse to do a certain job, the last called upon to do it is – yes, sir, you guessed right – is the drag of the rat-watch. He has to do it. If he prefers rather to go overboard or knife himself, he doesn't get any chance to do so until he has completed the job to the full satisfaction of the skipper or the chief; I mean the chief engineer.

As to dangerous jobs, it went like this: The chief told the second engineer, the second told the donkey, the donkey told the greaser, the greaser told the fireman, or the stoker if you want.

Said the fireman: 'Blast me somewhere, but that's not a fireman's job, I don't care a bitch who does it, but I am the one who of all the cracked nuts plumb sure won't do it, and not for twenty bucks either.'

Goes the second to the drag of the noblemen-watch, that is the watch from eight to twelve, where only stranded princes and dukes are on watch. Says the drag of this palace-watch: 'Not me, sir, and never mind the double pay and fourfold ration of rum. My great-grandmother is still alive and she is dependent on me.'

Goes the second to the drag of the golden middle-watch; that is the watch from four to eight. 'Me?' he answers. 'Don't come to me that way, sweety, I don't want to be the father of a never-born child. No, sir, my dame is still expecting something from me which I have to furnish and not leave her in the cold. Thank you just the same.'

Goes the second to the drag of the rat: 'Hey, you guy, hop on it and make it snappy. Steam is dropping like hell. No, you cannot leave now, no going out from here until it is fixed. Get at it and hell if you don't. Stinking son of a filthy beachcomber.'

After half an hour or so the drag of the rat-watch comes out bleeding all over, knuckles broken, bones freed of skin and flesh, body scorched and burned and scalded in fifty places, and he drops like dead.

Goes the fireman to the greaser and says: 'I have fixed it.' Goes the greaser to the donkey and says: 'I have done it.' Goes the donkey to the second and says: 'Sir, I did it, it is working fine now.' Goes the second to the chief and says: 'Well, sir, I wish to report I have done it, all is shipshape.' Goes the chief to the skipper and says: 'Sir, I wish to have the following reported in the ship's journal, please: Chief engineer risked his life in repairing bursted steam-pipe, while boilers were overheated and the ship was falling off schedule; and by doing so saved ship from serious disaster. Yes, sir, that is right. Will you please sign it? Thank you, sir.'

One day, when the board of directors of the company are reading the ship's journal, the president will say: 'Gentlemen, I think we ought to give this chief engineer from the *Yorikke* a more responsible position. He deserves it.' The chief gets it. As a matter of fact, it is less responsible than the position he had on the *Yorikke*, because these engines are almost new. But the higher responsibility means a higher salary, and that is the point which counts.

The drag has the report on his body and in his body; he is crippled for life, and the twenty or more burns will leave their marks in his face, on his hands and arms, on his breast and on his back. Now, of course, one should not take it so hard, because why did he do it? He could have said: 'Hell and devil alive, I won't do it.' But the answer is ever ready: 'Why, you man, you do not mean you are going to let the ship go to the bottom and have all your mates drowned and fed to the fish? You wouldn't do such a thing, would you? A brave and courageous man like you? You are not yellow, are you? Could you bear it on your conscience to have a ship with its men aboard go to the bottom and never come up again? There's a fine fellow, brave and smart, the true sailor.'

The chief would have to do it. It's his business to know something about boilers, and about repairing broken steam-pipes on the high sea. He has to know them and he has to know how to fix them; that's why he was made chief engineer and why he gets the pay for it. But he cannot throw his life away, can he? The life of a filthy coal-drag is no life at all. What does such a man know about life and responsibility and the welfare of the country and of economic competition? Don't let us speak about it. Oh, honey, fish him out, that dear little fly in the milk-pot; he might get drowned; please save his little life. A coal-drag? He is not like a fly who has fallen into the milk-pot. He is a filthy, dirty, lousy fellow, no soul, hardly human. He is just good enough for shovelling coal on a ship. He ought to do it just for the fun of it and for three square meals a day.

Yells the chief: 'Hey, coal-drag, come up here for a minute. Like a shot of rum?'

'Yes, sir, thank you.'

But he cannot have it, because the glass falls out of his hand, and the rum is over the floor. The hand is burned and cannot hold anything; yes, sir.

Supper was on the table. Right in front of me. I felt hungry. So I thought I might just as well eat the supper.

I looked around for the mess-gear; I mean for spoons, forks, knives, plates.

'Hey, you bird,' somebody cried at me, 'leave that plate alone, it's mine.'

'All right, all right. Where do I get a plate and a spoon?'

'If you haven't brought any, you will have to do without, son.'

'Ain't they supplied here on this tub?'

'All the supplies here have to be your own.'

'How, then, can I eat not having a plate or a spoon?'

'That's your business, not mine. Invent something new.'

'Listen here, you newcomer,' somebody cried out from his bunk. 'You can have my things to eat with, also my coffee-cup. Of course, you will have to wash them and keep them always clean for me in return for me being so kind to you.'

One man had a cracked plate, but no cup; another had a fork, but no spoon. When the grub was brought in, there usually started a fight about who might have the plate and spoon first. Whoever had them was the lucky bird who fished the best pieces out of the kettles, leaving to the others the meagre remains.

Whenever the *Yorikke* left a port, there were always spoons, forks, knives, plates, cups missing in taverns. Nothing mysterious about the disappearing of such things when the *Yorikke* was in port.

The liquid called tea was brown water. Usually it was not hot, but lukewarm. And then it tasted like – like – yes, sir, right you are, it tasted exactly like that. Another liquid, which was called the coffee, was served at breakfast and about three in the afternoon. This afternoon coffee I seldom saw, because I was at that time busy at the boilers. When I returned from my watch, there was nothing left of the coffee. Sometimes there was some hot water found in the galley to make your own tea or coffee. But if you have no coffee-beans it is rather tough to make coffee, no matter how good you are at it.

The more your coffee and tea are free from real coffee and tea, the more you wish to improve these wonderful drinks with milk and sugar, so as to liven up your imagination. Every three weeks each man received as his ration one six-ounce can of sweetened condensed milk, and every week one pound of sugar. Coffee and tea came from the galley without sugar or milk, just plain.

Upon receiving your can of milk you opened it, took out one teaspoonful, and with it you made a beautiful-looking cloud in your tea. After having done so, being an economical fellow, you carefully stowed away your can of milk to use for your next cup of coffee, because you knew that during the next twenty-one days you would not see another can of milk.

While I was at my watch, my can of milk was not stolen. Nobody stole anything aboard the *Yorikke*. But my can of milk was used up to the last drop by my fellow-sailors, who had used up their milk long before, and they were hungry. No hiding-place was so secret that it could not be detected, and since there were no doors in the wardrobes, you could lock nothing in, even if you had a padlock. Only once did my milk disappear without my assistance. The next time I received my ration of milk I ate it up at one sitting. I did not mind having a sour stomach. I had found out that the only sure and safe hiding-place for all such things was your own belly. Only what was inside your stomach was safe. After I had hidden my milk in this hiding-place I learned that every member of the crew did exactly the same. No one had ever been told to do so. No one had ever lost more than his first can of milk.

We did the same with the sugar. No sooner had you received your pound of sugar than you sat down and ate it up. Once we came to a gentleman's agreement. The sugar of the whole quarter was to be put together in one box. Whenever tea or coffee came in, each man was allowed to take one teaspoonful of sugar out of the box and sweeten his coffee. The agreement was all right, only the gentlemen were missing. Because it turned out that on the second day after the agreement was signed the entire ration of sugar had disappeared. All that was left was an empty box which I found on coming from my watch with the idea of sweetening my coffee; yes, sir.

Each day fresh bread was made by the cook. Something was always wrong with it. Sometimes it was badly kneaded, usually only half baked, often burned black. Each week every man got a cake of margarine. It was sufficient to last for a week. Yet nobody could eat it, no matter how hungry he might be. For it tasted like bad soap.

There were quite a few days when the skipper made his pocket-money, and then we had to close our eyes and shut our swear-holds and keep mum. On such days each man received a ration of two good-sized glasses of fairly good rum and half a cup of marmalade. These were the days when some mysterious business was going on.

For breakfast we had a thick barley soup cooked with prunes. Sometimes the breakfast consisted of black sausage with rice. Then again it was potatoes in their skins with salted herring; another course was beans with smoked fish. Every four days the same dish appeared again, beginning with thick barley soup cooked with prunes.

Never before had I known that all such things could be eaten by human beings, and that such strange mixtures could exist anywhere on this earth where ships with steam-engines had been seen.

The dinner on Sunday consisted of boiled beef with mustard sauce, or corned beef and a slimy gravy, and sometimes cabbage, but mostly potatoes. Monday dinner was salt meat which no one ever ate, for it was only a sort of meat-crust soaked in salt. Tuesday we had dried salt fish, which was always stinking. Wednesday it was vegetables, and prunes swimming in a paste of potato-starch. This paste was called the pudding. Thursday the dinner was again salted meat, which nobody could eat.

Supper was either one of the dinners or one of the breakfasts. Potatoes came with each meal. Potatoes were the backbone of all our eats. Half of the potatoes, however, were so bad that we could not eat them. Sometimes we had a cargo of fresh young potatoes, so-called spring potatoes. The cook stored up well from this cargo, and we had really excellent potatoes. But when we didn't have such cargoes, the cheapest potatoes the skipper could buy were served for our food.

For blinds not only potatoes were taken in, but also bananas, pineapples (real pineapples of course, not moonshine), tomatoes, dates, figs, coconuts, sweet chestnuts. Only on account of such cargoes was it possible at all for us to survive the food which was served to us. Men who had been for five years soldiers in the last war can well imagine how much a human being can endure before breaking down in health and spirit. Yet a man who has sailed on the *Yorikke* will know for sure what and how much an individual can bear and still not go overboard.

Supper over, I had to wash the kettles in which the food had been brought in. Also I had to clean the dishes that had been used on the table, at least those which I had used in common with the fellows who had been kind enough to lend them to me.

I looked around and I began to feel sick. I could not live in this dirt. It seemed impossible. I made up my mind to clean the quarter.

After the men had eaten, they let themselves drop into their bunks as if they were dead. While they had been eating, hardly one word had been said. One could easily get the impression that hogs were eating from their trough. But this impression I lost entirely before I was one full week on the *Yorikke*. Then I could no longer make any comparison. The capacity to make comparisons or to recall my former existence had been killed. I was positive that any newcomer on the *Yorikke* who still had a light cover of civilization would have thought precisely the same of me when seeing me eating as I had thought of my fellow-sailors when I saw them for the first time.

'No soap supplied,' somebody yelled from his bunk. 'And no scrubbers and brushes either. And for devil's sake keep quiet now and leave the quarter as you found it. Hell, I want to sleep, bigud, I need it. Shut your grub-hold.'

I rushed to the chief's cabin and knocked at the door.

'I want soap and something to scrub with. I want to clean up that – in the fo'c'sle.'

'What do you think I am? You do not mean to suggest that I have to buy soap and scrubbers for the crew, do you? Nothing doing here. Go to the captain.'

'All right, sir. But now what about me? I haven't got any soap to wash even my face. And I have to work in the stokehold, haven't I?'

'You are not a kid-sailor, are you? Don't look like it to me. You are an old salt. Ought to know better – any decent sailor provides his own soap. Part of his outfit.'

'Maybe. News to me, sir. Fine soap of course. But not ordinary soap. Soap for the black gang has to be supplied by the company. It's regulations. Also sweat towels. What sort of a bucket is this anyway? Every decent ship supplies mattresses, pillows, blankets, ordinary towels. And above all things plates, cups, spoons, knives, forks. We are no pigs.'

'Every man knows best what he is.'

'All these things are part of the equipment of the ship and are no part of the sailor's outfit.'

'Not here. Not with us. And besides, if you don't like it here, why the hell don't you go where you came from?'

'You dirty chunk.'

'Out of my cabin and stay out. I shall report you to the skipper.'

'In iron, hey?'

'Not us. We are not that crazy. I need the drags badly. And I need you even more badly. No, not iron. It will cost you two months' pay for subordination. We cannot afford iron or chains, see. And whipping neither. You cannot heave coal with a sore back.'

'You are a fine bunch,' I said. 'So low you even steal the poor sailor's pay.'

The chief grinned and said: 'How come stealing your pay? I didn't invite you to come here into my cabin and insult me.'

I could have socked him fine. But it would have cost me another two months' wages, and I could never sign off as long as I would not have money coming.

'I just wanted to see clear,' I said. 'I wanted to hear from you, from the chief, that we cannot have a cake of ordinary soap, and that we have to live here like hogs.'

'Tell all this to your grandmother,' he said; 'maybe she'll listen to that nonsense. But I do not like it at all. And now get out of here; and do not dare step in again until you are called. Out! You had better turn in. Your watch starts at eleven.'

'My watch starts at twelve. From twelve to four.'

'Who said so? Not here with us. And most certainly not with the coal-shovellers. You start at eleven and you heave ashes first until twelve. Understand?'

'Heaving ashes is overtime, of course?'

'Of course not. No overtime paid for clearing ashes. Not with us. It's part of your regular work. That's what you have signed on for.'

Which age was I living in? Among what sort of people had I fallen by accident? In ancient Rome and Greece even the slaves had certain rights.

My mind befogged, I staggered to the fore.

I leaned against the railing, trying to find myself back where I really was in the world.

There was the sea. That blue glorious sea which I loved better than I ever could think of loving a jane. That wonder of a sea, in which to be drowned as an honourable sailor when doing my duty I would have felt to be the greatest honour that could be bestowed upon me. That sea, that capricious woman whom alone I felt truly married to, that wonderful woman who can smile so charmingly, can sing such bewitching cradle-songs, that can rage so furiously, that can show such a savage and alluring temperament, and then fall asleep so sweetly and so dreamily that one could do nothing better than just kiss her and kiss her over and over again.

It was that same sea on which thousands and thousands of decent and honest ships were sailing at this very time. And I, of all sane persons on earth and on sea, I had to ship on this can that was suffering from leprosy. A bucket that was sailing for no other reason but that the sea might have pity on her. Somehow, I felt that the sea would not take this tub, which had all the diseases known under heaven, for the simple reason that the sea did not wish to be infected with leprosy and pus. Not yet at least. She, the sea, still waited for the day when the *Yorikke* would have to be in some port far out of the way and when this old maid, for some reason or other, would then burst or explode or fall apart and so save the sea from being used as cemetery for this pest of the oceans.

314

So standing against the railing and looking up to the star-loaded sky above me, before me the whitish glimmering waves of the sea that lullingly splashed against the ship's hull as the *Yorikke* furrowed her way, and thinking of my lost New Orleans and of my dear sunny Spain, a feeling I had never had before tried to get hold of me. I thought: What's the use? Make a clean short cut, old boy from Sconsin, chuck the coal-drag, and hop over; have done with that filth and dung. Make the hop and enter the good old sea while you're still a clean Yank sailor, and before you get soiled all over and make the sea ashamed of you when you come to kiss her good-bye. But then where is the salvation? It cannot be done that easily. Because there would be only another poor, overtired, ragged, starved, and tortured coal-drag who would have to go on double watch on account of your having kicked off. This fellow-drag of mine, left behind with a double watch, would make my last trip so unbearable that I could not stay below, and it might happen that I would have to come up again just to say: 'Hey, brother-sailor, I am sorry, please forgive me. Won't you forgive me, so that I may stay below?' Suppose he doesn't. What then?

Damn it, damn it all, and devil and hell. Now, listen here, boy from Sconsin, that pest *Yorikke* cannot get you. Not you. And all the consuls neither. Chin up and get at it. Swallow the filth and digest it. Quickest way to get rid of it. Some day there will be soap and brushes again, and plenty of them. Be it New Orleans or Galveston or Los An. All the filth is only outside. Don't let it go to your soul and spirit and your heart. Take the plunge head-first. That way you'll feel the cold less. And now away from the railing and away from that beast that is after you. Kick him right in the pants. Sock it right in the swear-hold. Spit it out, and do it well. Spitting out the filth you feel in your throat is all you can do now. But make a good job of it. Now back into your bunk.

When I was back in the quarters, which were filled with thick kerosene smoke, I knew, and this time for certain, that I was on a death ship. But I also knew for certain that it would not be my death ship, no matter what might happen to her. I shall not help the *Yorikke* make insurance. I shall not be a gladiator on her. I spit right into your face, Imperator Caesar Augustus. You have lost one of the slaves who greet you: 'The moribund salute you, hail!' Save your soap and crash it down your wind-pipe. I do not need it any longer. But you shall not hear me whine again. I spit into your face. I spit at you and at your whole damn breed. Swallow that. I am ready now for battle.

6

I could not sleep. The smoke from the kerosene lamp of the seven virgins became thicker every minute, and it filled the quarter with a heavy cloud. Breathing became difficult and I felt a piercing pain in my lungs. I had no blanket, and, since the nights at sea can be very cold, I was freezing.

Just when I had fallen into a light sleep, I was shaken up and somebody dragged me by force more than half-way out of my bunk.

'Up now. Eleven. Don't fall asleep again. I can't come again. At ten to twelve you go get up your fireman and bring him his coffee.'

'Don't know him. Won't know where he bunks.'

'Get going. I'll show you.'

I sprang up, and I was shown the bunk of my fireman, which was in the opposite quarter, at the port side.

'Hop on it. Go right away to the winch at the ash-pipe. We've got a hell of a load of ashes to heave.'

The man that had called me had come like a phantom, and like a phantom he disappeared. I had not seen his face.

The quarter was dark, for the virgin's lamp gave no light. It just glimmered along.

When I came to the gangway at port side, where the ash-tube led down into the stokehold, Stanislav was waiting. He held an open wick-lamp which he hung up on some hook near the ash-tube.

Stanislav was the coal-drag of the watch now on duty. He tried to explain to me how to handle the winch, a sort of a windlass, which was used to heave up the heavy ash-cans from the stokehold.

'Now look here, Stanislav, I don't understand anything at all here,' I said to him. 'I thought I was an old salt. Yet never have I seen a bucket like this one here on which the coal-drags have to work extra watches. Why and what for?'

'You tell me. What do I know?' he said. 'I am not a baby myself. Believe me, I have shipped on a good many wash-basins. On any

316

decent tub the fireman has to help his drag clear the ashes, so that every watch is just for itself. But here the fireman never gets a rest for a minute. The drag even has to help him stoke. Or the steam comes down to a hundred twenty just like that. Everything is busted and broken. Steam doesn't stay. See? Pipes are leaking. Furnaces rotten, see? On other ships of this size there are two firemen and a drag, or at least one fireman and a half besides the drag. Here the fireman cannot leave the fire alone for one minute. Anyway, I think by now you know where you are, my angel sailor.'

'Bet your sweet little sailor life, I am not going to become an angel on this kettle.'

'Going to skip next port, hey?' he asked. 'Doesn't work well. You will learn this pretty soon. Just make yourself comfortable, feel at home, you know. Get acquainted with the boats, I mean the life-boats. Take a good look at the one you would like to choose on a proper occasion. Talk it over with the cook. He is the grandfather on this bucket here. Warm up with him. He can be of great help to you, if you know how to take him. He doesn't know anything about cooking. But a swell guy. He has two life-jackets stowed away.'

'Why? Are there no jackets or vests for us?'

'Seen any?'

'Didn't look.'

'Better don't take anything for granted here. There isn't even a life-ring aboard. Of course, against the mid-castle you see four gilded rings, pretty to look at. Take my advice, don't touch any of them. If you stick your head through one of them you would be by far safer with your head stuck through a hole of a millstone. With a millstone you have a chance that a miracle might happen. But with these gilded rings around you even your mother would say, it serves you right, boy, you ought to know better.'

'How can that lousy dog do such a thing, leave us without life-vests or jackets? So used to see them in the quarter that I didn't notice that there were none.'

Stanislav laughed: 'You never shipped a box like this one. That's why. *Yorikke* is already my fourth death tub. In these days, I mean since the war is over, you can pick tubs like this one here at random. Never before seen that many.'

'Hey, Lavski!' the fireman yelled from below.

'What's up, fireman?' Stanislav cried through the ash-tube.

'Are you devils heaving ashes or are you not or you want me to come up and sock you in the grub-hold, hey?' the fireman answered.

'Shut up, down there. I have to teach the new drag how to work the ash-winch. Has never seen one in his life,' Stanislav explained.

'All right, get going and come below here. A bar fell out,' the fireman cried angrily.

'Let's heave the ashes first, the bar can wait. I have to teach the new one,' Stanislav cried back.

'What's your name?' he asked.

'Mine? Pippip.'

'Pretty name. Are you a Turk?'

'Egyptian.'

'Good to hear it. An Egyptian, eh? That's exactly what we were missing to be complete. You see, we have all nationalities here on this can.'

'All, you say? Yanks also?'

'I guess you are still asleep to ask such a silly question. The only two representatives of foreign nations that never ship on a death can are the Yanks and the Comms.'

'Comms?'

'Don't try that old trick on me, making me think you a baby. Playing the innocent kid. Not me, buddy. You know quite well what I mean. Comms, you ass. I mean Bolshes. Communists, you bonehead. Yanks do not hop on such a bucket, because they would die in that filth within twenty-four hours. Apart from that, Yanks are always well tipped off by their consuls. They have got the finest consuls on earth. Almost as good as are the British.'

'And the Comms?' I asked.

'Those guys are too smart, by far too clever. Cannot catch them. I tell you that they have got a smeller that knows right away what's the matter. If they see only the mast-head of a can, they can tell you offhand every meal that is served on that ship, and they guess the pay so close to the fact that you can bet six shillings on their being correct. Whenever there is a Comm on a bucket, no insurance money can ever be cashed in. They bury every insurance policy regardless of how well it is sugar coated. And if they smell something about the can, they right away start making a mess. No port inspector can get away with five dollars for closing his eyes. I tell you whenever you see a regular bucket on which are shipping not alone Yanks, but, what is more, Yanks that are Commses, why, man, you may say to yourself that you are sitting now fine and deep in real sugar. Right now I am sailing for no other reason than to get some day a chance to sign on for such a can. I certainly shall never leave it again, and I wouldn't even go ashore to have a shot, because

I'd be afraid that I might lose that can. I would be the lowest drag in the lowest rat-watch to be on such a bucket. And of all the ships in the whole world the best of all are those Yanks from New Orleans. That's the fortification of the Wobblies, and they sure know what they want. It would be paradise to have such a ship to sail on.'

'I have never seen a ship from New Orleans,' I said.

'A Yank from New Orleans would never take you on. Not even when you wait a hundred years for it. Not you. Not an Egyptian. They are particular. They don't look at you even if you have got a sailor's card like sweet honey, clean and honest. Well, now of course this dream, like so many others, is also gone. Any guy on earth that ever shipped on the *Yorikke* can never again get an honest tub. It's after you, all the rest of your life, like the stinky pestilence. Oh, –, let's get at it.'

He yelled down the ash-tunnel: 'Got it hooked, fire'm?' 'Fire'm' meant fireman, in the *Yorikke* lingo.

'Heave up!' the fireman cried.

Stanislav moved the lever, and the ash-can came up, rattling against the tunnel-walls. As soon as it appeared at the mouth of the tunnel, Stanislav moved back the lever, and the can swung out.

'Now take the can off the hook and carry it to the railing, and there you dump the ashes into the sea. I warn you, do it carefully or the whole can'll go overboard. Then we sit here and have to do the whole – with only one can.'

The can was so hot that only with pain could I get a good grip on it. Stanislav saw it and said: 'Hot, is it? You'll get used to that after your hands have been scorched enough, don't you worry. It won't be long.'

The can was heavy. Eighty or ninety pounds when full. I carried it, holding it against my chest, across the gangway, which was about twelve feet. At the railing there was a short wooden shoot through which the ashes were dumped into the sea. This wooden shoot prevented the outside hull from being soiled by the ashes. The ashes were swallowed up by the sea with a loud, angry, whistling hiss. I carried the can back to the opening, hung it on the chain, and Stanislav pushed forward the lever. The can went down the tunnel like thunder. 'Naturally,' Stanislav said, 'it's clear why the life-jackets and the rings are gone. They say the old man sold them to make some extra coin. I know better. It wasn't just for making that side-money. You see the whole thing is like this: if there are no life-jackets, then there can be no witnesses. And if there are no witnesses, there can be no proper hearing in the court of the shipping board, see? Guess you get me. Old trick. They never can depend on witnesses. Witnesses might have seen something or heard something, and then the insurance would get pretty sour with all the presidents and vice-presidents. You shouldn't miss looking at the boats some time. What was your name? Yes, what I said, Pippip, look at the boats. You can throw both your shoes straight through the cracks the boats have. No survivors. Sorry, no witnesses.'

'Don't tell me tales, young man. Doesn't the skipper want to get out safely?'

'Now don't you worry about the old man. Look after your own skin first,' Stanislav said ironically. 'The skipper will get out all right. Never mind him. Would to the devil that you knew everything as well as that. He will make it fine. Ought to see how he is fixed.'

'But didn't you come home safely from three death tubs already?' I asked.

'Yip. That's true. The last one that shuffled down I forgot, at the last port, to board, and so I let her go without me. You just have to figure out when and where is the best time to stay behind. As to the other two, well, you have to have a bit of good luck. If you haven't got luck, not any, you better stay away from the water by all means, or else you might get drowned even in a wash-basin when bathing your feet. They haven't invented yet any kind of useful water in which you can find hooks hanging around wherever you grasp.'

'Lavski! What for thousand devils are you doing up there?' the fireman yelled up through the tunnel.

'Oh chucks,' Stanislav cried, 'the chains have gone off the drum. I'll have them fixed in a minute.'

'Now, you try the winch,' said Stanislav to me. 'Take care. It kicks and hammers and jams worse than an overfed horse. It knocks your head off just like that if you don't look out.'

I pushed the lever forward and the can was shot up right against the top of the tunnel. It sounded as if the whole tunnel would go to pieces. Before I could snatch the lever to pull it back, the winch set in reverse by itself, and the can shot down into the stokehold, hitting the bottom with such a bang I thought the whole can must be smashed. The fireman bellowed that if I had any intention to kill him I should come down and do it like a brave sailor. I had not yet caught his words in full when the winch again reversed itself and the can, now half empty, thundered up the tunnel and again crashed with a bang against the top. When the can was just about to shoot down again into the tunnel, Stanislav grasped the lever. The can stood still as death the same instant.

'You see,' he said, 'isn't quite as easy as kissing the bride. You will learn that all right. Just get all your knuckles peeled off and then you will know how it is done. Tomorrow at daylight I will show you the trick. You better go now, shovel the ash into the cans, hang them on the hooks, and I will serve the winch up here. You might smash the winch. Should that happen, my boy – well, I would not wish it to you nor to me. Then we would have to carry all the cans up here on our backs. Don't you ever wish it, man. After we are through just with the ash of one watch, you would no longer know if the sky is above you or below. We would not walk, we would crawl instead. We sure would just roll from one place to the other. So better treat the windlass with love and kisses.'

'Let me try once more, Lavski,' I asked him. 'I will say Gracious Lady to her. Maybe if I consider that winch a person, then she will do it and work with papa.'

I yelled down: 'Hook on!'

'Heave up!' came the call.

'Hello, Duchess, come, let's do it together. Come, come, come, up with the shirt.'

Mohammed is my witness, she did it, and fine she came along. Like oil and soft flesh. Gentle like a lambkin. Papa is not without experience. I guess I know the *Yorikke* better than her skipper or grandfather, the wise cook. That winch was still the same that was used by old man Noah. And the *Yorikke* had been built after blueprints left over by the Ark-builder. This windlass, therefore, belonged to pre-Flood times. All the little goblins of those far-off times which were to be destroyed by the Flood had found refuge in the *Yorikke*, where they lived in all the corners and nooks. The worst of these little evil spirits had taken up quarters in this winch. Consequently the winch had to be respected and the goblins hidden within her had to be treated well. Stanislav had won over these ghosts by long practice. I tried to make them friendly with noble speeches.

'Hey, Your Highness, once more, get your legs going, please.'

And how she came, that winch! Smoothly and with a decent shame. The can stood like a soldier exactly where I wanted it to make my embrace more powerful and carry the ash to sleep in the sea.

Of course, the winch was not all the time good-humoured. More than a hundred times she played me nasty tricks. What else can you expect from women? If the lever was not pushed or pulled exactly at the right fraction of the right second at the right distance, the can shot with rattling thunder up against the top of the tunnel so that the whole ship seemed to shake in her bones. Pushing the lever in or pushing it out one thirty-second of an inch too far made all the difference in whether the can stopped exactly in the right position.

Stanislav had gone below to shovel the ash and the slags into the cans. After I had heaved about fifty cans, Stanislav cried up that we would leave the rest to take out during the next watch.

I felt like breaking down on my knees after having carried so many heavy cans across the gangway. Hardly could I catch my breath. But before I had time to get acquainted with my feeling of collapse, Stanislav bellowed: 'Hey, get ready, you, twenty to twelve.'

Partly crawling, partly staggering, I dragged my carcass to the fo'c'sle. There was no light on deck. Kerosene costs money. The company could not afford it on account of hard competition with other companies who offered still lower rates.

Several times I struck my knees and shins against something hard before I reached the quarters. Not easy to describe in detail everything that was lying about the deck. To make the description short I would say: everything possible under heaven was lying on deck. Even a ship's carpenter was lying there, drunk like a helpless gun with all its ammunition shot off. Later I learned that this carpenter got drunk in every port we put in, and that, for this reason, during the first two days after the ship was out he could not be used even to scrub the deck. The skipper always felt lucky when the A.B.s did not join the carpenter in his happiness, and when at least one A.B. was left sound enough to hold the wheel fairly by the course. The carpenter and the three A.B.s were, by the way, so thoroughly drenched in body and brain that the skipper could give them life-jackets without any fear of making them bad witnesses when riding out the insurance. They had lost every ability to gather and to assort their ideas of what they had seen and what they had not seen. All they knew about the economic welfare of civilized nations was the exact price of whisky in the various taverns of the different ports the *Yorikke* usually put in. The skipper mentioned frequently that he considered these four men real pearls of first-class sailors.

In the quarters I fetched the coffee-can, went with it to the galley, and filled it with hot coffee which stood on the stove. With this coffee-can in hand I again had to make my way across the dark

322

deck to the quarters. By now my shins and knees were bleeding, so often had I knocked them against boxes, hold-shafts, beams, chains, anchors. There was no such thing aboard as first-aid. The first mate played doctor. The medicine and other helpful material were stowed away well, so as not to make any extra expenses. With trifles like these – bleeding shins and knees and knuckles, anyway – one could not have gone to the first mate.

He would have laughed and said: 'Where is it you are hurt? Don't be silly. I can't find anything wrong. Rub in coal-dust – bleeding will cease then. Out of here.'

I had to get up my fireman. He wanted to break my neck for waking him up so early. He said he had missed two full minutes of sound sleep on account of me being such a sap. But when the bell rang out and the watch from the bridge was singing down the 'Ship all right!' my fireman wanted to smash in my head because I had called him too late and he sure would start his watch right away with a row with the second engineer, with whom he was not on good terms, he added. He gulped down his black unsweetened coffee, tore off a chunk from the loaf of bread that was lying on the table, pushed it into his swear-hold, and with a full mouth, while his eyes were swimming in red ink, he yelled at me: 'Go below. I'll come right after you. Get water ready for the slags.' His movements were heavy and tired. He did not sit upright at the table, but half lay on the bench. With his arms spread out on the table he pushed one hand forward as if in a dream to reach a knife he saw. He could not reach it with this movement. He gave it up. The knife was too expensive for him. So he grasped only the loaf of bread and tore off another chunk of it. Again he swallowed a gulp of coffee, and the bread in his mouth swelled up, compelling him to chew with his mouth wide open.

I drank half a cup of coffee. Before I could grasp the bread to cut off a slice, he said gargling to me: 'You better go now. I come right after you.'

Passing the galley, I saw Stanislav moving about inside. It was dark in the galley. Only the glimmering live coal of the stove gave an uncertain light. Stanislav tried to find and steal soap hidden by the cook. The cook in turn stole the soap from the steward. The steward took the soap out of the skipper's chest. Each of these persons was always surprised on finding his soap missing again. The rats were accused of being responsible for the disappearance of so much soap.

'Won't you show me off to the stokehold?' I asked Stanislav.

He came out of the galley.

We climbed up the upper aft deck of mid-castle. He indicated a black shaft and said: 'There you see an iron ladder leading below. You can't go wrong. I have not finished yet in the galley. Don't know where grandfather has hidden the soap this time.'

All around me was the clear night, deep black blue. Out of this surrounding beautiful night, resting upon the lulling sea, I looked down that black shaft.

The depth appeared to have no limit. At the bottom below I saw the underworld. It was a smoke-filled hell, brightened up by darting spears of reddish light which seemed to dash out of different holes and disappear as suddenly as they had come. Every other second this underworld was wrapped in bright fire, which broke out somewhere and swept this hell below all over and went off again, leaving behind thick clouds of smoke. This smoke stayed solidly in that hole, and the underworld could now be recognized only by a very dim yellowish light.

As if he had been born out of this thick smoke, the naked shape of a human being stepped into the centre of the hall. He was black from a thick layer of coal-dust which covered all of his body, and the sweat ran down him in streams, leaving glittering traces in the soot on his body. The man stood there for a while with arms folded. He stared motionless in the direction from which the reddish lights came flaring out. Now he moved heavily about and seized a long iron poker. He stepped a pace forward, bent over, and suddenly it looked as if he were swallowed up by the sea of flames which enwrapped him. He sprang forward with his poker, pushed and pulled with it as if he were fighting an escaped dragon. Then, with a swift move, he jumped back, straightened up his body, and put the poker against the wall. The flames had been quieted, and the hold was black and smoky more than ever, lightened up only with that ghostlike yellowish glimmer.

I tried to go below. No sooner had I set my foot on the fourth rung of the ladder than I felt myself being smothered by a blast of heat, by a choking oilish smoke, by thick clouds of coal-dust, and by heavy fumes of a mixture of steam, kerosene, and burning rags. I coughed and I jumped up to get fresh air into my lungs, which seemed to have become paralysed.

There was no hope of getting away from this job. I had to try it again. No matter what happens. Below there was a human being. A living soul could breathe there in that hell. Wherever any other human being can live and work, I can. I am no exception. I am no sissy either. I have to do it. The watch has to be relieved.

Hurriedly, so as to overcome the uncomfortable effects of a plunge, I stepped down again, and right away I took six rungs. There I stopped. I could go no farther. My lungs were bursting again. I had to take in once more fresh air to survive.

I made a third attack. This time I reached a landing about four feet long and two wide. From this stage another ladder led farther below. But I could not reach it. Because through a crack in the steam-pipe, shooting up right where you had to pass, a fierce blast of overheated steam hissed across the stage near the first rung of the second ladder. I tried to make it. But my face and my arms were caught in this hot gust and I was sure I should be scalded beyond recognition, and my eyes lost, if I went on.

I knew then that I had gone the wrong way and that there must be some other way to reach the stokehold.

Stanislav was still in the galley and still looking for the hidden soap of the grandfather.

'I shall go below with you,' he said willingly.

On our way he asked: 'You have never been part of the black crew, have you? Don't tell me. I knew it when I had the first look at you. How come you say Gracious Lady to the winch? If she does not work and go with you as you wish, just sock her. Most dames like it. And those who don't like it, let them go. Lots more in the world.'

I wanted to tell him that many things apparently lifeless have really souls like humans and that you have to treat them accordingly. Yet I thought there would be time enough to tell him my ideas of a sound philosophy.

So I answered only: 'Right you are, Lavski. Never been before a boiler. Can hardly remember that I have ever even looked down below into the stokehold. Have been cabin-boy, steward, deckhand, A.B., carpenter even. Never liked the smell of the black gang. Listen, comrade, won't you lend me a hand for my first watch before the boilers?'

'Don't talk nonsense. Of course I will. Know your trouble better than you do, baby blacker. It's your first death-mobile. I know these wagons all right. Believe me. But I tell you there are times when you will thank heaven and hell for a *Yorikke* putting in port. And you hop on with all the joyful feelings you have in store, making faces at the one or the ones that are hot after you. Just call on me, sweet innocent, whenever anything goes queer. I get you out of the dirt. I even break jail for a regular guy to get him out of a jam. You see, it's like this, old Egypt, even if we are all dead ones, all of us, it is not worth the trouble to lose heart. Don't get down on your knees. Blare them all in their stinking faces even when sighing your last. You cannot live beyond for a thousand years or a hundred thousand with the feeling eating at you that you gave in during your last hour. Don't lose heart. Stick it, and stick it hard. It can't come worse. I ought to know.

These, surely, were words to pep me up when I was so near to go bitch and ditch. However, it came worse. Much worse. One may ship on a death ship. One may be a carcase among the dead. One may be all wiped out of all that lives, one may have vanished from earth and sea, and yet there can happen horrors and tortures which you cannot escape no matter how dead you are. For when all means of escape are cut off, there is nothing left to do but to bear it.

7

Stanislav went to the shaft I had just left, which I thought was the wrong way below. He climbed down the ladder and I followed him. We came to the stage on which the steam had halted me.

I called to Stanislav: 'We cannot make this. Your hide will be scalded off all your bones.'

'Don't be funny, sailor son. I make this every twenty-four hours two dozen times. Course you have to know the trick. Tricks is the only assistance here on this pest-basin that you have to keep away from the bottom. There is no other way for us to reach the stokehold. The goddamned engineers, devil may have them for nothing, they don't allow us to go through the engine-hold. They say we are too filthy and stinking and leave in the hold a smell like skunks for weeks. Some day in hell we'll all stink together and I shall call them up then.'

I watched him throw his arms about his head to protect his face and neck against the steam sword. Then, more agile and swift than a young snake, he twisted his body through this labyrinth of hissing steam-pipes and darts of shooting steam rays, so that,

326

before I had caught my breath on seeing his elegant acrobatics, he was across to where the ladder went below.

All paddings of those pipes were rotten and in pieces, fittings burst, pipes cracked all over. Since the company had decided where to send the ship, it would have been a foolish expense to have properly repaired the steam-pipes, boilers, grates, or anything else aboard that was rotten, broken, burst, cracked, leaking. Repairs were done with the cheapest material, and done only when there was danger that the ship might go too early to the ground port. The ship had first to make some good money, by making excellent use of certain quarrels among peoples in rebellion against their protectors, who protected by mandate of sheer conquest or by mandate of friendly acts of the noble League of Nations.

When I saw Stanislav doing the snake-dance, I thought highly of his ability, and I felt that no one else could do it so elegantly. I learned soon that every member of the black gang could do the same. He had to. Because only the best snake-dancers survived the black gang. All others who had tried and failed were no longer alive.

I now understood also why we never got food enough to feel satisfied, why we had to be undernourished. Suppose we had been fed like a regular decent ship; we could not have done the snake-dance. Only men lean and without indigestion could reach the stokehold. There was a strict regulation aboard that we must never throw overboard anything which could not be eaten, but that, instead, all left-overs, even bones and crusts and rinds, had to be returned to the galley for the grandfather to make Irish stew, hash, goulash, and mock fricassee out of.

'That's the way you have to do it, brother,' Stanislav said. 'Don't hesitate. If you do, you are finished. You would not be the first one either. If you ever have seen a scalded guy, you won't fail to be good.'

I did not think at all. I imitated what I had seen. And there I was, through, caught only by a few hot shots.

'Don't feel sorry learning this elegant slip,' Stanislav said. 'Acrobatics like those may be of great help some day in your life. In particular if somebody finds your hand in a pocket which is not yours. Having been an excellent snake-dancer on the *Yorikke*, believe me, the iron bars have to be damned close together or they won't hold you for long.'

From the other side of that landing a long iron ladder, or, if you wish, gangway, led below, to the base of the underworld. This ladder, like the one I had passed already, had the rail not at the side, from which you could fall twenty feet and break your neck and bones; no, the rail was close to the brick wall of the boilers. So close, indeed, that you could hardly squeeze your hand between rail and wall. The boilers were covered with a thick brick wall in front and on all sides and on top, to keep the heat better inside. There was a reason why the rail was not outside the ladder, but against the boiler-wall. Suppose the winch that was used for heaving the ashes cracked up or otherwise went out of commission; the ash-cans had to be carried on one's back up the ladders. This would have been rather difficult, not to say almost impossible, if the rail had been outside, for the ladder was just wide enough to be used by a single man. If this man were to carry the ash-can on his back, he could not go straight up the ladder, but had to go sideways with his face against the boiler-wall, and the ash-can hanging outside the ladder.

When I touched the rail to get a hold on it, I found it was so hot that I had to let go. It was heated partly by the immense heat of the wall and partly by the heat of the streams of steam pouring out of the many cracks.

Stanislav had a way of using that rail that was really amazing. He touched it more lightly than he would have touched eggs. He did not *go* down, but he *flew* down, playing on the rail with his finger-tips just enough to keep his equilibrium. Only when for some reason or other he seemed to sway did he grasp the rail for the fraction of a second longer and more firmly, to balance himself. A piano-player could not do better on the keys than he did on that rail.

Everything would have been easier if the shaft had had proper light. But all the light there was came from the smoky yellowish glimmer which filled the stokehold below.

Not being used to this ladder, I had to feel my way step by step. The rail became so hot that I felt my hands getting scorched. The lower I came, the thicker, hotter, and more choking became the smoke. The fumes from burned oil and the coal-gas from the slags pierced my lungs like poison gas. I was sure that this could not be the hell I had been condemned to go to after my death. In hell devils have to live. Yet I could not imagine for a second how it would have been possible for the most savage devil to live here and do his work of torturing poor sinners.

I looked up, and there stood a man. Naked and covered with streaming sweat and soot. He was the fireman of the watch I was to relieve now. Human beings could not live here, since devils could not. But this fireman, he could, he had to. So had all the others of the black gang. They were dead. Without a country. Without nationality. Without birth-certificates with which to prove that they had been born of a mother belonging to the human race. Men without passports by which to prove that they were citizens of the earth, given by the Lord to all animals and insects and all human beings. They could not prove their existence to the satisfaction of consuls and immigration officials and passport-printers.

Devils could not live here, for some culture and civilization are left even among devils. Just ask old man Faust. He knew them personally. But men with no papers had to work here. They were not asked, they were ordered. They had to work so hard, they were chased about so mercilessly, that they forgot everything that can be forgotten. They even forgot more than that. Long ago they had forgotten their own selves; they had abandoned their souls. Whoever took the trouble to pick up their abandoned souls could have them for the taking. It would have been a feast in hell. But the devil is not hot after souls that he can have for the picking. Such souls are worthless. These humans here on the *Yorikke* forgot more than that; they went so far as to forget to think that it might be impossible to work in this hell.

Have I any right to despise the company which runs this ship and which degrades her crew to the lowest kind of treatment in order to keep down expenses and make competition possible? I have no right to hatred. If I had jumped over the railing, nobody could have made me work in this hell. I did not jump, and by not doing it I forsook my prime right to be my own master and my own lord. Since I did not take my fate into my own hands, I had no right to refuse to be used as a slave. Why do I permit myself to be tortured? Because I have hope, which is the blessing, the sin, and the curse of mankind. I hope to have a chance to come back to life again. Sooner or later. I hope to see New Orleans again and Baby waiting there, perhaps, I hope. I'd rather eat all that filth than throw my sweet and adored hope into that stinking mire.

Imperator Caesar Augustus: don't you ever worry! You will always have gladiators. And you will have more than you will ever need. The strongest, the finest, the bravest men will be your gladiators; they will fight for you, and dying they will hail you: *Morituri te salutamus!* Hail, Caesar Augustus! The moribund are greeting you, Happy? I am the happiest man on earth to have the honour to fight and die for you, you god Imperator.

8

Of course, sir, I can work here all right. Others are working here. Why can't I do the same? Man's aptness for imitation makes slaves and heroes. If that man yonder is not killed by the whip, then I won't be either. So let him whip. 'Look at that fellow there. My, what a brave guy! He goes straight into the machine-gun fire just like that. There is a great man. You are not yellow, are you?' Others do it, so I can do it. That's the way wars are fought and death ships run. All after the same idea. No invention of new ideas or new models is necessary. The old ones are still working smoothly.

'Hey, what are you brooding about? What's your name, anyway?'

My fireman had come below. He seemed to be in very bad humour.

'My name is Pippip.'

He brightened up a bit and said: 'Looks to me you are a Persian.'

'You guessed wrong. I am an Abyssinian. My mother was a Parsee. Those are the people that throw their dead to the vultures instead of burying them in the ground.'

'We throw them to the fish. It appears from this that your mother was a rather decent woman. Mine was an old whore doing it for half a peseta. But if you ever say to me son of a bitch, or, worse, *cabrón*, I sock you so that even your vultures won't find you. I respect my mother, don't you ever forget that.'

Now I knew he was a Spaniard.

The fireman of the other watch, now off duty, pulled out of the furnace a thick glowing iron bolt and stuck it into a bucket of fresh water to heat it. He began to wash himself with sand and ashes, because he had no soap.

The stokehold was lighted by two lamps. I call them lamps, but the word 'lamps' was all they had in common with a lamp. One of the lamps hung against the boiler near the water- and steam-

330

gauges. The other hung in a corner to be of use to the coal-drag.

In the world to which the *Yorikke* belonged, little was known of modern things. The only modern object the *Yorikke* ever saw was the suit the skipper wore. Nobody seemed to know that there existed on earth things like gas lamps, acetylene lamps, to say nothing of electricity.

The lamps used in the stokehold and in the engine-hold were the same the *Yorikke* carried when she was making old Carthage on regular trips from Tyre on the coast of ancient Phœnicia. In the British Museum one still can see such ancient lamps. They were iron vessels big enough to hold a pint. From the bottom of this vessel, going outside and upwards, a funnel was stuck in. Inside of this funnel there was a wick. The wick was as far from a real wick as this lamp was from being a lamp. The company did not supply wicks. We had to get them somewhere. When we knew the engineer was not in the engine-hold, we sneaked in and searched the box where the engineers kept the rags with which they tightened up leaks in the fittings. To explain it more clearly, the wicks were of the same kind that were used in the quarters and which had their origin in the woollen petticoats of the seven virgins who kept their candles burning all night to guard their worthless virtues. Suppose they had not had candles lighted at night; some guy might have mistaken them for pretty girls and gone off with their virtue.

The fuel for these lamps was the same famous diamond oil. But while the fuel for the lamps in the fo'c'sle still, sometimes, had a slight touch of real kerosene, the fuel we got for these stokehold lamps was pure burned-out and scratched-up oil and grease from the bottom of the engine-hold and from the catchers beneath the bearings and cushions of the engine.

Four times during one hour the wick had to be pulled out of the funnel because it burned off so quickly. You had to pull out the wick with bare fingers; no other instrument was at hand to do it with. After your first watch you left the hold with your nails half burned off and your finger-tips scorched.

Stanislav had already worked a double watch that day. Later it will be understood what a double watch on the *Yorikke* really meant, and then only will it be fully understood what kind of a guy Stanislav was when he decided to help me during my first watch before the boilers. He could hardly crawl by himself. None the less he stayed with me a full hour helping me shovel coal into the stokehold.

The fireman had to wait upon nine fires, three for each boiler.

331

Two boilers would have been sufficient to produce the necessary steam for the *Yorikke*. One boiler was meant to be the reserve boiler, to rely upon in case something happened to one of the other boilers. But since all pipes were leaking, too much steam was lost, and therefore the reserve boiler, which should be used only in port to feed the winches and windlasses, had to be used permanently, otherwise the *Yorikke* would never have had steam enough to weather off a rough sea and gales.

It was the duty of the drag to haul into the stokeroom all the coal needed to feed these nine fires.

Before the coal could be hauled in, there was a heap of other work to do. The fires, of course, did not take into consideration any other job save swallowing fuel.

So to complete all the work that was already waiting, quite a huge load of ready coal had to be held in reserve before the boilers. This heap of coal had to be furnished by the watch that was leaving now; that is to say, when the watch went off duty, it had to leave an amount of fuel ready large enough so that the new watch could work before the boilers one full hour without having to haul in more coal. When the present watch was relieved, it also had to leave behind a similar amount of ready coal, to be used by the next watch.

Only during the two middle hours of one's watch could this great extra supply be hauled in – in my case, from one to three. At three o'clock the drag of the relief watch came, and with his help the ashes that had accumulated in the stokehold were cleared out. For this reason at three o'clock there had to be in the stokehold sufficient fuel ready to serve the nine fires during the hour while the ashes were cleared, plus the fuel which had to be left over for the relieving watch. Naturally, during the two hours in which the hauling of the fuel went on, the fires of the ship under full steam were incessantly fed, eating and eating away from the heaps of coal you were hauling in. Whoever had not superhuman strength, a heart like a sledge-hammer, and lungs which worked like the sails of a racing yacht could not make it, regardless of how willing he might be. He collapsed for sure. In one case which I remember he never stood up again and died in less than six hours.

The back of the stokehold was towards the bow, and the boilers, lying parallel to the keel, were located in such a way that the doors of the furnaces looked towards the bow. The engine-hold was situated behind the boilers in the direction of the stern.

At the back of the stokehold there were two huge coal-bunkers.

When they were well filled, only the gates had to be heaved and the coal would fall right in front of the boilers. This was honey to the drag. There was practically no work for him to do – just shovel the coal still nearer to the furnaces to make it easier for the fireman.

The *Yorikke*, though, was obviously cursed, because whatever sort of work was to be done on her was the hardest work one can think of. Nothing was easy on her. If for some reason you had a sunny day, then you could be sure that the next fifty days would be only that much harder for you. So it is not to be wondered at that in those coal-bunkers, at the back of the stokehold, only very seldom was there any coal at all. And if there was, the second engineer, that devil of a pickpocket, locked the gates. He did not open them until all other coal in the ship, no matter where it was housed away, had been taken out first. In the meanwhile the *Yorikke* coaled afresh in some port, and the hard job of hauling in fuel from the farthest holds of the *Yorikke* began again. To be honest, hard as it was for us to haul fuel all the time from the far bunkers, there was some sense in keeping the gates to the stokehold bunkers locked. In heavy gales which might break upon us at any time, it would mean the safety of the ship to have fuel in reserve so close at hand. For in a very rough sea it might have been near impossible to haul sufficient coal from the other bunkers.

The regular work on the *Yorikke* for the fireman and the drag would have been considered on any decent ship the work of four healthy well-fed men. Since even galley-slaves develop pride, why shouldn't we? There are galley-slaves who are proud of being good galley-slaves. When the overseer who sings out the strokes walks up and down the plank with his whip in his hand, lashing here and there, and he looks with approving eyes on a husky fellow who is hauling out with long sweeping strokes, then that husky feels like a soldier called for at an honour parade to be decorated with a bronze medal by Mr Pershing. 'That's nothing,' says the worker close to a collapse, 'I can still do better; just watch me and see what a real guy can do.' All right, the medal is yours, keep it and be happy; some day you will tell your grandson how smart a slave you were. Honours are so cheap, you can pick them like fallen leaves in November.

The fireman stirred open three fires, skipping two of each boiler and going from one boiler to the next. After having worked boiler number three, he returned to boiler number one, breaking up fire number two, then going to boiler number two, breaking up fire number two, and so on. On each furnace door the numbers of the fires were written with chalk, beginning with number one and finishing with number nine.

Breaking up the fire was done with a long heavy poker. The slags and cinders were broken off the grate-bars to clean the fire and let it have all the draught it needed to keep it going with full force. Artificial fans were not known on the *Yorikke*. All the draught was provided by nature.

When the furnace doors were opened, a tremendous heat flared into the stokehold. The glowing cinders were broken off the bars and pulled out of the furnace. The fire inside the channel roared like an angry beast ready to jump at the troublemaker. The more cinder was broken off and cleared away, the wilder the fire seemed to act. In front of the furnace the glowing slags mounted until the fireman had to jump back, lest he be scorched. He yelled: '*Agua*, water, cool'm off.' I had to spray water over the cinders to kill them. With each spray a cloud of hot steam sprang up and filled the stokehold with a hot fog, making it difficult to see what was going on.

As soon as the fireman heard the hissing of the water on the slags, he hurriedly began to shovel coal into the furnace. He did it so quickly that one hardly could follow his movements. Before the steam cloud had disappeared, he was done with the job, and with a bang he closed the furnace door. He wiped his forehead with one stroke, jumped to furnace door number four, opened it, poked off the cinder, yelled: 'Get the water, hell and devil!' and began at the same time throwing up coal by the shovelfuls, wiped off the sweat, swore, and jumped to furnace door number seven, jerked it open, crashed off the slags from the grate-bars, howled: '*Agua!*' and threw in the fuel. Like a black tiger he jumped to boiler one, pulled open furnace door number two, and so the work went on: Jumping tiger-like, yelling for water, throwing up fresh fuel, closing the doors with a bang, swearing, spitting, wiping off the sweat, jumping again.

We wore only pants. On his feet the fireman wore a sort of cloth slipper. I had shoes. Now and then the fireman jumped back with a curse and shook off the cinders that leaped upon his bare arms and naked chest. There were no hairy apes around with lurking strains of philosophy for stage purposes. No time for thinking and looking under dames' skirts. Five seconds lost thinking of anything else but your stokehold might cause twenty square inches of your sound flesh to be burned away. A stokehold in a stage-play or in a movie is something different, at least more pleasant. People in

334

evening dress would not like to see the thing as it is and still pay for it.

More often than upon his breast and arms the embers sputtered upon his feet. Then he danced and swore and howled like a savage. The embers slipped inside of his footwear, where they scorched his flesh before he could even find them and get them out.

After three fires had been broken up, the poker became so hot that the fireman could handle it only by wrapping thick rags around his hands.

The cinders taken out from the furnaces and accumulated in front of the fires gave forth such heat that it became impossible for the fireman to go near the furnaces. That bowl of water shed upon the cinders and ashes when the fireman working at the furnaces sang out: '*Agua*, for devil's sake!' did not suffice to kill the cinders thoroughly. Only the surface got slightly cooled off for a few seconds, giving the fireman just a breathing-space to hurry up to finish this particular fire. When he was through with all nine fires, and the heat had become unbearable, the cinders had to be cooled more completely. The stokehold had almost to be flooded to accomplish this. They never could be cooled entirely until they were thrown overboard. For underneath the embers kept glowing and they spread the fire to any bit of coal among the ashes not fully burned.

This flooding of the stokehold brought up thick clouds of scalding steam, from which we could protect ourselves only by jumping into the farthest corners of the hold.

The stokehold was ridiculously small. The space between the boilers and the back of the stokehold was considerably shorter than the length of the fire-channels beneath the boilers. Pulling out the poker from the furnace could not be done straight away, because the end of the poker was out of the fire. Therefore the fireman had to go sideways and jerk the poker up and down to get it out. He had to do a real dance about the stokehold to handle the poker properly. In heavy weather, when the ship rolled hard and fell off big breakers, the dances the fireman had to do looked funny enough to anyone watching it. But there was anything but fun about it. The fireman was then thrown about; he fell with his face upon the red-hot poker, with his bare breast or back upon the heaps of white-hot slags, tumbled over the mounds of fuel against the open furnace, lost his clogs and stepped right into a hill of embers. Incidents like that happen on any ship in any stokehold when there's a rough sea. But in a good-sized stokehold the horrible consequences of such incidents can be avoided to a great extent. On the *Yorikke*, however, these dreadful burnings, scaldings, and scorchings could not be shunned, regardless of how hard one might try. Here they were part of the job. Working before the boilers meant getting burned, scalded, and scorched, all over.

Death ship; yes, sir. There are several kinds of death ships. In some the carcasses are made inside the hull; in others dead sailors are made outside. And then there are death ships that make fish-fodder everywhere. *Yorikke* made carcasses inside, outside, and everywhere. She was a model of a death ship.

While we were cleaning up the fires, the fireman of the former watch finished his bath. All the time he was washing himself in the bucket, entirely stripped, he was in danger of being burned or scorched either by the poker or by sputtering embers. He did not mind. He felt sure that since he was dead nothing could happen to him. From his face, after he had washed himself, one could see that he was really dead.

His face and body had been washed fairly well with the heap of white ashes and sand. But he could not rub the ashes into his eyes, and consequently his face was white while his eyes had big black rings around them. Perhaps this was the reason why he looked like a man with a death skull instead of a face. His cheeks were hollow, his cheek-bones stood out, and they were white and polished like billiard-balls. There seemed to be no flesh in his face.

He put on his pants and his torn shirt. He groaned a deep 'Ough,' which he meant perhaps as a good night. Tired and heavily he climbed up the ladder. When he had reached the landing, I just caught a glimpse of him doing the snake-dance.

Stanislav had meanwhile been busy dragging coal into the stokehold to build up a pile for me to have on hand until I had found myself.

When we were breaking up fire number six again, Stanislav came to me and said: 'Well, brother, I am sinking now. I can't do it any longer. I am finished. Guess I have to shuffle off. It's about half past one. I am on the spot now for almost sixteen hours. At five I have to hop on again and heave ashes with you. It's a great thing that we have you with us now. I could not have done it any longer. I have to make a confession which I should have made earlier. But you see, bad news is always told too early. It is like this, we are only two coal-drags on this bucket, if I count you in. That means that each of us has two watches with six hours each; and taking in each watch one hour extra for clearing ashes, it makes seven hours or, to make it quite clear to you, fourteen hours' tough work with every twenty-four hours, as long as twenty-four will last. Tomorrow we will have still more extra work. We have to clear the whole deck of the mountains of ashes left there while the can was in port. You know, in port no ashes must be cleared into the water. That's all left on deck until the can is in the open again. It will cost us another four hours' extra work.'

'Of course, all these hours more than the regular watch of four hours are overtime, aren't they?' I asked.

'Yes, buddy,' Stanislav said, 'you are right, all this is overtime. But it won't make you any happier. You may write it down on paper, all the hours you call overtime. Only you mustn't expect anybody to pay for it.'

'Oh, I settled that with the old man when I signed on,' I said.

'Now look here. Don't be a sucker. Whatever you settled here when you signed on or after has no value. Only what you have got in your pocket, that's what you may rely on, as long as it isn't pinched by somebody in the fo'c'sle. And don't you ever think that you get paid here. Not in your lifetime. What you get is advances and advances. Just enough to get drunk and get a dame under your legs. Sometimes there is just a bit left to buy a shirt, a pair of pants, or new clogs. You never get enough to buy you a complete outfit. You see, if you look like a respectable citizen, you might get some ideas into your head and walk off and become alive again. Nothing doing. Get the trick now? As long as you haven't got money, and as long as you are in rags, you cannot get away here. You stay dead. If you try, he orders you arrested for desertion and they keep you in jail until the very minute the *Yorikke* is putting out. Then they bring you aboard, and all the costs for jailing you are cut off your pay. And the old man fines you two or three months' pay extra for desertion. That's in the regulations. He can do it. And he does it. Then you go to the old man on your knees and beg for a peseta and you apologize. Because you must have likker. You can't do without. Or you go all nuts. You need the shots and the dames. Without, you can't stand it. Believe me, buddy, it's a lie that the dead has no feeling. You will learn how much a dead one still can suffer before he has become accustomed to it. I won't wash myself. I cannot lift my hands any more. Good night. All the luck, and I wish that no grate-bars fall out. That costs life-blood, Pippip. Good night.'

I could not answer him. I had no words. My head was humming. I saw him dragging his tired body up to the landing at the middle of the gangway. As in a dream, I saw him doing the snake-dance. For a second it looked as if he had lost his hold and was about to fall below. Then he climbed farther up and disappeared in the dark hole through which I could see a few stars sparkling in the black sky.

'Holy Virgin, *Santísima Madre*, *purísima en el cielo*. Thousand holy sons of skunks. Damn the whole – '

The fireman was howling as though bitten by a mad dog. He took a breath, and then he began again to curse whatever came into his mind, which for a long while seemed to be the meeting-place of degenerate individuals and animals with overanimated sex deviations. Nothing was left of the purity of the Heavenly Virgin, or of the holiness of the saints. They all were dragged by him into the gutter. If ever hell had held any horror for him, he now did not care any more. He smashed hell, with a few good words, into an insignificant dung-hole, and he cursed the devils to useless mongrels disrespecting their mothers. He was no longer afraid of anything on earth or in hell. He was in a state where he could not be punished by anybody or by anything. For when I asked: 'Hey, fire'm, what is up?' he beat his chest like a jealous gorilla and, with blood shooting into his eyes, he roared savagely: 'Hell is upon me, six grate-bars have dropped. Holy alligator-tail and ogress-mouse.'

9

The last word of Stanislav on leaving me had been that it would cost life-blood if grate-bars fell out. He had meant one bar. Now six had dropped.

I soon learned that to put them back into their berth not only cost blood, not alone flesh torn off, large pieces of skin scorched, but cost bleeding sperm, shredded tendons, and painfully twisted entrails. The joints of all limbs cracked like broken wood. The marrow in one's bones appeared to flow out like hot lava. While we worked like Egyptian slaves to bring the bars in again, the steam was falling and falling. Ahead of this hard work, we saw already crawling upon us the hard work that was to follow to bring the steam up again to its full pressure. The longer we had to work with the bars, the lower fell the steam. I may justly say, though, that since that night, my first night with grate-bars in the ash-pit, I feel myself standing above the gods. I am free. Unbound. I may do now whatever I wish. I may curse the gods. They cannot punish me any more. No human law, no divine commandments can any longer influence my doings, because no longer can I be damned. Hell is now paradise. However horrible hell may be, it cannot frighten me any more. There is nothing under heaven or in hell that can be compared with putting back fallen-out grate-bars on the *Yorikke*.

To know what it meant makes anyone understand that the swearing of my fireman was not swearing at all, but in fact only a sweet love-song. His language, rich as it was, could not meet the situation. No language, not even the Chinese, could possibly express in words the feeling any sane person simply had to have when confronted with a problem like setting in dropped grate-bars in the stokehold of the *Yorikke*.

Paradise, whatever it may mean, was for the black gang of the *Yorikke* not the opposite of hell, but was simply freedom from the obligation to set in their place dropped grate-bars.

The skipper never came into the stokehold; neither did the two mates. I have never heard that one of them ever even went below to the engine-hold. They even avoided passing too closely to the hatchway that led below to the stokehold.

The engineers dared enter the stokehold only when the *Yorikke* was snugly lying in port and the black gang was wiping and greasing and doing odd jobs about the boilers and the engine. Even then the engineers were soft-footed with the blacks. The firemen and the drags on the *Yorikke* were always, even in port, in a state of exaggerated anger, ready any second to throw at the engineer a hammer or a wrench. Prison, hangman, or the like did not mean a thing to any of the blacks. It would have been only liberation from the grate-bars of the *Yorikke*.

The engine was set up in a hold which was so small that the engineer on watch had to move about carefully to avoid being caught by the engine. Towards starboard there was in the engine-hold a heavy work-bench with tools for emergency work on the engine, the boilers, or the pipes. This bench could not be set up anywhere else. So it had to be in the engine-hold. Between the bench and the engine there was a space hardly two feet wide. On the other side of the engine, toward port, there was a space of only one foot, which had to be sufficient for the engineers when they wanted to go round the engine to look after the greasing. The slightest slip at either side would have been the last of the engineer. He would have fallen into the running engine. Both engineers were hard drinkers. They could get drunk like a Dane at the funeral of his mother-in-law. And they got soaked whenever the *Yorikke* was in port. But I have never seen either of them drunk, at least not in full, the same day or the same night the *Yorikke* was putting out. They knew that being drunk in the engine-hold of the *Yorikke* on high sea meant death surer than by the noose of a lynching party in Kentucky.

There was a good reason why the engine-hold was so narrow. On either side of the engine-hold coal-bunkers had been built in. Coal-bunkers must be. But since they do not carry any pay-load, they are built in any space that cannot be used for any other thing. At least so it was on the *Yorikke*.

From the stokehold, along starboard and along port side, a very low and narrow gangway led to these bunkers alongside the engine-hold. At the back of the boilers, toward starboard, an iron door led into the engine-hold. This door was supposed to be sea-tight to shut off the engine-hold from the stokehold in case water should break in. Since nothing was sea-tight on the *Yorikke*, no one expected this door to be tight. And it wasn't. It was this door that was used by the engineers when they wanted to enter the stokehold. When they wanted to go from deck to the engine-hold they had, of course, a separate hatchway.

This gangway was about four feet wide and so low that if you forgot about it you hit your head severely against the iron beams which strengthened the boiler-walls against the ship's hull. Like everything else aboard the *Yorikke* these gangways were dark like a coal-mine, day and night alike. Since they ran alongside the boilers they were so hot that a Turkish steambath seemed to be at freezing-point compared with their permanent heat.

We, the drags, could find our way in these two gangways just as easy as a drunken mole coming home at midnight. Because these gangways played a great part in the tortures that the coal-drags had to undergo on the *Yorikke*. Through these gangways we had to shovel and to haul and to squeeze numberless tons of coal toward the front of the boilers. So it will be understood why these gangways, and the labyrinths of the bunkers next to the engine-hold, held no secrets for us. Other people, among them our two engineers, did not know these gangways so well.

Suppose the steam, for one reason or other, began to fall. Then the engineer had to do something about it, because that was what he was paid for. Now, the first engineer never entered the stokehold when the *Yorikke* was on high sea. A broken shoulder would always remind him that the boiler-gang must not be molested when the ship is in the open. But since he had to do something about the falling steam, he went to the hatchway on deck leading to the stokehold, and from here he cried: 'Steam goes down!' No sooner had he spoken than he fled away from the hatchway like the devil from an open church. From below a yell sprang up: 'Damned greaser, go to hell and stay there. Just hop below, reception service is ready.' And right after this a mighty piece of coal was flung upwards towards where his face had been for a second.

No use to preach to the working man courtesy and politeness when at the same time the working man is not given working conditions under which he can always stay polite and soft-mannered. One must not expect clean speech from a man compelled to live in filth and always overtired and usually hungry. Well fed, and sitting in a deep soft seat in an Episcopalian church, it is a godly pleasure to listen to a high-powered sermon about the wickedness of an ever unsatisfied working class. Make all the wicked sailors and restless workers, after a good meal, sit in the same soft church seats, and they will listen with the same joy as do the others to the sermon about the lost proletarians who won't believe in God or heaven.

The second engineer, the one I thought a pickpocket and a horse-thief, was still rather young. Perhaps thirty-five. He was very ambitious and hoped to be, some day, first engineer on the *Yorikke*. His idea was that he could show his ability to make a good first engineer no better than by chasing the black gang, especially when the *Yorikke* was in port, for then he was in full command of the black gang. I, for one, did not think he had a chance ever to make a good first engineer – a chief, as we would express it properly. He learned very slowly. In fact, he could not learn at all how to get along with the black gang. At least not with a black gang like the one the *Yorikke* had. Maybe most of us were wanted, somewhere or everywhere, for murder, more or less, or the like, or pretty near the like. Who knows? But no matter what we had been before, and no matter for what reason we had to come to sign on for the *Yorikke*, the firemen and the drags on the *Yorikke* were workers such as hundreds of decent ships would like to have and would pay real gold to have.

There are chiefs by whom the black gang swears. I knew a skipper once who was worshipped by the boiler gang as no god would ever be adored by them. That skipper every day went in person to the galley: 'Cook, I wish to see and taste the food my firemen and coalers are to have today. Well, cook, this goes overboard. My blacks are no pigs. Understand. They have to get food. Real food. And when I say real food I mean it, or you and me are through. This steam-bucket is run by my firemen and by nobody else.' And when he met a fireman or a coal-drag occasionally on deck, he would halt him and ask: 'Fireman, how was the grub today? Enough to eat? Well, tonight you are to get an extra ration of bacon and eggs. By the way, does the boy bring you below regularly the iced tea I ordered for you? Just tell the truth. I cut his ears off if he doesn't do as he has been told to.' The natural result was that you could go a long way through trouble in the stokehold before you would hear the fireman or the drag yell a couple of sons of bitches or something to that effect. You could have invited the whole black gang to a Rotarians' luncheon, and the Rotarians would have thought that these boys had come straight from the reception given in honour of the ambassador of Wortisdansikan in Washington. Yes, sir. A worker only blares back when he is blared at. In his face you see the face of those who make him the way he is.

While the grate-bars were worked into the frame the steam was falling and falling. The second engineer, then on duty, crawled through the gangway and came into the stokehold. Or, to make it clearer, he stopped where he just could let us see his head. From there he said: 'Hell, what's the matter with the damn steam? The bucket will stop now any minute.'

At this moment the fireman happened to have in his hands the red-hot poker with which he was just about to lift the bars. When he saw the second peeping in, hearing him talk utter nonsense, blood shot into his sweat-covered eyes, and his mouth became frothy. He yelled some inarticulate row of sounds, straightened up, and then, with superhuman force, he ran the poker toward the second with the intention of running him through and pinning him against the boiler-wall. The engineer, having seen the move in time and the fireman, on account of the heavy weight of the poker, missed each other. The engineer fled, with all the speed he had, through the gangway back to the engine-hold. Since he was not so accustomed to this gangway as we were, he smashed his head several times against the iron bars.

342

The poker of the fireman went into that corner of the wall from which at that instant the engineer had disappeared. With so much power was the poker shot against the wall that a thick piece of that wall was broken off like so much pie. The fireman was not yet satisfied. He dropped the poker and ran after the engineer into the gangway. If he had caught him, not a pound of the engineer's body would have kept together. The second engineer, knowing that his life was forfeited if he failed to reach the door to the engine-hold, was by far quicker than I had ever expected him to be. He made the low door all right, though bleeding all over, and had just bolted the door behind him when the fireman bounced against it with a heavy bolt in his hand.

The second engineer did not report that attack. Perhaps he knew he would lose the case. As he, or anybody else on earth, would have lost the case against any member of the boiler gang of the *Yorikke* as long as one member of this gang was the only witness. What I would have done, any other of the gang would have done. If I had been asked to testify, I would have sworn, on any amount of Bibles, that the second engineer had come into the stokehold with a wrench in his hand to kill the fireman, because the steam had come down, and because the second was stink-full drunk. And why should I not testify against the trouble-maker? Right or wrong, my country. All right. Justified. Agreed. But then I am also entitled to say: Right or wrong, my fellow-worker; we work together, we suffer together, we laugh together, we die together. Now come on, who wants to blame me? My closest countryman is the one who burns his skin at the same furnace I do. After we have settled this relationship, then let's talk about nationality.

Next day the chief asked the second when and how he had received so many holes and bruises on his block. The second said that he had obtained them in the low gangway when making his get-away from the savages in the stokehold.

The chief, cleverer and with a better understanding of the worries of the blacks, did not report the case to the old man either. He ignored the case entirely, for he also knew it would be useless. For what could the skipper do? Lay us in irons? The *Yorikke* could not afford such a luxury. Every man was needed. In the trenches, when an attack is expected any minute, the soldier is at liberty to beat or to insult his officers as much as he likes. If you shoot him you may lose the trench. Here it was the same. If you laid a fireman in irons, the *Yorikke* in turn might never weather off a gale.

Said the chief in answer to the complaints of the second: 'Man, you are lucky. Don't ever try that again, if you want to live. When grate-bars have dropped, then don't go near the stokehold. Let the steam go down. They will bring it up all right as soon as they have a chance. But if you go in to bother them, or even to let them see your face, then I haven't to be a crystal-gazer to foretell your fate. You cannot get away if they catch you. They eat you up alive, they tear you to little pieces, and they put you into the furnace, and when the relief comes they throw you overboard with the slags. No one ever will know what has become of you. That's what you ought to blame, not the black gang, but the grates we have on this can. Try it once yourself. Ought to. And if I drop in and ask you why the steam is dropping, you will do exactly the same and throw me into the furnace without mercy. Better leave them alone. Well, I warned you. Keep out of their way when they are hard at it. That's all I can say.'

The second never again entered the stokehold when grate-bars were out. At times he would come in when the steam did not rise. He then just looked around without saying a single word. He would look at the steam-gauge, would hang around for a little while, offer the fireman and the drag each a cigarette, and then would say: 'A rotten cheap coal we have bunkered this time. There is no fireman on all the seven seas who is apt to keep up steam with stinking fuel like that.'

The fireman, of course, understood quite well what the second meant. He did his best to bring up the steam. He worked his whole body into rags to get the right pressure. Not alone the swell guys with money, but also working men, no matter how low they may seem, have got the true spirit for sport. They feel as proud of a job well done as the Harvard guys feel when they have won a football game. Only no one cheers up the black gang with Rah-Rahs when in a heavy sea, with all the dead-wind that can blow, they have to keep the steam up with a fuel which would not be good enough for Mother to cook a proper meal of corned beef and cabbage. Our quarter-backs in the stokehold of the *Yorikke* sure were filthy and dirty; but that does not mean that they were not quarter-backs as noble in spirit and as brave in work as any fine quarter-backs of Princeton. There would be no dukes if we all were princes.

No man could have a better college than the college represented by the *Yorikke*. Six months' shipping before the mast on the *Yorikke*, and you no longer had any idols left to worship. Help yourself and do not depend so much upon others, not even upon your union officials. Kick off the authorities who want to wisecrack at you and mould you to a uniform opinion of what is good for you. If you do not know yourself, nobody can tell you, no matter how much you pay to be a member of something.

Of all the schooling the *Yorikke* had to offer, there was nothing which could yield better results than fishing dropped grate-bars and setting them back into the grate-frame.

Each of the three boilers had three furnaces. Two of these furnaces were side by side, with a space of about two feet between them. The third furnace was squeezed in between these two, but above them. All three furnaces were actually located inside the boiler. The furnaces were not square, but cylindrical. The fuel rested upon a grate. This grate was a heavy iron frame along the length of which were lying nine bars which could be removed from the frame one by one. Each bar was about five feet long, about an inch and a half thick, and four inches wide. In front and at the back the frame had a rim upon which the bars rested. This rim was less than a half-inch deep. Hence the bars rested rather uncertainly. Neither in front nor at the back was there a higher rim against which the bars would have found a brace. It was only this three-eighths of an inch against which the bars could be fixed. Each bar weighed between eighty and a hundred pounds.

The grates were really simple affairs. Only the use of these grates made them such a horror. When the boilers and the grates had been new, which, as I figure, must have been about the time when the good old British Queen married, even then it must already have been quite a job to hold these bars in the frame, or to put them back after they had dropped. In the course of so many thousands of trips the *Yorikke* had accomplished to make money for her owners these rims had burned away.

The slightest disrespect of the fireman toward the grate when knocking off the slags was inevitably punished by a bar dropping into the ash-hole. As soon as this happened the fire had to be left alone, and the combined efforts of the fireman and his drag had to be exerted to set the bar back into its berth.

First thing to do was to fish the bar out of the ash-hole. This was done with the help of a pair of tongs which weighed about forty pounds. These tongs did not work the way the tongs a blacksmith uses work. They were, like all things on the *Yorikke*, the other way round. That is to say, if you pushed the handles together the mouth opened, and vice versa. It would have been too easy for us had it been otherwise.

The bar was red-hot, and the furnace was white-hot. One of us held the bar up with the tongs, the other steered the bar into the furnace and then steered it alongside of those bars still quietly resting in their berth, until the opposite end of the bar reached the rim at the back. There, with the help of the poker from beneath – that is, from the ash-hole – the bar was slowly and carefully moved into the rim at the back. Then we worked to get the bar into the front rim too. One push too much towards the back rim, or one very slight pull too much towards the front rim, and the bar said good-bye and dropped off again into the ash-hole. One of us lay flat on the ground to use the poker while the one that held the tongs tried once more to move, with tenderness, the bar back on to the rim. All this was done while the bar was red-hot, and while the open furnace roared into our faces, scorching face, hands, chest.

Now, of course, to set in one bar, hard and cruel as this job could be, was considered merely an interruption of the regular work. The real torture began when, on trying to set in one bar, other bars were stirred and pushed so that they also dropped, until five, six, or seven bars had dropped into one fire alone. If this happened – and it happened so often that we forgot how often – then the whole fire went out of commission, because all the fuel broke through into the ash-pit. The furnace had to stay open, for otherwise the bars could not be set in again. So after a while the whole boiler cooled off so much that the two remaining fires could not keep it working at even half its capacity. Consequently the boiler became practically worthless. The more time we had to spend at the bars, the less time we could afford for the two boilers which alone had to furnish the steam necessary to keep the engine running. No wonder these two boilers also began to slack and we had to leave the dropped bars for a long while and bring up the remaining boilers to a point where they were ready to explode any minute. As soon as we had them going far above their power, we again started to work at the dropped bars. Seldom did we get a bar in right at the first attempt. It dropped in again and again, often ten times, until we, finally, had them all in – to last only until they were ready to drop once more during the same hour or the next.

When, after long slaving, the bars were now in again, we had to build up the fires anew. Having accomplished this also, both of us dropped as if we were lifeless into a pile of coal or wherever there was any space free from embers and red-hot cinders. For ten minutes we could not stir a toe. Our hands, our arms, our faces were bleeding. Our skin was scorched; whole patches and strips had been torn off or burned off. We did not feel pain any more, we only felt exhausted beyond description.

Then a glimpse at the steam-gauge whipped us into action. The steam would not stay. The fires had to be stirred, broken up, and filled.

When bars were out I had to assist the fireman. One man alone could not put them back. While I helped the fireman with the bars I could not haul in coal. But whether I could carry in coal or not was of no concern to the fires. They ate and ate, and if they did not get enough to eat, the steam came down. So whatever huge piles had been in the stokehold just before the bars began to drop were all gone by now. To drag in the coal needed during one watch took all the hard work the coaler could give. There was hardly a free minute left to step up to the galley and bring below a drink of coffee or cold water to the fireman. The oftener bars dropped, the harder the drag had to work afterwards to pile up coal in the stokehold, which always, no matter what happened, had to be a certain load, of which not ten pounds could be cut off. Within four hours the fires of the *Yorikke* swallowed about sixteen hundred well-filled large shovelfuls of fuel. The fuel was in many instances so far away from the boilers that these sixteen hundred shovelfuls had to be thrown in four shifts before they reached the fireman, so that the real hauling for the drag was not sixteen hundred shovels, but sometimes close to seventy hundred shovels. Some of the bunkers were located close to the fo'c'sle, others close to the stern.

This work, unbelievable any place on earth outside of the *Yorikke*, had to be done by only one man, by the drag. It had to be done by the filthiest and dirtiest member of the crew, by one who had no mattress to sleep on, no pillow to rest his tired head upon, no blanket, no coffee-cup, no fork, no spoon. It had to be done by a man whom the company could not afford to feed properly on account of the competition with other companies. But the company had to stand competition, because it was very patriotic, and every company had to go the limit to keep a good record in shipping in favour of its country. The country had to be first in all things, exportation, importation, production, shipping, railroad mileage. All was done for the good and for the glory and for the greatness of the country. A company cannot take care of two things that are contrary each to the other. If the company wants to beat competition, the drag and fireman have to pay for it. Some way or other. Both the company and the crew cannot win. One has to be the loser in this battle, as in all other battles. Here on the *Yorikke* the biggest losers were Stanislav and I.

The *Yorikke* has taught me another big thing for which I am grateful. She taught me to see the soul in apparently lifeless objects. Before I shipped on the *Yorikke* I never thought that a thing like a burned match, or a scrap of paper in the mud, or a fallen leaf, or a rusty worthless nail might have a soul. The *Yorikke* taught me otherwise. Since then life for me has become a thousand times richer, even without a motor-car or a radio. No more can I ever feel alone. I feel I am a tiny part of the universe, always surrounded by other tiny parts of the universe; and if one is missing, the universe is not complete – in fact it does not exist.

The winch used for heaving ashes had personality, and it had to be treated accordingly. Everything and every part of the *Yorikke* had individuality and soul. The *Yorikke* as a whole had the greatest personality of all of us.

When once on a trip from Santander making for Lisbon we were caught in one of those terrible cross-gales in the Bay of Biscay, the *Yorikke* was thrown about so that we all thought she would never weather it out. When we – my fireman and I – came below to relieve the former watch, and I saw how the pile of fuel was thrown from port side to starboard unceasingly, I had only one thought: what will happen to us or the *Yorikke* if six bars should drop in one fire? If the steam in such a heavy sea is too low, the ship will easily get out of control, and it may be smashed against cliffs or helplessly driven ashore or upon sand-banks.

Any sailor who is not superstitious – which would be the rarest thing under heaven – would certainly become so after being on the *Yorikke* hardly a week. My fireman was no exception. So that night, when we came below, the fireman knocked his head three times against the boiler-wall, then spat out, and said: '*Yorikke* dear, please, don't drop any bar this night, please, just this night.' He said it almost like a prayer. Since the *Yorikke* was not something dead, but a ship with a soul, she understood what Spainy had said. You may believe it or not, but the truth is that for thirty hours, while the heavy weather lasted, not one single bar fell off. When we were near Lisbon and the sea had become fine again, the *Yorikke* joyfully dropped nine bars in our watch, four in fire number two, one in fire six, three in fire seven, and one in fire number nine, just to keep us from getting haughty. We did not mind the nine bars, hard as it always was to bring them in, and Spainy swore only fifteen times, while usually he never ceased to swear, nor did I, for a full hour after the bars were in.

My fireman was relieved at four. My watch did not end until six.

I went to call Stanislav at twenty to five. We had to clear ashes for an hour. I could not get him out of the bunk. He was like a stone. He had already been a good long time on the *Yorikke*. He had still not got used to it. People who do not know what hard work really means and do nothing but just figure out new laws against criminal syndicalism and against communist propaganda usually say, when they see a man at hard work: 'Oh, these guys are used to it, they don't feel it at all. They have no refined thinking-capacity, as we have. The chain-gang means nothing to them; it's just like a vacation.'

They use that speech as a dope to calm their consciences, which, underneath, hurt them when they see human beings treated worse than mules. But there is no such thing in the world as getting used to pain and suffering. With that 'Oh, they are used to that!' people justify even the beating of defenceless prisoners. Better kill them; it is truly more merciful. Stanislav, a very robust fellow, never got used to the dropped bars or to all the rest of the hard work on the *Yorikke*. I never became used to it. And I do not know of anybody that ever became accustomed to it. Whenever a fireman with fairly good papers, or on reaching his country, had a chance he skipped off; if he could do no better he skipped without waiting for his pay. There is no getting used to pain and suffering. You become only hard-boiled, and you lose a certain capacity to be impressed by feelings. Yet no human being will ever become used to sufferings to such an extent that his heart will cease to cry out that eternal prayer of all human beings: 'I hope that my liberator comes!' He is the master of the world, he who can make his coins out of the hope of slaves.

'You don't mean? Is it five already?' asked Stanislav. 'I just lay down. It cannot be five.' He was still as dirty as when he had left the fire-hold. He had no ambition now to wash up. He was too tired.

'I tell you, Stanislav,' I said, 'I cannot stand it. We had six bars out in one fire, and two in another. I cannot come at eleven to help you clear the ashes and then start dragging again at twelve. I am going over the railing, I tell you.'

Stanislav was sitting on his bunk. His face black. In the thick kerosene smoke of the quarter I could not distinguish his face well. He turned his head to me and he said with a swollen sleepy voice: 'Nope, don't you do it, Pippip. Don't leave me. I cannot do your watch also. I will have to make the railing also. No. Hell, I won't. I would rather bury two cans of plum marmalade in the furnaces and let the whole thing go to blazes, so that they could no longer catch lost souls to get their insurance with. I still feel something in my breast here for the poor guys who might come after us. Geecries, that game with the plum marmalade might be a pretty come-off. I have to think it over some time.'

Plum marmalade? Poor Stanislav, he was still dreaming. So I thought.

10

My watch ended at six in the morning with an hour's work clearing ashes with Stanislav. I could not leave any reserve fuel for him. The shovel dropped out of my hands. 'It's okay, Pippip, don't mind. We'll get even some day when I am down.'

I did not miss mattress, pillow, blanket, soap. I understood now why such things were not supplied on the *Yorikke*. They really were not needed. Covered with soot, dirt, oil, grease, as I was, I fell into my bunk. What meaning inborn cleanliness? All culture and civilization depend on leisure. My pants were torn, burned, and stiff from oily water and soot. My shoes and my shirt looked no better. Now, when we put in the next port and I stand at the railing and look down upon the pier, side by side with my fellow sailors, I shall not look any longer different from those who I thought were the worst of pirates when first I saw them. I, like the rest, was now clothed in striped garments, in prison clothes, in death-sheets, in which I no longer could escape without falling into the hands of the guards of the world of bureaucrats, who would pinch me and bring me back to where I now properly belonged. I had become part of the *Yorikke*. Where she was, I had to be; where she went, I had to go. There was no longer any escape to the living.

Somebody yelled into my ear: 'Breakfast ready.' Not even an ambassador's breakfast would get me up and out of my bunk. What was food to me? A saying goes: 'I am so tired I can hardly move a finger.' He who can say that does not know what it means to be tired. I could not even move an eyelid. My eyelids did not close fully. So tired they were. The daylight could not make my eyelids

350

close. No power was left within me even to desire that the daylight go away and give my eyes a rest.

And at that very instant when I had the feeling: 'Why worry about daylight?' the huge iron mouth of a gigantic crane gripped me, then tossed me violently up into the air, high up, where I hung for a second. The man who tended the crane had a quarrel with something or somebody; and, being a bit careless, the brake slipped off his hand and down I fell from a height of five thousand feet, and I dropped squashing upon a pier. A mob gathered around me and cried: 'Get up, you, come, come, snap out of it, twenty to eleven, heave ashes.'

After I had heaved ashes with Stanislav, there were just about ten minutes left. I had to hurry to the galley to carry dinner for the black gang to the fo'c'sle. I swallowed a few prunes swimming in the watery starch. I could not eat one bite more. The jaws would not work. Somebody bellowed: 'Hey, drag, where is my dinner? Hop at it.' It was the donkey-man, who had to be served separately in his own quarter. For the drags were the stewards of the donkey-man, who was their petty officer. He could have done all this alone, because he had practically no work to do. Yet he would have lost his dignity if he had to go to the galley and get his dinner himself. Hardly had I set the dishes on his table when the bell rang and the watch on the bridge sang out the watch-relief. I went below to help the fireman break up the fires and haul in the fuel from the bunkers.

At six in the evening I was relieved. Supper was on the table in the quarters. It had come in at five. It was now cold and everything edible had been picked by the other hungry men. I did not care to see what was left. I was too tired to eat anyway. I did not wash myself. Not for all civilizations present and gone did I care to have a clean face. I fell into my bunk like a log.

That lasted three days and three nights. No other thought entered my mind and my feelings but: 'Eleven to six, eleven to six, eleven to six.' The whole universe, all religions, all creeds, and my entire consciousness became concentrated in this idea: eleven to six. I had vanished from existence. Two painful yells cut into what had once been my flesh, my brain, my soul, my heart. These yells caused a piercing pain, as the feeling might be when the bared brain is tickled with a needle. The yells came, apparently, always from far away, falling up me like avalanches of rocks and timber, thundering into my shattered body like the onrush of a hundred express trains gone wild. 'Up, twenty to eleven!' was one of the yells. And the other: 'Holy sons of fallen saints, three bars have dropped! Turn to it.'

When four days and four nights had passed, I felt hungry. I ate heartily. Now I was initiated and a true member of the *Yorikke*. And I began to get accustomed to it. I had lost the last tiny little connection which up to this hour had bound me to the living. I had become so dead that no feeling in mind, soul or body was left. There were times when I felt that my hands were steam-shovels, that my legs and arms moved on ball-bearings, and that all the insides of my body were but running wheels.

'It is not so bad after all, Stanislav,' I said ironically to him when I came below to relieve his watch. 'The hash tastes all right. The grandfather is not so bad a cook. If, the hell of it, we could get only more milk. I say, brother, the pile of coal you are leaving me here in reserve isn't very much to brag about. We stoke it off in three fires without even saying so much as pem-pem. Listen, how do you think I can loosen the chief from a good shot of rum? Haven't you got a good tip?'

'Nothing easier than that, Pippip. You are looking sour enough. You will make it. Go right up and tell him your stomach won't hold, you spill it all at the fuel, and if you won't get a stomach-cleaner you cannot stand the watch through. Tell him you are spilling all green. You will get a good full-sized swinger from him. You can ride this same horse twice a week. Only make sure not to come too often. Then he gets wise and he may fill your glass with castor. Being used to good clean drainings, you won't notice it until you have shot it all in. Then it is too late. You cannot spit it into his cabin. You have to finish up and get it all down. It won't do you any good if, after having sipped the castor, you drop six or eight bars in your watch. Believe me, it sure would not be a sweet watch. Keep that prescription for yourself. If you spill it, it will be ineffective. The firemen have got one of their own invention. They don't give it away, those sinners. They often make as many as four, even five shots a week. But they don't know genuine comradeship, those knights in shining armour.'

The time came, though slowly, when I began to get my own ideas again, and this was when the two piercing yells ceased to have any corrupt effect upon me. No longer did I stagger about the bucket in a dazed and unconscious state. I began to see and to understand. Rebirth had taken place. I could now, without the slightest feeling of remorse, bark at the second that I would allow him to throw me overboard for bragging if I would not smash his head with a hammer and drill his back with the poker if he ever came into the stokehold again when we were on high sea, and bars were out, and the steam was falling to a hundred twenty. I swore to his face that this time he would not get away through the gangway safely like he did the other night. He could not have done it anyhow. Maybe he knew it. We had placed in the gangway a heavy poker, hung up in such manner that when, from a certain spot in the stokehold, one of us pulled a string, the poker fell down, making impossible the get-away of anybody in that gangway. Whether he, once trapped, got off with his life or only with a bleeding head and shins depended in the last decision not on what he had said to us but only on how many bars had dropped into the various ash-pits.

There were no regulations and rules for the firehold. Articles, of course, were signed when signing on, but the articles were never read to anybody as is required by law. Yet we had proof that people can live without laws and do well. The fire gang had built up among themselves rules which were never mentioned, but, nevertheless, kept religiously. No one was there to command, no one to obey. It was done to keep the engine, and so the ship, going, and at the same time give each member of the fire gang exactly the same amount of work and worry. Since there were nine fires to serve, each fireman left to his relief three fires elegantly cleaned of all slags and cinders. The first watch cleaned fires number one, four, and seven; second watch fires number two, five, eight; third watch fires number three, six, nine. The relief could depend on these fires being left clean by the former watch. Therefore no matter how much trouble the new watch had with their bars, they were sure to have at least three fires going at full blast. The relief, furthermore, found a certain amount of fuel ready in front of the fires. The former watch did not leave the stokehold until the ash-pits were drawn clear. Without this unwritten agreement in the black gang, work would have been nearly impossible.

Another important agreement was that the outgoing watch did not leave one single bar dropped. All bars were in when the watch was relieved. Sometimes a watch worked half an hour into the new watch just to bring in the bars which had fallen out ten minutes before the relief came.

Now let us have a heavy sea with all the trimmings. Such as we had once when sailing along the Gold Coast of western Africa.

The pleasure began with the heaving ashes. I released the heavy ash-can from the hooks, and, hot as the can was, I carried it against my chest across the gangway toward the railing. Long before I reached the railing, the *Yorikke* swung out on a swell roller, and I with my hot can rolled some thirty feet toward the bow. I had not yet got up on my feet when the *Yorikke* fell to the stern, and I, still with my can, had, of course, to follow the command of the *Yorikke*. After two of these rollers there was nothing left in the can, and the first mate cried from the bridge: 'Hey, drag, if you want to go overboard it's all right with me. But you'd better leave the ash-can with us, you really won't need it when you go fishing.'

In such a heavy sea it is considered a good job if you can get half of the ashes over the rail. The other half is strewn over all the decks. And since they are ashes, it is the job of the drags to clear the decks of this useless cargo.

Below, in the firehold, things are just as interesting as they are up on deck. The fireman is about to swing a beautiful shovelful into the furnace when the roller meets him square. He is thrown, and the whole shovelful of coal goes splashing right into the face of the drag. When the roller comes over from astern, the fireman, with his shovel, disappears into a pile of coal, out of which he emerges again when the *Yorikke* falls off from a fore.

Jolly dances take place in the bunkers. I have a huge pile of fuel, one hundred and fifty shovels, right near the hatchway to the firehold when a breaker throws the *Yorikke* over to port and the pile of coal goes the same way, back to where I had just taken it from. So this swell job has to be repeated. After a while one learns to time the rollers, and as soon as a certain amount of fuel is near the chute, one shovels it down into the stokehold so quickly that, before the bucket falls off to the other side, nothing is left that can go with her. A coal-drag has to know how to time the rollers correctly in heavy weather. He must therefore understand the principles of navigation just as well as the skipper does. If he could not time the moves of a ship, he might never get a single shovelful of coal in front of the boilers. But by the time a good coal-drag is through with his studies in navigation, he comes from his watch in a heavy sea brown and blue all over, with bruises and with bleeding knuckles and shins. What a merry adventurous life a sailor has! Just read the sea-stories. They can tell you all about it.

A merry life. Hundreds of *Yorikkes*, hundreds of death ships are sailing the seven seas. All nations have their death ships. Proud companies with fine names and beautiful flags are not ashamed to sail death ships. There have never been so many of them as since the war for liberty and democracy that gave the world passports and immigration restrictions, and that manufactured men without nationalities and without papers by the ten thousand.

A good capitalist system does not know waste. This system cannot allow these tens of thousands of men without papers to roam about the world. Why are insurance premiums paid? For pleasure? Everything must produce its profit. Why not make premiums produce profit?

Why passports? Why immigration restriction? Why not let human beings go where they wish to go, North Pole or South Pole, Russia or Turkey, the States or Bolivia? Human beings must be kept under control. They cannot fly like insects about the world into which they were born without being asked. Human beings must be brought under control, under passports, under finger-print registrations. For what reason? Only to show the omnipotence of the state, and of the holy servant of the state, the bureaucrat. Bureaucracy has come to stay. It has become the great and almighty ruler of the world. It has come to stay to whip human beings into discipline and make them numbers within the state. With foot-printings of babies it has begun; the next stage will be the branding of registration numbers upon the back, properly filed, so that no mistake can be made as to the true nationality of the insect. A wall has made China what she is today. The walls all nations have built up since the war for democracy will have the same effect. Expanding markets and making large profits are a religion. It is the oldest religion perhaps, for it has the best-trained priests, and it has the most beautiful churches; yes, sir.

11

Overworked and overtired men do not care what goes on about them. There may be corruption, robbery, banditry, gangsterism, piracy, all at wholesale, right in their neighbourhood. What do they care? They are the best people to govern. They never criticize, they never argue, they do not read papers, and they feel sure that everything in the world is just fine and could not be any better.

They are satisfied and they hail the ruler if sometimes they get an extra ration of pudding or rum. They only sleep, and sleep, and sleep. Nothing else interests them. That was the reason why I had been a good long time on the *Yorikke* before I got even a dim idea what the *Yorikke* was really doing and how she was doing what she did.

I was standing against the rail, rather sleepy. There were near us quite a number of feluccas, with their strange sails. They were around us as if they were about to attack us. This aroused my attention. They came and went, returned and sailed off again. Perhaps they were fishermen or smugglers. Great crowds of them often came in certain ports. There was a crowd that day when I looked at them with more interest than usual.

Suddenly I was wide awake. I could not understand at the moment what it was that had made me so. It had been like a shock. Fixing my mind upon this strange feeling, I noticed a great quietness. The engine had ceased to work. Day and night there is the noise of the engine; its stamping, rocking, and shaking make the whole ship quiver. It makes the ship a live thing. This noise creeps into your flesh and brain. The whole body falls into the same rhythm. One speaks, eats, hears, sees, sleeps, awakes, thinks, feels, and lives in this rhythm. And then quite unexpectedly the engine stops. One feels a real pain in body and mind. One feels empty, as if dropped in an elevator down the shaft at a giddy speed. You feel the earth sinking away beneath you; and on a ship you have the stark sensation that the bottom of the ship has broken off, and the whole affair, with you inside, is going right through to the opposite end of the globe. It was this sudden silence of the engine that was the cause of my awakening.

The *Yorikke* drifted swanlike upon a smooth, peaceful, glittering sea. The chains were rattling, and the anchor dropped with a splash into the water.

At this very moment Stanislav passed by, the coffee-can in his hand.

'Pippip,' he whispered to me, 'now we have to step on the gas. God damn it, below we have to raise the steam up to a hundred ninety-five.'

'Are you mad, Lavski?' I said. 'Why, we would fly up straight to Sirius without a single stop-over if you raise the steam to a hundred eighty-five. At a hundred seventy we are already twisting our bowels.'

'Precisely, that's the reason why I try to be up on deck as often as

356

I get a chance,' Stanislav grinned. 'Here, when the bucket goes up, you may have a chance to fly off and save your hide by getting a good swim. Below you are finished, there is no getting out. Trapped in for good until the police of the Last Judgement snatch you out of it. You see, Pippip, you have to be smart to go round the world in slippers. I mean, when I peeped so many feluccas hanging about us, then I knew the skipper is going to cash in. So below I worked like the devil to pile up a good heap of reserve fuel and so get my chance to be on deck as much as I can. I told my fireman I had got the colic, and that's why I had to beat it every four minutes. Next time you are in this mess you will have to find some other excuse. Or he gets wise to what is going on, and he won't stay below alone.'

'Now, spring it, damn, what is the trouble?' I asked.

'Don't make me sick with your innocence. The skipper is collecting the dividends. I have never in all my life seen such a silly fool like you. What do you think you are sailing? A mail-boat under the flag of lime-juicers? Your head is dumber than the clogs on my feet.'

'I know well enough that I am shipping on a death bus,' I said, defending my intelligence.

'At least something you have got clear,' Stanislav answered. 'But don't you ever believe that they are running down to ground port a bucket without music. Don't you misjudge them. The funeral of the *Yorikke* is well advertised and registered. The death ticket is all written up; they have only to fill in the exact date. You see, any man playing on his last string, and knowing it, may do as he pleases. Because it cannot come worse. The *Yorikke* may risk whatever she wants to. If taken in by a French chaser, before she reaches port of investigation, she sinks off, plugs out. The insurance is safe. No evidence found. Just send up a glance to the topmast head. What do you see? Yep, siree. The bos'n with the skipper's prisma-squeezer overhauling the horizon. Suppose he finds the air getting thick. Then, O boy of my dreams, then you will see the *Yorikke* hobbling off. Tell ye, you will be surprised to see how this old maid can raise a fuss when forced to and when willing to help her master across the lazy river. For the first fifteen minutes with that steam-pressure pepped up she makes twenty-two knots, and I bet you my black girl in Tunis free of charge that she makes even twenty-five when whipped into it. French chasers afraid to take such a risk with safety-valves under screws cannot come up with this old dame. Not during the first fifteen minutes. Of course, after fifteen minutes the old jane puffs and pants through all pissports and buttonholes, and as long as twenty-four hours you think she is going to fall apart at all her seams. For weeks afterwards she has got the acute asthma. But she made it. She wasn't pinched. And that's the only important thing, not to get pinched. Well, Innocent, I have hop below, or my fireman'll smell a deceased monkey.'

When caught in heavy weather we carried a hundred fifty-five pounds steam, while the ordinary pressure was a hundred and thirty. A hundred and sixty pounds meant *Attention*; a hundred sixty-five *Warning*; at a hundred seventy-five there was the thick red line *Danger* which meant: one pound more and the boilers will most likely go straight up to heaven, taking the *Yorikke* with them. Such a hasty leave from her earthly existence, though, was prevented by the proper functioning of the safety-valve, which opened automatically when the steam had reached that high pressure, and by doing so relieved the boilers of their dangerous fevers. At the same time when the safety-valve opened, the steam blew the warning whistle, and so the boilers howled out their mistreatment to the whole world. Then the ship would get in an uproar from the skipper to the last deck-hand, and the ship would become like a stirred-up beehive.

Now, of course, everything was different. The skipper wanted to make his collections. Therefore he had given orders to the donkey to prevent the *Yorikke* from crying by screwing tight her tear-ducts, so making it impossible for her to open her safety-valves when the steam-pressure threatened her life.

The feluccas swarmed closer. Two approached the *Yorikke* and made fast alongside. The gangway was lowered away.

The feluccas had fishermen of the Moroccan type aboard. These men climbed up the *Yorikke* like cats, swift and oily. On deck they moved about as freely and lightly as if the whole ship was theirs.

Three Moroccans, intelligent and distinguished-looking gentlemen, though garbed like ordinary fishermen, after very ceremonial salutations towards the second mate, were led by him to skipper's cabin. Then the second mate came out again and directed the unloading. The first mate was on the bridge. Every once in a while he would look up at the topmast head and cry: 'Orl korrect, bos'n? No nasty weather in sight?'

'All shipshape, aye, aye, sir!' answered the bos'n from the look-out.

Boxes and crates appeared from the holds like magic, and like magic they disappeared into the feluccas. Ants could not work better. No sooner was one felucca loaded and the cargo well covered with fish, than it pushed away from the ship and sailed lustily off. The second it was off, another one came alongside to take in cargo. Before you would have thought it fastened, it was already loaded and off on its way. Each sailed off in a different direction. Some even went seemingly towards parts where land could not be found. It would have been almost impossible for any chaser to catch more than three, at best, so widely did they stray.

The second mate had a pencil and pad. He counted the boxes. One of the Moroccans who had an air as if he were the supercargo of the outfit repeated the numbers the second mate sang out. All the numbers were called in English.

When the last felucca was loaded, the first were out of sight. They had sunk beneath the horizon or had been veiled by curtains of mist. The others had become tiny bits of white paper floating upon the calm sea.

One felucca which all the time had hovered about now came close and made fast. This one took no load on. It carried only the usual cargo of fresh fish.

The three Moroccan gentlemen who had been with the skipper came out on deck, accompanied by the old man. They all laughed and talked merrily. Then, with their beautiful courteous gestures, they took leave of the skipper and climbed down the gangway. They boarded their felucca, put the sail into the wind, and the gangway was taken in. The anchor chains began to clank, and soon the *Yorikke* was running wild as if chased by the hells of all religions.

The skipper had gone to his cabin. After about fifteen minutes the skipper came out and cried up to the bridge: 'Where is she?'

'Six off the coast, sir,' the first mate answered.

'Then we are out of the limit, mate?'

'Aye, aye, sir.'

'Give the course to the A.B. and come below to my cabin; let's have breakfast,' the skipper said, smiling.

Thus the finale of this strange comedy.

The skipper, however, was no miser. Eat and let eat, he thought. We all had the so-called after-weather dinner: fried sausages, bacon, cocoa, French potatoes; and each got his coffee-cup filled with rum. Besides this everyone received ten pesetas in cash paid out the same day at five o'clock.

No one had to tell us. We knew the after-weather dinner, the extra rum, and the cash were mum-pay – that is, offered us to keep our swear-hatches shut up. The skipper's and the mate's breakfast sure was rich. The richest part of which, naturally, was not to eat; it was to be put into a pocket-book and not into a belly.

We had no complaints whatever. With that skipper we would have sailed straight to hell if he had wished us to. No thumb-screw would ever squeeze out of us what we had seen.

Yes, of course, we had seen something. One engine, on account of being overheated, had become defective, and the ship had come to a stop, until the damage had been repaired. While we stood by for repairs, several feluccas had come alongside, offering us for sale fruit, fresh fish, and vegetables. The cook bought fish and vegetables, and the officers had bought bananas, pineapples, and oranges.

Swear to that? Of course, quite simply, because it is the truth and nothing but, so help me, lordy. Yes, sir.

You don't suppose a decent sailor gives his skipper away, do you? No, sir, certainly not. If pirates have got their honour, how much more so do decent sailors have theirs, if the skipper treats them like decent sailors.

12

Any man who is not overworked and not overtired begins to worry about things which ought to be of no concern to him. Right away he has ideas and an imagination which, when nursed and pepped up, might easily start to nibble at the very foundations of the state and of its sacred institutions and constitutions. Therefore a very good piece of advice to a sailor who wishes to stay an honest sailor runs thus: 'Remain where you are, at your wheel, and at your paint; do not think about how the world is run; then you will always be a good sailor, beloved by everyone. Trouble-makers are hated everywhere.'

The chief ordered open a coal-bunker which was right at the back of the firehold. More, the *Yorikke* coaled in the next port, and we had all the fuel so close at hand that we almost fell over it when at work before the boilers. This rare pleasure lasted three days and three nights. There were watches beautiful as holidays with money. Hardly any work at all. Just heaving ashes, and occasionally one bar to be set in.

While we were coaling through lighters, a mile and a half or so out of port, I noticed that, besides coal, other cargo was taken in. It must have been somewhere off the coast of Portugal, for the men bringing on the cargo spoke Portuguese. The loading was not so much different from the unloading that had taken place some time before.

Two men, clothed like simple fishermen, but who otherwise did not look like it, came aboard from one of the lighters. They went to the skipper's cabin. While they were talking things over with the old man, boxes were unloaded from the lighters. The boxes had been hidden under the coal. Smaller boats came alongside the *Yorikke*, and, taken out from under loads of fish and vegetables, more cargo was heaved in. Cargo in boxes, in barrels, in crates, in bales. It was loaded from starboard, while the port side was towards the coast. Therefore from the harbour nobody could have seen what was going on at the opposite side of the *Yorikke*.

As soon as all the coaling was done, the two gentlemen left the ship. The gangway was still lowered and the two gentlemen were barely in their boat when the anchor came up and the *Yorikke* went under full steam.

This time no after-weather dinner was served. We had only cocoa and raisin cake. Because there was nothing yet to swear about and tell the truth and nothing but.

Said Stanislav: 'And why should you have to swear, anyway? Suppose somebody comes aboard and starts looking around. Let him open the hatchway. What is he to find? Boxes and crates and barrels. Naturally, you cannot deny that. You cannot swear that there are no boxes aboard when the reeker has got his hands upon them. Only the skipper will have to swear what is inside and what he means to do with the contents. None of your business, Pippip. Never worry about the old man, he sure will know all right what he is going to swear about, bet your life and my black girl free of charge.'

Did we have elegant watches then? I should say we had. The ash-cans heaved and dumped off, the fires stirred, the slags broken off, and then you went just to the bunkers at the back, opened the gate, and the stokehold was filled with fuel. No dragging, no hauling, no shovelling, no pushing the wheelbarrow and knocking off your knuckles.

During one of these blissful watches I started to examine the holds so as to see if there was some loot loose. Sometimes there is genuine money in that game if you have a soft hand. Oranges, nuts, tobacco leaves, and lots of other things which any decent tavern-keeper likes to take for cash. At times one has to open a few boxes to see if there are shirts, or silk hose, or shoes, or soap. Man has to live. Morals are taught and preached not for the sake of heaven, but to assist those people on earth who have everything they need and more to retain their possessions and to help them to accumulate still more. Morals is the butter for those who have no bread.

The important thing is to close the boxes well after you have looked into them. It is not wise to put on the shirt and the shoes right after you have found them. You might make a bad impression on somebody, and you might even lead innocent youngsters to follow in your footsteps, which is a real sin. The best thing is not to use anything you should find for yourself, but to sell it honestly when you're in the next port. Any fine citizen will buy from you, because everybody knows the sailor always sells cheap, for he is not greedy for a big profit. He has no taxes to pay, no store rent, no light and telephone bills to bother about, so he can sell well below factory prices. If you need something good and really cheap, always try a sailor first. After this has failed, you may still go to the Jew.

Of course, it is not so that a sailor has no expenses at all. It is not always easy to go through the boxes and bales. One has to be a sort of snake. I had learned the snake-dances and I kept in good shape because I trained several times every day. If you made just one wrong step in your daily snake-dances, you felt it right away in the scorches and burns on your skin. What better training can anybody have? Going about the holds and looking intelligently for the most saleable goods has some difficulties too. It is not at all easy to make money, no matter where you try it and how. Here a box falls upon you, there a barrel comes down and squeezes you in and peels off your hide a strip of useful leather. There is no light in the holds at night. You may, if you are very careful, light a match for a moment. But suppose the mate on the bridge sees the flicker, it would not be so good for you. Better leave the matches altogether and rely upon your soft hands and your true feelings.

The *Yorikke* carried rarely goods of real importance. Highly valued merchandise was not trusted to her. These frequent loadings and unloadings, though, did not let me sleep. I knew the Moroccans and the Riffs. Furthermore, I had examined the lifeboats, and I had found that only one boat was in a seaworthy condition. It was the boat the skipper was supposed to man, with the chief, the carpenter, and two A.B.s. All the other boats were hopeless decorations. Since the skipper's boat was still dry and without water and provisions changed, I was convinced that the *Yorikke* had something in the hold too expensive yet to touch ground.

One quiet night I went exploring again, and I came upon little barrels which, as I could see by the light of a match, were labelled thus: *Garantiert reines unverfalschtes Schwabisches Pflaumenmus. Keine Kriegsware. Garantiert reine Früchte und Bester Zucker. Kein künstlicher Farbstoff verwendet. Erste und alteste Schwabische Pflaumenmusfabrik Oberndorf am Neckar.* Which when explained in a human language would mean: Guaranteed Genuine Plum Marmalade. No War Substitute. Pure Fruit and Sugar. No Artificial Dyes. First and Oldest Plum Sauce Packing Plant Oberndorf on the Neckar.

Now, what sort of boneheads are we? was my first thought. There we are pushing down with our bread some ordinary laundry soap which somebody calls margarine, while here the holds are overflowing with the finest and purest marmalade the German people can produce for the customers abroad. 'My, my, Stanislav, I always had figured you a smart guy with a lot of good intelligence; but now I see I was mistaken; you are the biggest ass I have ever known.'

What a feast this will be in the morning – to smear this wonderful marmalade thick and soft on the warm bread! The Moroccans sure knew what was good for them. They preferred pure and guaranteed German marmalade to their dates and figs – of which they surely sometimes became as sick as we back home were of cabbage and potatoes.

I heaved two of these small barrels and took them to the upper coal-bunker, where I could use the lamp without any suspicion from the bridge. No one could enter this bunker without my permission. Because a plank led from the bunker to the hatchway of the stokehold. None of the engineers ever ventured across this plank, for one roller of the ship or one false step would have thrown them twenty feet below. It took nerve to use this plank as a gangway when the ship was under weigh. What was more, the plank was not very strong, nor was it new; it might break any moment. When Stanislav or I crossed this plank, we did it flying. To be absolutely safe from any intruders, anyway, I drew the plank back into the bunker. I was now ready to get the barrel open and go at the marmalade.

The barrel was open. I must state that I felt a shock, because I was astonished really to find plum marmalade in the barrel. To tell the truth, I had expected something different; I had thought that the label was misleading as to the contents. But sure as daylight at noon, there was plum marmalade inside the barrel. One should not do such a nasty thing as be suspicious all the time of good old *Yorikke*. Why, she is as honest and decent a tub as any other – as any other – as any – now, wait a minute. What is that? The marmalade tastes like – Let me get this straight, hell. It tastes like – well, I should say it tastes rather good. Good? I don't know for sure. Now, I'll be damned, there is a taste of green copper in that marmalade. Haven't they put pennies in the sauce? Sure, they must have. Like Mother did back home when she was cooking preserves for the long winter; when she wanted to keep the string beans in good colour, she put in a penny. Old Norse custom I guess, invented by the good old Vikings who put into their preserves old copper nails left over from building boats. And here the label lies: No artificial dyes. I will try it again. Perhaps it is only imagination, while thinking of Mother's string beans. No, no getting away from the taste. It really tastes like brass, really all verdigris. I can't eat that on bread. Impossible. Rather prefer the laundry soap. I cannot get rid of this taste once it's on the tongue. It sticks against the gums.

The Moroccans must like this taste. They have got strange tastes anyway in lots of their eats, I know. Or maybe only the upper layer has got this brass taste. All right, boy, let's go deeper with your finger into the sauce. Hello, good morning, now, what of all the fallen angels is that? These Germans or Swabes were in a hurry when cooking this marmalade. They sure have left all the stones inside. It was too much trouble for them to stone the plums. I wonder what kind of people these Germans are, eating the marmalade with all the stones in. There sure are still some savages left among them in the Black Forest and in Swabia. Let's have a look at these stones. Funny shape. Let's take one and look closer at it. Oh, well, of course, that's why the strange taste. The stones are made of lead, covered with nickel lining, and put into an elegant little brass bottle. And inside the little brass bottle? Now, let's get this straight. Yes, that must be the pure sugar. Swabian sugar. Fine

364

little black glittering leaves. Pretty sugar they have in Oberndorf on the Neckar. That must be the plum stones and the pure sugar the Moroccans and the Riffs like; for which they sell all their dates and figs and horses. Swabian plum marmalade. The Moroccans like this taste.

Yorikke, you have won back my respect. I was seriously afraid you had cheated me. It would have broken my heart. I don't like women that cheat. If you want to go astray, all right, go ahead, but don't be lousy and cheat with dirt. And just to see how loyal good old *Yorikke* really was, I crawled back into the holds to look at other barrels and boxes. Label: Mousetraps. What do Moroccans care about a couple of mice, having all the harems full of them? And, sure enough, there were, in those boxes, as many real mousetraps as there was real plum marmalade in the barrels. But when I looked for the stones left in the marmalade, I found no mouse, but Mausers, named after the great man who invented them.

I found other boxes. Label: Toy Automobiles with Mechanism for Self-Running. When I saw where these toy automobiles were made, which was Suhl in Thuringia, I did not open them. Suhl in Thuringia is known as a town in which all the inhabitants live by making hunting guns and ammunition. I could have saved myself the trouble of opening the barrels of plum sauce had I known, what I learned a few years later, that in Oberndorf on the Neckar is not a single marmalade plant, but one of the greatest rifle and munition factories in Germany. To know something about geography is always a good thing, because then labels won't catch you so dumb. On a label you may print anything you like, the label does not object. On the other hand, it is rather unlikely that a well-established munition and arms factory will be converted overnight into a plum-marmalade packing plant. Therefore, if some grocer wants to sell you canned pork and beans made in Chic, better be careful, you might find anything inside, even Scotch or an automatic. Nothing strange about that. Who ever saw in Chic somebody raising pigs or beans?

It was not alone Germany that was well represented in the holds. Stepmother England also was there, partly with Sheffield, partly with Manchester. Belgium, not minding her neutrality in the boxing match between the Moroccans and the French government, had contributed sugar-coated fruits. The English merchandise was labelled: Tinned Sheet Iron, Galvanized Corrugated Iron, Frying-pans. On seeing the sugar-coated fruits of Belgium, shipped from Liège, you became sure that those fruits were so indigestible that if you were to swallow only one you would never need any castor oil until all graves open again and the real name of the Unknown Soldier is headlined in the New York papers.

The Moroccans are quite right. They have my sympathy. Spain to the Spaniards, France to the French, China to the Chinese, Poland to the Poles. What did Wilson chase the American boys into the European war for? Wasn't it for the simple reason that the Czechs should have the right to call their sausages in Czech instead of in the uncivilized Austrian lingo? We don't want any Chinese in our God's country, or other furreners either, to help us eat up our surplus wheat. Let them stay at home, where they belong. So I don't see any reason why I should get sore at the Moroccans. And, just for Wilson, as a good Yank I have to ship on the *Yorikke* and get things cleared up for democracy and for the liberty of small nations.

I feel as though I am going to fall in love with that hussy *Yorikke*.

13

'I say, Stanislav, haven't you got any pride left? I simply cannot understand how you can swallow all the time that marge. Ain't you ashamed a bit?'

'What else could I do, Pippip?' Stanislav said. 'Above all things I am sure hungry. You don't suppose I should boil my rags and thicken the juice that comes out to have something on the bread, do you? I have nothing on the bread save that stinking margarine. You just get cracked up eating all the time that stale bread without something on it. I feel like concrete in my stomach sometimes.'

'Now, aren't you just as dumb as I imagined? Man, don't you know that we are shipping right now the finest German plum marmalade?'

'Yep, I know.'

'If you know, why don't you loot a barrel or two?'

'That marmalade is no good for us.'

366

'Why not?' I asked innocently.

'Good only for the Moroccans and the Syrians, and, of course, for those who make it and those who sell it. The Frenchmen get all the time belly cramps whenever they eat it. Or let's say when it is fired into them. Then they run so fast that they can catch up with their grandfather and overtake him at his funeral.'

This answer made me wonder. 'Then you know what is inside?'

'What sort of an ass do you believe me?' He laughed. 'The two gentlemen of Portugal were still in the skipper's cabin when I was already through with my exploration. It would not be me, an old honest sailor, if seeing labels of Danish butter, or sardines, or corned beef, or chocolate, I didn't right away investigate the possibilities of a bargain sale at the next port.'

'This time you are mistaken,' I said; 'there is really marmalade inside.'

'There is always something inside. But this marmalade you cannot eat. Has got a horrible brass taste and a smell after black sulphur sugar. If you eat too much you may get belly poisoning. You may get green all over the face like the statue of a general. Last trip, before you were on, we had corned beef. It was genuine. Nothing inside. The finest stuff you can think of. Sometimes you are lucky. The skipper had to ship honest goods for a trip or two. He was sure he'd be brought up by French chasers. See? It was a thick layer. Going to Damascus. The Syrians were in dire need. They had some misunderstanding with the French governor as to the people they wished to trade with.'

'How were the stones beneath the thick layer?'

'The stones? You mean what was the true inside of the corned beef? Well, as I said, the layer was fine. For days I did not have to touch the galley vomit. Of course, if you went sufficiently deep into the corned beef you found excellent carbines. Made in U.S.A. Late model, had come out during the last weeks of the war and could not be sold because the armistice came too soon before they could cash in on them. They had to sell them. You cannot have them wait until the next war and then be stuck with them. Next war they have got a better model. Tell you, when we had landed those corned-beef cans without any trouble and the skipper had got all the syrup he had expected, we got two cups with real cognac, roast beef, chicken, fresh vegetables, and canned English pudding. Yes, siree. Because. Well, because, you see, it was like that. A French chaser got us up. The officers came aboard. Spying about, asking the crew, spreading francs and cigarettes just like old junk, expecting

367

some guy to spring a word or two. But they had to leave with a sour face, and they had to bow and salute to the skipper as though he was their admiral.'

'And no one gave the skipper away for the francs and the cigarettes?' I asked.

'We? On the *Yorikke*? We took the francs and the cigarettes all right. But give away somebody? We are filthy. And we are dead. Gone beyond hell. We would take in a little purse or a pocket-book of somebody who is careless about it and might lose it anyway when going along the street. We loot the holds and sell out at bargain prices. We would throw a hot bolt at the head of that second engineer when he comes bothering us about the steam and the bars. That's all honest and clean. But squeal to the police and the customs guards and the arms chasers? Not for a thousand pounds in cold cash, fine as it would be to have them. But, you see, what good would these thousand pounds or francs do to you? No good at all. What's the use of having a thousand pounds in your pocket and lose all the honesty of a decent sailor? You cannot look at your own face any more for the rest of your life.'

We were lying before anchor off the coast of a small port in Portugal. The skipper felt that the *Yorikke* was suspected. He was sure that as soon as he should be in French waters he would be stopped and searched. So he took in honest cargo for the next two trips. The cargo was not worth much. But anyway it was cargo, and he could get hold of the most elegant clearance papers. The French would have to pay good money for having molested him and for making him reach his port twenty-four hours late. After two such searches, and after having made so much trouble for the French government and getting a payment of some ten or fifteen thousand francs in damages, he then could afford again a half a dozen trips that really paid, without any fear of being molested.

On such occasions, when the *Yorikke* lay about, waiting to take in cargo, we knocked off work at five in the afternoon and were free until seven in the morning. Since we were at anchor off the coast, we could not get ashore. The boatmen charged too much, and the skipper refused to give any advance, being afraid that we might not be aboard when the *Yorikke* was ready to go under weigh.

So we now had time to sit together quietly and peacefully and just tell our stories and exchange our opinions of life and the world.

There were as many nationalities represented on the *Yorikke* as there were men aboard. I have not found a single nation as yet which has no dead citizens somewhere on this earth – I mean such

368

dead as still breathe the air, but that are dead for all eternity to their nation. Some nations have their death ships openly. These nations call their death ships the foreign legion. If he survives this death ship the legionnaire may have a new name and a new and legally established nationality with all the chances to come back to life again. Certain nations give citizenship to men who sail under their flags for three consecutive years. It was different with the *Yorikke*. The longer you shipped on the *Yorikke*, the farther away you sailed from any possibility of winning or regaining any citizenship. Even the Chinese or the Swahilians would not have taken you in, regardless of how many applications you might make and how many truckloads of papers you might fill in.

The *Yorikke* was a nation all by herself. She had her own language, her own established morals and customs, her own tradition.

In Algiers I once met a man who claimed to be a hundred and sixty years old. He was a Syrian, from Beirut. He looked like forty, and at the same time like two hundred. He told me that he had so far been on the *Yorikke* twenty-three times. The skipper knew him; and he admitted that he could vouch for the fact that this Syrian had shipped on the *Yorikke* at least four times. The Syrian, having invited me to a cup of coffee in a Turkish coffee-house, told me that he had shipped first on the *Yorikke* when he was rather young, as a kitchenboy. I asked him what the *Yorikke* shipped in those times. He said that while he was kitchenboy she was used as a transport ship for Napoleon, to transport his soldiers to Egypt. It was before he made himself emperor. Then, of course, as the Syrian told me, the *Yorikke* carried only sails and had no steam-engine, which, by the way, proved that the Syrian was entirely correct in his story. He could not have known what the *Yorikke* looked like in those days if he had not been on her.

I asked him how come he had shipped so often on the *Yorikke*. He told me that the *Yorikke* had always been his guardian angel, and that he would never forget the good service she had often rendered him. For, poor man, he was always in trouble with his wives. Each time, of course, it was another wife. He had consumed about nineteen, which accounts for the times he shipped on the *Yorikke*, taking into consideration that during the first trips he was still too young to be able to consume a healthy wife. It so happened that whenever he had a wife who was a real nag, he had no money to get rid of her. So he just waited for the *Yorikke* to come in port and off he went. When he returned he found his wife otherwise provided for, and he was free again for the next issue. The next issue, after the proper time had passed, proved a worse nag than the former. So he again had to make use of the *Yorikke* as an effective divorce lawyer.

I thought that now, since he had become rather old, he would no longer be in need of consuming wives, and that might be the reason why he had not been seen on the *Yorikke* for quite a while. But he said that this was only my mistake, not his, because he now had a new wife oftener than before. I said to him that very likely the women of Algiers were not the nagging type. He answered that in this I was mistaken again, and that he suspected that I had had no experience with women at all. He said he had to admit that the women of Algiers were a lot worse even than those of Damascus and Beirut. But the case is simpler dealt with in Algiers than in Syria. In Algiers, whenever he thinks that his wife is nagging too much, he has her put in jail, because these fine people of Algiers are of the opinion that a nagging wife cannot be considered sane, and besides it is a law with these people that the nagging of a wife is a criminal offence. So my Syrian said: 'Now you will understand why I no longer need the *Yorikke*. Algiers is heaven for me. And if I had ever been in Algiers during my early youth I would never have been on the *Yorikke* when she was in the midst of the battle of Abukir. There it happened that the middle finger of my left hand was shot off by some silly English gunner.' This finger was really missing. Therefore I do not see any reason why I should not believe his story. He finished his story by saying that if, and may Allah prevent it, the people of Algiers should ever change their humane law in regard to nags, he would see no other way out than to start again shipping on the *Yorikke*, even as drag.

I made up my mind that if I could get away from the *Yorikke* I would live in Algiers, where there are people who have their hearts in the right spot. And no alimony either. Gee, what a man with the true working spirit could achieve in such a place!

With so many different nationalities aboard, it would have been impossible to sail the *Yorikke* unless a language had been found that was understood by the whole crew. From that Syrian, who of all living people I have ever met knew the *Yorikke* longest and best, I had learned that the universal language used on the *Yorikke* had been usually the language most widely known at the time on the seven seas. When the *Yorikke* was still a virgin maiden the language spoken by her crew was Babylonian; later it changed to Persian, then to Phoenician. Then came a time when the Yorikkian language was a mixture of Phoenician, Egyptian, Nubian, Latin, and

Gaul. After the Roman Empire was destroyed by the Jews, through the means of a renegade puffed-up religious movement, with Bolshevik ideas in it, the language on the *Yorikke* was a mixture of Italian, Spanish, Portuguese, Arabian, and Hebrew. This lasted until after the Spanish Armada was knocked out. Then French influence became more dominant in the lingo of the *Yorikke*. At Abukir the *Yorikke* was on the side of the French, and old man Nelson took her as a prize. He sold her to a cotton-dealer and shipping agent in Liverpool, who in turn sold her to English pirates who worked the Spanish Main, then already in its declining glory. Anyway, from that time on until today the lingo of the *Yorikke* was English. At least that was the name the language was given, to distinguish it from any other language known under the moon.

Only the skipper spoke English that was without flaws. A prof of Oxford could not have spoken it any better. But the lingo spoken by the rest was such that Chinese pidgin English would be considered elegant compared with the Yorikkian English. A newcomer, even a limey, a cockney, or a Pat, would have quite a lot of trouble during the first two weeks before he could pick up sufficient Yorikkian to make himself understood and to understand what was told him.

Every sailor of any nationality knows some thirty English words, which he pronounces in such a way that after half an hour you may get a rough idea of what he wishes to say. Each sailor, though, does not have the same vocabulary as the others, and hardly two have the same pronunciation of the same word. Living together and working together, each sailor picks up the words of his companions, until, after two months or so, all men aboard have acquired a working knowledge of about three hundred words common to all the crew and understood by all. To this vocabulary are added all the commands, which are given without exception in English, but in a degenerated cockney flavoured with Irish and Scotch, the r's and ch's mostly out of place. This lingo, of course, is enlarged by words which are brought in by sailors who, owing to their lack of the right words, have to use occasionally words of their own home-made language. These words, used over and over again, are, after a while, picked up by others and used at the proper place. Since usually one fireman at least was a Spaniard, it had become proper to use for water and for fuel never any other words but *agua* and *carbón*. Even the engineers used these words.

We found ourselves able to tell each other any story we wanted to. Our stories did not need more than three hundred and fifty different words, more or less. And when a good story, born in the heart and raised in the soul and fattened on one's own bitter or sweet experiences, had been told, there was nothing left unexplained or misunderstood. They all could have been printed, but, of course, it must be added that no bookstore would have sold two copies and bookstore-keeper, printer, and publisher would have been in the pen for thirty years.

Regardless of how far from the academic the Yorikkian English strayed, the fundamentals remained English; and whenever a newcomer hopped on who spoke English as his mother tongue, the Yorikkian lingo once more was purified and enriched with new words or with a better pronunciation of words which by long misuse had lost their adherence to their family.

A sailor is never lost where language is concerned. He always can make himself fairly well understood, no matter which coast he is thrown upon. He surely will find his way to an answer to the question: when do we eat? Yet whoever survived the *Yorikke* could never be frightened any more during his lifetime by anything. For him nothing had become impossible as long as it was within reach of a courageous man.

14

Stanislav was called Stanislav, or, usually, Lavski, only by me and by the firemen. Everyone else aboard, including the engineers and the mates, called him Pole or Polack.

The majority of the crew were called after their nationalities. Hey, Spaniard, or Spainy. Portes or Portuguese. Russ. Dutch. Germy. Dansky. Taley the Italian. Finsky the Finn, who, by the way, when he joined the *Yorikke*, understood only a few commands, but otherwise knew no word of English; and since there was nobody aboard who understood Finnish, he was for months unable to say to anybody even so much as: 'May I have your spoon?'

That everybody was called according to his nationality was one of the great ironies of which there existed so many aboard the *Yorikke*. Their native lands and the authorities of their native countries had denied all of them citizenship, and therefore passports, for some reason or other. But on the *Yorikke* their nationality was the only thing they possessed to distinguish them from anybody else. Whether, however, the nationality they agreed to have was their true nationality was never proved. When a newcomer joined the crew and was asked what nationality he had, he gave one in answer; and hence he was called as he had answered and was believed by everybody.

Rarely if ever did anybody on the *Yorikke* reveal his real name. No one, not even the skipper himself, knew for sure if the name and the nationality given by a man when signing on were correct. The skipper was very discreet about what he wrote in the crew's record-book concerning a man. He was the kind of master who stuck to his men; and most likely he would never have given away a man of his to the authorities as long as he could avoid it. The true facts about a man came out only from the man himself, who told frankly all about his person and his past. Few ever did such a thoughtless thing. When a newcomer, after having signed on, left the skipper's cabin and stepped on deck and was met by the mate or the bos'n or the chief and asked his name, he usually answered: 'I am a Dane.' With this he had answered already two questions, his name and his nationality. Henceforth he was called: Dane! Nobody, officer or man, ever asked him again. The officers were sure that Dane was already a lie. Anyway, they never went deeper into the matter, because they did not want to be told more lies. It is an old rule, only not sufficiently obeyed, but a good rule: If you do not wish to be lied to, do not ask questions! The only real defence civilized man has against anybody who bothers him is to lie. There would be no lies if there were no questions.

One evening, while the *Yorikke* was at anchor off an African port, waiting for cargo and orders, Stanislav told me his story, and I told him mine. The story I told him was not my true story; it was just a good story, which he accepted. Of course, I do not know if the story he told me was true. How can anybody know if any story told or heard is true? Does even a girl tell her own mother always a true story about what she did last night between nine and twelve? She would be a fool and would have endless trouble if she did. And as to true stories in general: I do not even know if the grass is green; it may just happen that the grass causes within my brain an illusion which reminds me instantly that I was told, when I had no judgement of my own yet, that whatever looks like grass must be green. Besides, green is not something by itself, but grass is everything which I can compare with the colour of fresh grass. So how do I know whether the story Stanislav told me was the story of what he had experienced in fact, or whether it was the reflection in his mind of what he believed he had experienced? Another man than Moses, who was trained in an Egyptian priests' college, would have told the story of the creation of the world and the history of the Israelites in a way entirely different from what we now believe to be the only true story of the misleading of the human race.

But there were many reasons that made me feel that the story Stanislav told me was true, for the story did not differ much from all the other stories of men who sail death ships.

His true name, which together with his story I never betrayed to anybody on the *Yorikke*, was Stanislav Koslovski. He was born in Poznan, which then was the capital of the Prussian province of Poznan, or, as it was called by the Prussians, Posen.

In Poznan he went to school until he was fourteen. All instruction was given in German, but he knew a little Polish from his parents, who spoke it occasionally, mainly at church service. The German Poles, it seemed, had the idea that the Lord would not understand them if they addressed Him in German.

When he was about to leave grammar school, his parents wanted to give Stanislav as an apprentice for four years to a master tailor. A couple of hundred stories in imitation of Cooper's *Last of the Mohicans*, sold at a dime apiece, and another couple of hundred sea-stories and pirate-yarns, had ambushed his spirit, and he ran away from home, landing in Stettin, one of the greatest German ports in the Baltic Sea. Here he stowed away in a Danish fishing schooner and came to the Danish island of Fünen. The fishermen found him here half frozen and nearly starved to death.

He told them that he came from Danzig. He assumed the name of the bookshop-keeper where he had bought all the dime novels that he had consumed during his schooldays. He said (rather intelligent) that he was an orphan and that he was so mistreated and so cruelly beaten every day by his foster-parents that he had jumped into the sea to end his life. Since he was a good swimmer he could not die in the sea, however, and he swam for his life and reached the fishing schooner, where, not seeing anybody aboard, he stowed away to escape from his martyrdom. He finished his story, his eyes filled with tears, and said: 'If I am brought back to Germany I will tie my hands and feet and jump again into the sea and this time make a good job of it. I prefer rather to go to hell than to return to my foster-parents.'

He told his story so excellently that all the fisherwomen were bathed in tears over the terrible fate of a fine good German boy. So they kept him there.

Not only the German, but also the Danish and Swedish news-papers were full of stories about the tailor-apprentice who had mysteriously disappeared from Poznan, probably kidnapped by Jews who needed, for a religious ceremony, the blood of a Christian boy. A similar affair had happened not so many years before in Konitz, another town of the same province, where, according to police records, Jews had kidnapped and butchered a Christian college boy. All Germany, then already in the grip of anti-Semitism, believed this horrible story true.

The boy was sought all over Germany, and the most gruesome stories as to his possible fate were published in the papers. The Danish fishermen, having other troubles to worry about, did not read newspapers. And if they did, as the story was in all the Danish papers also, they never for a moment thought their boy from Danzig to be the tailor-apprentice from Poznan.

Stanislav had to work hard with the fisherfolk on Fünen. He ate nothing which he had not earned honestly. He liked it, neverthe-less, a hundred times better than sitting on a tailor's table. If he seriously meant to become a good sailor, he could have had no better schooling than he had with those fishermen. The Baltic Sea, looking often so calm and so smooth, is in reality one of the most capricious of waters. Four miles off the coast you think you can make it whistling and singing, and before you have got time to think what has happened a squall has got your craft so hard that, with the coast at arm's reach, you have to struggle for your life. If you can sail a plain fishing schooner from Svendborg on Fünen to Nykjöbing on Falster in any weather, and you bring the ship home again and no sail lost, you have got every right to call yourself a great sailor. Compared with this it means absolutely nothing to bring a transatlantic liner from Cherbourg to Hoboken. Any fool can do that and be thought a great captain.

No matter how hard the work was, when Stanislav thought of being a tailor-apprentice he lost all and every desire to send word home that he was still alive and not sacrificed in Jewish rites. His fear of being made a tailor was greater than the love of his parents, whom in fact he hated profoundly for their attempt to make an honest tailor of one who wanted to detect new straits and unmapped islands in the South Sea.

At seventeen he had become an A.B., a real able-bodied seaman. With the good wishes of the fisherfolk he left for Hamburg to look for long trips and so satisfy his craving for the great seafaring world.

He could not find the right ship going out on a big voyage. For a few months he took up work with a sail-maker. Having in mind to sail on real big ships under his true name, he went to obtain a legitimate sailor's identification book, or what they called a seaman's book, with which he could ship in the finest of German ships. German shipping was then at the peak of its glory. By working at this sail-maker's he had established his residence in Hamburg, and so it was easy to obtain true papers. He shipped for a few trips on honest great German merchants.

For a change he shipped on good Dutch vessels, with which he made several trips to the East Indies.

While on a Dutch the bloody dance about the golden calf started. His ship happened to be in the Black Sea. When it passed the Bosporus on its return to Holland it was searched by German officers in the service of the Turks. He and another German were taken off the ship and put into the Turkish navy under assumed names, because when arrested he did not, for some reason, give his true name. A Belgian sailor on the Dutch ship had betrayed these two Germans to the officers, but the Dutch master of the ship said he had nothing to do with this and added that he did not know their names and was not sure if they were Germans at all.

Two German war-ships, which had been in an Italian port and had evaded the English, reached Constantinople, and by order of the German government they joined the Turkish navy. So Stanislav served under the Turkish flag for a while.

Smart as he was, he quit the Turks as soon as he had an opportunity. He shipped on a Danish merchant. The ship was brought up in the North Sea by a German submarine. Stanislav, whom everybody on the Danish ship believed a Dane, had made the gross mistake of telling a Swede, also on the ship, that he was a German. So when the Germans examined the Dane, the Swede gave Stanislav away. Stanislav came to Kiel, the most important port of the German navy. He was put into the navy, again under an assumed name. Artillery service.

In Kiel he met, by chance, another coolie, as a gob was called in the German navy, with whom he had once shipped on a German merchant. By sheer carelessness, and not through betrayal by this

376

fellow-sailor, Stanislav's real name became known. Now he was in the German navy under his right name. Had he given his right name before, when in the Turkish navy, he could have been court-martialled for desertion.

Stanislav was at the sea-battle of Skagen, where two nations who were at war against each other came out victors at the same time and where the English lost more ships than the Germans, and the Germans more than the English. It depended on the papers you read.

The ship on which Stanislav was a gunner was blown up by a torpedo. Since the battle was off the Danish coast it happened that Stanislav was picked up by Danish fishermen after having been in the water for about thirty hours. They took him to their village. He knew how to get along with Danish fisherfolk, and so they did not hand him over to the Danish authorities, but helped him to hide. By his good luck Stanislav met a fisherman who happened to be the brother of that fisherwoman at Fünen who had picked him up first. With the help of this brother he was roaded to Esbjerg, where he was put as a Dane on a Danish ship, with which he again sailed for the great voyage. He had learned his lesson, and so he never told anybody his true nationality any more. He could laugh at all English, German, and French submarines whenever they searched the Dane. He never was caught again, and he kept himself out of the struggle for supremacy of the big banking firms.

The governments thought it wiser, finally, to make up again. Time had come when all governments were convinced it would be cheaper and more profitable to talk peace and wait for a better chance. The burglars and gangsters sat down to an elegant peace-banquet. The workers, and the little plain people of all countries, had to pay the damages – that is, the hospital bills, the funeral expenses, the tombs for unknown soldiers, and the bills for all the banquets and conferences which left everybody in the world, save the hotel-owners, exactly where they had been before. And all those little people, who had, not profits, but all the losses and all the deaths, were now allowed to wave flags and handkerchiefs at the victorious armies coming back covered with glory and everlasting fame. The others, who could greet only an army which had not been victorious on the battlefield, but which never had been defeated on the battlefield, did not wave flags and handkerchiefs, but cried instead at the tops of their voices: 'Doesn't matter at all. Next time it will be our turn. Hurrah! Hail!' The workers and the plain people became dizzy when presented with the bills they had to pay.

If they tried to rebel they were led to the tomb of the unknown soldier where they were lectured so long and with such deafening jazz that they could do nothing but admit their solemn duty to pay the bills and believe in the existence of the unknown soldier. In those countries where there was no unknown soldier to offer, a whole army was stabbed right in the back, and all the workers and plain people were kept busy smashing each other's heads to find the man who had stabbed the army in its back.

This was the time when in Germany one match cost fifty-two billion marks, while the expenses for making these fifty-two billion marks were higher than a whole truck-load of Kreuger matches. For this reason the Danish shipping company thought it most profitable to send her ships to the dry-docks of Hamburg to be overhauled. For twenty Danish kroner five hundred German ship-yard workers would work six weeks under the whip of a Socialist president who had ordered his Socialist secretary of war to break the bones of every German worker who dared strike for better wages. The German labour leaders, having sold every sound principle to satisfy their personal ambition, and having handed over the fate of a new-born republic to unscrupulous financiers like Sklarz and Barnat, had taken already their first successful steps in paving the way for the powerful foes of modern civilization.

The future, which lately had looked so very rosy for Stanislav, was darkened once more for him. He came with his Danish ship to Hamburg; and when it was docked he was laid off.

Thus he found himself again without a berth.

15

The more the Americans advertised all over the earth that the world had now been saved for democracy, the more narrow-minded became all nations, including the American. Only true Englishmen could hope to land a job in England if there was any. If you had not been English for ten centuries, you had to look elsewhere. Italy did the same; only good Italians were allowed to

378

work for the profit of Italian exporters. The States, feeling as nationalistic as the other nations, closed all the doors against immigrants, with the exception of the Russian grand dukes, and only Americans were sure to get a well-paid union job. If the great-great-grand-uncle of your great-grand-uncle had not come over on the *Mayflower*, there was little chance for you to be employed as a street-cleaner in an American city.

Since this fine spirit of human fellowship was enforced all over the world, it was not strange to see Stanislav, with his Danish sailor's pay-book, go in Hamburg from ship to ship and from agency to agency without the slightest chance of getting a job. All and everything was reserved for their own nationals. Even Danish ships did not want him any longer. Their shipping business had gone from bad to worse and was actually on bed-rock.

When he, then, came again to German skippers he was told: 'No Danes for us. To hell with the Danes, who have taken our Slesvig and who now want Holstein also. No Danes, off you go.'

While the pay for German sailors went down more each day, it was still the only hope he had, as Danish ships without a complete crew hardly ever put in port.

Stanislav had to look for a good German sailor's book.

Asking at the office of the seafaring bureaux where such papers were issued, he was ordered to go first to police headquarters and take out a certificate of good behaviour.

'I have got here my old sailor's book.'

'Let's see. That is Danish. We are not in Denmark, we are in Germany. We do not recognize what those people up there write or say.'

His Danish book had his assumed, not his true name. So he could not very well present it to the police authorities.

At police headquarters he gave his right name and asked for a certificate with which he could secure the sailor's book. 'Registered in Hamburg?' he was asked.

'No. I arrived here only yesterday, coming in with a Dane that went to dry dock and was laid off.'

'Then you will have to send first for your birth-certificate; without it we cannot certify you anything,' the police inspector said.

Stanislav wrote a letter to Poznan, asking for his birth-certificate. He waited one week. No certificate came. He waited two weeks. No answer. He waited another week. The certificate still did not come. He had sent a registered letter and put in two hundred and fifty billion marks to cover the expenses. All this was of no avail. No certificate was sent and no answer either.

He should have known better. What does anybody care about a jobless worker? It would have been different if he had been a banker or a railroad president. But just a bum sailor without money and without a job. Why doesn't he die or emigrate? And, besides, what did people care in Poland about the birth-certificate of a jobless man living in Germany? If he were a good Pole, why didn't he live in Poland and be decent and join the army? The Poles had other worries right then. There was for instance Upper Silesia, about which Poland was rather patriotic, because it had rich coal-fields and well-developed industries. Then there was Danzig, another worry of the patriots who wished to own all Germany up to sixty miles west of the river Elbe, which part of the world had been in possession of the Slavs two thousand years ago. And why not also take all Saxony, which had been ruled two hundred years ago by a Polish king, the strong man August? Once granted the right to be an independent nation, make use of it and take in all the world. Who knows anything about that goddamned birth-certificate of that drunken sailor? Let's go out and see the parade of the army in their new uniforms.

The money which Stanislav had brought from his Danish ship was long since gone. It was spent all over St. Pauli. There they knew, especially in those times, the exact value of genuine Danish kroner. Danish kroner were almost as good as dollars, and some-times even more welcome. No one in St. Pauli better knew the kroner, carried in the pockets of a fine-looking sailor, and appreci-ated them more than the janes. Didn't the gals of St. Pauli do everything to get just one Danish kroner from that swell-looking swanker Stanislav? I should say they did. And of course that's the way of all money in the world. It always goes so easily and friendly. After it's all gone and not a cent left, then you know how hard it comes in.

'Anyway, only dumb-heads and oxen heave coal and take any job,' Stanislav said. 'An honest trade will always keep a good man above the mud. Just take it up and stick to it.'

So it happened that occasionally a box or a crate would drop out of a freight-car of which the door opened too easily. 'All you have to do,' Stanislav said, 'is to be close to the spot at the time when boxes or crates are tumbling out of a freight-car. That's all there is to it. Easy, isn't it?'

'Looks like,' I said.

'What else could I do? Hell, how I wished to work honestly! Heaven knows, bigud. But simply you could not land a job even when you tried to hire out as a dumbwaiter. Other times, if you had a bit of good luck, a couple of bags of sugar or green coffee would open almost by themselves, and right in front of you. Now, if you happen along at the right moment with an empty knapsack and you hold the knapsack right under the spot where the bags ripped open, then, of course, the goods would drop into your empty knapsack. If you don't put something under the rippings, then the whole thing would go right to the ground to feed only rats and mice. Well, it surely is not my intention to fatten up rats. And if the sugar and the coffee, so useful for human beings, fall into the street-mud, man, it would mean an insult to God, who gave the goods that humans might enjoy themselves. And suppose the coffee or the sugar or whatever it may be has dropped, by chance, into your empty knapsack and you were fool enough to pour it out again, somebody might see you doing it and might think you stole it and call the cops to have you arrested for pilfering from freight-cars. You may get into such trouble quite innocently, see.'

There was also cocaine and salvarsan and such things. 'You must have a feeling for the poor, suffering beings badly in need. You can't help it. It is your heart that commands you. You don't realize what it means to be in need of salvarsan and then not have it. You mustn't be that kind, always thinking only about your own welfare. If you wish to be good, you have to think of other people who suffer.'

'You see, Pippip,' Stanislav explained, 'there is a certain time for everything. Then a time will come where you will say to yourself it's better now to think about something else for a change. You see, the big mistake most people make is that they do not say at the right time: 'Now you'd better hop down from the baby because the old lady is about to make a surprise visit with all the trimmings, before you can get out of the window." So I say to myself: now you have to get a bucket even if you have to steal one or you will find yourself in a tough spot.'

When Stanislav came to that decision he again went to the police and told them that his birth-certificate had not arrived yet.

'There you are,' the police inspector said; 'those damned Polacks, they do this just to make us mad. But don't you worry, we sure will make it hot for them when the great day comes. Let only the English in China and India, and the French in Africa, and the Italians in Albania, have their hands full of mud one pretty day,

381

and then we will show these stinking Polish pigs where they get off.'

Stanislav was not interested in the political opinions of the police inspector, but he had listened and nodded his head to make himself amiable to the authority that had the power to issue passports and sailors' books. After he had fully agreed with the killing of all the Poles he said: 'Where do I get my sailor's book, Mr Inspector?'

'Ever lived in Hamburg before?'

'I have.'

'Before the war?'

'Yes, Inspector.'

'Long?'

'More than half a year.'

'Properly registered with the police?'

'Yes, sir.'

'Which ward?'

'This one here, in this same precinct.'

'Everything fine,' the inspector said. 'Now you go to the head office of the police registration and let them hand you an application paper. You bring it with you and three photographs so that I may stamp it all.'

Stanislav obtained the application paper from the head office, and he came back to the station.

The inspector said: 'Application is all right. Yet how do I know that you are the person named in this certificate of registration?'

'I can easily prove that. You see, I may bring up here Mr Andresen, the sail-maker, with whom I worked when I lived in Hamburg. But no need to do that. There is a sergeant who knows me, right behind you, sitting on the bench.'

'I? Know you?' the sergeant said sourly.

'Yes, sergeant, you know me rather too well,' Stanislav explained. 'I have still to thank you for the nine marks' fine which I received on account of your reporting me for disturbing the peace when I was in a row. That time, of course, you carried a little fly-brush on your lower lip; you have shaved it off since then, I see.'

'Yep, yep. Now I remember you. So you are that guy. Well, how do you do? Grown up since that time. You were working with old man Andresen all right.' The sergeant came closer, and he smiled as though he were thinking of the good old soft times before the war. 'Yea, I remember all of you. We had lots of trouble with you. Poznan was looking for you. You had left home, and the whole world thought you butchered. We did not send you back to Poznan, because we had no right to. You were working here and there were no bad records on file. So Poznan lost all interest in you.'

'So I see,' the inspector said, 'all is in shape. Now of course I have no longer any objection to give you all the police identification stamps on your sailor's book application and on your photographs. As many as you wish.'

Happily Stanislav went next day with his application to the seaman's registration office.

The officer in charge said: 'Application and police registration are in perfect order. The inspector confirms personally that he identifies you, the applicant. So everything seems to be correct.'

Stanislav was smiling. He knew he would have his sailor's book inside of two hours.

'B-u-u-u-t,' the officer drew out to start a long bureaucratic explanation.

Stanislav lost his smile and looked anxiously up.

'But,' the officer said again, 'the nationality, the citizenship does not seem very clear in your case, as I see here, Koslovski. We doubt your citizenship as written here in your application. You say here: German nationality. You will have to prove this before I can give you a German sailor's identification book. We do not issue sailor's identifications to other nationals but our own.'

He had been told already at the police station that he might have to prove before the seaboard authorities his genuine citizenship.

Very politely Stanislav answered: 'But, officer, I have served the K.M., the Kaiserliche Marine, the Imperial Navy, and I have been severely wounded at the battle of Skagerrack and picked up and interned by the Danes.'

The clerk lifted his eyebrows high up. He felt himself growing to the size of a god. Before he spoke he made a gesture with his hands and with his head as though he wished to impress on a mortal in distress that the continued existence of the universe depended upon what he was to utter. From the attitude he assumed it could easily be expected that he might cry out: 'Be there no earth before me!' and the earth would disappear into a fluttering fog.

The great gesture finally materialized: 'That time, when you were serving the Imperial Navy – Hurrah for our poor great Kaiser! – then, of course, without the slightest doubt, you were a German citizen. Because we never allowed an alien to set foot on our Imperial battle-ships. And that glorious day when you were wounded at Skagerrack you were still a German citizen; it was then that we gave these perfidious sons of that even more perfidious Albion the licking of their lifetime. Those glorious times! I pray to the old God of the Germans that they may come soon again to finish those stinking dogs for good. In those times you surely were a German citizen of whom the country could be proud. But, understand this, my man, if you are still a German citizen you will have to prove it, and there's no way of getting out of it. As long as you cannot prove you're still a German citizen, sorry, my man, I can do nothing for you, and there will be no sailor's identification book for you. That's all, good-bye.'

'Pardon me, sir, where do I have to go to prove my German citizenship?'

'Police headquarters, Resident's Registration, Citizenship Department.'

16

Stanislav had to eat. He could not have a ship without proper papers. So he had to take up once more what he used to call his honourable profession. If all people had a decent job to occupy their minds, and regular meals to satisfy their hunger, most crimes would not be committed. Sitting in an easy chair, the belly filled with an excellent supper topped off with a pint of good Scotch, it is a pretty entertainment to talk about crime waves and the vanishing morality of the jobless. Standing in the shoes of Stanislav, the world and its morals look entirely different. Stanislav could not help it. It was not his fault that the world was as it was presented to him. No job was to be had at this time, not even as third assistant to a rag-picker. Everybody lay upon the dole. Stanislav had an aversion to living on unemployment relief funds. He preferred his honourable trade.

'You feel so terribly depressed,' he said, 'standing all the time among the unemployed to get your few cents. The whole world looks then as if only unemployed were still alive and as if every hope for any better time had vanished for ever. I'd rather look around to see if somebody's pocket-book is annoyed with its owner than stand in file with those jobless talking of nothing but their misery. Matter of fact, I respect everybody's property. But I assure you I didn't make this world. And I have to eat. Had these goddamned bureaucrats only given me a sailor's book, I would have been off on the great voyage long ago.'

He went to police headquarters, Department of Citizenship. He was asked: 'Where were you born?'

'In Posen, or what is now Poznan.'

'Birth-certificate?'

'Here is the postal receipt of the registered letter I mailed them weeks ago to send the certificate. They don't even answer. And the money I put in for expenses they have kept.'

'The identification stamps of the inspector of your district will do. I accept them. It is only the citizenship which is in question. Have you adopted for Germany?' the clerk asked him.

'Have I done what?'

'Have you adopted for Germany? I mean have you officially chosen German citizenship? Did you, within the proper time given, declare before a German authority, especially assigned to take such declarations, declare that you wish to retain German citizenship after the Polish provinces according to the provisions of the Treaty of Versailles were returned to Poland?'

'I did not,' Stanislav answered. 'I did not know that it had to be done. I always thought that if I was once a German I should always be a German as long as I did not take out citizenship for any other country. Why, I was in the K.M. I have fought for Germany at Skagerrack.'

'Then you were a German,' the clerk admitted. 'Because then Poznan belonged to Germany. Where were you when all the people born in the Polish provinces but living in Germany were officially ordered to adopt either country as their native land?'

'I was shipping on a Dane. I was likely then somewhere off the Chinese coast.'

'It was your duty to go to a German consul at the nearest port and make there your proper declaration.'

'But I did not know that such a thing had to be done. You see, when sailing, and working hard, out on the sea, you have no time or even thoughts to think of such things.'

'Didn't your captain tell you that you had to go see the German consul?'

'But I shipped on a Dane. It was a Danish master I was with. He

385

sure was not interested in any orders issued by German authorities.'

'Very bad for you, Koslovski.' The clerk sat back and seemed to work his mind for a solution. When, after long meditation, he had found one, he said: 'Bad for you, I say again. I think that is all. I can do nothing for you in this case. Are you rich? I mean do you hold any property?'

'No, mister, I am a sailor.'

'That settles it, then. Nothing I can do for you. Even the periods of grace for proper adoption have expired. Sorry, but you cannot even rely on the fact that a higher power prevented you from making the declaration when there was time. You were not shipwrecked. You called at many ports in which there were German consuls, or at least consuls of other nations who were authorized to represent German interests. The call for adoption was published profusely and repeatedly all over the civilized world. At all consulates there were the bulletins on the blackboards.'

'Sailors never read newspapers. When in port, one has other things to do than to go to the consulate and look at bulletins. Where could I get a German newspaper? Papers in other languages I do not understand well. Sometimes, by good chance, one may pick up a German newspaper. But I never saw any notice about this adoption thing.'

'I am not responsible for this, Koslovski. Sorry. Sure I would like to help you. Yet I have not the power to do so. I am just a clerk here, an official to do what I am ordered to do. Now, of course, it is not quite as bad as you imagine. There is still a way for you – make an application to the Secretary of State. He can do it. But this takes time. Probably two years or three. Since the war, citizenship has become a more definite matter than it used to be. Besides, the Poles do not show any consideration towards our nationals. Why should we be more generous? In a certain way you are a Pole. You were born on soil that is now Polish territory. I tell you, my good man, it sure will come to the point where the Poles, those stinking godless dirty pigs, will drive out of Poland all those Germans who have adopted for German citizenship. I assure you, Koslovski, we will do the same. The only way to deal with those bandits.'

Every official assured him that he would like so very much to help him, if only he had the power to do so. Yet, suppose Stanislav had talked loudly or without proper respect to any clerk, high or low in office, or he had dared to look sternly at the face of an official, he would have been thrown into prison without mercy for having insulted an official and for having committed a criminal assault upon the state. Then the official would become automatically the almighty state in person, endowed with all the powers, forces, responsibilities, and privileges of the state. The brother of the insulted official would pass sentence, another brother of the official would beat him up with a club, and still another brother in office would lock him up in jail and guard him there for as long a time as another brother of the official thought suitable for such a horrible offence. But none of all these brothers in office have the power to help a poor individual in distress. 'What, then, is the state and all its great apparatus good for if it cannot help a being in need?' Stanislav questioned.

'I can give you only one piece of good advice,' the clerk said, swinging leisurely in his chair: 'You'd better go to the Polish consulate general. The Polish consul, believe me, is simply under obligation to give you a Polish passport, with which you may easily obtain a sailor's book. If you bring us a Polish passport we will make an exception of you, having served the German navy, and having lived in Hamburg now and before the war. I will see to it, personally, that you get a German sailor's book upon presenting a Polish passport. That is the only advice I have in your case.'

Next day Stanislav was at the Polish consulate.

'Born in Poznan?'

'Yes, my parents still live in Poznan.'

'Speaking Polish?'

'Not very much; practically none.'

'Did you live in Poznan, or in West Prussia, or in any of the Polish provinces then under the rule of Germany, Russia, or Austria at the time when Poland was declared an independent and sovereign country?'

'No.'

'You did not live in any territory considered Polish territory between 1912 and the day of the armistice?'

'No. I was on high sea, mostly with Danish or German merchants.'

'What you were doing, where you were sailing, and on what ships you were at that time, I have not asked you. Answer only my question.'

'Stanislav,' I broke in while he was saying this, 'here was the right moment to grasp this nuisance by the collar, drag him across the desk, and land him the best you have in store.'

'I know, Pippip. I felt that way. But I was smart. I kept on

387

smiling like a gal at her first dancing party. You see, first I wanted my passport. Then, one hour before my ship would sail, I would come back to this guy and sock him until he went shreddy. And then out and off with the can.'

The Polish consul continued: 'You said that your parents are still living in Poznan.'

'Yes.'

'Since you are of age, we, of course, could not consider any adoption made by your parents on your behalf, even supposing they had done so. What concerns us is the correct answer to my question: Have you in person registered your serious intention to remain a Polish citizen before a Polish consul or any other person authorized by the Polish government to accept such declarations?'

'No. I did not know that I had to do this.'

'What you did know and what you did not know is of no importance to me. What I wish you to answer is: Did you register your declaration?'

'No.'

'Then what do you want in this office? You are a German and no Pole. Go to your own officials and do not molest us here any more. That's all. Good afternoon.'

Stanislav narrated this experience not in an angry tone, rather sadly and almost pitifully. He would have liked to express his ideas as to bureaucracy in true sailor's fashion. Yet it was too late for this now. The consul was not at hand.

I said: 'Now look how quickly those new-born countries have acquired Prussian officialdom. Some of those countries did not even have a complete civilized language of their own yesterday, and today they are doing even better than the big powers. You may be sure that these new countries that, so far, are not even sure of their own names, will go a long way to make bureaucracy their one and only state religion. You ought to know what America has achieved in the hundred and fifty years of her existence. How fast she works to surpass even Imperial Russia with passports, visés, restrictions of free movement. Limitations and mouldiness everywhere. All the world over, in consequence of the war for democracy, and for fear of communistic ideas, the bureaucrat has become the new tsar who rules with more omnipotence than God the Almighty ever had, denying the birth of a living person if the birth-certificate cannot be produced, and making it impossible for a human being to move freely without a permit properly stamped and signed.'

'They are all talking high-hat at conferences about the progress

388

of culture and civilization and the welfare of mankind,' Stanislav said. 'It looks fine on the front page of the papers. But it is all talk, with nothing back of it save hypocrisy, egoism, and an insane nationalism. There is hardly any chance to become alive again, once on the *Yorikke*. Not under conditions as they are today. The only hope you have to be free again in this world is that the can goes down to ground and doesn't take you along, but spits you out like a leper. And suppose you find yourself after such an affair at some shore again; where do you get off? Only on another *Yorikke*.'

Stanislav went again to police headquarters, Citizenship Department.

'The Polish consul does not recognize me as a Pole,' he said.

'You might have known this before,' the inspector explained. 'These stinking Polish pigs need a licking, that's what they need. The old German God in heaven is our witness, they will get it soon enough, and after that they will never come for more.' The inspector banged the desk with his fist.

When he was calm again, he said: 'Now, Koslovski, what can we do for you? You must have some papers. Otherwise you will never get a ship. Not in these days.'

'Certainly, Mr Inspector, I must have papers.'

'Right, right, Koslovski. Tell you what I will do. I shall give you a police certificate. Tomorrow morning you go with this certificate to the passport department. It is room – wait a minute – yes, it is room 334, here in the same building. You shall have your passport all right. With this passport you go to the sea board, seamen's registration, and there you will get your sailor's book. With a good sailor's book you will get the best liner the Hapag can afford.'

'Thank you, Mr Inspector.'

'That's all right. We do what we can for an old man of the K.M.'

Stanislav felt so happy that he wanted to embrace the whole world.

The Germans proved that, after all, they were less bureaucratic than all the other nations.

He went to the passport department, presented the police certificate and the photographs, stamped by the inspector as evidence that he was the person whose face the photographs showed, signed the beautiful new passport with the German republican eagle printed on it, paid seventy-five thousand billion marks as fee, and left the department with the most elegant passport he had ever possessed in all his life. With such a passport in hand he could even emigrate to God's own beloved country, and he would be received at Ellis Island with a brass band, and all the sirens singing. Yes, sir.

He could hardly believe he had in his possession such a fine passport. Everything in it was fine and perfect. Name, birthday, birthplace, occupation: Able-bodied seaman, honourably discharged from the Imperial Navy. Everything like a hymn. Now, let's see, what is this? Wha-a-a-a-t? 'Without country?' All right. It won't matter. He will get a sailor's book like a whiff. Well, well? What does this mean? 'Good only for the interior.' Maybe the clerk thinks that ships sail on the sands of Brandenburg, or on the moors of Lüneburg, or only on the river Elbe. Doesn't matter. The passport is a peach.

Next day Stanislav went with his beautiful passport to the sea board to take out a sailor's voyage book.

'You want a sailor's book?'

'Yes, please.'

'We cannot give you a sailor's book on this passport. You are without nationality. To have citizenship, properly established, is the most important thing for a sailor's identification book. Your passport is all right for Germany, but not for any foreign country. It gives you no right to a German sailor's book.'

'How, then, can I get a ship? Won't you, please, tell me this?'

'You have got a good passport. You will get any decent foreign ship with that passport. Only not a German ship. The passport says that you are living here in Hamburg, it tells who you are, where you come from, and all that. You are an old sailor with experience. Easy for you to get any ship. Any foreign ship. You make more money on a foreign ship than on a German, since our money is without any value.'

Stanislav found a ship. Two days later. A Dutch. An elegant merchant. Almost new. Was still reeking of fresh paint. Fine Dutch pay.

When the skipper saw the passport he smiled with lips lifted high, and said: 'Good paper. That's what I like, men with fine papers. Let's go straight to the consul, read the articles, sign on, and you get your advance. We sail with high water early in the morning.'

The Dutch consul registered his name in full: Stanislav Koslovski. A.B. Age, height, weight.

Then he asked: 'Sailor's book, please?'

Stanislav said: 'Passport.'

'Passport is brand-new. Ink still fresh. Only two days old. All shipshape. I know the officer personally who signed this passport,' the skipper said, and lighted a cigar.

The consul held the passport, satisfied to have in his hand such a wonderful piece of bureaucratic fine art. He turned the leaves and nodded approvingly. He was pleased.

Suddenly he stared. He stopped, and his satisfied smile froze on his lips. He turned the pages back and on again.

He took a breath and said shortly: 'You cannot sign on.'

'What?' Stanislav cried.

And 'What?' cried the skipper. He was so surprised that he dropped the match-box.

'That man cannot sign on,' the consul repeated.

'Why not?' the skipper asked. 'As I said, I know the officer who has signed the passport. The passport is correct.'

'No objection to the passport,' the consul said. 'But I won't sign on this man. He is without a country.'

'What do I care?' said the skipper. 'I want this man. My first mate knows him to be a first-class man at the helm. I know the ships he has been on, and I know their masters. Therefore I know what he is worth. So that's why I want to have him. I need men like him.'

The consul clasped his palms together and said: 'Listen, captain, since you say you like that man so very much, are you willing to adopt him?'

'Nonsense,' the skipper said.

'Do you take all the responsibility for this man after he signs off your ship again?'

'I don't quite understand you, Mr Consul.'

'I'll explain it. This man, no matter how good a sailor he is, may not go ashore in any country he wishes; he cannot stay in any country he would like. He may go ashore, of course, as long as the ship is in port. But if he is found ashore after your ship has put out, the company of your ship is made responsible for him. Your company has to get him out of this country again. Where are you, or your company, going to take him?'

The skipper was quick with an answer: 'He can always go back to Hamburg, where he comes from.'

'Can. Can. The truth is he cannot.' The consul began to talk like a judge sitting at his bench and pouring out stale moralities. 'He has got a German passport good only for Germany. Germany has no obligation to let him in again once he has left it. Now, of course, he might obtain a special certificate, independent of this passport, which would permit him to enter Germany and to live there whenever he wants to. Such a certificate, though, can only be issued by the German secretary of state. I do not believe that this German authority will give him such a paper, because it would equal a paper of citizenship, and that is exactly what was denied him, or else he would have obtained a passport without any restriction. Fact is, and so far a well-established fact, that he was born in Poznan, and that neither Germany nor Poland, for some reason or other, has acknowledged his citizenship. He may go to the League of Nations. But the League of Nations has no country to give him. So, whatever paper the League of Nations may issue on his behalf, the fact that he has no country to call his own would still be unsettled. Only if you are willing to make out an affidavit here that you take the responsibility for him after he leaves your ship – '

'I cannot do such a thing. I am only an employee of my company,' the skipper said.

'Then, of course, no other road for me. I do not sign him on.' Saying this, the consul, with a heavy double stroke, crossed out the name of Stanislav, already written in the registers, so indicating that for him the case was at end.

'Listen.' The skipper leaned over on the desk. 'Couldn't you make an exception here? I would like to have him. I cannot find a better man at the helm than he is. I can go to sleep and leave the whole ship to him and nothing would go wrong. He got the right sailing instinct with the first bottle of milk he drank. I know this. We have talked together for a couple of hours.'

'Sorry, captain. Very sorry indeed that I cannot be at your service.' The consul rose from his chair. 'My powers are extremely limited. I must obey my regulations. I am not the government. I am only her faithful servant.'

When he had finished he drew his mouth wide into his cheeks, as if he wanted to give a smile studied before a mirror. At the same time he lifted up his shoulders so that they almost reached his ears. His arms hung down flabbily, and they swung slightly at the elbows. He looked like a plucked bird with both wings broken. He made a sad picture, but it was a true picture of an excellent bureaucrat, who knows that by his word men may live or die.

'Damn it all, and to hell with it,' bellowed the skipper. With a powerful gesture he threw his cigar upon the floor, and crushed it with half a dozen steps, dancing like a savage Negro. He sent the consul a look as if this shrimp had been a deck-hand and been caught kicking a full pail of black paint over a washed deck. He stormed with two long steps to the door, jerked it open, went out, and banged the door so that the whole building seemed to shake.

Stanislav, having already left, waited outside in the corridor.

The skipper came up to him and said: 'What can I do now with you, Lavski? Nothing. Devil knows how much I would like to have you with me. I cannot get you now, not even under the emergency. That guy knows your name, and if he finds out, then I will find myself not in good shipshape. These goddamned scribblers, how I hate them! More than squalls on the Zuider. Well, here, take five gulden. Have a good time tonight. Now I have to run around to find another A.B. Good ones are rarer than sunshine on the North Sea. Good luck.'

The skipper was gone. And so was the elegant Dutch with milk and honey.

17

A ship. Stanislav needed it badly. 'Honourable trade,' he said, 'is all right for a certain length of time, provided this length is not too long. You see, here a box, there a crate, then yonder a bag with crude coffee or sugar – all this doesn't hurt anybody. This goes for overhead expenses and inevitable losses of the big merchants. They don't feel it, while it will help me well over water. The boxes and crates and bags may just as well have been broken or busted while being loaded. Anyway, this is not the point. The point simply is, one gets tired of the honourable trade.'

I said nothing and let him go on spreading out the inner part of his soul.

'Yep, believe me, Pippip, you get awfully tired and bored of this kind of business. There is something which is not true about the whole thing. And you feel it, see? You are just like living all the time upon somebody's pocket. Almost like living on a woman. So you feel dirty, see? For a certain time, well, you cannot help it. You do your very best to land a job, but you cannot get one, not even by selling your soul to the devil. You see, you want to do something. You wish to be useful. I do not mean that silly stuff about man's duty. That's bunk. There is in yourself that which is driving you on to do something worth while. Not all the time hanging on like a bum beggar. It is like this – hell, I can't explain what I mean. It is that you want to create something, to help things going. You – you – I mean, some day when you know it is all over, you wish to have the true satisfaction of having done at least something while you were alive on this crazy earth. What I mean is, to stand by the wheel, say, in the dirtiest weather hell and devils can think of and then, in such weather, keep the course straight. That is something which nothing in the whole world can be compared with. No honourable trade, no matter how thick and honey it may be, is like that. Damn my soul. There you stand by the wheel, and the old bucket kicks around and around and wants to get off the course by all means and by all forces under the thickest sky you can imagine. But no matter how hard she may kick, you hold the wheel by the course just like that, see?'

Stanislav grabbed me by the belt and with a powerful twist tried to throw me off my feet and around, just as if he had his hands clenched to the wheel.

'Let go,' I cried. 'I am no rudder.'

'Don't get sore. I only wanted to show you what I mean. See, when you get her through and out of that sour weather without losing so much as half a point off the course, I can tell you, your heart jumps like a fish in a frying-pan. Then you could just bellow loud, out of joy and satisfaction. Just think how powerful you feel – you, such a little mite of a human thing, you can hold a fifteen-thousand-ton-bucket in the heaviest gale straight on, as if it were a baby coming straight from mother, innocent like new-fallen snow. And then the old man comes along, or the first, and he glances at the rose, and he says: "Fine work, Koski. Man, you are some sailor, as I haven't seen many the last twenty years. Damned fine accurate work, my boy. Hold her this way and we'll still back her through and we won't lose even fifteen minutes off the schedule." Tell you, Pippip, then your heart knocks right in your throat, you can feel it. And you just could cry out aloud how happy you are and all the world around you. Believe me, the finest honourable trade, no matter how much you may get out of it, cannot beat such a feeling as holding old Caroline straight by the course.'

'I never stood by the wheel of a big can,' I broke in, 'but I had the rudder of five-hundred tonners all right. I suppose what you say is positively correct. Painting is just as pleasing often as standing by the wheel. If you can draw a green edge without breaking over into the brown layer, it sure makes you feel that you have done a great job. Because it takes a good time before you can accomplish this when the ship is in the open, and before you learn not to spit and splash the paint all over like a puppy does on mother's fresh-washed floor.'

Stanislav did not speak for a while. He was meditating. After a few minutes he spat in good fashion over the railing. He bit off a cigar he had bought an hour ago from a dealer who had come alongside with his boat and had sold tobacco, matches, postal-cards of acting couples, fruits, chocolate, chewing-gum, buttons, thread and needles, writing-paper, stamps, and all such things as are offered to crews by these small traders in row-boats.

Stanislav lighted his cigar, spat out again, and said: 'Perhaps you are going to laugh at what I am going to tell you. Anyway it is the truth. Now I am here on this can to shovel coal, to cart coal, to heave ashes, and to do the dirtiest and most miserable kind of work any rotten landlubber can do aboard a ship, while actually I am an A.B., and for sure a ten times better one than any of these three brazen drunkards here that think themselves such great guys. Maybe it is a shame, a real disgrace for me, a good sailor, to shovel coal here and all that goes with it. But maybe it is not. It has to be done to keep a can going, and somebody has to do it. I tell you, Pippip, even this has got its fun. You see, to throw into the tunnel, down to the stokehold, some six hundred shovels of coal and do it fine even in heavy weather, and then look at this mountain of fuel you have shovelled in, right in front of the furnaces, so that the fire'm stares at you in admiration, you feel so happy that you just could go and kiss that mountain of coal. Because it all looks so funny and so useful at the same time. That mountain also stares at you, and rather bewildered, for only a half hour ago it was still in the farthest corner of the upper bunker and now, without giving it any time to think things over, it is down here, ready to go into the furnaces and make steam for the bucket. Doesn't that make you happy and feel as if you had done something important? Sure it does. And even here, believe me, the best honourable trade cannot be compared with what you feel having this mountain of coal down in the stokehold. You feel so healthy and so sane that I think the skipper can't feel any better after having brought the ship home through a nasty sea.'

'Sometimes I feel that way also,' I said.

'And why is it that you have to do the honourable trade? Is it your fault? I should say not. You haven't got anything better to do. You can't lie in bed all day long or bum about and hang at the kerb-stones day in, day out. You get plumb crazy in your head if you do.'

'Well, and you forgot to tell me. What happened when the Dutch was gone?' I asked him.

'I could not stand it any longer. I had to have a ship and go out again. Or I would have gone nuts. That excellent passport I had, which was no good for me, I sold to a stranded American for twelve dollars. Then, one night near the freight depot, a sack of coffee burst open again and in that way I got some sugar; I mean, of course, dough. Coffee was high then in Germany. Occasionally I went with Danish fishermen, helping them getting brandy into Denmark. Denmark had extremely high duty on foreign brandy. This business paid well. When I, finally, had shovelled on enough money, I took the train to Emmerich, which is the border station on the German-Holland international line. I got across fine at night. Yet when I bought a ticket to Rotterdam I was caught, and in the dark of night pushed across the border back into Germany again.'

Surprised at such a yarn, I asked: 'You don't mean to say the Dutch secretly smuggle people at night across the German border?'

I was anxious to hear Stanislav's opinion of a case about which I thought I was an expert.

'They?' he said. 'They? Don't make me laugh. They do other things. Worse than such a trifle. Every night there is going on, at all European borders, a lively exchange of unwelcome travellers. Men and women and children. The Germans kick their Jews, and their undesirable foreigners, and Bolshevists and communists and pacifists, across the Dutch, the Belgian, the French, the Polish, the Swiss, the Danish border just like nothing. And, of course, the Czechs, the Poles, and all the others do exactly the same in exchange. They simply cannot do it openly. It would cost them milliards of money. Who is going to pay for that? It's being done on such a great scale that it has become almost a legitimate procedure. Everybody knows it, yet nobody admits it.'

Shaking my head I said: 'Stanislav, now don't you try to pull my leg over the table. I can't believe it.'

'They do it just the same, whether you believe it or not. That doesn't matter a bit. I have met scores of men along the Dutch line who have had experiences you sure would get the kick of your life out of if I told you about them. What else can the officials do? It seems still the most human thing to do under the circumstances. They can't murder them or throw them into the ocean. Those people haven't committed any crime or anything bad. Only they haven't got a passport. Some can't pay for it. Most of them have had trouble with their voting for adoption. Lots have lost their country altogether. Their country has been split and divided up between five or six different nations. Every country tries to get rid of all such people who have no passport and no established nationality, for these people are for ever causing trouble to any nation that harbours them. Now, of course, if all the nations would cut out passports and all such things and do as it was before the war, this trade in human souls and this kicking out and pushing about of people – often very decent people – all that would cease immediately and everything would stop that goes with it.'

'I have said this before, ' I interrupted him.

'I know you did. But don't you put into your head the idea you invented it. Thousands of people have said this before you. Whom do passports do any good? No one but the bureaucrats. As long as there are not at least five hundred million sane and decent persons found on earth who admit the same you say and I say, there will be no change. That's all I can say.'

Stanislav had been warned by the Dutch border officials that if he should ever try again to come into their country he would get the workhouse, or the chain-gang, or at least the prison camp. He did not mind. He wanted to have a ship, as a banker wants depositors. He was afraid of nothing. So the same night he crossed over into Holland again. He had learned how to avoid border patrols. So he worked more cleverly and with more intelligence. He reached Amsterdam. Four days afterwards he got an Italian, a real rotter. A death ship with all the trimmings. She was all set to make sailor angels or sailor devils as the case might be. He went on his first trip out on the reefs with her. He and a couple of fellow-sailors survived and landed on some shore. In rags he bummed and begged along the shore until he came to a port where after a few weeks he got another ship. Again it was a death can. When he found it out he skipped her in a North African port. He had reached the end of his possibilities for surviving when the *Yorikke* put in. He knew what she was and what she was after. But he had not eaten for days. And having tried his honourable trade several times again, the planks of the pier had become too hot for him, and he had to look for a hole to get out. The only hole was the *Yorikke*, just hauling in anchor. He hopped on and was welcomed. Safely on deck, he made faces over the rail at the police.

Now where is he? A man fine at heart and body, for ever willing to work true and honestly. Where am I? Where are all the deads to be some day? On a desolate reef. Or on a shore with another death ship the only future ahead of them. Nobody can sail death ships for ever and get away with it. Some day, no matter how far off it may be, everybody has to pay for his voyage. And the payment is always made on and with a death ship.

One day I said to Stanislav: 'I have been told that in the bunk on top of mine somebody was killed. Did you know him, Lavski?'

'Of course I knew him. We were almost like brothers. Was a German. Home in Mülhausen, in Alsace. I don't know his right name. Said name was Paul. He was called Frenchy aboard. Coal-drag. Once, in a night, when we were sitting in a coal-bunker, he told me all about himself. He was crying like a schoolboy.

'He learned the trade of a coppersmith in Strasbourg or in Metz. Don't remember which of those two towns. When he had finished his apprenticeship he went travelling, as most young German artisans do, so as to get an all-round experience of their trade. He went to France, worked there for a few months, then he went to Italy, where he also worked for a time at his trade.

'When that bloody trouble started, he found himself in Switzerland. He had no money and no job. Was caught as a vagrant and deported to Germany. There he was put in the army. Fighting on the Italian front, he was taken prisoner by the Italians. He escaped from the prison camp, stole civilian clothes, and bummed about in Italy. It was southern Italy, where he had worked before the war. So he knew that part well enough. Somehow he was caught. Nobody knew that he was an escaped prisoner of war; they accepted his story that he had bummed in Italy all the time. He was taken to a camp for civilian aliens.

'From there he escaped before the armistice and fled to Switzerland. The Swiss again deported him to Germany. Here he found well-paid work in a brewery. It was the time when they had some kind of communistic trouble there, which after a short success was quelled by the socialists. He was thrown into prison, and later deported as a Frenchman. The French, however, did not accept him, probably because he was thought a communist. All people today are afraid of communists, as in the time of the Roman emperors everybody was afraid of the Christians. Officially of course, the French refused him recognition on account of the fact that he had been away too long from Alsace, which was now French territory again, and that he had not declared his adoption to either country. What does a worker care about such nonsense? He has to

398

worry and to think about other troubles when out of a job and when running around like a hungry rabbit to find something to eat.

'The funny thing was, while the French, without saying so, did not accept him, because of his communistic ideas, truth is he did not know even the elements of communism. He had no idea at all what it was all about. What he talked was pure insane nonsense. Nothing behind. That's the trouble with nine hundred ninety-nine out of every thousand people – that they think they know something and really they don't know anything. If the capitalists would know the truth about communism I feel sure they would adopt this system overnight to meet their fear of depressions. Of course, it is by far better they do not accept it; they sure would spoil the whole thing just as much as the original Christian ideas were spoiled the very moment an emperor made them his state religion.

'The Germans, now, ordered him to leave Germany within forty-eight hours or he would be put at hard labour for six months with exactly the same deportation order meeting him at the prison gate after he had served this term. And so on until his death.

'What else could he do facing such a dilemma? He had to make France. Half a dozen times he had been at the French consulate without any success. When he came there for the eighth time, the consul did not receive him, but forbade him to set foot in his office ever after. He had lost his job long ago. At the French border he was held and sent back into Germany, where again he got six months' hard labour. The Germans warned him once more to beat it. He went to Luxembourg. From there he made France. He could not speak much French. It was not long before the French caught him. He swore he was a French citizen. Official investigation was made, with the result that it was established clearly that he had tried to acquire fraudulently a citizenship to which he had no legal right. Such doing is today considered a greater crime than a bank hold-up or taking a jane behind a bush without her full consent. He was to get five years or so for this crime. To punish such a crime with five years is only the beginning. The next stage will be, without question, the electric chair. God the Almighty can no longer bestow on human beings citizenship; any bureaucrat may set it aside if he wants to.

'The French left him a hole through which he could escape a couple of years of prison. So he went to the recruiting office of the Foreign Legion and came out a legionnaire. If he could stand it for nine years, the French would grant him a little pension and about one tenth of French citizenship.

'He could not stand it and to keep alive he had to run away. He told me it is not quite so easy as one may see it often in the pictures. Where can he go? If lucky, to Spanish territory. But the distance is too far. Then there are certain Moroccans who are greedy enough to get the money that is paid for capturing a deserter. He said that he would have rather killed himself than return to the legion a captured deserter. It is not so pleasant, what awaits them when they come back.

'Then there is another type of Moroccan, who does not return a deserter, regardless of how high the reward may be. He catches the deserter, strips him entirely, and then lets him lie on the sand in the boiling sun. If he happens to meet such a fate it would be still better to be brought back to the regiment. There are still others who take a legionnaire and torture him slowly to death with a refinement that takes a week or so before it is fully accomplished. With them nobody on earth is more hated than a legionnaire. Again, there are tribes who take the captured man and sell him for a good price to the farthest interior, far south of the Sahara Desert, to be used as a slave for the treadmills. Also very pleasant. There are so many reasons why the Foreign Legion has so astoundingly few deserters. The real legion, the comradeship and the honour of its soldiers, are not quite as pictured in the movies made for salesladies and for the profit of the film companies.

'This fellow, though, he had all the luck. He met Moroccans that first wanted to tie him to the tail of a horse and skin him. Yet he could make them understand that he was German. Now, the Germans are Christian dogs as well as the French. Not much difference. Nevertheless, the Germans had fought the cursed French, which was something to their credit. Exactly as the Germans are liked in Cuba, Nicaragua, Spain and all over Spanish America for having killed some fifty-five thousand gringos. To all the Mohammedans, including the Moroccans, the Germans have got one more point to their credit. They have fought side by side with the Turks, also Mohammedans. All prisoners of war of Mohammedan faith captured by the Germans were treated as they treated no other prisoners, because these prisoners were considered rather friends than enemies. This is known all over the Moslem world.

'Only it is so very difficult to make a Mohammedan who is not a Turk grasp the idea that somebody can be a German and then fight on the side of the French in their legion. An Arabian believes a German looks different from an Englishman or a Frenchman.

Seeing that a German looks almost exactly like a French, the Moroccan gets sort of suspicious against his captured legionnaire, and thinks he is being fooled.

'What happened to pass in the minds of those Moroccans who had captured Paul no one will ever know. They believed his word, however, that he had never fought against any Moroccans, and that he had joined the legion only because he had been facing years of prison in France, for some conduct of which he really was not responsible.

'So they clothed him, fed him, doctored his sores, and then handed him over from tribe to tribe and clan to clan until he reached the coast of Spanish Morocco. Here he was brought to the *Yorikke*, then right off the coast with special cargo for the Moroccans.

'Now, the old man was overjoyed to have him. Because we were badly in need of a coal-drag. Paul was happy to be with us. He did not know and had no idea that his situation had not changed at all since he had enlisted for the legion.

'It took him anyway only about two days to learn where he was, and that it was more difficult to escape from the *Yorikke* than from the legion. After he had passed a watch with three bars out in one furnace and five out in another, despite the fact that during this time all the fuel was rather close at hand, he said to me: "I wish I had not skipped the legion. This here, I tell you the truth, is ten times worse than our sweat company and the penal company combined. Compared to this, believe it, comrade, we lived like princes in fairy-tales. We had at least decent food, clean quarters, and soap and washed shirts and some leisure. I feel I'll go to the rats here in no time."

' "Now, don't talk like an old woman, Paul," I consoled him. "You get used to it. And there is still some fun, sometimes, when in port with some cash. Don't hang your head. Up the chin."

'It is likely that Paul had already caught something on account of his wanderings and hardships during his flight. Because it all happened rather rapidly,' Stanislav went on with his tale. 'He began to spit thick blood. Every day more and more. Then he vomited blood, pails of it. One night, when I came to relieve him, I found him in the upper bunker, lying upon a pile of coal, his face bathed in thick blood.

'He was not dead. I carried him to the quarters and put him into his bunk. I took his watch on, so that he could rest.

'In the morning, when I went to see him, he was dead. At eight

401

he went overboard on a greasy plank. The skipper did not even take off his cap and say a prayer for him. He only touched his cap and said: "Lower away." The boy was not clothed. He only had his rags on him, stuck on his body by his blood. A big lump of coal was tied on one of his legs to hold him down in the sea. I had the feeling that the skipper would have liked to save even that piece of coal. He looked that way.

'Paul had never been registered in the pay-book of the ship. He left the world like so much useless dust. Nobody ever knew his name. He was just Frenchy. A member of a civilized nation which had denied him legal existence.'

18

While Stanislav was on the *Yorikke*, more than one coal-drag had been taken, eaten, and digested by that can.

There was Kurt. He was from Memel territory, which was a part of Germany that had been taken away from the Germans after the war, without any other justification than to bite away from Germany as much as possible. Nobody had any idea what to do with or to whom to give this territory. So it stayed independent.

When the residents and the natives of Memel had to make up their minds what nationality they wished to adopt, Kurt was in Australia. During the war he had not been molested very much by the Australians. The war over, he got homesick and wanted to return to Germany.

He had been mixed up with a strike. In a battle with strike breakers one of those rats had been beaten up until he was left dead in the street. Kurt was supposed to have had a hand in this, and he was sought by the police. He could not go to the German consul. If he had done some damage to the Australian army, the consul would have done all in his power to help him out of the country. But being mixed up with a strike is a different thing. Labourers attacking the profits of capitalists are out. When a strike is to be quelled, all consuls work in unison, regardless if only a few months ago they would rather have liked to cut one another's throats. The consul, doubtless, would have handed Kurt over to the Australian police, or at least tipped them off. A consul is always on the side of order and state authority. A strike is always against the state, if led by the workers. When led by the leaders, one is never sure in whose interest the strike has been declared.

Kurt could make England without any papers, being helped by members of the seamen's union of Australia.

England is a tough spot, since it's an island. An island is always tough. You can hop on it easily. But it is not at all easy to hop off again if you have to do so within a given time. Kurt found himself like in a cage. He could not get off again. He had to go to see the consul. The consul wanted to know why he had left Sydney, or Brisbane, whatever town it was, without going to the German consul to get his papers in shape, and why, in particular, he had come to England illegally. Kurt could not tell his true story. He did not want to. England was in no way safer than Australia. The English would have sent him back to Australia without delay to go on trial there.

Stanislav could not remember exactly what town in England it was where Kurt had gone to see the German consul. When in the office of the consul, where everything, pictures on the wall, labels on drawers and file cabinets, the homely voice of the consul, reminded him of his country, which he had not seen for so many years, Kurt began to cry. The consul took his tears as an expression of the hypocrisy of a bum who wished to gain something by unfair means. So the consul bellowed that he had better cut that comedy because it wouldn't do him any good. Kurt gave him the only answer fit for such a situation. The German language is well provided for such needs. To make his meaning even clearer, Kurt took up an inkstand and hurled it against the consul's head. The consul began to bleed at once and he phoned right to the nearest police-station. Kurt did not wait for the police. He struck down the porter at the gate who wanted to hold him, and off he went out in the street, making a clean get-away.

Kurt had made a mistake anyway in going to the consul. He should have known beforehand that the consul could do nothing for him. He was from Memel, and since he had not adopted according to the regulations of the Treaty of Versailles, that masterpiece of the overwhelming stupidity of brilliant statesmen, no consul on earth could help him. He was neither German nor a citizen of this tiny little worm of a new nation that does not know,

403

and never will know, what to do with herself. The consul was only a paid servant of the state. He had no power to help a lost sheep get on the road again.

So Kurt was dead now for ever. Nevermore could he see his native country, his parents, his relatives. 'All seems so strange and ghastly. But so it is. Let all the political wiseacres try to find out if such things do exist in modern civilization. Of course they won't try, and dismiss even the thought of it by crying out loud that it's an exaggeration if not a brazen lie,' Stanislav interrupted his tale.

To Kurt a high official of state had said that his homesickness was only a bum's comedy. A bum cannot be homesick. Refined feelings are reserved only for men and women far up in class, who can take from their drawers every day two fresh handkerchiefs, silk, if you please, or at least genuine Irish linen.

I was homesick. I am homesick. All my struggling and roaming is but a dope to put to sleep my homesickness. It took me some time, and it cost me thousands of achings of my heart, before I learned in full that this thing which is supposed to be your native land, which God gave to you, and which no one, no emperor and no president, can take away from you, this homeland is today canned and put in files of passport departments and consuls' offices. It is now truly represented only by officials with credentials, by men who have the capacity to destroy your true feeling for your country so thoroughly and so completely that no trace of love for your homeland is left in you. Where is the true country of men? There where nobody molests me, where nobody wants to know who I am, where I come from, where I wish to go, what my opinion is about war, about the Episcopalians, and about the communists, where I am free to do and to believe what I damn please as long as I do not harm the life, the health, and the honestly earned property of anybody else. There and there alone is the country of men that is worth while living for, and sweet to die for.

Kurt, the dead boy from Memel, hopped on a Spanish ship which was leaving England exactly the minute Kurt needed a ship most. He could not stay long on the Spaniard. The crew was complete. He had to get off when she reached home. After switching from one port to another in search of a berth he finally, one day when very hungry and desperate, met the *Yorikke* going under weigh. He climbed up and landed a job as coal-drag. The berth as a coal-drag was always to be had on the *Yorikke*.

The *Yorikke* knew nothing about safety devices such as provide for the safety of the working men in all civilized nations. The

Yorikke could not have such modern nonsense. Because it costs money, in the first place; in the second place, safety devices are only hindrances to the work that has to be done. A death ship, everybody ought to know, is no kindergarten. Keep your eyes open and look around. If your skin is scorched off, your knuckles smashed, your chin bruised, your arm broken, it's only the lazy parts of your carcass that go off. Work, and work well, and you won't need any means to safeguard your limbs.

The crystal tube at the boiler which served as the water-gauge didn't have the wire screen that is demanded by the law, even in the interior of Afghanistan. One day, while Kurt had the watch in the stokehold, this tube burst.

There is on all boilers a valve which, with the help of a long rod, serves to shut off immediately the water-pipe leading to the gauge. As soon as this valve is closed, no steam can go through the broken gauge, and a new gauge-crystal can be set in without the slightest danger to the man who has to do it. There is nothing to it.

But the trouble on the *Yorikke* was that she had no such rod-valve, because the Phœnicians did not have it and so there was no earthly reason why the *Yorikke* should have it. There was only the regular cock directly under the crystal tube to shut off the steam and the boiling water that rushed out through the broken pipe. In less than half a minute the stokehold was so thickly filled with hot steam that one could not see the end of his arm, and it seemed impossible for any human being to stay there half a minute longer without being cooked all over.

But that was not to be used as an excuse for the man who had to shut off the pipe. It had to be done, for the steam went down so rapidly that the engine was liable to stall any moment. To bring the steam up again would take two hours. Suppose the bucket was then close to reefs or shoals, the whole ship would be a total loss if owing to the stalled engine the ship went out of control.

Who had to do the job and shut off the pipe? The coal-drag, of course. Who else? The dirtiest and lowest of her men had to sacrifice his life that the *Yorikke* might survive. In the sea-stories and in the pictures these jobs are done, of course, by the skipper himself, or at least by the chief, because somewhere in the background a girl is waiting with a kiss for the great hero. In real life it is always the other way round. It is the soldier, the private, who does it; on the ship it is the dirtiest and the most despised hand that has to do what is called in the log the most heroic deed of the chief.

Kurt shut off the pipe. The steam came up quickly again. The engine had not stopped for a second, and the mate on the bridge had not lost for a minute control of the ship.

Down below, however, Kurt had dropped upon a pile of coal. He had to be carried to his bunk by the second engineer and the donkey.

'I do not wish anybody on earth,' Stanislav said, 'no matter how much I hate him, to hear once in his lifetime the shrieking and screaming that we had to listen to from the bunk Kurt was in. It went on hours and hours without ceasing for a minute. Never before, not even when I went down with my battle-ship at Skagerrack, had I believed that any human being can cry so long a time without losing his voice. He could not lie on his back, nor on his belly, nor on either side. The skin hung down on his body in long strips and rags as if it had been a torn shirt. All over blisters, some as thick as a man's head. I don't think that he ever could have been saved, even if a hospital had been at hand. Maybe it could have been done by putting on his body new flesh some way or other. But sure the doctors would have needed the whole skin of a calf to cover all he had lost. And how he yelled and shrilled! I only wish that the consul who had refused him a passport could have heard his shrieking in his sleep. He sure would never have felt at ease again for the rest of his life, knowing that such a damned worthless little stamped paper as a passport was to blame for such a terrible fate of a young man supposed to have also a soul. But these guys sit at their desk, scratching and filing and polishing their fingernails and smiling crooked at you if you want something from them – maybe a paper to help you along. They feel so very superior to us working men. Easy to feel great a hundred miles away from the real life as it is out here.

'Bravery on the battlefield? Don't make me laugh. Bravery on the field of work. Here, of course, you don't get any medals; no mention in the report either. You are no hero here. Just a bum. Or a communist always making trouble and never satisfied with the conditions as ordered by the Lord himself to help the profits.

'He screamed himself to death. The mate had nothing in his medicine chest to make it easier for the poor devil. We tried to pour into him a cup of gin, but he could not hold it. Late in the afternoon he was sent overboard, the boy from Memel land. Can't help it, Pippip, I have to take off my cap, speaking and thinking of this boy. Damn it, don't look at me that way, I am not an old sissy. But here you have to sound taps. No getting away from that. Sent overboard like an escaped convict. The second engineer looked down over the rail when he disappeared in the water. Then he said: "Damn it all. Hell. Rotten business, short again a drag. Wonder when I will ever be complete." That was his prayer for the boy's last trip. And he was the man whose obligation it was to shut the cock. It's not the fireman's or the drag's business to look after repairs while the ship is out.

'Yes, this was Kurt from Memel. His name is not in the log either. The second had his own name written in as the man who had done it. The grandfather saw the book when he went lifting toilet soap from the skipper's chest. Yes, sir.'

19

With the rest of the crew I spoke very little. Most of the time they were cranky, cross, mad at something, sleepy whenever you saw them. In every port they got drunk, drunk as only sailors can get.

To tell the truth, however, I have to admit it was not I that did not speak to them, but they who did not speak to me or Stanislav. We, Stanislav and I, were but coal-drags. A coal-drag is not as high in society as a deck-hand, or, more, the great A.B. These are gentlemen compared with the coal-shovellers, who live in filth, in soot, in dirt, in ashes. You must not touch a drag; you will get so dirty that you won't be clean again inside a week. Take the bos'n, the donkey, the carpenter. These were the peers, before whom a coal-drag had to stand in awe when they passed by. Capitalists are too dumb, otherwise they'd find some new ideas on how to get along better with the workers. They would make use of the fine social distinctions of the workers for their own benefit. There are even nobles among them – that is, the union men. He who is not fit to join the union is looked upon as a Hunk even if born on the Emerald or right north of Aberrrrdeen.

The bos'n, the carpenter, the donkey-man, and that hang-around of whom I never knew what he really did on board, all these mugs were the so-called petty officers. They were, nevertheless, just as filthy and dirty as we were. None of them had any better experience in seafaring than we had. For the regular life of the *Yorikke* our work was by far more important than theirs. Yet we, the always overtired and overworked coal-drags, had to serve the donkey his meals on his tiny table in his little hole of a separate quarter. We had to clean up his cave, and we had to wash his dishes. What a great man he was, that we had to serve him! What was his work, anyway? When the ship is under sail, all he does is tinker around without any special aim or anything definite. He smears here a bit of grease on the engine, and there a drop of oil on a winch-shaft; he takes away here a little bit of dirt and puts it there. As the *Yorikke* had only two engineers, he occasionally went on watch in the engine-hold, particularly when the chief felt too tired or not yet perfectly sober, and when the weather was so calm that all the donkey had to do in the engine-hold was to sit on a bench, smoke his pipe, and read true confessions. When the bucket was in port, he was fireman and coal-drag at the same time; and he was in full charge of the winches used to hoist in and hoist out the cargo. For all these reasons he was so great a personage that he had to have his own quarter. He got the same meals we got. But, so as to let us feel that he was a person far higher in social standing than we, he received on Sundays rice pudding with marmalade, well watered by the grandfather to make it last longer and to make it look like more. The donkey also had twice a week our famous prunes in the bluish starch sauce. We received our pudding only once a week, and no rice pudding at all. Such elegant differences are made even in food to show that one person is worth more than another, not for his work, or talent, but for his social standing among workers. There sure would be no Caesar and no Napoleon without these petty officers, foremen and sweat-shop whips who have one foot on the first rung of the ladder that leads up to the rank of general. Petty officers who come from above are no good; they are failures. The best petty officers are those who come from the ranks, where they were whipped hard only as far back as yesterday. They make the best whippers today. Caesar can rely on them. They do the job best, and without them he is lost.

Next came the A.B.s – able-bodied seamen. Then came the deck-hands. All of them were higher in rank than we. Stanislav knew more about sailing than all the three A.B.s and deck-hands put together. Not only the donkey and the A.B.s, but even the deck-hands often put on airs when one of us passed by them, as if they were about to suggest that we first had to ask their kind permission. We expected any day that one of these haughty mugs

408

would utter such a demand. Stanislav and I wished they had.

We all were dead. All of us were convinced that we were on our way to the fishes. Funny that even among the dead these fine distinctions of rank and class do not cease to exist. I wonder what goes on night and day beneath the surface of a cemetery, particularly in the cemeteries of Boston, San Francisco, and Philadelphia.

There was, nevertheless, a certain bond that kept us together. We all knew that we were the moribunds. The destiny of all gladiators was ours. Yet we never spoke of it. Sailors do not speak of shipwrecks. It's no good doing that. If you don't want to have the wolf around, then don't call him. Don't even speak of the devil if you don't want to go to hell. We all felt the last day approaching, nearer and nearer. It made us often nervous. Maybe it is the same way that a condemned criminal feels in his cell when he knows the last week has arrived.

We did not like each other. We did not hate each other. Simply we could not and would not make friends or even comrades. But strange, when in port, none of us ever went ashore alone. We went ashore in bunches of from four to six.

Pirates who had not made a pinch for six months could not look as terrible as we. No sailor of any other ship in port ever spoke to us or said hello. We were too filthy and dirty, too ragged, for any decent sailor to admit belonging to the same honest trade as we. Suppose we tried to speak to other sailors; they never answered. They just hurried away from us as quick as they could. When hanging around in a tavern or in a saloon with dancing dames, we could say whatever we wished; we could insult any other guy that was present. They all pretended that they had not heard what we had said or that it had not been meant for any of them. By the way, this fighting among sailors in foreign ports, seen so frequently in the pictures, is just, like so many other things in the pictures, the bunk. It's a lie all over. Sailors do not fight one tenth as much as sea-stories and pictures try to make the paying public believe. Sailors have more sense than the movie-producers. Evidently no one ever wished to fight with us. We were too dirty and filthy even to be knocked down by a decent sailor. Perhaps he would have felt himself infected. Other sailors just finished their drink, paid, and left. Often they did not even drink, only paid and left quietly. They all belonged to the honest working class, the fourth rank in a modern state. We had the feeling that we did not even belong to the sixth rank, if such a thing exists in modern civilization. I suppose it does.

409

There was still another reason, I think, why no other sailor, or groups of them, ever tried to fight with us. They could see that nothing mattered to us. We would kill mercilessly, once entangled in a row. We could tear them to shreds. We would not leave one piece of their clothes good for use. It would have been expensive for them even if they had won the fight. What did we care? Prison or the noose? It was all the same to us. We could not be frightened by any punishment, because we knew what it meant to have six or ten grate-bars out in one watch. We had a Portuguese deck-hand who was only waiting to get a chance to knife a man to death. He had said so, and he had explained it by saying that he was badly in need of a vacation in prison, or else he would die like a dog on the *Yorikke*. He said the worst prison he had ever been in was in a small North African town. But he added that it was still better than to work for the food he got on the *Yorikke*. I am sure there were others on the *Yorikke* who thought the same way and who were waiting for their chance, only they never spoke about it so frankly as did that boy.

The crew of the *Yorikke* was known, let's say notoriously, in all the ports of the Mediterranean, save those of France and Italy, where we were never allowed to go ashore. All the ports of the west coast of Africa as far down as the French Congo were touched occasionally, when the skipper thought it wise to do so, or when some tribe or little nation tried the newfangled ideas of freedom and independence advised by our smart brother Wilson.

Wherever and whenever we stepped into a saloon, the owner would be nervous and eager to get us out as soon as possible, although we threw upon the bar all the money we had in our pockets or in our mouths. Often one of us had all his pockets torn, and in such a case the money was carried in the mouth or, if it was paper money, in the cap. We were good customers. The saloon-keeper knew it. Nevertheless, he did not for a minute let us out of his sight. Every step, every move we made was watched by him.

People in the streets frequently shrank away from us in horror when we crossed their way. The constant fight of the *Yorikke* to live and to prevent herself from being sent down to ground port was marked in all our gestures and movements. Women grew pale when unexpectedly we came into their path; and women who were waiting for child often shrieked pitifully when they saw us. They pressed both their hands against their belly and murmured prayers to protect their unborn children against the evil, and then they ran and ran without looking back.

Men who were just ordinary townsmen or peasants lost their self-confident manner when meeting us. Some of them plainly showed fear. Most of them just turned their faces away, so that we might not think for a moment that they meant to offend us.

Usually we were followed by one or two policemen, who did all they could not to lose us without coming too close and making it too plain that they were ordered to stay with us all the time we were ashore. Never did they wish us to know that we were under the vigilance of the police. They thought that if we were aware of this we might get wild and lay the whole town in ashes. In many ports there was a rumour that the *Yorikke* had in reality some two hundred men aboard, ready to take any town or any ship on high sea whenever ordered to do so by her master. In these parts of Africa there are hundreds of little ports whose inhabitants are still fed with stories of pirates of the times of the Phœnicians and Carthaginians.

The effect we had upon children was perhaps the most remarkable. Some of them, especially the older ones, cried for their mothers when they met us; some stood lifeless, as if touched with a magician's wand; some ran off like deer. The younger ones, though, stopped in front of us, gazed at us with eyes wide open, as if seeing birds of paradise. Others would follow us, overtake us, smile openly like little golden suns, and frequently they would say: 'Good morning, sailor-man! Have you a fairy ship to sail in?' They would shake hands and pray us to bring them little princes and maidens one inch high from the blue Yonderland. Then suddenly they would give us another look, and they would take a deep breath and show an expression as if they were waking up from a sweet dream. Then they would run away and cry without ever looking back again. It was on such occasions that I thought that perhaps we were already dead, and only the souls of children could see us as we really were.

20

The *Yorikke* went her own way – a way which very few other ships ever tried. Perhaps the skipper knew exactly what he was doing and what his orders were. From our point of view, however, it looked as if the *Yorikke* had no schedule whatever. I cannot recall many times when the ship made exactly the port it was bound for when it left the last port. France and Italy we avoided almost entirely. We did not put in at the greater ports of Spain, either. There we stayed a mile or so off the port, and the skipper signalled for a boat to take him in to get his orders and arrange his papers with the consuls and with the port authorities.

For this reason no death ships are known. It's just a yarn of bum sailors. Death ships belong to the period long before the American Civil War, to the times when slave-trading was a great business, and blockade-breaking could make a ship-owner rich with three successful trips. No, there are no longer any death ships today. They are things of the past. Any consul can tell you that. And a consul is a high personage of diplomatic rank. He won't tell you anything which is not true. No one knows death ships. No government recognizes them. After all, that which is not admitted does not exist, like the Russian revolution. Don't look at it, and then it disappears.

The seven seas are so full of death ships that you can have your choice of them! All along the coasts of China, Japan, India, Persia, the Malay Islands, Madagascar, the east and the west coast of Africa, the South Sea, South America, coming up as far as the Pacific coast of Mexico, where they land Chinamen and dream of artificial paradises by the truckload. Money is always useful, no matter how you make it. The point is to have it. As long as you have it, no minister will ever ask you where and how you got it; just rent, or better buy, a church seat, and pay something for the missions in China.

There is still room enough for a couple of thousand more of these

412

beautiful and useful ships. Making immigration restrictions does not help the shipping trade very much. So the ships must look elsewhere for a sound business. One cannot do away with all the bums of the world, because there might be a few artists among them, and writers, or cranky millionaires. So it is close to impossible to check white slavery, just because there might be among the slaves a few wives of men with influence and some daughters of great kings of finance who wish to adventure on their own account. White slavery makes more money for those fine men who are paid to investigate and prevent it than for those who are actually in the trade. One is just as good a business as the other. Difficult as it is to do away with all the bums, it is just as difficult to do away with all the death ships. There are not a few shipping companies who would go broke overnight if they had no death ships. Other companies could not survive boom or depression if they did not send down to the bottom a ship when it is time to do so for cold cash. Honesty is the best policy. But it must pay. Otherwise this saying is as good as the saying about having gold in your mouth if you keep silent. There are some respectable ships among the death ships, just as there are quite a number of rather decent women in the C'mon-up-some-time trade. Since this is so, it would be hard work to find all the death ships. Wherever there is a road or a kerb-stone, a bum may exist, regardless of how many bums you send up the river or down to the chain-gangs. After all, there is three times more sea-water than dry land. Therefore there is three times more room for bums at sea than on land.

Certain people think one can find somebody easier on a desert than in the bush, and a ship on the open sea easier than in a delta like the one down at New Orleans. It is, of course, not so. Five ships may go out to find one ship and never find it, not even when its position is fairly well known.

Nobody would ever have found the *Yorikke* if her skipper did not want her to be found. Often he had good reasons to be found, only to be safer afterwards. That skipper knew his peanuts. He could have been invited by the Marquese of Pompshundure and he would never have made a false step drinking his sherry or eating his fruit salad or asking the Marquese to dance the latest blues with him. He knew how to work himself and his old maiden out of any jam anybody had ever tried to put him in. The papers he presented were always in fine shape. Whether they were genuine was another question, which the guy who wanted to get him tight had not the guts to decide. No transatlantic liner could show better papers than he could when cornered.

A Spanish chaser, a gunboat, came up while the *Yorikke* was just bordering the five-mile limit. Suppose the skipper said that the *Yorikke* was outside the limit, and suppose the Spaniard said she was not; the Spaniard wins, because he represents the state. The state is always right, and the individual is always wrong.

Thus it happened. The Spanish gunner signalled with flags and whistles. The skipper did not heed. So the Spaniard got sore and he fired twice the stop-and-stand-by order. The shells fiffed about the mast-heads of the *Yorikke* so that the old maid started to dance, thinking it was still Abukir. The skipper was laughing. Anyway he could not make it and bring the *Yorikke* out of the limit. We were not prepared to choke down the crying throat of the old hussy. Well, the skipper gave the signal to the engine to stop and stand by. The *Yorikke* was within the five miles, no doubt. The skipper pretended to be out. They would have blown us straight to hell if the old man had not stopped.

Aboard they came. Much bowing and begging your pardon and excuses for troubling us. 'Yes, sir, excuse me, you are still within the limit. No, sir, we have just taken our position. If in doubt, may we take position together, sir, so as not to leave any question?' 'It's all right,' said the skipper.

'May we, please, examine your papers? Thank you, sir. Are in order. Only a matter of routine, you know. Would you mind, sir, may we, please, make a slight inspection of the cargo, sir? Won't take long, sir. Half an hour or even less, sir. Acting under orders, sir, excuse me, sir.'

Said the skipper: 'No objection, gentlemen. Am at your service, gentlemen. But, please, make it snappy. Or I will have to make your government responsible for all and everything. I am short already, gentlemen. We have had dead wind all the time. Go ahead, gentlemen, the ship is all yours.' The skipper laughed. He went on laughing and laughing. How this man could laugh! It was a sight and at the same time a feast for the ear. He changed his laughter from the bright and jovial to the ironical, then to the vulgar haw-haw of a fishmarket-woman; then he would chuckle and giggle like a high-school baby. He went through the whole scale and all the shades of laughter, while the officers were diving into the holds or ordering boxes heaved out of the holds to be opened on deck.

Every child on all the coasts of the Mediterranean knew the stories about corned beef from Chicago. Exactly as the husband

414

whose wife is known by all the men in town is always the last person on earth to hear something, so it is with governments. Not before the dumbest village idiot has long forgotten it will the government obtain official knowledge that the whole village was swept away during the flood last year. So the Spanish government, in the grip of a stern dictator, finally had word from an office-boy about the lively trade in corned beef from Chicago.

The officers of the gunner, supported by an experienced customs officer, went about the holds of the *Yorikke* like ants about a dead mouse. They were actually looking for corned beef. And the skipper laughed and giggled so that one could hear it from bow to stern.

The officers became nervous, partly because they did not find what they were looking for, but mostly on account of the laughing and chuckling of the skipper, of which they could make neither head nor tail. They thought of going straight to the bottom of things, and they asked the skipper: 'Pardon me, sir, have you any corned beef on board?'

The skipper narrowed his eyes and smiled at them as if he wanted to make love, and said: 'Of course, gentlemen. Excuse me, please. Por'guese, show the gentlemen to the galley and tell the cook to let the gentlemen inspect the corned beef from Chicago.'

The officer in charge looked at the skipper for a while, half-dumb, half-surprised. Then he said, saluting: 'Thank you, captain, this will do. I do not want to see it. I am not yet through here. It will take me only a few minutes more, if you don't mind, sir.'

'Not at all, sir,' the skipper said. He bowed and laughed again.

The experienced customs officer and two men more were still in the holds below, rumbling about.

The officer in charge went to the hatchway and pointed out several boxes to be hoisted on deck. The skipper ordered two of our hands to assist the officers.

Up came the boxes. The officer tapped them all off, some with his hands, others with his shoes, and still others with his closed pocket-knife.

'Have this one opened, please, sir,' he asked the skipper.

The skipper giggled, now drawing up his lips in an ironical manner. He ordered the Portuguese, who was ready with tools, to open the box pointed out by the officer.

When the box was open, one could see a row of cans sparkling in the bright sun.

The officer took out one can, then another. So did the skipper;

he picked out one and another one.

The officer looked at the label, and the skipper smiled. The officer read: 'Van Houten's Pure Hollandish Cocoa. Free of Oil.'

The skipper handed the officer one of the cans he held. He laughed right out and said: 'Why don't you open this can, sir, to make sure it is cocoa?' His smile became satanical now. I was watching him, and I thought if something should go wrong the old man might be capable of killing that officer like a rat, shut in the others still below in the holds, and try to make off, resting his luck upon the well-weighted safety-valves of the *Yorikke*. Later, knowing him better, I knew he was far too intelligent to do such a thing. He had brains enough to get himself out of any jam, regardless of how thick it might have come. Anyway, his smile stayed diabolical, but it changed again into a light chuckling.

When he offered the officer one of the cans he held in his hand, the officer looked him straight and searchingly in the face. He noted his ironical smile. The officer pressed his lips together and got pale. He seemed no longer able to control his nerves. His hands trembled. He knew something was queer about the ship. But he got angry with himself for finding himself outsmarted by the skipper.

He reached for the can the skipper handed him. Again he looked the skipper in the face like a professional poker-player. Then, with a resolute gesture, he gave the can to the Portuguese and said to the skipper: 'Please, sir, order him to open it.'

'Go ahead, Por'guese,' the skipper said.

The officer thought of corned beef from Chicago and expected to find it in this can labelled Van Houten's Cocoa. When opened, there was in it: cocoa. The officer looked rather disappointed, almost pitiful. But he came to and smiled at the skipper.

He knocked with his shoes against two more boxes and seemed to listen to the echo. He pointed out another box, had it opened, saw the cans with the same labels, pushed it aside, and ordered open the third box. When it was open the skipper looked at it, bent rapidly down, and picked out two cans, apparently at random. He held one of these two towards the officer and said, again using a nasty satirical smile: 'Won't you examine one of these, sir?'

The officer looked with a sort of consternation at the two cans in the hands of the skipper and for two or three seconds he seemed to hesitate. Unexpectedly, however, and as rapidly as the skipper had done before him, he picked out two other cans from the box.

The officer weighed them in his hands. Just when he was about

416

to give one of them to the Portuguese the skipper butted in and said: 'Sir, why don't you open this can from the bottom?'

The officer gazed at the skipper, saw his smile, got extremely nervous and said: 'No, sir, I'll have it opened from the top.' This time the officer had a smile which, no doubt, he thought looked satanical. But the skipper was a far better actor. His smile could look really diabolical, while the best the officer could achieve was a rather silly-looking smile.

He opened the box from the top by having the lid cut off. There was only cocoa in it, Van Houten's Pure Hollandish, Free of Oil.

The skipper laughed out loud. The officer, almost mad with fury, emptied the whole can. Nothing came out but cocoa, and the paper it was wrapped in to keep it dry.

The officer picked out four more cans, opened the lids, smelled at the contents, closed the cans, stood thinking awhile, and then gave orders to his companions below in the holds to come up, the inspection being over.

When all the men had come out and were standing at the rail to go down the gangway to their boat, the officer wrote out the receipts for the damage done, bowed to the skipper, and said: 'I beg your pardon, sir, for the trouble I have caused you, but these were my orders. We are, as you know well, at war with the Riff colony, and so you will understand why we have to examine occasionally ships sailing within our waters. Thank you, good-bye, and have a lucky voyage.'

'All right with me, sir,' the skipper answered, shaking hands with the officer, 'come again any time you wish, I am always your most obedient servant. Good-bye.'

Off went the shallop with the officers.

The skipper bellowed up the bridge: 'Get her going. Full steam to get her out of the five. Damn it. Close cut.'

He took a deep breath and forced it out with a whistling noise. His laughter was all gone. Now he got pale. After a while he wiped his forehead.

He stood still at the rail where he had said good-bye to the officer. Now he crossed over and came near the galley.

'Cook,' he hollered, 'full after-gale supper tonight, raisin cake and cocoa with plenty of milk, and for each man two cups of rum with extra tea at nine. Come here, get the cocoa.'

He took up the various cans the officer had opened, smelled at them, and threw them overboard, save one, which he gave the cook. Then he fingered about the open boxes, picked one out here,

417

and another there, rather confident in his picking. He handed them to the cook and said: 'Of course, special supper for the mess.'

'Aye, aye, sir,' the grandfather said, and hurried off with the cans.

'Por'guese,' the skipper called the hand, 'close the boxes and put them back where they came from.'

All this time I had been standing at the rail watching this elegant business. I hardly remember a picture which interested me so much as had this procedure. What wouldn't I give to know what went on inside the brain of the skipper when he offered the officer the cans in his hands, and, more, when he suggested to the officer that he open the cans from the bottom! I had more admiration for that skipper than ever before. What a pity, I thought, that the times of piracy are all over and gone for ever. With this skipper I would have gone to rob the whole English merchant marine. It's too late now, with wireless and all that.

Anyway, I thought, something must be done, when I saw those boxes full of cocoa put back in the holds again. One should never lose any opportunity when it knocks at your back door. A few boxes of this Hollandish cocoa mean real money in the next port. All people like to drink cocoa.

That same night, still well filled with the elegant supper, and feeling swell, I crawled into the hold and swiped five boxes.

When Stanislav came below to relieve me, I said to him: 'Hey, you smarty, did it ever occur to you that we sail a living gold mine? I am talking of cocoa, you dumbhead. Honourable trade. We can make at least three pounds easy money.'

'No such thing as easy money on this trip,' he answered. 'Still wrapped in diapers, kiddy? It would be a gold mine all right if there were cocoa in these cans. But there isn't. That's the only objection to the gold mine in this case. Are you still that dumb to believe in newspapers, advertisements, and labels? The labels are all right. Only they don't belong to these cans. Haven't you inspected them? Don't dream into your pockets any money so long as you are not through with the inspection. Haven't I told you a hundred times not to trust in the *Yorikke*, whatever she may show you? If you look closer you will see in these cans only cocoa-beans – beans I mean. But you won't find in any port any soul to buy these beans unless you can sell them at the same time the bean-mills to grind the beans with. If you have got the right mill and you try to grind the beans, they come out: pupp-pupp-pupp-pupp-pupp-pupp, like this and whoever swallows them won't need any cocoa any more, with milk or without. What an innocent lambkin you are! I don't understand myself how I can get along with such as ass.'

I was sure Stanislav was lying to put one over on me. I had seen the cocoa with my own eyes. So had the Spanish naval officer. It couldn't be all black magic.

I simply could not believe it.

Immediately I went up to the bunker and opened the boxes. Stanislav was right. There were cocoa-beans inside. Hard ones, with shiny brass shells. In all the five boxes there were the same kind of beans. I did not find one single can in which there was Van Houten's Pure Hollandish Cocoa. It all was Chicago, again. Behind the label Pork and Beans you sure find anything, even bent hoof-nails, but no pork and beans.

I closed the boxes and took them back into the hold. I was certainly not interested in the kind of cocoa-beans the Arabians and the Moroccans cook.

The skipper alone, that great magician, knew the word that turned cocoa-beans into emma-gee shells when needed. He was a great master of black magic, the skipper was. Yes, sir.

21

We were half a day out of Tripoli and met with real nasty weather. In the stokehold we were so thrown about that most of the time we did not know if we were at starboard or at port side or in which of the four corners and which of the two gangways of the bunkers.

Thrown upon a pile of fuel, trying to collect my limbs, I accidentally looked at the crystal tube of the water-gauge, and I marvelled how such a pretty-looking little thing could kill a grown-up sailor in the horrible way that it had done to Kurt from Memel. I questioned myself for a few seconds: would I jump at the broken tube and shut the cock and in doing so sacrifice my precious life?

I would not do it. I decided. Let anybody who wants to be brave do it. I don't care a tinkling about being brave and being called a great and regular guy.

But who is there who can say for sure what he will do on a given occasion, when no question is asked at all, but has to be answered by a quick move without time to think of what the consequences might be. The fireman might be right under it, and he cannot get away because he is entangled somehow or caught at the furnace door or blinded. Leave my fireman in the mud? Have him yell at me day and night for the rest of my life: 'Pippip, for hell's sake get me out, I am boiling to death. Pippip, come get me. I can't see a thing, my eyes are scorched out. Pippip, quick, or it's all over. Pip-pip-p-p.'

Just try that and live afterwards. Just try to save your own hide, and leave your fireman lying there whimpering. You hop at it and do it, even when you know that both of you won't stay alive.

On second thought, maybe I would not go. My life is worth just as much to me as is the life of my fireman to him. My life might –

'Pippip, the devil, jump back, don't look, port side and over, jump!'

My fireman howled so mightily that the noise of the engine seemed to be drowned away. Without turning my head or hesitating I jumped over to port and dropped on my knees, because I had tumbled over the poker against the wall. Simultaneously with my fall I heard a tremendous crash right behind me.

I saw the fireman get pale all over, so much so that even under the thick layer of soot and sweat on his face it seemed to be whitewashed. So I learned that even dead men still can get pale.

I stood up and rubbed my bruised shins and knees. Then I turned round to see what it was all about.

The ash-funnel had come down.

This funnel was a heavy tube made of thick sheet-iron, about three feet in diameter and about ten feet long. In, or, better, through it, the ash-cans were hoisted up on deck to be emptied into the sea. The funnel hung on four short chains against the ceiling of the stokehold. The lowest part of it was about eight feet above the floor of the stokehold. Perhaps the holes in which the chains were fastened had broken out or rusted away, or the chains had broken. Whatever the reason, the heavy sea we found ourselves in had hastened the break and so the funnel had come down. The weight of this funnel was a ton or so. Suppose someone is beneath it when it falls – he is severed in two, as if cut with a heavy knife, or only his head is cut off, or an arm or a leg or both, or he is cut deep into the shoulder. Who ever would have thought that this ash-funnel would come down? It had hung there since Queen Betsy had her first lover. Why couldn't it stay another three hundred years in its place? But in these revolutionary times, nothing is safe any longer; everybody and everything gets restless and wants to change positions and viewpoints. So the funnel drops.

'Yep, fire'm, this sure was a close jump over a razor-blade. Almost got me. I would have been well mashed-up. Nothing would have remained for Judgement Day. Well, anyway, I wonder what these guys, sent out at Doomsday to collect all the dead and bring them before the Judge, are going to do with the sailors fallen overboard or shipped over the rail and eaten by the fishes bit by bit – by thousands of fishes? I would like to see how they settle this affair of collecting all the sailors out of a hundred thousand millions of fish bowels.'

'That's why sailors are out anyway,' the fireman said. 'This is the reason why a sailor doesn't care if he swears all the hells he wants to and spits at the seamen's mission.'

This time there was no burial with a begrudged lump of coal at the feet, a disinterested tipping of the cap and the funeral prayer: 'Damn it, hell, now I am short again a coal-drag. Wonder when I ever can stay complete for a while.'

The water-gauge got its victim. The ash-funnel did not. I would like to know what will be next and who is next? Perhaps it will be that plank leading up from the upper bunker to the landing above the stokehold. It already crackles rather suspiciously when you walk across. Or if it is not the plank it might be the – What's the use of guessing? The finish will come some way, and likely it will be very different from what one figured.

Next port I'd better step out and skip. I knew, however, that there would be only another death ship after a little freedom. The deads have to go back to the graves, even though they may get at times a mouthful of fresh air to keep them healthy.

Stanislav's and my thoughts must have been somehow in the air. Because when we were in port again, we could not make a move without being watched by the police. At the first attempt to go to the outskirts of the town or to show signs of skipping, the police would have pinched us and taken us back to the bucket. The skipper would have got a bill for the cost of catching two deserters from a foreign vessel. We, of course, would have to stand up for the bill from our pay. And again we would have to be on our knees before the old man to let us have a little advance for drinks.

We tried it again at Beirut. We were in a tavern, waiting for the *Yorikke* to sail and leave us to our fate. But quite unexpectedly, when we felt sure the *Yorikke* had put out and was under weigh, in stepped two guys: 'Sailors, aren't you from the *Yorikke*?' We did not say yes or no. We said nothing. But these birds did not wait for an answer. They only said: 'Your ship has hoisted the P flag already and is about up and down. You are not going to miss your berth, gentlemen? May we show you the way back? If you do not mind, gentlemen, we are very much pleased to accompany you to your ship.'

After we had sadly climbed up the gangway these friendly fellows stood at the wharf waiting until the *Yorikke* was steaming so far off that we could hardly have made it swimming. I say there are really fine folks in some ports, bringing the sailors back to their ships and bidding them farewell as long as they can see the last cloud of smoke.

After all, Stanislav was right: 'No way ever to get off again, once on. If you really make it and have luck in skipping the can, they catch you within a day or two and take you straight to another death tub. What else can they do with you? They have to get you out somehow. Can't deport you. You haven't got a country to be deported to.'

'But, Lavski, how can they make me sign on? They cannot do that.'

'Yeah? Can't they? You should see how they can. The skipper, always in need of hands, even pays them a pound or two for bringing you in. He swears that he has signed you on by hand-shake in a tavern, and that he has given you two bobbies advance. A skipper, such a fine man, is always right; the sailor is always drunken and of course always wrong. You have never seen the skipper; neither has he seen you. But he needs you and claims you as a deserter. And don't you try the court. That's the curtains for you. The skipper swears and the birds that got a pound from the happy old man swear, and what of you then? Committing perjury? They fine you ten pounds, and leave you in care of the skipper. Then you work half a year without any advance just for the ten pounds fine the skipper had to pay.'

I stood aghast listening to this horrid tale of modern slavery. Those foolish white-slavery acts protect a woman, or claim to do so. Why not a sailor? He cannot wait for the Lord to protect him.

So I said: 'Lavski, so help me and bless my soul, there must be some justice in this world.'

'There is justice in this world. Heaps of it. But not for sailors, and not for working men making trouble. Justice is for the people who can afford to have it. We are not these people. Everybody knows well you cannot go to a consul. If you could, you would not be on a *Yorikke*. So whenever you come in port on a *Yorikke*, every child knows what you are and who you are. If you could go to the consul, then of course they would have no chance. But your consul is not for you. You cannot pay the fee, and you cannot rattle a hundred-dollar bill among the papers on his desk and forget it there.'

'Where is your Danish sailor's pay-book?' I asked.

'Now, look here, you sap. Sometimes I earnestly believe you haven't got any brains at all. A question like that! If I still had that Danish scrap I would not be here. No sooner did I have that beautiful passport from Hamburg than I sold the Danish pay-book for ten dollars American money. For the bird that bought it, it was worth a hundred. He had to get out of Hamburg by all means. You see, I was so sure that I could depend on that beautiful passport. It was just perfect. Reliable like a jane that has got three kids from you and is so ugly that you can't be seen with her in the daytime without feeling sick.'

'Why didn't you try your luck with that passport elsewhere, after the Dutch consul had said he couldn't sign you on?'

'Did I try, Pippip? I should say I sure did. I would be the last one not to have on full run such a brilliant front page. I got a Swede. The skipper had no time to take me to the consul, because he was already on his way to put out. When he asked me for my papers I produced my elegant passport. He fingered it, gazed surprised, and said: 'Sorry, sonny, nothing doing. I can't get you off my chest again. Can't make it.'

'The Germans would have taken you in,' I said; 'they could not refuse you with that German passport.'

'Tell you the truth, Pippip, I did. I got a fine Germ. The pay was dirty low. Yet I thought, well, to begin with, let's stick for a few trips. But when the mate looked at my passport, he bellowed right out: "We don't take stinking Polacks. Out of here, this is a decent German ship." Then I got a third-rater Germ. But I could not stand it. Workers, and all those what is called "proletarians of the world unite", they are more patriotic than the kaiser's generals ever could be, and more narrow-minded than a Methodist preacher's wife. I hardly ever heard anything else but: "Polacks out." "Won't you swallow the rest of Silesia also, Polack?" "Even pigs of the German peasants stink less than a Polack." "Where is that Polack swine of ours?" They never said it directly to me, right

423

in my face. But I heard it all around, whenever I came in sight. I was often near going over the rail. I sure can stand a lot, but this I could not. So I went to the skipper after the first trip back home in Hamburg. He was fine. He said: "I know, Koslovski, how it is, and how you feel. I am sorry. I can do nothing about it. You are a most realiable man. Sorry to let you go. But I understand you are going mad or you will kill a couple of the rest. Either wouldn't do any of us any good. I think it is best for you to go and look for a ship which is not German. You sure will find one." '

'Great guys, these fellow-sailors, and sure they are talking all the time about communism and internationalism and eternal brother-hood of the working class and whatnot. Bunk,' I said.

'Now, don't take it this way, Pippip,' Stanislav excused them still. 'They are educated that way. They can't help it. Was the same with them when war broke out. Karl Marx on their bookshelf, and the guns over their shoulders, marching against the workers of France and Russia. There will still have to pass five hundred years before they won't fall any longer for worn-out slogans. You see, that's why I like it on the *Yorikke*. Here nobody pushes down your throat your nationality. Because nobody has any to play. And don't you think the Russians are so much different. They are as jazzy about their Bolshevik Russia as are the hurrah nationalists of Germany. The Bolshevists shut their doors against hungry workers from the outside as close as do the American labour unions. Dog eats dog, and any devil is a devil for another. I rather go down to the bottom with that sweet old *Yorikke* than eat and live on a Germ ship. I don't want a Germ for a Christmas present, if you ask me.'

'Haven't the Poles now a merchant marine of their own?'

'They have. But what good does that to me?' Stanislav asked. 'I have it from a first-class Polish authority that I am not a Pole, while the Germs, on the other hand, take me only as a Polish swine. There you are.'

424

22

Month after month passed. Before I knew it I had been on the *Yorikke* four months. And when I came aboard I had thought I could not live on her for two days.

So I found one day that the *Yorikke* had actually become a ship on which I could live and even laugh. Occasionally we would have a great after-gale supper, sometimes one cup, frequently two cups, of gin. We would have raisin cake and cocoa cooked with canned milk. Sometimes, having picked out for the cook some extra-fine nut coal from bunkers, he would hand us in return an extra pound of sugar or an extra can of sweetened milk. Whenever we made a port where the skipper did not mind giving us shore leave we were provided with some advance to go and lift a skirt or two, and after that to get well drenched. My mess-gear – that is, the tools to eat with – had become complete. It was, of course, not a perfect unit, for one piece had once adorned a table in a tavern in Tripoli, another had come from a saloon in Smyrna, and another one from Tangier. I had even some surplus, in case one was nipped or got lost.

The filth of the quarters had become thicker, but I was now used to it. In this way the *Yorikke* once more proved an excellent teacher, making it quite clear that the saying: 'All civilization is only a thin layer of varnish on the human animal' has a lot of truth in it. The bunk I slept in was not so hard as I had thought when I lay down in it the first day. I had made a pillow out of cleaning rags swiped from the engine-hold. Bed-bugs, yes, we had them. But they are found in all the elegant cities of the world, like New York, Boston, and Balti, and Chic also.

Looking at my fellow-sailors now and then, I could not imagine how it had ever been possible that, seeing them for the first time, I had thought them the dirtiest and filthiest bunch of guys I had ever seen. They looked quite decent.

Everything became a bit cleaner, and more endurable every day that passed. It is like this: You look every day at the same thing, and then you don't see it any more.

No, sir, I have nothing against the *Yorikke*. She was a fine ship. Got finer every day. The crew was not at all so rude and sour as I had thought during the first month.

Stanislav was an intelligent guy, I might even say a real gent. He had knocked about the world a lot, he had seen many things and happenings, and he had gathered experiences such as I only wished every president of the U.S. could have had. The marvel about Stanislav was that he not only saw things but that he saw them clear, through and through, right to their very sources. Nobody could blindfold him with slogans and success yarns. From every experience he had had, from everything he had seen or heard of, he deduced a wisdom and philosophy which was worth more to him and to his understanding of world, matter and conditions than the finest and thickest book about philosophy written by a great prof and doc.

My two firemen, I learned, were not like automobile mechanics that understood only their trade, and outside of their trade knew nothing but how far a certain place is, how much gas they use per mile, and what chance you have to win a poker game against the boss who hires and fires. My firemen knew how to talk, because they had learned to think. The A.B.s and the hands – after knowing them better I found that none of them were the ordinary kind of human bugs. No ordinary man ever came to ship on the *Yorikke*. Ordinary men have their birth-certificates and passports and pay-books in fine shape. They never make any trouble for a bureaucrat. There would be no such thing as the Most Glorious God's Country if half of the pioneers and builders of the great nation could have produced passports and could have passed Ellis Island like the Prince of Wales. Ordinary people can never fall over the walls, because they never dare climb high enough to see what is beyond the walls. Therefore they can never ship on such a peach of a maiden as the *Yorikke*. Really good people believe what is told them, and they feel satisfied with the explanation. Therefore we can be at ease in Nicaragua, and cross the ocean to lick the Germans, and make the bankers the emperors of the republic.

It serves the guy right when he falls from the wall. Let him stay at home in the first place. Freedom? Okay with us. But it must be certified and stamped.

There came a time when the skipper held quite a bit of pay of mine. The question was where and when to sign off. My signing off

426

would not have been recognized in any port. Since I had not brought aboard any paper, the skipper was not obliged to give me a pay-book. Without one, and without being able to prove that I was once born somewhere, the port authorities would have shipped me off on the next death can that put in.

There was left only one kind of signing off. That of the gladiators. Signing off on a reef and going to the fishes' bellies. Still there might be some luck. A sailor without luck should not go sailing. So it might happen that I could reach the coast, somehow. Shipwrecked sailor. Poor wretch. Folks living along the coast take pity on a shipwrecked sailor and take him in and feed him.

Then the consul hears that there is a shipwrecked sailor somewhere. He gets hold of him. He is not a bit interested in the man. He is interested alone in the report how, when, and where the ship was wrecked, and, if you can give an account of it, under what circumstances the ship was lost. 'Now, my man, be careful what you say.' The report is of great importance, not to the world, but to the company that wants to collect. For if there is no report from an eyewitness the company may have to wait a couple of years to pull in the cash. After the report is made, sworn to, and signed, the shipwrecked sailor gets one pound and the news: 'Sorry, since you cannot prove your citizenship, I can do nothing for you. Anyway, don't you worry, an experienced man like you, you will soon get another ship. Quite a few ships put in here. Just hang around.'

The ship puts in all right. Yes, sir. The sailor, hungry and sick of sleeping on bales of straw, on park benches, in gateways, in the furrows of cultivated land right near the last house in the town, hops on the ship just getting under weigh. He tumbles to the fo'c'sle, reads what is written over the entrance of the quarters, and knows where he is again. So he learns that the shipwreck was only an interruption, and, at best, a change in the name of the ship and in the language of the skipper. The fish have patience.

We were at anchor off Dakar. Dakar is a decent port. Nothing doing. Full of French gobs, French marines, French didonks, and French colonial blues, and a lot of French hoppies or dames. But we had no money to look them under. I won't complain, anyhow, because the Arabian janes in Tunis and in Tripoli waiting to see us are just as good. It mustn't always be French. They haven't got any new tricks. The Arabian and Egyptian babies have, and that's that.

Boiler-scaling. That comes right next to setting in fallen-out grate bars. Boiler-scaling when the fire in that boiler was taken out only ten hours ago and the neighbouring boiler is still under full steam. But that's not all. Because it is done right near that section of the funny globe where you say: 'Hey, you, look there, see that green painted fence, with an E on it? Know what that is? That is the Equator, or what the scientists call "the imaginary circle" or the zero meridian.' But there is nothing imaginary about it, if you have to scale boilers there.

The imaginary circle. Don't make me laugh out loud. In the first place this fence is white-hot. If you only so much as touch it, your whole arm, as far up as your shoulder, is gone, scorched off like nothing. Put the heavy poker against this fence, and the poker melts like lard. Doesn't leave even a pinch of ashes. No, sir. If you put two thick bars of fine steel one against the other and you hold them on the fence, they get welded into one single piece so that you cannot even see the seam.

'You guys don't know the full story as yet, you dumbheads,' Stanislav said. 'But let me tell you what once happened when I crossed the E with the *Vaarsaa*, which was a rather fine Dane hussy. It happened about on Christmas Eve, as far as I remember. Now, old *Vaarsaa* got so white-hot while crossing the E that you just poke your finger or your pocket-knife through the iron hull, and wherever you poked, a hole was left. It was funny when spitting against the hull. Now, it sure is not decent of a regular sailor to spit against the bulwark of the ship he is sailing on. Anyway, we did it for fun just to see what might happen. Tell you, wherever we spit against the gunwale the spit went clear through and another hole was left. The skipper, who was on the bridge, saw what we were doing and he yelled down: "T'hell with you damned devils, don't you try to make a sieve out of my ship, or I put you all in irons." That's what he said. Then he ordered: "Close all those holes immediately or, hell, I feed you to the sharks." There wasn't much to it. We just rubbed with a piece of wood over the holes or with our elbows, and the holes closed like you would work with clay or with a fresh custard pie. You see, the hull had gone as soft as dough. The masts really made us quite a lot of trouble that day. They were good masts, all steel tube, see? But in spite of that we worked like young devils to prevent it, we could do nothing to keep those steel masts from bending over like candles you leave standing on a hot stove in the kitchen. We had to work fast to fix tackles high above the mast-tops and to hoist the masts and straighten them out while they were still soft. You see, it was like that, if we had waited until we had crossed the whole E they would have cooled off, then there would be no chance to straighten them until we docked

428

somewhere around a shipyard. But I tell you, you little birdies, one should never fool around with the E. It's dangerous.'

'Now, who would ever do such a nasty thing?' I said. 'But I wonder, Stanislav, how come that you, so smart a sailor, could ever ship on a can that had a skipper who would not take the slightest precaution when reaching the E. He must have been a queer miser. Sure, he wanted to save the tunnel expenses like the others who sail four weeks round Cape Horn to save the few pennies the American government charges for using the old Panama Canal. When we made the E on the *Mabel Harrison*, that was what you guys might call a regular ship, such as none of you has ever seen and never will, well, as I said, when we made the E we went right through the tunnel under the ocean, not minding a bit that old fussy Equator at all. Now, in this tunnel it is really cold; you would be surprised to find something so cold straight beneath the E. Not for a minute would you ever imagine you are sailing straight under the E. It's all well lighted up, almost like day.'

'Don't you think that I don't know that tunnel, you puppy,' Stanislav said. 'We stayed out because the company did not want to pay the expenses. They charge quite a bit. I figure it must be close to a pound a register ton. Sure, they make truckloads of money with that tunnel. But since I have never been in this tunnel I, for the world, cannot make out how the hell they get down the ships the size, let's say, of twelve thousand tons.'

'That's easier than you would ever think it is,' I explained. 'There is a huge hole in the midst of the ocean. Now, the engineers have put through this hole a pipe – 's matter of fact, several pipes; I reckon about twenty or so – to hustle up the traffic. As soon as the ship reaches the entrance to the pipe she bends over a bit and goes in bow first, glides down on well-greased rails. Now, after a while of gliding this way, she finally reaches the bottom, which is a mighty tunnel. There the hands are all ready to get her a carriage, which is drawn by heavy engines, all running on ten-inch rails. Some tunnels have no rails and carriages. There they have got water in and the ship goes along under her own steam. Here they charge a bit less, but it takes more time and it has happened that ships even sank and were a total loss. Now, when the ship has reached the end of the tunnel it is put in a sort of floating dry-dock and heaved up through the pipe until she comes out again to the open. Here the dry-dock is opened, and off she goes without any damage done by the E. If I had money, I tell you, I would buy only the shares of this company; they pay no less than twenty-two per

429

cent per share. And you have the shares rather cheap, because there are people who don't believe in the company and in the Equator.'

'I never thought it would be that simple,' Stanislav said. 'My idea was that they would put the ship in a kind of diver's bell and then haul her down, drag her along the bottom, and heave her up again on the other side of the E.'

'Of course, they could have done the whole job that way as well,' I answered. 'But, somehow, I think there must be a catch in why they haven't done it. Sure, they could not do it for a pound a ton. Because I figure it must be more complicated working a whole ship with a diver's bell. There would have been still another way to – '

'What for hell's sake is going on there?' The second had put his cone through the manhole and was yelling like a mad gorilla. 'Is this a sewing-circle for an African mission or what? Are you paid for scaling that goddamned boiler or do you get your money for shabbering like drunken monkeys. We will never get the boiler scaled. Turn to it, the hell, you stinkbones.'

'Hey, you grandson of two peaches, you come in here,' I hollered so that the boiler drummed. 'What did you say, stinkbones or what? Come in and scale your bitch of a boiler yourself, you thief. Wait until we are under weigh again, and then step in the stokehold; I swear we'll roast you in the furnace.'

From the thick dust of the scale and from the infernal heat I was nearly mad. I would have killed him like a louse if he had come in.

'He won't report you to the old man,' Stanislav said, 'just as during the war an officer never reported you for having spit in his face. They needed you and could not afford to have you in the guard instead of in the trenches.'

In the sweat of thy face shalt thou eat bread. Well, you who said so, you have never scaled a boiler of the *Yorikke* right close to the Equator with the fire out only ten hours and the boiler next to it under full steam! It must be done. Boilers have to be scaled or they go up to heaven, taking along the whole crew and all that is left of the ship.

We were sitting inside that boiler as active members of a nudist camp. The walls of the boiler were so hot that we could not touch them with bare hands, nor could we kneel at the bottom without a thick layer of rags under us.

There wasn't such a thing as goggles for boiler-scaling on the *Yorikke*. No goggles were known at Carthage, so why should the *Yorikke* have them? The dust of the scale sprang into your eyes and almost burned the light out of them. If you tried to rub it out it would only pierce so deeply into your eyelids and under them that you would have to pick the specks out with a pin or with a pocket-knife. You feel that you are going mad. You cannot stand it any more and you call on one of the other guys to get them out. He works with his dusty and clumsy hands about your eyes until he gets them clean, but your eyes swell under this torture and they stay swollen and bloodshot for a week.

Even suppose you had goggles, they would not do you any good. The dust darkens them to such an extent that you cannot see where you are.

The boiler inside has to be illuminated for you to see what you are doing, because it is as dark inside as it is in a coal-mine. If you had electric light it would be easier. But on the *Yorikke* we had only the ancient lamps of old Carthage. Five minutes, no more, and the boiler was filled with black smoke so thick that we could cut it like a cake. And the smoke stood as if chained and gummed.

The drumming, hammering, and knocking against the hull inside seemed to crack open your head and mash your brain to powder.

Hardly ten minutes' work and we had to come up and out to get air, exhausted each time like pearl-divers.

We would crawl out and dart under the air-funnel which reaches into the stokehold. The ocean breeze would strike our hot bodies, and then you feel as if a sword were thrust through your lungs. After fifteen seconds you feel like lying naked in a blizzard. To escape this terrific snowstorm, which in fact is only the soft breeze of the tropics, you hurry back into the hot boiler as if hunted, and go to work harder than before with the hope that the harder you work, the quicker you will be out of the inferno.

Before ten minutes have elapsed, however, you have to crawl out again into that blizzard of Saskatchewan, because you feel you are surely going to die if you don't have fresh air.

There is a moment where the nerves seem to burst. It happens when you feel that you have to go out that very second and you see your fellow-man squeezing slowly through the manhole. The boiler has only one manhole. The narrower it can be made, the better for the boiler. Only one man can crawl through at a time. The others have to wait until he is through and fully out. While he is squeezing himself through, which takes a certain time, the hole is entirely closed, and not one mouthful of air can come in. The two men still inside feel exactly like men in a sunken submarine. No difference.

It happened within these few seconds, when Stanislav was just out and I was next, that I looked back on hearing a bump, and I saw the fireman lifeless. With the last breath I had I cried: 'Lavski, the fire'm has dropped out. If we don't get him out quick he will choke to death in that poison smoke.'

'One minute, Pip –' Stanislav was snapping for air, 'let me just catch a noseful.'

The fireman was lying somewhere in the thick black cloud inside the boiler. We could not see him at first. But when I crawled back into the boiler I found him lying flat under the lower flue.

It is difficult for a living being to squeeze himself through the manhole. First your head through, then one arm, then you bring both your shoulders so far forward that your body takes on the shape of a cylinder. Now you get the other arm out and then you finally squeeze the lower part of your body through. Having tried this half a dozen times, getting bruised and scratched on both arms and shoulder blades, you can do it rather quickly and efficiently.

To get out a lifeless body is quite a job. We had to take a rope and sling it around the body and under the arms. With another rope we had to bandage the fireman mummy-fashion. After we had him out, his arms and shoulders were well peeled.

Stanislav wanted to take him right beneath the air-funnel into the blizzard. When I saw it I cried: 'Lavski, you are killing him. First he must come to and breathe well before we can do that.'

We blew into his face, beat his wrists and the soles of his feet, and worked him up with artificial breathing. The heart was throbbing so feebly that we could hardly hear it. But it was beating regularly. We poured water over his head and his chest, and we pressed a wet rag against his heart. Whether his face was pale or red we could not make out, because he, like Stanislav and me, looked blacker than a Negro. When I noticed that his breathing was slowly coming along, we carried him under the air-funnel, but put there only his head. The rest of the body we covered with rags. Stanislav had to go on deck to twist the mouth of the air-funnel into the breeze, because the wind had changed.

When we were entertaining ourselves a bit in the boiler, the horsethief was quick to put his cone through the manhole, choke away the little air that came in, and bawl us out. Yet now, when we were in need of somebody to help us and treat us to a good shot, he did not show up, but sat with the chief in the mess, lapping his coffee and blabbing about useless drags and lazy firemen. A cup of gin would have done the fireman good right then, and us too, if only to forget for a minute that grinding of scale dust between our teeth.

We had the fireman coming on fine. We carried him to a pile of coal to have him sit upright. He was still far away somewhere under palm-trees in southern Spain. It took him quite some time to find himself back in the stokehold.

'What of all the drunken lousy beachcombers is up again?' The horsethief, that second engineer, had come from the enginehold, through the famous gangway alongside the boilers into the stokehold, and he was standing right at the corner of the boiler wall, yelling at us, who were still working about the fireman. 'You are paid to work here, and not for sitting around and clicking your stinking swear-traps. Get to work, the hell with you.'

Stanislav or I could have said: 'Look here, sir, the fireman was –'

Yet both of us had, at the same second, exactly the same instinct. And it was the right instinct. Without saying one word we both bent down, grabbed a huge chunk of coal, and gunned it against the face of that pickpocket.

He was almost as quick as we. He had his arm up to protect his face the same moment we flung the lumps of coal. He flew off through the low, narrow gangway. But Stanislav had another big piece of coal ready, and quick as a weasel he was after him and hurled that chunk into the dark gangway with all his might so that it exploded into dust against the iron wall of the side-bunker, and he cried: 'You heap of dirty –, if you ever drop in here again you are going through the ash-pipe to feed the sharks, so help me geecries, and you may spit straight into my face if I don't do it. Now go to the old man and report me and have a month's pay cut off. But if you do, grandson of peaches, there will not be a square inch of skin left sound in your face when we get ashore.'

Stanislav had run to the steel door of the engine-hold, which the second had tightly closed behind him. But he listened to what Stanislav yelled through this door, and he took note of it.

All the time we were lying at Dakar, scaling the boilers, the second never came in again and never again said a word even if he did not hear the hammering in the boiler for half an hour. From that day on he treated us as if we were raw eggs. He, in fact, became more diplomatic than even the chief. So the *Yorikke* again had taught me something new, by which I mean: It works wonders for a labourer to have a hammer or a lump of coal at hand to use at the right time in the proper way. A working man that is not respected

433

has only himself to blame.

After the boilers were scaled and washed we got two cups of gin and a good advance. So we thought things over, went ashore, and gave the port the once-over. I could have stowed away on a French that was making Barcelona. But I did not take this opportunity because I would have left the skipper with my four months' pay in his pocket. I could not afford to enrich skippers. So I let the French sail without me. Stanislav could have got a Norwegian on which he could have gone as far as Malta. He had the same reason not to go I had. His outstanding pay was even higher than mine.

We just roamed about port and looked ships and crews over. Wherever a sailor goes or tumbles, he thinks he is going to meet somebody or something unexpectedly and so have a surprise without paying for it.

23

Looking at ships in port is practically the only thing worth while for a sailor to do after having seen the dames and if he hasn't enough cold cash left over to get his belly wetted. To the pictures you cannot go, because you do not understand the language. So there is nothing better to do than to criticize other ships, their looks, their crews, their grub, their pay, and to wonder whether it would be better to ship with this one or that one or stay where you are.

So we came at last to the *Empress of Madagascar*. She was English. Seven thousand tons or even close to eight; yes, sir. Seeing her, we thought she might be a fine can to get out on. A fine shippy. Clean and brilliant, freshly polished over. Almost new. Could hardly have more than four years. The gilded stripes and lines and patches were still shiny. The paint like from last month.

'Now, wouldn't she be a peach to have under your legs?' I said to Stanislav. 'She is so smart she has even painted eyelashes. Let's have a closer look at her. Trouble is we have no chance with her.'

Stanislav said nothing. He just looked at her as if he meant to buy her and find out the price for it.

If it were not for the four months' pay I'd have to leave behind I sure would like to try her. Wonder if I could make the chief fire me by getting so stiff that on coming aboard I would go to his cabin and knock him down. Then the old man might pay me off and keep only half a month's pay for socking the chief. Or I might go to the old man directly and tell him I am a Bolshevist, and I have got it in mind to get up the whole crew, and we would take over the ship and run her for our own benefit or sell her to Russia. Or I might go to the skipper and tell him the old story about my mother back home sick in bed and having an operation and ask for the biggest advance possible. Once I had this advance in my pocket, I would watch out for the *Empress* and hop on when she was hauling anchor. There is still the question of where she will set me off again, because she cannot take me with her to England. The British Board of Trade, having so many thousands of unemployed juicers to take care of, would be worried to death what to do with me.

Anyway, it costs nothing to work her a bit.

We went into port and there I left Stanislav in a place he found jolly and needed badly.

Then I strolled back to sweet *Empress*.

'Ahoy, there!' I yelled up, seeing a guy with a white cap leaning against the rail.

'Ahoy yourself!' he answered. 'What ye want?'

'Ain't a chance for a fireman?'

'Papers?'

'Nope.'

'Naaw. Sorry. Nothing doing, then, up here.'

I had known this before. A pretty innocent dame like this doesn't take a guy like me up with her. Here I have to bring the marriage licence or out you go. Mother is still holding her hand over mousy.

Along the dock I walk, down the whole length of the bucket. On the quarter-deck I see a bunch of the crew squatting, playing cards. I am close enough to understand almost every word they are saying. Now, that's some English they are talking! And on an English can on which the gilded stripes are still sparkling! There must be a ghost somewhere around here. They are playing cards. But they do not quarrel, they do not fight or argue or laugh or swear or accuse one mug of having drawn the wrong card at the right time or the wrong ace at no time, or debate who should have dealt and who not.

Shark-fins and ambergris! What is this? They are squatting as though sitting on their own graves and playing for their own worms. They seem to have the right grub. Look fed all right. Somehow something does not fit. Never seen sailors playing cards with troubled faces like these. Something is queer about the whole safari. A newly born ship. English too. What is she doing here in Dakar anyway? In a port all French – more French, I should say, than Marseilles? What's her cargo, anyhow? I'll be – Now, who could believe it? Scrap iron. On the west coast of Africa, close to the Equator. Maybe, she couldn't get cargo on her way home and took scrap iron on for ballast. Makes at least some coin for the company. Home, Glasgow. Maybe they are badly in need of scrap iron in Glasgow. As for ballast, scrap iron is still a better cargo than rocks. Nevertheless, strange that an English bucket with such elegant looks cannot get cargo from Africa to old England or Scotland.

Now, if I hung around here in Dakar a few days, I would find out what's the trouble with that hussy. She can't be a bobtail, can she?

Come to think of it, these birds squatting there are playing cards like deads on their graves. Like deads on – Hello, old masher! Dead ones. But no; it cannot be. It simply cannot be. A dame looking so elegant and innocent, could it be that she is already walking the street? No. No, I am just a bit sun-tipped. Must be the boiler-scaling. Cracks of scales still in my eyes. I haven't got my eyes clear yet. Seeing things. If I had money to spare, I would go and see the doc.

I walked back and met Stanislav.

'Let's go over to that Norske and have a little talk with them,' Stanislav said.

So we went to the Norwegian where Stanislav, yesterday, had made friends with a couple of Danes who came from a section of Denmark which Stanislav knew well. They had a can of fresh butter ready for us to take home. Living like real gents, that's what these guys do. I got a mighty lump of fine Danish cheese extra.

'Now, you two pirates, you are just in time to have supper with us,' one of the Danes said. 'Sit down on your buttocks and have a real old Danish supper. Quality, and I mean it, and, of course, quantity even more.'

So we sat down to a human meal, the kind we had not seen for so long a time that we for a while could not trust our eyes that such suppers still could exist somewhere in the world, and in particular in the fo'c'sle mess of a freighter.

'Has any of you sailors seen that lime-juicer yonder there? The what is she? I mean the *Empress of Madagascar*?' I asked while we were eating.

'Hanging around at the kerb-stone quite a bit,' one of the men said.

'Elegant dame,' I went on.

'Yip, elegant dame, silk outside, crabs underneath. Better stay off her.'

'But man, why?' I could not understand it. 'Why lay off her?'

'Silk all right. But if you lift the camisole you might easily find yourself in a garden of cauliflowers,' the Dane said.

Broke in another one: 'She is legal all right. She signs you on. With honey and chocolate ice-cream. Last dinner every day. With roast chicken and all the trimmings and pudding besides.'

'Damn your silly talk,' I said impatiently. 'Now come along with the low-down. What's her signal?'

Said the speaker of the house: 'You don't look like a John to me. Rather like a hopper with heaps of salt water inside the belly. I thought you would guess it for yourself on seeing her. Well, she is a funeral hussy. Next trip to bottom, with hell waiting for you.'

'Don't you think you are just a bit jealous?' I asked.

'Angel-maker and baby-farmer,' the Dane said. 'Help yourself to another cup of coffee. Another treat of beef? Just stuff it in. We don't have to be misers about milk and sugar. In the pot. As much as we want. Want to take home another can of milk?'

'You make tears come into my eyes with such a question,' I said.

'Well, I don't want to offend you, so I will take it.'

'Yip, sailor man. She has loaded dead men all right. But not dead soldiers from France to be taken home to mother across the pot. Not that. No, dead sailors still eating. But they may already write home to have their names carved in the lost sailors' plank in their village church back home. They can't miss it any more. If you wish to have your own sweet name on a plate in your church, if you have any, just go and sign on. It looks rather distinguished to have right by your own name such an elegant name as the *Empress of Madagascar*. Sounds a lot better than having gone down with an ordinary *Caroline*, or *Clementina Pumpstay*. *Empress of Madagascar*, boy, that looks like something great and swell, almost as if you had been her handy boy-friend.'

'Why should she try to make insurance cash?' Stanislav asked.

'Simple, honey, like making Swiss cheese around holes.'

'She can hardly be out of her diapers three years,' I figured.

'Now you got that straight and perfect; I see you can be trusted.

Exactly, almost to the day, she is three years old. She was built for East Asia and South American trade to beat the Germans, who are undermining rates again. She was to make sixteen knots at least. The gent who constructed her tried out, it appears, a new model, a new streamline, see, to raise her speed, but with less fuel expenses. As it happened, when she made the virgin hop she could reach four knots only, with asthma. With such a speed any clipper would beat her and she herself couldn't bring in even the pay for the crew, to say nothing of all the other expenses and a profit for the owners. With four knots she was scrap iron. Not even that.'

'She could be rebuilt.'

'Of course she could. You are a wise guy. But the owners thought of this before you came along and they did rebuild her. Rebuilt her not once, but twice. Each time she came out worse. She has to have the wind at the hams to make four knots now. So she cannot live, and she cannot die honourably. The owners cannot afford to sink her. It would break them. So nothing is left but to cash insurance.'

'And you think it will be on her next trip?'

'It has to be. She has tried to cash in twice already within less than three weeks. But she is so bully well that she did not even crack a leak. The first time she went upon a sand-bank. Pretty like a swan she was sitting. I am sure in Glasgow they already celebrated the insurance with champagne. But bad weather came up and with it high water, which embraced the lady and whipped her off fine, off into twenty fathoms, where her old man could not do anything better than steam her off on her way. The second time she tried the game was last week, when we were already lying here. She was sitting smoothly between reefs. Well done by the skipper. He is a smart guy and knows how to navigate a can on a two-inch stripe. Wireless station, of course, was smashed up at the right time, so that the old man had an excuse for not using it. But he had to set flags to keep face and to bake proper witness cakes for evidence. He had tough luck again. Just when he had ordered to lower away the boats, a French coastguard popped up. What that skipper must have cursed when he saw the coast coming! Sure, he had the log already charmed up, and now he had to work the rubber to make it blank again for another fill-in. He had gone between the reefs at low water. The coast sent him, calling by wireless, three tugs. As soon as high water came in again, the tugs got the lady out like on oiled roller-skates.'

'And what is she to do now?' I asked.

'Desperation. She has to take her last chance. If she reaches home safely, the Board of Underwriters will sure make an investigation. They will demand a change of skipper. A new skipper has to be worked up by the owners before he is reliable and trustworthy. It may happen that the underwriters back out of her, once she's home again. Then it will be too late for her to make good for her owners. So you see she has to do it on her trip out of here or she can never make it. Around this coast here she must go at it, because it is the safest part, free from the interference of ships rushing in too quick. Here it is silent. Farther north there is too much traffic, besides, there she cannot go off too far from the route, as she easily can do here without arousing suspicion.'

I wondered: 'Why is she hanging here such a long time?'

'No firemen.'

'Silly,' I said. 'I just passed by her and asked for a chance, saying I am fire'm.'

'Got papers?'

'Don't ask herring.'

'Without papers she cannot take you. She is English. Rules. Taking in dead ones would look suspicious under these conditions. The investigation might build up a case against her for taking on men without papers who may be inexperienced. She must have good men with clean papers. The firemen were smart. They burnt themselves well enough to be taken to the hospital. Care of the British Consul. They know why. Because they are the worst off when she cracks up. The water rushes into the stokehold, breaking in the hatchways and gangways, and so they are caught like rats in a trap and cannot get out. They are scorched to death, or drowned, or blown into rags when the furnaces get the cold shower and gun off. The firemen don't have to sign on again, once off. They make time in the hospital until the dame puts out of port.'

'How is that bucket to get out without firemen?' I asked.

'Don't you worry, sonny. They are ready for kidnapping, or for shanghai-ing, if you like that expression any better.'

'Horrible!' was all I could say.

Walking home to our good old *Yorikke*, I could not help thinking of this beautiful ship, with a crew on board that had faces as if they were seeking ghosts by day and by night.

Compared to that gilded *Empress*, the *Yorikke* was an honourable old lady with lavender sachets in her drawers. *Yorikke* did not pretend to anything she was not. She lived up to her looks. Honest to her lowest ribs and to the leaks in her bilge.

Now, what is this? I find myself falling in love with that old jane. All right, I cannot pass by you, *Yorikke*; I have to tell you I love you. Honest, baby, I love you. I have six black fingernails, and four black and green-blue nails on my toes, which you, honey, gave me when necking you. Grate-bars have crushed some of my toes. And each fingernail has its own painful story to tell. My chest, my back, my arms, my legs are covered with scars of burns and scorchings. Each scar, when it was being created, caused me pains which I shall surely never forget. But every outcry of pain was a lovecry for you, honey.

You are no hypocrite. Your heart does not bleed tears when you do not feel heart-aches deeply and truly. You do not dance on the water if you do not feel like being jolly and kicking chasers in the pants. Your heart never lies. It is fine and clean like polished gold. Never mind the rags, honey dear. When you laugh, your whole soul and all your body is laughing. And when you weep, sweety, then you weep so that even the reefs you pass feel like weeping with you.

I never want to leave you again, honey. I mean it. Not for all the rich and elegant buckets in the world. I love you, my gipsy of the sea!

THE THIRD BOOK

An old love-song
of an experienced sailor

There are so many ships on sea,
Some do come and some do flee;
Yet none can be so dreadful low
That none is found still further so.

1

I suppose this is a good rule: If you want to keep your wife, do not love her too much. She might get bored with you and run away with somebody who gives her a sound beating twice a week to keep her lively.

My sudden strong love for the *Yorikke* looked rather suspicious, I thought. But having heard right before a hair-raising story of a tough kidnapper, and carrying in one pocket a beautiful can of fine golden Danish butter and a can of milk in the other and a huge lump of rich Danish cheese in my hand, it will be easily understood why I could fall so deeply in love with *Yorikke* and chuck that silken hussy.

Nevertheless, I felt strongly that there was something strange about my growing love for the ragged *Yorikke*. Something was going to go wrong. Maybe the ash-pipe was waiting for me, or the plank across the top of the stokehold, or the water-gauge of the boiler. So, with all my ardent love for her, I began to worry and to feel uneasy. Something was hanging in the air for me.

The quarters were stuffy. I could not stand them right now, after having seen the clean quarters of the fine Norske.

'Come on,' I said to Stanislav, 'let's go off again for a while. We'll stroll along the docks and the water-board until it gets cooler. A fresh breeze is sure to come up soon, likely about nine. Then we go home and sleep on the poop, where it is coolest.'

'Right you are, Pippip,' Stanislav agreed. 'It's near impossible to sleep here now, or even sit around. One feels like getting dumb all over. We might give that little Dutch can a look. Sometimes you meet quite unexpectedly an old friend.'

'You don't mean to say you are still hungry?' I asked, laughing.

'Not exactly. But I might get a cake of soap and perhaps even a towel. Things which I really need, and I would sure welcome them.'

We hoofed leisurely on our way. It had by now become dark. The lamps of the port could be seen only dimly. No ship was busy taking in cargo or spitting it out. All the ships seemed to have gone to sleep.

'Say, that tobacco the Danes handed us isn't so great when you look closer at it,' I said, puffing.

Hardly had I spoken, and I was just turning my head towards Stanislav, when I received a terrific blow on my block. I felt the blow quite clearly when it came down, yet I could not move myself. My legs at once became strangely thick and heavy, and I fell. There was about me a dreadful humming and roaring, the cause of which I could not figure out. Anyway, I was sure that I had not lost my consciousness; at least, I had the impression that I saw and heard everything that was going on around me. That is what I thought.

This sensation did not last very long, it seemed to me. I came to again and rose and tried to walk off. On doing so, I ran against a wall which was iron. All about me it was dark, pitch-dark.

Now, where and what could this iron wall be? I moved to the left. The wall was still there. The same wall I encountered at the right. Also at my back. My head was still roaring and buzzing. I did not know what had happened and what it all was about. From so much thinking and figuring I became very tired. I lay down on the floor.

After some time, when I woke up again, I found the four walls still there. I could not stand up very well. I staggered and tumbled. Getting wider awake, I felt that I was not staggering at all, but that

442

the whole floor was swaying.

'Damn the hell and all the devils,' I said. 'Scram the whole outfit. Now I know where I am. On a bucket, and she is already well out on high sea. Jolly on our way to hell. The engine is knocking and stamping in regular time. Must be an hour or more since the can went under weigh.'

It was still dark about me.

With my fists and with my feet I began now to work the walls to see what would happen. Of one thing I was positively sure, I was not on the *Yorikke*, because on the *Yorikke* I knew every nook and corner, and that I might be in our chamber of horrors was out of the question, for I had had no quarrel with the skipper in regard to the pay for overtime, and the second would never lay me in. In the first place, he could not spare so good a drag as I had become during the last four months. Besides, he knew that he would land in the furnace the first hour I was out again and below in the stokehold.

For a long while nobody seemed to take notice of my bombing the walls or of my yelling, either. But then a ray of light fell into the box in which I was. The light widened, and I saw it came from above. It was a flashlight.

An ugly voice asked: 'Finished your snore, you funking drunkard?'

'Looks like, buddy,' I answered. 'Hey you, won't you help me out of here?'

Having said this, I knew where I was and what had happened. Shanghaied. I am on the *Empress of Madagascar*, to be fed to the fishes and to help sailing-insurance.

'The ole man wan's 'a see ye,' the jailer said.

He let below a rope and I climbed up the shaft. Looked to me as if I was below as far down as the bilge.

'You are a pretty bunch of peach-sons,' I said the very moment I stepped into the cabin of the skipper.

'Beg pardon?' the skipper said, with quite a distinguished air.

'Shanghaiers. Man-pirates. Kidnappers. Baby-farmers. Filthy sons of beachcombers, that's what you are, all of you,' I bellowed.

The skipper remained undisturbed. He lighted a cigarette and said: 'I fancy, my good man, you are still intoxicated. We shall put you for ten minutes under an ice shower to get you sober and to teach you how to address the master of a British vessel. More respect, my good man, when you have the honour to stand in the cabin of a British captain.'

I looked into his face and said nothing more. One should not try to catch hissing bullets with bare hands. It does nobody any good, not even the pistol.

The skipper pressed a button.

Then he said: 'Sit down.'

In came two men. Husky, bully, with horribly crumpled faces, and with the hands of gorillas, they looked like the animal-men roaming wild in mystery stories. The average woman meeting these two birds a quarter of a mile from an inhabited house would have fallen dead on seeing them.

'Is this the man?' the skipper asked.

'Yegh, t'as him all right,' one of the two said.

'What are you doing on board my ship?' the skipper asked me. He acted like a judge in an English criminal court; only the wig was missing. Before him there were papers on which he wrote as if he were at the same time his own court clerk. He asked again: 'What are you doing here on my ship, and how did you come aboard?'

'That's what I wish to know from you, sir, what I am doing here and how I came to be here.'

Now one of the mystery-story animals broke in: 'Twas t'is way, sir captain, and shoo 'twas t'at. We, my companero an' meshelf, we wae shus like order cleanin' ter hold namber eleven when wae fell on t'at man in she sleepin' an' much all drunk from whiskae.'

'Well, well,' the skipper said. 'No more questions needed. Everything is cleared up. You, my good man, wanted to stow away on a British vessel with the intention of being taken to England. I feel sure that you are not in a mood to deny this accusation. It is a very serious offence under the British law to stow away on a British vessel with the intention of entering illegally the British Isles. It will cost you no less than six months' hard labour, perhaps even two years, and deportation. I have every right to throw you overboard, charging you with intending to blow up a British vessel in the Straits of Gibraltar and with finding explosives in your possession when arrested. Of course, as a good and law-abiding British captain, I would never do such a thing. A man like you ought to be hoisted up the mast fifty times until you're well skinned, to remind you of the fact that a British ship is not made to help criminals run away from the police.'

What was there to say? If I had told him what I really thought of him and what I thought of the social standing of his mother, the mystery-story animals would have worked me for three hours. No longer, for I knew that my bones and my working ability were badly needed. But three hours in those gorilla hands would sure have been three very nasty hours for me, and, for the time being, I could not pay them back.

'You are not needed any more, leave us alone,' the skipper said to the huskies.

To me he said: 'What are you?'

'Good deck-hand. Painting and brass-polishing, sir.'

'You are a stoker.'

'No, sir, I am not.'

'What is this? You do not mean to lie to a British captain, do you, my good man? I am informed that, yesterday afternoon, you came around and asked for a stoker's berth, did you not?'

I did not answer. I only felt sorry that I had made that mistake of saying, the day before, that I was fireman. Had I said I was a deck-hand or a P.S., a plain sailor, they might have lost all interest in my carcass, and I would now be sitting snugly on my beloved *Yorikke*, scaling the second boiler or washing the engine-hold.

I could not wander far off with my thoughts because the skipper said: 'Since you are a stoker, you may call yourself very lucky indeed. Two of my stokers have become sick. Tropical fever. You may earn your passage and your bread on my ship. Ten pounds a month, one shilling sixpence an hour overtime when on high sea. Of course, I have no right to sign you on, since you are a stowaway. Upon reaching England, I am sorry, but I shall have to deliver you to the authorities. I shall speak a word or two in your favour in court, provided you obey orders here and do your work well. You may get off with only six months, and of course you will be held for deportation. However, as long as you are here on my ship and you behave as I expect you to, you shall be treated precisely like every other member of the crew. No distinction will be made against you.'

I let him have the pleasure of being pleased with his sermon. What else could I do anyway? Nothing; no, sir.

'We may get along fine, provided you do not make any trouble here. If we do not, there will be no fresh water, but plenty of smoked herring. For this reason we would do best to tolerate one another and accept conditions as we find them. Your watch begins at twelve. Watches are six and six hours, because I have no more than two stokers, you included. The two extra hours of each watch will be paid as overtime, at one and six each hour. That will be all. Good morning.'

Ahoy, ship! There I was. Fireman on the *Empress of Madagascar*. Well on my way to the wall of my village church. I had no village church, since the last burned down in Chic during the great fire or still earlier. So even this bit of honour finding my name next to that of the *Empress of Madagascar* on the wall of the church, was denied me.

I might become rich on this tub, for the pay was the up-to-date pay of the British firemen's union. But then there was England with six months of hard labour and two years' waiting for deportation day. The only trouble was that I would never get any pay in my hands. The fishes would get it. Suppose I should have the luck to get away from the reef; I would not get a bob, because I was not signed on. Since I was not signed on, I could not be called to testify in court as to the sinking. So I do not get any money from the insurance, or the board either. I have no proof that I was on the *Empress*. They might even put me in prison as an impostor claiming damages for the shipwreck.

Now, don't you worry, old boy. We won't make England. As to the ground, well, let's have a look at the boats as the best and surest indication of the date.

The boats are ready. Provisions in, and sails, and fresh water. Even gin packed away to keep us jolly. Well, *Empress*, it looks to me the wedding will take place no later than the third day from now.

I have to glance about the stokehold to see how I can get out easiest and quickest when the rush breaks in. At the first dim crackling my hearing-flap catches, I shall be up and out so fast that even the devil running after an escaped Presbyterian preacher will get yellow with envy.

2

The quarters are clean and new, reeking with fresh paint and a washing with chloride of lime. Mattress in the bunks, yet no pillows, no blankets, no sheets. The *Empress* is not quite so rich as she wishes to appear from the outside. It doesn't take me long to know where the pillows and blankets have gone to. The skipper is smarter than one might have expected. Why send the pillows, blankets, and all such things down to feed the fishes while there is still a market for them?

Most of the dishes are gone also. But enough is left for me to eat like a human being. The meal is brought into the mess by an Italian boy who chatters in a friendly way. The grub is excellent, beyond any criticism. Though I would have thought a last dinner ought to be better. At least it was better at the French fort where I was to be shot as a spy or something.

No rum ever, I am told. The skipper is bone dry and does not give out rum. Being on a ship on which no rum is handed out makes me feel as if I'm sitting in a mission and looking at the silly Bible phrases. How can you walk straight from bow to stern without having some rum laid down in your belly to hold you on your feet?

The mess-boy is calling all hands off duty for lunch.

Two heavy Negroes come in. The drags. Then the fireman comes in. He walks rather heavily and quite swanky.

Now, I have seen that face before. Somewhere. Don't know right now where. Seems to me I must have been once on the same can with him. Wonder who he is.

His face is swollen. Both eyes blackened and blood-shot. A bandage on his head.

'Stanislav, you?'

'Pippip, you too?'

'The same, you see. Caught and caged, and perfect. Looks like we're again in the same stokehold,' I said to him.

'You got the better of it, Pippip. I took them up. Had a damned fine row with them. Blacked them up and broke them half a dozen fingers. Sure. There is a palm-sized hole in the head of one of them. I got up right after I had the first blow upon my bone. You were lying flat and full out. You got a mighty buzzer under your cap. When I saw you dropping, I bent down the same instant, see. So that blow meant for me in full came on only sidewise. I got up and oared them as they sure never before had been taken. Four they were. But don't you think for a minute that they are still four. Each is only one quarter for permanent use. Want to see them? Go to the port-side bunks. They are still cooling off and plastering all over. I lasted to the last round. But then someone, the fifth, who came in later, got me from behind. I did not know that he belonged. I thought he was rather coming to get me out and give me a hand. So I got a damned hard one on the bean.'

'What was the story the skipper told you?' I asked while we were eating.

447

'Me? There came in two guys telling the skipper that I had been drunk ashore and that in a fight I had stabbed and killed a man, and then I had run aboard the *Empress* to hide and stow away because the police was after me for slaying an innocent citizen of the port.'

'Almost what I was told I had done.'

'Now,' Stanislav said, 'on the *Yorikke* we never lost our pay for so many months. Here we will never get a bent penny.'

'Won't last long,' I said. 'Hardly four days. He cannot take her to a better cemetery than the one he is over right now. And be sure it will happen when both you and I are on watch. We two are in boat four. I saw the list in the gangway. The firemen of the watch from twelve to four go into boat four.'

'Yep, I know it, I have seen it,' Stanislav admitted.

'Got a look at the stokehold? How to get out?' I asked.

'Twelve fires. Four firemen. The other two are Negroes. I guess from Kamerun or thereabouts. Speaking a bit English, and quite a bit of German. All the drags are also Negroes. Only the petties are white.'

'They, of course, will be in the right boat at the right time, especially if they are limeys.'

'Telling me. Those men sitting there and eating like dogs, those are the drags of our watch.' Stanislav pointed to the two bulky Negroes at the table gulping down their food without any other interest as to what we were saying or doing. Pitiful poor devils they were.

At twelve at night we went below to start our watch. The earlier watches had been served by the donkey, with the help of the Negro drags.

We found all the fires in very bad shape. For two hours we had to work hard to get the fires trim so that they looked like something worth speaking of. Nobody seemed to care here if the fires were going fine or not, or if the steam was holding on, or if it was low to slugging-point. The furnaces were sick with clogged and burned-on slags. The Negroes had no idea how to fire, how to break a fire, and how to clean it. They just threw in as many shovels of coal as the fire would hold, and after having done this they waited to see what would happen to the fire and to the steam.

There are so many firemen, even whites, who never realize that keeping a fire in shape is an art which some men never understand. Working five years before boilers on ships does not make a man a good fireman. If he does not know the art of it, he will be as uninteresting in the stokehold after five years as he was when he came below for his first watch.

We had little trouble with grate-bars falling out. The rims were new, therefore wide and strong, so the bars had a good hold on them. One might say it was often hard work to get them out at all, when they had burned away and had to be changed for new ones. It was almost a real pleasure to replace them.

The Negro drags, real giants, with arms like tree-trunks, looked strong enough to carry away on their shoulders the whole boiler and take it up on deck. Yet they dragged in the fuel so slowly that we had to pep them up and curse them to the limit to get sufficient fuel to keep the fires going. Not only were they, despite their huge bodies, unable to furnish the fuel we needed, they were whining all the time that it was too hot, that they sure were just about to drop dead, that they were choking and could not get any air, that they were going to die of thirst and hunger the next minute, and that their mouths were as full of soot and ashes as if they had died already and were now swallowing earth.

'Now, just look at these black Goliaths,' Stanislav said, 'dying of work which a cabin-boy might do without feeling overworked. What, compared to this, had we to drag in on the *Yorikke*? I would like to know what these mammoths really mean to do with their bones? One arm of theirs is thicker than my whole chest. Before they get in half a ton I would drag in six without even so much as wiping my sweat off. And here they have got the whole coaling-station right at arm's length. I can't figure that out. Not for ten dollars.'

'A pity,' I said, 'to have to leave behind the *Yorikke* right now, after we have scaled the boilers and have shovelled in all the coal from the most distant bunkers. Now comes the easy time on the *Yorikke*, with fresh fuel filled up right next to the stokehold, and the next five or six days there would have been sheer pleasure sailing – damn the *Yorikke*, we have got other things to worry about. So what's the good of crying about a dame you can't have any longer? Maybe she is going to the taxi dance. What do I care?'

I gazed about the stokehold, about all the gangways, hatchways and port-holes.

Stanislav followed my looks and said: 'I have viewed quite a bit already. What we have to do above all is to look for air-holes where to snap out quickest and easiest. We cannot reach the gangway. That much is certain. Usually they break off first thing when the crash comes. Just fly away from the pipes and boilers when you hear the faintest crackling. The gangway leading up and out is always liable to make a trap out of which you have no chance to escape. Once up, you mostly cannot come below any more on account of steam and boiling water. So better don't try the gangway at all.'

When I was through with my inspection I reported to Stanislav: 'The upper bunker has got a hatchway leading clear out on deck. We have all the time to keep the way to this bunker clear and the hatchway loose so we can't be caught. I shall take care to fix up a provisional rope ladder, which we'll keep here in good shape.'

Stanislav went to examine the way I had told him about. When he came back he said: 'You are smart, Pippip. I have to hand it to you. It is the surest and the only safe way out. All right, we will stick to that and make no other trial.'

Our work before the boilers was easy. We could have done all there was to do with one lazy hand. We didn't have to worry about heaving out the ashes. The two Negro drags did it.

The engineers never pestered us; in fact, they never popped in. None of them ever complained about the steam-pressure. As long as the engine was still moving, the engineers seemed satisfied. If the *Empress* was speeding or just tumbling along on her way to the last ceremony did not concern anybody.

The funeral could be arranged quite easily in the usual way. Half a dozen good-sized holes drilled into the hull near the bilge. All of them on port side, to make the can lie over softly but surely. The cargo of scrap iron would hasten the effect elegantly. Then it would only be necessary to give all the pumps a punch on the nose. The wireless station would be out of commission accidentally at the very minute the holes begin to suck. Wireless stations do such things. They are not perfect yet. Any shipping board will testify to that and accept it as evidence. A few members of the crew have to go along with the hearse. Otherwise suspicion will arise. The point is, every suspicion has to be avoided. The two or three guys who do the drilling of the holes and the boxing of the pumps must be safe. They are well paid, and if they say anything wrong before the board, they find themselves quickly confronted with three different traps out of which it is rather difficult for them ever to escape again. First, they are accused of being implicated in a crime. Second, they are accused, on account of having been bawled out by the skipper for something, of looking for revenge and trying to get square with the skipper by accusing him of a crime which everybody knows a British licensed captain would never commit. Third, the good old way, taking the guys for a pretty ride. Knowing all this, and keeping it in mind for the rest of their lives, these two or three undertakers keep mum. Anyway, it is not their money that is lost, and other people's money does not hold any interest for them.

There are still other ways. Ways often tried out, and just as safe. Who the hell knows how that bomb with nitro-glycerine happened to be in an innocent-looking case among the cargo? We had better arrest a couple of anarchists and well-known communists, search their lodgings, and find a few similar bombs right under their beds in an old leather bag. The judges and the gentlemen of the board and all the experts who testify in court hate anarchists and communists; they know that all communists do such nasty things, and so the insurance is paid. The judge does not pay. Nor do the gentlemen of the board. The underwriters pay. They also hate communists. So this case helps them to make better laws against communists and criminal syndicalists.

It was not our business to worry about which way it would be done this time. Fact is, we had no time to find out. The whole affair happened, even to us who were prepared, at a time and moment when we least expected it.

3

We had thought the music would start a day later. As it happened, it was only two days after we had been for the first time below before the boilers.

We had just relieved the former watch at midnight, and we were about to break up the fires when there was a terrific bang, and right afterwards a crash. I knew by instinct that the funeral was to take place when Stanislav and I would have the watch. Because then two white men who had every reason to wish the skipper the worst in court or out of court would be done away with. The Negroes, the Portuguese, the Italians from Malta, and the Greeks did not count. They were all tramp sailors who knew nothing about ships.

When the crash came, I was thrown against the furnaces. With the bump that followed I fell back into a big pile of coal.

I had a queer feeling, the cause of which I could not figure out for a second. For a moment I thought that I had gone partly nuts since I felt so strange. But then it dawned upon me that the boilers were standing up vertical, the furnaces above me. So I knew that the bow had gone down and the stern was high up in the air.

All this thinking and reckoning, of course, rushed like a flash through my mind. I had no time to reflect on this or anything else. For some of the furnaces, on which we had been still working when the crash came, had not been closed fully. They now broke open, and shed out their fires into the stokehold. As only a few furnaces had broken open, I found that I could step out of the mess by jumping between those heaps of white glowing coal and cinders. The electric lights went dim, and almost at the second when I reached the starboard hull they went out. There was still sufficient light in the stokehold from the heaps of glowing coal now spilling out faster and faster. I knew that it would be only twenty seconds or so and the boilers would explode. The steam-pipes would bust even before that, filling the stokehold with so much hot steam that you could never find your way out safely, because the steam would boil you and make you sightless and utterly helpless.

I did not see Stanislav. I made for the rope ladder leading up to the bunker. It was not necessary to climb up the ladder, because, since the bow was now down I could walk straight into the bunker and out through the hatchway as if on a plain floor.

When I reached the bunker I saw Stanislav already climbing out. At this very moment when I felt safe we heard a pitiful yell.

Stanislav, with one leg over the hatchway, turned around and called to me. 'That's Daniel, the drag. We can't leave him. Guess he is caught.'

'Damn it all,' I said, 'we have to get him.'

'Snappy,' Stanislav answered, 'come in again and get him. But, for all the devils, run or we are finished.'

In a whiff we were back in the stokehold. The boilers seemed still to hold on for a few seconds. The heaps of fires began now to fill the whole cave with smoke. But they were still glowing and rendering enough light so that we could make out where Daniel, one of the giant Negroes, was lying. With all this smoke and glow the stokehold looked like the underworld for ghosts.

Daniel was caught with his left foot under a heavy slab of iron broken off or fallen from somewhere. We tried to lift that slab, but we could not even move it. We tried madly to raise it with the poker. We failed.

452

'Can't make it, Daniel,' I yelled at the Negro, 'your foot is stuck and stays stuck.'

We tried to drag him out under the plate. We saw we should have to tear him apart to get him out this way. We could not leave him. And we had to go out or we would never make it.

It was then, when the hold brightened up from a flare of the open fires, I noticed the crackling of a steam-pipe, which was bent and upon which one boiler was sinking. The crack just began to hiss, and while not actually seeing it, one could feel that the crack was beginning to widen like the seam of a garment.

'Gadsake,' I hollered to Stanislav, 'the main pipe is coming.'

Stanislav gave it only a glance and yelled at the same time: 'Where is the hammer? Get it.'

Before he had ended his words I had flung the sledge-hammer into his hands. He grasped a shovel and with one mighty stroke of the hammer he flattened out the shovel so that it looked like a crude ploughshare with a handle. He set that ploughshare against Daniel's knee-joint, put the handle in my hand, and cried: 'Hold it this way, hell of it.'

I did. With another heavy stroke with the hammer upon the ploughshare he cut deep into Daniel's leg. He had to give it two more strokes before the leg was cut through. Now we could drag Daniel out into the bunker and then through the hatchway on deck. The deck, like all other things, was naturally no longer horizontal, but standing up vertically.

Close to the hatchway was Daniel's partner, the other Negro, drag of our watch. He had not cared about his brother. He had made his get-away as quick as he could. Now we handed him his crippled pal, and he took good care of him. That must be said.

The whole bow, and with it the forecastle, was under water. The stern was high up in the air. Such a position for the ship had never been tried out at the life-boat drills, which were held every Saturday at two o'clock sharp. Everything about the ship was in a position to which a sailor can seldom find himself accustomed.

The electric lights on deck were still burning. The engineer doubtless had switched the light over from the dynamo to the storage batteries. Apparently the batteries began to draw water, or their fluid had started to leak out. So the lights were getting fainter.

Climbing and crawling about the deck we saw the mates, the skipper, the engineers, the cook, and a few others whom I could not distinguish. They went about with lanterns and flash-lights, trying to get the boats clear.

I did not see anybody from the fo'c'sle. They had been drowned like mice in a trap.

The officers, with the help of the galley-boys and the cook, were working hard to get the boats below. Boat two tore off and was, at the same moment, carried away by the sea without a man in it.

Boat four could not be cleared at all: neither could boat six. Boat five could not be reached, and, besides, it was already so heavily battered that it would have been of no use.

So there remained only two boats with a chance to get off.

Boat one came clear. The skipper ordered the men who were to man it. I was not among them, nor was Stanislav. The skipper did not go with it. He was standing on the aft wall of the main-house on midship. He tried to give us the impression that he knew it was his duty to be the last to leave the ship. When such a gesture comes up in the investigation court it looks fine, and it always makes a good story for the sob-sisters. So the underwriters do not feel plucked, and they admit that it was the will of the Lord, against which we can do nothing, and therefore they pay the insurance in full.

Now, all the men still aboard, hanging and crawling against the vertical decks, tried to catch boat three, the last left for use. We got three clear and after much trouble had it jumping upon the waves.

The skipper ordered the manning. Stanislav and I were about to go with the boat, also two of the engineers, the Negro Daniel and his Negro partner, who carried and guarded him. Later there came with us the first mate, a junior assistant and the steward.

It appeared that the boilers were holding on boldly, obviously for the reason that some of the fires had fallen out and the others lost their strength since, owing to the position of the ship, they were no longer right underneath and within the boilers, but sideways. The stokehold, of course, was by this time so full of poisonous carbon gas, heat, steam, and boiling water that anybody caught there would be standing already outside the gate of – well, wherever he had to wait for the trumpets. If the boilers hadn't behaved so well, nothing of the ship or of us would still have existed.

The skipper, after hollering and whistling several times for any man who might still answer, finally ordered the boats to make off. He took his place in boat one. We had an emergency lantern, and so had the other boat. Besides, there were a few flash-lights still in the hands of the officers and the engineers. All together they yet gave only a dim and restless light.

We made our boat clear and pushed off. So did boat one.

The sea was not heavy. A sailor with a good ship under his feet would even have called it a sunshine sea. But it was rough, really rough. One had not felt it while the ship was under weigh. Yet in these small boats one got the feeling of a very lively sea. Close to reefs and rocks in the open the sea behaves in general rather differently from the way it does farther off the reef. While elsewhere the waves may reach a height of only from four to seven feet, near a reef and hidden rocks the waves may reach often three or five times this height, especially when, as often happens, two or three different currents meet at the rocks. The wrecked ship sets up another obstacle to the free movement of the sea, and therefore close to the wreck the sea acts even more unruly.

Taking into consideration these circumstances, it will be easy to understand why those peculiar accidents occurred which changed the whole pile of beautiful plans the skipper had worked out so carefully. It is safe to say that our strange position had never entered his reckonings.

Boat one struggled hard to come clear of the ship. It was a difficult thing to do. It might have been easier in full daylight. Perhaps. In daylight one may get the timing of the waves and try to make off on an outgoing one. Now, when the boat was about twenty yards off and the men were just about to stretch the oars and bring them into the water, a mighty wave crashed the whole boat against the hull of the ship.

Something else happened, right at the same moment when the boat was hard against the hull. One huge part of the ship broke loose and fell with a bang upon the boat, shattering it in uncountable pieces. We heard the cries and yells of the men. But as suddenly as these outcries had appeared, so did they drop into silence. I had a feeling that bang, yells, and boat had been swallowed in one single gulp by a giant sea-monster all at the same moment. Nothing more was heard of this boat. It sure was the most elegant insurance collection, because 'even the skipper had sacrificed his life to save the ship'. All persons present in court would rise and stand in silence for two minutes in honour of the skipper and his brave crew.

We had managed fine to get out of the crashing and sucking waters near the ship. But we had practically no skilled oarsmen with us, save the first mate. Usually mates do not know much about it, but Stanislav was a first-class man at the oars. I did my best to help him. Daniel could do nothing. He was moaning and begging for a shot of gin to dope his terrible pain. The other Negro had never had an oar in hand any time during his life. The steward was useless. The mate was out of practice. His strokes were brakes rather than pulls. So we could not make any speed.

The mate had a compass. He gave us the supposed direction towards the coast.

The sea was far more unruly than we had imagined. We were tossed high upon the waves and thrown into deep valleys. The oars, so badly manned, did not pull our boat in any given direction. We appeared to circle about the same spot.

Then all of a sudden the engineer said: 'Mate, I think we're on shoals or rock. Hardly more than three feet.'

'Can't be,' the first mate answered. He took his oar and sounded the depth: 'You are right, chief. Get out of here, you men, or we go to the devil.'

Before he could catch breath enough to say one word more, the whole boat was lifted high up upon a tower-like wave as though it were only a plank. When we were at the crown of the wave, the boat stood still for a fraction of a second and I thought that the wave would go out from under us and leave the boat hanging in mid-air. At that moment another mighty wave caught the boat in its huge fists, whipped it down, and crashed it heavily against the naked rock, and the boat was splintered into a thousand pieces.

No cry was heard, which made me feel sure that the others had been thrown so hard upon the rocks that they must have been left like fleshy rags.

I felt myself lifted up on another wave.

More to assure myself that I was still alive than to cry for help, which would have been silly anyway, I hollered: 'Stanislav, have you something to hold on?'

For a short while I heard no answer. But then, his voice still with that twang of a mouth full of water, Stanislav cried back: 'Not even a twig. Funk it all, the whole mess. Hey, listen, Pip, I am making back for the tub. Safest place right now. She sure will stay on for a day or two. She won't fall in two yet. Come along. Ride down the waves.'

Naturally, he did not say all this in one sentence. The flow of his speech was interrupted by the pails of sea-water which old man Neptune gunned into his swear-hold.

His idea was not so bad. It couldn't be. Because any other idea would have been without sense. I managed to keep my course to that dark tower which could be seen against the dimness of the horizon.

Both of us reached this goal, the dying *Empress of Madagascar*. It had not been easy. Dozens of times we had been thrown back and forth before we finally got hold of this haven in a restless world.

We climbed up, using the bulwark as a gangway. Reaching midship was quite a task, for we had nothing to hold on. We had to go a long way around up to the stern, and from there drop foot by foot until we dropped finally upon the wall aft of the midship-castle. This aft wall now was the deck, while everything else aboard had become steep walls. The two gangways, or corridors if you wish, the one at port side, the other at starboard, were in fact now shafts and no longer corridors. Going down these shafts, one had to climb from door to door, using the door-knobs and hinges for steps. The skipper's cabins and the officers' mess were at the end of the gangways towards the bow, now at the bottom of the shafts.

The *Empress* was standing like a strange tower firmly squeezed in between two rocks. Extraordinary as this position seemed to me then, I learned later that positions like that one have happened before, may happen, and do happen, although rarely. How she could have gone into that position only she could have explained. She stood so solidly that one might have thought she had become part of the rock upon which she had gone to die. She did not shake or tremble. One felt only now and then a sort of rumble whenever a particularly high and strong wave struck her and tried to lift her out between the rocks and throw her over, so as to give her the final shot of grace. At such times she quivered lightly, as if she were frightened of something terrible which she felt might soon take place. But after that she again stood rock-like.

There was no gale. Not even a strong wind. The unusually heavy breakers that came strolling along and pounded unceasingly against the ship seemed to come from a storm-centre far away. The outlook was for no heavy weather within the next six hours or so. The sky had been dark all night, without being really black. Just covered over with light, fluffy clouds, which seemed ready to change into mist.

We crawled round to the galley, which was open. We went in and slept there as best as we could.

The sky began to turn grey. The sun came up over the horizon and gilded the sea. Fresh and clean and golden she rose from her bath in the sea and went climbing up the firmament like an invincible warrior for ever fighting against the powers of darkness. I could not recall any time in all my life when a rising sun made such an impression of earthly glory upon me. It made me feel happy inside and proud of being man and living in an age when

457

such a sun was the lord of the world.

We looked out over the sea. Nothing was to be seen. Nobody seemed to have survived. I had no confidence that someone might come along and pick us up. Stanislav felt the same way. All day yesterday we had met no ship and had seen not even the faintest smoke-line of a ship passing in the distance. So we knew that the skipper had brought the *Empress* as far out from the ordinary routes as possible. His two former experiences had taught him to stay away from passing ships and coast guards and patrol-boats. He had hoped and worked for an easy burial, and then a fine get-away for himself and a few men. He had not taken into consideration that he might lose the whole crew of the fo'c'sle, all the men who were trained oarsmen. The A.B. standing by the helm had been thrown through the front windows out of the bridge and had disappeared. The two look-outs at the bow had gone down before all others. If the boats had been manned as provided for in the boat-lists, at least two boats would have gone off and away without any trouble.

4

By now daylight had become complete. We set out to explore. And for breakfast. We climbed down the gangways.

At the bottom we came into the two cabins of the skipper. I found a pocket-compass and took possession of it. But Stanislav had to keep it, for I had about me no pocket without holes. In the cabin there were two fresh-water tanks for the personal use of the skipper. In the officers' mess we discovered later two more tanks, which were larger than the skipper's. It was likely that we would not run short of water for a month or longer, if, as we were sure, the pumps in the galley would draw water from the ship's fresh water tanks, which certainly still held a thousand gallons. Of course it might be that these tanks had been cracked and were leaking.

On the *Yorikke* we had been familiar with every hidden hold. We could have found on the *Yorikke* the farthest and deepest nook without a glimpse of light. Here it was different. We knew nothing

458

about the ship. But no sooner came the question 'When do we eat?' than Stanislav, using his trained sense, found the storehouse. Looking at it, we were convinced that we could live for six months like Balkan kings in Paris. We would not even have to drink fresh water, for the store was well stocked with stout, ale, different sorts of wine, brandy, and a row of gallon-sized bottles with soda water and mineral water. And we had seriously believed the skipper a perfect dry. He would have been the first and only Scotch skipper whom I ever heard of as a dry.

We set up the stove in the galley and fired it. Now we could cook. We tried the pumps. One of them did not draw, but the other brought out fresh water in thick streams. It was cool; the refrigerator seemed to have worked well until the last minute.

We had an elegant breakfast. Nothing was missing. It was better even than I had ever seen on the *Tuscaloosa*. *Tuscaloosa*, New Orleans, Jackson Square. Well, let us not think. Thinking won't do me any good when I'm on a reef off the west coast of Africa.

After we had eaten and while we were smoking the skipper's cigars, I began to feel slightly sick. Stanislav too seemed not to be at ease.

For a while I thought there must have been something wrong with the food.

Then Stanislav said: 'Now, Pippip, what do you know about that? I am getting sea-sick. Has never happened to me since I sailed for the first time on a Fünen fishing-boat.'

I became worse than a lubber on his first trip in heavy weather. No explanation could be found. The ship was firmly bedded between the rocks. The heavy breakers thundering, now and then, against the huge mass of the *Empress* made her sometimes tremble slightly, but that could not be the cause of our sickness.

After thinking, Stanislav said: 'Now I can tell you what the trouble is with us. It's that idiotic position of the cabin, with the heavy breakers going up and down all the time while we are standing still. Everything is head under foot. See? We have to get used to that position, and after a day or two we will be fine.'

'Right you are,' I admitted.

We left the cabin, climbed up upon the aft wall of the main-house, then upon the bridge, and there the sickness left us, although we still felt funny having a ship in such a crazy position and set in a strange angle against the horizon.

The excellent cigars we were smoking made me a wise man. I said to Stanislav: 'You see, it's like this; only what you talk into yourself, only that makes you what you are. What I mean is this, I am sure that as soon as we learn to distinguish all that is imagination from what is established fact we shall realize very remarkable things, and we shall look henceforth at the whole world from a different point of view, without interference from any coined slogans or phrases or cheap ideas. I wonder to what far-reaching results such a change in thinking and general outlook might lead us.'

Stanislav did not follow me. I had thought all the time that he was a philosopher of high standing, taking things as they came and making the most of them.

He took up my last words: 'Lead. Right you are, Pippip. We could lead the most beautiful life any sailor has ever dreamed of or read about. We have here everything we want. We may eat and drink what we wish, even caviare and Chablis, or a good English smoked herring washed down with two quarts of stout. Nobody butts in here and cranks about what we are doing or talking. But what's all the good of it? The quicker we could get out of here, the better, I would feel. Suppose no bucket shows up, I figure we'll have to do something to reach the coast. Every day the same. That's what you can't stand. I sure do not believe there is such a thing in heaven or under heaven as what is called paradise. For I can't figure where the rich go. They can't go to the same place where the sailors go and all the communist workers. Anyway, I tell you, if there should be a paradise and I was unlucky enough to be shipped there, I would yell the most terrible blasphemies day and night and in the afternoon, just for the sake of being thrown out, so that I have not any longer to play the harp and always sing church hymns with stale Methodist sisters, and with seamen's mission preachers, and with mission librarians, and with those hussies that come aboard looking in the fo'c'sle for photographs from Spain to confiscate them and then sleep with them after much praying to save sinful sailors. Hell must be a pleasure to get away from revivals and collections for the salvation of the heathen.'

I laughed and said: 'Don't you worry, Stanislav, you and me, we won't get in there. In the first place, we have no papers, no passports. You may depend on that all right; they ask papers from you when you come to the gate. Stamped by consuls and passport-office clerks with the okay of an Episcopalian deacon. Or else they bang the door right in your face. And don't be short of papers that make a modern citizen, such as birth-certificate, vaccination-certificate, certificate of baptism, certificate of confirmation, marriage licence, income-tax receipts, receipts that you have paid your light-bills and for the telephone, an affidavit that you have no connections with criminal syndicalism or Moscow, and a certificate from police headquarters that there are no charges against you still pending. You think what I say is funny. But why the hell does a man need so many papers here on earth if no one would ask for them up there? Doesn't every preacher tell you everything on earth here is only a preparation for the beyond? So are all the papers and passports, only preparations to have them in good shape when knocking at the gate to be let in.'

'Now what you say, Pippip,' Stanislav answered, 'makes me think. The whole mess we are in does not fit me all right. Everything we have here is too good to last. It can't last, I tell you, I am suspicious of the whole safari here. Having such silly luck as we have, I think there must be something wrong. I simply can't stand by. All looks like as if this good luck and all this splendid grub and drinks has been shipped to us for the simple reason that something very tough is kept in store for you, and they wish to pep you up and fix you well before you get the finale done. I know that feeling. It was plumb sure exactly the same before we went into that fight off Skagen.'

'Shucks. Don't talk liver-wurst. You're the kind of guy who spits out roast chicken when it flies into your open mouth, to avoid meeting with tough luck. All nasty things come by themselves. They don't need any help from you. Live your life when you have it; you don't know a thing what will be hereafter, and there may be no way of making good what you lost while still here.'

Stanislav picked up his usual good humour. He laughed and shook off his depression and his German philosophy mixed with Slav fatalism. He whistled. But right after that he said: 'Damn it, a sailor whistling. Funking hell, I don't know what is the matter with me. Guess I have eaten too well. I am an old fool, that's what I am. Never before in all my life did I have such rotten ideas. Only today. It all started while we were sitting in the old man's cabin, in his easy chairs, at his table, drinking out of his glasses, using his mess-gear. And there it was that I thought: Now we are eating here like real gents, and right there, below your feet, almost touching them, there are swimming in the fo'c'sle all the guys you saw yesterday still alive. You have only to crawl down through a few feet of water, smash in the doors, and out they come floating, all dead, swollen already, with their eyes wide open. They won't allow us to sit here quietly and eat and drink like kings. They sure will call the unseen

461

visitor of the ships to come and get us off the table and join them. A ship is something alive, with a soul, and therefore she does not like to have in her bowels dead sailors, who give her indigestion. Corpses as a paid-for cargo, that is different. That is all right. But no dead sailors swimming and floating about, and no way to spit them out. I hate it.'

'What can we do about it?' I asked. 'Can we help it?'

'Exactly what I mean,' Stanislav said. 'We can do nothing. That's what makes it so bad. And look at this: All the others have gone fishing, while just we two have been left. Just we two. There must be something wrong somewhere.'

'Look here, Stanislav, what's the use of spitting like that? And if you don't get quiet, I shall change quarters. Yours will be the starboard gangway, mine the port-side one. And we won't even say hello when we meet. As long as I am still alive, I won't listen to such nonsense. There is plenty of time later when we are washed off here. Besides, if you seriously want to know my opinion as to that queer leaving us behind alone – but, boy, there is nothing to talk about. We simply did not belong. We were shanghaied, kidnapped, robbed, stolen. We were not here on our own account. We surely never wished anything bad to the *Empress of Madagascar*. She had never done us anything wrong. So why should we help her to her funeral? And she knows it. She had no reason to do us any harm. That's why we are still sitting here, whereas all the rest of them have gone off.'

'Why, for all the funking sons, didn't you tell me this before, Pippip? Of course, you are right.'

'I am not your legal adviser. Besides, you never asked me, and you are not paying for it either,' I said. 'And look here, Stanislav, really you should be less ungrateful towards fate.'

'What do you mean by that, Pippip?'

'What I said. You are ungrateful, that's what you are. You need a guy to tell you that. Destiny has made you half-partner of one of the latest issues of His Majesty's merchant marine. She is a bit slow. I will admit that. But so are others which are less beautiful. If somebody makes you a gift of a fine turkey, you wouldn't be so rude as to ask also for the cranberry sauce, would you? You are not only fifty-fifty on this most elegant British ship, you are also half-owner of a store the like of which you don't find in many ports along the coasts of western Africa. Caviare, jam, jelly, golden butter, milk, tips of asparagus, spinach, plum pudding, ten different kinds of soups, meats, fish, fruits, all the crackers you need,

462

biscuits, cognac, French wine, Italian wine, Port wine, Malaga wine. Man, Stanislav, you do not deserve what destiny has dropped into your lap. You are rich, Stanislav, did you ever realize that? You are a ship-owner. We may form the company right now. I vote for you as president if you vote for me as the vice-pres, yes siree. I mean it. Has the world ever seen an ungrateful guy like you? Owning an eight-thousand-register-ton ship and then still worrying about the running expenses. I guess I will go below and shake me up a cock. Just feel like.'

'That's right.' Stanislav was again the jolly partner he had always been. 'I am going with you and get drunk. Who knows, a can may hop along and pick us up, and for the rest of my life I would never forgive myself for leaving behind all these treasures without having even tasted them.'

So there now began a banquet which could not have been any better for the original owners of the *Empress* when it was newly born out of the shipyard. I think we got mighty soused. Whether we spent at this banquet one day or four I could never figure out. We got sober and drunk, and sober and drunk again. How many times this happened neither of us could tell.

Occasionally, to cool off our heads, we went up on deck and looked around for a passing ship. We never saw one. We felt sure none had seen us, or it would have come close to see what was up with our ship, standing on her head, with her buttocks high in the air.

'We are getting sour weather,' Stanislav said one afternoon.

He was right. It came up late in the evening. It was getting heavier and wilder every hour. Looked like one of the worst that came along those parts of western Africa.

We were sitting in the skipper's cabin, which was lighted up by a swinging kerosene lamp.

Stanislav went restlessly to the windows and then back again to his seat.

'What's the rag?' I asked. 'You can't do anything about this heavy sea coming up.'

He looked at me with a pretty worried face. He said after a while: 'Tell you, Pippip, if this weather comes up the way I see it coming on, it is very likely the *Empress* slips off the reef, is thrown over, and goes down with this heavy water-filled bows of hers like gliding off the rails of a shipyard. Then we will have hardly any time to get out of her suck-water. I tell you we'd better look in time how to get off her before she takes us for a ride with no return ticket.'

463

He found about ten yards or so of rope, which he tied around his body to have it ready and with him all the time. I found in a drawer a ball of strong cord about as thick as an ordinary pencil.

'Let's climb up on our deck,' Stanislav advised. 'It's better for us to sit there in the open than to stay inside. We would be trapped here in this cabin the same minute she makes off, and then we would have no chance to get clear. Being in the open and free to move, there is always a chance of getting away in time.'

We came up, and there we were sitting again on the aft wall of the main-house. The gale had become so hard that we had to hold on to the rings and hooks we found in the wall.

Wilder and wilder the gale came up. Breakers powerful as trains at full speed crashed against the main-house. We expected any minute to see the bridge break off and be carried away. The breakers came higher and higher until every third breaker reached us and washed us all over. The skipper's cabins and mess-cabins were now flooded with water.

'If this weather lasts all night through,' Stanislav said, 'there will be nothing left of the bridge and fore part of the main-house by the morning. Looks like the sea is quite ready to carry off the whole house on midship. We'd better work before that happens, Pippip. Let's climb up on the aft wall of the sternhouse, where the rudder machinery is. Seems the safest place. But good-bye, lordly eats and kingly drinks. The rudder-house has not enough left-overs to feed even a young mouse.'

'All right with me, Stanislav, let's go and make the rudder-house.'

'There is still the probability that, supposing the weather calms down, part of the main-castle will stay. The house does not go off with just one blow. It breaks off piece by piece. We may just still wait an hour before we try to climb up. Here we have a hold, but while climbing we are at the mercy of the breakers; if they whip us at the wrong time, we are all washed off.'

So we hung on waiting for our chance to start to climb.

Three gigantic waves, each of them seemingly ten times as heavy as any of those that had licked the *Empress* so far, whipped against the wreck with such a roar that we thought the end of the world was close.

The third of these gigantic breakers caused the *Empress* to rock heavily. She still stood firmly upon the reef, but we had the feeling that she had broken lose, or that one of the rocks between which she had been squeezed had cracked. She trembled as never before.

We no longer were sure that she was standing upon the rocks like a tower.

The sea seemed to know that the end of the *Empress* was near and that nothing could save her now from her fate. Dark thick clouds were tossed above us like so many torn rags. The storm seemed to grow into a greater rage so as not to be laughed at by the thundering and roaring waves.

Through these rags of clouds we could see, for a few seconds, the shining stars that, in spite of all the uproar, called down upon us the eternal promise: 'We are the Peace and the Rest!' Yet between these words of promise we could see another message: 'Within the flames of never ceasing creation and restlessness, there we are enveloped; do not long for us if you are in want of peace and rest; we cannot give you anything which you do not find within yourself!'

'Stanislav,' I hollered, 'the breakers are coming on again. There she goes. The *Empress* is dragging off.'

I saw, in the dim light of the stars, the first breaker closing in on the *Empress* like a huge dark monster.

Then it fell upon us. We felt its hundreds of wet claws trying to tear us away from our hold.

With all our strength we held on. But the *Empress* was lifted high up – standing for a while, it appeared to us, at the very peak of the bow – then she made a half-turn and stood quivering and trembling as though in terrible fright or in pitiful pain.

The second breaker leaped at us even more strongly, and we lost our breath under it. I felt that I had been thrown into the sea, but I still had iron rings in my hands, and so I knew I was still on the ship.

The *Empress* now moaned like a human being dying of horrible wounds. She turned around slightly. High up at her stern she staggered and began to lean over towards port side. We heard her hull cracking and heard hatches or masts breaking away. No longer did she stand upright with her stern straight up towards the clouds. Again she quivered all over. To see the death of a young woman who does not want to die cannot be more pitiful than watching the *Empress* resist so bravely the onrushing end. Strange it was that although my own end was as close as hers, I felt like a dying soldier on the battle-field who forgets his own death when he sees how painfully his buddy is making off to glory.

Suddenly, almost without knowing it, I roared: 'Stanislav, ahoy!'

I did not know for sure if he had yelled also. I think he must have done so, but I heard nothing.

The third breaker came on. It was the heaviest and most powerful of all. It came entirely conscious of its victory.

The *Empress* seemed to have become indifferent already. She showed no reaction any longer. It was as though she had died of fright.

The third breaker roared and thundered and raged. Yet it was a useless comedy. The *Empress* was dead. She did not tremble when this last breaker caught her, nor did she rock or waver. She lay down ever so gently. The little waves which run after the outgoing breaker like so many little tails caressed and kissed the *Empress* when she fell on to her knees and glided smoothly down into her last berth.

Another breaker rushed on like a hustling undertaker. The *Empress* was softly lifted up once more, she was whirled around in a half-turn, and without cracking or knocking her hull upon the rocks, she was laid on her side, and with a last gargle, ghostly against the uproar of the sea, she was buried.

Before she disappeared entirely, I heard Stanislav holler: 'Jump off and swim, Pippip, swim for your life or you will be caught in the wash down. Get away from her.'

It was not quite so easy to swim as Stanislav had suggested, for I had received a good knock on my arm by a broken mast or something that had broken loose.

I nevertheless swam with all my strength. A wave had caught me, and it threw me far enough out of the wash so that I could make off the sinking *Empress* without being in danger of being caught by her eddy.

'Pippip, ahoy!' I heard Stanislav yelling. 'Where are you? Are you clear?'

'I am. Come up here!' I hollered back. 'Come up here! I have got plenty room for you. No, here! Here, ahoy. Here I am. Hold on. Here, here, come on. Ahoy, hoiho!'

I had to holler some time before Stanislav could make out in which direction to swim to reach me.

After a long while he came close. He reached me. I lent him a hand and he climbed up where I was hanging on.

5

'Like to know what's this we are sitting on,' Stanislav asked.

'I don't know myself. I was thrown upon it,' I said. 'I couldn't even tell exactly how it happened. I figure it must be a wooden wall from one department of the bridge. Perhaps from the chart-room. Here are some iron rings set in with bolts and brass handles.'

'I didn't have time to look at the bridge cabins closely,' Stanislav said, 'or else I would know where this wall comes from. Anyway, it doesn't matter what it is and where it comes from. Lucky that there are still some parts on some cans that are still made of wood. Otherwise we should not be here.'

I agreed. 'Makes me think of the old story-books in which you can always see a sailor or a cabin-boy embracing a mast floating upon the high waves. Nothing doing in times like ours. Masts also are now made of steel. Just try to embrace a broken-off mast of a sunken ship today and see where you'll head at high speed. If you ever see another picture like that in a book or in the movies, just cry out loud that the book-maker or the movie-director is a cheater. Sock him if you can get him.'

'My, you have got a nerve to talk such silly nonsense right now under the conditions we are in.' Stanislav seemed to be sore at me.

'What do you expect me to do? Mourn about a bucket that went off under our feet? Sing hymns? Say my evening prayer kneeling before the bed? Or cry like mother's baby who has put his finger in the hot gravy? Hell, who knows where we shall meet within an hour or so? It's now maybe my last chance to tell you what I think about steel tube masts. And, mark my words, that sure is something which ought not to be forgotten, because it is very important indeed. Masts are no longer of real use to make a good story.'

Morning was still far away. The night was heavy and dark. The waves were high. We were thrown up and down. Hardly a star could be seen. It was cold. The sea was, on the other hand, lukewarm, as it is in the tropics.

467

'We are lucky, damn it. Clear off and safe like that,' Stanislav said.

'To the devil you go with your whining. Beseeching all the guys down at the bottom. You are a luck-killer. Waking up the whole safari to come up and get us. I wonder where you were raised. Unbelievers of heaven and hell. I say hell, that's what I say. And damned we are, all of us. No getting away from the outfit. – in the goldfish. If you are sitting pretty, don't yell about it. Knock wood. Oh, why did I ever in all my life put up with a blasphemous sailor like you? I don't understand the Germans at all, why they could ever take a guy like you for a gob. No wonder they could not make Skagen and had to go home. Well, they were saved only by leaving you to the Danes.'

'Won't you shut up and let us think a bit to make sure what we are doing?' Stanislav broke in.

'Think? Think? What do you want to think about? Tell me that. Sitting on a broken-off wooden wall in mid-ocean, and at midnight so I wouldn't have to see you any more. It makes me sick. Thinking.'

'What else can we do right now? If we fall asleep we are finished.'

How the world changes. For months and months we had to worry and be troubled about papers and identification cards. Then we had to worry about rats the size of huge cats. After this, or at the same time, we had to sweat and to bleed about dropped grate-bars. And now, all of a sudden, it does not matter any longer if there are passports in the world or if the world can go on without them. What does it matter if grate-bars fall out or not on the *Yorikke*? Sailor's identification cards or not. Whatever a being may own is of no importance, of no concern at all. It is gone and useless. All we have is our breath. I shall fight for it with teeth and nails. I won't give up and I won't give in. Not yet. Not to the ground port.

'My opinion of the merriments of life is different from what we have right here and now,' Stanislav broke up my reflections.

To this I answered: 'I think, Stanislav, to tell you the truth, you are again ungrateful to destiny. How changeable is human life! Just think. Yesterday you were half-owner of one of the finest ships of His Majesty's merchant marine. You were half-owner of the most elegant store, with caviare, Scotch, and champagne. Now all is gone, and you are fighting with the fish for their eats. What else, what more pleasure do you expect in our lifetime? You cannot have everything. Others have it only in stories. We have it in reality. Do you want to change places?'

'I don't know exactly. But I figure I might like to change places and rather read stories than live them. And if you talk any more of that kind and don't hold on well to the rings and the handles, you won't even have a chance left to live your stories.'

He was right, Stanislav was. As usually he was. I had nearly been swept off the raft. The breakers were not felt as when we were still on the ship. The breakers now just played with us, taking us high up and then down again fifty feet. Often we were for almost a minute entirely submerged. This helped us not to forget that we were still on high sea and not reading a story in bed.

'We must do something about it,' I suggested. 'My arms are paralysed. You know I got quite a crack on them. I am losing ground. I cannot hold on very much longer.'

'Same with me,' Stanislav said. 'We have still rope and cords about us. Let me have yours.'

I got the cord I had tied around my waist while we were still on the ship, and Stanislav helped fasten me to the rings and handles. With my lame arm I could not have done it alone. This done, he tied himself upon the raft with the rope he had brought along.

We were now ready to wait for the next adventure.

After a thousand hours, or so it seemed, morning came and brought with it a calm day. The sea was still high.

'See any land?' Stanislav asked.

'Nothing I would know of. I always knew that I would not have discovered America, not even if I had been washed against her shores. Well, I don't see anything. Not even a smoke-line.'

Stanislav suddenly made a jerking gesture: 'Man, are we lucky? Fine that you picked up the compass in the old man's cabin. Now we can sail.'

'Yes, we can sail now,' I said; 'at least we can now always make out in which direction lies the coast of Africa and which way America. All we need is sails, masts, a rudder, and the right wind. Little, isn't it?'

'Sure it is. But I have got the feeling we are going somewhere else. Neither shore.' That's what Stanislav said.

During the forenoon the sky had cleared. In the afternoon it became cloudy again. Before evening a slight mist began to settle over the sea. With this mist the sea calmed down and became rippled.

The vast distances towards the horizon and the immensity of the sea shrank when the mist closed in on us. The sea became smaller with every minute, until we had the illusion that we were floating on an inland lake. As time went on, even this lake narrowed more and more. Now we felt as if drifting down a river. We had a sensation that we could touch the banks with our hands. The walls of mist seemed only to veil dimly the river-banks.

We became drowsy. I dropped asleep and fell into dreams. When I woke I looked around and said: 'Stanislav, man look, there is the shore. Let's get off and swim. It's hardly a hundred yards off. Can't you see? There, right behind that misty wall. I knew we were close to shore.'

Somehow, both of us hadn't the will-power to loosen the cords, make off, and swim that stretch to the shore.

I simply could not, hard as I tried, get my thoughts clear and reason things out. There was something in my head or about my head that made my brain feel numb. Almost like being drunk. Or it was like I felt when I was bumped on the head by the shanghai-ing gang. I wanted to talk to Stanislav. I only wanted to talk nonsense so as to keep awake. But I could not manage it. I saw that Stanislav was drowsy again and was falling asleep. So I could not resist and I also fell asleep.

I woke up when water splashed into my face. Night had come.

The mist was still upon the sea, which had now become glassy. An indication that the mist might turn to thick fog. But the mist was not heavy. It was only upon the water. High above me I could see the stars twinkling. I thought I heard them calling.

Now I could see quite clearly the river-banks on both sides. We were still drifting down the river. It might be the Hudson or the Mississippi. How we had come there I could not figure out. It caused me pain to think. Then the mist banks opened. Great patches of it fluttered. Through these openings I could now see the thousands of twinkling lights of a great port. What a large harbour it was! It had skyscrapers and many other high office-buildings and apartment-houses. I saw the windows illuminated. Behind the windows there were people sitting and moving about. I saw their shadows. They all went about their own affairs, not realizing that here on this big river two sailors were drifting down helpless and out into the open sea.

The skyscrapers and apartment-houses grew higher and still higher. I had to bend my head down against my neck to see the top of the highest buildings. What a huge city this was that we were drifting by! Twinkling lights far, far away and close at hand also. The skyscrapers went on growing until they reached the very heights of the sky. So now the lights in the windows looked exactly like the stars in the firmament. Right straight above me, and in the zenith of the heavens, the tops of the skyscrapers closed in upon each other, so much so that they were bent, touching each other. I became afraid that these high buildings bent over to such an extent might cave in any minute and bury me under their ruins. I was filled with a joyful hope that it would happen, and that that way I would be relieved from all the pain I felt, and, more than from everything else, from the thirst. I shook off the thought of thirst and of fresh water. But I could not help it. It came again. In my soul I began praying that the skyscrapers might fall down upon me and make an end of the world.

A terrible fright caught me, and like mad I yelled: 'There is a huge port, Stanislav, look! Get ready. Must be New York, Stanislav, can't you see? Wake up! Hell, what are you so slow about?'

Stanislav stirred, woke up, scratched himself, shivered from the cold, shook off his sleepiness, looked around, gazed into the mist, tried to penetrate the veils around us, stared at the river-banks.

He made a gesture as though he had not seen right. He rubbed his eyes over and over again to get the salt out.

Then, having looked around at all sides, he said: 'You are dreaming, Pippip. Pull yourself together, old man! That's no lights of a port. It's only the stars that you are seeing. There are no river-banks. How could we be on a river? We are still out on the high sea. You can easily tell it by the long waves. We must be off coast no less than thirty miles. Maybe two hundred. Search me. Wonder if this damn night will never end.'

I did not believe him. I could not believe him. I still wanted to get off the raft and swim over to the river-banks. While thinking about how many strokes I might have to make before I would reach the bank I fell asleep again.

Thirst, hunger, and salt in my mouth woke me up.

It was bright daylight.

Stanislav was watching me. His eyes were red as if they were bleeding. The salt water had made my face feel as if covered with an iron crust.

Stanislav was moving his mouth in a strange way. I thought he was trying to swallow his tongue. His tongue was swollen and seemed not to fit any longer in his mouth. So I thought again that he might try to spit it out and relieve himself from this nuisance.

He looked at me as though scrutinizing my face. Blood seemed to run into his eyes in streams. He flew into a rage and yelled with all the might of his voice: 'You dirty liar, you dog! You have always said the fresh water on the *Yorikke* is stinking and pesty. You stinking rat, you funker! Water on the *Yorikke* is the finest water in the world, coming from the cool springs of Nampamptantin of Hamtinoa of the springs of the – of the – of the springs – the springs of the pine forest – of the fresh – of the water – of the crystal springs – of wandering in pine forest.'

I did not think that he was talking nonsense. It was all clear to me, like short commands from the bridge. I said: 'Right you are Stanislav, good boy. The water on the *Yorikke* was iced water from the pole, and the coffee was excellent. Have I ever said a word against the coffee on the *Yorikke*? I have not. Never will.'

Stanislav was working again with his tongue. It looked as if he were in need of breath or as though choking to death. He swallowed and made an effort to press his lips together. He closed his eyes and I thought he would fall asleep.

With a jerk he awoke and yelled somewhere into the far distance without giving me a glance: 'Twenty to five, Pippip. Get the hell up and out. Bring the breakfast. Sixty sixflytee ashes cans with ashes coal fuel boiler cans with ashes to be heaved. Heave up! Throw the lever around. Smash the pipe. Get the breakfast. Potatoes again and stinking. And smoked herring sick. The coffee. Much coffee. Much much more coffee. Where is the coffee? Water. Bring the water, cool the glowing cinder. The water. Water. Water.'

'I cannot get up,' I said. 'I cannot make it today. I am too tired. I am all in. You have to heave the ashes alone this morn. Where is all the coffee?'

What was that? Now? I heard Stanislav yelling. But I heard him yelling from three miles away. My own voice also was three miles away.

Three furnaces then broke open. Heaps of live coal were falling out. The heat – I could not bear it any more. I rushed up to the air-funnel to turn it round to catch the breeze and blow it down into the fire-hold. Spainy, my fireman, hollered at me: 'Pippip, for hell's sake, shut the furnace doors. The steam is falling. Steam is falling. Falling. Falling. All falling. Breaking. Hop away, Pip, ash-funnel is coming down. Smash your belly. Breaking.' The steam-pipes burst, and all the steam hissed in the fire-hold, and upon me, boiling me and scalding me. I rushed to the trough in which we kept the water to cool off the cinders. I wanted to drink that muddy water because I was thirsty. Devil, how thirsty I was! But it was all salty and thick. I drank and drank as if I'd never be filled up. The furnaces were still open. I could not shut them. They

472

were too heavy. I had to leave them open. They were high above me, and I saw it was the sun burning down upon me and I was lapping up water from the sea.

I got tired trying to close the furnaces and I fell asleep, dropping into my bunk as if dead. The fireman took up the trough and with a wide swing he threw all the water about the fire-hold. The water drenched me, I awoke, and a wave had come splashing over our raft.

'There is the *Yorikke*!' Stanislav yelled all of a sudden, pointing in some empty space above the waves. His voice was hundreds of miles away. Or my ears had lost the ability to judge distances. Stanislav began to yell louder. I could see it, that he was yelling as mightily as his voice would allow. Yet I could catch it only as a very thin sound, as far away as heaven. 'There, there! There is the death ship. She is standing by. The port. Do you see the Norske ship? There she is. All glory. All in golden sun. She has iced water from the fjords. Can't you see, can't you see, Pippip?'

He had partly risen, squatting upon his knees. With both his arms he was pointing into space.

'Where is the *Yorikke*?' I too began now to yell.

'Man, old man, can't you see her? Are you blind? There she turns about. Now standing by. Please, please, can't you see her?'

His voice became pitifully pleading.

'Can't you see, Pippip? The devil, six grate-bars have dropped. Damn the whole – . Now funking eight. Get me the can with the plum jelly put into the furnace and finish the grate-bars. Where is the coffee? Why didn't you leave me a drop? That's no Chinese laundry soap, it's butter, golden butter, you funking liar. Get me the tea! God damn, where is that coffee again? Eat the whole can of milk in one seat, Pippip. They steal it. All highwaymen. Another shot. Straight, I said; can't you hear me? Off your skirt, you little hussy, sweety! Get the coffee!'

I, not knowing if I was in my mind or out of it, watched Stanislav. It came to me, thinking what power he had, how he fought before breaking down. He hammered the raft with his fists. He worked his whole body, still bound by the rope. He threw his arms and his upper body into all directions, pointing here and there, yelling at me and asking if I did not see the *Yorikke*, once under full steam, then turning about, then standing by and lowering away anchor.

I became indifferent to everything. It began to hurt me to turn my head to see the port or to watch the manoeuvres of the *Yorikke* coming up to reach us.

Stanislav, unceasingly watching something on the sea which he believed real, started hollering again: 'Hold her, hold her! Pippip, we are drifting away. She cannot make it after all. I must now get her. All the bars are out now. Do you see the fireman? My fire'm is in the boiler. Where is the water? I have to hurry now to run along and hop on or she makes off.'

He worked on the rope with which he had fastened himself to the raft. He had lost his ability to loosen knots. He worked at them like a monkey, not knowing any longer how to pull them open. In fact he tightened himself up more while he thought that he was getting out.

'Where is the shovel? Hell, let's cut the leg for once. Or I am going down. The water is rushing in already.' He went about the rope more hastily, yet with still less skill. Of course, the rope, not very strong from the beginning, rubbed and torn constantly against the iron rings and brass handles and worked at with the hard hands of Stanislav, could not last long. It finally began to break and to loosen. With a last hard jerk Stanislav freed himself of his entanglement.

'The *Yorikke* is sailing. She is off. Quick, quick, Pippip! The Norske has iced water. See the guys standing at the rail waving the coffee-pot? I won't stay on a death ship. I won't. I won't.'

Stanislav trembled in excitement. He got wilder every minute. His feet were still in a few slings of the rope. He noticed it with the last flicker of his dying mind. He pulled his legs out of these slings. Then he sat on the raft with his legs hanging down in the water.

All this I saw and took note of as if it were happening a hundred miles away and as though I watched it through a field-glass. I had no personal concern in it. Such was my feeling, strange as it may seem.

'There is the *Yorikke*. The skipper is saluting us. See him, Pippip? He tips his cap. Lump of coal at the leg. Why don't you come?'

I stared at him. I could not grasp what he was saying. I could not form his words into an idea. They were just words.

'Hop on, Pippip! Tea and raisin cake and cocoa and aftergale.'

Now I saw, he was right. Yes, no doubt, there was the *Yorikke*. Floating above the waters in a sort of majestic silence. She made no wash. I could see her quite clearly. I recognized her by her funny-looking bridge, which always hung high up in the air.

Sure, there was the *Yorikke*. They were having breakfast now.

And prunes in a bluish starch paste for pudding. The tea was not so bad. It was even good when there was no milk no sugar. The fresh water did not stink, and the tanks were clean as if new.

I got busy to loosen the knots of the cord I was tied with to the raft. My fingers, however, did not obey me. They were just fumbling, doing nothing I wanted them to do.

I called upon Stanislav to help me untie the cord. He had no time. He did not even pay attention to my calling him. I do not know how he had managed it, but I noted that his feet were entangled again in the slings. He was working hurriedly to free himself once more.

His yelling and his ceaseless working at the rope had caused his wounds to break open. The wounds on his head which he had received when fighting the shanghai-ing gang. Thick blood broke out of those scars and trickled down his face. It did not concern him. He didn't notice it at all.

I tore and pulled at my cord. It was too thick, and it had been tied up too well by Stanislav. I could not break it, nor rub it through, nor was I able to wind myself out snake-fashion. Whenever I thought I had won a few inches, I only found that I was fastened better than before. The water had tightened the cord so much so that the knots were as if soldered. I looked round for an axe, a knife, a shovel. This reminded me that some years ago, on one occasion, I had helped flatten out a shovel to cut a mast which caused a Negro to cry. Anyway, the compass fell into the water again, and I had to fish it out with a grate-bar that was still red-hot. I was still working at the cord. It refused to let me out. This made me think I was wrangling with a policeman who had searched my pockets right in front of the American consul, who asked if I wanted a meal-ticket. The knots of the cord got tighter. This made me mad, and I cursed whomever I could think of, even God and my mother.

Stanislav, quite cunningly, had got his legs again into the water, but was still sitting on the raft.

He turned around to me, but looked not at me but by me. He shook his head. Then he yelled: 'Come here, Pipplav Pap Pip. Only twenty yards' run. All sand. Just run. Grates are all out. Water minutes to seven engineer. Get up. Below all full of ashes. Get up. Shake out of it!'

Then the gangway was shrieking: 'No *Yorikke*. There is no *Yorikke* . It is all fluttering mist. There is no – no – '

The noise hurt me, and I hollered as loud as I could: 'There is no

Yorikke! It is a hellish lie. There is no *Yorikke!*'

I grabbed the cord with all my strength, because I looked around and saw that the *Yorikke* had gone far away. I saw only the sea. I saw only the waves rolling from horizon to horizon like eternity in movement.

'Stanskinslovski, don't jump! For God's sake, stay on!' I howled. I became terribly frightened. I felt as though I had lost something which I had found and could not have any more, no matter how much I might want it. 'Stanislav, don't jump! Don't jump! Stay! Stay on! Hold on! Never give up!'

'She is heaving short. Hauling in. I am running to the death ship. I have to run to catch the *Yorikke* by the buttocks. Running. Running. Hundred yards. Fünen, ahoy! Com'a! Come'a!'

He jumped. He did it. He jumped. There was no river-bank. There was no port. There was no ship. No shore. Only the sea. Only the waves rolling from horizon to horizon, kissing the heavens, glittering like the mirrors of sunken suns.

He made a few splashing strokes in no definite direction. Then he lifted his arms. He went down. In deep silence.

I looked at the hole through which he had slipped off. I could see the hole for a long while. I saw it as if from a great distance.

I yelled at the hole: 'Stanislav. Lavski. Brother. Comrade. Sailor. Dear, dear comrade. Come here. Ahoy! Man, ahoy! Sailor, ahoy! Come here. I am standing by. Come on!'

He did not hear me. He would have come. Sure he would. He did not come up any more. There was no death ship. No port. No *Yorikke*. He did not come up any more. No, sir.

There was something very remarkable about it. He did not rise. He would have come up. I could not understand.

He had signed on for a long voyage. For a very great voyage.

I could not understand this. How could he have signed on? He had no sailor's card. No papers whatever. They would kick him off right away.

Yet he did not come up. The Great Skipper had signed him on. He had taken him without papers.

And the Great Skipper said to him: 'Come, Stanislav Koslovski, give me your hand. Shake. Come up, sailor! I shall sign you on for a fine ship. For an honest and decent ship. The finest we have. Never mind the papers. You will not need any here. You are on an honest ship. Go to your quarters, Stanislav. Can you read what is written above the quarters, Stanislav?'

And Stanislav said: 'Aye, aye, sir. He who enters here will be for ever free of pain!'

The Bridge
in the Jungle

1

'Stick'm up, stranger!'

'?'

'Can't you hear, sap? Up with your fins. And you'd better snap into it!'

Through my sweat-soaked shirt I distinctly felt it was not his forefinger nor a pencil that was so firmly pressed against my ribs. It was the real thing all right. I could almost figure out its calibre – a .38, and a heavy one at that. The reason why I had been slow to obey his first order was that I believed it a hallucination. For two days while marching with my two pack mules through the dense jungle I had not met with a single human being, white, Indian, or mestizo. I knew I was still far away from the next rancheria, which I expected to reach about noon tomorrow. So who would hold me up? But it happened. From the way he spoke I knew he was no native. He fumbled at my belt this way and that; it was quite a job dragging my gun out of my holster, which was as hard and dry as wood. Finally he got it. I heard him back up. The way he moved his feet back on the ground told me that he was a rather tall fellow and either fairly well advanced in years or very tired.

'Oke, now. You can turn round if it pleases your lordship.'

Fifty feet to the right of the jungle trail along which I had come, there was a little pond of fresh and not very muddy water. It had glittered through the foliage, and from the tracks of mules and horses leading to that water hole I knew that it must be a paraje where pack trains take a rest or even spend the night. So I drove my tired mules in to water them. I needed a short rest myself and a good drink.

I had not seen anyone near nor had I heard anything. Therefore I was astonished when, as if coming from a jungle ghost, the gat was pushed between my ribs.

Now I looked at him, who, as I had rightly guessed, was taller than I and slightly heavier. Fifty or fifty-five years. An old-timer,

479

judging from the way he was dressed (which was not much different from my own get-up), cotton pants, high boots, a dirty sweat-soaked shirt, and a wide-brimmed hat of the cheap sort made in the republic.

He grinned at me. I could not help grinning back at him. We did not shake nor tell our names. Telling other people your name without being asked for it seems silly anyhow.

He told me that he was the manager of a sugar plantation about thirty miles from where we now stood, but that he preferred to manage a cocoa plantation if he only could get such a job. I told him that I was a freelance explorer and also the president, the treasurer, and the secretary of a one-man expedition on the lookout for rare plants with a commercial value for their medicinal or industrial properties, but that I would take any job offered me on my way and that I hoped to find, maybe, gold deposits or precious stones.

'I should know about them, brother, if there were any around here. See, I'm long enough in this here part so that I know every stone and every rubber shrub and every single ebony tree you'll ever see. But then again, that goddamned beautiful jungle is so big and so rich – well, what I mean to say is, there are so many things that can bring money home to papa if you only know how to use them and how to doll them up when selling them, and besides that you may actually find not only gold but even diamonds. Only don't get tired looking for them.'

I felt the irony he had not put into his words but into the corners of his nearly closed eyes while speaking.

Having watered his horse, filled his water bag, and gulped down a last drink from the pond, scooped up with a battered aluminium cup, he tightened the straps of the saddle which he had loosened so that the horse might drink with more gusto, mounted his beast, and then said: 'Two hundred yards from here you can pick up your gat where I'll drop it on my way. I'm no bandit. But you see, brother, what do I know about you? You might be in some kind of new racket. You seem to be green around this section of the globe. At places like the one we have had so much pleasure together – I mean this one here – a guy that's in the know doesn't take any chances, if you get what I mean. That's the reason why I relieved you of your rusty iron for a while – just to keep you from playing with it. You might have taken me for a bum after your packs and beasts and you might have slugged me just for fear of me. I know greenies like you who get dizzy in the tropics – specially if they're trailing alone through the jungle without seeing a soul or even a mole for a week. Then they see things and hear things and they talk alone to themselves and listen to the talk of ghosts. Sure, you get what I mean. In such cases the first who has his iron out is the winner, you know. I'm always happy if I can be the winner over a greeny like you. Because it's the greenies I'm ten times more afraid of than a hungry tiger. A tiger, I know what he wants if I meet him, and maybe I can trick him, but a greeny who has been three days alone on a jungle trail, you never know what he might do when he sees you suddenly standing before him. Well, so long, brother, and good luck in discovering a new kind of rubber shrub.'

I went after him and I saw him drop my gun. This done, he spurred his horse and two seconds later the jungle had swallowed him.

When I found myself once more alone with my mules, a strange sensation came over me that I had dreamed the whole intermission. I tried to think it all through and then I knew that every word I had heard him say, whether in my imagination or in reality, was a true statement of facts. You can easily fall victim to any sort of hallucination when you're travelling alone through the jungle, if you're not used to it. I decided to be on my guard against the jungle madness he had talked about. I also decided that the next time I met someone in the jungle I would do my best to be the winner – by doing exactly what the man had done to me.

Three months later, in an entirely different region, I was riding across the muddy plaza of an Indian village when I saw a white man standing in the portico of a palm-roofed adobe house.

'Hi, you! Hello!' he hollered at me.

'Hello yourself!'

It was Sleigh.

He invited me into his house to be introduced to his family. His wife was Indian, a very pretty woman, with a soft, cream-like, yellowish skin, brown eyes, and strong, beautiful teeth. He had three kids, all boys, who easily could pass as American boys from the South. His wife was at least twenty-five years younger than he. The oldest of the kids was perhaps eight years old, the youngest three.

His wife fried me six eggs, which I ate with tortillas and baked beans. For drink I had coffee, cooked Indian fashion, with unrefined brown sugar.

On my entering the house his wife had greeted me: 'Buenas tardes, señor!' accompanied by an almost unnoticeable nod of her

481

head, which wore a crown of two thick black braids. After this short salutation, nearer to suspicion than to friendliness, I did not see her again. Neither did the children come in again, although I heard them playing and yelling outside.

The house was as poor as could be. There was practically no furniture, save one cot, a crude table, three crude chairs, and a hammock. Besides these things there were two trunks in the room, old-fashioned and besprinkled with mud. The house had two doors, one in front, the other at the back leading to a muddy and untidy yard. Yet there were no windows. The floor was of dried mud.

Sleigh, whose first name I never learned, did not invite me to stay overnight. It was not that he was ashamed that he could not offer me a bed; it was simply in accordance with the rule that a man travelling by horse or mule over the country knows best when to stay overnight and where, and therefore he is not urged to change his plans. If on the other hand the traveller were to ask whether he might stay overnight, he is sure to meet with unrestricted hospitality.

I did not ask Sleigh what he was doing here and how he made his living, nor did he by word or gesture indicate that he was curious to know what sort of business brought me through that little native village so far out of the way of regular communications.

2

One year later I was making a rather difficult trip on horseback on the way to the jungle sections of the Huayalexco River, where I hoped to get alligators, the hides of which brought a very good price at that time. My task turned out to be far tougher than I had expected.

At certain places along the river-banks the jungle was so dense that it would have taken many days of hard work with the help of natives to clear the banks sufficiently to enable me to approach the points where alligators were supposed to be found. Other parts of the region were so swampy no one could pass them to reach the banks. I then decided to ride farther down the river, expecting to locate territory easier to hunt in. Indians had told me that on my way downstream I would meet with a number of tributaries which at that time of the year were likely to abound with alligators.

One day while on this trip down the river I came to a pump-station practically hidden in the jungle. This pump-station was railroad property. It pumped the water from the river to another station many miles away, from where it was pumped on to the next railroad depot. For about a hundred miles along the railroad there was no water all the year round save during a couple of months when the rainy season was at its height. Hence the need to pump water to that depot. Part of this water served the engine. The greater part, though, was carried by train in special tanks to the various other depots and settlements along the railroad track, because all the people living there would have left the depots and the little villages if they were not provided with water during the dry season.

The pump-master, or, as he liked to be called, el maestro maquinista, was Indian. He worked with the assistance of an Indian boy, his ayudante. The boiler was fired with wood, some of it brought in from the jungle by an Indian wood-chopper on the back of a burro, the rest carried, in the form of old, discarded timber and rotten sleepers, from the depot.

The boiler looked as if it were ready to burst any minute. The pump, which looked as though it had been in use for more than a hundred years, could be heard two miles away. It shrieked, howled, whistled, spat, gurgled, and rattled at every nut, bolt, and joint – and the first day I was there I stayed a safe distance away in the fear that this overworked and mistreated dumb slave might throw off its chains and make a dash for freedom. The railroad, however, was justified in using this old pump until it broke down for good. To dismantle it, take it to the depot, and ship it to a junk yard would have cost more than half the price of a new pump. So it was cheaper to keep it where it was and let it work itself to death. Owing to the difficulties of transportation and mounting, it would have been bad economy for the railroad to bring down a new pump at this time, especially since the railroad expected that any day now an American company would strike oil near by and that this company would then take care of the water problem for a hundred miles along the track.

About seventy yards from the pump a bridge crossed the river.

483

This bridge, built and owned by the oil company and made of crude heavy timber, was wide enough so that trucks could pass over it, but it had no railings. The oil company had considered railings an unnecessary expense. Had there been railings on the bridge, perhaps this story would never have been told.

'We have lots of alligators in that river, montones de lagartos, señor, of this you may be assured,' the pump-master said to me. 'Of course, you will understand, mister, they are not right here where the pump is.'

I could understand this very well. No decent alligator who respects established morals would ever be able to live near that noisy pump and keep fit to face life's arrows bravely.

'You see, mister, I wouldn't like them around here, never. They would steal my pigs and chickens. And what do you think, and you may not believe it, but it's true just the same, they even steal little children if they're left alone for a while. No, around here there are very few if any and these are only very small ones, too young to waste a bullet on. Farther down and also upstream, three or four miles from here, you will find them in herds by the hundred – and bulls, dear me, I think they must be three hundred years of age, so big they are.'

I nodded towards the opposite bank. 'Who lives over there? I mean right there where the huts are.'

'Oh, there, you mean. There is prairie, mucha pastura. In fact, it's sort of a cattle ranch. Not fenced in. All open. It belongs to an Americano. After you pass that prairie there's thick jungle again. If you ride still farther through that jungle about six or eight miles, you'll find an oil camp. Men are drilling there, testing holes to see if they can find oil. So far they haven't, and if you ask me, I think they never will. That's the same people what have built this bridge. You know, if they want to drill for oil they have to get all the machinery down here from the depot. Without a bridge they couldn't pass the river with such heavy loads. They tried it a few times during the dry season, but the trucks got stuck and it took them a week to get them out again. The bridge has cost them a lot of money, because the timber had to be brought fifteen hundred miles, and, believe me, mister, that costs money.'

'Who lives on that ranch over there?'

'A gringo, like you.'

'That's what you told me before. I mean who looks after the cattle?'

'Didn't I tell you right now? A gringo.'

484

'Where does he live?'

'Right behind that brush.'

I crossed the bridge on my horse, pulling my pack mule along behind me.

Behind a thick wall of tropical shrubs and trees I found about ten of the usual Indian chozas or jacales – that is, palm-roofed huts.

Women squatting on the bare ground, smoking thick cigars, and bronze-brown children, most of them naked, a few dressed in a shirt or ragged pair of pants, were everywhere. None of the little girls, however, was naked, although only scantily covered by flimsy frocks.

From here I could see across the pasture which the pump-master had called the prairie. It was about a mile long and three-quarters of a mile wide. On all sides it was hemmed in by the jungle. The tracks where the oil company's trucks had passed over the prairie were still visible.

It was quite natural to find an Indian settlement here. The pasture was good and there was water all the year round. The Indians need no more. The pasture was not theirs, but that didn't bother them. Every family owned two or three goats, two or three lean pigs, one or two burros, and a dozen chickens, and the river provided them with fish and crabs.

The men used to cultivate the land near their huts, raising corn, beans, and chile. But since the oil company had started to exploit its leases, acquired twenty years before, many of the men had found work in the camps, from which they came home every Saturday afternoon, remaining until early Monday morning. The men who did not like the jobs, or who could not get them, made charcoal in the bush, which they put into old sacks to be transported by burro to the depot, where it was sold to the agents who came once a week to every depot on the railroad line.

Neither the women I saw nor the children paid any attention to me as I passed them. During the last two years they had become used to foreigners, because whoever went to the oil camps by truck, car, or on horseback stopped at this settlement, or at the pump-station, even if only for an hour or two, but frequently for the night if they arrived at the bridge late in the afternoon. Everyone, even the toughest truck-drivers, avoided the road through the jungle at night.

Among the huts I noted one which, although built Indian fashion, was higher and larger than the rest. It was located at the end of the settlement, and behind it there was a crudely built corral. No other hut as far as I could see had a similar corral.

So I rode up to that hut which boasted a corral and, obeying the customs of the land, halted my horse respectfully about twenty yards away to wait until one of the inhabitants would notice my presence.

Like all the other jacales, it had no door – only an opening against which, at night, a sort of network of twigs and sticks was set from the inside and tied to the posts. The walls were made of sticks tied together with strips of bast and lianas. Therefore if a visitor didn't wait some distance from the house until he was invited in he might find the inhabitants in very embarrassing situations.

I had waited only a minute before an Indian woman appeared. She looked me over, said: 'Buenas tardes, señor!' and then: 'Pase, señor, this humble house is yours.'

I dismounted, tied horse and mule to a tree, and entered the hut. I found the Indian woman who had greeted me to be the wife of my old acquaintance Sleigh. After recognizing me she repeated her greeting more cordially. I had to sit down in a creaking old wicker chair which was obviously the pride of the house. She told me that her husband would be here any minute now. He was out on the prairie trying to catch a young steer which had to be doctored because it had been gored by an older bull and now had festering wounds.

It was not long before I heard Sleigh ordering a boy to open the gate of the corral and drive the steer in.

He came in. Without showing even the slightest surprise he shook hands with me and then dropped into a very low, crude chair.

'Haven't you got a paper with you? Damn if I've read or seen any paper for eight months, and believe me, man, I'd like to know what's going on outside.'

'I've got the San Antonio *Express* with me. Sweat-soaked and crumpled. It's five weeks old.'

'Five weeks? Hombre, then I call it still hot from the press. Hand it over!'

He asked his wife for his spectacles, which she pulled out of the palm leaves of the roof. He put them on in a slow, almost ceremonious manner. While he was fixing them carefully upon his ears he said: 'Aurelia, get the caballero something to eat, he is hungry.'

Of each page he read two lines. He then nodded as if he wished to approve what had been said in the paper. Now he folded it contemplatively as if he were still digesting the lines he had read, took off

486

his specs, stood up, put the glasses again somewhere between the palm leaves under the roof, and finally pushed the folded paper behind a stick pressed against the wall, without saying thanks. He returned to his seat, folded his hands, and said: 'Damn it, it's a real treat to read a paper again and to know what is going on in the world.'

His desire for a newspaper had been fully satisfied just by looking at one, so that he could rest assured that the people back home were still printing them. Suppose he had read that half of the United States and all of Canada had disappeared from the surface of the earth, I am sure he would have said: 'Gosh, now what do you make of that? I didn't feel anything here. Anyway, things like that do happen sometimes, don't they?' Most likely he would not have shown any sign of surprise. He was that kind of an individual.

'I'm here to get alligators.'

'After alligators, you said? Great. There are thousands here. I wish you'd get them all. I can't get them away from my calves and my young steers. They make so damn much trouble. What's worse, the old man blames me. He tells the whole world that I'm selling his young cows and pocketing all the money, while in fact the alligators get them and the tigers and the lions, of which the jungle is packed full. I can tell you, the old man that owns this property, he is a mean one. How can I sell a cow, even a very young one, or anything else, without everybody here knowing about it. Tell me that. But he is so mean, the old man is, and so dirty in his soul, that's what he is. If I wasn't here looking out for his property, I can swear he wouldn't have a single cow left. But he himself is afraid to live here in the wilderness, because he is yellow, that's what he is.'

'He must have money.'

'Money, my eye. Who says money? I mean he hasn't much cash. It's all landed property and livestock. Only, you know, the trouble is there is nothing safe here any longer, no property, and cattle still less so. It's all on account of those bum agraristas, you know. Anyhow, I absolutely agree with you that you can easily shoot a hundred alligators here. Whole herds you can shoot if you go after them. There are old bulls among them that are stronger than the heaviest steer, and they are tough guys too, those giant alligator bulls. If one of them gets you, man, there isn't anything left of you to tell the tale. But, come to think of it, why don't we first go after a tasty antelope?'

'Are there many antelope here too?' I asked.

'Many isn't the right word, if you ask an old-timer. You just go into the bush over there. After walking say three hundred feet, you just take down your gun and shoot straight ahead of you. Then you walk again a hundred feet or so in the same direction and there you'll find your antelope stone dead on the ground, and more often than not you'll find two just waiting to be carried away. That's how it is here. I'll tell you what we can do. Stay here with me for a few days. Your alligators, down the river or up it, won't run away. They will wait with pleasure a few days longer for you to come along and get them. What day is it today? Thursday. Fine. You couldn't have selected a better day. My woman will be off tomorrow with the kids for a visit to her folks. I'll take them to the depot. Day after I'll be back again. From that day on we'll be all by ourselves here, and we can do and live as we like. The whole outfit and all the house will be ours. One of the girls of the neighbourhood will come over and do all the cooking and the housekeeping.'

3

On Saturday morning Sleigh returned. In the meantime I had been fishing, with not much result.

'Tonight there will be a dance,' Sleigh said. 'The party is to be on the other side of the river, on that square by the pump. It's the pump-master who has ordered music.'

'Out of his own pocket?'

'Of course. You see, it's this way: he has also ordered two cases of bottled beer and four cases of soda and lemonade from the general store at the depot. That's how he will get his money back for the music.'

'How many musicians?'

'One fiddler and one with a guitar.'

'That music can't cost much.'

'Certainly not. But he won't get rich on the beer and soda either. He'll make a little profit all right, which he deserves since he takes the risk of bringing the music out here.'

488

The Indian girl Sleigh had talked about had come already and was busy about the house. Although she was hardly out of her baby shirt herself, she had with her a baby of her own.

'The guy she got the brat from has left her,' Sleigh said.

She was not a pretty girl; in fact, she was ugly.

'It seems to me,' I said, 'that man saw her only at night or when he was drunk, so when he saw her for the first time by daylight or after he had sobered up, he got so sick that he couldn't help but run as far as his feet would carry him. Somehow, I think that girl would be grateful to the night when it happened. Without that dark night she might never have had a baby. Now, since she has one, it's not unlikely that another guy might get interested in her, believing her possessed of rare qualities which can't be seen from the outside.'

Sleigh eyed me for a while with a quizzical look, as if he had to think out what I had just said. When he got the point or at least thought that he had caught up with it, he nodded and said: 'There is something in what you say. She certainly has had her fun. And if you ask me I am sure she is not a bit sad about it that this guy left her. It isn't that. It is only that she can't have the same fun every night that worries her.'

We sat down and ate tortillas and frijoles while the girl was baking the few fish I had caught early that morning. She just laid them upon the open fire and all she did was to watch that they didn't get burned.

The hearth was a simple affair. It consisted of an old wooden box, three feet by two, which had been filled with earth and put on four sticks.

In the afternoon I rode with Sleigh over the prairie to look at the cattle. We also searched for fresh tracks of antelope. As I had expected, there were no such tracks.

'They must have migrated,' Sleigh said. 'They sometimes do and then you can't possibly find any tracks.'

Early in the evening when we were eating dinner I asked Sleigh whether only the people who lived in this settlement would be at the dance. He explained that at least eighty, even a hundred, other people would join the party. They would come from all directions, from settlements, hamlets, and huts hidden deep in the jungle, and they would come from little places along the river-banks and from ponds and creeks in the bush. Many would travel from five to eight miles on horseback, on mules or burros; some would come from even farther away.

'How does the pump-master advertise this party?'

489

'No difficulty at all,' Sleigh said. 'Whichever native comes this way is told that on this Saturday or that there will be a dance at the pump-station, and that music has been ordered already. So every passer-by takes the word wherever he goes and the people who receive the word repeat it to their neighbours and friends and whoever comes their way. It's remarkable, I tell you, how quickly such a notice reaches twenty miles in every direction.'

4

Night had fallen and we were on our way to the pump-station on the other side of the river.

While passing Sleigh's neighbours, I observed that one hut had a lantern tied by string to a post in its portico. When I came closer I saw an Indian sitting on a bench and playing a fiddle. He seemed to be about forty-five years old. A few silky black hairs, so few that one could easily count them, framed his brown chin. I was sure that because of these few hairs his friends called him the one with a beard. He played pitifully badly, but he tried hard and with some success to keep time.

'What's that?' I asked Sleigh. 'I thought you said the dance would be at the pump-station.'

'Sure enough. Well, the fact is I don't know. Anyway, I don't think the dance will be here.'

'Then why should these people here have cleaned up the whole front yard? And here's this elegant lantern. They don't look to me so fat that they'd use lanterns just for the fun of it.'

'In a minute we'll know all about it. The pump-master will tell us. Anyway, why shouldn't they have their own dance if they want to? There are always two or three parties going on around here. Perhaps he has had a row with the pump-master and wants to have his own party.'

We had reached the opposite bank. On one post of the portico of the pump-master's hut there also was a lantern hung up. The light it gave was less bright than the one we had just seen at the fiddler's.

This lantern was smoking and the glass was not cleaned. But the square in front of the pump-master's hut was well swept.

Six Indian girls who were constantly giggling about nothing in particular tried to sit on a rough bench which wasn't long enough for three. They were already made up for the dance. Their beautiful thick black hair was carefully combed and brushed. They wore it hanging down their backs, reaching almost to their hips. On their heads, fastened to their hair, they had crowns made of fiery red wild flowers. Their brightly coloured muslin dresses were clean and neatly ironed. A heavy odour of cheap, strongly perfumed soap surrounded them. When they saw us coming, they stuck their heads together, hid their faces behind their shawls, and chatted and giggled even more than before, as if every one of them knew a good story about Sleigh or me.

The pump-master was leaning against the post from which the lantern was hanging.

'Now, what's the matter?' Sleigh asked. 'Do we get a dance or do we? If not, say so, and I'll turn in.'

The pump-master scratched his head, coughed and spat several times before he said: 'I wish I knew myself. First thing, to tell you the naked truth, the orchestra hasn't come yet. Frankly speaking, I don't think they'll come at all. It's too dark now. They are afraid to ride through the jungle after dark. I don't blame 'em. Por Jesu Cristo, I'm afraid myself to ride through that goddamned jungle at night, and I know every trail and every vereda for twenty miles around. These two guys promised by all the saints that they would be here by five in the afternoon. I'm sure they've been caged by another party right at the depot and have been promised better pay. So these lazy sticks said to themselves: "Why should we ride through that nasty jungle for hours and under that blazing sun if we can stay right here at the depot and get more money?" You would do the same, mister, or would you?'

'Since you ask me, Don Agustín, I don't care and I can't even play *Dixie* on a comb, still less a mouth-organ. Christ, I'm tired and I'd like to turn in.' Sleigh yawned as wide as his mouth would permit.

'Have a cigarette.' The pump-master offered Sleigh the little tobacco bag. Sleigh pulled out a corn leaf, shaped it, pressed it between his thumb and forefinger, poured the black tobacco on it, wetted it, and began to roll it.

'You wouldn't like our cigarettes,' the pump-master said to me while helping himself. 'Take one of these here, they'll suit your taste better. You gringos prefer to be fooled about real tobacco.' He pulled out of his other shirt pocket one of our most advertised brands imported from back home. 'I never smoke that sissy stuff,' he said, 'I only carry them for the oil people who come this way to make them feel at home and sell them a few bottles of beer.'

'What's going on at Garcia's over there?' Sleigh asked. 'Is he throwing a competition party or doing a dance all his own?'

'Perhaps he is. How should I know? The fact is, his big boy, his oldest son, I mean, has come home for the week-end. He came all the way down from Texas, where he works in the oil fields some-where between San Antonio and Corpus Christi, as he tells me, and he is making good money too. He looks like a prince, the boy does. So maybe the old man is celebrating that event. He is always on the spring for an occasion to show what he can do on the fiddle.'

After this talk, seeing that the party seemed far off, we returned to Sleigh's place. He was, as he told me on our way back to the other bank, concerned about a certain cow that hadn't come home yet.

Garcia was still sitting in the portico of his jacalito, whimpering on his violin and putting all his soul into it.

This time I saw the big boy from Texas sitting beside his father. He was about twenty, for an Indian rather tall, clean and carefully combed. From the creases that were still in it I could see that the shirt he wore was brand-new. In a way his attitude was that of a rich uncle paying a visit to poor relatives. His face showed clearly how happy he felt to be the spoiled member of his family. On his left knee he held an enamelled cup full of black coffee, as I learned a minute later when part of it was spilled over the ground. On his right knee he rested his elbow and in his right hand he held an enchilada – that is, a tortilla filled with cheese, onions, chicken, and chile. From long experience he had learned how to eat without moving his arms and hands more than absolutely necessary. Had it not been for his laughter and his happy face, one might have thought that an automaton and not a human being was having supper. He was preparing himself for a ten-hour dance, so he tried his best to avoid any waste of man-power. He would not worry whether the music arrived or not. As long as there was a fiddle around and a few good-looking girls, there was sure to be a party also.

At the very moment when we were just in front of Garcia's the loud and over-excited voice of a child could be heard: 'Ay, alloh, Manuelito, what's the trouble with you? Still not ready?' And as if

492

he had been shot from a catapult a little boy sprang from behind the hut into the portico. With the agility of a young leopard he jumped straight upon the neck of his big brother, so that coffee and enchilada, or what was still left of them, tumbled over onto the sand.

Once the little boy was firmly settled on his brother's neck, he began savagely mussing the hair that had been so carefully oiled and combed for the dance. When the hair looked like that of an enraged madman, the little boy's fists started hammering the neck, the head, and the shoulders of his brother so furiously that the poor victim of that terrific onslaught finally had to stand up. With heavy, good-natured laughter he tried to shake off the little cat riding on his neck. Carlosito, the little brother, now no longer able to hold on, glided down his brother's back. Hardly had he reached the ground when he took a boxer's position before his brother and challenged him to a fight. Manuelito accepted, saying that he would teach the little one how a real prize-fighter boxes.

Carlosito, however, was not fully himself. Accustomed to stand, walk, and run barefooted since he was born, he now felt unsure on his feet. He had the feeling that his feet were clamped to the ground when he tried to lift them and that they were wrapped in iron so tightly that they could get no air. All the flexibility and lightness of his feet, which heretofore had made him feel like a young antelope, he had suddenly lost without knowing why. So when he tried to fight, his little body swayed and wriggled.

Manuel had brought along with him, as a present for his kid brother, a pair of genuine American shoes. The soles of these shoes were polished and they were smooth as glass. Carlosito, of course, had to put on his new shoes to show the giver how much he liked them. Never before in his life had he worn shoes on his feet. So it was only natural that he should feel the way he did about the heaviness and insecurity of his little feet.

Garcia scratched his fiddle untiringly, not in the least bothered or molested by the noise.

'The kid is pitch crazy about his big brother,' Sleigh said to me while we were walking to his place. 'It's funny how things are in this world. These two boys are only half-brothers. The big one and another about fifteen years old are the ones Garcia had by his first wife. The second, the one who is fifteen, is not quite right in his mind. At least that's what everybody here, me included, thinks. He has the craziest ideas and he does the most stupid things. The little one Garcia had by his second wife, the one he is living with now. She is very young, more than twenty years younger than he. Yet they seem to be very happy, never have a row. Manuel, the big boy, has come here for no other reason than to see his kid brother, who is as mad about him as the big one is about the kid. He has spent practically all his savings just to make this trip to bring the kid a pair of new shoes and a little ukulele. The trip alone takes more time than he can spend here. The second one – I mean the one who's half-witted – is absolutely indifferent about his two brothers and about his father and his stepmother too. Often I get the idea that he is jealous of the kid, I don't know why, and that he's waiting for a chance to do the kid some harm. He has already played many nasty tricks on him – burning his feet when the kid was asleep, or pulling out a tuft of his hair, or throwing snakes at him, or putting ticks all over him. That's one of the reasons why we all think him screwy.'

We had arrived at Sleigh's hut. In one corner of the large room, the only room the hut possessed, the girl had arranged her bedding on the earthen floor. It consisted of a petate, a sort of bast mat. An old blanket full of holes – her cover – lay on the mat. Over this simple bed a mosquito bar was hung.

Hardly had we entered when Sleigh again left to see if the missing cow had come home.

The girl, not minding my presence at all, squatted on the floor, pulled down her dress almost to her hips, and let her baby drink. As soon as the baby was satisfied, she pulled her dress up again and, holding her baby in one arm, crawled beneath the mosquito bar. From the movement of the netting I judged that she was undressing. Then I heard her stretch out her limbs while she uttered a long sigh, by which she obviously meant: 'Well, folks, I think I deserve my rest, so leave me alone.' The fact was that the work she had done during the day had been so easy that a child could have accomplished it. To her it meant nothing whether the world outside her mosquito bar was heading for a gay night with music and dancing or for a tragedy. She had her baby, her eats, and a dry place to sleep in. That was all she wanted on earth.

5

It was dreary in the hut. The little lamp – a tin container filled with kerosene, with a strip of wool stuck in it for a wick – smoked and gave only a spark of light, which made this gloomy, primitive room seem ghostly – a place that gave you no hint that there was civilization somewhere in the world. Any minute I expected to see phantoms of dead Indians and strange animals appear. Everywhere in the hut there were little shadows dancing about, as the smoking flame fluttered in the soft breeze that came in through the walls. I thought I saw big spiders, tarantulas, and huge black scorpions crawling along the wooden rafters on which the palm roof rested.

Frequently the flame got so low that through the walls I could see the flicker of lights in the near-by jacales. The knowledge that there were other huts inhabited by people close by did not make me feel easier in the least. I did not know these people. They all were Indians and if, superstitious as they were, they thought I might bring them or their children harm, they would sneak in and kill me, then throw me into the river; and before Sleigh returned, every trace of what had happened would have been washed away.

Beetles, moths, mosquitoes, and night butterflies bigger than my hands entered the open door. Flying around the little lamp, they deepened the ghostliness of the room rather than brought life into it.

Now and then a gurgling or a gulping sound would come from the river, whose bank was less than twenty yards away. Not only the air around me, but also the ground seemed to be filled with a never tiring sobbing, whistling, whining, hissing, fizzing, whimpering. A burro brayed plaintively in the prairie. A few others answered him, as if they wished to encourage him against the dangers of night. Then a cow mooed. A mule came running close to the open door, chased by a real or perhaps an imagined enemy. On looking into the hut and seeing a human being sitting quietly inside, it recovered from its fear or dream or whatever it was, sniffed at the earth, then calmly walked back to the pasture.

Now and then I heard fragments of speech and hushed voices. A shrill laugh cut the night, reached me, and vanished at the same moment. From another direction came a woman's yell. For a second her yell hung in mid-air, then fell to the ground and was swallowed by the whining jungle. It left behind it a deeper night, a more intense gloom. A few trembling notes from a fiddle floated on the breeze. They came as if they were dancing through the night, but before they actually came close to me they were adrift again.

And there, suddenly, like a shadow, Sleigh stands in the entrance to the hut. All I can see of this shadow is the face. His sudden, silent appearance makes me gasp. I am glad in a way that he cannot see my face at this moment.

'Hell, I wonder if that lazy piece of a girl has left me a gulp of coffee.' His words give me back my breath. 'The devil, I am thirsty.'

The girl, that lazy piece, knows no English, but coffee she has understood and from the questioning tone in his voice she knew what Sleigh wanted.

So from under the mosquito bar she says: 'There is some left on the fire on the hearth.' Of course, she answers in Spanish.

While Sleigh was away she had slept profoundly, as I gathered from her deep, quiet breathing. Nevertheless, with the excellent hearing of an Indian, she had been aware of Sleigh's coming, while I, fully awake and facing the entrance, had heard nothing.

'De veras?' Sleigh says. 'That's almost as good as a diamond found on the prairie.' In a tired manner he goes to the back of the hut where the enamelled pot full of coffee had been left on the smouldering ashes of the hearth.

'How about you, Gales? Have 'nother cup of coffee?'

'No. Thanks all the same.'

The girl snores already. As quickly as she had come out of her dreams, so quickly had she returned to them.

Sleigh sat before me. After a time during which he seemed to doze he said: 'Damn the whole outfit. I can't find that devil of a cow. Not for a thousand dollars could I bring her home. She has got her calf here in the corral, that damn devil has. Every evening she comes home all right without any trouble. Also at mid-day when it gets too hot and the cattle are plagued by horseflies, she comes in with all the others to lie down under the trees. I'm plum sure we've got a lion around. Maybe even a couple of lions. Perez, one of the neighbours, he has a fine goat, a milker, she hasn't come home for days. He too is sure we've got lions. The fact is that goat will never come home again. It's gone for good. The cow has always been very punctual, almost like a clock. Something is queer about the whole damn machinery, that's what I tell you. Well, we'll see tomorrow. Now, in such pitch-dark night, I can do nothing about it, not a thing.'

A minute later he's asleep. In spite of his being asleep he nods, frowns, murmurs, smiles at what I say, just as if he were awake.

'Hi, you!' I shout suddenly. 'Listen, you, if you wish to sleep, all right, then, sleep, only don't let me talk here to the walls.'

'Asleep? Who is asleep? I asleep?' he yells as if I had insulted him. 'I'm never asleep. I don't sleep at all. That's just the trouble here. I haven't got no time to sleep. I've heard every word you said. That thief Barreiro you are talking about. Gee, I've known him for years. Didn't I know him when I was on that cocoa plantation down near Coacoyular? He's a thief all right, and a killer too, if you ask me.'

'What's the matter with that dance?' I asked him. 'The whole day long we've heard nothing else but the dance tonight. Is there a dance or is there? If not, well, I'll turn in. I'm sick of that babble about a dance which never happens.'

'All right, all right, don't get upset about that dance. Here we take our time and don't hustle. Let's go once more to the pump and see how things are. I'm sure the pump-master has got the problem solved. He doesn't want to be stuck with his beer and his soda.'

Without hurrying Sleigh pulled down his leather pants, looked around until he found a broken comb, combed his hair as butchers and saloon-keepers used to wear it twenty-five years ago, put on a pair of yellow cotton pants, and then said: 'Well, I'm all set now for the dance. Let's go. If I only had the faintest idea where that damned cow might be!'

When we passed Garcia's home I noticed that the lantern was still hanging on the post in the portico. Garcia, though, was no longer sitting on the bench. Nor did I see the two boys. Through the wall I got a peep at Garcia's wife, making up by the dim light of a lamp like Sleigh's.

'Well, well!' I said to him. 'There will be a dance all right. The señora is putting on her very best for the great event.'

497

6

The night is thick with blackness. None of the stars that are so bright in the tropics is visible.

At the river-bank we have to feel our way to the bridge. From the opposite bank the pump-master's lantern gave us a vague indication of our way. After some groping, more with our feet than with our hands, we finally hit the heavy planks.

'Christ!' I suddenly yelled. 'That surely was a narrow escape from a bath in the river. Seems to me, one has to be as careful here as if walking a tightrope. Only an inch to the left and I would have toppled off that damn bridge.'

Sleigh showed no excitement about my adventure. He only grumbled passionlessly: 'Yes and God knows you have to be extremely careful at night trying to make the bridge. If you're drunk you have no chance. There is no rail you know.'

'How deep do you think the river might be here near the bridge?'

'Between eight and fifteen feet. The banks are low. On the average I should say it is eight feet deep. Right in the middle of the stream, if you want to call that lazy current a stream, it is about fifteen feet.'

'Deep enough to disappear forever,' I said, 'and even suppose you are a good swimmer, if it is as pitch dark as it is tonight, you can swim around in a circle without realizing it and never reach either bank.'

Talking to Sleigh and thus not paying much attention to how I was walking, I had marched straight ahead, when all at once I saw right beneath the tips of my boots another light. This surprised me so much that I halted with a jerk to examine that great marvel of a light in the water. However, my surprise was shortlived, for I quickly realized that the light in the water was but the reflection of the pump-master's lantern. My right foot had struck the rim, which was about six inches wide and six inches high – just high enough to prevent a truck from gliding off the bridge when the planks were covered by slimy mud during the rainy season. Had I walked a bit faster I would undoubtedly have lost my balance on striking the rim and I would have tumbled over and into the river.

On reaching the end of the bridge we found several Indian youngsters sitting on the planks. They were singing Mexican songs, and also American ones translated into Spanish. Their legs dangled over the edge, swinging in time to the tunes they sang. Mostly they stayed within a range of only seven notes. Yet presently and without warning their voices jumped up two full octaves. As they could not sing notes that high, they shrilled them at the top of their voices. Anywhere else under heaven such singing would have sounded insane. But here in a warm tropical night, surrounded by a black and forever threatening jungle, noisy with thousands and thousands of voices, whispers, melodies, and tunes blended with the gentle sound of the river, their singing seemed proper and in harmony with the whole universe.

To the left of the bridge was the pump-station. To the right was a wide, open sandy space, with very coarse grass trampled down in patches. A pack-mule caravan had arrived only ten minutes before and was now camping on this site. It consisted, as I learned later in the evening from one of the mule-drivers, of sixteen pack mules, three riding mules, and one horse. The caravan brought merchandise from the depot to villages in the jungle and in the sierra beyond the jungle. The muleteers were Indians, of course. There were three of them, who at the time we arrived were unloading the mules, while a boy of twelve was building a fire.

The pump-master's place looked a bit more colourful and lively than it had an hour ago. The pump-master was cleaning another lantern and when he thought it fine enough he hung it to a second post of the portico.

The music had not arrived. Every hope that it might still come had vanished by now. In the meantime, though, many men, women, and girls had appeared.

All the women were gaily dressed in bright-coloured muslin gowns of the cheapest kind. They all wore stockings and high-heeled shoes, although on their way through the jungle they had taken off these fancy garments. None wore a hat. Yet most of them carried shawls, rebozos, or thin black veils to wrap round their heads on their way home in the cool and misty morning.

The men were clothed as always. Many were barefooted, a few had shoes, a few wore shabby puttees, while most of them had the ordinary home-made huaraches or Indian sandals on their feet. All their children had come with them.

Since these people had come for a dance, or at least to spend a jolly time, something had to be done.

Garcia had found an audience at last. Sitting on one of the few improvised benches outside the portico, close to a post from which a lantern was hanging, he fiddled continuously, going from one tune to another without any noticeable intermission. Nobody danced to the music he produced. He did not mind. He seemed fully satisfied, even happy, that there were people around who could hear him play and who had to listen whether they liked it or not. No one yelled at him to stop the almost unbearable scratching and squeaking of his fiddle.

Everybody was waiting, but no one could say what he was waiting for. It looked as though all were expecting a great musician to arrive, who would provide a motive for an assembly of so many people, for the presence of these visitors now seemed without reason or sense.

Why, all the women had gone through really arduous pains for the occasion. They had washed themselves with perfumed soap; for hours and hours they had combed and brushed their hair; every rag they wore was clean; they had dressed themselves in the finest garb they owned, although their gauze dresses were the cheapest the Syrian peddlers carried – in spite of the fact that they cost so much that for many months the Indians would have to economize on everything. Then they had adorned their dresses and their hair with the most beautiful, the rarest flowers they could find. And then, to top it all, there had been the long, hard trip on mule or burro for five, six, eight miles through the steaming jungle, crossing swamps and wading rivers. And now all this seemed to have been in vain! It simply could not be. Everybody wanted to go home in the morning with many things to talk about for two months, it is so very lonely in those little settlements and hamlets hidden deep in the bush and jungle.

No one blamed the pump-master. He could not help it. He had done everything in his power to get the music. Besides, it would do nobody any good to blame anybody or anything for the failure of the party. It had to be: destiny's orders.

7

The married women sat around on benches, on planks, on old sleepers, on gas drums, chatting and laughing.

The girls were giggling, watching the boys pass by, criticizing them, making fun of them, telling stories and exchanging bits of scandalous gossip about them. Now and then two or three girls would get up to stroll after some favoured pair of boys, or they would pretend to pay no attention to them and walk in a different direction, knowing quite well that the chosen boys would follow them. After a while the girls would return and take their seats again. And when they sat down, other girls would arise to play the same game, the oldest in the world and the one that is still best liked, with or without motor cars and campuses, radios and night clubs.

The children were fighting, running around, rolling on the ground, chasing one another, crying, howling, watching the muleteers in their camp. A boy who had thrown stones at the others and hurt them was called by his mother; and he received a thrashing in public. While he got his ointment he howled so much that the people around thought he was going to be butchered. No sooner was he set free than he hurried away to knock down the boys who had complained about him. This time, however, he kept out of reach of his dear mother's voice.

The bigger boys, those between twelve and fifteen, sat in groups, boasting of their strength and their abilities in general, and also about the size of the snakes, tigers, and lions they claimed to have met in the jungle when looking for stray goats or burros. Then they showed each other remarkable tricks – what they could do with their fingers, hands, arms, and bodies, how they could twist and contort them. Some were admired because they could turn their eyes in their sockets so that only the whites could be seen. Others told gruesome stories to the younger ones of how they had been swimming in the river and while diving had been caught by the leg by a bull alligator, and then they showed by throwing themselves on the ground and rolling about how they had freed themselves and what sort of fight they had had to go through before they found safety on the bank.

Everybody was smoking, men, women, children. But not the girls, because the boys say that a kiss from the tobacco-stained lips of a sweet girl is the ugliest thing in love. They smoked cigarettes made by rolling black tobacco in corn leaves. Mothers with their babies at their breasts blew tobacco smoke into the babies' faces to protect them against the mosquitoes.

The men lounged around in smaller groups, talking, laughing, boasting, and occasionally buying a bottle of beer for themselves and a lemonade for their womenfolk. They always had one eye on their women and daughters.

With Sleigh, the pump-master, and an Indian who worked with the oilmen, I stood mid-way between the bridge and the pump, slightly nearer to the river than to the pump-master's hut. I looked towards the river, but I could see neither it nor the bridge because of the blackness of the night.

From where I stood, by turning my eyes to the left I could see the fire of the mule-drivers' camp, where the boy at this moment was throwing coffee into the tin kettle by the fire while the men were toasting tortillas and cutting cheese and onions.

Dim lights shimmered through the brush on the opposite bank. As the soft breeze moved the shrubs, these little flickers now appeared, now disappeared in quick succession. These were mostly lights from the huts yonder where the women were making up for the dance, but some came from the big, tropical fireflies which were everywhere about us.

The boys sitting on the bridge at this end were still singing. Their stock of songs seemed inexhaustible, but the tunes seemed to be always the same. There were differences, though, and the Indians recognized them.

Wherever I looked there was animation and laughter and the noise of children at play.

8

'I tell you, they are going to cement again, and they'll do it next week,' Ignacio said importantly. He was the man who worked in the oil camp and was now standing with Sleigh and the pump-master and myself.

'How deep are you down now?' Sleigh asked.

'About twelve hundred feet, I think.'

'At that depth there is no reason why they should cement the hole.' The pump-master, who in fact knew nothing about oil, wished to impress us with his wisdom. He had picked up a few phrases which he had heard from oilmen passing by, so he went on bravely: 'Why should they cement at twelve hundred? There are holes where they drill down to four thousand feet.'

'You're telling me,' Ignacio said, with the firmness of an old expert. He had been working with the oilmen only about three months and his principal job had been carrying iron pipes on his shoulders. 'But, believe it or not, they are going to cement Monday or Tuesday. On that I'll bet any of you guys.'

Garcia was still scratching his fiddle, but nobody paid any attention to his plaintive invitation to dance.

The singing of the boys on the bridge was getting thin, as if some voices had fallen out or as if all of them had at last become tired.

And at that moment something strange happened. I had the feeling that the air was invaded by a mysterious power which hovered over us like a huge winged beast. A kind of lethargy overcame the crowd. People began to yawn. And, as if by command, everyone suddenly stopped talking and laughing. There was a sense of tiredness and depression about us.

'You'll never make me understand why they should cement at twelve hundred feet.' The pump-master brought up the question once more. To me it seemed that now he was not at all interested in what the oilmen were doing here or anywhere else in the world and that he was talking only to break that strange silence which was spreading around us.

None in our group accepted the pump-master's invitation to talk. The air was heavy, burdened as it is just before the break of a thunderstorm.

And then, when everybody was on the verge of opening his mouth to say something to end that horrible silence, there came the sound of a heavy splash from the river, which during the last fifteen minutes had been so quiet that not even the softest gurgle could be heard.

That plunge was very short, but distinctively characteristic in its peculiar sound. Yet nobody seemed to have noticed it. Nobody paid any attention to it. It was the sort of splash that occurred perhaps a dozen times every day.

I, however, felt as though the river had cried out: 'Don't forget me, folks. I am still here and I shall survive all of you!'

I looked Sleigh straight in the face. He looked at me in the same manner. I knew he was thinking something and I wondered whether he might not be thinking the same thing I was. He had heard the plunge, but he tried to give the impression that he was paying as little attention to it as the others.

Now let me think. What was that sound? Could it be that one of the boys sitting on the bridge had jumped into the river just for fun? No, it was not that. I would have heard somebody swimming or paddling through the water. Yet there was no such sound after the big splash, nor was there any of the laughing or howling with which the other boys would inevitably have greeted such a plunge.

Perhaps it was a stone or a log thrown into the river by someone.

Garcia was fiddling again. His fingers must have been tired by now, but he fiddled on.

Perhaps it was a big fish jumping out of the water to catch a mouthful of mosquitoes. No, it was no fish. The sound was entirely different. If I could only find a simile for it! But I simply could not place it.

'Why are they going to cement?' Ignacio now said. 'I'll tell you. They have already cemented two holes deeper in the jungle. You see, here's the way they work, those gringos. What they are actually doing is robbing our poor country, leaving us poorer still and making themselves a thousand times richer than they are already. They drill until they reach oil. No sooner do they get in than they right away cement the hole tight to keep the oil inside. Once they have it under control and locked up, then they come out and say that they have not found one drop, not even a noseful of gas. That's what they are doing, these damned foreigners of Americanos.'

The pump-master shook his head. 'No, that's something the gringos won't do. I know them too well. If they get to the oil, then they take it out, to the last crippled drop; they even dig out the mud and filter it for the oil left in it. What do you think, Don Nacho, how much does it cost them to drill a hole two thousand feet or perhaps deeper? That will cost them at least around thirty thousand dollars, and good American money too. Some holes cost them still more, up to fifty thousand dollars Americanos. Do you think they would throw their good money away? If their money were pesos, maybe they would. But believe me, their money is good money, all dollars. So that's all squash about them drilling a hole and cementing it tight after they find oil.'

Perhaps it was a dog. No, the dog is out. A dog would make lots of noise in the water. The boys would holler after him from all sides to make it tough for the animal, confuse him as to the shortest way to the bank. Yet there was not even the slightest noise after the plunge. Even a cat would have struggled and made some noise. But there was just the one brief, sharp splash, and nothing followed.

Ignacio laughed. He knew all the secrets of the American oil companies. 'Only you, Don Agustín, because you are a maestro maquinista and have never had any experience with oil people, only you can talk the way you do. Can't you see, hombre, why they cement the hole at twelve hundred feet instead of going down to three or four thousand? Easy to see for one who is in the know, as I am. It is because they have struck oil already at twelve hundred, so they don't have to go down farther. That's why they cement now.'

Manuel, the big brother from Texas, was standing by a girl, talking to her almost incessantly while she just giggled. He was different from all other boys she knew. She could see that. That was because he worked in Texas. He sees the wide world, and so he knows a pretty girl if he meets one. Out there in Texas he has learned how to tell the pretty and clever girls from the dumb ones. She let him understand clearly enough that she was willing any time he said so. Next time he came for a visit he would surely bring her a fine dress such as the gringo women in Texas wear all day long. He had become a genuine pocho up there in Texas, he even spoke American, and so she was immensely proud that he had chosen her for the dance tonight.

'Well, Don Nacho,' the pump-master said, 'you shouldn't really tell me such things about gringos. As for me, all gringos may go to hell straight away. I don't give a peanut for any of them. Only you

505

musn't tell me that they are stupid. Whatever they are, even godless heathen who don't believe in the Holy Virgin, stupid they are not.'

'I never said that they are stupid, Don Agustín. You mustn't turn my words round. I mean it just the opposite way, see? They are too smart, that's what they are. And that's exactly what I meant to say. If they would get no oil at twelve hundred, why should they cement? They would go down at least another twelve hundred to make sure. Otherwise they'd lose all that good money the hole has cost them so far. And now I'll tell you why they cement. It's a secret, but it's true just the same. You see, they have found oil and lots of it at twelve hundred. Now they cement it tight, but stake it as their legal property. They then say that they have struck nothing, not even a sneeze of gas. Why do they deny it? Because they haven't yet got leases on all the land around. If they now can make landholders believe that there is no oil on their properties they will get all the leases they want and they'll get them for a few hundred dollars. Otherwise companies with more money would come down and whip the prices for leases so high up to heaven that this company would have to let it go or spend a hundred times more than they spend now. As soon as they have got possession of all the leases they are after, then they return and break open all the cemented holes, and then you'll see the oil flowing like rivers in the rainy season.'

The pump-master was convinced that he had underestimated the wisdom of his friend and neighbour Ignacio. His eyes widened, he looked admiringly at him and said: 'Well, Don Nacho, I have to hand it to you. You are right after all. What you have told me right now, that must be correct, because it's exactly what I always expected that these gringos would do to us. Stealing not alone all our oil, but also all our land, that's what they do. For if they buy the leases for a hundred dollars instead of paying ten thousand, which is the real price, that's what I call a goddamned robbery. The government should know about that and of such dirty doings. Yet, as I've said before a hundred times over, stupid they're not. I see this clearer every day. They are not stupid, though I frankly admit that they are a damn bunch of bandits, and cabrones too.'

'There you see, Don Agustín,' Ignacio shouted triumphantly, 'there you see, what did I tell you? You have only to open your eyes and ears when you're near them and you'll learn quickly and easily how they make big money. Yet they can't bedazzle me. Not me. None of them. I know those thieves all over.'

That these people who were so very courteous by nature should, in the presence of Sleigh and myself, talk in such a way about Americans was proof that they did not count us among the gringos and thieves, simply because we were not oilmen, and therefore, in their opinion, we had no relationship with the race from which the oilmen come.

A man had meanwhile seated himself near Garcia. He had taken the fiddle away from him and put it against his breast, Indian fashion. All the girls looked up with hope in their eyes, because that man grasped the fiddle so resolutely, as though he were going to show Garcia how a fiddle should be played.

He played the first twenty notes so astonishingly well that the girls pulled at their dresses and stroked their hair, while the boys turned their faces quickly towards the benches and sleepers where the girls were sitting. Just when the boys were about to jump to their feet to dart over towards their partners, the tune got confused, and as abruptly as the music had begun, it finished with a pitiful moan. The new fiddler, trying to make good, started once more on another tune, but there was now no doubt that he was ten times worse than Garcia, who could at least keep time.

Garcia took his fiddle back with a smile. Tuning it, bending down to put his ear to the strings, he looked around at the crowd as if he wanted to say: 'Well, now you can see for yourself who the really good musician is hereabouts.'

He began playing again, and obviously influenced by the lively notes he had just heard, he fiddled with more energy. Two girls got up and started to dance. Garcia was in heaven when he saw that somebody was going to take his music seriously. After twenty passes or so the girls realized that it was impossible to dance to the mixed-up melodies Garcia was composing. If there were only a guitar at hand to accompany the fiddle, bad as it was, it might have been possible to obtain some sort of dance music.

Nobody thought of leaving the party. And what is more, no one showed any sign of disappointment. In fact, not a single person considered the party a failure. Real music to dance to would have been a good thing to liven up the party, but since it could not be had, everybody made the best of the gathering.

Most of the people there had come a long way. They couldn't return in so dark a night through the jungle; and since they were here anyway, everybody was sure that something would happen, because something had to happen to justify the trouble they had taken to get to the place. Where so many people are gathered together, something is bound to happen, and nobody and nothing can prevent it. It is nature's law.

We two, Sleigh and I, did not break into the discussion that was being held in our group, save occasionally to exclaim: 'Zat so?' or 'Really?' or 'Maybe,' or 'No doubt!'

Ignacio, the man with the great knowledge of the way in which oil magnates make their millions, left us. He went looking for another group before whom he could show off. That he could win the admiration of the highly respected maestro maquinista would live in his memory for years to come, and the pump-master might now ask him for whatever he wished and he would get it. Men are devoted to those who admire them.

9

A young and very pretty woman came towards us. She was dressed in a cheap sea-green gauze frock. Through it one could see her white cotton petticoat, richly trimmed with lace. Two big red flowers adorned her thick black hair, combed and done up neatly, almost meticulously. A little bunch of wild flowers was pinned to her breast, and another was fastened at her girdle. One could see that she had good taste, for the flowers matched the colour of her dress so well that a delicate but natural harmony was achieved. Her lips were painted a shade less than dark red. While many of the other women powdered their faces startlingly white, this woman had used ochre-coloured powder. But like all the others she carried with her the heavy odour of the strongly perfumed soap bought from Syrian peddlers.

'Have you seen Carlosito?' She asked the question lightly, unconcernedly, as though she were not in the least interested in our answer and was asking it only to say something friendly. 'He hasn't had his supper yet. He is too much excited because of Manuel's being here for the week-end. The kid forgets eating and everything.' She laughed loud when she recalled the boy's fervour and she tried to imitate the way he acted. She waved both her arms through the air, and her feet were tripping and dancing on the ground. 'Buenas noches, mamasita!' and 'Adiosito, mamasita!' and 'Cómo estas, mamasita linda, cielito?' and 'I've got to run after my hermanitito Manuelito!' . . . 'So he comes, so he goes, so he runs hither and thither, not for one minute remaining quietly in the same place. Off like the wind. I can't catch him and I can't grasp him. Well, that's the way kids are. Only he ought to have his supper, but he won't die if he skips it, will he?' She laughed not only with her face but with her whole body. 'A happy mother if there is any,' I said to myself.

The pump-master yawned, openly bored by the woman's fuss about her brat. He said: 'He wasn't around here. I've not seen him since late in the afternoon when he came over to the wife to buy one centavito's worth of green chile.'

'Yes, that's right. I sent him over here to get chile. That was long ago. He has been in the house since then twenty times or more. I'll catch him, never mind.'

Sleigh looked around as uninterestedly as the pump-master did when he said: 'I reckon he was here chasing other boys. Perhaps he wasn't. Well, the fact is I haven't noticed him, what with so many brats about.'

'Never mind, caballeros, never mind at all. It isn't very important anyhow. When he's hungry he'll come home all right. He knows where he finds his beans ready waiting for him. It was only to say something. Forget it, caballeros.'

The woman leaves us with a happy smile on her face.

A man walked slowly up to us, greeted us, and started to talk about the new boiler that had been promised the pump-master two years ago and which had not come yet and would probably not come for another two years.

Gazing after that pretty woman, I noticed that she was going to Manuel, whom she spotted standing with his girl a short distance away from us. He listened to her and I saw him shake his head. Paying no further attention to the casual interruption, he talked again to his girl, whose happiness over having him for her companion did not diminish.

Without asking Sleigh, I now knew that this young pretty woman was the Garcia woman, the mother of the little Carlos and the stepmother of Manuel, who was only three or four years younger than she.

She walked over to the portico where her man was still sitting on the bench. He was not playing his fiddle at this moment, but he was rolling himself a cigarette. He listened to her unimportant question with the mien of a man who has to listen to the same question a hundred times every day. While wetting his cigarette he shook his head, as if to say: 'Don't bother me about that kid now, I've got other things to worry about at present.'

For a minute the woman stood outside the portico, under one of the lanterns. She was obviously undecided what to do or where to go next. From the stillness of her body I judged that she was brooding over something, no doubt recollecting where and when she had seen the kid last, what he was saying or doing or telling her as to where he meant to go.

Now she slowly moved on, mixed with the crowd, looked this way and that, fixed her eyes on the boys of the age of Carlosito.

The farther away from the weak light of the two lanterns the men and women were, the more ghostly they appeared. Their deep bronze-brown faces blended with the surrounding darkness so perfectly that their faces vanished and only their hats and white clothes remained. One often got the impression that only clothes were walking about, over which hats were mysteriously hanging in mid-air.

Here and there I saw the Garcia woman walking among the groups. It seemed to me that she was now moving about slightly nervously and that she jerked her head this way and that, pushing her face forward.

Garcia had taken up his fiddle again. Others had also tried to play during the last half-hour, but it was clear that Garcia was the best fiddler in the place.

Out from somewhere in the deep night the wailing tunes of a mouth-organ could be heard. Again girls aroused enough courage to try to dance, and again they realized, to their chagrin, that it was useless.

The pump-master woman, who had been sitting on a crude chair near the portico chatting with two other women, stood up, took down one of the lanterns, and went inside her hut.

With half the illumination gone, the square became darker and ghostlier than ever.

The campfire of the mule-drivers was nearly extinguished, and the three men and their boy came to the square to mix with the party. Right away they met several acquaintances and soon they were partaking in the general conversation.

The Garcia woman, coming from the direction of the bridge, stepped up to us at this moment. She walked fast now, as though

510

she were in a real hurry. She said to us: 'The kid isn't here and he isn't there. He isn't anywhere. I can't find him. Where do you think he might have gone?'

Her face, which only a quarter of an hour ago was so full of smiles and happiness, and ten minutes ago looked rather businesslike, had by now taken on an expression of worry and uneasiness. Yet it was not fear. She raised her eyebrows, opened her eyes wide, and with those staring eyes she gazed at us, searching the face of every one of us. And for the first time since I saw her, there appeared in her eyes a suspicion that we might know something or imagine something, and that we might be withholding our knowledge from her for some reason or other, perhaps out of sheer pity for her.

Helplessly, like a wounded animal that is down and can't get on its feet, she looked at us again, almost piercing our faces with her burning eyes. Finding nothing, she shook her head and folded her hands against her breast.

Another change came over her eyes. The slight foreboding she had felt only a few seconds earlier had now become half a certainty. With all her power she tried to fight off that feeling, but she couldn't.

Well! The Great Music-Master had arrived. Here at last! He was ready to play. The dancing that all had been waiting for would begin. It would be a wild and whirling dance, to be sure. It would be a dance at which the trumpets and fanfares of Judgment Day would blare.

Slowly the dancers began to take their positions.

'Don't you worry, Carmelita,' the pump-master said in a fatherly way. 'That kid got tired out, so he has laid himself down somewhere as kids will do. There's nothing strange about that.'

'He isn't at home. I've looked everywhere. I've searched every nook and corner.'

'He'll be in another choza with other kids; sure, that's where he is.'

'No. I've asked everywhere in all the jacales.'

'Don't get hot, Carmelita. Perhaps he has crawled beneath a blanket or a petate or hidden in a heap of old sacks. He may have climbed up on the roof, where it is cool, and fallen asleep there.'

The Garcia admits she has not thought of the roof. Frequently he climbs the roof of their hut or that of another, alone or in company with other boys. Why, only last night he slept on the roof. It is not comfortable to sleep on an inclined roof, but then, boys have their own ideas about comfort.

Hope entered the woman's mind. She hurried back across the bridge to the other bank.

The pump-master woman returned with the lantern. She hung it up again and once more the square was bright and the shadows retreated to the jungle.

10

Garcia fiddled. He was not troubled by what was happening around him. A hundred times before, the kid had failed to come for his supper. And a hundred times he had had to search for him in the most unthinkable places where little boys may hide themselves. A dozen times if not more the boy had taken a burro and ridden away just for the fun of it. And he had done so knowing perfectly well that on returning he would be greeted with a good spanking.

Those womenfolk, hell, they always have their buttocks full of fear for no reason as soon as they haven't got their brats hanging at their skirts! Damn it! Although nobody tried any more to dance to his fiddling, he did not feel offended. Not at all. If someone thinks he can play any better why doesn't he show up? That's just it. There is nobody here who can play better. He would willingly and with pleasure lend him his fiddle, Garcia would. But there is no one. He alone can play. He knows all the foxtrots, all the one-steps, all the danzones, all the bostons and blues. They are, sorry to say, all mixed up a bit, one with another. You have to listen carefully for a while before you can make out what he is playing or what he means to play. If after hearing a dozen notes you are convinced he is playing a waltz, you realize that in fact he is playing a two-step. Never mind that, it is music all the same.

Now and then somebody played a mouth-organ again. You couldn't see the player. But you didn't have to see who it was that was performing in the darkness to know that the mouth-organ was going from one mouth to another, because between tunes you could hear the voices of the players. Often one heard what they were saying: 'Caray, you burro, let me have it, you know nothing of

512

music, a dumb ox plays better than you, you don't even know how to hold it the right way.'

The boys on the bridge were singing no longer. From where I was standing I couldn't see whether they were still sitting on the bridge. Perhaps they were telling stories to one another. It might be that they had been attracted by the mouth-organ players and that they had joined them to try their skill as musicians.

Since we – Sleigh, the pump-master, another man, and myself – were standing between the bridge and the pump-master's, it was only natural that anybody coming from the bridge should pass us on the way to the hut. When the Garcia returned from her search and walked up to talk to the pump-master woman, she saw us and stopped.

Her face had taken on the shimmer of fear. It was no longer mere anxiety, as it had been ten minutes before. Her wide-open eyes were fixed upon us questioningly. There was a tiny last flicker of hope still somewhere in the corners of her staring eyes. She did not want to ask the question lest that last shred of hope flutter away. She expected to hear from us that while she had been back at her hut we had learned something new about the whereabouts of the kid. None of us could resist her questioning gaze any longer. It almost pierced my very soul.

I avoided her eyes and looked at her head. Her beautiful hair, combed and neatly done up when I had seen her first, was now deranged. She had climbed the roof and she had obviously crawled through shrubs near the hut.

'He isn't on the roof either, señores.' We felt relieved of her eyes and we now breathed again as she spoke: 'The neighbours also have searched for him in their homes. They haven't found him.' This she said with the peeping voice of a little girl about to weep. 'No, he isn't over there on the other bank.' These last words were spoken as if each were weighted down by a heavy load.

For a few seconds she seemed not to know whether to expect an answer from us or not. She took a deep breath and walked over to her husband. Her steps had become less youthful.

While he fiddled unceasingly she talked to him with excited gestures. Suddenly she stopped and looked at him, anxiously awaiting his opinion.

He drew a last long stroke. Then, still holding the fiddle pressed against his breast above his heart (which is where every Indian musician holds his violin), he turned his head, and with his great, sad, dreamy eyes stared at his woman.

Suddenly his whole body grew tense. An Indian, considerably older in life and experience than she, he saw in her eyes far more than she wanted to let him see. She did not want to appear ridiculous before her man. It would be against the nature of an Indian woman. But he knew now what she could not and would not say. He opened his mouth and his lower jaw dropped as a dying man's does. Slowly, apparently without knowing what he was doing, he took the fiddle from his breast and let it rest on his left knee. And while he was putting down his fiddle he saw the Great Music-Master come and take it out of his hand. Garcia knew there would be music now, more music than he could stand.

The kid had been missing less than one hour. Many times he had been away from home for half a day, and for hours and hours nobody would know where he was roaming during that time. Yet never before had Garcia seen his woman with so much fear in her eyes.

'Manuel!' the woman called out.

Manuel came right away, shouting a few jolly remarks back to his laughing girl.

The laughter still in his voice he asked: 'What is it, mother dear?'

'We can't find Carlos,' she said with trembling lips. She looked sternly into his eyes, hoping to hear from him the only word that could relieve her of the growing pain in her heart.

The big smile on Manuel's face became a few degrees brighter when he said: 'Why, mother, I saw him only a short while ago.'

'Where?' the mother cried out, her face immediately lighting up as if a wreath of a hundred thousand sun-rays had fallen upon it.

'Where?' Manuel repeated. 'Where? Why, right here. He wanted to blow his nose in my silk handker. He did it all right. Then he pushed it back into the hip pocket of my pants. Here, it's still there. Then he beat my legs with his fists, jumped with his new shoes on my toes to make me angry and make me box with him, and right then he was off again swift as a young coyote.'

'You said only a short while ago, Manuelito.'

'Of course, mother. Just now – only a few – I mean – just – wait. Or – '

'Or what? Or what? Speak up, muchacho.' The woman shook him violently by his arm. He was half a head taller than she.

'Or – wait – well, come to think of it, it might have been ten minutes, I should say, or fifteen.'

The woman fixed her eyes on his lips to catch every word quicker than her ears would get them.

'Let me think, mother. I was talking all the time to Joaquina. And considering how much we talked in the meanwhile, well, it might be half an hour since I've seen the kid. Perhaps even longer. I believe, yes, I do believe it is longer still. Even an hour. Since then I haven't seen him. Not around here anywhere. That's right, mother, it may well be almost a full hour.'

The face of the woman darkened. Then it seemed to shrink as if it were about to wither. Now her words tumbled out of her trembling lips: 'After he had been here with you he came over once more. He gave me the thread I asked him for to tie up this little bunch of flowers on my dress. This happened after you had seen him.'

In her growing fear she forced herself to think clearly and sum up every little detail she could remember and she tried to fit each into its proper minute, believing perhaps that by so doing she might find the exact minute when the kid had slipped away, as if knowing that exact minute might make it possible to find him. 'Yes, yes, yes, this was afterwards. I know for sure it was later. Because he told me that he had pulled your handker out of your pocket and that he would have liked very much to steal it from you because it is such a beautiful silk handker and that he surely would have stolen it were it not that you are such a very good Manuelito whom he loves too much to steal anything from.'

Manuel looked around the square, hoping to see his kid brother pop up that very second from the depth of the darkness to make faces at them. So vividly was the kid in Manuel's mind that he could not believe that anything serious had happened to him. Something so lively and so full of pep as that kid couldn't disappear like a feather. There must be a trace or a fight or a yell or something.

Garcia stood up slowly. For a while he did not know what to do. He had laid his fiddle on the bench. Feeling something in his right hand he looked down and saw that it was the bow. He turned around and laid it close to the fiddle. Then he stared with empty eyes into the night.

The pump-master woman came up to Manuel and his step-mother. A few women followed her, and two men walked up to hear what had happened. So far only Garcia's family and we four men knew that the kid was missing.

The pump-master woman reasoned with the Garcia. She had children herself, she said, and there was not a day in the year when she didn't have to work to find one or the other, and more often than not in places where no Christian soul would ever think a child might be. Why, they had even been found inside of hollow trees, and no one on earth knew how they wriggled in, since the hole was too small and they had to be cut out with an axe. 'Children, dear me, don't tell me anything about children, least of all about little boys. Once we found our Roberto inside the boiler and it was only by a holy chance that the boiler was inspected before water was poured in and the fire started.'

Other women, all mothers, made fun of the Garcia woman's fear, telling her she wouldn't worry so much if she had a dozen brats and not just this one. 'Don't tell me anything about these little rascals,' one woman said; 'these little vermin and good-for-nothings return home always. That's just the trouble with them. I wish some of mine would stay away for good and look out for themselves. Don't you get excited, Carmelita. As soon as he gets hungry he will be back and will make a big row if he doesn't find his frijoles and tortillas ready for him. A boy like that can't just fly off like a mosquito, seen by nobody. You'll see him soon enough and then give him a good whipping so that he knows where he belongs. They are like puppies, that's what they're like.'

Manuel had walked away. After a few minutes we heard him calling in the darkness: 'Carlos! Carlosito! I've got candy, Carlosito! Where are you? I got candy, Carlos. Carlosito!' His voice went farther into the night and finally was heard no longer.

Talk ceased. Everybody listened for an answer from the kid. Yet there was only the whining, the singing, the chirping, the humming from the jungle, at intervals interrupted by Manuel's distant shouts.

Stirred up by Manuel, other groups on the square became interested in what was going on. They all began to move, to fall in line for the dance to which the ghostly music was playing faster every minute.

The pump-master went to the open shed where the pump and the boiler were located. With lighted matches he peered into every corner. Those who were near him watched his every move and expected him any minute to drag out the boy from some hidden retreat behind or under the pump. On seeing him return empty-handed, everybody thought it very silly to have believed the kid to be under the pump or inside the boiler or in the ash pit.

The Garcia looked pitifully from one to another. Holding one fist against her mouth, she nibbled thoughtlessly at her fingers. Her eyes were like an animal's which sees some danger approaching and finds itself without means of defence. A certain thought entered her mind. She took her fist away from her face and hid it in the palm of her left hand. For a while she pressed both hands against her breast. With a jerk she turned around and hurried towards the bridge. After a few paces she stopped. In utter despair she let her head drop. Slowly her arms glided down her body until they dangled lifelessly. She turned away from the bridge and with heavily dragging feet she came back to our group.

Old man Garcia was standing with us, and not knowing what better he could do, he began rolling a cigarette.

'Carlos! Carlosito! Carluchito!' Now from this direction, then from that, sometimes nearer, sometimes far away, Manuel's strong voice could be heard calling his kid brother.

Only the jungle answered with its whining.

The boys, spurred by Manuel's anxious search, formed half a dozen groups of two and three and scattered in all directions. Soon from everywhere one heard 'Carlosito!' After each call there was silence for a few seconds so that little Carlos might have his chance to answer, were it ever so faintly. It seemed that even the jungle fell silent for a moment as if it wanted to help save a little child.

11

'Señora! Señora Garcia! Señora Garcia!' The bright and jubilant voices of two boys broke the monotony of the calling of the child's name. These young voices freshened up the heavy atmosphere like a cool breeze wiping the depressing glow off a treeless plain at the height of a midsummer day. And again those animated and exultant voices blared through the night like the cornets of a military band. Running like devils, the two boys, shouting and yelling all the time, were now crossing the bridge.

'Well, well! Now, there, there! There is the boy at last,' the pump-master woman cried out, and blew a deep sigh of relief. 'Haven't I said a hundred times that a healthy boy like him can't get lost? Well, thanks to heaven, that's all over now!'

All faces lost their funny distortions and became ordinary

human faces again. Hurriedly uttered words were flying about all groups. Everybody wished to say something very quickly and wanted to confirm that he had said so long before. Some even went so far as to boast that they had known all the time where the boy had been hidden.

A few youngsters and girls left the centre of the square, bored now with all that noise about nothing. It was pure nonsense, the whole excitement was, for how could it be possible that a boy would disappear with a hundred people around?

The Garcia swallowed something which had been in her throat for a long time. Then she licked her dried lips. After this she took a deep breath as if she had not breathed for an hour. Somehow, though, she was not fully taken in by the joy and relief shown by all the others. There was hope rising in her soul, but doubt remained the stronger emotion within her. So hard had she worked her mind into the certainty that her boy was lost that now she had some difficulty in giving her thoughts a new direction. She was perhaps not clear as to her true feelings at this moment. Yet deep in her heart there was something in which her doubts found nourishment. One could read it from her eyes, in which doubt and suspicion mingled with bits of hope and a slight expectation of the best.

The two boys arrived at our group. Breathlessly they said: 'Señora Garcia, you are looking for your chiquito, for your little Carlos, aren't you, señora?'

'Yes, yes, of course, she is. We all have been looking for him a long time.' It was not the Garcia who answered the boys; it was other women in our group who pressed the boys for a quick report. 'Well, where is he? Come, come! Out with it.'

The Garcia was staring at these two boys as if they had come from another world.

'Carlos has ridden to Tlalcozautitlan, that's where he has gone,' the elder of the two boys said, stumbling over his own words, so hurriedly and breathlessly were they spoken.

'Yes, that's true,' confirmed the younger one, 'that's absolutely true, Señora Garcia, cross my heart and soul.'

'Well then, everything is all right now,' the pump-master woman said, slapping the Garcia on her shoulders in a neighbourly way.

'Didn't I say so long ago?' another woman broke in. 'A boy can't fall out of the world just like that.'

The men said nothing. Most of them left us to go back to other groups where they wanted to take up their interrupted discussions.

The Garcia frowned as if she had great difficulty thinking. Holding both her hands against her abdomen, she looked at the two boys without speaking.

The boys were getting slightly irritated under this piercing stare and they tried to run away. The Garcia, however, grasped one of the boys by his arm and so the other boy remained also.

'You say he rode to Tlalcozautitlan?'

'Yes, señora, he really and truly has.'

'On what did he ride to Tlalcozautitlan?'

'On a horse, señora.'

'On whose horse? On whose horse can he have ridden away?' The Garcia questioned the boys with a deadly calm, almost frightening voice. A woman condemned to death, with only one hour to live, might question in this calm, direct way a newly discovered, very important witness on whose testimony the governor's decision for a stay depended.

'Whose horse was it?' She repeated her question, since neither of the boys had answered yet.

Now the elder said: 'A boy bigger than me was coming this way, and he was riding on a beautiful white horse.'

'Yes, that's right, señora,' the younger one said, 'he was sitting on a beautiful white horse and Carlos was standing right here by my side and the big boy on the white horse said – '

' – and the boy on the white horse said,' the elder boy took up the tale again, 'he said: "Won't you come with me, Carlos? I am riding very fast." '

'And what did Carlos answer?'

' "Are you riding to Tlalcozautitlan?" Carlos asked. To this the boy on the white horse said nothing and only nodded his head. Then Carlos said: "That's fine, because then I might ride with you to Tlalcozautitlan and buy myself lots of candy; you see, I have twenty centavitos given me by my big brother who has come today for a visit from the far Texas land." So then the boy on the white horse said: "All right, let's go, my horse is a very fast one, awfully fast, we will be there in no time." And saying so, he helped little Carlos up on his horse, and the very moment he had done so, the horse was away like nothing and we couldn't see it any more.'

Whenever one of the boys telling the story stopped or hesitated, the other one took up the tale and went on with it. From all appearances the story seemed to be true. Two boys of their age are not able to tell a false story the way these two boys were narrating it.

The Garcia searched the boys' faces. The boys looked into her eyes with frankness. Then the Garcia looked at the faces of the people standing by, glancing from one to another although their faces could not be seen clearly.

Manuel arrived at our group. A few boys had gone after him and told him there was news at the pump-master's.

The Garcia woman looked at him. Then she turned violently round to the two boys and said, almost yelling: 'I don't believe it!' Again she shouted: 'I don't believe it. Carlos does not ride away from home, not when Manuel is here and when he knows that Manuel has to leave early Monday morning. He will not miss a minute to be with Manuel. And if he really wanted to go to Tlalcozautitlan he would have come first to Manuel and told him so and made him go with him.'

'But it is true, señora, he rode away with that big boy,' the elder boy insisted.

'Who was that boy?' the Garcia asked suddenly.

'We don't know.'

'Is that so? You don't know him, you don't even know that boy?'

'No, we don't know him, señora,' the elder boy repeated. And the younger answered: 'I saw him once pass by here with a loaded burro, but he didn't stop here, not even for a drink of water did he stop, as all the travellers coming this way do.'

The pump-master came close and asked: 'What did the boy on the horse look like?'

Up to now the two boys had been very clear about everything they had been describing. But in trying to answer this new question they became more and more confused and even contradicted each other. Neither remembered exactly what that boy looked like. Asked if he was an Indian boy or a Mexican or a white, they said they had not looked closely enough and it was too dark to see whether he was Indian or white, and that they had looked more at the beautiful horse than at him. They could not, when questioned further, even describe the saddle on which he was sitting. The younger boy insisted the horse had no saddle, while the elder said it was saddled. Nor could they say anything about how the boy was dressed. Then again, the time they gave as to when the boy invited Carlos for the ride, fitted into the time when the kid had last been seen. According to the two boys, it was now one hour since Carlos rode away. This would mean it had been eight o'clock. And it was exactly eight when the child left the hut and ran as fast as a weasel towards where he knew Manuel and his father were. Since that moment his mother had not seen him again.

All those present save the mother believed the story of the two boys, especially since a dozen men declared that they had seen several men riding by, some of them riding in the direction of Tlalcozautitlan. Everybody added that the two boys had no reason whatever to tell such a story and in so serious a situation, that they gained nothing by telling it except maybe a good thrashing if they were found out to be lying deliberately.

Garcia wakened from his lethargy. He looked for a horse to take him to Tlalcozautitlan. It was quite possible that the boy on the horse was travelling farther than just to that little town and on reaching it he might have left Carlos there all by himself. Boys play such tricks on other boys, especially smaller ones. They never think of the consequences of such tricks. All the stores in that town were closed by now and there was never any light in the streets. Little Carlos was perhaps at this moment sitting in a dark corner, forlorn and either crying or asleep. If perchance he were picked up by good people he couldn't even tell where he lived. Because this settlement had no name and was not to be found on even the best map. It was just 'Huts by the River,' and of such places there are thousands in the republic.

Garcia's activity – saddling the horse, mounting it, listening to a score of opinions as to which was the shortest and best trail, for there was no road – filled the Garcia woman with new hope. At least she thought it was hope, while in fact it was only that for a few minutes her thoughts were moving in another direction. She felt easier knowing that her man was on the way to find the boy at the place where everybody assured her he was. She sat down with other women on a bench and soon she joined their talk about everyday things.

Manuel leaned against a tree-trunk. He, at least for the present, had no desire to mix with the girls, as all the other boys were doing now that the excitement was over. But after ten minutes he walked slowly back to his pretty girl, and both soon disappeared where the shadows were deepest.

Sleigh had shown little interest in the whole affair. I wondered what could get him aroused to some sort of enthusiasm. Sometimes I thought him just brain-lazy. Then again I thought him a wise man who had learned that nothing matters, not even his own death. He was interested in his cattle. That was true. But I often doubted even that interest, for he probably showed concern about the cattle only because he was hired to attend them. Yet maybe he really loved the cattle and did not wish anybody to know it. When the excitement was at its peak he said to me that he had better go to his house to see whether the missing cow had come in. He returned in time to hear the two boys telling their story. After this he helped Garcia fetch a horse and saddle it.

Now he was again standing with me, telling me in his slow drawl that the goddamned cow had not come home yet and that he would give anything to know where that cow might be at this time of night.

12

A boy called for Manuel. After a while Manuel came out of the dark and I went closer to hear what the boy wanted of him.

'It isn't true at all, Manuel, that Carlos rode to Tlalcozautitlan,' the boy said. 'I know that Carlos and another boy have ridden to Pacheco, and they did not ride a horse, but just a burro.'

'Did you see that?' Manuel asked sceptically.

'Sure, I saw it or I wouldn't be telling about it. Do you think me a liar, or what?'

'Why didn't you tell it before?'

'Simply, I didn't know that those two boys had told you Carlos had ridden to Tlalcozautitlan.'

The Garcia heard his last words. She jumped up and ran over to us.

Shaking the boy wildly by his shoulders, she cried: 'What did you say right now?'

The boy repeated his tale and swore by all the saints that he had seen Carlos riding away with another boy on a burro and that they had taken the trail which leads to Pacheco.

The Garcia let her head sink between her shoulders. Her whole body shrank. Her mouth was wide open and her eyes flickered like a madman's.

The pump-master grasped her by the arm and shook her. He said: 'Now, don't you get excited over nothing Carmelita, please, calm down. Don't let your worry eat you up. Wait until your man is back from Tlalcozautitlan. There is nothing, absolutely nothing you can do until he has returned.'

The woman said nothing. It was obvious she had heard not a word.

One of the mule-drivers who were camping there said: 'I know the way to Pacheco. It's an awful trail by day and ten times worse at night. If you don't know it very well, you have no chance to return at night. Now, I say, if somebody will lend me a mule – a horse won't do – I'll ride over to Pacheco and look for the kid. Our mules are tired, they can't make it, not that trail, tired as they are.'

A mule was offered immediately. When he mounted, a boy riding a burro came up and said that he wished to accompany him because he, too, knew the trail.

'Have you guys enough matches?' the pump-master yelled after them. They would have to make torches to light them across difficult stretches on that hard trail.

'We've plenty,' they shouted.

The Garcia looked into the darkness into which those two had just disappeared. She dug her fingers into her hair and turned round to face again the pump-master's hut. The little shred of hope she had had for a few minutes, when everybody was so confident that the kid must be in Tlalcozautitlan, was gone entirely. Her hope was never very strong anyway. That certainty she had had the first minute she missed the boy seized her again. What nobody else under heaven could know, she, his mother, knew right away, that the boy was never coming back. Her heart and her instinct, that instinct of a primitive, of an Indian mother, told her the truth. Everybody else here might doubt, but she no longer doubted. In fact she had never doubted. She had only been playing so as to keep herself from going mad.

And now, being certain, she became herself once more. The flickering disappeared from her eyes. She pulled herself together as if by a resolute decision. There was work to do now. She had to do something for her baby. She had to get busy. Whatever might have happened, she had to see her darling once more, once more she had to hold him in her arms, press him against her heart, and cover his sweet little face with kisses. She had to get him, even if she should have to drag him out of the clutches of hell. But she had to get what was left of him.

With firm steps she hurried across the bridge back to her hut. One minute later she was crawling with a lantern in her hand among the shrubs along the opposite bank of the river. Now she disappeared deeper into the bush, now she returned to the bank. With the lantern dangling from her hand she stretched her arm over the river to light up the muddy water. She called her baby by the sweetest names she could think of or her heart was able to invent. Seen from this side, where I was standing, every move she made looked ghostly. Everybody expected soon to hear a cry which would be horrible and gruesome.

For half a minute she stood still by the bank, thinking of what had to be done. Her arms were hanging motionless. In her right hand she held the lantern. It lit up her dress. But her face was partly in shadow, and it resembled no face I ever saw before. It might have been a face created by an insane sculptor who had tried to outsmart nature.

On this side people were gathered close to the bank, looking at the lonesome mother who, with a lantern, wanted to get back her baby. Two enemy camps divided by the river, two worlds opposed to each other. One world was in deepest sorrow and pain, the other world ready to help yet none the less happy, in a way, that it was the other world which had been floored by a merciless fate.

A few men crossed the bridge to join the lonely mother. Aimlessly they crawled through the shrubs and brush. They didn't really believe they would find the kid there. They merely wished to show the mother that they were willing to do all in their power to lessen her sufferings.

The mother came back towards us. As she crossed the bridge she held the lantern over the river, but the light hardly penetrated the muddy yellow water.

The pump-master woman walked over to her, put one hand upon her shoulder, and said: 'Let's wait, Carmelita dear, and see first before we worry so much. Come, sit down by me on the bench and don't worry and break your head to pieces. The kid has really ridden away with that boy, I'm sure of it. We may worry later a good deal if the men come back without having found a trace of him. Yet they'll find him all right. With all that worry now we can do nothing. Just wait and see.'

'Carlos hasn't ridden away,' the Garcia said, firmness and conviction in her voice. 'He does not ride away when Manuel is home.'

'Tut, tut, Carmelita! There, there! Children, dear me!' The pump-master woman laughed loudly. 'You have got only that one. What do you know about these brats? I know better, I've five. What you never even dream of, that's exactly the first thing they'll do.'

The Garcia put her lantern on the ground by her feet. She turned her head towards the river and with tired, heavy eyes looked into the darkness. Then she faced again the group of women she was standing with, and looked from one to another without saying a word. Though she was in the midst of neighbours and friends, she felt utterly alone in the world. Her head dropped and she closed her eyes for a few seconds. Then suddenly her body stiffened and she cried out: 'The boy is in the river! The boy has been drowned!'

Everyone present stood aghast, as if lightning had struck near by. Some women crossed themselves. The pump-master woman fought to catch her breath, and finally gasped: 'Carmelita, for heaven's sake, by the Most Holy Virgin and Her Holy Child Jesu Cristo our Lord and Master, don't commit such a horrible sin against God. How can you say such a terrible thing? Have you gone mad, woman? Come to, come to, woman!'

The Garcia uttered a deep sigh. She felt relieved of the thick lump in her throat which had been trying to choke her for the last half-hour. She stretched her neck and moved her head round in a wide circle to free herself still more from that nightmare. Her eyes became sober, almost brutally sober. She was at last herself.

While everybody was still dumbfounded, the Garcia started explaining, so clearly and fluently that one might think she had memorized it. She was getting rid of all her anxiety by talking fast, by summing up all her thoughts concerning the whereabouts of her baby.

'How excited that kid was this evening and the whole afternoon! Never have I seen him like that. Wild, swift, uncatchable. I might have chained him to a post and he would have broken away, so wild he was. He had practically lost all sense of what he was doing and where he was running. I couldn't keep him in the house for more than two minutes at a time. He had to run across to Manuel again. And off he went like a whirlwind. He knows the way to the bridge, and the bridge itself, well enough – better perhaps than any one of us – because ever since he could run at all he has been running across that bridge two hundred times every day. So he ran back again without even thinking that he might ever fall off the bridge, because he could run across it blindfold. But now he had the new shoes on his little feet, those pretty shoes with polished and lac-quered soles that he was so proud of. With these shoes on his feet he was not the same any more. But how could he know that? No longer was he sure about his way, and no longer did he have his feet under control the way he used to when he ran barefooted. How could he, a child, know the difference it makes on your feet when you have shoes on? Now, when I crossed the bridge tonight, I almost tumbled over. I saw the lantern hanging here at the pump-master's and went straight towards the light. Only when I stumbled against the rim and almost lost my balance did I remember that the bridge doesn't lead straight towards the choza here, but more to the right. When this happened to me, right then my first thought was that should the kid run so wildly and thought-lessly across the bridge, as he surely did because of his excitement, there is every chance that he might tumble over the rim and fall into the river. That's why, on coming over here, my first question was about the kid. Otherwise, if this had not happened to me, I would not have thought of him, not until I saw him here again. And believe me, all of you, when I asked for the boy and nobody had seen him, I knew instantly that it was too late already, for my heart was full of a sudden pain.'

Nobody interrupted the mother in her long speech. For many minutes no one said anything. They were thinking of what they had just heard. There was so much good sense in what she had said that most of those present were beginning to believe that what had happened was just as the mother had explained it.

The pump-master woman was the first to speak. 'Now listen, Carmelita, be reasonable. What you tell us is absolutely imposs-ible. It can't be. Somebody would have heard it when the kid tumbled over and fell into the river. There would have been a splash, sure there would.'

Tumbling over. Falling into the river. A plunge. A splash. I looked sideways and my eyes met those of Sleigh, who was looking at me at that very moment. Neither of us had any desire to say anything.

'No, no, that's quite impossible,' a man said, 'we would have heard it. If such a boy falls into the water he splashes, doesn't he? Has anyone heard such a splash? I, for one, haven't. Besides, a boy of his age doesn't tumble into the water and disappear immediately just like that. He would shout and yell like hell. He would beat and kick around and make such a terrific noise that you could hear it a mile away. No, don't tell me he is in the river, not me.'

'Naturally, he would make an awful noise,' the pump-master remarked. 'I know that kid, I do. There wasn't a day in the year when he wasn't in the water swimming and splashing and making such a row that you would think he owned the whole river all by himself. In the water he is like a fish, the kid is. He would have got

526

out just like that, shoes on or no shoes on. And if he had met with some difficulty he would have hollered like the very devil himself, that's what he'd have done.'

The Garcia had listened to every word; not once had she interrupted the talk. Now, however, she felt that she had to defend her boy. 'Certainly he would have worked himself out of the river, and all alone, and he would have yelled, too, if he couldn't get out. But how could he yell? He was wearing his new shoes, so he wasn't safe on his feet. Running across the bridge fast as he could and not thinking of anything but of Manuel. And so he stumbled with his shoes against the rim. Had he been barefooted, he would have got hold somehow. But the soles were smooth and polished like a mirror. Before he even realized what was happening to him he had already tumbled over and had knocked his head against the rim or against a post. So he became unconscious instantly, and before he could come to, he was already under the water with his belly full and his windpipe choked. He never got any chance to make a noise.'

Having told her story so as to make everyone see that she was not out of her mind, the Garcia had nothing more to say. Nobody could convince her that the kid might be somewhere else. She knew he was in the river and she had to get him out. That was all she was thinking of now.

13

The men and women were by no means satisfied with the Garcia's narrative. They said she was just seeing things because she was not herself any more. Someone remembered the boys who had been sitting on the bridge and singing at about the time when Carlos was supposed to have fallen into the river. These boys declared that they had seen nothing and heard nothing, and that they were sitting at the end of the bridge on this side, facing the water and thinking only of their songs; but they were positive that the kid could not have fallen in the river without their seeing or hearing it.

Of course, they added, the night was so black that they could not have seen the kid if he had been half the length of the bridge away from them. They would have paid little attention to a splash because they were fully occupied with their singing. After all, fish jumping out of the water to catch flies and mosquitoes make the same noise.

'Now, there you can hear it for yourself, Carmelita,' the pump-master said; 'these youngsters have been sitting here near the spot during the whole evening and they haven't heard a thing, not the slightest splash. So you see you are just making up a story which has no foundation. It simply couldn't have happened the way you imagine.'

The Garcia was silent.

Everyone produced another idea with which to convince the Garcia that she was wrong. No one supported her.

A couple of men, noticing that I had not joined the discussion, asked me bluntly what I thought of the Garcia's tale. I knew where the kid was. Sleigh knew it too. I saw him shrug his shoulders as if he wanted to answer on my behalf. Then I spoke. 'What can I say, amigos? I don't know all the nooks and corners, holes and trees and tunnels around here where a little boy might hide himself. So what can I say? Anybody might fall in the river; why not a boy?'

'Well, then, do you really think he may have fallen in the river?'

'I've told you my opinion. It's possible. Anything under heaven is possible. Therefore it is also possible that the kid may have fallen in the water. Where there is water, anybody may fall in any time, whether he wants to or not. That's the way with all water.'

'The señor is perfectly right,' a man next to me said. 'Don't you folks remember – it's only a year back – when in this river, only two miles farther down, the Egyptian was drowned? – I mean that Egyptian who had his choza there and who planted onions and lettuce for the market.'

'Yes, I remember it well,' another stated, 'but the circumstances were entirely different. That Egyptian was taking a bath in the river and he unexpectedly reached a deep washout or some sort of whirlpool into which he disappeared and never came up again.'

An old Indian was nearing our group. He came close and asked me: 'What do you think, señor, what we might do and what we should do?'

Half a hundred people were talking and denying and talking again, yet none had suggested anything practical. The old Indian was the first to do so.

'Since you ask me, I would advise that the river be searched along both sides of the bridge and also for a hundred fifty feet or so down the stream. If the kid really is in the water, then we'll find him and so we'll know at least where he is. What is more, if the men who have gone in search of him return and have not found him in either place and in the meantime we have not discovered him in the river, then we will know that we have to search the whole jungle.'

The Garcia had crossed the bridge again. With the lantern in one hand she was standing at the other end of the bridge. After a while she went close to the rim and held the lantern as far out over the water as she could. Suddenly she let out a horrible scream.

A few boys ran across to her.

They came back right away, tapped their heads, and said: 'The señora must have gone nuts, for nothing is in the water.'

It was hardly necessary to tell us that, for even if the kid were in the water at that particular spot, the Garcia would not have been able to see him, so muddy was the water, so dim the light of the lantern.

Nevertheless, the Garcia now yelled continuously. No sooner had she finished one of those long plaintive cries than she uttered another, still more plaintive, still longer. It was the crying of a primitive Indian woman bewailing the death of a loved one. It wasn't weeping, it was a howl which seemed to accuse the heavens. It was the howl of an animal whose mate or child has been killed. But I recognized in that almost savage howl the same deep sorrow that one finds in the silent weeping of an American woman.

If all the women here had been convinced that the kid had been drowned, they would have joined the Garcia in her lamentation. And they would have joined her with all the compassion that mothers and wives are capable of when they open their hearts and souls to the suffering and pain of another mother or another wife. For only a mother and wife knows what a mother and wife suffers when bemoaning the loss of someone beloved. Because what befalls one mother, the same befalls every other mother on earth at the same moment, wherever she may live, for in all eternity it is never just one single woman, a Garcia woman in a Central American jungle, who is in deep pain, but it is always all womanhood that suffers and weeps.

No other woman here was sure of the kid's death. They remained quiet. Some called their little ones to them as if they might be in danger, and they held their babies against their breasts as the safest place on earth they could offer them.

Two men crossed the bridge and, ever so delicately and lovingly, led the Garcia woman back to this side and made her sit on a bench in the pump-master's portico.

The pump-master woman gave her water to drink, sat beside her, and, in a motherly way, stroked her hair and occasionally dried her tears with the ends of her shawl.

The men were standing around, once more wondering what to do and how to behave in this situation. They were uneasy in the presence of a mother who had lost her baby and who, in spite of all the sympathy shown her, was alone in the world. They had a feeling of guilt, they shuffled about and tried to hide themselves. No one spoke. Whenever the woman cried out again, the men's faces became distorted. Their uneasiness became finally so unbearable that they began to do what every man on earth does when he finds himself superfluous. They got very busy about nothing in particular.

Without uttering many words and without waiting for a leader, they ran like ants this way and that. Some carried timber, others took their machetes and went into the bush to get more wood. Huge fires were lighted on both banks and arranged so that both sides of the bridge were illuminated. One stripped and waded into the river. He started diving alongside the bridge. It was a daring job and might easily have cost the diver his life.

The river-bed was boggy and covered with all sorts of plants, partly tropical water shrubs, partly shrubs and bushes torn away from the banks far upstream and caught by the bridge posts when they were carried down by the current. This marine jungle was infested with water snakes, crabs, and young alligators, not to mention the hundreds of other tropical underwater creatures.

The swimmer who keeps to the surface will rarely be in danger, but a diver may easily be caught. Yet, a few minutes later, another man stripped and started diving too. Soon there were six bronze-brown human bodies in the water. Women and girls lined the river-banks and the bridge to watch the naked men searching for the kid. The lean, brawny bodies, which looked youthful in spite of the fact that most of the men were fathers, seemed to be covered by a metallic gold film. Their thick, long, wiry hair appeared still blacker and thicker when their heads popped up on the surface. Breathing deeply, they gazed up to the bridge, where men and women were watching them, and said not a word. But one could easily read in their dark brown eyes the answer to the unspoken question: 'Nada! Nada! Nothing, nothing!'

Among the men in the river there now appeared a very old Indian with white hair. His body, while still well formed and lean, was less brawny, less agile and flexible than those of the others. His skin was less golden. And his chest was not so strong. Hence he could not stay under water as long as the young could. Yet whenever the others, the young ones, showed signs of getting tired, he was the one who fired them on again.

Carrying a long iron hook tied to a lasso, the pump-master strode up to the bridge. Slowly he walked along the rim, constantly throwing the hook and dragging it along the bottom. Whenever he thought he had caught something, he pulled it up – to find only some weeds or twigs.

Sleigh was standing near the pump.

I went up to him and said: 'If we only had a boat, more might be done. A pity that the pump-master hasn't got one.'

'There is a boat down the river that belongs to a Dutchman who raises chickens and grows tomatoes there and never makes any money. He has a boat all right, home-made. But it is at least three miles from here, if not four. And what is worse, the trail can't be made before the sun comes up.'

We walked together to another group where Sleigh started talking about things which had nothing to do with the kid. He was right. One cannot talk all the time about the same thing; you have to go on living, boy dead or no boy dead.

14

It was a picture – a picture exuberant in its greatness, in its truthfulness, in its liveliness, in its colours, in its constant changes.

On both banks huge bonfires were flaring. They threw their flames high up into the air and flickered in the mild breeze. A hundred different shadows, long and short, bulky and thin, darted now this way, now that, now playing upon the ground, then sweeping over the water or along the bridge, until at last they were swallowed up by the jungle walls – only to shoot out again two seconds later. On the bridge a score of men and boys were lined up, holding torches and flaming sticks over the water. Others were running like deer up and down the banks to start new fires or to bring light to a diver who was shouting for it. Long pennants of smoke followed these torch runners.

Bronze-brown men and youngsters were hurling fresh fuel into the fires. Swarms, thousands, millions of sparks rose towards the dark sky.

Here and there boys were kneeling on the bridge, leaning with their torches far over the rim, and a black head dripping with water would appear on the surface of the muddy river.

Women and girls gaily dressed in their cheap but bright-coloured dance gowns, with crowns of beautiful wild flowers on their heads and with little bunches of flowers fastened on their breasts and girdles – many of the women carrying babies in their arms, others leading children by the hand – were wandering back and forth across the bridge. Now and then half a dozen people would suddenly run to a definite spot on the bridge, where some-one was shouting as if he had seen or found something of impor-tance.

Little clouds and flags of smoke were flying over our heads like strange night birds, like fairies, like ghosts trying to materialize and falling apart at the same moment.

The surface of the river seemed to be bedecked with thousands of floating gold coins. Into that river of gold, naked human bodies were diving. Here they came out again, swam to a bridge post, wiped the water off their faces, and shook their thick black hair. There one diver was hanging on to the post with one hand while with the other he pulled thorns off his legs. One diver left the water and went to a fire to warm his hands and feet, which had become numb. With his back to the river and his face to the flames, he stretched out his arms to the fire and closed and opened his hands quickly, while a friend of his put a lighted cigarette between his wet lips.

A child that had been asleep awoke and whined. Another child, awakened by the first, began to cry. Their mothers ran up to feed them from their breasts.

Most of the children had fallen asleep. They lay on the ground near the portico, huddled together in groups to keep warm and feel safe. Some of the children were wrapped in a blanket as if they were sticks. Others were covered with ragged pieces of cotton cloth. Some were lying on mats of the kind put between the saddle and the back of a horse. Others were sleeping on old sugar sacks. Many were stretched out on the bare sandy ground.

The bigger children were, of course, having the time of their lives. Here they were watching the divers. There they were betting on which of the divers would stay longest under water. Others were more interested in the bonfires and torches. A few practical jokers of the next generation were playing nasty little tricks on smaller boys and girls. Some boys who had never had a chance were now at last testing their skill as musicians on the mouth-organs snatched from the trousers left ashore by the divers.

So it appeared that everybody had his own kind of fun and was making the best of a party which two hours before had looked like a complete flop. Even the mules of the caravan were partaking of that lively affair in their own fashion.

They were grazing near the banks. Now and then they brayed sadly into the night and were answered by others out on the prairie. Frequently, when they got in the way of the men who were busy near the river, they got kicked in the hams. Yet they took it as a friendly gesture and did not move – until they themselves decided to change places, which is the way the stubborn always win.

The night was getting cool.

Aided by a neighbour, the pump-master woman was in her kitchen making coffee. A very fine kitchen it was. All the neighbours agreed to that. The kitchens of all the huts in the settlement on the opposite river-bank were far less luxurious. No one else had his kitchen separated from the main room, which in all the homes was the only room. The fact that the pump-master had a separate kitchen proved that he was of a higher class. The hearth was a wooden case filled with earth, like Sleigh's. The pump-master and Sleigh were the only people in the community elegant enough to possess that last word in stoves. But the pride of the pump-master woman's kitchen, and the reason why everybody thought it the finest and classiest in the world, were the various pots and dishes she could boast of. They were all earthenware, but they were richly ornamented with all sorts of fancy designs. On many vessels these designs represented flowers, bees, squirrels, butterflies, antelopes, birds, tigers, lions, dogs, coyotes. Yet of all these flowers, insects, birds, and animals, not one looked natural; they were creations of an Indian artist who was in no way satisfied with the work of the Creator and thought he could do a lot better if he were given the power to create life. Some of these pots were neatly arranged on a shelf, others were hanging in rows against boards nailed to the posts on which the roof rested. Whenever a woman visitor came to see the pump-master woman, she just stood in front of these rows of pots and gazed at them with shining eyes as if she were beholding paradise. All the other families in the settlement used pots and vessels of the crudest sort, most of them broken or cracked. Two families, and the Garcia family was one of them, owned only potsherds. So very high class was the pump-master woman that she actually used these beautiful vessels and did not keep them just for decoration.

The coffee was cooked with crude brown sugar. In another pot black beans were being boiled. A piece of sheet iron about twenty inches square leaned against the wall – to be used to heat tortillas. In a reed basket tied to a piece of rusty wire dangling from a rafter, the tortillas left over from an earlier meal were kept. There were other foodstuffs in that basket. In fact, it was the pantry of the house.

The Garcia had gone once again to her hut. What she was looking for or what she expected to find, she herself would not have been able to say if she were asked. When she returned, carrying the lantern which seemed to have become a part of her, she watched the divers for a few minutes as if they were fishing for something she was not the least interested in. Then she walked with dragging feet, as if in a dream, towards the pump-master's.

Manuel was sitting on a bench, gloomy and brooding. He saw his mother standing beside him. With wide, glassy eyes he stared at her. An idea entered his mind. He jumped up, crossed the bridge, and, along the sandy path which passed through the jungle to distant villages, he walked into the night.

15

The pump-master was throwing his hook untiringly into the water. Like an expert, he carefully sounded the bottom, trying to get the right feel for the shrubs and for what might be the kid's body. Occasionally he pulled out a load of dripping weeds.

The divers began to show fatigue. Less and less often did they dive, and longer and longer did they hold on to the bridge posts before diving again. A few did not go to the bridge posts at all, but swam or waded to the banks where they could stand on their feet.

The old white-haired man had to give up. Soon all the others swam to the banks, dressed, and went to the fires. Some of them were blue-lipped and had sickly white faces.

The fires, too, seemed tired. No longer did they blaze so lustily. The men and boys who had gone into the bush to get fuel were also tired and were now resting. Gradually the fires died down and soon they were only heaps of embers. The flaming sticks and branches used for torches had turned into black clubs set with sleepy sparks.

One lantern at the pump-master's had burned out. A boy was sent across the bridge to ask the neighbours for kerosene.

Two divers were standing by a fire smoking cigarettes. They were dressed in only a shirt tied round their loins – ready to dive again if somebody asked them to.

Because of all the work in and around the river, many people had in the meantime come to believe the Garcia's story true. Those who refused to believe it did so for no other reason than that they believed that no human being, not even a little boy, could die without any noise. To them death was so great an event that it could not occur silently, safe in bed, from old age. Through their experiences they connected death with much shouting, yelling, swearing, shooting, knifing, clubbing, the falling of a horse, the crash of a tree, the sudden descent of a rock. If one fell into the river or a lake one cried for help. There was always noise when a man died. Therefore they did not believe it possible that death could walk among so many grown-up men and women assembled for a gay dance without a leaf stirring. Death never worked that way! They had searched the river merely to show the sad mother that she must not think herself all alone in the world, that she was surrounded by friends, and that every one of them would willingly sacrifice anything he possessed to bring the kid back.

Someone now had a new idea. Two men searched for a long pole. Having found one, they began sounding the bottom along both sides of the bridge, insisting that if the kid were there they would feel him with a thin flexible pole.

Once more the picture changed entirely.

Around the dying fires, some standing, some squatting, men and boys were talking and smoking. The low fires illuminated them so little that only mere shadows of figures could be seen. Near

535

one fire a heated discussion was going on, but only half sentences and broken incoherent phrases could be heard, though violent and impressive gestures could be seen through the dancing smoke.

A few men and women were sitting on the bridge. Boys were snatching gleaming sticks and branches out of the fires and swinging them through the air to sketch fantastic figures against the black walls of night.

A mouth-organ was being played somewhere. Two girls were singing in a mournful manner from a place hidden behind bushes. From behind the pump-shed the giggling of a young woman was heard, joined by the half-suppressed but animated and eager voice of a man. From another place deep in the darkness of night, there came the harsh voice of a woman quarrelling with a man. A gush of light breeze carried a man's voice saying in a hushed tone: 'Don't shout; they can hear you,' and a woman answered: 'Be quiet, you burro.' Someone was whistling beyond the camp of the caravan, and his whistling was arrogant and boastful, like that of a man who has just conquered a difficult situation.

On the square in front of the pump-master's, groups were slowly forming again. They talked, but in a rather tired way, because whatever one said or wanted to say had already been said a hundred times before.

Women and girls were walking about or sitting on benches and on piles of logs and rotten sleepers. Many of them went over to the kitchen, where the pump-master woman served them steaming hot coffee in little enamelled cups and in small earthen pots. The coffee was black. In each case, when the hostess offered a guest a cup of coffee, she nodded her head in the direction of a sugar bowl. It was meant for those who wanted the coffee sweeter than it was already.

Each woman or girl drank only half a cup and handed the rest to someone else, so that everyone might have at least a few gulps. The night had become still cooler and the hot coffee was welcomed. No guest pushed or jostled to be served first. Everyone awaited his or her turn.

On the bridge several men were still sounding the river in the hope of finding the kid there.

The roosters began to crow for the first time. It was one hour before midnight.

16

The pump-master had ceased casting his hook into the river. He joined our group and talked of other fatal accidents he had witnessed. The kid was practically forgotten. No one mentioned him any more.

The Garcia was the first to whom hot coffee was offered. She was the guest of honour of the pump-master woman. That meant very much.

In this little settlement hidden in the jungle the pump-master woman was considered more or less the same as a duchess is in a European principality. She could read and also write fairly well. Therefore she was regarded as a highly educated woman. Her children had no lice – at least not as many as the other children had. What is more, her children did not run about naked. The boys wore a pair of ragged pants and the girls a patched-up, cheap, rather flimsy skirt. As for herself, the pump-master woman owned five muslin dresses, all alike in style, but different in colour. Furthermore, she possessed five shirts, which she did not call chemises, because she insisted that a shirt is just a shirt and nothing more. Every woman in the settlement knew that she had two blue and two yellow pairs of bloomers and two pink step-ins. Two of the bloomers and one step-in, however, could no longer really be counted. They were worn out. Then she had earrings of genuine gold. She also owned a Spanish comb set with little pearls which looked real, but she was honest enough to admit that they were only of paste and that the little stones in the comb were also false.

Her husband was the owner of a special suit for Sunday – and it included a coat. A suit with a coat, that's the thing – where everybody's suit consists only of a pair of cotton pants.

They had a clock, an alarm clock at that. Furthermore, they had a real mirror, which was framed. For their table they had a knife and two forks, not to mention the spoons, of which they had seven. But the greatest thing they owned was a real mattress, with springs, and a bed made of iron, with big brass knobs at the four corners. Who else in the world, everybody asked, had such a bed and such a mattress? Perhaps the president of the republic.

Of course, the pump-master could afford all that luxury. Wasn't he an employee of the railroad? Railroad employees were the greatest men under heaven. Whatever the pump-master woman said was worth ten times as much as anything the priest said. He who was befriended by the pump-master woman did not need the queen of England, whoever that might be. It is still doubtful that the queen of England owns two pairs of silk stockings, as the pump-master woman does, and whether the queen of England possesses three silk handkerchiefs and one of lace; that would have to be proved before anybody here would believe it. For what people said about the riches of kings and queens and presidents and such gentry, well, it wasn't always true. On the other hand, everything said about the riches and the luxury of the pump-master woman was absolutely true, because everyone had seen it.

While the women were hanging around the pump-master's kitchen, gossiping and chatting, there was suddenly great excitement in one of the groups. One heard rapid speech interrupted by a flood of questions.

One of these questions finally came to us very clearly: 'What did you say? The kid wasn't there?'

The mule-driver and the boy who accompanied him had returned from the nearest village, where they had gone because of the boy who reported that he had seen little Carlos riding in that direction, towards Pacheco.

'No, he wasn't there. And no one has seen him.'

'Have you asked everywhere, in all the huts?'

'Of course we have. Everybody was asleep when we arrived. Yet we went to every choza and asked every family we found at home if they had seen the kid. None had.'

'Did you also ask if the boy might have passed through the pueblo alone or with somebody, a boy or a youngster?'

'We certainly have. The whole day long no one from Pacheco has come this way and no one who is not of the village has been seen there any time today or tonight. The dogs would have barked if somebody had passed through the pueblo at night.'

'Now what about the trail? Have you looked well at the trail?'

'No fresh tracks on the trail, I'm sure. We lighted the trail twenty times and at different sites too. No fresh tracks of any sort of horses or burros or anything save cattle which marched home from the bush and the pastures in the evening. We're absolutely sure that if the kid went away alone or with some other boy he certainly did not go that way. I know all the side trails and the veredas going in other directions off the main trail and we've looked them over too, and very carefully. No tracks on them either.'

The muleteer gave the mule he had been riding to a man standing near by, asking him to return it to its owner. Then he walked to his camp, followed by the group which was still asking questions.

The mule-driver noticed the Garcia woman sitting on the bench in the portico. He went to her, for until now she had not known of his return.

She stood up and looked at him, and his eyes immediately began to wander from one to another of the men who had followed him. He could not bear her stare. He wanted to say something. But she sat down again before he opened his mouth. She knew his report. The mule-driver turned his back to her and faced us. He looked as though he were guilty of the kid's disappearance. Not until he had gone far enough away from her and had mixed with the men in the crowd and lighted a cigarette did he feel well again.

Not knowing what else I could do, I went to the bridge, where one Indian was still sounding the bottom. Suddenly he turned to me and said in a low voice: 'Señor, I have him. There, touch the stick yourself and you'll feel him all right.'

'Be calm, Perez,' I said to him; 'if you make any noise now, we'll have the whole crowd around in a second and then we can do nothing. Let's be sure first before we say a word. Keep the stick fixed where it is now.'

With utmost care I took the pole from his hands. Inch by inch I sounded the bottom, moving the stick lightly. No doubt there was something at the bottom, but it could have been the body of an animal, a pig or a dog, or a goat. Again I pushed the stick slowly down against whatever it was that was lying on the ground and again I felt that body very distinctly.

'Well,' Perez asked, 'what do you make of it?'

'I am not so sure yet. We'd better not stir up the people, not yet. We would make ourselves only ridiculous if we howled and afterwards found it was a heap of mud.'

I tried to measure the mass, its length and width. So far we had touched only something which might be a chest or a belly. Sounding to one side I found that the body had no length and nothing I felt could be taken for legs or arms. It was a body with the same extension in every direction. So I was convinced that the thing we had found could be nothing but a thick ball of grass or a pack of accumulated twigs, held together by a few big branches or by lianas. Whatever it was, by no means could it be the body of a boy. Perez admitted his mistake. He dropped the stick and let it lie on the bridge. While I was walking off I looked back and it seemed to me that the pole had taken on an expression of accusation. Perhaps I was only tired. It was near midnight.

I went to the pump-master's, where I was offered hot coffee, black beans, and tortillas. It was now the men's turn to be served.

The bridge was entirely abandoned. Women and girls were chatting gaily. The coffee, it seemed, had given all the visitors fresh energy. All that had occupied their minds during the last three hours was apparently forgotten or at least cast aside for the time being. It was obvious that the weariness of these people who had been on their feet since sunrise was growing and their emotions were getting dull. Even the Garcia was seen to laugh a few times. As the kid had not been found in the river, she tried to convince herself that he had not tumbled in, but that in fact he had ridden to Tlalcozautitlan as the two boys had said and that he would be found in that small town asleep in some nook.

Everyone agreed to wait until Garcia returned from Tlalcozautitlan. If he returned alone, with no news as to the kid's whereabouts, they were all going to stay here the whole night and as soon as morning arrived the river would be searched more thoroughly. Their mood was rapidly returning to normal. If there had been music, they would soon have gone on with the dance.

A few men, tired of standing around and talking about the same thing over and over again, slowly walked back to the bridge, where they picked up the hook and the long stick and started fishing again, after lighting a fresh torch.

For five minutes the Garcia watched those men on the bridge. Suddenly she yelled and with her lantern swinging in one hand ran to the bridge.

Holding the lantern over the water, leaning forward on tiptoe, she cried wildly: 'Chico mio! My little one! Carlos, my darling! Mi nene, mi nene! Come back to your mother, who loves you so dearly! Oh, come back to me, Carlosito! Where are you, chiquitito mio? Carlosito, my sweet little boy!'

The pump-master and another man hurried up to her and grasped her by her arms to prevent her from jumping into the river. She seemed to have lost control of herself. Kicking, pushing the two men away from her, using her feet and arms and even the lantern for defence, she yelled at them: 'Let me go! Caray, let me go! What do you want from me? What have I done? Leave me alone, for God's sake or for the devil's, but leave me alone!'

17

On this side of the river-bank, not far from the end of the bridge, a group of men began to attract attention. There was excited talking, nodding of heads, animated gesticulation. On coming closer I saw that the speaker was the same old white-haired Indian whom I had observed earlier in the night. The group, with that old man in its midst, marched off to the pump-master's.

And once more the bridge became a very lively scene. Boys had broken away from the group after receiving certain instructions and they were now on the bridge preparing something which I could not make out, for I, too, was going to the pump-master's to find out what was happening.

All over the place people began to hustle, scattering in all directions. It was obvious they had a definite purpose in spite of the fact that they looked like ants running around aimlessly. Most of the people, however, did not know the cause of all that liveliness, because it seemed that those in the know had no time to stop and answer questions. People asked one another what was going to come out of that sudden agitation. While no one mentioned it, everybody realized that the kid was the centre of the noise and bustle.

The two men, who, a little while ago, had started fishing again were now working faster than ever. Two others joined them at this moment.

At the pump-master's choza I heard the old Indian say to the woman: 'Yes, señora, a thick candle it must be.'

'Sorry; I've only a few thin ones, but you are welcome to them,' the pump-master woman answered.

'That won't do.' The old Indian looked around and asked: 'Who might have a thick candle around here? Does anybody here have a good thick candle?'

'I don't think that anybody has that sort of candle,' the woman said; 'they are all thin ones, the same as I offered you. Of course, I know they are not of much use, since they bend over so quickly because of the heat.'

'If we could only get a good strong candle that would stand up,' the old Indian repeated, looking vaguely around as if he expected such a candle to fall out of the skies.

'Olla, wait a minute,' the pump-master woman shouted triumphantly. 'I'm sure I've got a good strong candle. It's only,' she added in a sad voice, 'it's only that this candle is a consecrated one, one specially blessed by the señor cura. I've kept it in the house since the Corpus Christi celebration in Rio Lodoso.'

'A consecrated one?' the old Indian gasped. 'A consecrated one, a real consecrated one! Woman, be thanked, that's exactly the very one I'm looking for. Now we can't fail. Bring it! Quick! Hurry! Please let me have that candle, señora!'

The pump-master woman took a lantern from the post and disappeared in her hut. The old Indian explained to the men: 'A consecrated candle is a thousand times better than any other, no matter how beautiful it may look or how costly it is. But this one, being blessed, will work in no time.'

He looked around and discovered a wooden case. It was an ordinary box in which canned milk or soap might have been shipped, but it was weather-beaten, so its exact origin could not be made out.

The old man drew the box into the light of the lantern. Carefully looking it over, he finally selected a board which he broke off. It was half an inch thick and perhaps twenty by ten in area.

He pulled out all the nails. Then he balanced it, held it up to the light, and judged its evenness, for, as he explained, all four corners had to be exactly on the same level; if the board were bent even slightly, it would be useless. After looking at it from every angle he said: 'This board will do, if any.'

The pump-master woman came out of her house holding in her hand a fairly thick candle half burned down and adorned with a little cross of gold paper. It was the sort of candle which the children of the poor carry to their first communion. The children of the rich carry thicker and longer candles, richly decorated to show the Lord and His Virgin Mother, who otherwise might not know that the parents of these children can afford to be more generous – so far as candles are concerned, for in other things it does not matter, because nobody can see it.

Having laid the board on the ground, the old man took the lantern the pump-master woman was holding and put it beside the board. With his fingernails he marked the exact centre of the board. Then he lifted it up, put the tip of his forefinger at the marked centre, turned the board upside down and balanced it on his forefinger. Satisfied with this test, he again laid the board on the ground.

He lit the candle, allowed a few drops of the hot paraffin to fall on his centre mark, placed the candle firmly on these drops, waited a minute, and then touched the candle to see whether it would stand. He worked with great patience and still greater care. From all sides and angles he looked at the candle to be sure that it was standing absolutely straight. 'If it were inclined towards one side even only slightly, success would be doubtful,' he explained while admiring his job as an artist would.

A score of men and women watched every move the old Indian made. The longer they observed what he was doing, the more they showed an expression of awe in their faces. They might lose all their fear, even all reverence towards their Catholic priests. But they could not lose their deep-rooted fear, reverence, and awe for anybody of their own race who was considered gifted with divine powers and with a knowledge of nature's secrets. If the old man had said: 'Now I need the bleeding heart of one of you,' half a dozen men and youngsters would have stepped forward to offer it. Not so much out of sheer joy or of a faint hope of becoming saints in the hereafter, but merely because they had lost their own free will and had become spellbound. None of them would offer his heart or even a hand to please a Catholic priest. Their brujos and medicine men still held immense power over their souls and minds – in most cases for their own good.

Everybody knew without asking that all of the old man's strange and mysterious manipulations had something to do with the missing kid. No one spoke. No one interrupted the old man with questions. The more patiently he worked and made his tests, the bigger became the circle of people surrounding him. But they were no longer standing close, in their neighbourly intimacy, as they did half an hour ago. The old man was growing into something which made him seem different and difficult for them to comprehend. Everybody was sure that he was trying to get in touch with the beyond on behalf of the child.

He now lifted the board from the ground. As carefully and devotedly as a priest carries the monstrance, he carried the board towards the river-bank. All the people followed as if it were a procession.

Those who were still on the bridge remained there to watch and learn what it was all about. The few who were still fishing with hook and pole also took notice and ceased working. They dropped their tools and came slowly forward.

18

An old, old Indian woman with a thousand wrinkles in her face, who was surely more than a hundred years of age, was squatting on the bridge. Like all the others, she watched the procession, but she showed little interest, let alone curiosity. She was smoking a thick cigar and puffed away with great gusto. Seeing her calm and philosophic serenity, I realized that it must be a very great thing to be a hundred years old and not an inmate of an institution for the aged, but rather the honoured and respected chief of a family or a clan.

After each puff she contemplated her cigar, apparently brooding over the sad fact that everything good on this earth must end sooner or later, even a good cigar. And a good cigar it was, no doubt, because its leaves had not been cooked, cured, toasted, perfumed, cooled, sweetened; and a shipload never coughed as long as you left it alone. From her lack of interest I conceived the idea that besides the old man she was the only one who knew what was going to happen.

I squatted Indian fashion beside her.

'Caray!' I said to her. 'That cigar of yours is a good one. It smells like paradise.'

'You're telling me, me who made it! And besides, my young man, mind your own goddamned business. Get me?'

It was too late to mind my own goddamned business. I could take it. So I went on: 'What are they doing there with that candle on the board?'

She looked at me with half – no, with almost fully closed eyes, and the wrinkles on her face trebled in number. Then, obviously satisfied with my bearing, she blew out a huge cloud of smoke, brooded over the loss of tobacco, and then said: 'If you must know, damned gringo, if you must know how we do our things without asking your advice or permission, well, they're searching for that good-for-nothing bastard of that lousy hussy – lazy bitch that she is – and if she had looked in time for her brat and what he was doing, we would not have to look for him now and call heaven and God and the devil for help. Never mind, young man, they will get him all right. Now they will get him out of the dirt and mud, now that at last they're searching the proper way, as they should have done four hours ago and not waited until he is eaten up by the crabs.'

'How do you mean, señora, searching the proper way?'

'Searching. Yes, that's what I said, searching. If that brat is in the river and nowhere else, they'll have him in a quarter of an hour, provided there is not much current.'

'How can he be in the river, señora? We have searched the river for hours and we have not found him.'

She grinned at me ironically. Her teeth were thick, large, and of a brownish-yellow colour. The gums had retreated so far that her teeth were laid bare to the roots, which made them look even longer. 'What did you say? Oh yes, you said you searched for hours. What people call searching in these days, that's what you have done and nothing better. How smart and clever you are, all you people of today! Talking of superstition and never knowing a goddamned thing about what is behind the world you see with your eyes – or you think you see while in fact you see nothing because you are blind and deaf and dumb and you can't even smell. That's the trouble you people suffer from. The way you and the others have been searching, well, my young man, you may be sure that you could search that way for seven days and you wouldn't find the brat if he didn't come up by himself. If you had waited until the morrow, there wouldn't have been much of him left to show his father, that damned drunkard, when he comes back from that useless trip which anyway he made only to get booze. Every sane person knows that the little devil is in the river and nowhere else. The trouble is, there is not one single sane person around, myself not excluded, because I am just as mad and crazy as all the others. I tell you, my young man, they are all crazy here, waiting for the music to come and none realizing that the music has been here and playing for hours already. But they are deaf and blind, that's what they are.'

'I think you are right, señora. Only you see I can't understand the meaning of that board with the candle on it. We have looked and searched with torches and huge bonfires for light. If we couldn't find him with so much light, how do they expect to find him with that little candle?'

'Borregos, yes, that's what you are, muttonheads. You and your iron hooks and poles and sticks and lanterns, which are good for a dog but not for a human. The candle alone will find him as surely as it's night now and there'll be day tomorrow. All the old man has to do is watch where the candle goes, and wherever it stops, there below is the kid.'

'How can the candle find him if we didn't?'

She puffed her cigar, blew out huge clouds, contemplated the cigar with dreamy eyes, and then scanned me all over from top to bottom to see whether I was worthy of being talked to any longer. It had all come out in bits which I had had to arrange in the right order myself to catch what she wanted to say. That was difficult because she mixed words of the Indian idiom with her poor Spanish. But she accompanied her words with vivid facial expressions and with an occasional gesture, so it was not so hard after all to understand her. Her eyes often opened wide and then they would sparkle like those of a young woman telling her intimate girl friend of her honeymoon experiences.

All my attention was now concentrated upon the activities at the river-bank. I forgot to ask the old woman more questions, but I was aware that she was watching me, catlike, to learn what I might think of the strange performance I was witnessing. I was sure she was taking note of every move or gesture I made. No doubt I was gaining her confidence every minute. The fact is I was taking the whole rite, or whatever it was, very seriously; I would under no circumstances make fun of it or joke about it. After all, every religion is right and proselytism is always wrong.

On the bank, a score of men were again forming a circle around the old Indian. He held the board with the candle on it before him. The flame of the candle was on a level with his eyes. I think the old Indian priests of the ancient Aztecs and Toltecs must have looked as he did at that moment if one forgot his simple peasant clothes. About him there was the dignity and the aloofness of the high priest who is about to celebrate a mysterious rite. Perhaps he would evoke the gods whom he knew and recognized in his heart, for the Lord to whom he and everyone of his race prayed in church dwelled on their lips only and never reached their hearts.

From the corners of my eyes I saw that the old woman did not cease watching me. And still I had no reason to disapprove of what those men were doing. It was their business, not mine.

The old woman, guessing correctly what I was going to ask her, suddenly said: 'The kid is calling all the time. Can't you hear it?'

Perhaps I dreamed those words. Yet there they were. Rather dazedly I said: 'I am sorry, señora, I can't hear him calling. Did you say the kid is calling?'

'That's exactly what I just said. And you don't have to be sorry that you can't hear him calling. I can't hear it either, the way we hear ordinary things. No human ear can hear him calling the ordinary way. It is the light of the candle which is hearing his calls. We can only watch and see the calling, but not hear it ourselves.'

'The light of the candle? Did you say the light of the candle?' I was still not sure that I wasn't dreaming. Or perhaps I did not really understand what the old woman was saying in her corrupt Spanish mixed with Indian lingo. So I asked once more: 'Do you really mean to say the light hears the kid calling?'

'Yes, and don't make me believe you are too dumb to understand plain language. I'll tell you something else. So far no one knows if the kid is actually in the river. But if he is, and I am sure he is, then he'll call the light close to him. The light will follow his calling and it will come to him as sure as there is a God in heaven. And the light will stand by because the light has to obey his calls and it cannot do anything on its own account or of its own free will. Not in such a case.'

It was night. It was a pitch-black night. It happened in a tropical jungle. I was in the midst of Indians, very few of whom I knew, and even those few I knew only superficially. What was it the old woman had just told me? What she had told me was something out of their everyday life, an ordinary thing. I wondered which of us was mad. One of us surely was. Anyway, in such a night, in a jungle, among Indians, whatever else the old woman might have told me would have sounded unnatural. The old woman simply could not talk any other way than she did. It was in harmony with everything. I saw clearly what the men were doing on the river-bank, so it could not be a dream. I was awake. And I remained squatting beside the old woman. She spoke no more, enjoyed her cigar immensely, and with a bored look in her eyes she watched the group of men preparing the mysterious ceremony.

The old Indian began to speak in a loud, chanting voice. What he said I could not understand, because I was still on the bridge.

Now he ceased speaking and moved the board before him three times up and down and three times sidewise and then once more up and down. After a short silence he raised his voice and again chanted a few lines. This time his chant was taken up by a dozen of the men standing around him and they repeated these lines as a kind of response.

All the men had taken off their hats. Everybody near followed the ceremony with solemn zest.

I leaned forward to try to catch the words, for I would have liked to know them. But I preferred to stay away even if I had to miss the words. Theirs was a religious service to which I had not been invited, so I considered it rude to go close when everyone was aware of the fact that I was not moved by faith, but by curiosity.

I could pick up some phrases. I learned that in the main it was Spanish they spoke. Yet this Spanish of theirs was blended with words and phrases taken from the Indian idioma, which was still spoken by hundreds of families in that jungle region. However, the expression 'Madre Santisima!' was used so frequently that it stood out clearly. I felt, however, that they prayed to the Most Holy Virgin only with their lips while with their hearts they were calling upon their ancient holy mother, perhaps to Cioacoatl.

This ceremony lasted about ten minutes. The old Indian raised the board high above his head. The light of the candle was reflected in the water. While holding the board in this position, he chanted a few lines more. The audience joined him before he ended. And they all finished together. I listened carefully, but there was no Amen, only a sound like an owl's hoo-oo.

Quick as a flash Perez stripped. He stood in the water for a while. Then with arms stretched forward he strode slowly towards the old Indian, who also came forward until he too was standing in the water. With a solemn gesture he handed Perez the board and mumbled a few words. Perez gestured with his right hand over his chest and then over the board. Perhaps it was the sign of the cross that he made – perhaps another sign. When he received the board he also said a few words in a low voice as a response to the old man's chant. As soon as the board was in Perez's hands, the old Indian made similar gestures with his right hand over the board and then over his heart. After this he stepped back to the bank, walking backwards with his face to the board.

Perez carried the board high above his head. He waded into the river until the water reached his chest. Now he stopped and waited until the water had calmed down again. Then he set the board upon the water with infinite care. When the board was floating he waded slowly back to the river-bank, facing the strange little raft as he did so.

19

The board rests quietly on the water as if it were deciding which way to go.

Perez wraps his shirt around his loins and steps back from the river-bank. With his eyes fixed upon the board he keeps walking backward, then turns to the bridge, from where he can see better what is happening. As I was told later, the board might go straight to its goal, but it might also merely wobble, and in that case the right direction could be determined only by an expert.

All the people present are spellbound. For moments on end they forget to breathe and then have to catch up suddenly, so that a ceaseless moaning comes from their lips. They seem to force themselves not to wink and their eyes redden and widen, which gives the crowd the appearance of being in a deep trance.

Some men hold their hats in their hands; others have thrown theirs away. Nobody smokes any more. Not a word is heard, not even a murmur or a whisper. Only the singing, chirping, and fiddling of the jungle fills the night. This great jungle symphony is at times unexpectedly interrupted by a deep silence, as if the jungle insects were ordered to stop for two or three seconds, for no other reason than to break out again louder and more intensely than before. These sudden intervals in the jungle music deepen the mystery of the night and heighten the tension of the people who are waiting almost ecstatically for the miracle to happen. No one knows whether the miracle will take place tonight as it took place, according to their traditions, five hundred, yes, ten thousand years back under similar circumstances. All present have a faith which no power could shake. There is not one in the whole crowd who even for a second thinks the light could fail to obey the call of the lost boy. Of course, it would fail if the kid is not in the river, for then he could not call, and the light has no will of its own; it can only go if it is called. It will float down the river and disappear if the boy is not in the water.

Suddenly that multi-headed body utters a cry and takes a deep breath as though there were only two very huge lungs in that body.

The board has started to move.

With infinite slowness it begins to sail away from the bank towards the middle of the river. Now it stops, wobbles, sways, trembles slightly. Then it takes again the same direction.

The bridge is crowded with people. Those along the rim are kneeling, tightly pressed against each other, their heads reaching as far over the edge as possible. With burning eyes they stare at the slowly moving board. Nobody breathes more than absolutely necessary, partly because of tension, but more because their breathing might throw the board off its course.

I stand on the bank near the end of the bridge, from which point I can see the face of everyone kneeling along the rim. This row of eager faces is lighted by the new bonfires on the banks. The fact is I am far more interested in these sixty or seventy faces and in these bronze and dark-yellow bodies than in what the board is doing at this moment. The board I am sure will do its job all right. If it does not, it will be of little concern to me. Yet during the rest of my life I may never again behold such a grandiose picture, such a huge human body with threescore and more heads, all thinking the same thought, all concentrated upon the same hope, all charmed by the little flame of an ordinary candle. Their deep brown eyes reflect that little flame as if each contained a tiny, forlorn star. There are half-naked bodies, stark naked bodies, bodies clothed in rags only, and bodies covered with white shirts and white or yellow cotton pants. So thick is their black wiry hair that it looks as if these men had heavy fur caps on their heads.

Against the simple and natural clothes of the men the women's dresses from modern sweat-shops make a pitiful contrast. What sin have these women committed that providence could allow Syrian jobbers to hang upon those beautiful bodies dresses designed by immigrant watch-repairers starving in New York's East Side? In their simple week-day skirts, even in their rags, these women are in harmony with the jungle, the river, the bridge, the asthmatic pump, the pack train, the alligators, the earth, the whole universe. Now they are aniline-dyed ghosts, foul bastards of the land, nobody's daughters. Thanks to a merciful God and to Nature with its eternal good taste, beautiful wild flowers still grow and blossom in jungle and bush, and these women can pick them at their hearts' desire and with them cover the ugliness of modern products. And it is only on account of the wild flowers and orchids of the jungle that these women do not lose all their contact with the earth which has borne them.

The mysterious performance of which I am a witness, the crowd's belief that the miracle will happen, the dim light of the lanterns in the pump-master's portico, the licking flames of the bonfires, the torches held by boys on the bridge, the floating board with the lighted candle in the river, that huge body of excited beings who are not my race, at this moment breathing as one, their eyes gazing without winking and each with a tiny star in it, the gloomy silence of that mass of men, the never ceasing whining of the jungle – all this depresses me and makes my heart heavy. My throat is parched. My tongue feels as though it were wood. Where is the world? Where is the earth on which I used to live? It has disappeared. Where has mankind gone? I am alone. There is not even a heaven above me. Only blackness. I am on another planet, from which I never can return to my own people. I shall never again see green meadows, never again the waves of wheat fields, never again shall I wander through the forests and around the lakes of Wisconsin, never again shall I ride over the plains of Texas and breathe the air of desolate goat ranches. I cannot come back to the earth, my true mother, and never shall I see the sun rise. I am with creatures I do not know, who do not speak my language, and whose souls and minds I can never fathom. One, only one out of this crowd has to stand up at this moment, only one has to point his finger at me and yell: 'Look at that man! Look at him! He is the white, who has not been invited to come here, but he came nevertheless. He is the guilty one. By his blue eyes and by his skin of the pale dead he has brought the wrath of our gods upon us poor people. He is a gringo. He has brought us misfortune and sorrows. He has come only yesterday and today our little boy had to leave us, driven away by that white man and making the kid's mother weep like the skies in the rainy season. He has been here only two days and the river, which hates him, has robbed us of our beloved little child. Look at his eyes and you will see that with those eyes he is poisoning our children and bewitching all of us!'

If I never come back again, if I am sacrificed here and now, tonight, nobody, no consul, no ambassador, no government will ever know what has become of me and where my bones are bleaching under the sun. The buzzards won't leave anything of me that could be identified. 'Disappeared on a trip through the jungle.' Or perhaps: 'Caught by alligators on a fishing trip in swampy territory.' This will be the last the old folks at home will hear of me.

Why do I feel uncomfortable? There, only a few yards away, there stands Sleigh, my fellow citizen, white of colour like myself, thoughts the same as mine, brought up in the same traditions, speaking the same language. He is standing behind the men who are kneeling on the bridge, and he too has his eyes fixed upon the board slowly floating on the river. Suppose this crowd, stirred up by somebody gone mad, were to jump at me to make me pay for the lost kid, Sleigh would be my guardian angel, my life-saver; he would protect me with his very body. Certainly. Most certainly. Because he is my fellow citizen, singing with me the *Star-Spangled Banner*. He would save me. He would cock his hat slightly, with a lazy gesture, and he would say: 'Why, now, see here, you folks, you can't do that. That is stupid. He didn't throw the kid in the river. I'm plumb sure he didn't. He is a mighty good fellow and nobody can deny that.' Having said this, he would turn to me and say: 'You must excuse me, I've got to look after that goddamned cow. Christ, if I only knew where to find that damn bitch. Perhaps she has come home at last. I'll go and see.' So he would go and leave me alone with that frenzied mob. After I have been torn to pieces he would return and talk to the neighbours, telling them that the cow has not come home yet and that surely a pair of tigers or lions must be roaming in the vicinity. Then, on seeing the last ragged shreds of me, he would say: 'Well, you men, you shouldn't have done that. It isn't right. I told you so before. Anyhow, who would have thought that of him? He seemed to be a fine chap. I don't think he threw the kid into the river. You shouldn't have done that. Well, well, who would have thought such a thing of him?'

Sleigh. Who is Sleigh? What is he to me? He was born in the same God's great country I was. Nevertheless he is farther away from me than our president. Sleigh. He has lived more than half his life among these Indians. He is married to an Indian woman. His children don't speak one word of American, they know only Spanish and quite a few phrases of the Indian idiom. Sleigh. The meals he eats are Indian, and he eats as the Indians do, without using a fork, shovelling up his meat, beans, and gravy with a torn-off bit of tortilla, wrapping the whole thing up and pushing it into his wide-open mouth, swallowing the food and eating the tortilla-made spoon simultaneously. He lives in an Indian jacal on an earthen floor under a grass roof. He would feel most uncomfortable in a house or a bungalow. Without moving an eyelash he would stand by and look on should this crowd become infuriated and hammer me into a pulp. I am absolutely alone among these people. And I also know perfectly well that whatever might happen to me, no battle-cruiser will steam into this jungle with a crew yelling: 'Hip, hip, hi! Everything is under control, we have the situation well in hand!' It is a very good thing to know that. One thus becomes a fatalist. The more fatalistic I become, the closer I get to understanding these people. They could not bear life were they not all fatalists.

20

The board is some fifteen feet from the river-bank. It stops for half a minute. Now it begins to whirl slowly and, still whirling, drifts farther towards the middle of the river, gradually nearing the slow current. For five feet or so it moves along that current. Then it stops again. And again it whirls as if it were trying to get out of the stream.

After a few minutes it again follows the current for a short distance. Then it stops abruptly. It begins whirling again. At first it does so very slowly, then quicker and quicker still, and at the same time it starts moving back towards the bridge and now, as can be clearly seen, it moves contrary to the current. I personally cannot see any miracle in that, because all rivers have currents of two or more different directions, although usually only for short stretches.

Nor does the crowd regard it as something miraculous or even strange that the board is moving against the current. Only they have a different reason for being calm about it. To them it is something long anticipated. It convinces everybody that the kid is in the river, that he is calling the light, and so the light has to answer his call. Further, it is proof that the body has not been washed downstream.

Which of us, the crowd or I, will be right in the end?

The board floats towards the bridge. It sails so slowly that its movements can be judged only by watching the candle against a fixed mark on the opposite bank.

Now it stops and wobbles on the surface. Apparently it has been caught by a plant or a shrub in the water. That at least is my explanation. Strange as it may seem, the board struggles to free itself.

The crowd is watching that struggle with more tension and excitement than they would a cockfight. Many faces show disappointment. One young man gets ready to wade into the river and help the board out of the tangle. The old Indian commands him to leave the board alone. 'No shrub, no branch, nothing that grows or lives in the water can keep the board from going where it has to go. Mind that, muchacho,' he counsels him.

The old Indian has told the truth. A few minutes after he spoke the board wobbles faster, begins to whirl, twists itself out of the entanglement. Slowly it sails nearer to the bridge.

It now has reached the bridge and here it touches the seventh post. That post repulses it and, while keeping directly under the rim, it wanders towards the sixth post, where it stops for several minutes.

'There, now it's stopping for good! There is the boy! That's the sign!' A score of men are shouting excitedly.

'Hold it! Hold it!' the old Indian cries. 'Go easy, you folks. Let's wait and see first before we make any mistake and stir up the water and lose our best chance. The light is not perfectly quiet yet. I'll give you the word!'

Hardly has he said that when the board starts wriggling. It moves away from the sixth post and sails, whirling all the while, towards the fifth post, still remaining under the rim of the bridge. On the way it is caught by the slight current and carried out for a foot or so. But each time it pulls itself out of the current and struggles back under the rim as though forced to do so by some strong power.

It has reached the fifth post. It hangs on for a few minutes. Then, still clinging to the post, it moves around and sails away from it straight under the bridge for about one and a half feet.

The people kneeling on the rim lean far over and stick their heads under it to watch the board's movements. Everyone in the crowd now thinks himself very stupid for not having fished for the kid under the bridge instead of only along its edge. Several men crawl over to the upstream side of the bridge and put their heads down there. Others lie flat on the planks and watch the miracle through the joints and knot-holes.

The board in the meanwhile has wandered farther under the bridge, but always in a right angle to the fifth post. Now it is under the middle of the bridge. From here it sails towards the fourth post, though only for about a foot.

And here it stops as if it were nailed to the water. It does not mind the current nor the light breeze that sweeps softly across the surface of the river. The manner in which the board has halted is entirely different from that in which it stopped before. Now and then it trembles slightly, as if something were breathing against it from below. But it no longer whirls.

In fact, its behaviour is so clear, so definite, that nobody can doubt any longer that the board has found its final destination.

A long-drawn-out groan comes from the crowd as if from one mouth. A hundred heavy sighs fill the air and almost drown out the million voices of the jungle. Many men and women seem covered with thick pearly sweat, while the sweat runs in streams down the faces and bodies of the others. No one bothers to wipe it off. Here and there whispered words float through the night.

The board begins softly to dance as if impatient. It seems that it wants to be relieved of its torture. It wriggles, swings about itself, though it does not move as much as two inches. One might think it is trying to go down to the bottom.

The old Indian watches the board like a hawk watching a mouse. He has an infinite calmness of manner. Four or five minutes more he waits, and now he gives the long-expected signal. 'There, you may dive now. There is the little one. He is in the river all right. Poor mother, may God save and bless her!' He goes a few paces nearer the bridge.

It is a spot nobody has thought of. Who would have thought that a boy who has tumbled over the rim should be looked for under the middle of the bridge? It seems impossible.

Perez is already in the river. Two men follow him. He is the first on the spot. He pushes the board gently aside so as to have room to dive.

Only a few seconds he is under the water, then he comes up, spits, and says in a thick, sad voice: 'He is there! The kid is there! I've touched his little body.'

The people on the bridge look at Perez. He has swum to the fifth post, to which he clings with one hand while with the other he wipes from his face the water dripping down from his hair. His face, dimly lighted by the flickering bonfires on the banks, shows an expression of horror mixed with mental pain. He looks up to the bridge and lets his eyes wander over the whole crowd. Everybody knows that he is looking for the Garcia woman, yet none calls her.

At this moment, coming from nowhere at all, the Garcia walks with heavy dragging feet along the bridge to where Perez clings to the post. Everybody steps back to let the woman pass freely. She has heard Perez. Her mouth is wide open. She wants to yell, perhaps she even thinks that she is yelling. But somehow she cannot do so, because her throat is tight as if in a cramp. She raises one hand, makes a fist, and stuffs that fist into her open mouth as deep as it will go. Horror haunts her eyes. Fear flutters over her face with jumping shadows as if huge unseen birds were flying around her. She is trembling with fear of the final sentence. She wishes to hold fast to the last little bit of hope and doubt. Perhaps Perez has erred. Perhaps he has felt only a pack of balled grass. Would to Almighty God that he has erred as have all others before him! Her eyes are slowly moving upwards to heaven. Yet half-way she turns them into the direction of Tlalcozautitlan, where her husband has ridden and where her last glimmer of hope now rests. The kid has surely gone to Tlalcozautitlan with that boy on the white horse. It must be so or the world cannot be right and there can be no God in heaven.

Nobody says a word. Only a shuffling of feet on the bridge is heard. And the singing of the jungle.

Perez has dived again, accompanied by one of the other two men. Soon both come up, their hands filled with wet and rotten shrubs and branches and twigs all dripping with water. They push them away, and down again the two men go.

Bubbles boil on the surface. Torn water plants, branches, bits of shrubs rise and float on the water. One of the two men comes up. One cannot see who he is because only part of his face is visible and that is covered with his matted, dripping hair.

A few seconds later something black is seen rising to the surface. It comes up slowly until it can be identified as the thick hair of Perez. Now his head is fully out. He shakes it as a dog shakes his pelt to free it of water. He blows, breathes heavily, swallows, and rises farther, treading the water with all his power. He is not using his arms this time. In his arms he holds the little Carlosito, whose knees are seen before anything else. His knees protrude high above the rest of his body because they are bent in an unnatural angle so that the heels are only a few inches away from the small of his back.

One might think that the kid had been sitting on his heels all during the time he was on the bottom.

Strange. The new American shoes on his little feet draw everybody's first look in a verily obtrusive and arrogant manner, as if they were the most important part of the whole body.

Perez does not look up to the bridge. Partly swimming, partly wading, he makes for the bank.

'Chiquito mio! My baby!' the Garcia yells. She darts to the bank and awaits Perez.

Perez walks up the low slope of the bank. Entirely naked he now stands before the young mother. Still in her cheap sea-green gauze dance dress, with fire-red wild flowers in her hair, on her breast, and in her girdle, she receives Perez with arms stretched out towards the little burden he is carrying.

With an indescribable nobility and solemnity, and in his eyes that pitiful sad look which only animals and primitive people possess, he steps slowly foward. And Perez, the man whose daily task it is to fell the hard trees of the jungle and convert them into charcoal, lays that little water-soaked body in the outstretched arms of the mother with a tenderness that makes one think of glass so thin and fragile that a single soft breath could break it.

21

At this moment many women uttered a shrill, plaintive wail full of reproach.

That wail, which pierced the blackness of the night as if it meant to break through and rise to the sun in the sky, swelled until all the women fell in. Then it sank and became a low moan. The women wrapped a piece of cloth, be it a rebozo, a black veil, or a shawl, around their heads. Their faces hidden, they wept bitterly.

It was no longer only the death of the Garcia woman's child that they bewailed. By his untimely death the little boy had become every mother's baby. Only a mother knows how a mother feels. No one else, not even God in heaven with all His immaculate wisdom, with all His stern serenity, can feel as a mother does when her baby has been taken away from her.

The Garcia held her baby in her left arm against her breast. With her right hand she squeezed his wet and already shrivelled little hands.

Perez stole away from her. He no longer wished to be seen by her, as though he were guilty of an unforgivable crime.

A middle-aged Indian walked up to the mother, bowed his head, and spoke to her. She handed him the little body; he received it very gently. Then he stepped back a few paces. Resolutely and unsentimentally, like an old country doctor, he now grasped the kid firmly by his feet and held him up with the head hanging perpendicularly. He shook the body several times. Only watery blood dripped out of the kid's mouth.

The body was already stiff. In spite of the weight of the body hanging by its feet, the knee joints stretched very little.

While the kid still hung upside down, a thick bruise became visible on the forehead above the left eyebrow. The nose and mouth were swollen and the upper jaw was partly smashed in.

I went near and lifted his head slightly because I wished to see his eyes by the light of a lantern. Holding his head in the palm of my hand, I felt, with the tip of my middle finger, a little hole in the back of his skull. I turned the head round to the light, and from its size I decided that this hole was caused by a fairly thick nail.

The Indian who was holding the body by its feet winked at another man. This man pressed the little body between his hands, moving from the belly down to the chest inch by inch. Even then surprisingly little water came out of the kid's mouth. Yet there was still that trickling of thin blood.

Huge pearls of tears formed in the eyes of the mother, and when her eyes could not hold them any longer, they tumbled down, running down her cheekbones, over the corners of her mouth, down her chin, finally dropping upon her breast. They fell upon the flowers she had fastened on her dress slightly above her heart.

She snorted as though pushed from the inside of her chest, and through her nostrils she blew violently a loud hiss which, it seemed, she had suppressed for hours and which now at last was released in a second. Her nose was running. She looked around vaguely. Then she looked down along her own body, lifted up her green dance dress, and blew her nose in it.

It pained her to see her baby hanging head down, almost like a slaughtered goat. She stared at this lifeless body and, obviously thinking it might hurt him to hang that way for so long a time, she took his head and lifted it. Her eyes fell upon his bent knees. She let the head go and tried to press the joints into a more natural position. While doing so, she blew her nose several times in the folds of her dress and in her sleeves. Again and again she worked at his knees, which would not stretch. Despite her grief she was already thinking of the beautiful ceremony of laying out the body for the funeral. The body had to be presented to the mourners and visitors before being buried. For this occasion it had to be pretty. It was the last thing she could do for her baby, for she did not want him to go to heaven looking like a pauper.

The man who had tried to press the water out of the body understood the mother's desire and made it his job to straighten the knees. By pulling, massaging, kneading, pressing the joints between his labour-hardened hands, he achieved some success at last. While he was working at the knees the mother gently stroked the new shoes on the kid's feet. These shoes had still preserved, in spots, their original brilliance. She pressed the little shoes, caressed them as if they were part of his body, because she remembered how much he liked them. And while she caressed them she doubtless wondered about the mysterious ways of destiny, that this token of brotherly love should have become the cause of the kid's destruction. Overwhelmed by these thoughts she forgot to breathe and her suppressed weeping now almost suffocated her. She tried to gasp for fresh air, opened her mouth wide to let the air in, but instead she yelled so fiercely that it seemed the night of the jungle would be rent into pieces by the scream of a wounded mother accusing the universe of injustice.

There followed a few seconds of silence during which time the world seemed to vanish. Again the mother yelled.

The men standing by felt depressed and shy. They dropped their eyes and fumbled with their hands as little children do when they are ashamed. In the face of the mother's distress the men became little, worthless, poor, and empty in their souls. None dared touch her, none consoled her for fear of doing the wrong thing.

The pump-master woman came up, and without saying one word she embraced the mother as if she meant to crush her ribs. She covered her face with kisses, kissed away her rolling tears. She lifted her own Sunday dress and with it she dried the mother's tears and wiped her nose. Then she kissed her again and again. The two women wept and sobbed together so that it could be heard all over the wide square.

Who would ever have thought that the pump-master woman, that very proud woman, as highly respected as if she were the president's wife, that this haughty woman could let herself go that way and lose all her composure. The mothers. The mothers. That's what mothers are like. They understand each other when one of them is grieved.

The men felt themselves getting still smaller and poorer on seeing these two women weep together as one. More and more did they feel ashamed of – they did not know what. They had only one wish at this moment, the wish to be able to weep as these two mothers wept. How they envied the two who had busied themselves with the little body!

Sleigh came up. He touched the kid, ran his hand up and down the whole body, and finally said: 'He's a goner all right, and I'll go and make coffee. The Garcia woman certainly will like to have something hot in her belly.'

The pump-master woman wormed herself very gently out of the Garcia woman's arms and looked at the kid, who was still hanging head down while the two men worked on him. She lifted his head, stroked back his wet hair, and softly patted his cheeks. The watery blood trickled over her hand. With her dress she cleaned his bleeding mouth and blood-smeared nose. The blood still trickled forth.

The kid wore not only new shoes but also new socks, which, like the shoes, were the first he had ever worn and which were also a gift from his big brother. His short pants, reaching only to his knees, were worn out, patched in a dozen places, and still full of holes. He had no suspenders. Instead he wore a string fastened to one button in front, running across one shoulder, and tied to one button at the back of his pants. The upper part of his body was covered with a torn white cotton shirt which was already too small for him.

While the man holding the body by the feet shook the kid once more in the hope that at last the water would come out, a little wooden whistle fell out of one of the pants pockets. Before it reached the ground his mother caught it. She stared at it and began to weep in a soft and woeful manner. She wiped the tears off her face to have another look at the whistle, then she hid it in the bosom of her dress.

'Didn't he have a hat?' one man asked.

The men who had heard this question got excited. A job was at hand. They could now do something useful. They could jump into the water and fish for the kid's hat.

560

This hope, though, vanished quickly. If there had been a hat it would have been seen and found long ago or it would have drifted off downstream.

Then the Garcia said that the hat was in the hut, and that this was what had made her doubt that the kid had ridden away, because he would have taken his hat along, for he would have needed it badly on the return trip in the daytime when the sun is high and hot. Half of what she said one had to guess because her speech was constantly interrupted by her blubberings.

We were still standing on the bank not far away from the bridge. Someone was holding up a lantern, and by its light this part of the bridge could be seen clearly. I was looking up, thinking of Sleigh, who had said – it seemed to me a week ago – that he was going to make coffee for somebody. I saw something walking on the bridge towards us. That something was walking slowly and heavily, like a very old man. If it lifted a foot it did so as if it were nailed to the planks and had to be torn off by force. Its head was bent deep upon its breast. Before I saw the face I recognized that strange something by the Texas sombrero it was wearing: Manuel.

He had now reached this end of the bridge. For almost a minute he remained standing there. Then he came up to us without lifting his head. He was pale, as pale as the brown colour of his skin would allow. His face had become very small and narrow. Were it not for the hat, I might not have known for a long while who he was, so much had he changed. His eyes were dull and glassy as if they had lost their light.

The Garcia stared at her big stepson. Her eyes were filled with balls of water. She opened her mouth to say something. But the lips closed slowly and stayed closed.

Manuel was now standing by the two men who were holding the kid. They looked at him as if he were a ghost.

It was obvious that he did not wish to see anything. He stretched out his arms, while his head remained hanging. And in his outstretched arms the little brother was gently laid.

No word was spoken. The men and boys who had put their hats on took them off once more while this ceremony of handing the kid to his brother went on.

For a few minutes Manuel stood thus, statue-like, holding the kid in his arms as if he were offering the kid as a sacrifice to the gods. He was the only one with his hat on. It was this wide-brimmed sombrero on his mournfully bowed head, hiding his face, that made this simple act appear like a mysterious rite.

561

The whole incident became unbearable to me. I was caught by the same fear I had felt for a minute or two while the board was floating upon the water. Any second I expected to see all eyes fixed upon me as having been found guilty of magic or witchcraft and so responsible for the misfortune which had befallen that poor settlement of peaceful natives.

Not so much to help but merely to keep my nerves from going to pieces, I assured myself that I was still alive and sane and healthy by forcing myself to act – even though my action might have drawn everybody's attention to me and perhaps caused the very thing I was afraid of. At the very moment that Manuel was about to turn around to carry the little body to his home, I stepped quickly forward, touched Manuel's arm, and said: 'Por favor, amigo, one moment only.'

Whether Manuel had heard what I had said I did not know, but he remained standing. I put my hand on the kid's chest, pushed his shirt away, and put my ear above his heart. For a long time I had known that the kid was dead, or at least unconscious and nearly dead, before he reached the water and that he was surely dead five minutes after I had heard the splash. No, after I had heard a fish jumping high into the air to catch a mouthful of mosquitoes. That splash had been caused by a fish. I would swear it was a fish. And I would stick to that story until the end of my life. I did not wish to be haunted all my life by the sound of the splash I had heard early that night.

As I was saying, five minutes after that fish had made a heavy splash the kid was dead and beyond help. There was the bruise over his left eye, there was the little hole in his skull, and there was the smashed upper jaw. He was dead long before he was missed by his mother.

The little body which I touched with my ear was as cold as ice. There was not the faintest throb of that little heart which only five hours ago had been beating so happily. No one here had expected me to declare that the kid was still alive. Yet they let me do as I liked. I lifted the head. Everybody looked at me with a question in his eyes. As though I had not been absolutely sure of my first examination I laid my ear on the clammy chest once more. This time I listened longer and more attentively. I felt the repugnant coldness of death only that much more, and only that much more did I realize the helplessness of man against death. When I raised my head I did not look up; instead I turned away from the crowd, which, I knew without seeing, had their eyes fixed on me, obviously expecting to hear me promise a miracle. But my silent turning away convinced everybody that no miracle, not even something unexpected, would happen.

My fear had gone. That painful agony which had gripped me twice that night had disappeared entirely. By my careful examination of the kid's heart, useless though it was, I had shown that I was willing to help. So I had been accepted as one of the mourners.

22

Manuel, with the kid resting in his outstretched arms, marched slowly across the bridge in time to the unheard strains of some funeral hymn.

The mother walked beside him, leaning against the shoulder of a woman who had put one arm around her neck. Both were sobbing.

Behind them the men marched, hat in hand, followed by the women.

On reaching the point on the bridge from which it was supposed the kid had tumbled over, Manuel stopped for half a minute. As his head was still bowed, it could not be seen whether he said a prayer or whispered: 'Behold, O Lord, what you have done!'

The Garcia screamed horribly. The woman by her side put both her arms around the mother and talked to her in a low, soft voice. One man stepped to the edge of the bridge and with a few heavy strokes of his machete cut a cross in the rim as a sort of monument.

The procession marched on, arrived at the opposite bank, reached the opening where the settlement was located, and came to a halt at the clean-swept front yard of the Garcia's hut, where in the early evening old man Garcia had been fiddling and Carlosito had had a boxing match with his big brother Manuelito.

Following Manuel and the two women, we entered the hut.

This home proved to be one of the poorest I had ever seen. No table, no chair, no bench, no cot, no furniture of any sort, not even of the cheapest kind. Save a box, there was absolutely nothing which could be used as furniture. In the farthest corner four posts were stuck in the earthen floor. On these four posts there rested a network of thin sticks interwoven and held together by vines and lianas from the jungle. On this flimsy construction there was an old, threadbare blanket and an armful of prairie grass which was used as a pillow. That simple thing was the bed of Garcia and his wife. The kid's bed was a petate, a bast mat, spread out on the earthen floor and now shoved under the bed. Frequently, though, the kid had slept on the grass roof with a ragged piece of cloth for a blanket. His mother had always been afraid that a scorpion would sting him, but he had not minded, preferring the roof for a reason he had been unable to explain.

Several women had hurried to the hut before Manuel and all the others. These women had brought candles, put them into empty beer-bottles loaned by the pump-master, and set them on boxes which had also been obtained from the maestro maquinista. Owing to these preparations, the hut had a solemn aspect which, when the Garcia entered and observed it, caused her to break out crying again.

This time, however, she shook off her despair quickly and resolutely. She found herself confronted now with the tasks of a hostess, let alone her duty to prepare the funeral for her baby. The many obligations she faced helped her to forget her grief. And it was surely a very good thing that she had to get busy around her household. It would save her from becoming morose perhaps for the rest of her life. It is the first twelve hours that count. If one can survive them and keep one's reason under control during this time, one can find life worth while again in a few weeks.

At first she did not know what to do and where to begin. In the machinery of her daily life a very important bolt had been broken and she had to find a substitute for it before that machinery would run perfectly again. So far she knew only that she had to be busy and work hard for the next ten hours. She began with pushing the boxes to places other than where they had been put by the women who had brought them. Each box was moved and all the candles were taken out of the bottles and stuck into others and then the bottles themselves were moved from one box to another. When she was through changing those things around, it was found that everything was in practically the same place as before.

Now she started running from this corner to that. Here she picked up something which she put down in another place, only to take it away from that place and carry it back to where it had first been. There was not much she could move around: one pot, several potsherds (all in use), a spoon, a rag, a bundle. For a while she stopped altogether. Holding one fist against her mouth, she stood thinking. Then she hurried to a corner. She bent down upon a wooden box made into a sort of trunk, which was the wardrobe of the family. She opened it and with both hands she rummaged around inside it, having obviously forgotten what she wanted. After much aimless digging into that box, picking things up and pushing them back again, she finally dragged out a bundle of marine-blue cotton goods, all crumpled and wrinkled and partly smutty and stained. Holding it up against the light, she turned it round and round without saying a word about what she meant to do with it.

All this time Manuel was sitting on an old sack half full of corn-cobs. His chin resting on his breast, his hat covering all of his face, his dead kid brother lying in his outstretched arms, which were lying on his knees, he sat there motionless and serene as if he were a god made of bronze.

Sleigh appeared in the open entrance. On his head he carried a table, the only one he owned. He worked it through the narrow doorway and put it on the floor in the middle of the hut. Then the pump-master woman stepped forward and spread two bed-sheets over the crude table.

Manuel now rose, went to the table, laid the kid gently on it, and walked out into the night without once looking back.

The Garcia ran to the table, took the cold, wet, crumpled hands of her baby into her own, and pressed them together as though she wanted to fill them with new warmth. She noted that his head hung down on the table with the chin sticking up and she saw that blood was trickling out of his mouth and nose again, leaving little pink ribbons from the corners of his mouth down his chin and neck. It was strange that out of this body that had been dead so long, after having been in the water for more than four hours, there should still flow blood. But the blood was getting more and more watery.

It hurt the mother to see the little head in such an awkward position. She went to her bed, took a bunch of grass, and returned with it to the table. Half-way back she stopped, looked at her baby, and let the grass drop. A woman hurried out of the jacal and came back in a few seconds with a small soiled pillow.

The pump-master woman ransacked the Garcia's box, picked up a few green rags, sewed them together as a bag, stuffed grass from the bed into it and pushed it under the kid's head, so that instead of one he now had two pillows, and the head was now in the natural position of sleep.

On the two pillows and the bed-sheets watery pink blots soon appeared, which widened slowly into large stains.

The mother took off his shoes, which, I noticed, covered the ankles and were therefore more like low boots than shoes. I understood better why that kid had felt helpless in such stiff, heavy shoes. The Garcia also took off his new socks, his short pants, and she pulled off his shirt, which was so small for him that it couldn't be buttoned anywhere.

The pump-master woman searched for a comb. At first she parted his hair at the left. She looked at her job, did not like it, and parted the hair at the right.

The roosters crowed for the second time during the night. It was one hour after midnight.

Picking up from the ground the piece of blue cotton goods which she had dropped some time before, the Garcia spread and flattened it, and it turned out to be a cheap little sailor suit. It was the kid's Sunday suit and he had been very proud of it, because not even the pump-master's boys had anything like it.

The mother now dressed her baby in that sailor suit.

When this was done I looked at the kid, and horror crept down my back. In his torn and patched-up pants and in his dirty shirt with half a hundred holes in it, and with that funny-looking bit of string across his shoulders, the kid was very prettty in his way. In fact he was a real and natural-looking child of the jungle. He belonged here. But in that cheap sailor suit he no longer looked like a son of his native land. Yet somehow the clean-cut, noble features of a full-blooded Indian finally triumphed over the pale-faced, flat-footed Syrian jobbers and peddlers who had to sell cheaper and cheaper still if they wanted to sell at all.

While alive the kid had worn that suit only once, at a feria more than a year ago.

Neither the coat nor the pants could now be buttoned. In the first place the kid had outgrown the suit; in the second place his body was swollen with water. His mother was trying again and again to get the suit properly fixed. In vain. After many fruitless attempts she suddenly got impatient and began to twist and press the body until finally she was able to button the suit. The suit was now so tight that I expected it to burst any minute. She wrung out the wet socks and held them up to the little fire burning on the earthen floor. When the socks had dried she put them on his feet. Then she put on his new shoes.

During the time she was working on the kid she sniffed audibly and blew her nose every ten seconds or so into her fingers. Then she moaned and sighed deeply. Now and then she blubbered, but no one could understand what she said. Frequently she looked around the room, picked up a rag, and blew her nose into it. Her body trembled every once in a while with inner convulsions. But she uttered no more loud cries, perhaps because she forgot to do so in her concentration on her job of dressing the kid for his last trip.

The people inside the hut whispered, murmured. She paid no attention to anyone. It seemed that she thought herself entirely alone in the room. Whatever she did was done correctly. Nevertheless one got the impression that she was in a dream and that she acted automatically.

On one wall of the jacal there was a crude shelf. On it stood a little picture of the Holy Virgin of Guadalupe painted on glass. On either side of that cheap picture there were other, smaller pictures of saints. No image of the Lord could be seen anywhere. The pictures of the saints had short prayers printed on the back, which neither Garcia nor his wife could read. In front of the Holy Virgin there stood an ordinary drinking-glass, slightly cracked, which was filled with oil on which floated a tiny paraffin candle, no bigger than a match, stuck through a piece of tin the size of a dime. This tiny candle was lighted and it burned day and night to illuminate with its faint flame the picture of the Madre Santisima. The light was supposed to burn day and night, but often the Garcias did not have the few centavitos for oil because other things less eternal were needed more urgently. There was no oil in the glass when the pump-master woman had come to look after things. One of her first acts had been to fill the glass with fresh oil and light the candle. What would all these people have thought of the Garcia family if they had found the light for the Holy Virgin dead? They would have thought the house inhabited by pagans or, worse, by a godless gringo. The light was no more than just a glimmer, yet it satisfied the faithful and no devil could come in now to snatch a soul away.

The little shelf, at least to the Garcia family, was not only the house altar. It was at the same time the place for miscellaneous secular things needed in the house. On it were standing withered flowers in several broken pots. There, also, wrapped in a piece of newspaper, were what the Garcia called her sewing utensils – that is, a few rags, a few partly rusty needles, a few pins, and pieces of white and black thread wound around a strip of brown packing paper. There were also a comb, a dozen hairpins, matches, and

Carlosito's toys, including a broken tin automobile worth a dime, a fish-hook, a sling made out of a piece of automobile tube, a broken cork, a small, brightly coloured glass ball used as a marble, two brass buttons, a few coloured pictures of the kind one finds in cigarette packages. And there was the little ukulele, his treasured gift from Manuel, with which he had wanted to form a dance orchestra with his fiddle-playing father. From one corner of the shelf a cheap rosary dangled. In a little cup which once had belonged to a doll's kitchen, a few centavos were piled, and a few more bronze coins were lying near it. The total could not have been more than thirty-five centavos, the whole fortune of the house.

From a thin wire tied to a pole in the roof, a reed basket was hanging. It contained the family's few provisions, two little cones of unrefined brown sugar, a few ounces of ground coffee wrapped in greasy paper, a pound of rice of the cheapest kind, a few pounds of black beans, and half a dozen green and red chile husks. Two bottles were tied to the basket. In one of them there was salt – crude, large grains which looked old and dirty. One third of the other bottle was filled with lard, which in this region never hardens and must therefore be kept in bottles. If it were kept in an open vessel it would be found full of drowned ants. As in all the other homes, this basket was hung up to protect its contents from rats and mice. But the rats in this region were such excellent acrobats that they climbed down from the grass roof along the thin wire without difficulty, and, of course, stole the provisions; for the Lord in His infinite wisdom has so made the world that no one is so poor that he cannot be robbed by another, and no one is so strong that he cannot be killed by somebody else.

On the earthen floor near the wall a fire was smouldering. It was the family hearth. An earthen pot filled with coffee stood close to the fire. Obviously it had been left there early in the evening so that Garcia would be able to gulp hot coffee in the morning when returning from the dance. Next to the fire, leaning against the wall, there was the usual piece of sheet iron on which to heat tortillas. Then there were three earthen pots, two earthen vessels, none of them whole, an old, rusty iron pan, and the metate, the big concave stone in which boiled corn is ground for the dough out of which tortillas are made.

The choza had a second, very small room. It was formed by a wall made of sticks tied together with lianas. This wall was about six feet high and ran parallel to the outer wall, forming a separate compartment five feet wide and three-fourths of the hut in length.

That narrow side room was filled with old sacks, a shabby Mexican saddle, two home-made, wooden pack saddles of the most primitive kind, many old ropes and lassos, an old basket for the hens to lay their eggs in. The few chickens the Garcias had roosted in a near-by tree, as no other shelter was provided for them. From a spike in this compartment the Garcia's week-day dress was hanging. It was very ragged and very dirty.

On the floor of this narrow side room there was a bast mat on which lay a fairly good blanket. This was the bed in which Manuel slept while he was here. In the camp in the Texas oil fields where he worked he was provided with a decent cot, two clean sheets, and two clean army blankets, but, like all his fellow workers, he would grumble daily about the stinginess of the rich oil companies. Of course, there he worked and helped the company make millions of dollars, while here he was on vacation having a good time. And that made all the difference, which lots of people can't grasp.

23

More candles were brought in by friendly neighbours. They were lighted and two were set near the boy's head and two near his feet. Two had been set in front of the picture of the Madre Santisima. Because of these candles, and because so many people were coming in and going out and moving around inside the house, and especially because the women were dressed in their best, the jacal had lost its poor appearance. It looked almost like a little country chapel on Christmas Eve.

The majority of the people stayed outside. Anyway, there would not have been room enough in the choza for the hundred or more persons who were now here. They squatted on the ground outside the hut, where they smoked and chatted in low voices. Now and then a few women or men entered the hut, while others left to make room for the newcomers.

Manuel's younger brother, the one who was considered half-witted, squatted on the ground, right by the entrance, where he was weeping quietly. No one paid any attention to him. Nor did he pay any to the people passing by, although occasionally they pushed him unintentionally. It was not clear whether he wept for his little stepbrother or because he saw the women weeping or because for the moment he did not know what else he could do. No one asked him anything and no one consoled him. He was the only stranger present, now that I had been accepted by the crowd as a fellow mourner.

Manuel entered as though he were sneaking in. He looked at the kid, went to the shelf, took the tin comb, and parted the kid's hair at the other side. For this simple job he took a long time.

The pump-master woman, standing between the body and the shelf, was working with strips of gold, silver, red, blue, and green paper, which she had produced from the devil knows where, to make a little crown which would be set on the kid's head. When that crown was ready a little cross was fastened to the top. A man had cut this cross out of an old tin can with his pocket knife while the pump-master woman was making the crown. With a few drops of hot paraffin from a candle the cross was covered with gold paper. Repeatedly the woman measured the kid's skull with a thread to make sure the crown would fit. Her tears rolled down her cheeks and dropped on the coloured paper, and every once in a while she had to dry her tears because she couldn't see through them. Whenever she put the little crown on the kid's head to see whether it fitted, the crown looked more beautiful than before, and she smiled under her tears. And each time she took it off she had a new idea how to make it still more beautiful.

The two men who were busy stretching the kid's legs finally shaped them to everybody's satisfaction. A board on which rested a heavy stone was laid across the knees to prevent them from returning to their unnatural position.

I noted that his mouth was wide open. It did not disturb me a bit. Why, I thought it only natural for a little boy who looks suddenly at another and entirely different world to open his mouth wide for sheer astonishment. No one he would meet on his trip would take offence on account of it. His mother, however, thought differently. She wanted to have a beautiful dead baby. She tried to close that little mouth, but it would not stay closed. I asked for a strip of an old shirt. Having obtained it, I tied it round his face so that the lower jaw was kept firmly pressed against the upper, and I made a sort of tie under his chin, so that the meaning of the strip was concealed.

570

If any of the neighbours or visitors got busy on the kid nobody paid much attention. But as soon as I went near the body and touched it, all the people came around and many from the outside hurried in. It seemed they thought that I might still be able to perform a great miracle, even bring the kid back to life. A foreigner is always, everywhere, believed to be gifted with strange powers. That I might do any harm to the kid, even now after his death, no longer occurred to them. I had known them only three days, but I learned a few days later that they had known me for a long time. My fame rested on a story told about me far and wide which also had to do with a dead Indian; it was said that after he had been dead for seven hours he was brought back to life by me, or, to tell the truth, was nearly brought back to life by me. At least I had made him breathe once more and, in the opinion of all the Indians concerned, I would have raised him from the dead had it not been for a gachupin, a most hated Spaniard, who entered the scene at the crucial moment and ordered a treatment contrary to the one I had applied. Everybody in the Indian village where that had happened was convinced that I could raise Indians from the dead if I was left to do it my own way.

The dressing of the kid's jaw was approved by everybody in the hut and I was raised in the estimation of the mourning community.

With the help of a man, the pump-master woman now folded the kid's arms across his chest and tried to put the hands in the position they would take in prayer. Neither the arms nor the hands obeyed. Apparently the pump-master woman had learned from what she thought was my invention, for she and her helper tied strings around the little arms and hands. The strings cut deep into the swollen, spongy flesh.

The kid had the crown on his head by now. It was really astonishing how the pump-master woman had been able to make a very becoming piece of headware, a little work of art, out of such primitive material. If one did not look closely, one would not believe that the crown had been made of paper. Were it not for that horrible sailor suit, a suit which made one laugh and weep at the same time, the child would not look like a little boy who had been born and brought up in a poor Indian choza, but more like the son of a dethroned Aztec king of old whose high rank and dignity had been restored after his death.

The pump-master woman contemplated the body for a while with a smile on her lips. A new idea entered her mind. She found him not quite beautiful enough for her taste and her neighbourly love. She left the hut and then returned with a thin stick, around which she wound gold paper. When everything was done, a golden sceptre had been made, with a little golden cross at the top. This she put in the kid's right hand after loosening the strings.

Just as she finished this job, old man Garcia returned from his trip to Tlalcozautitlan and entered the choza. For a long while he remained standing at the door. Then, without showing by any gesture what was going on in his mind, he looked at his little prince. He took off his hat and stepped up to the table.

The kid was to him not just a boy; he was not just the youngest and therefore the most petted and the most beloved. This little boy meant far more to him than his other two. Having had the luck to be loved by a pretty woman who was half his age, he had seen in that child the assurance of a happy life with his young wife, permanent proof to her and to all the other men that she had made no mistake when she had married him.

All the people present in the hut stared at him to see how he would take it. Everybody knew how much he loved that kid of his, the only one he had had by his young wife and most likely the last he could expect.

He looked at the body with empty eyes as if there were nothing before him. He did not understand it, could not grasp the cold fact that the kid was dead and that he would never again hear him bustle about the house and climb up his back and ride on his neck when he returned from work in the bush. He turned around and gazed at the floor as if he were looking for something. When he raised his head again, thick tears like little crystal balls were running down his cheeks. He did not ask when, where, or how. He stood for a minute near the door, his head leaning wearily against the door post, then left the hut.

A few men, his intimate friends, went after him. He did not see them. He left the yard, mounted the horse on which he had come, and rode out into the darkness.

24

As there was nothing I could do inside at the moment, I too left the hut. Outside, in the yard, men, women, and children were lying all about, huddled up and asleep. Others squatted on the ground talking. Others were walking around. Out of every choza in the settlement dim lights were shining.

Burros brayed plaintively in the prairie. The jungle was singing its eternal song of joy, love, sadness, pain, tragedy, hope, despair, victory, defeat. What did the jungle or the bush care about the things which had happened here? To the jungle, men are of no account. It does not even accept men's dung, leaving it to flies and beetles. But it does take men's bones after the buzzards, ants, and maggots have been satisfied. What is man to the jungle? He takes a few trees out, or a few shrubs, or he clears a patch to build a jacal and plant some corn and beans or a few coffee trees. If man forgets that patch for but three months, it is no longer his; the jungle has taken it back. Man comes, man goes, the jungle stays on. If man does not fight it daily, it devours him.

I walked over to Sleigh, whose hut was only about thirty yards away. He was blowing on the fire and his face was red. The coffee seemed to be ready. It was not good coffee. It was stale, ground weeks, if not months, ago.

'Won't you have a cup?' Sleigh asked the moment he saw me.

'You'd better take some over to the women first, mister, they need it badly, they're breaking down.'

'Okay, if you say so. It's your loss. Never mind, I'll cook another pot and you can have as much as you like of that. The women left two pounds with me. Anyway, I think we need some hot coffee just as badly as others do.'

The girl lying on her petate spread out on the ground and hidden under her mosquito bar, slept soundly. Perhaps Sleigh had told her about the kid. She did not care. He was not hers. She had hers in her arms – and what else was there to worry about? She made no pretence that she might also belong to that great world community of mothers. She was on her own.

'Get those cups, please, and help me carry them over to the women.' Sleigh winked at a box on which were standing seven enamelled cups of different sizes, four of them battered so badly that no enamel was left. Two were leaking, Sleigh explained, and he said the people who used them would have to gulp like hell if they wanted to get some coffee.

'By all means leave two here for us. I don't like to drink coffee out of my hat if I can help it. Let's hoof.'

I took the cups and we returned to the Garcia's. Sleigh put the cups and the pot on the floor, poured coffee, and offered the Garcia woman the first cup. Automatically she drank the hot coffee with one gulp. The pump-master woman and a few others took some sips. None drank the whole cupful, but only part of it, handing the rest to the woman next to her.

The pump-master woman rolled a cigarette. Then she handed the little bag with black tobacco to the Garcia, who also started smoking after rolling her own. She did not sit down, but kept hustling without doing anything definite. The truth was that there was nothing anybody could do now.

After the women had sat around for some time smoking cigarettes or cigars and sipping hot coffee, they felt that they had to get busy. Using old shirts and dresses and bright-coloured rags, they designed coverlets and fancy ribbons to adorn the kid and the coffin in which he was to be laid.

Sleigh winked at me, seeming to feel out of place now, as I did too. So we went back to his hut.

There we sat near the smoking little tin bottle which was his lamp. I blinked at the fire on the hearth, on which had been set an old enamelled pot full of water to make fresh coffee.

'Listen, Sleigh, where do you get the water you consume in your household?'

He eyed me as if he had not heard me well.

'Yes, I mean the water you have in that bucket.'

'Well, my eyes, such a question! That water? I guess it's big enough for you to see where the water came from.'

'You don't mean to tell me that you get the water out of that river?' I repeated the question, spoke very clearly, because I saw him staring at me as if he doubted my sanity.

'And what do you think? You don't expect me or anybody here to order water in sealed beer-bottles from Kansas City or by air mail from Yosemite Valley, do you? You shouldn't ask such a dumb question because I always believed you were a guy with some brains – sometimes, I mean, not always. Don't misunderstand me. Look here, wise guy, when I met you the first time down at that stinking pool in the jungle where I had to stick you up to save my skin from a jungle-mad greeny, didn't I see you lap up that stinking water as if it were ice-cold beer, or did I? That time you didn't ask who had spit in it or what mule had let go into it only half an hour before. You drank it all right, and you were pretty happy to have found that muddy hole with some water still in it!'

'All right, all right, you win. But now how about the water for our coffee out of that river?'

He grinned at me. 'All the water you have drunk since you came here was from the river. You don't expect me to boil the water first or, as you would call it, deseenfaict it before we drink it? Don't make me laugh.'

'You know pretty well what I'm talking about. I'm not referring to the water I drank yesterday or today. I'm talking of the water in which only a few hours ago and only a hundred or a hundred and fifty yards from here that kid was drowned.'

'And what of it? Was that kid poison or what? His mother drank the coffee we brought, didn't she? And she liked the coffee, didn't she? Well, she didn't ask me that damn foolish question of yours – where I got the water for the coffee she drank! She knew what water that coffee was made of, and if she, the mother, can drink the coffee, you aren't too good to criticize it. We're thankful to the Lord for giving it to us and that we have water all the year round, while there are hundreds of thousands of families in this republic who have no water for months and have to leave their homes and fields in search of it, taking along all their chickens and goats and what have you.'

Sleigh was right. He might not be interested in reading a full column in a newspaper at one sitting, but he was right. I should not have thought of that little spongy body and of the blood dripping out of his mouth, his nose, and his skull.

After a long silence Sleigh said: 'God, I say all this doesn't interest me a damn bit. Water is water, and as long as I can drink it without getting cramps in my belly, I consider it good water and I thank God for it, if He wants me to, even on my knees. No, it isn't that. What interests me about that water is quite another thing. What I mean is that board with the candle on it. That's what got me shivering all over. I'm still not feeling very comfortable along my spine, frankly speaking. It's a remarkable thing, that board and the candle on it. My woman has told me about it before. They also do it where she comes from. She belongs to another region and another sort of people or what you may call another tribe. But they do it just like here. And I tell you, man, that candle always finds the drowned.'

'Always?'

'Always, that's what I say. My wife has told me that the board can even sail upstream against a very strong current if the drowned man lies in that direction.'

'I doubt that and nobody can make me believe it.' I meant it. 'No Indian can do anything more than we can do, and no Indian knows more than we. No coloured man, no man of any other race, no Chinese, no Hindu, no Tibetan can perform miracles we cannot perform. That's all nonsense. We think other races mysterious only because we don't understand their language well enough and we don't understand their customs and their ways of living and doing things. It's because of this lack of understanding them that we believe them capable of performing all sorts of miracles and mysterious acts. I personally have found out that on a long march through the jungle or the bush I can stand thirst and hunger just as easy as my Indian boys, and many times even better.'

'That may be so. Anyway, it has little if anything to do with what I'm talking about,' Sleigh said. 'I've got my experiences too, and as far as I know, you are right in what you speak about. We've got more energy, or, better, more strong will – still better, we've got a better-trained will than the primitive. These people don't think it worth while to have a strong will. It's only we, who want to exploit them, who wish to train their wills and energies so that we can enslave them easier and get better workers and force them into the trap of installment slavery so that they are never free and have to do our bidding because we've got the better-trained will and energy. But to come back to the point, you'll admit that there are Indians who let themselves be bitten by a rattler half a dozen times, or let themselves be stung by scorpions or what have you, and it doesn't do them any harm. On the other hand if a rattler bites you or the red scorpion gets you, there is a dead guy in less than twenty hours.'

'Not every one of them is immune against such poisons. I've seen Indians die of snake-bites as quickly and surely as any white man.'

'Right. That's because not every one of them knows the proper medicine.'

'Exactly. That's just it. If we knew the proper medicine we

would be as immune as some of them are or pretend to be. And you know that they die from calenture and other fevers and diseases in most cases quicker than a white man who just takes ordinary care of himself.'

Sleigh nodded pensively. 'Why not, I ask. Why not? They're humans, or ain't they? So they have to die somehow or other.' He stood up, went to the fire, stirred it up, blew at it, and pushed the pot closer to the flames.

Having sat down again, he said: 'All right, all right, if you wish to insist that no mysterious and hidden powers have worked in this particular case – I mean powers and mysteries which only the natives know about and can command – then perhaps you can explain why that board sailed to the kid and actually found him where no man had looked.'

'I admit I don't know. Not yet. Perhaps I can find an explanation some time later. I have to think it over. I only deny any mystery whatever behind it. It is absolutely natural, the whole thing. So far I don't even know in which direction to go to find out the truth.'

While vaguely thinking about where I could find an explanation of how the board was made to sail towards the body, there came to my mind another method by which a drowned man could be found, which I remembered having seen once back home in the States.

So I said: 'Look here, Sleigh, I'll tell you that we are not so much dumber than the Indians. I remember a time, when I was a boy, that a drowned man was found in a way which at first looked very mysterious to me. Later, however, when I had time to think it over, I found the explanation. It seems a man had drowned in a lake when fishing. His canoe had turned over. The lake was searched for two days and the body could not be found. So on the third day cans filled with dynamite were let down in the lake and blown up. The body soon came to the surface. I still remember that every-body talked of supernatural powers which had been at work to give the body back to his family for a Christian burial. The minister didn't overlook the chance to mention it in church, telling the congregation that the finding of the body was the visible result of the ardent prayers of the bereaved family and that the mighty and merciful hand of the Lord could easily be seen in that mysterious occurrence. The people explained it in a different way. They said that the lake likes to be quiet and calm, so when it is stirred up violently, it will immediately spit out the body to get back to its quiet condition. When I became older I learned the truth. Any drowned human or animal body, even a dead fish if it is big enough, will and must come to the surface sooner or later, sometimes inside of twenty-four hours, though sometimes it may take three days. But if that body is held down by water plants or shrubs or by heavy clothing, or if it is stuck in the mud, it cannot come up. In that case if the bottom of the lake is stirred up by a bomb, the body is freed and comes up.'

'Well,' Sleigh said, 'there is no mystery about that. Anyone can see that. I could have told you so before you explained it. Dynamite will blow up anything under heaven, even huge mountains and rock, so why not a human body? Don't tell me bedtime stories. In this case here, man, it won't be so easy for you to explain why that board sailed to the kid as if a captain were sitting on it. And you may believe me, Gales, I've lived long enough among these natives – now a generation, I would say – and I've seen things, my God, remarkable things and strange things which no professor of any American or even Bolshevik college could ever explain, no matter how smart and learned he may say he is. I won't tell you all the things I've seen here. It would be a waste of time, since you wouldn't believe any of them, as I know you don't believe in anything. You are one of the wise guys. Why, I'm sure you don't even believe in ghosts. I do and I could tell you lots about them. But what's the use with a guy like you? The mother of my woman can speak with her dead relatives. What do you say now? – It's no use. Forget it. Want another cup of coffee? Help yourself. There's plenty of it.'

He was right, Sleigh was. It was no use discussing such things with him. He had been living too long with these people and so he had accepted all their beliefs. He believed anything strange he saw or heard of, the same way the Indians did. He wanted to believe them and he never tried to find any sort of natural explanation. That was why such arguments with him moved in a circle and never got beyond. The fact is I was not interested in explaining what I had seen that night. All the events were clear to me. No mystery of any sort. I was under no spell and there was no auto-suggestion. I was not even sleepy or tired. I was fully awake and my mind was fresh. Of course I had no witness. Sleigh was no witness. His criticisms, as far as he criticized anything at all, did not count when dealing with affairs in which Indians were the actors. He thought all Indians possessed mysterious powers and great knowledge of the supernatural. He believed everything they told him or that he heard from his wife. He might doubt the virginity of the

Lord's mother, but he never doubted the beliefs of the Indians.

Perhaps it was the environment. Perhaps it was his unshakable faith. I was surprised to find myself beginning to dodge an explanation and I felt a certain comfort in not trying to think things through to the end. And why should I not have let the whole matter rest? One lives easier, happier, more in harmony with the universe, if one does not work one's brain continually about things of which the explanations and analyses cannot make us any happier, usually not even richer, if it is riches we are after. Take life as it is. Here in the jungle, perhaps all over the world, that is the whole meaning of life. What else do you want? What else do you expect? Anything else is negation of life and it is nonsense besides. It is the nonsense out of which grow every heartache, every grief, every evil in the world.

25

Looking up, I saw that Sleigh had left the hut and that he had taken with him the little lamp.

In front of me, on the creaking wicker chair that was so old and shaky that it was sheer wonder how anybody could sit on it without breaking through, sat Perez, the Indian who had fished the kid out of the water. How he had come to be sitting there so suddenly, so unexpectedly, I did not know. I must have been dreaming or asleep while trying to make the world a better place to live in happily. My first impression was that by some magic Sleigh had been changed into Perez.

'Listen, Perez, you promised me two yellowhoods, two young ones, this morning. When do I get them?'

'I haven't been in the bush for some time. I won't go next week either. No time, you know, mister.' He was sitting with his legs spread wide apart and his hands dangling down between them.

'Why don't you go in the bush, Señor Perez? Don't you burn charcoal any more?'

'Well, now see here, mister, it's this way. The gringo that is living up there on the hill where the best trees for charcoal are to be had and where I know the finest yellowhoods you've ever seen in all your life are nesting, well, that goddamned gringo, may he go straight to hell, well, he says, that liar says, that I've stolen one of his mules. That's a lie. It's the biggest lie I've ever heard in all my life. And he says that I'm a damned bandit and a bandolero and a cabrón too and that my poor mother is a damned bitch, that's what he says, and he calls himself an educated gringo that has gone to school. But the worst of it, I tell you, mister, is that I, poor Indian as I am, I can do nothing against him, absolutely nothing. I have to suffer it. So you see here, señor, there is no chance to get you the two yellowhoods I promised you, which would learn to speak in no time. That's why I told you that redhoods are no good. It must be yellowhoods. But it's a big damned lie. I am no bandit. I can swear it.'

'I don't think you're a bandit, Señor Perez, and I don't believe that you ever stole a mule.'

'That's the naked truth, mister. And I can see that you are an educated caballero. I can swear by the Most Holy Virgin in heaven and by the Holy Child also that I know nothing of a stolen mule. If I were a bandit, I tell you, I'd go to hell myself and of my own free will. That gringo up there, he isn't honest. He says he has seen the tracks of my feet right beside those of his mule, which he can recognize, so he says, by the iron shoes, and he says he has seen my tracks and those of my mule right together outside the fence of his pasture and he says he has followed these tracks – I don't know where to, because he doesn't say. Never in all my life did I ever go where he says he has seen my huaraches beside the irons of his mule. How do I know who has stolen his mule? It's none of my business.'

'Well, Perez, I've been told that Mister Erskin has said the mule he lost is worth around two hundred and fifty pesos.'

'Bueno, señor, right there you can see what sort of liar that gringo is. Do you know what I've been offered for that mule? Forty pesos I've been offered, and not a single red centavito more have I been paid for that mule by those miserable robbers down there in Llerra. This I swear is the truth. And then this gringo tells the world the mule is worth two hundred and fifty pesos in cold cash and en efectivo. That's the kind of gringos we have around here, who we have to suffer humiliation from. I can only laugh, that's the only thing I can do. And now, to make things still worse, that Americano comes along and says I've stolen his mule. You must admit that's no way to treat poor inoffensive people like us, and in our own country too. But what can we do? Nothing. Just suffer. That's what we can do.'

While he was sitting before me and talking, I could barely see him, because all the light we now had in the hut was the fire on the hearth. And that was not much.

Perez rose, went to the fire, and lit the cigarette he had been rolling while telling me the story of the stolen mule.

Sleigh returned with the little tin bottle lamp and an earthen pot filled with fresh milk.

'The cow has come home at last,' he said on entering. 'The damned devil may know where that poor animal has been all night.'

From a soiled paper bag he dug out coffee with his bare hand, which was dirty from handling the cows. Two handfuls of coffee he threw into the boiling water. The coffee foamed and ran over into the fire, which sizzled angrily. He took hold of the pot with a rag and set it down on the floor beside us.

'You'll get my cup in a minute,' he said to Perez.

'That's all right by me, don't bother,' the Indian answered.

'Listen, Perez, was that kid lying flat on the bottom or what was his position?' Sleigh asked.

'No, he wasn't exactly at the bottom. He didn't even touch the bottom as far as I could make out. His feet and hands were stuck in water shrubs. He was, in a way, sitting in the shrubs. If you ask me, I don't believe he would ever have come up if we hadn't dragged him out. The plants held him like the many arms of an ugly monster.'

'How did you know, Perez, that the kid was stuck just at that place and in no other?' I asked.

'That was very easy to know,' he said. 'There was no mystery about that. The light was standing right above him. You could see that for yourself. Anyone could have fished him out after the light had settled over him.'

'Yes, I saw the light standing there above him. Only the question is, how did the light know he was there?'

'Nothing simpler than that, mister. The kid was calling the light to come to him and show us the way. So the light had to obey, and it came. There is nothing strange about that. It's quite natural. Anyone can see that.'

Sleigh laughed right out. 'Well, there you heard it with your own ears. Are you satisfied now?' He grinned at me. 'Any more foolish questions now? I told you so before. It's all quite natural. Nothing strange about it. That's the whole mystery. In fact, there is no mystery at all. Here the Indians can't practise any more magic than you can or me. The kid calls the light and the light has to obey orders and goes to him. Everything is as clear and bright as sunlight. That's all natural. That's what I told you all the time.'

No use. So I spoke again to the man who seemed still to be the saner of the two. 'Well, Perez, now what about the two young yellowhoods?'

'I don't go up in the bush. Besides there would be no reason for going there now. They started to sit only a few days ago. I know it. A friend who had been up there told me. Why should I crawl through that damn thorny thicket if I can't get any. Because there are none to be had just at this time of the year. Two months later it will be easy and you can have a half-dozen if you wish.'

He had his coffee now and was sipping it slowly like a critical connoisseur of drinks. Sleigh poured me another cup and took the rest of the pot over to the Garcia's party.

After a short while he returned, went to the hearth, and lit a new cigarette. Then he squatted Indian fashion on the floor facing Perez and me, who were sitting on his rotten wicker chairs.

The baby of the girl under the mosquito bar whined softly. From the movement of the bar and by the gleam of the fire I saw the girl giving her baby a drink. Before the baby was satisfied, while he was still suckling, the girl snored again so heavily that the hut trembled.

Both Perez and Sleigh got sleepy, let their heads drop upon their chests, and blinked into emptiness. In his sleep Sleigh sensed that his cigarette had gone out. He rose swaying as if he were drunk and walked in a shuffling manner to the hearth. His cigarette again lit, he leaned against a post and dozed off again.

He slept only a few minutes. He woke up and walked to the door. Looking up to the sky, which had begun to clear and in which a few stars could be seen now, he said: 'It is just past two. I thought it later.'

I looked at my watch and said: 'Twenty past.'

'I'll have to go to milk the cows now or they'll get restless and start for the prairie. Perez, are you coming with me?'

'Of course, vamonos!' He was so fast asleep that his cigarette had dropped without his being aware of it. Now he looked for it, lit it, and followed Sleigh, who, with a bucket in one hand, had already walked off to the corral.

He shouted back: 'Hey, Gales, why don't you turn in for a coupla hours? You must be dog-tired and it will surely do you lots of good. Don't you bother about me, man, I've got to get busy with them cows, you know. Hi, Perez, where are you? Are you coming?'

Perez, just leaving the hut, said: 'Now, don't you holler, amigo. Here I am, always on the spot, just call on me for any trouble. Who, por la Santisima, put that damned log right in my way? Anyone could break his neck here, what with all sorts of sticks, logs, and stones lying about.'

26

As Perez had taken the little lamp with him, the hut was dark once more. A few forlorn embers gleamed on the hearth.

I was left alone and since I did not know what better I could do, I groped my way towards the corner where the bed I had slept in last night and the night before was. It wasn't a bed in the true sense of the word. It was more like a corrupted hammock.

The bed in which Sleigh and his wife slept was shoved against one wall. It was similar to the one the Garcias had, but the network was made more carefully and the mattress consisted of a softer fibre. The corner in which the family bed stood was separated from the main room by a wall of sticks six feet high. The sticks which formed that wall were so far apart that one could put his finger between them. To get some privacy Sleigh's woman had put up on this wall a few pieces of threadbare cotton goods.

Well, I was tired. I took off my boots, unfastened my belt, and, sailor fashion, crawled into that hammock, which only the greedy landlady of a cheap boardinghouse would call a cot.

Bridges, rivers without a downstream current, mule-drivers yelling for more coffee, alligators, asthmatic pumps which cough, queens of England waving a ragged handkerchief, bodies of little babies, naked Indians (some of them armless), black-haired heads popping out of prairie grass, lighted candles swimming under water like fish, cows with cougars on their necks, mouth-organs which play by themselves nailed to bridge posts, bandits riding on white burros, a picture of the Holy Virgin singing on a fiddle, Canada vanished from the earth and leaving mere emptiness behind, a few blurred lines from a Kansas City paper printed in Texas on a goat ranch, an oil well cemented with a splash in the water caused by a jumping bean, a girl with flowers in her hair dancing with a steel spring mattress which belongs to the president, a young woman with wreaths of fire-red flowers wound around her knees bent in an awkward position and crying: 'No, no, I won't, I won't, don't you dare, no, no, I say no and no,' battered enamelled cups without bottoms but full of hot coffee and flying across a white table on which a sailor suit is weeping bitterly, a five-gallon hat walking through the night with no face under it – no, to hell with it, I could not sleep. Maybe it was the coffee. My head whirled. Yet I was as tired as a coal-heaver on a death ship. At last I dozed off, but not for long and I saw Mr Erskin lying at the bottom of the river moving his hands and shouting: 'Bring me a lantern which will obey orders, a lantern, please, a lantern for all my mules!' The water was very deep, twenty feet past two in the morning, but still I could see him because the water was lighted at the bottom. I didn't know Mr Erskin, I had never seen him, yet I knew it was he who sat on eggs and hatched grown-up yellowhoods which sang a song about oilmen who made cigars out of cement. Nobody but me could see Mr Erskin lying in the water and I shouted to the people: 'There are two little American boots in the river.' Nobody listened and they said: 'We'd better put a crown on his head and say it is a sceptre of the Toltecs.' Chinamen were coming and there was an explosion in the lake and a coffee pot drowned in a sack half filled with corn-cobs and held fast by alligators jumped high up in the air and a man dropped out of the pitch-dark clouds. He was an aviator milking a cow which had come home late and drunk, telling a little tin bottle lamp that two tigers and two lions went to a dance with the musicians stuck deep in the mud. And again dynamite was thrown in the lake and it exploded with a hundred reverberations.

It was this explosion of dynamite that awoke me. There was another explosion, and still another and another. I was fully awake now and I heard shots being fired outside the hut.

I got up and put my boots on. There was no longer any hope of getting some sleep.

It was still night. Peeping through the wall, I saw the little flame of the tin lamp by the corral where Sleigh was milking the cows and Perez, holding the lamp, squatted beside him. I could hear their voices, although I could not understand what they were talking about.

Boots on and belt fastened, I went to the door.

At the Garcia's yard there was a huge bonfire throwing its flames high up into the air. By this light I saw a score of Indians dismounting from their horses and firing their guns at the dark sky.

I went closer to see what was up.

The news of the kid's disappearance had already travelled more than ten miles in every direction, in spite of the night, in spite of the fact that the nearest telephone was a hundred miles from here. Although old man Garcia was one of the poorest Indians of the region, he was beloved by all, for some reason or other. Therefore as soon as the people had heard the news, they had left their beds and homes and come to offer their help. So far they knew only that the boy was missing. Nevertheless they had all brought fireworks to be used in the event that the kid should be found dead.

Among these Indians it is customary to ignite heaps of fireworks if a child dies, so that the angels in heaven will take notice that a new angelito is on his way up. Fireworks burnt at the death of an adult had the opposite consequences; that is to say, on hearing the fireworks the devil would wait close by the gate and look the newcomer over to see whether he might not be on his list. If it is a child, the angels, aroused by the fireworks, meet him half-way; and it does not matter whether the devil is at the gate, because he can do nothing with a child; an innocent child is not allowed to be registered on the devil's list, for he is still without sin.

The fireworks which had been brought were received and taken care of by the second brother, the half-wit. From this moment on he no longer had any interest in anything but the fireworks. He had long ago ceased to weep. For him the more joyful part of the funeral had now come.

The newly arrived had already heard that the kid had been found. One after another, with their hats off, they entered the hut to look at the kid and say a few consoling words to his mother. While in fact not much interested in how it happened, every one of them asked the mother to tell the story. Not from curiosity. Very wise men, they merely asked the mother in order to get her mind off the body.

Once she had started, the Garcia liked to tell the story from the very beginning. She told it over and over again, and always with the same words and with the same tone of voice and with the same emotions displayed at the same episode. By being repeated so often, it became more and more an ordinary story of everyday life. Even the emotions at the various points in her tale got to be almost like those of a bad actress, the oftener she recited the narrative. She herself began to feel a certain distance from the event. She reached a point where she could tell it like a story she had heard from somebody else. It became impersonal to her. Her emotions were getting dull and leaving her heart and soul clearer every minute. Finally, when she was telling it for the twentieth time, she heard her own words sound like mere gossip.

She was beginning to take leave of her baby, without realizing it, at this moment.

She looked at him. To her astonishment she imagined that the boy lying dead on the table was not her baby any more. Her Carlosito was an active, lively little boy, forever talking and shouting and full of all sorts of mischief, who had to be spanked twice every day to keep him sensible and save him from himself. He was restless from the minute he opened his eyes in the morning until he closed them at night. That lump of ugly, clammy flesh with the smashed-in jaw and its arms held stiff across its chest, that could not be her baby. That had to be somebody else's baby, perhaps the baby she was just talking about. Hers wasn't so ugly. Everyone had told her how beautiful her Carlos was, one of the finest-looking kids for twenty miles around. The sailor suit, the crown, the sceptre had made him a stranger to her. God knows where that child had come from. 'What is he doing in my house, anyway?' she asked herself.

She wept now. And while she wept she realized, in sudden bewilderment, that she no longer wept only about her baby. She was now weeping about herself more than about the kid. She believed herself badly treated by fate, and unconsciously she began to hate many of the women present simply because they had babies at their breasts. She lamented the sad fact that she no longer had a child on whom she could heap her motherly love.

All these thoughts were running wild in her mind while her mouth was telling the story that was stale from so much repeating. But through her thinking and brooding and analyzing in her primitive manner her thoughts, emotions, pains, and heartaches, she came to realize that she was not at all an exception. She looked around and noted the presence of seven other women who she knew had also lost children as dear to them as her baby had been to her. So she became conscious of the fact that she was but an average mother and not a mother selected by fate to suffer something extraordinary. What she suffered tonight, thousands, millions of mothers had suffered before her, a thousand were suffering the same in this very hour, and thousands of millions of mothers would suffer when she herself would again be happy.

Perhaps it was because she was so very tired, so exhausted, from worry, pain, and weeping and yelling, that she began to be herself once more.

27

The Garcia's front yard was a sandy square open on two sides, while the other two were fenced in by thorny bushes. The hut was framed by a row of old rusty kerosene cans and broken vessels filled with earth in which flowers had been planted, some of which were now in full bloom. That conglomeration of old cans and potsherds with flowers in them was considered the Garcia's garden. Close to the hut on one side there was a wild chile shrub which daily provided the family with green pepper. Because there were so many visitors present, the bushes, thorny shrubs, and magueys were decorated with hats, diapers, shirts, rags, and blankets.

The whole place looked like a camp. Men, women, and children were sleeping on the ground or just dozing. Some were lying on mats, others on blankets, but most of them on the bare ground. Some people had put up mosquito bars, which looked like little tents. Bits of music played on mouth-organs fluttered about. The place was lighted by torches and campfires. There were also a few small lanterns and half a dozen of the usual open tin lamps.

Many boys were helping the half-witted son shoot off the firecrackers. No one was allowed to shoot them off but himself. The others were only permitted to stir up the fire and try out the firecrackers which had failed to go off the first time. The stepson's great day had come at last. He felt like a dictator among the boys who had to humiliate themselves before him to get the privilege of firing one occasionally. Two days later he would get his reward by being beaten up by all those whom he now refused a share in the game.

Many of the visitors had brought bottles of mescal, that very hard brandy distilled of mescal juice and tasting like rubbing alcohol blended with unrefined kerosene. Sometimes this brandy travels under the name of tequila; at other times it is called aguardiente, then again comiteco, also cuervo, or viuda, in some parts herradura, but whatever its name, it is always the same stuff.

The bottle went from mouth to mouth. One man, obviously with a heart of gold, took a bottle, entered the hut, removed his hat, and offered it to the Garcia woman. She looked at it, but she did not hesitate long. She took a shot of it that was equal to no less than three fingers of a hard-working peasant. Any sane white man who would whip into his belly a portion like the one the Garcia lashed down her throat, would be floored as if he'd been clubbed.

Among the Indians who arrived at this moment there was a very poor peasant. He was practically in rags, but they were clean. His horse had no saddle but a bast mat. He entered the hut with the others. He ran his eyes over the kid, then went up to the mother and told her how beautiful the kid was and how prettily dressed, like the Holy Child of the Madre Santisima in church, and that he was positive that the kid was already with the angels, so sweet did he look. The Garcia smiled proudly, straightened her whole body, and thanked him and the other men for their admiration and praise.

When that poor peasant came out of the hut, he looked around and found a bench that was not occupied at the moment. He sat down and drew out an old book which looked like a prayer book. For a few minutes he leafed through it as if to find the right page. Then he began to sing.

Unable to read, he knew by heart all the words he sang. He looked into the book only because he had seen people in church looking into such a book when they sang.

Most stanzas he repeated two, three, or even four times before he went on to the next. Perhaps these were the stanzas he liked or knew best. Whenever he began a stanza that was known by the people, many men and practically all the women who were awake fell in and sang with him.

Now he sang the second stanza and all the women inside the hut, including the pump-master woman, took up the song, at first hesitatingly but after a while with full voices. At times only one man sang because the others were rolling a new cigarette or greas-

588

ing their throats from the bottle. Some got tired of singing and talked on without being disturbed by those who preferred the song.

The ragged peasant, however, sang all the time. He refused to take a swallow from the bottle which was offered him every once in a while. He was an agrarista and thought himself a communist. In his hut in the little village where he lived he had a little house-altar with a picture of the Holy Virgin in the middle and on one side a picture of Saint John and on the other side a little picture of Lenin, who he believed sat next to the throne of the Lord like Saint John and all the other saints. His demands from communism, like those of all the other agraristas in the republic, would be fully satisfied the moment he was given from ten to twenty acres of fairly good land free and with the assurance that it would not be taken away from him or his family. He was the kind who makes you wise about politics and makes you believe that communism can be boiled down to one simple formula: give men food, plenty of it, and assure them that they will always have a job. Keep the bellies well filled and provide lots of movies, admission one cent, and there will be no more preaching from soap boxes and never any talk about a revolution.

The singer was paid by no one. He sang out of pure love for the bereaved mother, to help her get over her loss without too many scars. The kid would be buried without the blessings of a priest and without a death certificate from a doctor. Priest and doctor cost money. Even if all the mourners contributed half the money they possessed they could not raise enough to meet such expenses. Moreover the burial could not wait two days. Despite the fact that the night was cool, the body had already started to decompose.

The agrarista sang only church hymns. But nobody who knew Roman Catholic hymns would ever think that these songs were really church hymns. Perhaps Catholics used to sing that way when the first monks came wandering through these jungles to bring the true faith to the poor pagans of the Americas. But whatever the original tunes might have been like, they had since been blended with worldly songs, including American dance melodies of more recent times. Once a year, or once in two years, the people might go to church and listen to a real hymn, and a little of it would remain in their memory. And then there were the dances in the settlements and villages where the musicians brought new tunes which had been picked up in the nearest large town, where they were considered the latest hits just arrived from Broadway, while in fact in New York no one could remember them any more, because they must have been crooned about the time when the best-dressed American was running for mayor. And so here in the jungle after each dance new tunes were added and the former ones were dropped as obsolete. Moreover, the uneducated Indian couldn't and wouldn't sing the way we think songs should be sung. In all their songs there was a certain pagan motif and frequently an almost savage one, which seemed to be a heritage from their forebears. In their hymns, sung without any accompaniment, save perhaps the beating of high drums and the plaintive sound of a home-made clarinet, this strange native motif was often so strong that it carried the whole tune and left hardly ten notes of the original hymn.

This funeral singer was known far and wide in the whole jungle region. He was considered the best of his kind and everybody admired him. He was their movie star and radio crooner all in one, because on other occasions, at weddings or at Saints'-day festivals, he sang corridos – that is, native ballads. He could not sing corridos as well as the professionals who visit the ferias and who bring to the people who cannot read newspapers the news of the latest political events and love tragedies in the form of ballads sung in the open places. As a funeral singer, however, this agrarista was far better than any of the corrido singers.

The greatest ambition of all the boys in that jungle region was to become a railroad man, as this was the highest position in the world they could think of and was certainly far higher than working for an oil company. But when the agrarista came and sang his hymns the boys changed their ambition and wished to be nothing better than a funeral singer as great and as famous as the agrarista.

When the first stanza had started, the Garcia, in her hut, screamed as if she were going mad. The women around her took her in their arms and kissed her. She grew quiet and only sobbed after a while. But when other men and women joined the singer and the whole yard was filled with the voices of the visitors, she was again overwhelmed by her grief. She fell into a terrible rage and with both her fists she hammered her skull. Grasping her hair, she pulled it so fiercely that the scalp seemed about to be torn off. Suddenly she threw the whole weight of her body upon the table, which answered with threatening cracking sounds. Two men jumped close and held the legs of the table straight. Over and over again she threw her body upon her baby. Had he been alive she would have crushed his ribs, so violent was her outburst. And she yelled: 'Chico mio, my little beloved! My sweet only baby! Why?

590

Why did you go and leave your poor mother alone? Why? Why? Oh, Holy Mother of the Lord, why did you do this to me? Why? Why?' Whereupon she began to swear in the most horrible manner, cursing all the saints in heaven and the devil in hell. With her fists she hammered upon the kid's chest as if she meant to punish him for what he had done to her. When she did this a man seized her, dragged her back from the table, pushed back her head so that her mouth was straight up, and with his other hand grabbed a mescal-bottle. He forced the mouth of the bottle between her teeth, pushing the bottle in so that she could not turn away from it. She refused to take the brandy and struggled against both man and bottle. But another man went behind her and pressed her arms down, so that now she was defenceless. After that she got her mouth so full of that aguardiente that she could not help swallowing it in big gulps. The man did not let go until the bottle was nearly empty.

This medicine, however, was of little use. The woman didn't even get dull from the drink. And whenever she again became aware of the people singing hymns, she again got wild.

The women inside the hut could no longer resist the temptation to sing also, and so they fell in with the crowd singing in the yard. That caused the Garcia to shriek more than ever. Her crying was so loud and penetrating that for many minutes it drowned the voices of the singing women inside. Then she got weak and had to calm down. The women went on singing, considering it their duty to do so whether the mother spoiled the hymns by her yelling or not. The Lord would forgive the mother for her almost sacrilegious behaviour.

By now the mescal which had been poured into the Garcia began to show some effect. She was getting a bit foggy. Stroking back her hair, she glanced around and tried to remember what had happened. With blank eyes she looked at the women and apparently wondered what these people were doing here, how they came to be here, and what they wanted. She made a gesture as if she were going to say: 'Out of here, all of you! Get out of my house and leave me alone!' Then she shrugged her shoulders as if to say: 'What do I care? Let them stay here; perhaps they have no place to go while it is still night.' She turned to the table and gazed at the body, and then she said: 'Who is that kid, anyway?' The women stopped singing.

Hardly had she spoken thus when her whole body jerked. She blew her nose with a gesture of anger. Now she said in a very low voice: 'Oh, my little baby, why didn't you wait for me? We would have crossed the bridge all right had you only waited and let me take you by your hand.'

She looked at the women, who had stopped singing, and said: 'It's in fun, isn't it? Say it's all in fun, please say it.' No one answered.

The pump-master woman rose from her knees, took the Garcia woman in her arms, kissed her, and murmured: 'Don't be that way, Carmelita, you'll soon have another one. God will send you one right from heaven.'

Through her sobs the Garcia answered: 'Don't say so, woman, I never wish to have another one in all my life. I'll kill it before it ever comes to light.' She wept bitterly and said to the pump-master woman: 'Forgive me, comadre, I didn't mean to say that. You see, here in my heart there is so much pain. I really don't know what I am saying. The kid pained me so much when he came, and now it pains a hundred thousand times more when he goes. Forgive me, please. Tomorrow it will be different. It's only now, tonight, that I can't get over it. Only a few hours ago he was shouting and laughing and running, and now look what is left of him. And only a few hours.' She sobbed on the breast of the pump-master woman.

If the singing stopped for a while, the cracking of the fireworks outside reminded the Garcia anew that the kid was awaited by the angels. She never got a chance to forget.

The singing, when it was a new entertainment, had aroused the people, but now it had lost its attraction; everyone got sleepier than before. Many threw themselves flat on the ground. Others squatted, embraced their knees, and put their heads on them and then fell asleep immediately. A few men and women stayed awake, not because they were not sleepy but because there was still something left in the bottles – and it is an old saying that he who sleeps cannot drink.

Inside the hut the women were no less weary and sleepy than the people in the yard. Two women had already taken possession of the corrupted shakedown which the Garcias called their bed. Fully dressed, they lay there snoring like soldiers after a battle.

The little fire on the floor of the hut smouldered lazily. If it had been a cat it would surely have yawned. A few pots were standing close to it. Nobody cared what they were for, what was in them, or who had set them by the fire. Nobody asked. Indeed, nobody seemed to be interested in anything. Sleep, or at least the desire to sleep, ruled the scene.

28

During the past half-hour the agrarista had sung with difficulty. He had become hoarse. All who were still awake shuffled about and tried to sneak out of the hut without hurting the Garcia's feelings. Some were talking just to keep awake.

The agrarista and the men who had come with him entered the hut. They looked at the kid for the last time. They shook hands with the mother and told her again how sorry they were and then praised her for being so brave.

The Garcia said to each one of them: 'Muchas, muchas gracias, señor! Vaya con Dios! The Lord be with you on your way home! I thank you for your visit and for the beautiful songs you have sung in honour of my baby. Adiós, señores!'

When the last of these men had gone, the Garcia remained standing limply and stared vacantly at the door. The men went to their horses and, with many loud adioses, rode off. The Garcia still gazed after them.

The misty gown of the new day slowly descended upon the earth. Millions of pearls gleamed on the grass, on the leaves of the trees, and in the folds of the flowers, all of which were awaiting the kiss of the sun. Then the morning breeze dissolved the mist, and the new day was born.

The Garcia shivered in the cool morning wind. She went to the door and ran her eyes over the crowd sleeping in the yard. She felt alone and forgotten.

A golden spark leaped into the air from beyond the prairie. It seemed but a moment later that the sun rose over the jungle.

The Garcia turned around and saw that her hut was filled with daylight, in which the smoking, flickering candles looked ghostly. Although the daylight entered the hut only through the open door, it changed the whole interior, leaving nothing in it untouched.

The light of the few candles had been unable to reach the corners of the hut and so everything which otherwise would have looked

593

ugly had been mercifully hidden. The home had not been without a certain beauty – like that of a very poor chapel – but the daylight destroyed the illusion. The hut now looked gloomy and unpleasant.

The Garcia's face was haggard and swollen from so much weeping; her eyes were dry, dull, and inflamed and they were sunk in deep black hollows. She looked like a wax mask carved by an insane sculptor. She was still wearing her green gauze dress. The flowers at her girdle were torn and withered. The flowers in her hair had fallen long before. At night the dress had seemed quite becoming, but now it looked as if it did not belong to her. It only followed her, but was not worn by her. The woman was still the mother of the kid, but the dress no longer covered the mother. It was a stained, ugly corpse of a dress which trailed after her wherever she went.

The kid, who had been a very beautiful sight at night, was now an ordinary carcass – a carcass dressed up in a monkey suit. His mouth was green, and matter was running out of his smashed jaw. The strings which held his hands together were cutting deep scars into his wrists. His little folded hands looked as if they had been tied together by a professional tormentor.

The rays of the sun came like spears through the sticks of the walls.

The Garcia saw the rays touch the body. For the first time she now saw what all the others had seen long ago, that her baby was gone, was no longer with her in the hut. The little heap of flesh lying on the table could no longer be kissed. The morning breeze, blowing through the walls and coming in through the door, brought the odour of death to her nostrils. She shuddered, turned away from her child, and moaned in despair.

When she looked at him again she noticed that big green flies were beginning to settle on the body. She hurried to pick up a piece of cloth to cover the little face. But after that she could look no more at her child.

Luckily for her, she had no time to sit down and brood over things which could not be undone. For with the new day a great number of new visitors had arrived and more were expected. The news of the drowning and the miraculous discovery of the body had spread. No sooner did the people hear the story than they mounted their burros, mules, or horses and left home to visit the unhappy mother, to tell her that everybody loved her dearly and that whoever had a soul and a heart was weeping with her. Since it was

Sunday it was easy for people to come, and the crowd was growing bigger with every half-hour.

The men dismounted, helped their womenfolk and children off the animals, tied the animals to posts, trees, or shrubs or let them roam on their own, rolled cigarettes, and started talking to the other men.

The women, one after another, entered the hut. Here they greeted the mother, embraced her, kissed her, and then looked at the little body. Their eyes became wet. The Garcia shrieked: 'Why did this have to happen? Why, tell me, why? Isn't there any longer a God in heaven?'

She took the cloth off the face so that the newcomers could look at the kid. Although they were terribly shocked on seeing the ugly face, they suppressed their feelings, and invariably they said: 'He looks beautiful! Such a sweet little angel he is now! Doesn't he look sweet and beautiful?' And the other women answered: 'Yes, indeed, he is a little angel, un angelito muy lindo.'

Many of the women now arriving brought armfuls of flowers; other brought wreaths hastily made of twigs and covered with gold and silver paper. They put the flowers and wreaths aside without mentioning their gifts so as to spare the Garcia the pain of thanking them. These poor people, so very sincere in their sympathies, did not know the custom of the civilized of putting engraved cards on their flowers so that the family would know who gave what and who gave nothing, and so that the names of the mourners might be properly spelled when they were printed in the social columns. Here no one cared who brought flowers or other gifts and who did not. If one did not give something it was because he had nothing to give. But he was honoured just as much as those who had brought things. Whatever the visitors, the mourners, the neighbours did, they did out of pure love for the mother.

'Yes,' repeated a woman, 'yes, it is true he looks beautiful, the little Carlosito does, just like an angel, only with his wings not fully grown yet.' Another one said: 'To tell the truth, I've never in all my life seen such a beautiful little boy.'

The Garcia woman had already heard the praise. But she was a woman even in sorrow; she waited for more praise. She stopped her sobbing, grasped the hands of all the women around her, and said: 'Muchas gracias! O mil, mil gracias for your kindness. You women make me so very happy, very, very happy, thank you ever so much!'

She meant it because she was really grateful for the admiration rendered her dolled-up baby and she accepted the approval as if it were given for something she herself had achieved.

The exclamations of the women were not empty flattery. They praised the kid partly out of an inborn courtesy, but to some extent they felt as they said they did. To them the little prince with the golden crown on his head and the golden sceptre in his hand was something quite beautiful. He reminded them of the crowned little Jesus child held in the arms of His Holy Mother, which they saw in church and knelt before in prayer.

All the visitors were unbelievably poor. The women who had just arrived were barefooted. Their bodies were covered with thin, worn-out cotton dresses that were full of holes. The thorns take no pity on the poverty of an Indian woman who has to ride through the jungle. They wore black gauze shawls on their heads to protect them against the sun.

Most of the women had brought their babies with them. Sitting by the corpse, they pulled down their dresses and gave their babies to drink. At the same time they wept and sobbed. At intervals they interrupted their lamentations to blow their noses and ask the Garcia how it had happened and how the kid had been found.

The Garcia had covered the kid's face right after the last woman had paid him her respects.

Staying in the hut was becoming a real torture as the sun rose higher. The stench of death was making breathing difficult. Two women with child got pale and had to be led out to recover. The smoking candles, the heavy perfume around the masses of flowers which were dying so painfully and which refused to die so soon, the drifting smoke produced by the bonfire outside, the smell of mescal, coffee, and tobacco, and the odour of the many unwashed men and women crowded in that small hut, all this thick, almost suffocating air accumulated under the grass roof and could not drift away. But the people stayed there, out of politeness and out of respect for the suffering mother.

In two hours the morning breeze would cease. After that, until eleven in the morning, there would be not even the slightest bit of wind. By that time the interior of the hut would resemble a furnace in which a carcass had been burned. But whatever happened and no matter how unbearable the air in the hut might become, as long as the Garcia stayed inside, all the others would stay too.

The men who had come with the women and who were still outside had finished their cigarettes. They took their hats off and entered the hut. They came like frightened little boys late for school. One went to the body and took the piece of cloth away from the face. All the men came close, gazed at the corpse, stood around for two minutes, and left again. It appeared they were not sure whether they should shake hands with the mother or ask her how it had happened or talk to her about nothing in particular or keep silent altogether. But the fact was that none was really embarrassed. These people were very seldom or never embarrassed. Their behaviour was determined by one thought only: what to do to make the mother forget her loss. So in this case they had decided not to shake hands with the mother and not to ask questions which they were sure the mother had had to answer a hundred times already and they had also decided not even to tell the mother how beautiful they thought the baby looked. His mother knew that well enough. That was the reason they kept silent, and by so doing they were convinced that they had shown best their deep sympathy for the mother.

Whatever these people did or said, nothing was a cold formula which had been taught them. It all came out of their hearts. Their hearts were speaking, their hearts were ordering them to go on a long trip to console the mother, their hearts were commanding them to be silent when they felt it showed deeper sympathy to be silent. On leaving his host none would say: 'I've had a lovely time,' if he did not feel that way. In such a case he would rather say: 'Sorry, I think I've got to beat it now, for work is waiting back home. I hope to see you soon in my humble house, which is yours and where you're welcome whenever it pleases you to come.'

This knowledge of their good taste and of their delicate tact when meeting their fellow men had come to me bit by bit during the past twelve hours through observing them and taking notice of all their doings and sayings. When I had first come here, I had seen in these people the simple Indian peasants with ordinary courtesy such as one might find all over Spanish America in places where American tourists had never come to ruin the landscapes and try to make natives understand how glorious civilization is and tell them ten times a day how dirty and filthy they are and how badly organized their country is. It seemed that an occasion such as the one I had witnessed was necessary if one wanted to see those people as they really were, to see not only their dirt and their rags, but, what was more, their hearts and souls, the only things in man which count. Radios, Fords, and speed records do not count at all; they are but garbage when it comes to the final balance sheet.

It is religion that makes men love their neighbours and that dries

597

the tears of a mother who has lost her baby and that makes you who have two shirts give one to the poor who has nothing with which to cover his nakedness. Is it religion? Death is usually an occasion for lip religion to show off in all its splendour. And here, where death marched silently into a gay party all set for a merry week-end of dancing, I could not see a glimpse of the white man's great religion. I had heard no prayers so far. Nobody had fingered a rosary. The singing of hymns by the communist agrarista was only very superficially connected with the Catholic religion because his singing had the eternal worldly meaning of good will to all men, and the Holy Virgin was called upon merely to inform her of what was happening, not to come down and help a poor Indian mother out of her sorrows. And it was because religion as we understand it had not entered either the hearts or the inner minds of these people that they could preserve hearts and souls overflowing with kindness and love.

I was sitting on a box a few feet from the door. Whoever came in or went out had plenty of room to pass by without disturbing me in the least. Nevertheless everybody, man, woman, or youngster, who passed stopped in front of me and said: 'With your kind permission, señor!' And only after I had answered: 'Pase!' or 'Es su propio!' would he go out or enter. He did not do so because I was a white man. If an Indian peasant in rags had been sitting on this box, all the people passing by him would just as seriously have asked his permission to do so. To them it was impossible to cut through the breath of a human being without having his permission to do so. Of course, I did the same thing when passing an Indian. Suppose I should be as courteous back home as I was here; everybody would believe I had come home with a tropical disease. Back home I bleat exactly as do all the other sheep. I know it is easier on the nerves if you don't try to lift people up to your own standard and it makes you only yellow in the face or gives you high blood-pressure to insist on reforming people who are convinced that they know better than anybody else what is good for them. One becomes a philosopher by living among people who are not of his own race and who speak a different language. No, no matter what happens, you had better stay firm in the belief that there is no better country in the world than God's own great land of the free and then you will feel fine and be a respected citizen. Aside from the fact that that philosophy actually pays if you know how to handle it right, experience has taught me that travelling educates only those who can be educated just as well by roaming around their own country. By walking thirty miles anywhere in one's home state the man who is open minded will see more and learn more than a thousand others will by running round the world. A trip to a Central American jungle to watch how Indians behave near a bridge won't make you see either the jungle or the bridge or the Indians if you believe that the civilization you were born into is the only one that counts. Go and look around with the idea that everything you learned in school and college is wrong.

29

As I was feeling hungry I went to see what Sleigh was doing.

The girl had long been up. She had ground the boiled corn on the metate, toasted tortillas, cooked black beans, and set the coffee on the fire.

'Coffee isn't ready yet,' Sleigh said the minute he saw me. 'We'll have to wait a quarter of an hour or so. It would be different if my wife was here. Hell, I'm sleepy. Christ, I should say, I am damn sleepy, that's what I am.'

He dozed off. Right away he was awake again and asked me: 'Haven't you seen the boy? I mean that lazy stick that works with me. He has to carry the milk to the store.'

'He is at the fire helping the half-wit along with the fireworks.'

'So that's where he is. I'll kick him in the pants. He knows he has to attend to the milk or it will turn sour in that blazing sun before he gets it to the store.' He rose from his seat and both of us walked back to the Garcia's.

On arriving at the yard we saw Garcia returning from his mysterious trip.

Out of his bast bag dangling from the saddle horn he took a bundle of candles, a package of oily ground coffee, four cones of crude brown sugar, and three quart bottles of mescal. One of the bottles was half empty. Of course, there was a good excuse for that. The way was long, and he was heart-broken, old man Garcia was. So there was nothing to wonder at that he had such brilliance in his eyes. His face was red and had a spongy appearance. He was honest and did not pretend to be sober. Right away the bottle was handed to the friend who was holding the horse while he dismounted. The friend took a shot and then the bottle went the rounds.

When he had arrived at the general store, Garcia had had only a few pesos in his pocket, but because of his sad loss the storekeeper had been willing to charge up what he needed for the funeral. Garcia would have felt humiliated if he had had to celebrate the funeral of his son without mescal, coffee, sugar, and sufficient candles. The storekeeper knew, of course, that while other debts might be difficult to collect, the expenses incurred on account of the funeral would be paid as soon as Garcia had the money. As all prices at this general store were more than twice as high as in the town stores, the storekeeper would make an excellent profit out of this sale; in fact, the cash Garcia had paid amounted to practically four-fifths of the storekeeper's costs for these goods. As elsewhere, no battlefield is so sad and horrible that some men cannot make a good profit out of it. Everything under heaven can be turned to dollars or pesos. It really does not matter whether it is the tears of the mother or the laughter of a child or the sufferings of the poor, there is always money in it. Man has to pay for his grief as well as for his joys, for his stumblings as well as for his dances. Even his last little cave under the ground, where he no longer will be in anybody's way, has to be paid for, or he goes into the ashcan, unless a kind student of medicine takes pity on him and relieves him of such a shameless finale. Were it not so, the world would be a lot less entertaining.

'Muchacho!' Sleigh shouted. 'What about the milk?'

'Estoy volando, jefe, I am flying already,' the boy yelled back.

'Hurry up! And no maybe from your lips. Señor Velasquez will beat the hell out of you if you bring him sour milk.'

In spite of his harsh words Sleigh was not a bit worried or angry about what might happen to the few quarts of milk, and he was still less concerned about what Señor Velasquez might say or do. Señor Velasquez was the owner of the general store in a village located near the depot. Should Señor Velasquez complain about the milk when Sleigh visited him to check the accounts and collect the money that had to be sent to the owner of the ranch, Sleigh would lend a deaf ear to him. He would turn his back on him, mount his horse, and ride back home. If Sleigh loved anything at all, it was the cattle he was in charge of, but he did not care a rap about his boss, or about Señor Velasquez, or about the milk. In his opinion it was only incidentally that his boss or Señor Velasquez or the milk had anything to do with the cattle.

We returned to Sleigh's hut to breakfast on an old kerosene box. A not very clean newspaper served as a tablecloth.

Sleigh looked the table over as if something were missing from it. He then said to the girl: 'Fry each of us another coupla eggs.'

'Si, patrón, ahoritito!' the girl answered.

She went to a dark corner of the hut where a basket was tied to the post which supported the roof. A sleepy-eyed hen was sitting comfortably in this basket, obviously brooding over nature's whim which made her sit there while all the other hens could go about and wink at the rooster. The girl snatched the hen by the neck, threw her out of the basket, picked up four eggs, and returned with them to the hearth. The hen cackled noisily and ran around the hut violently. She jumped on our table, kicked over our coffee cups, flew up, glided down again, and ran back to her basket, where for a while she sat on the edge and looked inside. Then she hopped in, moved the eggs around, counted them with her claws, and, finding none missing, sat down quietly and closed her eyes, once more satisfied with the world. She was happy and satisfied with everything on earth because she could not count correctly. It is the ability to count correctly that causes so many tragedies among men. Since counting-machines have made mistakes practically impossible, tragedies resulting from counting have become more intense and greater in number.

After we had had our breakfast, we thought it time to get some sleep.

30

Music awoke me. The two musicians who should have been here last night and who, if they had come then, might not now be needed to play for the funeral, were presenting a lively foxtrot as an introduction.

Sleigh had arisen long ago. He was crawling through the brush because a calf had broken out of the corral. I washed up, shaved, gulped down two cups of hot coffee, swallowed a few spoonfuls of beans wrapped in hot tortillas, and then went over to the Garcia's.

Here I found a great and animated assembly. To every tree, shrub, or post a horse, a mule, or a burro was tied – some with the saddle still on, others without. Women dressed in their Sunday garments, men clothed as on week-days were standing around or squatting on the ground. A crowd of children filled the air with shouts and shrieks. Most of them were naked, the rest half naked, the latter being mostly girls.

More fireworks had been brought by the new visitors and there was a cracking and shooting and a tremendous noise all over the place.

The musicians who had played the whole night through were now no longer playing. They preserved their strength for the long march through the bush to the cemetery.

A few men were lying about drunk. Others were still sleeping here and there on the ground. Nobody disturbed them.

The sun was high and blazed down without mercy. The drunks caught in this broiling heat became uneasy, woke up, crawled to the shade, and fell back into stupor. One or two failed to reach the shade, dropped, and remained lying like shapeless bundles.

Goats and hogs were running around freely and getting in the way of the people, who kicked them and pushed them without any result. A multitude of dogs were constantly fighting each other or playing or chasing the hogs. Chickens were fighting with turkeys over worms and crumbs of food. The horses, burros, and mules which were not tied up or which had freed themselves were walking among the crowd looking for a green leaf which had not yet been trodden into the ground. Yesterday there was much green to be seen near the broken-down fence and in the corners of the yard. Now the soil looked as if locusts had passed over it.

All these animals were a nuisance to the people, but nobody got seriously angry over the annoyances they caused. Now and then an animal would be kicked. A woman would shout: 'Hi, you perro, you miserable dog, get away!' Another: 'Hog, don't push me down!' Occasionally a boy was called to chase a dog or a hog away. Or a stone would be thrown, but so gently that it could not hurt the animal. It was meant to be only a warning, not a punishment. But if a dog or a hog was fresh enough to try to get away with the whole morral, the little bast bag in which the family carried their provisions for the trip, a club or a big stone thrown at the thief would remind him to have more respect for other people's property.

Some groups were all laughter. Other groups entertained themselves with animated conversation. Groups of youngsters sang and played mouth-organs. Here and there men were appraising horses and mules. Some women were telling others about the troubles they had with their children or with their relatives or their neighbours. It wasn't all love and kindness. They told how greedy a sister-in-law was or an uncle, and what a beastly neighbour Don Chucho was.

Any outsider who had come along here at this time would never have thought for a minute that the assembly was there for a funeral. But now and then people were reminded of the fact and they became serious as befitted the situation. At such moments groups suddenly ceased being jolly or loud. Someone would then say: 'Well, all of us have to die some day, one sooner, another later, and some will die before they are out of their babyhood. That's only natural. Poor mother! She'll have to bear it and live on.' And a sigh from all the women in this group confirmed the truth of that philosophical statement.

Again, in another group which had become too noisy, a man's voice would be heard saying: 'Get quiet, all of you! You ought to be ashamed of yourself making such a row and laughing as if you'd burst. Don't you know that there is a dead baby close by, and that woman crying out her guts? You've not got a bit of decency left, that's what I say.'

In many places blankets had been spread over sticks planted in the ground so as to make little roofs for protection against the sun. There were few trees in the yard big enough to give any real shade.

Usually a fresh breeze would come up at about eleven in the morning. Today this breeze had failed to come.

Now the shadows of humans, animals, trees, and posts were right at their feet and could hardly be noticed at all.

I took off my hat and entered the hut to see what changes had taken place.

The hut was crowded with women who were fanning themselves with pieces of cardboard and with fans made of pasteboard on which were printed advertisements of cigarettes, beer, tequila, habanero, and dry-goods stores, and kissing couples with titles of moving pictures. The women fanned themselves automatically, as if their hands were moved by a little machine.

All candles were bent and at every candle a woman worked to keep it upright. This constant attention to the candles not only kept a number of women and youngsters very busy, but also served as a good show for the mourners, because each candle had its individuality and each attendant had a different way of handling the candle she was in charge of.

The kid had become a very poor side-show and was not attracting any real interest.

Then the Garcia once again took the cloth off the kid's face. The face could no longer be recognized. It had become almost formless. The wound in his jaw had become an enormous ugly opening. His teeth were exposed like those of a skeleton. The gums were greenish. The little wound on his skull had also widened and the bared bone of the skull had become visible.

It was not only the tropical climate that accounted for such rapid destruction; the process was also hastened by the water from the tropical river which had entered the body. The water of a river in the tropics contains billions of the most hungry, most voracious microbes, which attack a lifeless body a hundred times more savagely than those which infest water in the temperate zones. I for one could explain in no other way such a terrific and horrible decomposition in so short a time. I wondered what the body looked like under the sailor suit.

But the sailor suit was no longer visible. These primitive women had perceived the ugliness of that monkey dress. They had better taste than the jobber who had shipped a gross of these suits down here in the belief that they were the right clothes for little Indian boys who lived in the jungle where nobody knew what a ship looked like and where nobody understood why sailors had to wear this sort of suit and why they could not do their work just as efficiently in overalls. Of course, intelligent people know that it is the uniform that accounts for a good sailor's smooth and effective work. But while this may be known to the women in every port in the world, it is not known to the people in a tropical jungle.

The women had covered the admiral's overalls with a sort of frock made of red, green, blue, and yellow paper. This frock which had been made by simple Indian women had given back to the little Indian boy his dignity. I was surprised to see at least a dozen identical frocks on the kid. Soon I found the reason for this unnecessary abundance.

Almost every woman had brought something with her to be used for dolling up the kid. There was no possibility of exchanging ideas over the phone before leaving their homes. Many had brought a dozen sheets of coloured paper. Others had made paper frocks as soon as they had received the news of the tragedy. Since every woman had offered her gift with all her sympathy and love, the mother accepted them all with thanks and, with the assistance of each giver, dressed the kid in the new frock even though he had more than one on already.

Fortunately, not all the women had brought frocks. Many offered little stars and crosses, some of them cut out of tin cans, others out of coloured paper. These stars and crosses were pasted on the uppermost frock as extra decorations. A few women who had nothing better to give had brought brightly coloured rags and ribbons, which were also pinned to the frock.

A woman I knew entered. She was the mother of the boy whom I would have raised from the dead but for the Spaniard pushing me aside and applying another method. I was still pondering over the question whether I would be as highly respected today in that village if the Spaniard had not interfered with my handling of the dead. Well, perhaps the people of that village would admire me just the same, because working on a corpse with all sorts of rescue methods for six consecutive hours will always be highly appreciated even if the result is failure.

The woman greeted me before anyone else, and she did so in a very friendly manner. She had brought a pretty crown made of gold paper, but it had not been made with such good taste as the one made by the pump-master woman last night. She naturally believed, however, that her crown was lots prettier than the one the kid already had on his head. She stepped up to the body, and without asking anybody's permission she took off the old crown and put on the crown she had made.

The pump-master woman saw her do this, but did not interfere. When she had made that crown, with her tears running down over it, I had noticed how much kindness, neighbourly love, and compassion for another mother in distress she had been weaving into it, and I also saw how happy she had felt when she had finished her job and examined it with the satisfaction of an artist whose work has surpassed his intentions. I shall never forget the look in her smiling eyes, still wet from tears, when she put that crown on the kid's head and almost worshipped him as if he had now become a little saint.

Now she glanced at her rival and for a moment I was not sure that a fight might not start. She made a gesture as if she meant to prevent the unceremonious exchange of crowns. But she stopped, and over her lips a kind smile fluttered. She put both her hands over her breasts and watched the somewhat rude exchange without anger. Being a mother, she perhaps realized that the other woman was also a mother and that only recently that mother had lost a beloved son and what she was doing at this moment was but showing her sympathy for the young mother. And so, the pump-master woman thought, why start a fight over the crowns? The first crown had served its purpose, so let the second crown have its turn.

The woman with the new crown had thrown the old one aside as if to say: Well, what sort of junk is that? The pump-master woman picked up her discarded crown, crumpled it in her hand so that nobody would pay any attention to it, left the hut, and threw it into the bonfire.

31

Suddenly excited voices were heard outside the hut. Right away a man entered carrying under one arm the little coffin which he himself had made as his last gift to the kid. With his free hand he took off his hat.

The moment he put the coffin on the floor the Garcia woman broke out into a fit of hysterical shrieking. All the other women in the hut and outside in the yard joined her as if they were all mad.

The coffin-maker wiped the thick sweat off his forehead with the backs of his hands and then dried his neck with a large red handkerchief.

Three men came in and went straight to the table. The Garcia woman yelled: 'Don't take him away from me! Let him sleep here only a few hours more, please, don't take him away!' She wrung her hands and ran around the hut, pushing her head here and there against the posts which supported the roof, shrieking and yelling all the time. Finally two women cornered her and took her in their arms.

In the meantime, with a short businesslike 'Con su permiso!' and ignoring the shrieks and lamentations of the women, the men pushed the women out of their way and got to work.

Sleigh was one of the three who had just come in.

The coffin was only a very crude box made of rotten boards taken from different kinds of old cases. Not a bit of this coffin was planed. The outside was covered with blue and red paper to give it a more decent appearance. The inside had been filled with dry grass and corn leaves, on top of which pieces of limestone had been laid.

The coffin was set on a box. Without any ceremony the four men grabbed the little body and tried to lift it from the table. While lifting it the head dropped with a jerk as if it would break off. I jumped forward and held the pillow under it for support. The beautiful paper dresses spread apart and the whole laboriously achieved make-up turned into something horrible. But at last we got the body into the coffin. The pump-master woman jumped up and with her quick, expert hands arranged the dresses to give back the body its former illusion of beauty.

The coffin was then put on the table. At once the Garcia threw herself over her baby to kiss him good-bye. She was just about to press her lips to his mouth when she realized that his lips were all gone. Then she smelled the odour rising from the poor little body. She gasped for fresh air and drew back, almost falling over the woman sitting there.

She stood five feet away from her baby. She flung her arms up, waved them violently, then dropped them with a gesture of fatigue. Now her hands fumbled at her face, ran up and down her breasts, and finally glided down her belly, where she moved them around as if she were searching for something hidden there. Then her fingers climbed up her face like little snakes until they reached her hair. She pulled at her hair so savagely that two women fell into her arms to keep her from tearing her scalp off. Her eyes flickered about helplessly. She broke away from them, screamed, and dropped to the floor as if she had been struck by a club.

The women lifted her head, poured water between her tightly pressed lips, and tried to force open her clenched fists. First her lips and then her face got blue – but only for a minute. Slowly she came to. She opened her eyes, sat up on the floor, wiped her face, looked around, recognized her friends, and tried to smile at them.

That was her last good-bye to her beloved baby.

Her husband came in. Staggering towards her, he dragged out of one of his pockets, with great difficulty, a bottle of mescal and pushed it into her hands with a gesture of love and sympathetic understanding.

The Garcia, holding the bottle in her hands as if it were something very sacred, rose from the floor and disappeared into the little storeroom. I could watch her through the sticks which formed the wall and I saw her take a swig which would have knocked an old Norwegian sailor straight under the table. She took the bottle from her mouth, looked at it, and then took a shot that was not quite so big as the first one, but was still more than two fingers of a quart bottle. Having taken her consoling medicine, she came out and, good and honest wife that she was, returned the bottle to her lord and master. She wiped her mouth with the back of her hand with a satisfied look in her hollow eyes.

Since the bottle was out of his hip pocket and since it had been so hard to get it out, old man Garcia thought the occasion very opportune and he too whipped a fine shot down his throat. Fiestas must be celebrated on the day they fall.

The coffin-maker dragged a hammer out of one pocket and out of another two thick rusty nails. He considered this gesture more suggestive than a speech about what he was now going to do.

The Garcia immediately understood the meaning of that gesture. She went up to the coffin, took off the cloth, and looked at what was still left of the face which had only yesterday been so full of life and joy. She stared in horror and covered her face hastily.

She stood there for a minute as if she were waiting for something. Then she walked with quick steps to the little shelf on which the picture of the Holy Virgin was standing, removed the little ukulele, and put it in the coffin beside the kid. Then she pondered again over something she wanted to remember. Once more she returned to the shelf, gathered together all the kid's playthings – the battered tin automobile, the fish-hooks, the strings, the broken cork, and the few other silly items which her boy had treasured so highly – carried them to the coffin, and put them in too. And in a very low voice she said: 'He mustn't feel lonely, he mustn't.' And after standing there a few seconds more, she said: 'Adiós, Carlitos! Adiós, Carlosito mio!'

Nobody in the hut moved, nobody said a word, nobody mumbled, nobody even seemed to breathe while the mother was talking to her baby.

She bowed her head, turned around until her back was to the coffin, and walked towards the wall through which she could see the bonfire outside.

Quickly the coffin-maker put the lid on the box and with a few light blows of his hammer nailed it loosely so that it could be taken off again before the burial.

32

From now on, everything happened in a hurry. Four youngsters, each about fourteen years of age, lifted the coffin, and the funeral train was on its way.

Men, women, children followed the pall-bearers. The women carried their babies on their backs wrapped in rebozos.

In no time the train had reached the spot on the bridge from which the kid was supposed to have tumbled over.

Here the pall-bearers instinctively halted.

All the men took off their hats. The Garcia wept bitterly, but she did not yell. Her tears stirred the hearts of all the mourners more than her yells had, honest though they had been. The pump-master woman kissed her. 'There, there, now,' she said, 'weep if it helps you. Here, blow your nose in this.' The pump-master woman pressed her handkerchief against the mother's swollen face.

The pall-bearers marched on again.

Sleigh had stopped on the bridge with the others for a minute. Then he turned around and went home as soon as he saw the procession move on. He did not say so, but I was sure he had to find a cow which had strayed.

The crowd left the bridge and passed the pump-station. On this rough, occasionally swampy trail through the bush, it would take almost the whole afternoon for the procession to reach the little cemetery.

Naturally, the mourners did not march in good order.

Garcia staggered between two friends who had difficulty keeping him on his feet, especially since they themselves were no longer very sure of their faculties.

The mother walked beside the pump-master woman, on whose right arm she was hanging. She still wore her sea-green gauze dress and apparently she did not know it. Aside from her week-day rags she had nothing else to wear on such a great occasion. The dress was streaked with blood and mud. It had many holes in it and was ripped wide open at various places. The flowers had fallen off, but the safety pins by which they had been fastened were still there.

The pump-master woman, like practically all the other women, also wore the dress she had worn the night before, but her dress and those of the other women were less soiled and not torn.

After the people had left the bridge they all began to feel more comfortable. A new world opened before them and that sinister bridge would soon be forgotten.

After having walked in silence for a quarter of an hour, the crowd slowly began to get lively. A heavy burden seemed to have been removed from everyone's chest.

The musicians – one fiddler and one guitar-player, both Indians – lifted their instruments. They did not know that there were such things as funeral dirges, death marches, and nocturnos which allure ghosts to come out of their chimneys and attics and dance before a pleased audience. That hymns existed they knew because they had heard them in church. Yet they could not play them, and for some unexplainable reason they would not have played them even if they had known how. What in the world were the American jazz compositions for if not to be played any time and on any occasion, whether a wedding, or a baptism, a saint's day, a dance, or a funeral? Music was music anywhere and to have different tunes for different occasions was silly and befitted only people who knew no better – perhaps because they had degenerated and needed a rough-fisted bolshevism to put them out of their misery. Be this as it may, the little boy had to be buried with music, and any music would do, since he was already on his way to heaven.

I was afraid that they might play something like *Home, Sweet Home* or *My Old Kentucky Home*. But no, these good Indian musicians were not that far away from the path of civilization. They were far nearer to us. I could see here very clearly that international borders and colours of skins weren't barriers against the spread of our mighty culture. The dynamic force of our crooners, torch singers, and night-club hostesses had actually made it possible for our Vallees, Berlins, Whitemans, and Crosbys to reach even the depths of American jungles. Over this trail blazed by our dance songs, there would soon arrive Fords, vacuum cleaners, electric refrigerators, air-conditioned grass huts, jungle-coloured bathrooms, windmill-driven television, canned alligator stew, and pulverized hearts of young palm trees.

So it was that the tune played (as befitted the sailor suit) was *Taintgonnarainnomo*, which was the latest around here.

It was a long time since I had heard that tune. And since the time that tune was the rage back home, we Americans, tough guys that we are, have happily survived weddings of painted dolls, sonnyboys, and mammies crooned by poor devils suffering from St Vitus's dance; we had also had to swallow the strange news that only God can make a tree, a fact which none of us ever knew until we were told so by night-club entertainers. Then there was the coming (two hundred times every day and night) of the moon over the mountains with my mem'ries of you. Then we took our sugar to tea, asked for just one more chance, and incorporated the little innocent cucaracha, which used to be sung by Mexican revolutionists under the fire of machine-guns, but was sung by us under the fire of booze.

Everything in its right place and the world will be a better location to live in. No, it won't rain any more. This elegant song was played by Indians who for nine months had had no drop of rain and by whom rain was considered God's greatest blessing.

We reached these people so easily with our sailor suits, with our polished shoes and our yeswehavenobananas. Would that we tried once in a while to reach them, not with puffed rice and naked celluloid dames going with the wrong man in the right bed, but with the Gettysburg address, which next to God's rain would be the greatest blessing to all these so-called republics if we would take the trouble to make the people understand the true meaning of the greatest, finest, and most noble poem any American has produced to this day.

Yet the simple fact that the taintgonnarainnomo tune was played here as a death march was ample proof that this vomit of our civilization had, at least in this part of the world, met a wall it could not break. Death is understood by these people, but the hypocrisy with which we, the followers of Christ, bury our dead they cannot understand. Therefore American dance tunes could not confuse their feelings, while hymns and nearer-to-thees would only upset them as something not quite befitting that great mystery which is the extinction of life.

What does it all matter anyhow? What does the sun above us care about the dead, about weeping mothers, about funerals, about American foxtrots and hair-removers? What does it care whether there is a genuine culture or faked civilization, whether good music or noise with brass tubes? That glorious sun doesn't give a rap for anybody's anger about the white man's dumping the contents of his ashcans over the heads of people he believes inferior. Whatever woe, pain, and sorrow we may have, real or imaginary, the sun stays mighty and dignified in the universe. It is a god, it is the only god, the redeemer, the saviour, the only visible one, the always present, the ever young, the ever smiling god, forever an exulting song of eternal creation. It is the creator, the maintainer, the begetter, and the producer. It gives and wastes at the same time, never ceases to bless the earth with fruit and beauty, yet never asks for prayers or worship, nor for thanks. And it never threatens punishments.

What did the sun above us care about our funeral? It stood directly above and its flames struck us. We staggered along our dreary way, stumbled over roots and logs, fell into holes, and sank into swampy furrows. We squeezed ourselves through thorny brushes and beat our way through the high, wiry prairie grass.

For hours and hours we marched in this blazing heat. The crowd was chatting, laughing, yelling, squeaking, singing, whistling. Now and then the music played. Foxtrots, one-steps, two-steps, blues. Occasionally they played the *Jesusita en Chihuahua* and the *Reina de mi jacal* and *Amapola del camino* and *Adelita* for recreation, because these tunes they could play in their sleep. But if they had gone on playing these beautiful songs, the mourners would have believed them old-fashioned, and so that they should not be thought narrow-minded, doing only what their grandfathers did, they discarded their fine folk-music to show the crowd how Americanized they were. And there came floating through the boiling air the sounds of that musical glory of the century, the great American Te Deum, *Taintgonnarainnomo*.

The coffin swayed dangerously on the shoulders of the youngsters who carried it. If now and then one of them tripped over a stone or a root or sank into a hole, the entire crowd yelled: 'La caja, la caja! The box, the box!'

Those walking near it jumped closer and supported the case, for otherwise it might easily have gone down the scarp which bordered the trail. I did not wish even to imagine what might happen if that coffin had really gone down there and burst open.

On both sides of our trail buzzards accompanied us, some flying ahead of us, others following, some of them dropping into a tree or a bush to perch there for a minute, then arising again and coming close to us. They never came very close – just close enough so that we could clearly see their hungry eyes and their dry beaks.

We came up to a row of termite-eaten fence posts. From a few of them pieces of rusty barbed wire were dangling. A dozen buzzards took possession of this row and perched on the posts. It was a ghastly sight, considering that we were going to bury a dead child, for these buzzards sat in a file like sentinels. A mourner tried to make a wisecrack and remarked: 'With their black frock coats they look like undertakers.' Another one said with a giggle: 'That one looks exactly like our cura, who baptized our brats last fall.'

I too thought they looked more like ministers than undertakers – like ministers who could never forgive an error and who were at their best when preaching of hell-fire and Satan's sadistic pleasures.

In front of the coffin the second brother marched. He was surrounded by a bunch of shouting and shrieking kids. One of the boys was constantly swinging a thick stick, the end of which burned slowly, to keep it aflame so that it could be used to light the firecrackers which were exploding every minute. When the first crackers went off like rifle-shots, the buzzards got frightened and left our procession to hide in the depths of the bush. But now they were accustomed to the noise and they went with us all the way. Nobody throws stones at buzzards here or hurts them intentionally. The law protects the birds. But even if there were no law for the preservation of buzzards, the people would protect them, for they know them to be their health department, which disposes of carcasses.

Manuel marched all by himself as if he did not belong to this procession. Twice I went up to him and talked about Texas and about his job there. He answered and even tried to force a smile. When I saw how it pained him to talk, I left him alone for the rest of the way.

Old man Garcia stopped every once in a while, dragged the bottle out of his hip pocket, and took a shot. Both his friends who were helping him reach the cemetery on his own feet also helped him finish the bottle. Now and then another of his friends came up and was served. Garcia could afford to be generous, for should this bottle give out, he carried a second one in another pocket.

The mother walked in the midst of the crowd. Seeing her now, one would not believe her to be the principal mourner. No longer did she hang on the pump-master woman's arm for support. The heat and the rough trail would not allow it. The pump-master woman, however, still walked by her side, and a few other women were marching close by so that the mother could never feel alone, not even for a moment. They all chatted to shorten the trip and to forget the blazing sun. They were talking of a thousand different things, but not of the kid. They were walking back to ordinary daily life.

The youngsters started to fight about whose turn it now was to carry the coffin. None of the boys wanted the honour, which before had been much coveted. The stench near the coffin had become unbearable even for the toughest of them. All had their handker-chiefs tied over their mouths and noses to protect them as much as possible from the horrible odour emanating from the box.

It was certainly a marvel how bravely the Garcia marched among the crowd, considering that she had not closed an eye during the past thirty-six hours, that she had received the most cruel beating from fate that any mother on earth could suffer, that for twenty hours she had wept, yelled, and lamented as never before in her life, and that she had eaten nothing since late afternoon the day before. Hers is a race which has a great future, provided it is not taken in by installment plans for buying things they can do with-out.

And there was another marvel, the musicians. The whole night through they had played dances, one right after the other without an intermission. If Indians dance, then they dance – there's no sitting out, and no gazing at the moon, either. They have time enough for staring at the moon when there is no music around.

Looking objectively at this show, I almost wondered whether anybody still considered it a funeral train. All were marching to the cemetery, no doubt, yet somehow it appeared as if the dead one had been dismissed long ago and the march now received its meaning solely from the music which was played. In spite of all my silent protests and solemn curses, American dances and torch songs had won after all, dominating all the senses and feelings of the mar-chers, who apparently preferred this music to that of their own land. My noble thoughts had made me but a preacher in the desert and I was positive that if I were to yell my disapproval of our night-club achievements, they would have believed me crazy from the scorching heat.

Perhaps they were right after all. Why should anybody have thought of death and of funerals? The world around us was green and full of life. The sky was blue, the sun golden. Butterflies by the thousands, some as big as two hands and others prettier than precious jewels, fluttered against the dark wall of the bush. Birds hidden in the thicket twittered noisily. The jungle fiddled, sang, chirped so intensely that for seconds the music was drowned. Life was all around and everywhere and we maintained the silly notion that we were on a funeral march. Why didn't we leave that kid in the river, forget him, and have done with it? Why all the fuss? Wasn't he better off in the river than in a hole in the cemetery where dogs and hogs would dig him out and eat what was left of him? God gave him the river to play with, so we should have let him stay there and allowed him to be happy in his own way. Why did we interfere with the burial the Lord had prepared for him? Of course, since we had learned to be Christians we could no longer act like heathen and we had to do what was considered our Christian duty.

What the hell, if I only could concentrate on the march and not let my mind wander off all the time – and that's the reason why now I was stuck in a swampy hole and everybody was laughing at me! I wanted to be decent too; that's why I was marching and tripping over roots for a silly idea.

Long live the world which is so very funny to live in! What meaning to the living world had that little box of decomposing flesh? None. How insignificant is man in the universe, how insignificant his worries, his wars, his struggles, his ambitions, his trying to outwit his competitors! What is left of the great Cæsar? There would be one Rome just the same, Cæsar or no Cæsar. Perhaps it would not be on the river Tiber, but there would be one Rome. What will be left tomorrow of the dozen little Cæsars of today who think that they can build up a new world and terrify mankind? What are all the wars and dictatorships and bolshevisms for if finally men always end up by doing what is best for them, great men or not? So then why not enjoy life, love, merriment? And if some day you cannot enjoy them any longer, die and be forgotten and leave no ghosts behind. That's paradise.

33

There, at last, the village was in sight. Huts, palm huts, grass huts, and one rotten imitation of an American bungalow. A multitude of naked children were running about. Chickens, hogs, turkeys, mules, goats, dogs in front of the huts, between them, inside them.

The people came out of their huts and in deep silence awaited the procession. And in deep silence they let it pass them. The men took off their hats as soon as the first mourners came near. Even the naked children stopped their playing and yelling and stared at us with wide-open eyes. A woman holding a baby in her arms shrieked when the marchers passed. Another woman looked around with harassed eyes, grasped her child playing at her feet, lifted him up, and folded her arms around him as if he were to be taken away from her. Then she cried out plaintively, and many of the women marching, among them the Garcia, joined her and howled in the same manner, as if they were answering calls of their kind.

Out of the general store a man staggered. He was dressed in a cheap white cotton suit, with a coat on, which is something I had not seen for weeks. In his right hand he held a twig which he swished aimlessly through the air. He could hardly keep on his feet.

He was the teacher in the next village. Only for two months would he be in that village school, because the government paid that village only two months' salary for a teacher – a salary of seventy-five centavos a day. More than two months' salary the government could not spend on that Indian village. When the job was over, the teacher would return to town, where his family lived, and he would wait there for another assignment, which might come soon, which might come late, which might come never. It all depended on the teacher's personal friends and on their good standing with a diputado or another politician. Usually the teacher had to get the money for his return ticket by going from hut to hut and asking for as much as the parents of his pupils could spare; and as they were all very poor Indian peasants, it was not very much. After he had paid for his simple board and lodging in the village and sent the rest home to his wife and children, nothing of his salary was left for a ticket. But as a government employee he was entitled to a reduction of fifty per cent on a railroad ticket used in his capacity as a returning or outgoing teacher. This treatment of the teacher was caused not so much by a faulty government as by the fact that the resources of the republic are very limited and, as often happens in richer countries also, expenses for education and for schools in general come last. Soldiers always first. Another reason is that, just as elsewhere, politicians take twenty times more from the nation's income than is their legal share.

The school he taught in was a large room in a palm hut. No chair, no bench, no table could be found in the class-room. The children squatted on the earthen floor and put the paper on which they wrote upon their knees. Only the teacher had a crudely made chair, and a box for a table.

I had known the teacher when he taught in an Indian village about a hundred and twenty miles from here. I had been living there for a few months, and as I had had plenty of time, I had accompanied him on his Saturday excursions with the children to teach them the elements of geography, botany, insect life. In that village there had been only five or six persons who could write and read, and no more than a dozen who could write their names.

Each grown-up pupil had paid him one peso a month, which considerably bettered his small income. I had visited this night school chiefly to get acquainted with my fellow students, to make friends with them and be welcome in their homes. This had been worth more to me than learning how to write my name without a mistake and learning whether the Spanish word for work is spelled with a v or a b. I had known ever since that he was a good teacher and that he deserved a better lot than being chased around from village to village.

That he had got pupils for his night school had not been due to the ambition of the people in the village, but to communist agitators who twice every month visited that village and told the young men that if they did not learn how to read and write they would never amount to anything and would be exploited by American imperialistic companies and by Spanish hacendados and German coffee-planters, and if they did not learn quickly, the United States would come and take the whole republic away from them and teach them the English language by force. The fact was that, because of the constant preaching of the communist agraristas, practically every young Indian had gone to night school and many of them had learned reading and writing fairly well in four months.

Seeing that teacher now, one might think him a common drunkard. I knew that he was as sober a man as any teacher anywhere. He was not Indian, more likely of Spanish descent with a heavy dash of Arabian blood. That he was drunk today was something which a hilarious fate had obviously prepared in advance. I knew something was going to take a different turn from what was expected. I only wondered what it would be and how it would come out. Fate was at play, or the teacher would not have been drunk.

Friends of the Garcia family who lived in that village had begged

617

the teacher to come and say a few words over the kid's grave. The teacher knew the kid because the kid had gone to his school for a week when his father had had a job with the railroad. The job had lasted only a week, but during that week the kid's mother had sent him to the school near by, where the kid had learned to say: 'An I which has no dot over it is no I.'

The teacher had accepted the invitation to speak at the grave and had come to the village where the cemetery was. Here he had met the fathers of his pupils. On arriving, and not knowing any other place to go, he had stepped into the general store, where he had asked for a soda. In had come a man who was the father of two of his pupils. The father greeted the teacher and invited him to drink with him just one little copita of mescal. Beer was too expensive, and since there was no ice to be had, the beer was warm and therefore had no taste. To say no to such a kind invitation would have made the father believe that the teacher was too haughty to drink with an Indian. The teacher had a good heart. He knew how the father would feel if he were to refuse to drink with him. Even a soda or an orange crush costs more than a copita. So the teacher had drunk the hard mescal. The father of another pupil had then come in, and since he had accepted a drink from the first father, he could not refuse a drink from the second. Another father who had heard that the teacher was in the village stepped in and another drink was knocked down. Never more than just one little copita of mescal. But no matter how you count, a certain number of copitas make a pint. The heat did the rest. God in heaven, how drunk that teacher was!

The procession marched on. Many of the villagers joined the mourners and went along with them. Far behind the rest the teacher was staggering along. He needed the whole road for himself. On his left arm hung that friend of Garcia who had invited the teacher to speak at the grave. This man was even more loaded than the teacher, whose knees might be weak, but some of whose senses were intact. But to drag along a drunken companion who did not make the slightest effort to keep on his own feet – that, surely, was a dangerous task for one who had to fight hard himself against those spirits which are so very friendly to man the first three times, but are nasty fellows after the tenth.

The teacher tried his best to show that he was a dignified personage. His companion, however, walking practically upon his knees, dragged and pulled the poor teacher every few paces down to the ground. That drunken friend stumbled and tripped and fell, and the good-natured teacher had to lift him up again to his feet. That job made the teacher seem more drunk than he actually was at the time the mourners arrived at the village.

34

The procession reached the cemetery. What a cemetery! It was one more proof of the fact that Christianity had not yet come to the Indians, but instead a degenerated, corrupted religion dolled up with empty ceremonies borrowed from the Roman Catholicism of the first half of the sixteenth century.

The gate consisted of two lattice wings made of sticks. The gate was purely for decorative purposes because one could enter the place at either side of the gate, where the fence had rotted and collapsed; from the posts hung rusty barbed wire, some of which was lying on the ground.

From the top of the centre gate post a cross greeted the visitor. Three little hillocks covered with withered flowers and simple crosses without names on them were the only signs that this place was supposed to be a cemetery. Everything else looked like what the earth will look like on doomsday late in the afternoon.

There were a great number of little mounds. None had the shape of a grave. All these mounds were overgrown with wiry grass and thorny bushes which had been trampled upon, and most of the mounds had been dug open, obviously by dogs, hogs, and wild beasts searching the ground for tasty morsels. Bones were strewn all over the place, but mercifully hidden by the high grass. Rotten boards from decayed coffins were lying everywhere. A score of crude crosses were lying flat on the ground. And this ground was richly decorated with the dung of cows, horses, burros, mules, and dogs wherever you looked or walked. The funny thing about that cemetery was that I liked it immensely. If I cannot be dropped into the sea, which by all means I prefer, I should like to be buried silently in a cemetery of that kind, and, please, send no flowers.

We make too much fuss over our dead. We believe them holy or saintly and treat them accordingly. A dead one is dead. He has left us and we ought to leave him in peace. He should be forgotten the moment he is covered with earth or sent up in smoke. The billions we spend on our dead would serve mankind better if they were spent on more hospitals, on prepaid doctors' fees, and on more research on disease. It would be more human and surely more civilized if instead of wasting billions upon the dead we spent that money on the living to keep them sane and healthy and so have them longer with us. Just on the flowers that are thrown to the dead, who cannot see or smell them, we could save enough money to take care of ten thousand babies every year and make their mothers happy.

I wondered if that teacher and his companion would ever reach the cemetery. Now he was floored, now the other was.

At last we were standing before the open grave. There were no grave-diggers about. The grave had to be dug by the father or a relative or a neighbour. In this case Manuel had dug the hole. He had done the job early in the morning when it was cool. Then he had hurried back on horseback to be ready to follow the procession.

The coffin was put on the ground a few feet away from the hole. The coffin-maker pulled out the two nails and took off the lid so that the mother could see her baby for the last time. It was also the law, which ordered that a coffin must be opened just before it is let down so that the mourners may convince themselves they have the right corpse and are not by mistake burying the wrong one. It was furthermore the last chance for the dead to come back to life if he thought he was not yet fully dead and could afford to hang on a while longer. With the coffin open, practically nothing of the body was visible. The box was apparently filled only with a mass of coloured paper, a golden crown, and a sceptre from which the paper was already peeling off. The face was covered by the crown, which had dropped over it and hid its ghastly ugliness. The bared teeth grinning out from under the crown were the only evidence that the crumbling mass of wet coloured paper hid the remains of a human body.

With a terrific outcry the Garcia threw herself across the open coffin and embraced the whole box. Her crying ebbed to a long, bitter whimpering.

And while her body shook violently from inner convulsions, the little wooden whistle, which she had caught when it had fallen out of the kid's pants' pocket after he had been fished out of the river, dropped at this moment out of the bosom of her dress. The whistle fell on the ground. She stared at it, ceased whimpering immediately, picked up the whistle, pressed it against her lips, and quickly, as if she might forget it, she hid it inside the paper frocks and said in a low voice: 'Here, mi nene, chiquito mio, don't leave your whistle behind. And forgive me, chiquitito mio, my beloved darling, that I spanked you because you wouldn't stop blowing your whistle all the time right into my ears, and that made me so very angry. You forgive me, won't you, Carlitos mio?'

All the women, on hearing her speak to her baby as if he could still hear her, started sobbing.

Garcia, half staggering, half stumbling, came up to the grave. He leaned against the two men who had supported him. He could no longer stand up by himself, because his second bottle, which he had kept in reserve, had in the meantime been finished.

He considered it his right to stand before all the other people beside the open box, for he was the father, drunk or not. He opened his mouth to say something to the crowd. Perhaps he wished to cry, but only a little squeak came out. With one hand he wiped off the thick tears which were rolling down his cheeks. In spite of his drunkenness and all the numbness in his head, he realized fully that his little boy was leaving him forever.

All the women were weeping bitterly as if the child were their own. The pump-master woman, assisted by another woman, went close to the box and lifted the Garcia up from the ground on which she had fallen exhausted.

No sooner did the coffin-maker see the box freed from the mother's attention than he put the lid on, and in a few seconds it was nailed fast – this time for good.

Then it was carried to the hole.

35

Now everybody turns his head around towards the gate and waits for the teacher to appear. He is still outside. Ashamed to meet the weeping mother and the crowd of mourners in his present condition, he refuses to enter the grounds. But his companion finally pushes him through the gate. When the teacher still resists going further, that fellow, despite his being so drunk, has sense enough to wink to another man, who immediately approaches and leads the teacher to the grave.

After much labour and time the teacher is at last standing at the edge of the open hole. All look at him in anticipation of his speech.

Swaying dangerously, he stares at the mother. His eyes get moist and with an energetic twist he turns around and runs away. His companion, the friend of the Garcias, wakens from his torpidity just long enough to note the teacher's retreat and he yells after him to come back immediately and keep his promise like a real he-man and look the goddamned world bravely in the face. As the teacher does not heed his yells, he starts to swear terribly, until he is stopped by two men who slap him straight upon his hatchway, which censure astonishes him so much that he forgets what he was doing and why he was yelling.

A few other drunks take up the call and holler to the teacher not to be a deserter of the poor and ignorant. Sober men try to quiet the unruly shouters, telling them to pardon the teacher, as they could see what a state he is in. This fails entirely, and one of the drunken callers, just to show the crowd that nobody on earth, not even that goddamned son of an old hussy – the president of the whole damned republic – can tell him what to do, he now roars like an angered bull and insults the teacher in the most filthy manner.

Well, it is about to become a lively funeral after all.

The sober men, seeing no other way to calm the drunks, and too decent to give them a well-deserved thrashing right here in the graveyard, go after the teacher and beg him, please, to come back and just say a few little palabras, muy pocas palabras, which will do all right, and never mind the condition he is in, because everybody understands that and all of us are human and nobody thinks himself fit to blame or reproach his fellow men.

The teacher cannot answer audibly. He only jabbers incoherently. Turning around, he struggles clumsily to free himself from those who want to bring him back. While still struggling he suddenly sees the weeping mother, who silently and tearfully looks straight into his eyes. He immediately stops his struggle and stares at the mother as if he were awakening from a dream. Perhaps just because his brain is befogged, he detects something in the stare of the mother which others cannot see. For a few seconds he stands still as if listening to something which speaks to him from the inside, while his eyes are firmly fixed upon the mother's face. Then

622

he goes slowly to the grave.

Once more he stands in front of the hole, his body swaying in every direction. Both his arms gesticulate for a while before he opens his lips. Still holding the twig in his right hand, he looks savagely around as if he were going to fight an invisible enemy who is defending himself with a sword. His dull and glassy eyes gaze into emptiness. The hundred or more faces before him must surely be making a horrible impression upon his numb mind. He apparently sees in this lake of faces a monster creeping towards him, because his features are distorted with terror.

It cannot be stage fright, for I have heard him speak on a national holiday, and from that occasion I know that he is a fairly good orator who is not afraid of speaking before a crowd.

And now all of a sudden he throws both his arms up, opens his mouth, and then closes it almost automatically. This he does several times. It seems he thinks that he is speaking, yet not one word can be heard.

Now he shouts with great force: 'We all assembled here are very sad. Very, very sad indeed, that's what we are, all of us who are gathered here, God and men know why and what for.'

These words he shouts so loudly that if there were six thousand people present, all scattered over a wide plain, they could be heard by everybody.

Again he yells, and this time as if speaking to twenty thousand: 'The little boy is dead. He is completely dead. I am sure of that. We'll never see him again. We shall never, as long as this world may exist, never more hear his innocent and happy laughter.'

Tears well in his eyes.

All this was nothing. He now lifts his voice as if he had a good mind to split open the skies: 'The mother of that little boy of ours is very sad too. Yes, you folks, believe me, she is very sad, because she is the mother and she no longer has her baby with her to play with.'

He looks over all the people without seeing one in particular and he yells: 'I tell you, folks, the mother is grief-stricken. She weeps. You can see that for yourself. She has been weeping all through this terrible night, the mother has, and you people, you have to believe me.' While thus shouting, he grasps his twig firmly and whips it through the air with all his might as if he meant to slay anyone who dared doubt that the mother is very sad and that she weeps for her baby.

That stroke at his invisible enemy, whom he apparently considers the mother's enemy also, was well meant and it surely was an honest stroke. But it was too much for his wavering body. He tumbles over, straight into the hole in front of him. He does not quite reach the bottom, though, thanks to the two poles laid across the hole on which the coffin should be standing. Fortunately for him, it had not yet been put there. Owing to the long fight to get the teacher back to the grave, this part of the ceremony had been overlooked and the box is still on the opposite edge of the hole.

The teacher had grasped one of these poles and now is hanging from it helplessly. With his legs he struggles ridiculously to reach the edge and climb out. His fight proves vain, and if at this precious moment brotherly assistance had not come to his rescue, he would have fallen down to the bottom, from which he could never have got out until the next morning.

And now a very strange thing happens.

The fall of the respectable teacher, his pitiful and clumsy struggle to get out again, his hanging on that pole like an old, lame monkey – all happening at such a moment – makes the funniest show I can imagine. But not a single person, man, woman, girl, or boy, laughs at the teacher. I, for one, usually have great difficulty keeping from laughing. It has happened to me more than once, that I have had to leave a church quickly to avoid a scandal, because practically every minister, with his pretended dignity and his silly sermons, makes me giggle and after a while break out into open laughter. I cannot help it that I see most things in a funny way, and if I fail to see fun in supposedly sacred performances or speeches, then I can see only the irony in them. And yet here I do not laugh; even were I tickled I would not have laughed, for I can see neither fun nor irony in the situation. Instead, it makes me cry for the first time since the kid was fished out of the river. Years have passed since those twenty-two hours when the Great Bandmaster was down on earth to play the music for one of the wildest and hottest dances I have ever seen. And still to this day I cannot laugh at this apparently funny situation. No one laughed. I know today as I knew then why no man laughed. Nobody laughed; neither did I, because I was one of them, and it was my boy who was to be buried just as he was the child of everybody present. No teacher was struggling to come out of a grave into which he had fallen. I saw only a great brotherly love for his fellow men which had dropped into the grave and was struggling so hard to get out again. I can laugh at a thousand things and situations – even at the brutalities of fascism, which as I see them are but a ridiculous cowardice without limits. But I can never laugh at love shown by men for those of their fellow men in pain and sorrow. This love I witnessed was coming straight from the heart; it was honest and true as only love can be for which no one expects thanks because every one of us gathered here, not excluding the teacher, had lost a beloved baby.

And the teacher once more stands at the grave, the twig still in his right hand. Even while he struggled he had not let go of his twig, which seems to be the staff on which he leans for his safety in a cruel world.

He stands there looking as if all that had just happened had nothing to do with him, but had happened to somebody else whom he does not know, and he stands there as if he were waiting for the disturbance to cease so that he can go on with his speech.

Yelling much louder than before, he says: 'The father who is with us on this unlucky day is also very, very sad. Yes, my friends, believe me, the father is very sad and weeps as does the mother. You have to believe that, folks.'

Again his twig slashes the air. But this time he has taken better care of himself. He stays about three feet away from the grave, far enough so that if he should trip again, he would not fall in. Besides, this time he does not whip forward. He has learned from his first mistake. This time he whips along his right side as if he were sitting on a horse. So he does not fall towards the grave, but merely whirls around a few times. Then he gets set firmly on the ground again.

He faces the crowd. Nobody laughs.

'The little boy had to die so soon,' he yells, and whips the air. 'The good little boy had to die so very soon, and he is dead. We have all loved him very much. We have been happy when he was with us. Now he is gone. For this we feel very sorry and blame none. It had to be. He is dead. Now we will bury him. Adiós, my little boy, adiosito!'

Would that the buzzards had taken the whole funeral somewhere else. I weep and howl like the old watchdog of a haunted castle in Scotland at midnight when visited by the ghost of an old duchess who had been changed into a rattling lamppost. I weep and howl and the whole crowd weeps and howls; the whole crowd, men, women, children, and even the crumbs of the dry soil shed tears and blubber. It is no longer the shrieking of the night. It is a mournful weeping as if it were over something which had happened centuries ago and was now recalled to mind by a well-written narrative.

What do I care about that kid? An Indian boy whom I hardly

noticed, whom I have known only for a few hours. None the less I weep over him. Perhaps he is my own boy after all, my boy as well as the boy of all the others here, my boy as well as the boy of every mother everywhere on earth. Why should he be somebody else's boy? He is my boy, my little brother, my fellow man, who could suffer as I can, who could laugh as I can, and who could die as I shall die some day.

36

Two men try to lower the coffin with lassos, but the poles on which they are standing shake, wobble, and roll over and there is some difficulty getting the lassos straight.

On seeing this confusion a man jumped into the grave.

'Give me that box,' he says in a businesslike manner to those standing above.

The man climbs up again.

Mother and father are throwing handfuls of earth into the grave.

Manuel then does the same, but he has very little soil in his hands.

And now earth is thrown in from all sides and from every hand.

The musicians step up to the spot where shortly before the teacher had made his speech. Surely they will now play *Ave Maria* or *Nearer, My God, to Thee*, or something like that. I am honestly afraid that they will commit such a sin. After all, they are only Christians and are supposed to do what is considered right and decent.

God Almighty, I thank You, because I feel relieved of a pain. The musicians have excellent taste. I knew I could trust them. They know how to press the right button at the right time. They are not hypocrites and they will do nothing which does not come out of their sane hearts. True children of the jungle, they call everything by its right name and give back to nature what belongs to nature.

And so these admirable men are playing once more the great,

immortal funeral march of mankind, *Taintgonna*. I frankly admit that I could embrace them.

While they are playing the song of songs with enthusiasm and fervour, youngsters are shovelling earth into the grave. Women arrange the flowers and wreaths. The mother, softly weeping, is surrounded by a crowd of women who, one after the other, embrace and kiss her while telling her how dearly loved she is by everybody. The men cover their heads, roll cigarettes, and wait patiently. No one leaves the graveyard until the mother gives permission to do so by leaving first.

What to do now? Something should be done while everybody waits.

The musicians, having finished their piece, are waiting too. As the pause lasts longer than they expected, they think it would be highly appreciated by all if they played another piece until the grave is covered, the flowers all placed on it, and the mother ready to leave. So they remember the other funeral march, that of about sixteen years or so back, which was produced by exactly the same brain disease as was the first.

Well now, let me see, isn't that the beautiful song which was invented soon after the day when soldiers home from France tried to collect on that wonderful promise: 'Your country will never forget you! Others have joined, why not U! Do it now! Your country will never never – '? So help me God, how could I forget? Because it *is* the song all right, the song which kept in check the angry fist which was threatening to do some face-lifting on the old world. It is the song all right. It came then at the proper time as it comes now to this Indian country. *Yeswehavenobananastoday*. Yea, my good man, yes, I cannot give you a job today, or food, or a coat, or anything at all; but you see I can sing you a song which will fill your belly with beans of lead should you ever try to eat without having a job. Yes, of course, we have nobananas.

Adiós, my beloved little boy! Adiós! Worms and maggots are going to live and fatten. But you, my little boy, you had to die. Adiós! No king was ever buried the way you were. Adiosito!